Seeds
of
Betrayal

BOOKS BY DAVID B. COE

Available from Tor Books

A TOM DOHERTY ASSOCIATES BOOK
NEW YORK

Seeds
of
Betrayal

✦

DAVID B. COE

Book Two
of
Winds of the Forelands

SEEDS OF BETRAYAL: BOOK 2 OF WINDS OF THE FORELANDS TETRALOGY

Copyright © 2003 by David B. Coe

Edited by James Frenkel

Maps by Ellisa Mitchell

A Tor Book
Published by Tom Doherty Associates, LLC
175 Fifth Avenue
New York, NY 10010

www.tor.com

Tor® is a registered trademark of Tom Doherty Associates, LLC.

Library of Congress Cataloging-in-Publication Data

Coe, David B.
    Seeds of betrayal / David B. Coe.—1st ed.
        p. cm.—(Winds of the Forelands tetralogy ; bk. 2)
    "A Tom Doherty Associates book."
    ISBN 0-312-87808-7 (acid-free paper)
        I. Title.

PS3553.O343S44 2003
813'.54—dc21

                                                    2003041018

First Edition: May 2003

Printed in the United States of America

0 9 8 7 6 5 4 3 2 1

For Bill, Liz, and Jim.
Now they have *to read it. . . .*

Many thanks as always to my agent, Lucienne Diver; my publisher, Tom Doherty; the wonderful people at Tor Books, in particular Fred Herman, Jenifer Hunt, Irene Gallo, and Peter Lutjen; Carol Russo and her staff; Terry McGarry for her thorough copyediting; my terrific editor and good friend, Jim Frenkel; and Jim's staff, in particular Steve Smith and Jordan Zweck.

Once again, I am most indebted to Nancy, Alex, and Erin for their love and support, which make possible all that I do, and for their uncanny ability to make me laugh, which keeps me from taking any of it too seriously.

—D.B.C.

The Forelands

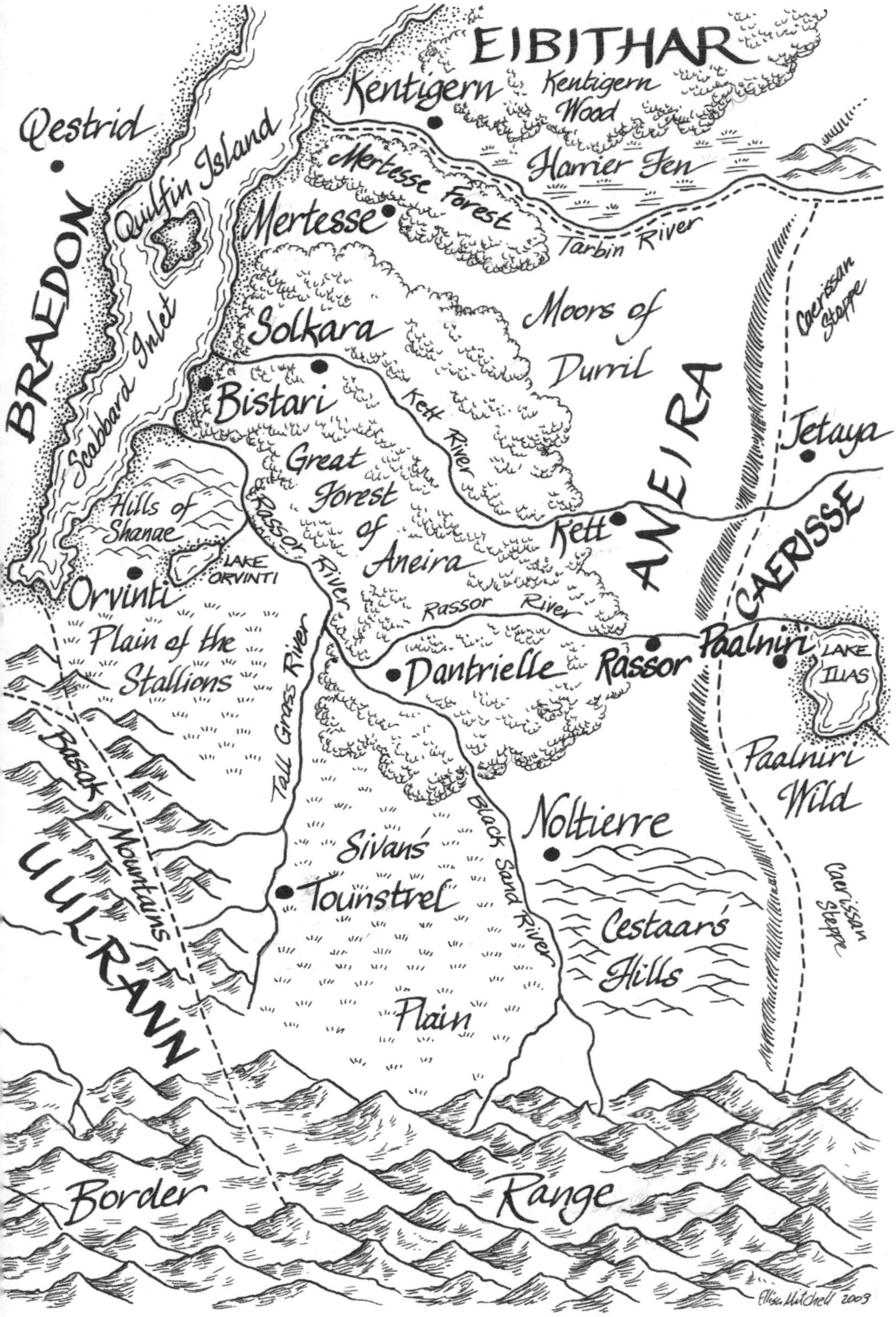

EIBITHAR
Kentigern
Kentigern Wood
Harrier Fen
Qestrid
Quilfin Island
Mertesse Forest
Mertesse
Tarbin River
BRAEDON
Scabbard Inlet
Solkara
Moors of Durril
Caerissan Steppe
Bistari
Kett River
Jetaya
Great Forest of Aneira
Rassor River
Hills of Shanae
Kett
ANEIRA
CAERISSE
LAKE ORVINTI
Orvinti
Rassor River
Plain of the Stallions
Tall Grass River
Dantrielle
Rassor
Paalniri
LAKE ILLAS
Basak Mountains
Paalniri Wild
Black Sand River
Noltierre
UUL-RANN
Sivan's
Tounstrel
Caerissan Steppe
Cestaar's Hills
Plain
Border
Range
Ellisa Mitchell 2003

Chapter
One

✦

Bistari, Aneira, year 879, Bian's Moon waning

The duke rode slowly among the trees, dry leaves crackling like a winter blaze beneath the hooves of his Sanbiri bay. Massive grey trunks surrounded him, resembling some vast army sent forth from the Underrealm by the Deceiver, their bare, skeletal limbs reaching toward a leaden sky. A few leaves rustling in a cold wind still clung stubbornly to the twisting branches overhead. Most were as curled and brown as those that covered the path, but a few held fast to the brilliant gold that had colored the Great Forest only a half turn before.

Even here, nearly a league from Bistari, Chago could smell brine in the air and hear the faint cry of gulls riding another frigid gust of wind. He pulled his riding cloak tighter around his shoulders and rubbed his gloved hands together, trying to warm them. This was no day for a hunt. He almost considered returning to the warmth of his castle. He would have, had he not been waiting for his first minister to join him. This hunt had been Peshkal's idea in the first place, and they were to meet here, on the western fringe of the Great Forest.

"A hunt will do you good, my lord," the minister had told him that morning. "This matter with the king has been troubling you for too long."

At first Chago dismissed the idea. He was awaiting word from the dukes of Noltierre, Kett, and Tounstrel, and he still had messages to compose to Dantrielle and Orvinti. But as the morning wore on with no messengers arriving, and his mind began to cloud once more with his rage at what Carden had done, he reconsidered.

Kebb's Moon, the traditional turn for hunting, had come and gone, and the duke had not ridden forth into the wood even once. More than half of Bian's Moon was now gone. Soon the snows would begin and Chago would have to put away his bow for another year. He had the cold turns to fight Carden on his wharfages and lightering fees. *Today,* he decided, pushing back from his worktable and the papers piled there, *I'm going to hunt.*

When Peshkal entered the duke's quarters and found him testing the tension of his bow, he seemed genuinely pleased, so much so that the Qirsi even offered to accompany Chago.

"Thank you, Peshkal," Chago said, grinning. "But I know how you feel about hunting. I'll take my son."

"Lord Silbron is riding today, my lord, with the master of arms and your stablemaster."

"Of course. I'd forgotten." The duke hesitated a moment, gazing toward the window. Moments before he hadn't been sure whether or not to go, but having made up his mind to ride, he was reluctant now to abandon his plans. "Then I'll hunt alone."

Peshkal's pale features turned grave and he shook his head. "That wouldn't be wise, my lord. There have been reports from your guards of brigands in the wood. Let me come with you. I have business in the city, but I'll meet you on the edge of the wood just after midday." The Qirsi forced a smile. "It will be my pleasure."

Still Chago hesitated. As white-hairs went, Peshkal was reasonably good company. But like so many of the Eandi, the duke found all men of the pale sorcerer race somewhat strange. If the object of this hunt was to calm him, riding with the first minister made little sense.

Then again, neither would it be wise for him to ride alone; he'd heard talk of the brigands as well. In the end, Chago agreed to meet Peshkal in the wood, and a short time later, he rode forth from his castle, following the king's road away from the dark roiling waters of the Scabbard Inlet toward the ghostly grey of the forest. His bow, unstrung for now, hung from the back of his saddle along with a quiver of arrows. But even after he entered the wood, he saw little sign of game. Not long ago, the forest would have been teeming with boar and elk, but each year, as the cold settled over central Aneira, the herds moved southward and inland, away from the coastal winds. Chago would be fortunate just to see a stag this day; there was little chance he would get close enough to one to use his bow.

Again, the duke felt the anger rising in his chest, until he thought his heart would explode. He could hardly blame the king for a poor hunt, yet already he was counting this cold, grey, empty day among the long list of indignities he had suffered at the hands of Carden the Third.

He couldn't say when it began. In truth, his own feud with the Solkaran king was but a continuation of a centuries-old conflict between House Solkara and House Bistari that dated back to the First Solkaran Supremacy and the civil war that ended it over seven centuries ago. During the next two hundred and fifty years, the Aneiran monarchy changed hands several times, ending with the Solkaran Restoration and the establishment of the Second Solkaran Supremacy, which persisted to this day. It was a period of constantly shifting alliances, all of them based on little more than expedience and cold calculation. But throughout, Aneira's two most powerful houses, Solkara and Bistari, always remained adversaries.

In the centuries since, when circumstances demanded it, the two houses managed to put their enmity aside. During the many wars the kingdom waged against Eibithar, Aneira's neighbor to the north, men of Bistari fought beside men of Solkara. But the wars ended and the crises passed, and always when they did, one essential truth persisted: Chago's people and those of the royal house simply did not trust each other.

Of course, rivalries among houses of the court were common in Aneira, and, from all Chago had heard, in the other kingdoms of the Forelands as well. When one's enemy was the king, however, the royal court could be a lonely place. Chago had friends throughout the kingdom. Bertin of Noltierre journeyed to the western shores each year and stayed with Chago and Ria. And though he hadn't seen Ansis of Kett in a number of years, he still counted the young duke among his closest allies. In most matters of the kingdom he could expect to find himself in agreement not only with Bertin and Ansis, but also with the dukes of Tounstrel, Orvinti, and Dantrielle.

Unless he was at odds with the king.

It was not that the others were blind to Carden's considerable faults, or that they agreed with every decree that came from Castle Solkara. But Solkaran rulers had made it clear over the centuries that those who opposed their word, especially those who sided with Bistari in doing so, would suffer for their impudence. Raised fees, restrictions on hunting, increases in the number of men levied for service in the king's army—all were measures used by Aneiran kings to punish what they viewed as defiant behavior. And no house had borne more of this than Chago's own.

It was a credit to his strength and that of his forebears that Bistari had retained its status as one of the great families of Aneira despite the abuses of the royal house. A lesser house would have crumbled long ago; Bistari had thrived, all the while taking pains to keep its rivalry with House Solkara from manifesting itself as anything that could be interpreted as an act of treason. Bistari's dukes paid their fees, though they were far greater than those paid by any other house. They sent soldiers to the king's generals, though their quotas were too high. They hunted the forest only when they were allowed, though their season was nearly a full turn shorter than that allowed in Dantrielle, Rassor, and Kett. Let the Solkaran kings play their foolish games. Bistari was the rock against the tide, the family blazon a great black stone standing against the onslaught of the sea. Chago's people endured. And this made Carden's most recent affront that much more galling.

The increase in the lightering fees he could accept. Kings had always taken their share of profits from trade and it was too much to expect that Carden would be any different. But no fair-minded man could doubt that the wharfage fees were directed almost solely at House Bistari. To be sure, several of Aneira's houses were located on water—almost all of them really. But Bistari was the only one on the coast; the others were on rivers or, like Orvinti, on a lake. Their wharves were in little danger of needing replacement any time soon. Bistari's, on the other hand, had to be rebuilt every few years after the passing of the cold turns and the powerful storms they brought to the Scabbard Inlet. Carden's latest fees covered the entire kingdom, but since the wharfages applied only to newly constructed wharves, Bistari would bear the brunt of this new levy.

The king knew that. Chago was certain of it. This was merely one more reprisal for an imagined slight that should have been forgotten years ago. How long did Chago and his people have to suffer for the fact that Silbron had been born within a day of when Carden's father, Tomaz the Ninth, died? Ria had nearly lost her life giving birth to the boy, and for the next several days, Chago refused to leave her side. True, it was a short ride to Solkara, and he was the only one of Aneira's dukes who did not attend the observances honoring the old king. But this was his son, his heir, and, as he had tried to explain to Carden several times since, he had come within a hairsbreadth of losing the woman he loved. No reasonable man would have done different. The Solkarans, though, had never been known for being reasonable.

A woodpecker drummed in the distance, the sound echoing among the trees, and two crows flew silently overhead, black as vultures against the grey sky. Chago reined his mount to a halt and surveyed the forest. At first he saw nothing, not even a jay. But as his eyes came to rest on the path just before him, something caught his eye. He swung himself off his horse to take a better look, his pulse quickening. Elk droppings, just as he had suspected. Squatting beside them, he saw that they were fresh.

The duke stood again, glancing around, his entire frame taut, as if for battle. He stepped carefully to his bow, removed it from the saddle, and shouldered his quiver. Resting one end on the ground and bracing it with his foot, he bent the smooth wood until he could slip the bowstring into place at the top. Then he drew an arrow from the quiver and nocked it.

It was hard to say which way the beast had been traveling. Chances were that it had crossed the path rather than followed it, but Chago couldn't say more than that with any confidence. After a moment's pause, he started south. A small stream flowed through the wood not too far from where his horse stood. Perhaps, he thought, the elk was headed there. Had it not been for the blanket of dead leaves covering the forest floor he might have found tracks, but as it was, the ground told him little. Before long, however, he came to a small tree with tooth marks on it, where the elk had eaten off much of the bark. The marks appeared as new as the droppings he had seen on the path. He heard something moving in front of him, the dead leaves betraying each step, and he stepped forward as quickly as he dared, craning his neck to see beyond the thick trunks just before him.

For an instant he caught a glimpse of the beast, the warm brown of its coat flickering amid the grey trees like candle fire on a moonless night, then vanishing again. He couldn't see its head, but the animal certainly appeared large enough to be a stag. He hurried on, bow half-drawn, expecting to come face-to-face with the creature at any moment. He spotted it briefly once more, farther ahead than it had been a moment earlier. It almost seemed to be drifting among the trees like a wraith. Running now, he tried to catch up with it, but all he saw was grey.

The duke stopped again, straining to hear over the whispering of another gust of wind. Nothing, at least not from the elk. Far behind him, his mount snorted and stomped. Chago felt the hairs rise on the back of his neck. And then he heard it, too.

Singing. It was so soft at first, so ethereal, that the duke thought he must be imagining it. Who, in his right mind, would be singing in the wood on a day such as this?

Who, indeed?

The thought made him shudder, as if another chill wind had knifed through his cloak. His sword was still strapped to his saddle, and though he carried his bow, he preferred to face an assailant with his steel. Turning quickly, he started back toward his horse, fighting an impulse to run. For just an instant the duke lost his bearings and halted again, feeling panic rise within him like bile. Then his bay nickered and he strode toward the sound, cursing his lack of nerve. As he made his way among the trees, he scanned the wood for the singer, listening as the voice grew stronger.

It was a man, with a voice both strong and sweet, rich and high. As the man drew nearer still, the duke even recognized the song: "The Blossoms of Adlana," a Caerissan folk song that Chago had learned as a child. It struck him as an odd choice for such a chill, dreary day. But it set his mind at ease somewhat and he slowed his gait. A moment later, he spotted his bay and could not keep a relieved smile from springing to his lips.

By the time the singer came into view, the duke had his sword in hand and was securing its sheath to his belt. Armed now, and within reach of his mount, the duke was able to laugh at the dread that had gripped him only moments before. This was no brigand, not with a voice like this, and seeing the singer's face, Chago felt what remained of his fear recede like the tide after a storm. The man was lean and bearded, with long dark hair that fell to his broad shoulders and pale eyes the same color as the silver bark on the maples that grew all around them. He smiled kindly at the duke as he walked toward him and he nodded once, though he continued with his song. His glance fell briefly to Chago's sword, but the smile remained on his face.

Chago thought him vaguely familiar and wondered briefly if he had ever sung at Bistari Castle, perhaps with the Festival. He almost stopped the singer to ask him. But though the man was clearly a musician, they were still alone in the wood, and the duke thought it wiser to let the stranger pass.

He offered a nod of his own as the singer stepped past him, but he kept his blade ready and turned to watch the man walk away. Only when the singer had disappeared among the trees, his song fading slowly, did Chago sheathe his sword and allow his mind to return once more to the elk.

He would have liked to track the animal; given time, he knew that he could find it again. But Peshkal would never find him if he left the path.

Where could his first minister be? It had to be well past midday. The Qirsi should have been there already.

"Damn him," the duke murmured.

The bay whinnied softly, as if in response, and Chago froze. The wood was silent. Even the wind had died away. More to the point, though, the singing had stopped. Or had it? The man had been walking away. Had the song ended? Had he just covered enough distance to be beyond the duke's hearing?

Chago stood, still as death, listening for the singer's voice, much as he had listened for the elk a short time ago. He was being foolish, he knew. Surely the singer was too far away to be heard by now. Besides, Chago had his bow and his sword, and he knew how to use both. He had nothing to fear from a musician.

Yet he continued to stand motionless, waiting. This time he heard no song. Only a footfall, soft and sure, and closer than it should ever have been. It had to be the elk again. Still, the duke reached not for his bow, but for his blade.

Before he could pull the weapon from its sheath, before he could even turn to face the sound, he felt someone grab him from behind, a hand gripping his right arm at the elbow, and a muscular arm locking itself around his throat.

The duke struggled to free his sword, but the man holding him was remarkably strong. He opened his mouth to scream, but the singer—it had to be he—tightened his hold on Chago's throat until the duke could barely draw breath.

"My apologies, my lord. But it seems someone wants you dead."

He's an assassin then, Chago thought, *not a brigand.*

Not that it mattered. He was going to die here in the wood, not even a league from his castle.

Where in Bian's name was Peshkal?

The realization came to him so suddenly, with such force, that his knees actually gave way, forcing the man to hold him up. He had been hearing the rumors for nearly a year now, long enough and from so many different sources that he no longer doubted their truth. But though he had little trouble believing in the existence of a Qirsi conspiracy, it had never occurred to him to question Peshkal's loyalty.

The sorcerer had been with him for eight years now, the first several as an underminister, the last five as his first minister. Chago would never go so far as to call the Qirsi his friend, but he had paid the man handsomely, relied on his counsel without hesitation, and trusted him with the well-being of his dukedom, the safety of his family, and his own life. Until this day, Peshkal had given him no reason to do otherwise.

The hunt had been his idea. So had Silbron's ride for that matter. He had contrived every circumstance so that the duke would be hunting alone. And then he had made certain that Chago would be at this very spot at precisely this time. He could hear the minister's words once more—he could see the man's smile. "I have business in the city, but I'll meet you on the edge of the wood just after midday." Indeed. The Qirsi had killed him, and Chago had made it far too easy for him.

All of this occurred to the duke in a single instant. The assassin still held him fast, and now he pried Chago's fingers off the hilt of his sword and drew the weapon himself.

"A pretty blade, my lord," he said, tossing it aside as if it were a trifle. "Where is your dagger?"

Chago said nothing, and the man began to crush his throat.

"Tell me."

"My belt," the duke rasped.

The man ran his hand along Chago's belt until he found the blade. This, too, he threw to the side. Both of Chago's hands were free, and he straightened, bearing his own weight again. If he moved fast enough . . .

Before he even formed the thought, the point of a dagger was resting against the corner of his eye.

"This can be done quickly or slowly, my lord. Painlessly or not. It's your choice."

"I'll do whatever you say," Chago whispered. "Please, not my eyes."

The man said nothing, though he did remove the blade.

"You don't have to do this," the duke said. "Just tell me what you want."

The man shook his head. "I've already told you, someone wants you dead. It's not my choice."

"No, it's your profession."

The singer offered no response, though it seemed to Chago that he pulled something from his pocket.

"Were you hired by the Qirsi? Can you tell me that much?"

The man stopped what he was doing. After a moment he turned the duke around and looked him in the eye. Chago and the assassin were almost the same height, and looking at him again, knowing now that he was more than a mere singer, the duke saw much that he had missed before. The man had a small scar high on his cheek, and there was something cold and uncompromising in those pale eyes. Without the smile he had worn as he sang, he had the look of a killer.

Their eyes remained locked for another moment, and then the assassin raised his hands. He held a garrote, the cord wound around his fists and pulled taut between them. For centuries, the garrote had been the weapon of choice for assassins sent by Solkaran kings.

"Is it Carden then?" the duke asked. "Is that who sent you?"

The assassin said nothing, and Chago backed away. He stumbled, fell backward to the ground, tears running down his face.

"Please," he said again, as the man came toward him, pulling the garrote taut once more so that it thrummed like a hunter's bow. "I have gold. I can pay you more than whoever it was that hired you."

Incredibly, the man seemed to waver.

"Just tell me how much you want," the duke went on, feeling bolder now. "My treasury is yours."

Cadel had never considered such a thing before. People paid him to kill, and he killed. In his profession, failure meant death. If by some chance he had forgotten this over the years, the loss just a few turns before of Jedrek, his partner, had served as a bitter reminder. But what if he refused to kill? What if he chose to let this man live?

Would the Qirsi try to kill him? A part of him wished that they would try. He had been working for them for too long, and had grown far too dependent on their gold. He longed to strike back at them. It was far more likely, however, that they would try to destroy him while stopping short of killing him. Somehow they knew his true name. They knew of the circumstances that had driven him from the court of his father in southern Caerisse when he was little more than a boy. And, of course, they knew of every murder he had committed on their behalf. They could keep him from ever working again. With a mere word uttered to the right person, they could turn him into a fugitive.

All of which made the gold offered by this duke cowering before him that much more attractive. Before they died, many of his victims tried to buy his mercy—his employers were wealthy and powerful, and, not surprisingly, so were those they wanted dead. Always in the past he had refused. But something in the duke of Bistari's plea stopped him, probably the fact that he knew who had paid for his death. It had come to that: he so hated working for the Qirsi that he saw in their newest enemy a possible ally, or at least a way to break free of the white-hairs and their gold.

In any case, the duke had Cadel's attention.

"You don't want to do this," the man said, still sitting on the ground, his cheeks still damp with the tears he had shed.

Cadel opened his mouth, then closed it again. Some things were best left unspoken. "You offered me gold," he said instead. "How much?"

"More than you can imagine. My dukedom is the wealthiest in Aneira. Only the king has more gold than I."

"I wasn't asking how much you have, I was asking how much you'd give me."

"As much as you want. All of it, if that's what it takes." He faltered. "I'm not a brave man, and I fear dying more than anything else."

Cadel closed his eyes for just an instant, cursing his own stupidity. Jedrek would never have allowed him even to begin this conversation. What had he been thinking? No duke would offer all of his gold, even out of fear. Bistari had no intention of actually paying him.

"And I suppose after you give me all this gold, you'll send your soldiers to ride me down, cut out my heart, and retrieve your money."

"No, I'll let you go. You have my word."

But Cadel felt his hope slipping away. Perhaps there was still a way for him to regain his freedom, but this was not it. Not with this man and his promise of gold. He should have realized it from the start. Jedrek was dead, killed by an enemy of the Qirsi men and women who had been paying him. That his friend's killer was Qirsi as well struck Cadel as ironic, perhaps even funny in a way Jed himself would have appreciated, but it changed nothing. If Cadel wanted to find this man, he would need the help of the white-hairs. Even if the duke of Bistari's offer had been sincere, he was in no position to accept it.

He smiled, extending a hand to the duke. The cord of the garrote was still wound around his fist, but the duke didn't seem to care. Chago took Cadel's hand and let the assassin help him to his feet, smiling broadly, as if they were old friends. He started to say something, but Cadel, still gripping his hand, spun him around and in one powerful, fluid motion wrapped the cord around the duke's neck and pulled it tight. The man's neck snapped like a dry twig, and Cadel felt the duke's body go limp.

He laid the duke down on the forest floor, pulling the garrote free as he did. Then he reached into the pocket of his trousers and pulled out a small strap of leather that was frayed at one end and adorned at the other with golden trim and a carving of the Solkaran panther. It had been given to him, along with half of his payment, by an older man, a Qirsi merchant in Dantrielle. Cadel had not bothered to ask how the white-hairs had gotten it, though he wondered. There was little chance that the man knew, and less still that he would answer the question if he did.

He placed the strap in the duke's hand, with the golden edging facing up so that it gleamed brightly, despite the grey shadows of the wood. Cadel even went so far as to break off one of the duke's fingernails and bruise the man's hand by squeezing his palm closed with the strap and its trim pressed awkwardly within.

They had said to make it look convincing, and given what they were paying him, he could hardly do less.

He stepped back, looking down on the body and the surrounding area to make certain that he hadn't forgotten anything or left something foolish for one of the duke's men to find. Satisfied that all appeared as it should, he started walking back toward the east, away from Bistari and the Scabbard Inlet. He had only walked a few strides, however, when he heard someone approaching. Concealing himself behind a broad tree, Cadel watched as a Qirsi rode into view on a small grey mount.

The man wore his hair shorter than did most Qirsi and the yellow of his eyes was so bright that they almost seemed to glow. He had on ministerial robes and his riding cloak bore the blazon of House Bistari. The first minister.

Cadel was so confident of this that he stepped out from behind the tree trunk. The man's horse snorted and the minister's eyes fell upon him. The Qirsi reined the mount to a halt and stared at Cadel for several moments. Then he glanced toward the duke's body, faced the assassin again, and nodded.

Offering a nod of his own, Cadel turned and started walking eastward once more, resuming his song as he strode swiftly among the silver trees. He had three days to reach Solkara, and though the distance wasn't great, he could ill afford to be late.

Chapter
Two

✦

Solkara, Aneira

oli crossed her arms over her chest and stepped as close to the hearth as she dared. She was wearing the heaviest of her black robes and soft woolen undergarments beneath it. But they weren't enough to keep the frigid air from chilling her frail bones, nor, she soon realized, was the fine fire built for her by the clerics.

She would have given nearly anything to be able to close the doors to the sanctuary. But this was Pitch Night in the turn of Bian, god of the Underrealm, and she presided in the Deceiver's temple. She could no more close the doors than she could extinguish the candles that burned on the god's altar.

It was early yet—the sun had been down for but an hour or two—and already she longed for this night to end. The cold, the constant stream of worshipers, the repeated offerings; it was too much. Yoli had never been a proud woman, and she wasn't above admitting that she had grown too old for this. It was time to pass the robe to one of her clerics. Several of them had been with her for the requisite twelve years, and of those, at least two or three seemed ready to lead the sanctuary. Perhaps when the snows ended and the warm winds returned, she would step aside.

But that did her little good tonight. She had barely managed to warm her hands before she heard the next group of suppliants approaching the shrine, their footsteps and hushed voices echoing off the domed ceiling.

Visitors came to the sanctuary every Pitch Night of the year, for in Bian's shrine, no matter which turn, one could always meet his or her beloved dead when both moons were dark. In the same way, on the Night

of Two Moons in Bian's Turn, one could encounter lost loved ones anywhere in the land. Pitch Night in the Deceiver's turn, however, was
unique. On this one night, the wronged dead roamed the land. This was
not a time when young widows came to cry for their dead husbands, or
bereft parents offered blood and shed tears for children taken from them
too soon. This was a night of fear, rather than grief, a night when the dead
sought vengeance rather than solace. Tonight, the sanctuary opened its
doors to mercenaries, executioners, and brigands, healers whose errors had
cost lives, and lovers whose passion inflamed their tempers to deadly violence. As prioress of the god's sanctuary Yoli could turn none of them away,
no matter how justified the wrath of their dead. On this one night she
thanked the gods for her failing eyesight. For though she could sense the
darkness in their hearts, she had no desire to see their faces.

She met them at the altar, raised her knife to spill their blood into the
stone bowl, and gave them leave to pass the night within the walls of the
shrine. Their dead could still reach them here, but many of them found
comfort in the offerings and the presence of Bian's prioress and the shared
company of others who had killed.

The newest to arrive were mercenaries, broad-shouldered men with
Caerissan or Sanbiri accents—Yoli had never learned to distinguish the
two. They had white hair and their arms, once thick with muscle, had
grown flaccid with the years. Still, they endured the edge of her blade sto-
ically before moving off to a distant corner of the shrine to cry like babes at
the sight of those they had cut down in some long-forgotten battle.

Yoli watched them walk away from the altar, dark, blurred shapes in
the candlelight that vanished into the shadows beyond the flickering
flames. She swirled each bowl so that the blood covered the entire surface,
then left the altar once more for the warmth of her hearth. She hadn't gotten very far when she heard another footfall in the shrine.

"Mother Prioress," a man called to her gently, his voice accented as well.

She turned wearily and forced a smile as she watched him approach.
He was tall and lean, with long dark hair. Her eyes were too weak to see
more than that. He stopped a few paces from where she stood and bowed
to her.

"You wish to offer blood?" she asked.

"I do."

Something about him—the accent, the gentle voice . . .

"You've been here before."

He hesitated then nodded. "Yes, several times."

"Come," she said, returning to the altar. The bowls were already empty; the god had a mighty thirst tonight.

The man pulled up his sleeve and turned his arm up to her blade.

"Is it my skill with the knife that brings you back?"

"You have a deft touch, Mother Prioress. But it's your beauty that draws me here."

Yoli laughed out loud. "Serves me right for asking."

She thought she saw him smile.

"Is there anyone in particular for whom you would like to make this offering?" she asked.

Once more he faltered, and in that moment she understood the true reason why he returned to her shrine. She shivered again, though not from the cold.

"No, Mother Prioress."

She nodded, but would not look at him again. Instead she raised the stone knife.

"Hear me, Bian!" she said, closing her eyes. "A man comes to you offering his life's blood. Deem him worthy and accept his gift."

She dragged the blade across his arm, catching his blood in one of the bowls. When the bleeding slowed, she placed the bowl on the altar and bound his arm in a clean cloth.

"Thank you," he said, flexing his arm and examining the bandage.

"You're free to remain here through the night," Yoli told him, her eyes fixed on the bowl of blood. "Whatever comfort there is to be found within these walls is yours."

"Again, my thanks." He started to turn away, then stopped. "Have I given offense, Mother Prioress?"

She shook her head. "No."

He stood there another moment, before giving a small shrug and turning again to leave her.

"I know why you come here," she said, surprising herself.

He halted, appearing to stiffen, but he kept his back to her.

"Shall I leave then?"

The prioress wasn't afraid, though perhaps she should have been. She was too old and had served the Deceiver for too long to fear death. Besides, this man came to her sanctuary precisely because he didn't have to harm her.

"I accepted your offering." She glanced down at the bowl and saw that his blood had vanished. "And so has Bian. You're free to remain or leave as you choose."

"Do I have reason to fear you?" he asked.

"You know you don't."

After a brief pause, he nodded once. "Then I'll stay."

"As you wish."

Still, he didn't move. "Mother Prioress," he said at last, facing her once again. "There is someone for whom I'd like to give blood. Will the god accept two offerings from one man?"

"Of course. Come forward, the knife and bowl await."

The man returned to the altar, pushing up his sleeve again.

Yoli began to repeat the invocation, then paused. "What is this person's name?"

"Is that necessary?"

"It's customary, when offering blood for someone."

He lowered his arm. "Isn't there any other way?"

"I suppose if you have this person foremost in your heart and your mind, Bian will know."

"Thank you, Mother Prioress. That would be . . . easier."

She finished the invocation and cut him a second time. Afterward, when she had wrapped the wound, and swirled the blood in the bowl, she looked the man in the eye as best she could.

"You've been kind to me," he said. "Perhaps kinder than I deserve. I won't forget it."

"I've done no more or less than the god would expect of those who serve him."

He dropped his gaze. "Of course."

"If you return here next year, you'll probably find someone else wearing the robe."

He looked up again. "Are you ill, Mother Prioress?"

"No, just old."

"I see. And why are you telling me this?"

She shrugged. "I just thought you should know that there will be a new prior or prioress. I don't know yet who I'll choose, but whoever it is will be far younger than I."

He grinned, and after a moment nodded as well.

"You're an extraordinary woman," he said. "I wish I could have met you when you were younger."

The prioress couldn't remember the last time a man had made her blush, but she knew that she had missed feeling this way.

"When I was younger," she told him, "I wasn't nearly this wise."

"I'm not sure I believe that." He paused, his smile slowly fading. "I'm grateful for the warning, Mother Prioress. I'll keep it in mind next year at this time."

"Good. In the meantime, I hope that you find some comfort in the shrine."

"As do I."

He bowed to her a second time, then left the altar.

Yoli watched him walk off, and despite what she knew of him, she truly wished him peace on this night. She felt certain, however, that there was nowhere he could go to escape the wrath of his dead. She sensed that he realized this as well, that the most he could hope for was the comfort of knowing that the prioress who took his blood was too old and too blind to see his face.

Walking to the farthest corner of the shrine, Cadel couldn't keep himself from shaking his head. For the second time in recent days, he had revealed far more of himself than he had intended, to a virtual stranger. The duke was dead, of course, and he didn't believe that the prioress posed any threat, but he had been far too careless. He might have expected Jedrek to act this way, but he demanded more of himself.

He stopped in midstride.

Jedrek. Could that be the problem? For the first time in nearly two decades he was alone, wandering the land and killing without a partner. Could it be that he was lonely? He nearly laughed aloud at the very idea of it. It didn't help that he now found himself trapped in a dangerous alliance with the Qirsi, but had Jed still been with him, the white-hairs wouldn't have mattered, at least not as much.

"I need a new partner," he said, his words echoing off the stone walls.

He glanced around to see if anyone had heard him, then remembered that it didn't matter. Everywhere he looked, men and women spoke as if to themselves, confronting their dead, sobbing like children, cowering like beaten curs. Even if they had taken notice of him, they wouldn't have thought it odd to see him speaking to himself.

He hurried on. It wouldn't be long before his own dead found him and began their torment.

As if prompted by the thought, a wraith appeared before him, indistinct at first, but white and luminous as if it were made of starlight. Slowly the figure took form, like the lead soldier of some great army emerging from a mist. It was a man, tall and lean with white hair and dark eyes. Cadel would have recognized him immediately even without the odd tilt of his head and the dark thin bruise encircling his neck. It had only been three days.

"You know me," the duke of Bistari said, his voice as bleak and hard as the moors during the snows.

Cadel nodded.

"Do you fear me?"

"No," he said evenly.

The duke gave a terrible grin. "Of course not. An assassin learns to live with his wraiths. Isn't that right?"

Cadel shrugged. "What choice do we have?"

Another figure emerged from the shadows, a knife wound in his chest. The marquess of Tantreve. Cadel had killed him a bit more than a year ago, near his castle in northern Aneira.

"What about him?" the duke asked.

"No, not him either."

Others stepped forward: Filib of Thorald, his throat slit and his ring finger cut off; Hanan of Jetaya, unmarked save for the contorted expression the poison left on his features; Cyro of Yserne, the angle of his head and the mark on his neck so similar to those of the duke of Bistari that they might have been the twin sons of some cruel demon from the Underrealm. Soon there were dozens of them. Cadel couldn't even recall all of their names, though he remembered each kill as clearly as he did the garroting of Chago.

Yet, he felt no dread. He could hear worshipers wailing all around him, begging for forgiveness, or at least mercy. He had heard stories of mercenaries clawing out their eyes on the Night of the Dead, so desperate were they to rid themselves of their wraiths. Several years ago he had been in the Sanctuary of Bian in Macharzo when a man used the prior's blade to take his own life. Maybe the others knew something he didn't. Maybe he should have been scared. But he had been paid to kill these men, and while they might not have deserved death, they would have been more than happy to pay him to do the same to their enemies had they thought of it in time.

He spent the Night of the Dead in Bian's Sanctuary each year not out of fear of his wraiths, but rather out of respect for the god who sent them to him. If the Deceiver could bend the rules of life and death in this way, didn't he deserve such homage? That was why Cadel came.

At least until this year. Because unlike all the years before, there now was one whom he did not wish to meet, one whose face he couldn't bear to see again. He had known it would be like this almost from the moment he saw her. It had been the middle of the planting season, a warm clear night in Kentigern, but even then he had been prescient enough to know how difficult this night would be because of her. If only he had been hired to kill her father, the fat, foul-tempered duke, or, better still, the spoiled boy to whom she had been betrothed. But Filib of Thorald had already been killed, and Cadel's Qirsi employers worried that the death of another heir to the Eibitharian throne would raise suspicions. They insisted that it be the girl.

He had heard tales of her beauty and her kindness, but only that night on the tor, when he met her in the duke's great hall, did he truly appreciate how little justice these tales did Lady Brienne of Kentigern.

She had worn a dazzling gown of deepest sapphire that made the yellow ringlets of hair spilling down her back appear to have been spun from purest gold. Though Cadel posed that night as a common servant working under Kentigern's cellarmaster, the duke's daughter favored him with a smile so warm and genuine that he would have liked to run from the castle rather than kill her, though it meant leaving behind all the riches promised to him by the Qirsi. But it was far too late for that. The white-hairs had paid them a great deal, and Jedrek was already spending the gold they were still owed. And then there was all the Qirsi seemed to know about Cadel's past—his family name, the disgrace that had driven him from his father's court. What choice did he really have?

"None of the dead you see here can touch your heart," the duke of Bistari said, gesturing with a glowing hand at the other wraiths who stood with him. "Is that what you want us to believe?"

"It's the truth," Cadel said, "whether you wish to believe it or not."

A small smile touched the dead man's lips, so that with his head cocked to the side, he looked almost like a mischievous child.

"There is one though, isn't there? One that you fear?"

Cadel shuddered, as if the air had suddenly turned colder. He wanted to deny it, though it wouldn't have done him any good. The dead could sense the truth.

"Yes. There's one."

The duke turned to look behind him, and as he did, the mass of luminous figures parted, allowing one last wraith to step forward.

He had known that she would come, of course—why should she have spared him this?—but still Cadel was unprepared for what he saw.

She wore the sapphire gown, though it was unbuttoned to her waist, as it had been that night. Her skin glowed like Panya, the white moon, and her face was as lovely as he remembered, save for the smudge of blood on her cheek. But Cadel's eyes kept falling to her bared breasts and stomach, which were caked with dried blood and scarred with ugly knife wounds.

Lord Tavis's dagger still jutted from the center of her chest, its hilt aimed accusingly at the assassin's heart.

He had wanted to make her murder appear to be a crime born of passion and drunken lust. He had succeeded all too well.

"You stare as if you don't recognize your own handiwork," Brienne said, her voice shockingly cold. "Don't let my lord's dagger fool you. It was your hand guided the blade."

Cadel started to say something, then shook his head.

"Do you deny it?" she asked, her voice rising, like the keening of a storm wind.

He looked up, and met her gaze. Her grey eyes blazed like Qirsi fire and tears ran down her face like drops of dew touched by sunlight.

"*Do you?*" she demanded again.

"No." It came out as a whisper, barely discernible over the sobs of the other worshipers.

"Did I deserve to die like this?" She gestured at her wounds and the blood that covered her. "Did I wrong you in some way?"

"No, my lady."

"Was I a tyrant? Is the world a better place without me?"

Cadel actually managed a smile. "Surely not."

"Then why?" the wraith asked. "Why did you do this to me?"

"I was paid, just as I was paid to kill most of those standing with you."

"You murder for money."

"Yes."

"Why?"

He blinked. "What?"

"Why would any person choose such a profession?"

Cadel stared at her a moment. With all that had happened, and the way she glared at him now, he found it easy to forget that Brienne was just a girl when she died. When he killed her.

"It pays handsomely, my lady," he explained, as if she were simple.

"Of course it does," she said. "I'm not asking why you do it now. I want to know how you started down this path. Certainly you didn't go to your Determining hoping that the stone would show you as a hired blade."

He felt his mouth twitch. Perhaps she wasn't such a child after all.

"It started when he killed me," came a voice from among the other wraiths.

Another man came forward. A boy actually; the young court lad who had been his rival for Venya's love. His name was Eben. Cadel killed him with a blow to the head. The assassin didn't need to see the matted blood behind the wraith's ear to remind him of that. He could still feel his fingers gripping the rock. He could even hear the sound the stone made against the boy's skull.

"Is it true?" Brienne asked, as Eben halted beside her. "Was he the first?"

"Yes, he was."

"Did you kill him for gold as well?"

Cadel shook his head, a thin smile springing to his lips. "No, my lady. I killed him for love. Or at least what I thought at the time was love."

"We were suitors for the same girl," Eben said icily. "He surprised me on the farming lane west of Castle Nistaad, a lonely, desolate stretch of road. Few venture there, and I thought I was alone. I never even saw him."

Brienne narrowed her glowing eyes. "And you enjoyed it? You decided to make it your life's work?"

It was all I could do, he wanted to say. *The only skill I had. I had fled my father's court rather than face judgment for my crime. I needed gold to make my way in the world. What else was there other than killing?* But he had never told any of this to another soul, and he wasn't about to now, not even to this wraith standing before him, so deserving of answers.

"Why does this matter?" Cadel said instead, looking away. "What possible reason—?"

"I want to understand!" the wraith said, her voice rising like a gale. "I'm dead, and I want to know why."

"You're dead because someone hired me to kill you. Isn't that enough?"

"No, it's not! Who was it? Whose gold bought my blood?"

Cadel faltered. "Why would you want to know that?"

"I already told you. I want to understand why you did this to me."

"But surely—"

"Answer me!" the wraith said, the words seeming to echo off the walls and ceiling of the shrine, though among the living only Cadel could hear her.

"No," he said. His hands were trembling abruptly, and he thrust them into his pockets. "I won't tell you. Someone gave me gold and I killed you. That's all you need to know."

"Did they want a war? Is that why they wanted you to do it? So that Tavis's father and my father would go to war?"

"I don't really know. Perhaps."

"Were they Qirsi?"

Cadel felt his face color. She was a wraith, a servant of Bian. Yes, she was crying, and her face was lovely, almost flawless. But this was no girl standing before him. He had to force himself to remember that.

"I won't tell you any more."

The light in her eyes danced like fire demons and she grinned, as did the other luminous figures standing with her. Some of them even laughed.

"You already have," she said. "And I intend to tell my father, and Tavis, and every other living person who can hear me."

He shook his head. "It won't matter."

She stared at him a moment. "The way you say it, one might think that this saddens you, that you'd like me to stop them."

"I take their gold. That's all. It doesn't mean that I share their cause."

"But you protect them. Why?"

"You wouldn't understand."

"You don't know that," the wraith said gently. "Explain it to me."

"No," he said again, his voice resounding through the shrine much as hers had a few moments before. He shook his head. "No," he repeated, more quietly this time. "They live in this world, my world. They know how to find me. I'm not going to risk my life telling you anything."

"So you're afraid of them."

"Yes."

"More than you are of me."

Cadel hadn't thought of it that way before, but there was little use arguing the point. He feared the Qirsi more than he did anything or anyone in the Forelands. It wasn't just that they knew so much about him and his past, it was also that they possessed powers he could scarcely comprehend. His Eandi enemies, even those he respected, didn't frighten him. He knew how to wield a blade, how to shatter a man's larynx with a single blow, and, when necessary, how to blend into his surroundings, be they the crowded marketplace of a city or the dense, silent shadows of a wood. But for all his dreams of striking back at the Qirsi who now so thoroughly controlled his life, he knew that he could never bring himself to risk their wrath.

"More than I am of you, my lady," he finally said. "You may be of the Deceiver's realm, but I only have to see you once in a year."

She nodded, gazing at him silently for several moments. Then she raised a hand and gestured for him to step closer.

"Come to me," she said. A sound like a soft wind rose from the other wraiths, as though they had all sighed as one.

Cadel stood motionless, drawing a grin from Brienne.

"Surely you're not afraid. You wouldn't hesitate to stand beside one of the Qirsi who pays you so handsomely."

He swallowed, and took a step toward her.

"Closer," she said, her grin broadening.

He took another step so that he stood only a few hands' widths from her, close enough to take her hands, close enough to lean forward and taste her lips.

"Now touch me," she whispered. The other wraiths murmured their approval, but Cadel hardly noticed.

A part of him longed to do as she said. He could almost smell the soft, sweet scent she wore the night he killed her. It would have been so easy to caress her cheek with his hand or kiss her smooth brow. Except that it would have meant his death. She could not touch him—as he understood such matters, Bian forbade the wraiths from doing so. No doubt had he not, those who died by Cadel's hand would have taken him long ago. But when the living reached out to touch their dead, they crossed over to the god's realm and were forever lost to the living world.

Brienne's image wavered briefly, as when a tranquil lake is swept by a gust of wind and then again is still. An instant later she stood before him whole and unbloodied, her dress fastened and the dagger gone.

"Touch me," she said again. "Take me in your arms."

"You know that I can't."

"I know that you'll die, if that's what you mean. But wouldn't that be easier than the dark death that awaits you when you leave this shrine? Already Lord Tavis hunts the land for you. I've told him that he should restore his good name and be done with it, but he'll never leave it at that. He's vowed to avenge me, and I've no doubt that he will."

Cadel should have expected this. Perhaps he would have, had it not been for Jedrek's death and his own quest for vengeance against the Qirsi gleaner who killed his friend. He had heard rumors of Tavis's escape from the dungeons of Kentigern and he knew that somehow, so far, the Eibitharians had managed to avoid the civil war that Brienne's murder was supposed to spark. But it had never occurred to him that the boy would come after him. Here was one more reason to find a new partner, and soon.

"He'll die in the attempt, my lady," Cadel said, knowing how his words would hurt her, and regretting even this. He gestured at the wraiths standing with her. "As you can see, I've killed men who were far more formidable than your lord. You'd be wise to warn him off his pursuit before it's too late."

She gave a wan smile. "If you were in my lord's position, would you heed such advice?"

Cadel stared at her, wondering if she asked the question in innocence, or had divined his thoughts. For he was in Tavis's position.

Grinsa jal Arriet. The name repeated itself in his head like the litany of some overzealous cleric, clouding his thoughts by day and keeping him from sleep at night. Cadel knew almost nothing about him except that he was a Revel gleaner who somehow had managed to kill Jedrek.

He might have been more.

The Qirsi woman, another gleaner, had told him as much in Noltierre several turns before, just moments after telling him of Jed's death. Looking back on their conversation now, Cadel wished that he had stayed with her long enough to learn more. She had paid him for Brienne's murder, and had admitted that she sent Jed after Grinsa when the gleaner left the Revel to go to Kentigern. He felt certain that she knew the man far better than she had let on. Still, even the little she did tell him should have been enough to keep Cadel from going after the gleaner.

It's possible that he had other powers. Mists and winds, perhaps others. There were seven Qirsi standing among his dead. Three he had killed in their sleep, the others he had taken in the back. None of them had seen him coming. And in all these cases he knew what powers they possessed before he approached them. How was he supposed to fight Grinsa when he wasn't certain what magic the man wielded? It was suicide. But Brienne was right. Like Lord Tavis of Curgh, who was already hunting the land for the lady's killer, Cadel couldn't keep himself from trying.

"You see?" the wraith said. "You're more like my lord than you care to admit."

"Perhaps," Cadel said. "But if he finds me, I'll still have to kill him."

"Have you ever fought a man who was intent on vengeance?" she asked.

He considered this for some time. "No," he said at last. "I don't suppose I have."

She nodded sagely, as if death had given her wisdom beyond her years. "I see."

A number of the other wraiths laughed appreciatively.

Cadel heard the city bells ringing in the distance. It was too early yet for the midnight tolling. This had to be the gate closing. The night was just starting, and already he was weary.

"Perhaps you wish to sleep?" Brienne asked, sounding as innocent as a babe.

He merely shook his head, as the wraiths leered at him hungrily. Few of the living ever slept on Pitch Night in Bian's Turn. The dead could not touch a man to kill him, but there was nothing to keep them from huddling so close to his sleeping form that the slightest movement on his part—a mere gesture in the throes of some horrible dream—might send him to the god's realm.

"Well," Brienne said, "you won't touch me, and you won't sleep." She flickered like a candle once again so that she stood before him as she had when she first appeared, scarred and half naked. "How do you propose we pass the rest of the night?"

"You could leave me," Cadel said. "Grant me peace and silence."

The ghost smiled. "Why would we want to do that?"

The other wraiths came closer, crowding around him like eager buyers in a marketplace pressing to see some wares. Cadel held himself still, closing his eyes and readying himself for what he knew would come next. It was said to be common—something that all the wraiths did on this night. It even had a name: the Excoriation. Usually it began immediately, with nightfall and the appearance of the first wraiths. But tonight had been different, perhaps because of Brienne. Not that it mattered. This night's Excoriation, like all of them, would last for hours.

They all began to shout at him, berating him for what he had done, not only to them, but to their loved ones. Their voices buffeted him like storm winds on the Scabbard coast, the din they created making his head pound. Yet, perhaps due to some power the wraiths possessed, or through some trick of the god who had sent them, Cadel could hear each of them. Brienne upbraided him for Tavis's suffering in the days after her death, when her father tortured him in Kentigern's prison. Chago told him of the tears shed by his son and wife in the few days since his death in the Great Forest. Eben blamed him for his mother's descent into madness and his father's suicide. On and on they went, and Cadel had no choice but to stand and listen.

Most of it he had heard before—the lament of the dead did not change much over the years—but that did little to make the night pass faster. They would continue this until dawn, as they did every year. Telling him all that they had dreamed of doing with their lives, of that which he had denied them with his blade, his garrote, or his poisons. If they ran out of things to say, they merely started over, forcing him to hear every word again. But he didn't have to look at them anymore; at least he didn't have to see Brienne.

He stood motionless, save for his trembling hands and the twitching muscles in his legs. He felt sweat running down his face, making his skin itch. But he dared not move, even to wipe his brow. He didn't have to open his eyes to sense how close the wraiths had gathered around him. His skin prickled at the mere thought of it. He could almost feel their breath stirring his hair, though he knew this was impossible.

There was nothing for him to do but endure their abuse and cling to the knowledge that dawn had to come eventually. He tried to occupy his mind with song, but their voices drowned out his own. He called forth an image of Jedrek, who had come to him as a friend earlier in this turn, on the Night of Two Moons. But the dead would not allow him any diversions. Their words demanded his attention, and he hadn't the strength to resist them.

He could not have guessed the time—if the midnight bells rang, he didn't hear them. But after what seemed a lifetime, Cadel realized that the voices had stopped. Slowly, reluctantly, he opened his eyes. Brienne stood before him looking young and sad, despite her bloody wounds. The rest of the glowing figures had vanished.

"It'll be dawn soon," she said, her voice low. "The others left me to see you to the end."

Cadel didn't know what to say. His dead had never done this for one of their own before. Just as they had never waited to begin the Excoriation. In his mind, he saw once more how they had parted to let her come forward when this night began. Even the wraiths could see how special she was, how undeserving of this fate. *What have I done?*

"You said earlier that you only have to face me once in a year, that you feared the Qirsi more because they were a part of your world."

Cadel nodded. "I remember."

"I believe this will be the only time in your life when you will have to face me in this way. By this time next year, I expect you'll be dead and we'll be together in the Deceiver's realm."

He felt a chill run through his body, as if some unseen ghost had run a cold finger down his spine.

"Is that prophecy, my lady," he asked, fighting to keep his voice steady, "or an idle attempt to frighten me?"

The ghost shrugged. "I'm merely telling you what I think. You can make of it whatever you will."

"You'll forgive me if I hope you're wrong."

"I will. It's the only forgiveness you'll ever have from me."

"And still it may be more than I deserve."

"Yes," she said. "It may be."

In the next instant she was gone, and the first silver light of dawn touched the stained-glass window at the farthest end of the shrine. Cadel closed his eyes briefly, reaching out a hand to steady himself against the nearest wall, and taking a long, ragged breath. The dawn bells tolled in the city, the sound drifting among the stone pillars of the sanctuary with the morning devotions of Bian's clerics. It was time for Cadel to be leaving.

He straightened and began walking toward the main doors of the shrine. Before he could reach them, however, he found himself standing before the prioress.

"I heard you cry out once or twice," she said. "It was a difficult night?"

The assassin gave a wan smile. "Yes."

"More difficult than most?"

"More difficult than all that have come before."

She raised an eyebrow. "I'm sorry to hear that. I hope our sanctuary brought you some comfort."

"It did, Mother Prioress. I wouldn't have wanted to endure last night anywhere else."

A smile touched her lips and was gone. "That's kind of you to say."

She turned away and Cadel started toward the doors once more.

"If last night was so difficult," she said, stopping him, "it may be time you considered a new profession. Much of what the god teaches us can only be gleaned through patience and contemplation. But on occasion, his lessons are as clear as the new day."

He gazed at her briefly, then nodded. "Thank you, Mother Prioress."

She smiled again, but Cadel could see in her eyes that she had little hope he would heed her words.

He left the shrine as quickly as he could. He had much to do, he told himself. Lord Tavis was hunting the Forelands for him, and Cadel himself had quarry to pursue. And before he could turn his mind to any of that, he wished to pay a visit to a tavern in Dantrielle. It was called the Red Boar, and it was there, nearly eighteen years before, that he had first met Jedrek. He could only hope that this visit would bring him such good fortune.

In any case, he had no more time to waste in Solkara.

Or so he wanted to believe. He knew, however, that the truth lay elsewhere. He wanted to put as much distance as possible between himself and the sanctuary, to rid himself of the memory of the previous night, to be sure, but also to get away from the half-blind prioress who seemed to see him so plainly.

Chapter
Three

✦

Orvinti, Aneira, Bohdan's Moon waxing

T he four dukes raised their goblets, the shifting flames in the hearth reflected on the polished silver.

"To Chago," Brall said. "May Bian grant him a place of honor and may the Underrealm shine with his light."

"To Chago," the others said as one.

They sipped the wine, then settled back in their seats, Brall still holding his cup so that it balanced on the arm of his chair.

Another gust of wind made the shutters rattle and stirred the tapestries hanging on his walls. He loved to see the hills covered with snow, Lake Orvinti shimmering with their reflection. But judging from the winds that already blew down from the Scabbard, this year's freeze was going to be harsher than most.

Fortunately, the growing turns had been generous. His people wouldn't starve, and there was plenty of food and wine to share with his guests. Such company was a rare luxury this time of year, and though he regretted the circumstances that had brought the other men to western Aneira, he was glad to have them in his castle just the same. Most dukes chose not to travel in the colder turns; usually they spent the waxing of Bohdan's Turn preparing for the god's festival on the Night of Two Moons.

Had it not been for Chago's death and the funeral in Bistari two days earlier, Brall too would have been busy with the celebration. As it was, he had been eager to return to Orvinti. Storms struck the Hills of Shanae every year around this time, and the last thing Brall needed was to be blocked from his castle so close to Bohdan's Night. So, after Chago's funeral, when Pazice insisted that he invite the dukes back to Orvinti, he was more than happy to comply. Most refused, as he knew they would. It would have taken many of them farther from their homes and at least a few of them—the duke of Rassor came to mind—didn't like him very much.

Those who did come, Ansis, Bertin, and Tebeo, were friends and allies of both Bistari and Orvinti. To the extent that any duke in Aneira trusted another, they trusted each other. It almost seemed to Brall that the god had granted him an extra gift this turn: for this one night, he was surrounded by friends.

"It was a good service," Ansis said, his pale eyes fixed on the fire.

Bertin shook his head. "It was a load of dung, just as I knew it would be from the start. Maybe if Carden had allowed Chago's prelate to preside, there would have been a measure of truth in it. But with the king's prelate controlling everything . . ." He shook his head a second time, a look of disgust on his square face. A moment later he drained his wine, then held out his goblet so that one of Brall's servants could pour him more.

Ansis frowned, looking even younger than usual. "I just meant that it seemed to do Ria and Silbron some good to hear so many people speak of Chago so fondly." He glanced at Brall and then at Tebeo, as if pleading with them to agree.

"I was surprised that the king allowed me to speak," Tebeo said. "I didn't expect that, not after I sided with Chago in their dispute over the road fees."

"He wouldn't allow me to speak," Bertin said, raising his cup again. He had consumed a good deal of wine this day. "And he refused Tounstrel's request, too. He couldn't very well keep all of us silent."

Brall cast a look at the duke of Noltierre. "I'm sure he was tempted to try."

Bertin grinned and nodded. "I wouldn't doubt it."

"Even Carden wouldn't have gone that far," Tebeo said. "He might have considered it, but he knows better."

"He didn't hesitate to have poor Chago killed," Bertin said. "Why would he care about the rest?"

Ansis sat forward. "Precisely because he had Chago killed. He couldn't silence all of us without making himself look guilty."

"Don't be an idiot!" Bertin said, rolling his eyes. "He had the man garroted. He wanted us to know who was responsible. It was intended as a warning to others who'd be as bold in opposing him as Chago was."

Ansis chewed his lip briefly. "Is that what you think, Tebeo?"

The duke of Dantrielle looked at Brall before answering. With Chago gone, the two of them represented the greatest threat to Carden's rule. Bertin hated the king more than either of them, as did Vidor of Tounstrel, but neither Noltierre nor Tounstrel was counted among the kingdom's more powerful houses. Kett, like Noltierre, was at best a middle-tier house, and even had it been more, Ansis's youth would have kept him from exerting much influence within the court. Until recently Mertesse had wielded a good deal of power. Its army was considered one of the finest in the land, and its treasury rivaled that of Bistari and Orvinti. But the dukes of Mertesse had allied themselves with House Solkara long ago, and with Rouel's death during the siege at Kentigern several turns back, the dukedom had passed to Rowan, an unproven and unimpressive youth.

Among the great houses, only Solkara, Orvinti, and Dantrielle were still led by men of experience. Surely it had not escaped the king's notice that both Brall and Tebeo had, at one time or another, sided with Chago in taking issue with his decrees.

All of which made Tebeo's answer to Ansis's question that much more significant. Though he was among friends in the privacy of Brall's quarters, the duke would have to choose his words with care. Still, even knowing this, Brall was surprised by Tebeo's reply.

"I might have seen it as a warning," he said, "had I believed that Carden was responsible."

Bertin nearly choked on a mouthful of wine. "*What?* 'Had you believed—'? You mean you don't?"

"I'm not as certain of it as you are."

"You saw his body before they lit the pyre! Good as he was, the embalmer couldn't hide the marks on Chago's neck. And as if that wasn't enough, the captain of Bistari's guard told me that they found a broken strap in Chago's hand bearing the Solkaran crest."

"I heard that as well," Tebeo said.

"So isn't it clear to you what happened?"

"I think," Brall said, "that Tebeo finds it a bit too clear." He faced the duke. "Is that right?"

Tebeo nodded. "Precisely." He rubbed a hand across his brow, staring at his wine as if searching the goblet for the correct words.

Of all of them, Tebeo looked least like a powerful noble. He was short and portly, with a kind, round face and large dark eyes. Pazice had once remarked that he resembled an alemaster more than he did a duke. But Brall, who had never been shy about complimenting himself on his own intelligence and foresight, thought Tebeo the wisest leader in Aneira.

"In all likelihood you're right, Bertin," the duke said at last. "Vidor showed me the message Chago sent to him and I understand that you and Ansis received similar ones. I'm certain that Carden heard about them as well. Chago made no secret of how angry he was about the fees; I have no doubt that he would have challenged the king openly at the first opportunity. And knowing what I do of Carden, I'm also certain that he would have found Chago's defiance galling. No king is above murder, ours least of all." He paused, shaking his head slowly.

"Then what?" Bertin asked.

Tebeo took a breath. "We've all heard talk of the conspiracy. I've even heard some say that Qirsi were behind the unrest in Eibithar."

Bertin snorted. "The Eibitharians are animals. They don't need any help butchering themselves."

"Perhaps not. But coming so quickly on the heels of their troubles, this just strikes me as . . . odd. They say it was Chago's first minister who found him. That makes me wonder as well."

"I can't believe what I'm hearing," Noltierre said. "Carden's reek is all over Chago's body, and you're trying to blame the white-hairs." Bertin turned to Brall. "And what about you, Orvinti? Does Tebeo speak for you as well?"

Brall sipped his wine, not quite certain how to answer. He shared Tebeo's suspicions, but he wasn't ready yet to give them voice. He would have been happy to pass the night in silence, allowing the duke of Dantrielle to carry the burden of this discussion. But more than that, he was troubled by the extent to which he found himself fearing the Qirsi. His own first minister had been with him for six years—not a long time, but enough to have nurtured a good deal of trust on his part. Fetnalla had offered him wise counsel since coming to Orvinti. As a younger man he had thought it impossible that he would ever consider any Qirsi a friend, but in recent years he had come to see the minister that way, as had the duchess. He didn't think it in her nature to betray him. Until the last few days, however, he would have said the same thing of Peshkal, Chago's first minister.

"Well?" Bertin prodded.

"I'm not certain what I think," Brall finally answered. "It appears that this was the king's doing, and we all know that Chago gave House Solkara reason enough to want him dead."

"But?"

Brall turned toward the voice. Ansis was eyeing him closely, looking young still, but not frightened as Brall might have expected.

"But I also agree with Tebeo that it all seems a bit too easy."

"What of the garroting?" Bertin asked. "What of the scrap of leather in Chago's hand?"

"That scrap of leather is part of what bothers me. Had Chago really pulled it off the murderer's belt or baldric, wouldn't the other man have noticed? Wouldn't he have retrieved it?"

Bertin threw up his hands. "It was a Solkaran garroting on behalf of the king! Why would he bother with a useless piece of leather? Everyone was going to know who killed the man anyway."

"What if it was the Qirsi?" Ansis asked in an even voice.

"It wasn't the Qirsi."

"What if it was?" the young duke said again, his voice rising as he glared at Bertin. After a moment he faced Brall again. "What could we do about it?"

"Do about it?"

"Well surely we'd have to do something. Warn the king and the other dukes. Interrogate our ministers and Chago's as well."

"Warn the king of what?" Tebeo asked. "I promise you, he's heard the same whisperings as we. We might as well warn him that the snows are coming. And as for the ministers, what would you ask them in these interrogations? Would you ask them what they've heard about this so-called conspiracy, or would you come right out and demand to know if they're traitors?"

Ansis gazed toward the fire. "I don't know," he said quietly, shaking his head. "But even if we just suspect that the Qirsi might have been involved in Chago's murder, we ought to do something."

Tebeo let out a sigh. "I probably shouldn't have said what I did, Ansis. The Qirsi have been on my mind a good bit lately, but I have no reason to think that they killed Chago. Had anyone other than his minister found the body, I never even would have considered it. Bertin's right: it was most likely one of Carden's men. And if it wasn't there are a hundred other possibilities I'd consider before I blamed the white-hairs."

"Like what?"

The duke shrugged. "Thieves. The wood's crawling with them."

"Not this time of year," Ansis said. "And whoever did this left Chago's jeweled dagger and sword untouched. I saw Silbron wearing both of them at the funeral."

"Maybe another duke, then," Brall said, "someone who wanted Chago dead for some reason, but wanted the king blamed for it."

Bertin shook his head. "Only the duke of a major house would have much to gain from such a act. Rowan of Mertesse is as loyal to the Solkarans as his father, and even if he wasn't, he's not clever enough to try this." He looked first at Brall, then at Tebeo, a small smile tugging at the corners of his mouth. "That leaves the two of you, and I've seen no evidence suggesting that you're clever enough, either."

All of them laughed, though Ansis quickly grew serious again.

"The truth is," he said, "there are no other explanations, are there? Either Carden had this done, or the Qirsi. Those are the only possibilities."

Tebeo said nothing. Brall kept his silence as well, drinking what was left of his wine and watching the others.

"The king did this, boy," Bertin said quietly. "I don't like it any more than you do. But that's just the nature of the man. He doesn't like rebels and he liked Chago least of all. The poor old fool just pushed him too far this time."

Ansis turned to Dantrielle. "Tebeo?"

"Carden hated him enough to do this, and he wouldn't hesitate to have any of us killed if he thought we were threatening his sovereignty." He started to say more, then stopped himself. "He certainly didn't look aggrieved at the funeral," he went on a few moments later.

Bertin sneered. "Of course he didn't. The bastard got just what he wanted."

Ansis sat back in his chair and drank some wine. "He did look awfully pleased. I guess I'm not certain which bothers me more, the idea that our king could do this, or the possibility that Chago was the victim of some white-hair conspiracy."

Brall had been thinking much the same thing and he almost said so. But the matter seemed to have run its course, and he saw no sense in rekindling the discussion, at least not just then.

Bells rang in the city, and Ansis sat forward again.

"Is that the gate close, or is it midnight already?"

"That's only the gates," Brall said.

The young man grinned. "Good." He stood and stretched his legs. "Still, I've a long ride awaiting me in the morning. I should sleep."

Brall rose as well. "Of course, Ansis. One of the guards will see you back to your chamber." He stepped forward and kissed the duke lightly on each cheek. "I'm glad you came. I hope next time it's under kinder circumstances, but I'm glad just the same."

"As am I," Ansis said. "You'll thank Pazice for me?"

"You can thank her yourself in the morning. We'll accompany you to the city gates."

"I'd like that."

"Wait a moment, boy," Bertin called, as Ansis stepped to the door. "I'll walk with you. I've got a journey ahead of me as well." He nodded to Brall. "Always a pleasure, Orvinti. Good food, good wine, and I always enjoy seeing the hills and lake, even this late in the year."

"You're welcome any time, Bertin. You know that."

Noltierre give a quick smile. " 'Til the morning then."

Brall closed the door and looked at Tebeo.

"Are you going as well?"

Tebeo shook his head. "I've a shorter ride than they do."

Brall nodded, knowing that wasn't the real reason his friend chose to stay. Dantrielle may have been closer than Kett or Noltierre, but it was still more than thirty leagues from Orvinti. It would be several days before the duke reached his own realm. Brall didn't say this, of course. He merely had the servants bring another flask of wine before dismissing them for the night.

Even after they were alone, the two dukes merely sat for some time, sipping their wine and watching the fire, which had burned low. Wind lashed the shutters again and Brall knelt by the hearth to place another log on the glowing embers.

"Our young friend may have a point," Tebeo said as the duke lowered himself back into his chair. "It may be that one of us needs to speak with the king."

Brall grinned. "One of us?" It would have to be him, and they both knew it. In the eyes of the king, Tebeo had been too closely allied with Chago. By siding first with one and then the other, Brall had managed to keep House Orvinti from becoming entangled in the dispute between Solkara and Bistari.

"All right," Tebeo said, smiling as well. "You should speak with him."

"To what end? You don't expect me to ask him if he had Chago killed."

Tebeo shrugged, the smile lingering on his round face. "Why not? As Bertin said, the murderer did everything but write 'The king did this' on Chago's neck. If it was Carden's work, he meant for us to know it."

"And if it wasn't Carden's work?"

Dantrielle's smile vanished. "Then we have a problem."

"The Qirsi."

"This is not just idle talk, Brall. The conspiracy is real. I'm certain of it."

"What have you heard?" Brall asked, not really wanting to know.

"Rumors mostly. Speculation. But I've heard similar tales from so many quarters that I can't dismiss them anymore. In the past few years, Eandi nobles have been murdered in nearly every kingdom in the Forelands."

Brall forced a grin. "That's hardly unheard of, Tebeo. As Bertin said, the Eibitharians don't need any help butchering themselves. Unfortunately, that goes for the rest of us as well. Court assassinations are as old as the throne itself."

Tebeo shook his head. "These are different; at least some of them are. Take the incident in Jetaya early last year."

"Jetaya? You mean Hanan? He was poisoned by men from Rouvin. The two houses have been rivals for centuries."

"He was killed with sleeping camas—seems his food was laced with it."

"So?"

"Camas works slowly, and its symptoms are subtle compared to most. In most cases, the victim is in a death sleep before those around him suspect anything."

Brall raised an eyebrow. "I had no idea you were so well versed in the ways of poison. I'll have to remember that the next time I'm asked to a feast in Dantrielle."

"This is no joke, Brall."

He opened his hands. "I'm sorry, Teb. I guess I don't see your point."

"My point is this: Hanan was killed with a poison that must be used in large doses. It's rare and costly, works slowly, and is difficult to spot. Whoever killed him went to a great deal of effort and did so with some skill. Yet within a day of his death, guards in Jetaya found a vial that had held sleeping camas and were able to determine beyond question that it came from Rouvin. Doesn't that seem a bit strange?"

Brall had to admit that it did. "But that's only one—"

"Cyro of Yserne was garroted, just like Chago. And just like Chago, he had recently challenged the authority of the royal house."

"All that proves is that the queen of Sanbira is no more tolerant of dissenters than our own king."

Tebeo eyed him briefly before looking away and raising his goblet to his lips. Again they sat in silence for a time.

"Earlier this evening you were agreeing with me," the duke finally said, his voice so low that Brall almost couldn't hear him for the wind and the snapping of the flames. "What happened?"

Brall wasn't certain how to answer. The truth was, he did agree with much of what Tebeo had said this night. He was neither blind nor a fool. Nobles in the Forelands were dying in strange, terrible ways, and in numbers that chilled his blood. But talk of this conspiracy disturbed him even more. Qirsi ministers lived in every castle and served every noble in the Forelands, from the lowliest baron of Wethyrn to the emperor of Braedon.

Even if a mere fraction of the white-hairs were party to this plot, the danger to all the Eandi courts would be immeasurable.

In a way, though, that thought troubled him far less than the notion that Fetnalla could be a traitor. Had she deceived him all these years? Had she been treating him with respect and kindness, while in secret thinking him an ass whom she could use for her own purposes? Worse, if she was allied with these renegade Qirsi, hadn't she proved him to be just that? Better that Chago had been killed by the king, or thieves, or a madman who chanced upon him in the wood. Anything but this.

"Nothing happened," Brall said after a long silence. "I still agree that there was something a bit transparent about Chago's murder. I'll grant as well that recently there have been too many murders of a similar nature throughout the kingdoms. I'm just not ready yet to blame each one on some white-hair plot to rule the Forelands."

"I don't want it to be true either, Brall. But if we ignore our suspicions out of fear, we help their cause."

Tebeo had always been a bit too clever for Brall's taste.

"What would they have to gain by killing Chago?" Brall asked, knowing how foolish he sounded.

"Come now, my friend. You're smarter than that. If the Qirsi did this, they didn't do it to rid themselves of Chago. They did it to divide the kingdom, to deepen the rift between Chago's allies and those of the king. That's what alarms me so. Chago's murder threatens to weaken Aneira; the garroting of Yserne has already emboldened those who would oppose the queen of Sanbira; Lady Brienne's murder almost caused a civil war in Eibithar, and still might. Perhaps there's nothing tying these murders to one another. From all I've heard, it certainly seems that the Curgh boy killed Kentigern's daughter. I can't help but notice, however, that each death further weakens the Eandi courts. It's been nearly two hundred years since any kingdom in the Forelands suffered through a civil war. Yet right now, at least three kingdoms, including our own, appear to be moving toward some kind of conflict. Doesn't that strike you as odd?"

"So you think they want to rule the Forelands? You think they plan to weaken every court north of the Border Range and conquer us that way?"

Tebeo shook his head, looking grave, and older than Brall had ever imagined he could. "I don't know. It may be that simple."

"Simple?" Brall repeated, giving a short, breathless laugh. "What you're talking about would require a conspiracy so vast . . ." He stopped, shaking his head as well. "I don't believe it's possible."

"Actually, it wouldn't take nearly as many people as you think. All that they've accomplished so far could be done by fewer than a hundred men and women, provided they were placed properly."

"But eventually they would need more. Or do you think that a hundred Qirsi sorcerers can defeat the combined might of our armies?"

The duke stared at him sadly. "Don't you understand? If this keeps up, they won't have to worry about the combined might of the Aneiran army, much less all the armies of the Forelands." He turned his gaze to the fire once more and sipped his wine. "Besides, it's probably far more than a hundred. And if it is, they must have a leader, someone who'll be able to bring them together when the time comes."

For all the thought he had given to the possibility of a Qirsi conspiracy, Brall had never imagined a single man or woman leading it. He had been foolish, of course; he saw that immediately. If such a movement was real, it would naturally have a master, someone whose vision and will inspired the rest and bound them to one another in a single cause. Still, like everything else Tebeo had told him this night, the image of this Qirsi leader, this white-haired sovereign-in-waiting, though faceless and nameless, served only to deepen his dread.

"You think they've chosen someone already? A would-be king or queen?"

Tebeo gave a wan smile. "I think it's much worse than that," he said. "They won't have chosen this person; he or she will have chosen them. The Qirsi don't follow nobles or monarchs. They follow Weavers."

If Tebeo had intended to scare him into acting, it worked. He could think of no response except to say, "I'll ride to Solkara before the snows begin. I'm certain Carden will see me."

"Thank you," his friend said. "If I thought the king would hear me on this matter, I'd gladly go myself. But under the circumstances, I believe you're the best choice."

Brall nodded, but said nothing.

They lapsed into another lengthy silence, both of them gazing at the flames and occasionally lifting their goblets to drink. After a time, Tebeo sat forward and rubbed his hands together.

"I should return to my chambers," he said softly. "My ride may be short, but I'm still an old man, and I want to be back in Dantrielle before the wind blows any colder."

"Of course."

Still, neither of them moved.

"Have you spoken with your ministers about any of this?" Brall asked.

Tebeo looked up from the fire. "Not yet, no. I've wanted to, but I wouldn't know how to start such a conversation. Particularly with Evanthya. Approaching my underministers will be difficult enough, but she's been with me a long time."

"I've been sitting here thinking the same thing. How do I ask Fetnalla about a Qirsi conspiracy without making her think that I'm accusing her of betraying me?"

"I suppose we just have to ask them. This matter is too important to let our fear of offending them keep us silent."

"Offending them?" Brall said. "I'm worried about ending up like Chago."

Evanthya woke with first light, and reached to the other side of the bed before remembering that she was alone.

"Appearances," Fetnalla had said the previous night, pulling away with one last kiss and dressing in the candlelight. As if a single word could explain everything. That they were two women in love would have raised eyebrows among some, particularly in the noble courts, but that was not why they concealed their relationship.

"I think you look fine," Evanthya said, trying to keep her tone light.

"That's not what I mean and you know it. Our dukes may be allies now, but that can change. They shouldn't know about us. Certainly Brall shouldn't. He'd be . . . displeased."

Evanthya wasn't sure how her duke would feel about it, but that hardly mattered. Fetnalla had made up her mind long ago. They could steal away for a few hours at a time, but whether in Orvinti or Dantrielle, they always spent their nights alone.

Early as it was, Evanthya could already hear the voices of Orvinti's guards through the shuttered windows. She swung herself out of bed, pulled on her riding clothes, and slipped silently from her chamber. Stepping lightly through the castle corridors, she made her way to the nearest of the winding stone stairways and hurried down to the garden, where they were to meet.

Her duke had returned to his chamber late the previous night, and though she knew he would be impatient to begin their ride back to Dantrielle, she was certain that he would not be ready to leave Orvinti much before the midmorning bells. She would have liked to rest a bit longer herself, but this conversation couldn't wait.

The winds that had buffeted the castle through most of the night had died away. Still, the air was cold, and a fine, chill mist hung over the ward.

Too late, she wished she had worn her cloak. The garden was empty—Fetnalla had not yet arrived—and she briefly considered retrieving the cloak from her chambers. But she didn't want to risk waking the duke, who was sleeping in the chamber next to hers. Better to be cold. She crossed her arms over her chest and began to walk slowly among the hedgerows and empty flower patches.

She had seen the gardens of Orvinti in Amon's Turn, just after the last of the rains, so she knew how brilliant they could be. During milder winters when she visited the castle, some of the hardier blooms had still been in the ground. But this year the only color that remained in the garden came from the spidery blue flowers of the hunter's hazel, which clung to the otherwise bare limbs of the trees lining the castle walls, heedless of the cold. A pair of ravens hopped on the brown grass at the far end of the ward, near the entrance to the kitchen tower, fighting over scraps of food and croaking loudly at one another. Another joined them, gliding to the ground like a winged shadow in the grey mist. A moment later, a fourth landed nearby. Evanthya shivered. According to the Mettai, the Eandi sorcerers who lived in the hills and forests of the southern Forelands, four ravens were a death omen.

"The Mettai legends don't apply to the Qirsi."

Evanthya turned at the sound of the voice, smiling despite the cold. "I didn't know that. Is that what the Mettai say, or only the Qirsi?"

Fetnalla tipped her head to the side and grinned, her pale eyes, the color of fire, seeming to gather all the light this grey morning had to give. She had her hair pulled back the way Evanthya liked, and her pale cheeks were touched with pink. She wore a heavy cloak, much like the one Evanthya had left in her room, but even with it draped over her shoulders and tied at the neck, she looked slender and graceful, like the tall white herons Evanthya saw in the shallows of the Rassor during the warm turns.

"It's common knowledge," Fetnalla said, walking toward her. "I'm surprised you hadn't heard."

She stopped in front of Evanthya and kissed her, her lips soft and cool with the mist. Evanthya returned the kiss hungrily, but then made herself pull away, glancing around to see if anyone was watching, though she knew they were alone in the gardens.

"There's no one here but us," Fetnalla said, still grinning. "And the high windows are all shuttered."

Evanthya shrugged, feeling her face color. "I know. But as you've said so many times, 'appearances.' "

Fetnalla started to say something else, but then shook her head, appearing to think better of it. "It's not worth arguing about." She flashed a quick smile. "Not right now at least."

Evanthya nodded, knowing what was coming. It had crept into all they shared, hanging over them like a cloud since early in the year. They had danced around the issue for the past few days, since Evanthya first reached Bistari for the duke's funeral. They hadn't spoken of it since coming to Orvinti, but Fetnalla had never been one to let a matter drop before having her say, particularly a matter of such importance.

"I'm still not certain I can do this," Evanthya said, turning to stare at the ravens.

"We can't stay out of it forever, love. These are Qirsi men and women we're talking about. It's not out in the open yet, and may not be for another year or more. But make no mistake, they're fighting a war for the future of the Forelands. Now, we can watch from the towers of our castles, or we can do something about it."

She had learned long ago that there was little to be gained from arguing with Fetnalla about almost anything. But Evanthya could be headstrong as well, and in this case she couldn't stop herself.

"And what about our dukes?" she asked. "You worry about Brall learning that we're lovers. That's a trifle, next to this."

"If we do this right, our dukes will never know."

Evanthya took a breath. *If we do this right.* When it came right down to it, most of this burden would fall on her shoulders, not Fetnalla's.

"We're going to be paying someone a good deal of gold. People tend to notice such things. Even assuming that we can find enough money, keeping it quiet is going to be hard."

Fetnalla produced a small leather pouch from within her cloak and handed it to her. It was quite heavy and it jingled like bells on a dancer's shoe.

"That's nearly sixty qinde," Fetnalla said. "It's most of what I have, so be careful with it."

"This is your money?"

Fetnalla nodded.

"I can't take this. There must be another—"

She tried to hand the pouch back to Fetnalla, but the minister merely shook her head.

"Please, love. I'm asking a good deal of you already. I have no choice in the matter. Orvinti is too remote for me to do any more. But at least I can take care of the gold. You may have to add a gold piece or two, but this should cover most of it."

Evanthya stared at the pouch chagrined at having felt overburdened a moment before. "I'll guard it with my life," she said softly.

Fetnalla laughed. "Well, don't go that far. It's only gold. Just don't go wagering it on a game of dice."

She smiled and looked up, her eyes meeting Fetnalla's. "I promise."

"You know where to go?"

Evanthya nodded, the smile leaving her face as quickly as it had come. "There are a few places, one in particular. It shouldn't be a problem. A person can buy anything in the alleyways of Dantrielle."

Fetnalla grinned again, the same crooked grin Evanthya remembered from their first meeting in Solkara so many years ago. "I'm counting on that."

They fell silent, their eyes still locked, and Evanthya longed to kiss her again. But at that moment, she heard a footfall behind her and the jangling of a guard's blade.

"Good morrow to you, First Minister!" the man called.

Fetnalla didn't take her eyes off Evanthya, but she raised a hand in greeting. "And to you," she answered. "Is the duke awake?"

"He is, First Minister. And the duke of Dantrielle also. They're asking for the two of you."

She finally looked at the guard, and Evanthya turned as well. He was a large man with a thick neck. Eandi, of course. They all looked the same to her.

"Let them know we'll be along in a moment," Fetnalla said.

The man nodded once and retreated into the castle.

Fetnalla gazed at her again. "We probably won't have another chance to speak alone before you ride. Is there more we need to discuss?"

"Are you sure about all this, Fetnalla? I know you want to do something, but this . . ." She shook her head, uncertain of how to finish the thought. "There are other paths we could take," she finally said.

"I know there are. But we've already waited longer than we should have. Everything else we talked about would take too long. It's time, love. We can't delay anymore."

Evanthya nodded. She had known just what Fetnalla would say, but she had to ask. "All right then. I'll take care of it."

"I know you will. Anything else?"

"Yes," she said, smiling. "When will I see you again?"

Fetnalla smiled as well. "Soon."

Evanthya raised an eyebrow. With the snows coming, it was likely to be several turns at least before one of their dukes traveled to see the other.

"Well, as soon as I can find some excuse to suggest a journey to Dantrielle."

Evanthya reached out for Fetnalla's hand and gave it a squeeze, unwilling to chance more with the dukes awake and guards moving about the castle. "Think of something quickly."

They made their way back to Brall's hall, where they found the dukes and Orvinti's duchess preparing for a formal breakfast. As was customary at such functions, the two first ministers were seated together, but both of the women made a point of speaking with their other seating partner. Evanthya carried on a pleasant but empty conversation with Brall's wife, and Fetnalla ended up speaking at length with Orvinti's prelate, for whom she had privately expressed nothing but contempt.

By the time they finished their meal, servants had gathered the duke's belongings and carried them down to the stables where their horses were waiting, already brushed and saddled. Brall and Tebeo kept their farewells brief, leaving their ministers little choice but to do the same, though they had already said their goodbyes.

Evanthya, Tebeo, and the rest of the duke's party climbed onto their mounts, offered one last word of thanks to the duke and duchess of Orvinti, and rode out the castle gate. The last Evanthya saw of Fetnalla, she was merely standing beside Brall, gazing back at her and looking lovely in the silver-grey light, her white hair, dampened by the mist, clinging to her brow.

The road out of Orvinti wound around the south end of the lake before following the River Orvinti northward toward the Rassor. However, Tebeo chose to leave the road almost immediately so that they might cross the northeast corner of the Plain of Stallions, thus shortening their journey. The company rode in silence for some time, Tebeo seeming lost in thought, though he never strayed from Evanthya's side. The day remained grey and the wind began to rise again, knifing through Evanthya's cloak and tunic as if they were made of parchment.

"I noticed you were up and about the castle quite early this morning," the duke said abruptly, as Evanthya watched a falcon soar over the plain.

"Yes, my lord."

"You were speaking with Fetnalla?"

She glanced over at him, but he continued to face forward.

"I was, my lord."

"What about?"

"We were speaking of Lord Bistari, my lord. His assassination has us both concerned."

It wasn't a complete lie, though it was far from the plain truth. Still, Evanthya surprised herself by the ease with which she deceived him. Fetnalla would have been proud.

"Concerned?"

"Yes, my lord. Concerned for our dukes, as well as for our kingdom. Both of you have opposed the king in the past. If this can happen in Bistari, what's to stop it from happening in Orvinti or Dantrielle?"

"So you feel certain that the king is responsible."

She turned to him again and this time he met her gaze. The look they shared lasted only a moment, but that was long enough for her to see fear in his dark eyes, and something else that made her chest ache.

"All the evidence suggests that he is, my lord. Don't you agree?"

Tebeo didn't answer immediately, and they rode wordlessly for a time. The falcon still glided above them, darting and wheeling in the wind like a festival dancer.

"You've heard talk of a conspiracy?" His eyes flicked in her direction for just an instant. "A Qirsi conspiracy?"

A denial would have raised his suspicions. "I have, my lord."

"Do you believe what you've heard?"

Again, what choice did she have but to be honest with him? "I do. Such stories have come from every kingdom in the land save Uulrann. It would be dangerous to dismiss all of them as idle rumors."

Tebeo nodded but offered no response. He seemed to be waiting for her to say more.

Evanthya took a breath. The question hung between them, waiting to be given voice. Better she should ask it and hear his reply, before he turned the question on her.

"Do you think the Qirsi killed Lord Bistari?"

The duke gave a small shrug. "With all I've heard, I have to think it possible. You said yourself that you fear for the kingdom. I fear for Sanbira as well, and even for Eibithar. It seems to me that every murder in the past year has moved one of our neighbors closer to a crisis. Now it's our turn. Eandi nobles are dying throughout the land. Whom should I blame but the Qirsi?"

Evanthya conceded the point with a single nod. She had never for a moment doubted her duke's intelligence, but she was surprised to hear how much thought he had given these matters. He hadn't mentioned any of this to her before today. She could guess why.

"I'm sorry to have to ask you this, First Minister, but are you party to the conspiracy?"

She looked at him, her gaze steady despite the pounding of her pulse. "No, my lord, I'm not. But as your first minister I have to advise you not to believe me. If you have any doubts at all about my loyalty, you should remove me from my office and appoint someone in my place until you're satisfied that I can be trusted."

That of all things made him smile, albeit wanly. "I'm sure that's wise counsel. But for now you'll remain my first minister."

"As you wish, my lord."

"You never really answered my question, Evanthya. Do you think the king had Chago killed?"

Her hands were sweaty in spite of the cold, and she had to keep from wiping them on her breeches. "I don't know, my lord."

The duke glanced at her and nodded once more, his round face pale and that same fearful look in his eyes. "Do you want to know the real reason I won't replace you?" he asked a moment later.

She just stared at him, not certain that she did.

"I wouldn't know who else to turn to. I'm afraid to trust any Qirsi right now. At least I know you."

Chapter
Four

✦

Kett, Aneira

H e went out of his way to be kind to her, showing her courtesies she was certain no one else enjoyed. He hadn't forced her to climb to the top of the rise since her fourth turn, and recently he had appeared to her before she walked more than a hundred paces. On the other hand, as her time approached he entered her dreams more and more frequently, until she found herself too weary to do much of anything during her waking hours. It almost seemed that the Weaver believed himself to be the child's father, so concerned was he with Cresenne's well-being. That was impossible, of course; she and the Weaver had never even met outside of her dreams. But he often asked what she had eaten the previous day, chiding her when the answer she gave failed to satisfy him. One night during the previous turn, he had spoken to her at length of what a glorious future awaited her baby.

"Your child will grow up in a land ruled by the Qirsi," he said that night, sounding almost breathless with excitement. "Rather than aspiring to be a gleaner or a minister, he or she will grow up dreaming of being a noble, a duke or duchess, perhaps even more. No Qirsi child born in the Forelands has ever had that before."

Cresenne had entertained such thoughts herself almost from the day she realized she was pregnant. But she nodded and agreed with the Weaver as if with his help, she had glimpsed this possible future for the very first time.

Still, she might have been flattered by the interest the Weaver had taken in her and her child had it not been for the utter terror that she felt whenever she spoke with him. And she might have believed his interest genuine and unselfish, had he not asked her the same one question during each conversation.

On this night he barely made her walk at all, appearing as a great black form against the same blinding light that stabbed into her eyes every time. She was heavy with child by now—she could hardly believe that she would have to wait two more turns before giving birth—and the Weaver said nothing for some time after she stopped before him. It seemed to Cresenne that he gazed at her, admiring her belly, though she could see nothing of his face.

"I have never seen any woman look so radiant as you do now," he said at last. She thought for a moment that he might reach out and touch her face, and a shudder went through her body. She would have preferred his wrath to this.

It took her a moment to realize that he was waiting for a reply. "Thank you, Weaver," she said, dropping her gaze. "I don't deserve such kind words."

"Of course you do, child. Tell me, what was your supper tonight?"

"Stew and bread, Weaver, with a plate of steamed greens." Actually she had barely touched the greens. For several turns she had been sickened by their smell. But the Weaver didn't need to know that.

"Splendid," he said, much as she imagined her own father would, had he been alive. "Have you gleaned anything about the child? Do you know if it will be a boy or girl?"

"No, Weaver. I've seen nothing." True, but she had a feeling. She hadn't shared this with anyone, however, and she certainly wasn't going to share it with this man.

"There's still time, child. Perhaps you will before long, if Qirsar destines that it should be so."

She nodded.

"You're in Kett. Still with the Festival?"

He was like a wolf, circling his prey, each pass bringing him just a bit closer to the kill. She knew where this was headed. The question. It was only a matter of time before he asked her.

"Yes, Weaver."

"You've been gleaning?"

"Yes."

"Anything interesting?"

"Not so far."

A pause, and then it would come. It always did.

"Have you found him yet?"

Just once she wanted to ask innocently, *Who, Weaver?* But the kindness he had shown her had its limits, unlike his ability to hurt her, which had none.

"No, Weaver. Not yet. I've asked throughout the city, as I did in Bistari, Noltierre, and Solkara. No one has seen him."

"It may be time you moved on to Caerisse."

"I still believe he's in Aneira."

"So you've told me before," the Weaver said, his voice hardening. "Yet you've nothing to show for the four turns you've spent there. Thus far, your instincts on this matter have served you poorly. You're searching for a Qirsi man and an Eibitharian noble whose face is covered with scars. They shouldn't be this hard to find. If they were in Aneira, you'd have heard something by now."

Not necessarily, she wanted to say. *He's smarter than you think. He may be smarter than you.* But all she could manage was "He may be avoiding the larger cities. I've yet to search the countryside."

"He wouldn't go to the smaller towns. You told me yourself that he's probably searching for you, which means he'll go where the festivals go."

Again Cresenne nodded, though she felt her heart clenching itself into a fist. For the first several turns she had assumed that Grinsa would come after her. He didn't know that she carried his child, but he had loved her, and that should have been enough. She knew there was a new king in Eibithar and she had no doubt that Grinsa had gone to the City of Kings to see him invested. The Revel had been there too, of course, so Grinsa would have learned from one of the other gleaners, probably Trin, that she had left the Revel. At the time she told Trin that she intended to return to Wethyrn, but Grinsa was too clever to believe that. He'd head south.

Or so she thought. Because recently it had become clear to her that he hadn't followed her at all. He should have found her by now. She had done everything she could to lead him to her. She found the assassin she had hired to kill Brienne, she joined the Festival, she sat in every Qirsi tavern between Mertesse and Noltierre. Everywhere she went, she asked about him, and not subtly. She had done all the things he might expect her to do, and more. She had done everything but stand in the sanctuary bell towers and yell, "Cresenne ja Terba is here!" A blind man could have found her. If he'd been looking.

He loved her. She was certain of it. It had to be the boy's fault, that stubborn, spoiled brat of a lord. But for all the times she told herself this, there were twice as many when her chest ached as if someone had buried a dagger there. Even now, speaking with the Weaver, when she needed so desperately to hide her feelings, she could not keep the hurt from welling up again, like blood from a wound.

"What is it, child?" the Weaver asked, clearly trying to mask his impatience.

She shook her head, cursing the single tear that ran down her cheek. "Nothing."

"You're worried that I'm angry with you."

Cresenne said nothing. She might be able to lie to him, but if he caught her, he'd kill her right then. And the baby, too. Not for the first time, she used her fear of him to mask her true thoughts.

"I'm not," he said. "I want to find this man, that's all. I don't believe he's in Aneira."

"I—I don't want to go to Caerisse," she said in a small voice.

He exhaled slowly, as if struggling to keep his ire in check. "Why not?"

"The winds are already blowing cold from the north. The snows are going to be fierce this year. And I don't want to be up on the steppe when my baby is born."

There was enough truth in this to conceal her real reason for wanting to stay in Aneira. Snow had already fallen on the steppe, and the cold turns up in Caerisse promised to be brutal. If she was going to travel with one of the festivals after her child came, she preferred to be at least somewhat comfortable.

Besides, she knew that Grinsa was near. She sensed it, just the way she sensed that this baby she carried was going to be a girl. She'd gleaned nothing. She'd had no visions of Grinsa or the Curgh boy. But her body and her heart told her what her mind couldn't. He was in Aneira. Perhaps she should have explained this to the Weaver, but she feared that he would understand all too well.

"All right," he said at length, just as she knew he would. When it came to this child, she could get him to agree to almost anything. "Remain in Aneira. Continue your search there. When the rains come and the air grows warmer, you'll go to Caerisse."

"Of course. Thank you, Weaver."

He seemed to stare at her again, his wild white hair stirring in the wind, his features still masked by shadows from the brilliant light behind him.

"If you have a girl," he said, his voice softening once more, "I hope she looks just like you."

She will. "Again, thank you," Cresenne said, making herself smile.

"We'll speak again soon. If you find him, or hear anything of his whereabouts, remain in Kett, even if the Festival leaves. Make some excuse, but stay there. I don't want to have any trouble finding you."

The dream ended abruptly and Cresenne opened her eyes to a room so dark she could barely see to the edge of her bed. The inn was quiet, as was the street outside her window. It must have been well past the midnight bells.

"Damn him," she whispered in the blackness. She needed to sleep more, but already she had begun to sift through her conversation with the Weaver, searching for anything that might tell her who he was and where she could find him.

She felt the baby move and smiled, placing a hand on her belly.

"Are you awake, too?"

She sat up, propping up her pillow against the bedroom wall and leaning back against it. These encounters with the Weaver always woke the child. Cresenne thought it must be because of how her body reacted to fear—the quickening of her pulse, the tightening of her stomach. How could the baby not notice? A part of her wanted to believe that he or she woke up to offer comfort. Certainly nothing made Cresenne forget the Weaver and all that he represented faster than feeling that tiny body turning somersaults in her belly like a festival tumbler.

"Don't you know it's the middle of the night?"

A tiny foot pushed against her hand, then a second.

"So you know, but you just don't care."

The feet moved away, but an elbow dug against her side.

"Where's your father little one? Is he really in Aneira, or am I just fooling myself?"

Not too long ago she had been ready to concede that she must be wrong, that Grinsa couldn't be in Aneira. But then she heard of the assassination of Bistari's duke. Immediately she knew that it had to have been the work of the Qirsi. Others were not nearly so quick to reach that conclusion, and she gathered from what she had heard that the use of the garrote and the scrap of Solkaran uniform had succeeded in fooling Eandi nobles and Qirsi ministers alike, including the duke of Kett. Of course, they didn't know the movement and its tactics as she did. Cresenne thought it had been poorly done, the signs pointing to the king too heavy-handed. To her mind, it bespoke a dangerous overconfidence. More to the point, however, she felt reasonably certain that the murder had been carried out by the same man she sent to Kentigern. Cadel, whom she last saw in Noltierre when she told him of the death of his partner. The killing so closely resembled an assassination he had been hired to carry out in Sanbira a year or two before that she thought it had to be his work.

And since he had pledged himself to finding and killing Grinsa in order to avenge Jedrek's death, the fact that he was still in Aneira gave her some cause to hope that the gleaner was as well. It wasn't much. It was pitifully little, really. But taken with the nameless sense she had that Grinsa was nearby, it was all she needed.

The baby's movements began to grow more gentle and infrequent. Cresenne lay down again and hummed a lullaby that her mother used to sing. Eventually, she must have fallen asleep herself, because when she next opened her eyes, sunlight streamed through the window and the mid-morning bells tolled from the city gates.

"Demons and fire!" she whispered, sitting up so fast that her head spun.

She should have been at the gleaning tent already. No doubt the line of children wound almost completely around the tent by now. Aneira's Eastern Festival had other gleaners, but she had promised to be there early today, having taken the later gleanings the previous two days.

She threw on her clothes and walked as quickly as she could through the narrow winding streets of Kett until she came to the tents and peddlers' carts of the Festival.

Meklud had already started the Determinings for her, and he glared at her as she entered the tent, a scowl on his narrow, pale features. A small girl sat across the table from him, gazing at the Qiran, though the stone showed nothing yet.

"I'm sorry," Cresenne said, standing in the tent opening.

"I should think."

"Do you want me to start now, or wait until you're done with her?"

His mouth twisted sourly. "You might as well let me finish this one. I've already had her tell me most of what I need to know."

"All right. As soon as you're done with her, come outside and find me. I'll do the rest."

She stepped back into the sunlight, only to find several of the children watching her.

"Are you the gleaner?" a boy asked.

"One of them, yes."

A girl stared at her belly. "Does that mean you know what your baby is going to be?"

Cresenne almost laughed aloud. Why was everyone so interested in her baby? Everyone except its father.

"No, it doesn't. I'll be just as surprised as any other mother."

"My mother says that Qirsi babies are born so small that they can fit in the palm of my hand."

Cresenne stared at the girl, fighting an urge to slap her. It was true that Qirsi women gave birth to smaller babies than did Eandi women. Indeed, romances between Qirsi women and Eandi men were forbidden by the gods and prohibited by law in most kingdoms because Qirsi mothers were too frail to give birth to the children of such unions. More often than not, the women died in labor. The sin of the moons, it was called, for Panya and Ilias, a Qirsi woman and Eandi man who defied the gods and loved each other anyway, only to be punished by Qirsar, the Qirsi god, who placed them in the sky as moons so that all might see how they suffered for their love.

Still, though Qirsi babies were small, they were not abominations, as the tale repeated by this girl implied. For centuries the Eandi had told such stories about her people, perpetuating ancient fears of the Qirsi and their magic. No matter what she thought of the Weaver, Cresenne still shared his desire to see the Eandi courts destroyed.

"Your mother is wrong," Cresenne said, unable to keep the ice from her voice. "And she ought to be ashamed of herself for filling your head with such dreadful lies."

The girl gaped at her, her eyes wide as an owl's. Cresenne turned away and merely stared at the tent opening, waiting for Meklud to finish with the gleaning. The old man would be furious with her if he learned what she had said to the girl—Festival gleaners were supposed to be courteous to all the Eandi, no matter how they were treated—but she didn't care. Let him throw her out of the Festival. At least then she'd have an excuse to defy the Weaver and leave Kett in search of Grinsa.

Meklud stepped out of the tent a short time later, fixing her with a look that made it clear he would have liked to replace her, even without knowing what she had said to the girl.

"You're ready now?" he asked, arching a pale eyebrow.

"Yes. Again, I'm sorry for being late."

"I was supposed to replace you at the midday bells," he said, leaving the thought unfinished, but looking at her expectantly.

You bastard, she thought. *It was only one or two gleanings.* But he left her little choice.

"I can continue for a time beyond the bells."

"To the prior's bells?"

Enough was enough. "No, Meklud, not to the prior's bells. I'm with child and I have to eat and rest. I'll go four gleanings beyond midday, but that's all."

He frowned, but after a moment he nodded. "Very well."

The old Qirsi stomped off without another word, but at least he didn't have a chance to speak with the girl.

Cresenne glanced at the boy who stood at the head of the line. "I'm ready for you," she said, stepping into the tent.

They were afraid of her now, but she didn't mind that. It tended to make the gleanings go faster.

The rude Eandi girl was the fourth child to enter the tent. She came in reluctantly, as if pushed by some unseen hand, but then hurried to the empty chair across the table from Cresenne, her eyes lowered and her cheeks pale. The Qirsi woman watched her for a time, saying nothing and allowing the girl's discomfort to build. It would be some time before this Eandi child said something hateful about her people again.

"What's your name?" the gleaner finally asked.

"Kaveri Okaan. But everyone calls me Kavi."

"Is that what you want me to call you?"

The girl shrugged. "I guess. What's your name?"

The Qirsi hesitated briefly. Most of the children were too afraid of her and the stone to ask. "Cresenne."

"That's a pretty name."

Cresenne had just been thinking the same thing about Kaveri, her hand straying to her belly.

"Thank you," she murmured. "What do your parents do, Kavi?"

"My father is a cooper in Tabetto, and my mother works sometimes for the village tailor, though usually she just takes care of us. She's going to have a baby, too."

Cresenne had taken a few moments when she first entered the tent to read the list of names given by the city elders to Meklud. The list included the last name of all the local children who were in their twelfth year and thus old enough for their Determinings. Next to the names of some of them—all the boys and a few of the girls—were written the words "wheel-wright" or "blacksmith" or "seamstress," the professions chosen for them by their parents. Cresenne and the other gleaners were expected to steer the children toward these professions with the images they summoned from the gleaning stone. That way the children could begin their apprenticeships now, while they were still young enough to master their trades. Cresenne had seen the name Okaan on the list, but as with so many of the girls, the space next to Kavi's name had been left blank. She was expected to be a wife and mother, but beyond that her parents had few expectations.

"Is there anything you want to ask the stone?"

The girl looked up for an instant, her pale blue eyes widening once more. Looking at her now, Cresenne realized that she was quite beautiful, with fine features and olive skin. She had long black hair that she wore to her shoulders, and her clothes, though roughly made, were clean and fit her well.

"I want to know what my husband will look like. Will he be handsome like my father?"

Cresenne suppressed a smile. "Anything else?"

She shrugged again. "Will he be rich?"

"Only the stone knows," Cresenne said. "When you're ready, speak the words."

The girl nodded, swallowed. "In this, the year of my Determining," she began, her eyes falling once more to the stone and her voice dropping to a whisper, "I beseech you, Qirsar, lay your hands upon this stone. Let my life unfold before my eyes. Let the mysteries of time be revealed in the light of the Qiran. Show me my fate."

There was nothing on the list, nothing she was supposed to show the girl, and so Cresenne merely offered her magic to the Qiran, opening herself to whatever the god might send through the stone.

Slowly the white glow of the stone began to change, greens and blues and reds spreading from the center like petals on a blossom opening for the first time. As the image took form, Cresenne saw Kavi, grown to womanhood, standing at its center. She was pretty still, though the years had left their mark upon her. Her fine black hair hung to the center of her back and her face was round and flushed. But there were tiny lines around her eyes and the smile on her lips seemed forced, as if pain lurked behind it. She was nearly as heavy with child as Cresenne. Two small children played nearby, one a girl who looked remarkably like young Kavi, and the other a boy with wheat-colored hair and dark eyes. The house behind them appeared solid and large enough for a family, but something about the vision troubled Cresenne.

"Is that really me?" Kavi asked, a smile touching her lips.

"She certainly looks like you. Don't you think?"

The girl nodded, her eyes never straying from the stone.

Cresenne continued to look as well. And then it hit her. In the image, Kavi and her children wore light clothing and stood amid flowers and green trees. But the windows of the house were shuttered. There had been a death within the last turn. Kavi's husband, no doubt.

The gleaner's eyes flew to the child sitting before her, but Kavi didn't notice. The image in the stone held her, and the small smile lingered on her face. Cresenne looked into the stone again, hoping, against all she knew to be true, to see a man emerge from the house. None came.

Fool! she railed at herself. This was an image better suited to Kavi's Fating, four years from now. The girl was far too young to learn of such a dark fate. It would have been so easy to create a vision for her, to give her a handsome man and beautiful children, to put them all in a big house. She conjured such images all the time for children of Determining age—all the gleaners did. Thinking that perhaps it wasn't too late, the gleaner tried to alter the image. How hard could it be to add a husband to the glowing scene before them?

But the stone would not allow such a thing. Maybe if she had used her magic to create the image in the first place, as she usually did for Determinings, she could have changed it. Once she summoned the power of the stone, however, Cresenne was helpless to do anything more than watch and hope that Kavi would not notice the closed shutters and the look of loss on her own face.

Finally, mercifully, the image began to fade, retreating into the white glow of the Qiran as if swallowed by a mist. When it was completely gone, Kavi looked up at Cresenne, blinking once or twice.

"I was almost as big as you are," she said. "I was going to have another baby."

Cresenne nodded, eyeing the girl closely, searching for any sign that she had noticed. "I saw that."

Her head spun slightly, and her stomach felt hollow and sour. It occurred to her that she had eaten nothing all morning. The baby kicked once and rolled over lazily.

"Did you see my daughter? She looked just like me."

"She was quite pretty."

"Did you see the house?"

Cresenne held herself still. "What about the house?"

"I think someone died. The windows were all closed, the way they are when a person dies."

The gleaner took a breath, making herself hold the girl's gaze. "Yes, they were."

"I didn't see my husband. Do you think he's the one who died?"

"I don't know, Kavi. People shutter their windows for a lot of reasons. Maybe a storm was coming, or maybe you were getting ready to leave your home for a time. And even if they were closed because someone died, that doesn't mean it was your husband. Sometimes we close windows when the king dies or a duke."

"I looked sad," the girl said. "I'm not sure I'd look that sad if the duke died." She looked down at her hands, as if ashamed of what she had said. "You won't tell anyone, will you?"

"No. And just between us, I know what you mean."

Kavi smiled again, though she kept her eyes on her hands. "Do you have a husband?" she asked.

"No, I don't."

"Did he die?"

Cresenne nearly laughed, though she felt tears stinging her eyes. Grinsa wasn't dead, though she had done her best to have him killed, sending one assassin to keep him from reaching Kentigern Tor after he left the Revel, and then giving his name to the assassin's partner, who all but vowed to avenge the first man's death. She didn't want him dead—in truth, she never had—but she had pledged herself to serving the Weaver long ago, and his desires ruled her own. Even now she searched for Grinsa, not knowing how she could find him without betraying him to the Weaver and thus endangering his life a third time.

"I don't think he's dead," she answered, looking off to the side. "To be honest, I don't know where he is. We had . . . a fight, before I knew about the baby, and he left."

"Does he know about the baby now?"

This conversation had gone on long enough. "That's not any—"

"If he doesn't know, you should tell him. It might end your fight."

Cresenne's head was beginning to hurt. She closed her eyes and rubbed her temples. *I need to eat.* The baby kicked again, as if agreeing with her.

"Are you all right?" Kavi asked.

"Yes." The gleaner opened her eyes and made herself smile. "I'm sorry about your Determining, Kavi. I shouldn't have—" She stopped herself. Most children had no idea that a gleaner could make images appear in the stone. They assumed that like a Fating, a Determining came only from the stone and the god, as this one had. "I wish it had shown something different."

Kavi shrugged. "That's all right. Maybe you're right: maybe it was the king or someone else."

"Maybe. I hope so."

She waited for the girl to stand and leave, but Kavi just sat there.

"I don't mean to be rude," Cresenne said, "but I have more gleanings to do this morning."

She nodded, but still she didn't move. "I'm sorry for what I said about your baby," she said at last, her hands twisting together in her lap. "I wasn't trying to be mean."

"I know," Cresenne said quietly. "I didn't think you were."

"But you think my mother is mean."

"I don't know your mother."

"She's not," the girl said, her voice rising. "She's not mean and she's not a liar!"

Cresenne felt her anger returning and she almost responded with the first words that came to her mind. But once again her baby moved within her, and the gleaner realized that she would want her child to defend her just as passionately.

"Your mother must be a good woman," she said instead, choosing her words with care, "if she can raise a daughter like you who loves her so much."

Kavi eyed her suspiciously. "She is a good woman."

Cresenne allowed herself a small grin. "I'm willing to say that I was wrong about her before, if you'll admit that she was wrong about Qirsi babies."

The girl smiled. "All right."

"Now go. There are other children waiting."

"Thank you, gleaner."

For what? Insulting your mother or revealing your dark fate four years too early? "You're welcome."

The child stood and walked to the tent entrance. Cresenne closed her eyes again, resting her head in her hands.

"Are you sure you're not sick?"

She looked up. Kavi was still there, watching her from the tent opening.

"I'm just hungry. I'll be fine."

"Want me to get you some food?"

"No, thank you. I'll eat later."

"I don't mind."

Cresenne hesitated. It would be hours before she would be able to leave the tent, and the pain in her head was growing worse, settling at the base of her skull.

"Really?"

"Sure. What do you want?"

The gleaner dug into her pocket and pulled out two silvers.

"Anything you can find. There's a Sanbiri woman on the west end of the commons who sells spiced breads and dried fruit. That would be perfect."

Kavi took the money, seeming pleased to be able to do something for her, though Cresenne couldn't imagine why.

"I'll be back soon."

"Thank you," the gleaner said, watching her leave.

She put her hands on her stomach, but the baby had grown still again, one of its feet pressed against the center of Cresenne's stomach.

As she had so many times in the past few turns, the gleaner found herself thinking of her mother and the time they spent alone together after Cresenne's father died, traveling with Wethyrn's Crown Fair. There had been one night in particular when, after a performance in Strempfar, her mother offered to let her join the rest of the Qirsi gleaners and performers when they went to a tavern. Cresenne had just turned fifteen, and was reluctant to go anywhere with her mother, but tempted nonetheless by the thought of spending time with the older Qirsi.

"I suppose I could go with you for a little while," Cresenne told her, trying her best to mask her eagerness.

"Oh, I won't be going," her mother said. "I'm tired tonight. You go and tell me about it in the morning."

Only later, when she was older and her mother long dead, did Cresenne understand that her mother hadn't really been tired at all. She had merely known her daughter well enough to see that Cresenne would enjoy the experience more if she was alone.

Her mother, it seemed, always knew exactly how to take care of her. It didn't matter that her husband was dead, or that they had little money. She just knew.

"And I just told a twelve-year-old girl that she's going to be a widow before her third child is born."

She felt panic rising in her chest like a cresting river. What did she know about caring for a baby? What did she know about children at all? Aside from these gleanings she did every day, she never spoke to them. She didn't know how they thought, or what they feared, or when it was time to treat them as adults rather than children. She wasn't even certain what to feed her baby once it was weaned.

"I'm going to be a mother in less than two turns," she said softly, gazing into the glowing stone. "I'm not ready."

She could almost hear her mother's reply. *You have to be.*

She took a long breath and looked down at her body, smiling at the changes she saw. Not only her belly. Her breasts had grown large and firm, so she knew the child wouldn't starve. And even in the midst of her fear, she could feel as well that she already loved this child. Perhaps for now, until she found Grinsa, that would be enough.

At least I've found a name, she thought. *Kaveri.*

She stood, stretching her back and legs before walking to the tent opening. The other children were waiting, and she couldn't look for the baby's father until these gleanings were done.

Peering out from the tent, she saw that the line had grown longer since she started the gleanings. There must have been thirty children waiting now, some of them twelve, others sixteen. So many faces, so many expressions, so many shades of fear and wonder and excitement. Had their mothers been as frightened as she was?

"Is it my turn?" the girl at the head of the line asked.

Cresenne nodded. "What's your name?" she asked, as the child stepped past her into the tent.

"I'm Sunya Kilvatte."

The gleaner smiled, following the girl to the stone. Sunya. That was a pretty name, too.

Chapter
Five

✦

Solkara, Aneira

astle Solkara stood on a small rise of the southern bank of the Kett River, just downstream from Bertand's Falls, a broad cascade that roared in the shadows of the Aneiran forest. The great red towers of the castle, bathed in the golden sun of late day, loomed above even the tallest oaks and elms of the wood. Banners, one of them red, black, and gold for House Solkara, and the other bearing the yellow and red sigil of the Kingdom of Aneira, flew from the towers above the east and west gates.

The city of Solkara sprawled on either side of the fortress, its formidable walls following the slow curve of the river and arcing back toward the forest to the south. Soldiers stood on the walls and in the towers that watched over each gate.

Sitting atop his mount just to the south and west of the city, Brall could not help but admire the scene. Solkara might not possess the land's most beautiful castle—that distinction belonged to Bertin's home in Noltierre, or perhaps the castle in Tounstrel. But there could be no denying that the fortress standing before him befitted a king.

If anything, it sometimes seemed to the duke that Aneira's king was not worthy of the castle. He still remembered the joy and hope he felt when Carden's father, Tomaz the Ninth, took the throne more than twenty-two years earlier. Brall himself had just become duke of Orvinti a few turns before and he looked forward to serving under his friend, who promised to be a fine king. Carden was but a boy then, only a year past his Determining, but already Brall saw in him signs of the quick temper and ruthlessness that would characterize his reign. He both hoped and expected that the boy would have time to outgrow these traits. Brall and Tomaz had been relatively young men, and the duke assumed that Tomaz would rule the land for decades. He never imagined that the king would die of a fever only nine years after his investiture, leaving Aneira to his eldest son.

It would have been too much to say that Carden had diminished the throne. He was a competent leader, whose hard manner and fierce reputation served Aneira well in its dealings with Braedon and the other kingdoms of the Forelands. But a king could be strong with his allies and foes while still caring for his people. Carden, it often seemed, saw the people of Aneira as a burden, and the nobles who served under him as potential rivals and nothing more. Brall's father once told him that the secret to being a good ruler was knowing when to raise a fist and when to extend a hand. He offered this as a lesson in leading the dukedom, but Brall knew that it applied with equal force to ruling an entire kingdom. Carden ruled only with his fists, and the land had suffered for it.

Since his conversation with Tebeo six nights earlier, Brall had given a great deal of thought to Chago's murder and the possible explanations for it. In the end he had decided that, one way or another, Carden shared responsibility for the duke's death. Even if Qirsi gold paid the assassin, Carden's past actions had made their deception possible. More than that, though, Brall also realized that regardless of whether Carden ordered the killing, the king would do nothing to dispel the notion that he had Chago killed. He drew his power from the fear he inspired in those who served him. Admitting that others were responsible, that the Qirsi had used his reputation to their advantage, was not in his nature.

Brall intended to speak with the king anyway. He had made a promise to Tebeo, and he believed that he could divine the truth even without an honest response from the king. But he dreaded this encounter, and he sensed that by approaching Carden so soon after Chago's death, he was placing his own life in danger.

Fetnalla rode with him, as did a small complement of guards. Before he left Orvinti, Pazice urged him to bring his taster as well, but one did not bring a taster to the king's castle, even while a fellow duke's ashes were still settling over the land. With brigands roaming the forest and common thieves on the king's road, the guards were a necessity. And no duke traveled without his first minister. But to arrive in Solkara with a larger company of servants and guards would imply that the king lacked the means or the good grace to make him comfortable and guarantee his safety.

"Shall we continue, my lord?" the first minister called to him.

Brall turned to look at her and the soldiers perched on their mounts behind her. They looked cold, and eager to ride on to the castle. The horses stomped impatiently, the vapor from their breath rising to the bare tree limbs in pale swirling clouds.

"I suppose," he said, his voice low as he looked at the castle once more. Not for the first time, he found himself thinking that this had been a bad idea.

"My lord?"

"Yes," he said, riding back to the king's road. "Let's get on with it."

They resumed their approach to the city, four guards riding in front of the duke bearing the Orvinti banner, a white bear on a green and blue field. Fetnalla rode just behind Brall, and eight more soldiers followed her. They had ridden this way for four days, speaking little save for what was necessary to get them through the days and nights. Fetnalla made it clear from the first day that she felt the duke should send a message to the king before journeying to Solkara, but Brall didn't want to give Carden too much time to prepare himself. He was far more likely to give something away if Brall surprised him.

The duke hadn't explained this to the first minister. Indeed, he had told her almost nothing about why he wished to speak with the king, except to say that it pertained to Chago's death. After his conversation with the duke of Dantrielle, Brall was afraid to tell her more, lest he make himself a target of the Qirsi as well as of the king.

For the first half of their journey, Fetnalla asked him repeatedly why he wished to speak with Carden at all, and what he hoped to accomplish by riding to Solkara rather than sending messengers. Each time she raised these matters, the duke tried to change the subject, or offered only vague responses, or just refused to answer her at all. Finally, after nearly two days of this, the minister gave up, lapsing into a brooding silence that troubled him nearly as much as her relentless questioning.

Seeing Castle Solkara, however, seemed to embolden her again.

"It's not too late for us to dispatch one of the guards as a messenger, my lord," she said. "It would probably only delay us a short while."

He nodded, not even bothering to look back at her. "Perhaps. But I'm not willing to delay at all. We'll ride to the city gates. That will give the king ample time to prepare for our arrival."

The minister kicked at the flanks of her mount so that she caught up with him. She had bundled herself in her riding cloak, though she still looked cold and weary. She was tall for a Qirsi and uncommonly graceful. But on a mount, she appeared uncomfortable, even awkward. No doubt she had little desire to make this journey, but at no time had she complained of her discomfort. It was not in her nature to do so. She deserved more from him than he had given. Yet, he couldn't rid himself of the suspicions planted in his mind by his late-night talk with Tebeo.

"My lord, please!" she said with a fervor he had rarely seen in her. "If I've done something to give offense, tell me and be done with it! But don't punish me by endangering your own life!"

"Is that what I'm doing?" he asked.

"It seems so to me."

"I'm not angry with you, First Minister, and I'm not trying to punish you."

"Then why suddenly won't you answer my questions? Why do you ignore my counsel?"

Because I don't trust you. "I'm not ignoring your counsel. I'm just not heeding it. There's a difference."

"There's more to it than that. You refuse to speak with me. You've told me almost nothing about why you wish to speak with the king."

"Must I explain myself to my ministers now? Is that the duty of an Aneiran duke?"

"Of course not, my lord. But my duty is to advise you, and I can't do that if you won't talk to me."

It was a fair point, though Brall was not willing to admit it just then. "What would you have me say?" he asked instead.

"You could begin by telling me what we're doing here."

"We're going to see the king, of course. There are matters I wish to discuss with him."

"What matters, my lord? What is so important that we have to brave this cold and the dangers of the wood?"

"That's between the king and me."

Fetnalla sighed heavily and shook her head. "Very well, my lord. Do as you will. I won't trouble you with questions any more. But I will say this: your dissembling does an injustice to both of us, as well as to House Orvinti. By treating me this way, you not only dishonor our friendship, you also serve your people poorly."

"You forget yourself, First Minister!" he said so sharply that the soldiers riding ahead of the company turned to look back at him. "I will not be spoken to that way, especially not by a Qirsi!"

The minister's face reddened as if he had slapped her. She turned away, looking straight ahead. After a few moments, she dropped back into place behind him.

Brall let out a long breath and cursed his temper. If she hadn't betrayed him yet, she would soon. He had given her every reason to. He almost called her back to his side so that he could tell her everything. But his fears wouldn't allow it.

Instead they rode, covering the remaining distance to Castle Solkara without speaking another word. Reaching the city walls, they turned eastward until they came to the nearest of the gates. There they were stopped by the king's guards in their red-and-gold uniforms, the panther crest on their baldrics.

"My Lord Duke," one of the men said, bowing to Brall, his sword drawn and raised to his forehead. A gold star on his shoulder marked him as an officer in Carden's army, perhaps a captain. "We weren't told to expect you."

"The king didn't know I was coming."

The captain raised an eyebrow. "You didn't think to send one of your men ahead so the king could prepare for your arrival?"

Brall felt his ire rising again. It was one thing to be questioned by Fetnalla, who had served him so well for so many years. But a duke did not explain himself to a soldier, not even to a captain in the king's guard.

"I'm here now," Brall said, anger seeping into his voice. "Do you care to inform the king, or shall I ride on to the castle unannounced and let him see for himself how careless his soldiers have become?"

The man paled. "Of course, my lord." He turned smartly and barked an order to the men standing nearby. Two of them started running toward the castle, while the rest took positions on either side of the city road, drew their swords, and raised them to their brows.

"I'll accompany you to the castle myself, Lord Orvinti," the captain said. "Please follow me."

He led the duke and his company past the soldiers, who stood motionless in salute, and through the marketplace of Solkara. Seeing Orvinti's colors, which Brall's guards still held high, the people of the king's city paused in their business to stare. Some of them even clapped. Children pointed at the flags and at the swords carried by the duke's men. They pointed as well at Fetnalla, staring wide-eyed at the Qirsi minister and whispering to each other.

"They must think you're the duke," Brall said, glancing back at her, hoping to draw a smile.

But she merely shook her head, her expression unchanged. "No, my lord. They just know that I'm a sorcerer."

He stared at her a moment longer, then faced forward again, not knowing what to say.

DAVID B. COE

They reached the south gate of the castle a few moments later. Four of Carden's soldiers stood before the gate, two of them bearing Aneiran flags, and the other two bearing the banners of Solkara and Orvinti. As they stood there, a group of musicians emerged from the castle and began to play "Amnalla's March," which had been written to celebrate the investiture of Queen Amnalla, the first Aneiran ruler to come from House Orvinti. It was not Brall's favorite Orvinti anthem, but for six centuries it had been the choice of Solkaran kings to honor dukes of Orvinti to the castle, no doubt because Amnalla's Rebellion ended the First Bistari Supremacy.

When the musicians finished, a second group of guards, also bearing banners of Aneira, Solkara, and Orvinti, stepped through the gate, followed by Queen Chofya, the king's archminister, and Solkara's prelate.

Brall swung himself off his mount and took a step forward. He turned briefly, intending to tell Fetnalla to do the same, but she was already there, just a step behind him, as was fitting. *She deserves better,* he thought.

An instant later he dropped to one knee, as did the minister, and bowed his head to the queen.

"Rise, Brall," Chofya said, smiling at him. "Welcome to Solkara."

She was still beautiful, with a full sensuous mouth, olive skin, and eyes so dark they appeared black. But Brall thought she looked weary, and there were more lines on her face than he remembered. She was dressed in a pale blue gown, her long black hair held back from her brow by a circlet of gold. She wore a single red gem at her throat that sparkled in the sun like morning dew on a rose petal.

The duke stood, then bent to kiss her hand.

"You honor me, Your Highness."

"You do us the honor with this most . . . unexpected visit."

The queen then offered quick introductions of the prelate and the king's Qirsi, before leading Brall and his company through the first gate of the castle. From there, they continued up the long, narrow ramps that ran between the great stone walls of the castle's outer defenses, and finally stepped into the vast inner courtyard of the king's palace.

Carden awaited them there, standing in front of what must have been five hundred soldiers in full battle uniform, all of them with their swords raised. The king wore plain battle garb, a warrior's sword, and a fur cape clasped at the neck with a simple gold chain. He stood taller than most of his men, with long golden hair and an angular face worthy of a hero from the ancient legends. Even without the carved gold crown on his brow, no one looking out across the courtyard would have wondered for long which of these men was king. Still, like the queen, Carden wore a slightly pinched look.

Four soldiers stepped forward and raised shining silver horns to their lips to play a Solkaran battle anthem, and the king's beautiful young daughter opened a small cage, releasing twelve white doves that circled the courtyard once, then flew to the highest tower of the castle. Whatever his doubts about Carden and his methods, Brall could not help but be impressed by this greeting, which the king and his servants managed to prepare in a matter of moments.

Once more the duke knelt, his head bowed and his hands resting on his bended knee. The rest of his company did the same, Fetnalla close enough to him so that he heard her whisper, "One might almost think that he knew you were coming anyway."

"Stand and be welcome, Brall," the king said, striding forward and embracing the duke briefly.

Brall returned the embrace and stepped back. "You're most gracious, my liege. I'm humbled and overwhelmed by this welcome."

Carden smiled. "Nonsense. This was nothing. If we'd known you intended to come, we might have offered a true greeting."

The duke smiled in return, but something he saw in the king's dark blue eyes made him wonder if this display had been intended as a warning as well as a welcome. *Take me lightly,* the king seemed to be saying, *and I'll destroy you.* Once more Brall found himself wondering if he'd been wise to make this journey.

"You must be hungry," the king went on a moment later. "Come, we've a meal waiting for you." He glanced past Brall to Fetnalla. "You're welcome to dine with us also, First Minister. I'm sure the duke doesn't want you far from his side."

Brall and the minister shared a look. It was a strange remark, made all the more awkward by the harsh words they had exchanged on the road to Solkara.

"Your Majesty is most kind," Fetnalla said.

Carden started walking toward the great hall on the north side of the courtyard, gesturing for Brall to follow. Chofya fell into step beside them and Fetnalla followed, along with Pronjed jal Drenthe, Carden's archminister. The king's daughter walked a few paces behind, staring shyly at the ground before her. She was the image of her mother, with black hair and eyes, though hers was a softer beauty. There was little in her appearance to mark her as Carden's child.

The central table in the hall had been set for six places. Two flasks of wine sat on the table, along with bowls of spiced stew, plates of fowl, mutton, and steamed silverweed root, and a basket of freshly baked breads. A fire burned high in the hearth and torches lined the walls, brightening the hall despite the failing light of late day. The meal at least did not reveal any foreknowledge of Brall's arrival. A king and queen ate thus every day, with enough extra for ministers or the prelate. An Orvinti banner hung on the wall over the hearth, but it was uneven, as if placed there in haste.

"Please forgive the meager table we've set for you," Chofya said. "If we'd had more time . . ."

Brall shook his head and smiled. "Not at all, Your Highness. It's a finer meal than I would find anywhere else in the land. Your generosity is exceeded only by your beauty."

Carden laughed, though there was a brittleness to it. "Spoken like an Orvinti. I remember your father having Bohdan's tongue as well. My father always said that he could charm a Wethy trader into giving away gold."

"I'm not sure I'd go that far," Brall said with a grin. "But it is said to be a family gift."

Fetnalla cleared her throat. "Speaking of gifts, my lord."

The duke nodded. "Of course. I'd almost forgotten." He pulled a small pouch from his belt and removed two objects wrapped in cloth. One was a glasslike crystal, about the size of a sourfruit, worn smooth so that it was almost a perfect orb. Such stones were found in Lake Orvinti and were called Tears of Shanae, for the woman who saved the Orvinti clan from northern raiders back before the Forelands were divided into the seven kingdoms. He handed the stone to Chofya.

"For you, Your Highness, from the people of Orvinti."

She smiled, taking the stone in her slender hand. "Thank you, Brall. My father gave me one of these years ago when I was just a girl. I'll put this one with it, and think always of you and your lovely home."

Brall inclined his head. "Again, Your Highness, you honor me." He pulled the cloth from the second object, revealing a small glittering dagger, with a silver handle and a blade carved from the same clear stone. "And for you, my liege, also from my people."

The king took the dagger and held it up to the torchlight, examining the carvings on the handle and the honed edges of the crystal blade.

"I've never seen a finer weapon carved from stone," Carden said. "This was made in Orvinti?"

"Yes, my liege."

The king nodded. "I'm impressed." He stared at the blade for another moment before laying it on the table. "Thank you, Brall. It will find a place of honor in my collection."

"You honor my people, my liege."

One of the servants poured out five goblets of wine and with the king's first sip, the meal began. For some time they said little, until Brall began to feel the burden of their silence. It almost seemed that Carden was waiting for him to begin a conversation, or perhaps to explain his sudden arrival in Solkara. The duke complimented both the king and his queen on the fine food they were eating, but Chofya only smiled, and Carden hardly did more than grunt in agreement.

When at last the servants removed what remained of the stew and roots, replacing them with a large platter of dried fruits and cheeses, and a flask of honey wine, Carden looked up from his meal and fixed his gaze on the duke.

"So why are you here, Orvinti?"

Brall cleared his throat, discomfited by the abruptness of the king's question. He glanced for an instant at Fetnalla, but given how little he had told her, he knew that he would find no support there.

"I'll be happy to tell you, my liege. But it might be better to wait until we can speak in private."

The king eyed him briefly, his mouth twisting sourly.

"Leave us," he said, turning to Chofya.

"But the fruit and cheese have only just arrived."

"Take Kalyi and the ministers and go to my private hall. You can finish your meal there."

The queen looked as if she wanted to argue the point further, but instead she said, "Yes, my lord," dropping her gaze. Recovering quickly, she flashed a thin smile at Fetnalla and the king's Qirsi. "Won't you join my daughter and me in the king's hall?" she asked. "It's not quite as spacious, but the food and wine will taste just as good."

"Of course, Your Highness," Fetnalla said, rising with the queen.

Pronjed cast a look at Carden, who nodded once. The Qirsi stood and followed Fetnalla, the queen, and the young girl out of the hall. A pair of servants approached the table and began to gather the empty plates, but the king waved a hand disdainfully.

"Leave them," he commanded. "Leave us."

The servants hurried from the hall.

"Now," Carden said, facing Brall once more, torchlight reflected in his dark eyes. "Answer me. Why have you come?"

The duke took a breath. He would have given all the gold in Orvinti's treasury to be back in his castle just then, enjoying a quiet meal with Pazice.

"I wish to speak with you about Chago," he said, relieved to hear that his voice remained steady.

"Chago," the king repeated. A smile stretched across his face, though it didn't reach his eyes. "What about him?"

"I . . . I wish to know if you had him killed."

For a moment Brall thought that the king would rage at him for even raising the matter. But Carden merely gazed at him for several moments, before picking up the crystal dagger and toying with it, the same half smile on his lips.

"You've always struck me as a cautious man, Brall, not at all the type to take chances. Coming here unannounced and uninvited, asking me such a question—this all seems much more like something one of your friends would do. Bertin, perhaps. Or maybe Tebeo. Did one of them put you up to this?"

"No, my liege."

"You're certain. They didn't suggest that you come to me, knowing that if one of them asked me the same question, I'd have him executed as a traitor? Think hard about this, Brall. Because I really am curious. Isn't it possible that they asked you to speak with me, perhaps while all of you were together in Orvinti a few days ago?"

Brall licked his lips, which were suddenly dry as sand. A part of him wondered how the king knew that the others had been with him in his castle, but he didn't dare ask. It mattered little at this point. The king had implied that his question was tantamount to treason. He'd be fortunate to ride out of Solkara alive. Still, having come this far, he wasn't about to betray Tebeo, even to save his own life.

"No, my liege. I did speak with the others about Chago's death. We had just come from his funeral, and were—" He stopped himself, uncertain as to how to finish the thought. He had taken great pains to keep himself apart from Solkara's feud with Bistari. He risked offending the king if he admitted that he and the others were grieving for a lost friend, particularly if Carden had ordered the assassination.

"It's all right, Brall. You and your friends were mourning his loss. I expected as much."

The duke exhaled. "Thank you, my liege. Whatever Chago's faults, we had all known him a long time."

"And you think I had him killed," the king went on, testing the edge of the dagger with his thumb. "Why?"

Brall faltered. "The garroting, my liege. And the Solkaran crest found in his hand."

The king looked at Brall as if the duke were a fool. "I mean why would I have him killed?"

"Your houses have been rivals for centuries, my liege. And you and Chago had more than your share of disagreements, most recently about the wharfages and lightering fees."

"Do you think I'd kill a man over lightering fees? Is that the kind of king you think I am?"

Brall closed his eyes briefly. If only he had listened to Fetnalla, and given this journey more thought.

"I think," he said slowly, "that any king must guard against those who would incite opposition to his authority. Chago was angry about the fees, and he may have gone too far in his efforts to fight them."

The king's eyes widened. "So you think he deserved to die. Did you come all this way to congratulate me on his murder?"

"Of course not, my liege."

"Well, Brall, I'm afraid you have me confused. First you imply that I'm a murderer, and then you seem to suggest that I was foolish to let the man live as long as I did. Which is it?"

The duke hesitated again, feeling like a prentice doing battle with a master swordsman. "Neither," he finally said. He took a breath. "Perhaps I should leave, my liege. I've offended you, which was not at all my intent. Unless Your Majesty wishes to imprison me, I should best be starting back to Orvinti tonight. After what I've said, I don't deserve your hospitality."

"What was your intent, Brall?"

There was little use in trying to be circumspect any longer. Best just to say it and be done, no matter the consequences.

"To find the truth, my liege. We—" He winced. "I feared that perhaps a darker force was at work here. There's been talk of a Qirsi conspiracy. I worry that Chago's murder might divide the kingdom against itself, and I've wondered if others were responsible and tried to make his death appear to be the work of House Solkara."

For the first time that night, Carden looked afraid. It lasted but a moment, like the flickering of a candle in a sudden wind. In that one instant, however, he was no longer the ruthless Solkaran king, but rather a young noble seemingly out of his depth. Brall had his answer.

Carden drained his goblet. A servant hurried toward the table from the doorway, as if intending to refill it, but Carden waved the boy away and poured his own wine, not bothering to offer any to Brall. And though it might have been a trick of the dancing torch fire and the shadows cast by the blaze in the hearth, it seemed that his hand trembled.

"I don't know if you're the bravest man I've ever met, or the most foolish," the king said a moment later, taking up the dagger once more. "You must realize that I can't offer you any answers. I would never admit to anyone that I had one of my dukes killed, even if it was clear to every man and woman in the land that I was responsible. Nor would I ever concede that I had allowed myself to be blamed for the crime of another."

"Of course, my liege. I understand."

"You understand, and yet you came here hoping that I would acknowledge doing one or the other."

"I came hoping that I could glean something from our conversation. I never expected you to admit anything."

"And what have you gleaned, Lord Orvinti?"

He might have been a fool, as the king said. But his foolishness did not run that deep. "Nothing, my liege. I will return to my castle as confused as I was when I left."

The king smiled thinly. "I'll take that as a compliment." The fire popped loudly, and the king glanced toward the hearth. "I will tell you," he continued, "that I share your concerns for the kingdom. For better or worse, Chago's death has angered my enemies, though it's forced them to quiet their voices for a time."

"Have you heard talk of the conspiracy, my liege?"

The king's mouth twisted. "I have, and it . . . concerns me as well."

"So you believe what you've heard?"

Carden gave a wan smile. "Do you honestly think that a year ago I would have sent my archminister from the room, even at your request?"

It was a more frank response than the duke had any right to expect, and he found himself wondering if perhaps he had judged the king unfairly.

Carden fell silent, staring at the crystal blade.

"I should leave you, my liege," Brall said again. "I'm deeply sorry if I gave offense."

The king made a vague gesture and shook his head, but he didn't give the duke leave to go.

"Do your friends think I killed him?" he asked.

"The other dukes harbor the same questions I do, my liege. There's much uncertainty in the land."

Carden looked up, meeting his gaze, a small smile on his angular face.

"Come now, Brall. You mean to say that Bertin hasn't been denouncing me as a murderous tyrant?"

Brall couldn't help but grin. "It is true that there may be somewhat less uncertainty in Noltierre."

The king actually laughed, though it lasted only a moment or two, and seemed to leave him in an even darker mood than he had been in before. "I don't doubt it. The man's an old goat. My father always thought so, too."

"In his own way, he's as loyal to Aneira as any of us, my liege."

"Don't worry, Brall. I won't be sending assassins to Cestaar's Hills any time soon." He paused, eyeing the duke. "Nor will I be throwing you in my dungeons, as you suggested before. Fool or not, you showed some courage coming here today. And I admire the loyalty you've shown your friends. In times like these, a loyal man is more valuable than gold."

"Thank you, my liege."

"You're free to go when you like, but the nights get cold this time of year. Why don't you take a chamber on the west side of the castle. That's where the queen will put your Qirsi."

Brall stood, sensing that the king had just ended their conversation. "Very good, my liege. Again, my thanks."

He stepped away from the table, and started toward the doorway leading out of the great hall.

"What about your Qirsi, Brall?"

The duke stopped and faced the king once more. "My liege?"

"Do you trust her?"

"I brought her with me, my liege, so I must trust her some. But I never told her why we were riding to Solkara."

Carden nodded once, but said nothing. A moment later, he raised his goblet again, as if bidding the duke goodnight.

"Forgive me for asking, my liege," the duke said. "But are you well?"

"Am I well?" the king repeated. He emptied his goblet again. "Do you fear for me, Orvinti?"

"I am your loyal subject, my liege. Like any good Aneiran, I wish for the good health and heart of my king."

Carden poured more wine, smiling thinly. "Of course you do." He took a long drink, nearly draining his goblet once more. "It's not your concern, Brall. For all matters that pertain to you and your people, I'm well enough."

"Yes, my liege," Brall said, knowing better than to pursue this any further. He turned once more to leave.

"Brall."

He looked back at the king.

"Don't ever come here unannounced again. I'm not one of your earls to be caught unawares. If you ever again arrive at my gates without first sending a messenger, I'll crush you as I would an attacking army. Do I make myself clear?"

"Perfectly, my liege."

The king stared at him a moment longer, then shifted his chair so that he faced the fire and raised his goblet to his lips.

Maybe he should have been angry. No matter the answer Brall expected him to give, the question itself bordered on impudence. Add to that the duke's admission that he hoped to glean something from their talk—as if a king might just give away information without intending it—and Carden would have been justified in having the man garroted right there in the great hall.

For an instant he had been tempted to do just that. It might have taught Tebeo, Bertin, and the others a lesson. A frightened duke was a timid duke, and in these times Carden felt far more comfortable knowing that his dukes feared him. He understood, however, that a king could take this too far. While Chago's murder might have tamed his more rebellious dukes, killing Brall as well would only serve to make him appear scared. The last thing he needed was for all Aneira to know how frightened he had grown these last few turns.

Besides, Brall was far more valuable to him alive than he ever could have been as a cautionary corpse. Despite his friendship with Chago and Tebeo, the duke had proven himself loyal to the crown. Indeed, he had managed to maintain ties to both House Bistari and House Solkara, no small feat given how much Carden and Chago hated one another. The king needed allies just now, particularly those who had mastered the finer points of statecraft. For Carden had not, and the duke might well be his only bridge to those nobles who hated him.

Now more than ever, he needed such a bridge. Because the truth was, he had nothing to do with Chago's murder. Had he wished for the duke's death? Of course, a hundred times over. Had he come within a hairsbreadth of giving such an order? Again, more times than he could count. But the words never passed his lips, and angry as he was with Chago's fulminations about the lightering fees and wharfages, he viewed them as an annoyance, not as a threat to his power. No one in all Aneira could have been more astonished than he to learn of the assassination, particularly when it became clear that the duke had been garroted. Still, only when he heard of the scrap of leather found in the dead duke's hand did the king fully grasp the implications of Chago's murder.

Just a few moments before, when Brall asked if he had heard rumors of a Qirsi conspiracy, Carden nearly laughed aloud. Who hadn't heard such talk? A person couldn't go anywhere in the Forelands without hearing of the Qirsi threat. No one seemed to know what the Qirsi wanted, or which of the white-hairs were involved, but that didn't stop people from talking. For all he had heard, however, the king never thought that the Qirsi would strike at him. Yet that was just what they had done. Chago was dead, but Carden had no doubt that he had been their target. Nor could he deny that their aim had been true. As he told Brall, he couldn't very well admit to all the Forelands that he had allowed himself to be made a fool. He knew that they were responsible, that the land was under attack by the sorcerers, but to raise the alarm among his people was to humiliate himself. They wanted him weakened, so he accepted the blame for Chago's death and made himself appear strong. They wanted his dukes and his people to hate him so that when they came back to finish him off, like a hunter circling back to kill a wounded stag, no one in Aneira would come to his aid.

He grinned darkly, his eyes still fixed on the low fire smoldering in the hearth. *Let them try,* he thought. *Let them bring their armies and their magic. If they believe one duke's death is enough to destroy me, they know nothing of House Solkara.* He had been hated for a long time now. It no longer bothered him.

Carden lifted his goblet, only to find that it was empty again.

"More wine!" he bellowed, his voice echoing off the ceiling and walls of his great hall.

After a few moments a young servant appeared carrying two flasks, one holding Sanbiri red, and the other the golden honey wine that was served after the main meal. Carden couldn't remember which he had been drinking most recently.

"I didn't know which to bring," the boy said, cowering as he approached the table.

"Both," the king said, sitting forward and gesturing for the boy to move faster. "Now leave me alone."

"But the hall—"

Carden grabbed the red and filled his goblet. "You can clean tomorrow," he said facing the fire again. "I don't want to be disturbed."

"Yes, Your Majesty." The boy bowed quickly and hurried out of the hall, closing the heavy oak door behind him.

The king took a long drink and closed his eyes, feeling the room pitch for a moment, as if he were on a merchant ship sailing the Scabbard. It was late to be drinking, but he wanted to be certain that Chofya was asleep before he returned to his chambers. On most nights like this he might have gone in search of one of his wife's court ladies to pass the time. But he had no more interest in a tryst than he did in his marriage bed. Not tonight.

He should have been thinking about Chago, and the white-hairs, and how he would crush them when they brought their army to Aneira. Perhaps he should have been confiding in Brall. With Chago's death, Orvinti had become the most powerful duke in the land.

Yet, his mind kept returning to his conversation with the castle surgeon earlier that day.

It shouldn't have surprised him. Kalyi, his only daughter, was nearly ten now, and Chofya hadn't been with child since. In his mind, Carden had blamed the queen for this. But he could no longer ignore the fact that there were no bastards either. Surely if it was her, there would have been bastards. The surgeon agreed, suggesting that his seed was defective in some way. "Sterile." That was the word he used.

Blaming the surgeon had been foolish. Having him executed had been the act of a coward. But no one could know of this, except Chofya, whom he'd have to tell at some point. Kings weren't sterile. Kings were powerful; they ruled men and led them to war. They passed their kingdoms on to their sons. Even in Eibithar, where the ascension of kings defied simple explanation, one principle remained clear: the eldest son of a king followed his father to the throne. To call a king sterile unmanned him. It invited challenge from his enemies, be they within the realm or on its borders.

He was fortunate to have the one daughter, the surgeon told him. She was a gift from Ean, one for which he and Chofya should have been thankful. But though Kalyi was his light and his music and his treasure, she was not enough. There hadn't been a ruling queen in Aneira for more than two centuries, since Edrice the Second abdicated to her brother in order to avoid a civil war and assure her son of the throne. Carden would have been happy to see Kalyi rule the land, but the other houses wouldn't stand for it. He needed a son. House Solkara needed an heir.

"There will be no heir," the surgeon had told him. "If you want House Solkara to hold the crown, you'd best choose a successor from among your brothers' children."

He had three brothers. Two were jackals and one was a fool, and their sons gave little indication of amounting to more. His best hope—and Aneira's—lay in the possibility that Kalyi would marry young and bear her husband a son. This ruled out a union with the son of another major house, any one of whom would expect to give his name to the child. She would have to marry within the Solkaran dukedom. A price to be sure, but a small one under the circumstances.

He drank, draining his goblet once more. How many times had he dreamed of raising a boy to be king, just as his father had raised him? What had he done to offend the god so?

"I'd gladly trade all I have for an heir," he murmured.

"Your Majesty?"

The king looked up sharply and saw Pronjed, his archminister, standing in the doorway. He felt his face grow hot with shame.

"What do you want?" he demanded.

"I saw the duke had returned to his chambers, Your Majesty. I was curious to know what he wanted."

He stepped into the hall, pulling the door closed behind him.

Carden shifted uneasily in his chair. He had no desire to speak with the white-hair right now, particularly about this.

"It was nothing of consequence," he said. "He had concerns about the new fees."

The Qirsi walked to the table and took an empty chair. "He came all this way to speak of lightering fees?"

The king felt his mouth twitch and wished he hadn't drunk that last cup of wine. "After Chago, he was afraid to leave the matter to messages, lest their be any . . . misunderstandings."

"I see." The Qirsi eyed him for a moment. "Are you well, Your Majesty?"

"Of course I'm well," Carden said, looking away. "Why does everyone keep asking me that?"

"You seem uneasy. And I heard of the surgeon's execution. You're certain everything is all right?"

"It doesn't matter," the king said. He cast a dark glance at the minister. "It's none of your concern."

"Very well."

They lapsed into a silence, the king watching Pronjed, whose pale yellow eyes flitted around the room like a sparrow, coming to rest at last on Orvinti's crystal dagger.

"That's a fine blade the duke brought," he said.

"Yes, it is."

"Pick it up."

Before he knew what he had done, the king held the dagger in his hand.

"You've ordered the servants away for the night?"

He wanted to lie, or better yet, to call the servants back to the hall, but all he could do was nod. "Yes."

"Good. Tell me what you and the duke discussed."

"He wanted to talk about Chago," the king said, unable to stop himself. "He wanted to know whether I had him killed, or if I thought it was the Qirsi."

Carden struggled to his feet. He didn't know what the minister was doing to him, but he had to get out of the hall.

"Sit down."

He sat.

"What did you tell him?"

"Nothing. Either way I look like a fool."

Pronjed smiled, the shadows in the hall making his thin face look almost cadaverous. "True. Turn the blade around."

He tried to fight the Qirsi's will, but his hands seemed to belong to someone else, someone who now had a blade aimed at his heart.

"The surgeon said you'd have no heir, didn't he?"

"Yes."

"I thought as much. Does anyone else know?"

"Not yet."

"Not even the queen?"

"No." The king tore his eyes from the point of the blade to look at the minister. "Why are you doing this?"

"For my people, of course. For the Weaver."

"But why does he want me . . . ?" He licked his lips. "What have I done?"

"Nothing. But you have no heir, and so Aneira will suffer. And by having the surgeon killed today, you made it so easy." Pronjed stood and stepped away from the table. "Do it."

He tried to resist. Ean knew how hard he tried. But his hands were no longer his own. He strained to take control of his body, reaching for his hands with his mind, summoning all the strength he thought he possessed. But none of it was enough against the magic of his Qirsi. He could only watch, despairing and utterly helpless, as he plunged the dagger into his own chest.

Chapter
Six

he duke had them up early the next morning, which dawned grey and cold, the air damp from a late-night rain. Fetnalla knew that Brall wished to be back in Orvinti for the celebration of Bohdan's Night, the Night of Two Moons in Bohdan's Turn, which was only five nights away. If they left that morning, they'd just make it, barring an early snow in the wood.

The duke had returned to his quarters shortly after she did the night before, offering a brief word of greeting to the guard standing by their rooms as he opened his door. The minister heard him from within her chamber and briefly considered going to speak with him. She still wondered why he had come to Solkara, though she had some idea, and she hoped that perhaps, having spoken with Carden, her duke would be ready to confide in her again. She had reached her door, and was resting her hand on the handle, when the memory of his harsh words on the road to the city stopped her.

Since the death of the duke of Bistari, she had noticed a rift forming between them, and with all that happened the day before, it had grown into a chasm. Astounded though she was by the speed with which their rapport had crumbled, she had no doubt as to the cause.

"I will not be spoken to that way," he had said, "especially not by a Qirsi."

Never before had he said such a thing to her or made her feel that the color of her eyes mattered to him beyond the powers it gave her to serve him. Certainly he had never given her the impression that he feared her.

Somehow, the murder in Bistari had made Brall suspicious of her, perhaps of all Qirsi.

In a sense, his refusal to answer her questions about this journey to see the king told her precisely why they had come. Her duke knew of the conspiracy, and while she hadn't thought him bold enough to take such action, Fetnalla suspected that he had come to Solkara to ask the king directly if he had ordered Chago's assassination. She would have given nearly anything to know Carden's answer.

Unfortunately, the morning found Brall as withdrawn as he had been the previous day. Aside from instructing her to gather Orvinti's soldiers in the castle courtyard and have the stable hands prepare the horses, he said nothing to her. He barely even looked her in the eye.

When all was ready for their departure, Brall led Fetnalla toward the king's hall, intending to find Carden and Chofya, thank them for their hospitality, and bid them farewell. They were still in the courtyard, however, when the bells in the castle's cloister abruptly began to toll, the sound echoing loudly among the stone walls. Almost immediately, the king's guards swarmed into the courtyard, surrounding the men of Orvinti and demanding that they drop their swords.

"What is this?" Brall asked, striding toward one of the older men, who wore a captain's star on each shoulder.

"My apologies, Lord Orvinti," the man said. "I know only what I was told by the archminister."

"And what was that?"

"That I was to raise the alarm and then find you and your men." He glanced at Fetnalla, who had followed only a step behind the duke. "The minister, too."

"You don't know why?"

"No, my lord."

Brall glanced back at Fetnalla, a question in his pale blue eyes.

"You say this came from the archminister?" she asked the captain.

"Yes."

"Where's the king?"

"The king is dead," came a voice from behind them.

Fetnalla and the others turned to see Pronjed walking toward them, accompanied by perhaps twenty more guards. His white hair fell unbound to his shoulders and his face looked wan and lean. Wrapped as he was in a fur-collared cape, he looked like some yellow-eyed buzzard from the southern moors.

"Ean save us all," Brall whispered.

"How did he die?" Fetnalla asked, shuddering slightly, as if Bian had brushed her cheek with a frigid hand.

"It would seem that he took his own life," the archminister said. "Though I find that difficult to believe." He faced the duke. "He used the crystal blade that you gave him last night."

All the color drained from Brall's face, leaving it as white as Fetnalla's hair. "I'm so sorry," he breathed.

"Are you?" Pronjed asked. "Perhaps you'd like to tell me what you and the king discussed last night. What did you say to him that would make him do something like this?"

"Nothing that I can think of," the duke said, looking past the minister toward the windows of the great hall.

"What was it that brought you to Solkara, Lord Orvinti? What did you and the king talk about?"

Before Brall could answer, Fetnalla laid a hand on his arm and pointed toward the doorway at the base of the cloister tower. The queen was there, stepping into the courtyard with the prelate. He held one of her hands, and had his other arm around her waist as if he were supporting her. But it almost seemed to Fetnalla that she led him, and that he was the more frail of the two. Chofya's face looked pale, but her cheeks were dry and her eyes clear. If she had been weeping, she hid it well. She still wore her bed robe, which she pulled tightly around her shoulders, and her dark hair was still tangled with sleep.

Seeing Brall, Pronjed, and the soldiers gathered in the middle of the courtyard, the queen hurried toward them, concern knotting her brow.

"Your Highness," the archminister said gravely, bowing low.

The others did the same.

"We grieve with you, Your Highness," he went on a moment later, "as does all of Aneira. We have lost a great man and glorious king."

"Thank you, Archminister," the queen said, her voice even.

Brall stepped forward and knelt before her. "Your Highness, I don't know how to express to you how sorry I am for your loss, and how much I regret my role in this tragedy."

Chofya stared at him, clearly puzzled. "Your role, Brall? Carden did this to himself."

"With the dagger I gave him."

She actually managed a smile, looking more beautiful in that moment than Fetnalla had ever seen her.

"He wore a blade on his belt as well, Brall. If the one hadn't been at hand, he would have used the other. Now please stand. Your obeisance isn't necessary."

The duke stood slowly. "You are kind, Your Highness. The kingdom is fortunate to have you."

She glanced around at the soldiers, her eyes coming to rest at last on Pronjed. "Why are all these guards here, Archminister?"

"The king is dead, Your Highness, and Lord Orvinti and his company were preparing to leave Solkara. I wished to speak with them before they did."

"Do you intend to take them as prisoners?"

Pronjed's eyes darted briefly to the duke before returning to Chofya's face. "No, Your Highness. But the duke was the last man to see the king alive."

"I thought a servant brought the king wine after the duke returned to his quarters."

"Well yes, but—"

"So you don't believe the duke is guilty of any crime."

The Qirsi's face reddened. "No, Your Highness."

"Then dismiss these men."

"I must object, Your Highness," the archminister said, his voice rising. "Even if your husband was alive when the duke left him, Lord Orvinti was the last person to speak with the king before he killed himself. I think we ought to know what he said that might have caused His Majesty to do this."

"I don't believe the king killed himself because of anything the duke said."

"But you don't know that for certain."

The queen straightened. "I don't wish to discuss this in front of Carden's men, Archminister. Please send them away."

Pronjed nodded reluctantly, then commanded the captain to dismiss the guards. As the men slowly dispersed, a wind knifed through the courtyard, making Chofya shiver.

"Perhaps we should discuss this in the castle, Your Highness," Brall said. "You should be by a fire."

The queen shook her head. "I don't want to go in there."

They lapsed into an uncomfortable silence, still waiting for the soldiers to leave the courtyard. Fetnalla kept her eyes fixed on the queen, but she was conscious of Pronjed standing beside her, his hand resting lightly on the hilt of a short sword. She had known the archminister for nearly six years, and in all that time, she had never once felt at ease in his company. In part, this was because of his position. She might have been first minister in Orvinti, but he was the most powerful Qirsi in the kingdom, and he carried himself like a man acutely aware of his own importance. But more than that, he struck her as having more in common with Eandi nobles than any man or woman of her race she had ever known. Her mother would have said that he had a warrior's heart. Like a young Eandi court lad new to his power, Pronjed always seemed to be eager for a fight, be it with another minister, another Aneiran house, or another kingdom. Most Qirsi in the courts of dukes and kings in the Forelands found themselves tempering the aggression of those they served. Pronjed, she was certain, had fueled it. It might have been why Carden chose him as archminister, but Fetnalla couldn't help but think that he was a man to be feared, a man whose fundamental instincts were at odds with the needs of the kingdom.

"You may have heard, Lord Orvinti," the queen began, when the four of them were alone in the castle ward, "that the castle's master surgeon was garroted yesterday."

Brall's eyes widened. "What?"

"My husband ordered it. At the time I didn't understand why he had done it, except to guess that the surgeon had given the king cause to grieve. There's an old expression: 'When a Solkaran grieves, others will as well.' "

"Was the king dying, Your Highness?" Fetnalla asked.

The queen let out a brittle, desperate laugh that chilled Fetnalla as much as the wind.

"It would seem so, wouldn't it? Carden and I barely spoke after the surgeon was killed, but how else am I to explain all this?"

Brall shook his head. "But to take his own life . . ."

"My husband was a proud man, Lord Orvinti. Too proud to allow himself to grow weak and frail at so young an age. I think he decided it was better to choose the time of his own death than to linger while the kingdom watched him fade."

"You truly think that he'd kill himself?" Pronjed asked.

"You surprise me, Archminister," Chofya said. "You knew the king nearly as well as I. All he did was driven by his pride and his belief in his own power. Without those, he would have been lost. It may not have been your solution or mine, and perhaps if he hadn't drunk so much wine, he would have thought better of it. But that was Carden, for better or for worse. I'd be lying if I said I could have expected him to . . . to do what he did. But I'd also be lying if I told you that I was astonished by it." She looked at Brall again. "This was not your doing, Lord Orvinti. Neither your blade nor your words killed my husband. Be at ease, and mourn with the rest of us."

The duke bowed his head. "You have shown me nothing but kindness since I arrived here, Your Highness. I am your humble servant. If there is anything I can do on your behalf, you need only name it and consider it done."

"My thanks, Brall. As it happens, there is something."

"Your Highness?"

"Perhaps we can speak of it later," she said. "For now, I have a funeral to see to, and messages to dispatch to the other dukes. Worst of all, I have to try to explain to Kalyi what's happened." She paused briefly, staring back at the castle, her expression pained. Then, as if remembering the rest of them, she looked at Brall again. "You and your company are free to remain here until the funeral. As our guests, of course," she added, with a sidelong glance at the archminister.

"Thank you, Your Highness. With your permission, I'll send word of . . . of what's happened to my duchess and have her inform the other nobles of my dukedom."

Chofya nodded absently, as if her thoughts had already turned to other matters. "Yes, Brall, that will be fine. We'll speak again later."

She turned to Pronjed, giving the impression that their conversation had ended.

Brall led his company a short distance from the queen and archminister and looked at his soldiers, his brow furrowing as it often did when he was thinking. "Return our mounts to the stables," he said at last. "Then report to the captain of the king's guard. Tell him that your duke has placed you under his command for the next few days, to be used as he sees fit. You're to consider an order from him as coming from me. Do you understand?"

The senior man among the Orvinti guards nodded. "Yes, my lord." The soldiers bowed to him, before leading the horses back to the stables.

"What about me, my lord?" Fetnalla asked, fearing for just an instant that he might assign her to Pronjed.

"I want you with me," the duke said, much to her relief. "We have a good deal to discuss."

"Very well. You wish to return to your chamber."

Brall hesitated. "My father used to say that no conversation was ever private in a castle. Why don't we walk?" He gestured toward a stone path and they followed it through the central ward to a smaller courtyard, which held the castle gardens. Nothing grew there now, of course, and the pools had been emptied in anticipation of the snows, but the courtyard was empty, and sheltered from the fiercer winds.

Fetnalla watched her duke, waiting for him to speak, but for a long time, he merely stood by one of the dry stone pools, seemingly lost in thought. She guessed that he was still shaken by news of the king's death, but when he finally spoke, he surprised her with the direction his musings had taken.

"Something about this bothers me," he said, his voice low, as if he had forgotten she was even there.

"My lord?"

He looked up at her. "The time for games has passed. Aneira's king is dead, as is its most powerful duke. I can't spend my days wondering what to share with you and what to hide. I have to know right now, can I trust you?"

She felt as though he had kicked her in the chest. "You have to ask?"

"Yes," he said. "In these times, every noble in the land has to ask. Are you a part of this conspiracy I've heard so much about?"

Fetnalla wanted to cry, but she refused to let him see how much he'd hurt her. She would have liked to rail at him for doubting her, or better yet, to just leave her life in Orvinti, never to return. She and Evanthya could go to Caerisse or Sanbira and find a noble who wished to employ both of them.

Instead, mustering what pride she could, the minister met his gaze and said, "No, I've no part in the conspiracy. I have served you as well as I could for six years, and will for as many more as you'll have me."

"I want to believe you," he said.

"Then do. What cause have I given you to doubt me?"

The duke shrugged. "You're Qirsi."

"And you're an Eandi noble. Does that mean you're just like the king, or Mertesse, or the dukes of Eibithar? Not every Qirsi is a traitor."

"Some are."

"Yes. And some nobles are tyrants."

"It's not the same. A tyrant makes himself known with every act. He's easy to spot. A traitor is more insidious, and therefore more dangerous."

She started to argue the point, then stopped. Thinking of it from the perspective of an Eandi and a duke, she had to concede that this was probably true. "I'm not a traitor," she said after a brief pause. "But if you don't believe me, you should find another Qirsi to serve as your first minister."

Brall looked away and shook his head. "I'm not certain that would solve anything."

This she understood as well. Until the conspiracy was defeated—or until it succeeded—every Qirsi in the Forelands would be viewed with even more mistrust than usual, whether or not it was deserved. The duke had little choice but to keep her as his minister.

"Why don't you tell me what you meant before when you said something was bothering you," she said, as if coaxing an answer from a reluctant child.

His eyes met hers for an instant and darted away. "It's probably nothing. I don't know what to believe anymore, even when it should be obvious."

"Just because I'm not part of the conspiracy, that doesn't mean it's not real, or that it can't strike here in Aneira."

"Do you think it has?"

Fetnalla hesitated. She didn't know anything for certain, and she and Evanthya had agreed that they should do nothing to alarm their dukes until they had more information. But if she wanted Brall to trust her, she had to start confiding in him.

"I fear so, yes," she admitted.

"Chago?"

The minister nodded.

"Tebeo and I think so as well."

Her eyes widened at that, and she wondered if Evanthya had already spoken of this with her duke.

"And now you think the king has fallen victim to it as well?" she asked.

Brall rubbed a hand across his brow. "I don't know. I find it hard to believe that he'd take his own life."

"The queen believes it."

"Yes," the duke said. "And so does the archminister. I'm probably just being foolish. But even if he was dying, why would he do this so soon, before he had the chance to name a successor? As it is, he's placed the very future of the kingdom at risk. It makes no sense."

"Much as I agree with you, my lord, I must also say that such a death would be difficult to fabricate. If he did take his own life with a blade, there would be blood on his hands, his clothes, his knife. There are far easier ways to hide a murder, my lord, even for a skilled assassin."

"You're right. But when I spoke with him last night, he didn't seem like a man who was about to kill himself. Talk of the conspiracy had him worried, and clearly something was troubling him. I even went so far as to ask if he was well."

"What did he say?"

Brall shook his head. "Very little. And having spoken with the queen, I now understand why. But still . . ." He shook his head a second time.

"My lord?"

The duke smiled thinly. "You'll think me a fool." He took a breath and then said, "He threatened me."

"What?"

"Maybe that's too strong a word. It was more a warning than a threat. But he told me never to come to him unannounced again. Why would a man who intended to take his own life as soon as I left him bother with something like that?"

It seemed so small a matter as to not merit consideration. She would have expected the king to comment on Brall's sudden appearance at the city gates—his pride would have demanded no less. Yet, she had no answer for the duke's question. It did strike her as odd that a man intent on killing himself would concern himself with matters of propriety.

"You think I'm making too much of it," the duke said, watching her closely.

"I agree that's it odd," she said slowly. "But I don't think that this one comment is enough to prove anything."

"You're probably right. But tell me this: given what we know of his death, is there any way that Qirsi magic might have killed him?"

After all that had passed between them since their departure from Orvinti, Fetnalla could not help but hear an accusation in the question. Immediately, she shook her head. "No, my lord. None at all."

The duke frowned. "I see."

But already, the minister's mind had moved beyond this first response, the direction of her thoughts turning her stomach to stone. For there was a way. It was one of the rarer magics, possessed by Weavers and only a few of the most powerful Qirsi. Those who did wield it almost never admitted as much, not only because it often made them objects of fear, but also because if a would-be victim knew of it, he or she would be less likely to fall prey to its powers. Still, the duke had asked only if there was any way magic had killed Carden, and indeed there was.

"Actually, my lord," she said quietly, "I spoke too quickly." She looked away, so as not to see how his eyes narrowed. "There is one magic that we call 'mind-bending.' A Qirsi possessing such power might have been able to do this."

"Mind-bending," he repeated, his voice thick.

"It allows the person who wields it to control the mind of another, though only for a moment or two." Fetnalla swallowed, knowing how he would respond to what she had to say next. "We also call it delusion magic because it allows one Qirsi to lie to another without fear of discovery. But long ago my people learned that with your people, this magic could do more. It could actually twist the Eandi mind, so that those upon whom it was used could be controlled, instructed to do the Qirsi's bidding."

The duke had paled and he appeared to be holding himself still, as if fearing what she might say next. "So a Qirsi couldn't have done this to another Qirsi. Only to one of us."

She nodded. "That's right."

"Do you have this power?" It wasn't an accusation; she could tell. He was simply afraid of her, of what she was, and of what else she might be. In a way, it was worse.

"No, I don't. And it's hard to know who does," she added, anticipating his next question. "If one Qirsi knows that another has delusion magic, she can guard herself against it. The Qirsi usually tell as few people as possible what powers we possess, but this one in particularly must be kept secret to be effective."

"I see," he said dully. "So you could be lying to me."

This was too much. "I'm not!"

"But you could be! Don't you see, Fetnalla? I have no way of knowing for certain, particularly now that I know of this mind-bending power. Even if you were using this magic on me, I wouldn't know, would I?"

She conceded the point with a single shake of her head. "But your king would have," she said. "A lie we can hide. But if someone took control of his mind long enough to make him pick up the dagger and thrust it into his own chest, he would have known. He just would have been powerless to help himself. It also would have had to be someone he knew, someone he would allow to get close. This power won't work from a distance."

"Pronjed," the duke whispered. "It had to be Pronjed."

"We don't know that, my lord. The king had other ministers. Besides, this is all conjecture. We know nothing for certain, and it would be dangerous to accuse the archminister before we do."

The duke stared at her, until she feared that he would accuse her of some new crime. Instead, he said the one thing she couldn't deny. "You're afraid of him."

"Deeply, my lord. As we all should be if he truly did this."

It was well past midday before someone finally removed the king's body from the great hall. Pronjed ordered soldiers to do it early in the morning, but the queen, at the urging of the damned prelate, insisted on having priests and priestesses of Ean bear him from the hall to the castle cloister. Of course, they had their morning devotions to see to first, and then they had to pray over the body for a time. All of which made it impossible for the servants to begin cleaning the table of the king's blood until just a short time before the ringing of the prior's bell.

Under most circumstances, the archminister wouldn't have cared one way or another. But the longer the king remained there, hunched over the bloody table, the more likely it was that others—in particular the duke of Orvinti and his first minister—would think about how the king had died, rather than merely accepting that he was dead. So, claiming to be concerned for the queen, Pronjed kept the hall locked, opening the doors only for the men and women of the cloister, and the servants who were to clean the mess.

As it happened, the queen appeared to be just fine. She had yet to shed a tear in front of him, and she had already begun preparations for the funeral, dispatching messengers to all the dukedoms with word of Carden's death. She was a model of strength and courage, more worthy of the circlet she wore on her brow than her husband had been of his crown. All of which made Pronjed's next task that much easier.

Killing the king had been his idea. The Weaver, he felt certain, would have approved had there been an opportunity to discuss it with him first. But it only occurred to him at the evening's meal, when Orvinti handed him the blade. He had heard of the garroting of the surgeon—everyone in the castle was speaking of it—and he could guess the reason. He was no fool. The king's daughter would turn ten during the snows and there had been no child since. Not even a stillbirth. It should have been obvious to everyone, especially the king. The greater surprise was that they had a daughter at all. It was enough to make one wonder if Chofya had strayed all those years ago. But the others in the castle were either too circumspect to speak of it, or too dull-witted to see it. Whatever the reason, their silence and the king's made the previous night's murder possible. In the light of morning, the garroting of the surgeon looked less like the pique of an over-proud king and more like the desperate rage of a dying man.

More important, the king's death assured Pronjed of great power and influence when the Qirsi finally put an end to Eandi rule of the Forelands.

The Weaver hoped to divide the land by killing the duke of Bistari and setting the king's foes against House Solkara and its allies. Brall's unexpected appearance at the city gates gave the minister cause to think that this plan might have worked, given some time. But that was the problem. Such unrest would build slowly. It could have taken a year or more to under-mine Carden's power enough to put his house at risk. Killing the king accelerated the process. House Solkara stood now with neither a leader nor an heir. Bistari's duke was dead as well, leaving the field open for others to grasp at the crown. Mertesse, Dantrielle, Orvinti, even Rassor and Noltierre; any one of them might be bold enough to think that he could rule Aneira. If all went well, the land would be at war with itself before the plantings. Surely the Weaver would be pleased.

Only one piece of his plan remained.

Glancing into the hall once more, he saw that the servants had almost rid the table of Carden's blood. Pronjed nodded his satisfaction and made his way through the castle corridors to Carden's quarters, where he knew he would find the queen.

He very nearly let himself into the room without bothering to knock. With Carden dead, the minister almost felt that Castle Solkara belonged to him.

Smiling at the misstep, he knocked once on the door, waiting until the queen called for him to enter before pushing the door open.

She sat at the king's desk, reading through the messages and scrolls piled upon it. Throughout his reign, her husband showed little patience for matters of state, preferring the pageantry and swordplay that came with the crown. The fees that aroused such resentment in Bistari had been levied at Pronjed's suggestion. The archminister couldn't help but think that he had done the people of Aneira a great service the previous night. No matter who ascended to the throne next, it had to be an improvement over Carden. Of course, the next reign promised to be quite brief. Once the Weaver rose to power, he would assign Qirsi to all the thrones in the Forelands.

"Archminister," the queen said, looking up from the papers. With the windows shuttered against the cold, the room was dark, save for two lamps burning on either side of the desk. "I'm glad you're here. Do you know if all the dukes have paid their fees for this turn? I see messages here from every dukedom but Bistari and Tounstrel. I can understand if Chago's son might be late with his tribute, but I don't want Vidor thinking that he can delay out of anger. Particularly now."

Truly she was a wonder, as brilliant as she was beautiful. Dressed in a black gown, with her dark hair held back by the golden circlet on her brow and her oval face paler and thinner than usual, she looked every bit the grieving young queen. This was a woman who could win the hearts of a kingdom. If Aneira's dukes took her lightly, she would crush them. But first she had to be convinced that she wanted to.

"Archminister?" she said again, frowning slightly.

"Yes, Your Highness. The fees. I'm not certain who has paid and who hasn't, but I'll speak with the treasury minister."

"I'd be grateful." She gestured at a chair with an open hand. "Please."

"Thank you, Your Highness," he said, stepping to the chair and sitting. "You're to be commended for your attention to these matters, Your Highness, but surely they can wait. Shouldn't you be with your daughter?"

She stared at the desk. "Perhaps. I was with her for a time earlier. She's still in the cloister, crying for her father and praying with the prelate."

"That's to be expected, Your Highness. She's suffered a terrible loss. As you have."

"It's harder for her."

"Only because she's young, Your Highness. You've lost the man you love."

She pushed herself out of her seat and began pacing behind the desk. "Stop playing games, Archminister. We both know better."

Pronjed prided himself on knowing all that went on in Castle Solkara, be it in the feasting halls and working chambers, or the corridors and sleeping quarters. But this caught him utterly unprepared. "Truly, Your Highness, I don't understand."

"You know what kind of man he was. He didn't marry me out of love any more than he married me to please his father."

This much at least, the minister knew. Chofya came from an earldom in Noltierre, the daughter of a insignificant noble. Tomaz, Carden's father, had wanted his son to marry the daughter of a duke, preferably one from Dantrielle or Kett. Such a marriage would have gone a long way to healing the rifts that had already started to divide the kingdom. But while journeying to the south for a hunt, Carden saw Chofya and, Pronjed had always believed, fell in love with her. When he returned to Solkara the young prince insisted that his father arrange the marriage. For a time, the king refused, but Carden was not to be dissuaded and finally Tomaz relented.

"I was a prize, Archminister," she continued after a few moments, and to his surprise there were, at last, tears on her face. "I was a jewel to be worn so that he might dazzle others. The same pride that led him to take his own life made him want me as his queen. He wanted me for my beauty, and I wanted him for his power and his wealth. Our marriage was a calculated matter for both of us. I wouldn't call it loveless, but neither would I call it loving. He had his dalliances, and it may surprise you to know that I did as well. So let's not speak of love and other trifles. There are more important matters at stake here."

"Such as?"

"The future of the kingdom, of course."

Pronjed had to suppress a smile. Just a few moments before, walking through the castle corridors, he had wondered how he might turn their conversation to this point. He never imagined that she would do it for him.

"I believe, Your Highness," he began, as if misunderstanding her, "that you are the future of Aneira. Whether or not you and the king loved each other, you are the queen. All the land sees you that way." He waved a hand at the desk. "Already you're applying yourself to the task of running the kingdom. It might not be easy to convince the dukes, but I can think of no better choice to succeed your husband."

Chofya laughed. "You flatter me, Pronjed. Even I know that I can't rule Aneira. There's no Solkaran blood in my veins, nor even the blood of one of the other major houses. I'm from a low family. If I tried to claim the throne for myself, the other houses would band together and destroy me. No," she said, shaking her head. "I'm not Aneira's future."

"If not you, then who? Brall? Tebeo of Dantrielle? The boy in Mertesse? None of them is worthy, Your Highness. We both know that."

"I agree," she said, surprising him again. "But there is one who is worthy, and who would continue the Solkaran line."

It was more than he could have hoped. She had taken him just where he intended to take her. The minister found himself wondering if he had misjudged the queen. He knew how clever she was, and how long she had worked to educate herself in the ways of the court. But he hadn't realized just how ambitious she was.

"Who, Your Highness?" Trying not to sound too eager.

"Kalyi, of course. I want my daughter to rule Aneira."

"She'll make a fine queen, Your Highness, but what I said about you applies to her as well. The kingdom hasn't been ruled by a queen since the Time of Queens centuries ago, and that ended with the other dukes threatening rebellion."

"I know that. But she's Carden's only heir, and as such has a legitimate claim to the throne."

"You'll need a regent, of course. That complicates matters as well. The dukes may oppose you."

"Some might. But I believe I can convince Brall to support me in this, and if so, perhaps he can win over some of the others."

"You've given this much thought, Your Highness."

"I've thought of little else all day. The hardest part, as you say, will be choosing her regent. Obviously, I can't be selected. It will have to be one of Carden's brothers."

Pronjed raised an eyebrow. "Ah, the brothers."

"You know them?"

"Well enough, Your Highness. If I may be permitted to speak freely, I don't think much of any of them."

"Neither do I," the queen said. "And neither did Carden. The Jackals and the Fool, he used to call them."

"I remember."

"I wouldn't trust the Jackals with my daughter, not for a moment. Numar, the Fool, on the other hand, will be more easily turned to our purposes."

Our purposes. Pronjed nearly laughed aloud. Already she counted him as an ally in this.

"Numar is the youngest, Your Highness. All Aneira will expect us to turn to Grigor. Tradition demands no less."

Chofya stopped her pacing, shaking her head with such vehemence that Pronjed half expected the circlet to fly from her brow. "Grigor is a dangerous man. He'll do everything he can to take the crown for himself, even if it means killing Kalyi."

"Then we'll have to watch him with great care. Against one of us or the other, his designs might bear fruit. But against both of us he won't have a chance."

She smiled at him, looking so relieved and so grateful one might have thought that he had already placed the Scepter of Tomaz in the girl's hands.

"Thank you, Pronjed. All of this will be much easier with you at my side."

Chapter
Seven

✦

City of Kings, Eibithar

t all comes back to Thorald, Your Majesty," Wenda said, her eyes fixed on the king, who stood motionless before the fire. "In that respect nothing has changed. As long as Tobbar continues to support you, and remains above the dispute between Curgh and Kentigern, you should be able to keep the houses from going to war."

Dyre sat forward, his pale eyes flicking from Wenda to the king and then to Keziah. "But Tobbar isn't well. If he dies before these matters are resolved, there's no telling what Thorald will do."

"Actually, it seems quite clear to me," Paegar said. "Tobbar has two sons in Shanstead, both of whom have much to gain from Thorald's return to supremacy. I expect that if Tobbar dies any time soon, they'll immediately throw the weight of their house behind Aindreas." He turned to Gershon. "Wouldn't you agree, swordmaster?"

Keziah might as well have not been in the room. She might have been archminister to the king of Eibithar, but to Kearney's other advisors, she was nothing. Wenda, Paegar, and Dyre had all served as ministers under Aylyn the Second, the late king. Natan jal Samara, Aylyn's archminister, left Audun's Castle when the old king died, having served him for nearly seventeen years. One might have expected the other ministers to do the same, but Kearney chose to keep them on, and at the time it seemed a wise decision. Kearney, the former duke of Glyndwr, ascended to the throne under the most extraordinary of circumstances, agreeing to lead the land after it became clear that this was the only way to avoid a war between

Javan of Curgh and Aindreas of Kentigern. Recognizing that some might question his claim to the throne, since under Eibithar's Rules of Ascension he was not the rightful king, Kearney thought it best to continue the practices of his predecessor as much as possible.

But rather than raising Wenda to archminister, making Paegar and Dyre his high ministers, and bringing in his own Qirsi as underministers, Kearney made Keziah his lead advisor, just as she had been in Glyndwr. No one could find fault with the king for doing this. He also made Gershon Trasker, his swordmaster in Glyndwr, the commander of the King's Guard. Such was the prerogative of a new ruler.

While the other Qirsi accepted the new king's choice, however, they did not accept her. When she spoke, they listened, and when Kearney agreed with her counsel, they yielded to his judgment. But they never asked her opinion, and they never deferred to her in discussions such as this one, though it would have been proper, given her position. They wouldn't even look at her, unless it was to glare at her responses to the king's questions. In recent days, over the past turn or so, Paegar had begun to show some signs of accepting her. But this was just a beginning, and a small one at that. Kearney had made her the most powerful Qirsi in the kingdom, and Keziah found herself afraid to so much as speak without leave from the king.

Gershon, who distrusted all Qirsi, hated her most of all, and did nothing to help her. Indeed, he seemed to relish her discomfort. While they still lived in Glyndwr, Kearney and Keziah had been lovers, sharing a dangerous and forbidden love for which the swordmaster blamed her and not his duke. Keziah had hoped that coming to the City of Kings might force them to put their differences aside and allow them to build on the progress they made during their ride to Kentigern, meager though it was. But if anything, the swordmaster had grown more protective of Kearney and thus more hostile toward her.

For his part, the king appeared to be oblivious of the politics of his court, or perhaps he just felt that it was up to Keziah and the others to make peace with each other without compromising their oaths to serve him. Their love affair ended with Kearney's ascension—it was one thing for an Eandi duke in the remote highlands of Glyndwr to love a Qirsi woman, he explained at the time, but it was quite another for a king to do so. She still remembered their last night together, in the Glyndwr Highlands, shortly before Kearney's army marched to Kentigern, with a vividness that made her skin tingle.

"I agree that Tobbar's sons have less interest than he in recognizing

Glyndwr's claim to the throne," Gershon said, glancing at Paegar before turning his gaze to the king. "But they have much to lose if this comes to civil war."

Kearney looked up from the fire. "Explain."

"When you ascended to the throne, we assumed that both Javan and Aindreas had abdicated in your favor. That's what you and the others agreed to in Kentigern. And so it followed that your investiture was consistent with the Rules of Ascension. But since then, Aindreas has claimed that he never agreed to this, that the bargain struck that night involved only you and Javan. In effect, Kentigern claims that you and Curgh stole his crown, and he's convinced the duke of Galdasten of this as well. In their eyes, with you as king, the Rules of Ascension are dead. This leaves them free to challenge your authority and even wage war against you without it being treason under the law."

Dyre nodded. "It also allows the lords of Galdasten to lay claim to the throne again, without waiting any longer."

Keziah had to agree that this made a good deal of sense, though she still found Aindreas's deception infuriating. Not only did it allow Aindreas to justify his defiance of the new king, but it allowed the House of Galdasten to move beyond the tragedy of 872, when a madman brought the pestilence to Galdasten Castle, killing the duke and duchess as well as their children. Under the Rules of Ascension, the House of Galdasten would have had to wait four generations before being recognized once more in the Order of Ascension. Abandoning the rules ended their wait.

"All this may be true," Wenda said. "But where does that leave Thorald?"

"Under the Rules of Ascension," Gershon answered, "Thorald has been Eibithar's preeminent house. Tobbar's sons, particularly the older one, won't be inclined to give up that standing."

Keziah cleared her throat awkwardly, drawing their gazes, including Kearney's. Feeling their eyes upon her, she nearly held her tongue. *I'm archminister,* she told herself. *I have a right to speak here, and a responsibility as well.*

"With the deaths of the elder and younger Filib," she said, "Thorald has no immediate claim to the throne either—that's why Javan was in line to be king. Won't Tobbar's sons be as willing as the duke of Galdasten to turn away from the rules?"

"Maybe," Gershon said. "It depends upon whether their own ambitions outweigh their loyalty to the house and their ambitions for their children. Their situation is different from that in Galdasten. Kell of Galdasten had no brother. His death nearly killed the entire family line. Filib the Elder had Tobbar, so the damage wasn't as great. Tobbar's sons can't claim the throne, but they need only wait one generation more. Marston's son can rule the land, and if he does, the younger boy's son becomes duke of Thorald rather than merely thane of Shanstead."

Keziah nodded, then rubbed a hand across her brow. Since Kearney became king, she had spent a good deal of time poring over the Rules of Ascension, trying to anticipate ways in which Glyndwr's enemies might seek to subvert the house's new power. Yet she still found the rules arcane beyond comprehension. They were inordinately detailed, providing for nearly every contingency, and therein lay their strength. The rules assured that the noble houses of Eibithar would always have a method by which to select a new king, even under the most trying of circumstances. At the same time, they allowed for some sharing of power among the kingdom's major houses, so that one family would not be able to hold the throne for centuries at a time, as had the Solkarans in Aneira and the Enharfes in Caerisse. Recently though, Keziah had begun to wonder if all the time the nobles of Eibithar spent fighting over the rules did more to undermine the kingdom's stability than the rules did to guard it.

"Do we have someone speaking with Tobbar's sons?" the king asked, looking first at Gershon, and then at the ministers, his eyes finally coming to rest on Keziah.

"We send messages to Tobbar regularly, Your Majesty," the archminister said. "We rely on the duke to see to his sons."

Kearney frowned. "But the duke is ill. From all I've heard, he may be dying. Wouldn't we be foolish to ignore the sons until after the father is dead?"

"It would be . . . inappropriate for us to send messages directly to either the thane of Shanstead or his brother, Your Majesty," Wenda said. "It might imply that we distrust the duke. At the very least it would indicate that we no longer consider him the leader of the House of Thorald."

Kearney threw up his hands. "Then don't allow the message to come directly from the throne. Use one of our allies. Use Lathrop."

"The duke of Tremain, Your Majesty?"

"Yes. Ask him to contact Marston. He shouldn't mention that he's acting at my behest, but we need him to get some sense of where the thane and his brother stand."

"Tobbar will see through that immediately," Gershon said.

"No doubt," the king agreed. "But he'll also understand why we're doing it. We don't need Thorald and his sons as allies in this. As long as

Thorald refuses to take sides, Aindreas can't challenge us. But if the brothers Shanstead sympathize with Kentigern and Galdasten, we need to know, so that we can make plans to defend ourselves and the houses standing with us."

Wenda nodded. "That seems a wise course, Your Majesty."

"Will you see to it, Archminister?" Kearney asked, facing Keziah once more. "I'd like the message dispatched before nightfall."

"Of course, Your Majesty."

"Very good," the king said. He glanced around the chamber. "Is there anything else?"

No one spoke, and after a moment Kearney gave a single nod. "Then we'll meet again in the morning."

The ministers stood and started to leave, as did Gershon.

"Archminister," the king called as Keziah reached the door. "A word?"

She cast an uneasy look at the others, all of whom were staring at her. "Of course, Your Majesty," she said, returning to her chair.

"You understand what I want in this message?" the king asked when he and Keziah were alone.

"Yes, Your Majesty," she said, knowing this couldn't be the only reason he had called her back.

Kearney opened his mouth as if to say something, then shook his head and turned away, looking hurt and just a bit angry.

He had told her several times that he didn't like her calling him "Your Majesty."

"It makes me feel that I've lost you," he told her on one occasion. "When we're with others, I understand that you have to. But when we're alone . . ."

When we're alone, she wanted to say, *it's the only way I can remind myself that you don't love me anymore.* He still looked the same, with a youthful face and brilliant green eyes beneath a shock of silver hair. They still saw each other every day and she still dreamed of his touch at night. Yes, they were in Audun's Castle, and yes, Kearney wore the jeweled circlet on his brow, but it would have been so easy for her to forget that their love had ended. She needed to address him formally for the same reason Kearney hated it: so that she'd know she had lost him forever.

"I trust you're well," he said after a brief silence.

"Yes, Your—" She let out a slow breath. "I'm fine."

"Good." He glanced at her briefly, looking uncertain. "Do you think Thorald can be convinced to support us?"

"Only if it serves them. You're a young man, and you have an heir. Under the rules, Glyndwr will hold the throne for as long as the line of heirs continues uninterrupted. Already they can see that their wait will be a long one. Gershon may believe they'll be slow to abandon the rules because of Thorald's position among the houses, but I'm less certain."

"Why didn't you say so earlier?"

She shrugged, gazing toward the fire. Five turns ago she could have explained it to him, but now he had other burdens. Her problems paled beside those of Eibithar and her king.

"It's not like you to lower your sword, Kez, especially where Gershon is concerned."

Keziah smiled. He hadn't called her that in a long time.

"I saw no reason to argue the point," she said. "The truth is, none of us knows what Tobbar will do, much less Marston and his brother. Perhaps after we've heard back from Lathrop we'll have a better sense of what we can expect from Thorald and Shanstead."

The king nodded, his brow furrowing beneath the violet jewel on his crown. "Perhaps."

They fell silent again, the king standing near his desk, and Keziah watching him from the chair. Whatever it was he had called her back to discuss clearly made him uneasy. But it wasn't until he finally spoke that she understood why.

"Have you had word from your friend?" he asked, his eyes flicking in her direction for just an instant.

"My friend?" she repeated.

"The gleaner."

It took her a moment to realize that he meant Grinsa, who was more than just her friend and a good deal more than a mere gleaner. Grinsa jal Arriet was a Weaver, a Qirsi who could bind together the powers of many Qirsi and wield all their magic as if it were his own. Such was the fear of Weavers among the Eandi that ever since the Qirsi Wars centuries ago, Weavers and their families had been executed upon being discovered. This explained why even Kearney, whom Keziah still loved as she had no other man, only knew Grinsa as her friend. In fact he was her brother, though, because of Qirsi naming customs, by which sons carried their mother's name, and daughters their father's, this was easy to conceal.

When Kearney first met Grinsa in Tremain during the growing turns, the king had sensed the power of the love they shared, and had actually been jealous. Keziah couldn't help but notice, just from the way he asked about Grinsa, that a residue of that jealousy remained to this day. Maybe she hadn't lost him entirely after all.

"No, I've heard nothing from him in some time."

Kearney twisted his mouth, as if uncertain whether to be relieved or disappointed.

"I thought maybe with the Revel in the city . . ."

"He's not with the Revel anymore. He's with Lord Tavis."

The king nodded. "I know. Do you have any way of contacting him?"

He contacts me in my dreams, as Weavers do. "No, I'm afraid I don't." She watched him as he squatted to stir the fire. "You're concerned about Tavis?"

"Of course," the king said without looking at her. "But more than that, I'm eager to learn if they've found Brienne's killer. If they can prove Tavis's innocence, we might end this conflict between Curgh and Kentigern before it turns to war."

"I suppose we might," she said, though she found herself wondering if it was too late for that. Even if there were a way to prove beyond any doubt that the Curgh boy hadn't killed Lady Brienne of Kentigern, her death and all that followed it had left scars on both houses. Their hatred for each other ran deep; bridging that rift would take time.

"Isn't there any way to find him?" Kearney asked, looking back at her, his face ruddy from the heat of the fire. "Is there no one to whom you can send a message?"

"I don't even know where they've gone. Before he left, Grinsa said something about going to Aneira, but he didn't tell me more. And while I may be archminister to Eibithar's king," she added with a small smile, "that doesn't carry much weight with the Aneirans."

Kearney tried to smile, but he just looked pained, like a man too aware of his own powerlessness to find humor in the limitations of those who served him.

"If you hear anything, you'll let me know?"

"Of course."

They remained that way for several moments, their eyes locked. Finally Keziah stood, looking away as she did.

"I'll see to that message," she said. "The one to Lathrop."

"Thank you."

She crossed to the door quickly and pulled it open. Glancing back one last time, she saw that Kearney was stirring the fire again, his lips tightly pressed together. She couldn't begin to guess what he was feeling, which scared her more than anything else.

*   *   *

There were times, more often than he cared to admit, when Paegar felt like a coward in his first battle. Standing by the door of his quarters waiting for the archminister to return from her conversation with Kearney, the minister smiled ruefully at the image. It wasn't just that he wanted to survive what he knew was coming. Above all else, he wished to make it through each day without being noticed by anyone, neither his allies nor his enemies. If he could have made himself invisible, like some mischievous demon from the Underrealm, he would have done it in an instant. Failing that, he did all he could to appear as ordinary as a chair or a table. He never allowed himself to arrive late for the king's daily discussions, but neither did he reach Kearney's chambers too early. He said little, but he always said something, so as not to make himself conspicuous with his silence. Most important, he did everything in his power to avoid the Qirsi healer with whom he had conspired to kill King Aylyn during Adriel's Turn.

Murdering the old king certainly had been a coward's act. Aylyn had been so weak, so lost to life already, that it barely counted as a murder at all. Paegar might have placed the pillow over the king's face to smother him, but the old man offered no resistance. For all the high minister knew, Aylyn may have been dead already.

Still, that night had haunted his sleep ever since. He dreamed of the murder quite often, and every time it was the same. He laid the kerchief over the king's mouth and nose, lifted the pillow, and placed it down on Aylyn's face, pressing harder and harder until he was leaning on the old king with all his weight. At first, just like the actual murder, Aylyn offered no resistance. But then suddenly, a mind-twisting pain ripped through Paegar's gut and he staggered backward to find the king's dagger buried hilt-deep in his belly. Looking up, he saw the pillow and kerchief fall away, revealing the king's face, his eyes wide open and a fierce grin on his pale lips.

Invariably the minister awoke soaked with sweat, his heart pounding against his chest and tears dampening his cheeks. Sleep was lost to him for the rest of the night. All he could do was sit in the darkness, choking back his sobs and hoping that no one passing by his chamber door would hear. He dreaded the dream as the wife of a drunken brute might dread a beating; the longer he waited, the more certain he grew that it would happen again soon.

Yet, when he lay down to sleep each night and prayed to Shyssir for gentle visions, it wasn't this dream he had in mind, but rather another that he feared even more. The vision of the Weaver. The leader of the Qirsi movement had only appeared to him twice, once to ask the minister to join his cause and a second time to tell him that the king had to die. To this day, he wondered how the Weaver had known to find him. Certainly one of the others had mentioned his name, but that didn't really change the question. How had they known that he would take their gold and betray his king? How could they have known that his loyalties to both Aylyn and Eibithar were so tenuous when he hadn't realized it himself? He still recalled the night he returned from one of the city's sanctuaries—he no longer remembered which one, though he often tried, thinking it important somehow— to find a small leather pouch on his bed. It was filled with five-qinde pieces, sixteen of them, more gold than he earned in an entire year as the king's minister.

That night he fell into a vision of a windy plain, and on that plain, at the top of a steep rise, he found the man who would thereafter control his life. At first he thought it a simple dream, a fantasy brought on by the mysterious gift, and even after the Weaver spoke to him of the gold, he failed to grasp that it was anything more. Only when the Weaver hurt him, wrapping an unseen hand around his throat and squeezing until Paegar thought he would die, did he understand that all of it was real. When he dared to ask why he had been chosen, the Weaver said only that he was one of the fortunate ones, that he had a choice. His service to the cause would be rewarded with riches; his refusal to serve would result in a slow, painful death.

For a time he served merely by giving information to others who contacted him on the Weaver's behalf. In return, he received small payments of gold. The night after he killed Aylyn, he found more than one hundred qinde in his chamber. He still didn't know who paid him or how the courier delivered the gold. But the Weaver remained true to his word— Paegar served, and he was paid. He could only assume that if he ever defied the Weaver he would die.

Thus, he lived in constant fear of having to take another life on behalf of the cause. For though he managed to murder an ailing old man who was already on his deathbed, and who had no wife or young children to mourn him, Paegar couldn't bear the thought of having to kill this new king. The minister owed nothing to Kearney, nor did he care if it fell to one of the others to assassinate him. But he hadn't the stomach for it himself.

It no longer bothered him that he was a coward. In his youth it had been the source of much shame, but as he grew older he began to accept it as a part of who he was, like his intelligence and his various magics. If nothing else, Paegar knew, it would allow him to live a long life, at least by Qirsi standards.

Unless the Weaver had other plans for him. He felt certain that the Weaver would see no virtue in his cowardice, but rather would view it as an impediment to Paegar's ability to serve the movement, perhaps even as cause to rid himself of the minister. So Paegar had decided that he needed to make himself indispensable to the Weaver. Not as a killer, since his talents didn't lie there, but in some other way. And he had to do so quickly. It was only a matter of time before the Weaver came to him again. Too much time had passed since their last conversation, and as with his disturbing dream of Aylyn's murder, Paegar knew he would have to wait only so long for the next one.

For more than a turn he had struggled to find some task that would keep him in good stead with the Weaver. The gold left for him after Aylyn's murder had been payment for the killing, but he knew the Weaver well enough to understand that it had also been intended as incentive to do more.

"I want those who serve the cause to go beyond my instructions," the Weaver told him the very first night they spoke. "I expect them to work on behalf of this movement at all times."

He knew better than to hope the Weaver would never ask him to kill again. If he found another way to serve the movement, however, one that even the Weaver himself could not have imagined, he might forestall the next murder for at least a short while. But what?

The answer finally came to him by chance, after he overheard a conversation between Gershon Trasker, Kearney's ill-tempered swordmaster, and Leilia, the queen. Gershon and the king's wife were in the corridor near Kearney's quarters, and Paegar had just descended the stairs of the prelate's tower. Hearing them speak, he kept himself in the shadows by the doorway and strained his ears to listen. Much of what they said held little interest for him. There was to be a feast the following night, and Gershon, always concerned for the king's safety, had asked to arrange some of the seating. Near the end of their discussion, however, Leilia said something that caught the minister's attention.

"I assume that the Qirsi whore will be there."

"Yes, my lady," the swordmaster answered.

"I want her as far from me and as far from Kearney as possible."

"The king is welcoming the duke of Aratamme, my lady. The duke will have his first minister by his side, and it's customary for the king's archminister to sit with the ranking Qirsi of a visiting noble." He seemed to hesitate briefly. "I assure you, my lady, their . . . trysts are over."

"I don't care if they're over, and I don't care if the queen of Sanbira herself is coming!" the queen said, her voice growing shrill. "I don't want that woman at our table!"

"To have her sit anywhere else would raise questions, my lady, questions that might be . . . awkward for both you and the king."

A long pause followed. At last Leilia muttered a most unqueenly curse. "Fine," she said. "Just put her at the end of the table. I don't want to have to see her, much less speak with her."

"Of course, my lady."

Their conversation ended a short time later and they walked off in opposite directions, the queen heading toward her chambers and the swordmaster entering Kearney's. Paegar had been on his way to speak with Keziah, Wenda, and Dyre, but he remained where he was for a long time, hidden in the shadows, his back leaning against the rough stone of the tower's inner wall.

One didn't have to be a scholar to make sense of what he had just heard. The king and the archminister were lovers, or at least they had been. From what he knew of the king, Paegar found it hard to believe that Kearney would have risked a forbidden love, even as the duke of a remote house on the Caerissan Steppe. But much of what he had observed of the king and his minister over the past several turns made far more sense in the context of a failed love affair. There was a sadness to Keziah that went far beyond anything that could be explained by the treatment she had received from her fellow ministers. For his part, the king's gaze often seemed to linger too long on the archminister during their discussions. On several occasions, Paegar found Kearney staring at Keziah's face long after she had finished speaking. He hadn't given it much thought before. Keziah was a beautiful woman, with a round, pretty face, pale yellow eyes, and long white hair that she always wore tied back in twin braids. Paegar had allowed that the king might be taken with her, as he himself was. But until this day, he had never guessed that they might share something more. Once confronted with the possibility, however, the minister could only rail at himself for failing to see it sooner.

Here was the prize he could offer to his Weaver. Wouldn't the leader of the Qirsi movement be interested to know that the archminister of Eibithar's new king had been the man's lover? Wouldn't the Weaver find some way to use such information, and wouldn't he reward handsomely the man who first brought it to him?

But his thoughts didn't stop there. What if Paegar could do more? What if by the time the Weaver entered his dreams again, the minister had already started turning the archminister to the Qirsi cause? Perhaps the king had ended their love cruelly, or maybe the hostility of the other ministers had left her resentful of both them and the king they served. He could see already that she and Gershon mistrusted one another, and no doubt she hated Leilia as much as the queen hated her. As far as Paegar could tell, Keziah lived as an exile, friendless, loveless, and joyless. To this point, he had done nothing but contribute to her pain. The other ministers resented the king's decision to pass over Wenda and make Keziah archminister, so Paegar had treated her with disdain as well. To befriend her would have been to draw attention to himself.

Now, though, he saw how much might be gained by making himself the archminister's confidant. There still were risks, but the possible rewards seemed too great to be ignored.

He started slowly, so as not to appear too obvious. Two days after overhearing the queen's remarks, when Keziah arrived for their daily audience with Kearney, Paegar allowed his gaze to meet hers and nodded a greeting. Even this small kindness seemed to surprise her, and she hesitated for an instant before nodding in return. A few days later, the minister arranged what would appear to Keziah to be a chance encounter in the castle corridors. Again, he didn't do much—he had to build her trust slowly, as one might win the affections of a feral cat. He merely nodded to her as they passed one another, adding, "Good day, Archminister," almost as an afterthought. Keziah murmured a reply, and Paegar found himself wondering if he had already pushed her too far too quickly.

The following day, however, when they met again in Kearney's chambers, the archminister nodded to him first, offering a small smile as well. Paegar struggled to keep himself from looking too pleased as he returned the nod. But his heart raced like that of a young man in love. It had begun. He no longer wondered if he could win her trust; the question now was how soon.

Fighting his excitement and his eagerness to build on these successes, the minister forced himself to avoid her. For much of Bian's waning, he refused to speak with her again. He even went so far as to argue a point with her in front of the king and the other ministers, though it required that he take the lead role in that day's discussion. Early in the new turn, however, he began once more to extend small kindnesses to her. He nodded to her at the start of each audience, and occasionally offered a smile if something in the discussion struck him as humorous. A second "chance" encounter, this one near the ministerial chambers, included not just a "good day," but a "hope you're well," besides. The following day he managed to arrive at the king's door just as she did and, bidding her good morning, held the door open for her, smiling as she stepped past him into the chamber.

All of which led to this day. He would have preferred to build to this over a few more days, but hearing the king ask Keziah to remain with him after the audience ended, Paegar realized that he could wait no longer. If Kearney began to turn to her for more counsel, or—gods forbid it—rekindled her passion for him even in the smallest way, all would be lost. He had to take the next step now.

Her quarters, like those of all the king's ministers, were on the same corridor as his, albeit at the far end. If she returned here directly from Kearney's chambers, she would pass by his bedchamber. So Paegar stood by the door, waiting and listening. For a long time he heard nothing, until he began to fear that he had miscalculated and that she had gone elsewhere after speaking with the king. At last, however, he heard the faint slap of footsteps on the stairs of the nearest tower. A moment later, she stepped into the corridor.

He waited until she had just passed his door before pulling it open and stepping out of his chamber.

Keziah turned at the sound and offered a small smile, though clearly something troubled her.

"Archminister," he said, smiling in return as he closed his door. He rubbed his arm and frowned. "These corridors get rather cold this time of year. Especially when the wind blows off the steppe."

She nodded, appearing unsure as to how to respond. "Yes," she finally said. "I suppose they do."

"Is everything all right, Archminister?"

"Yes, of course. Why?"

"You seem . . . distracted. And after the king asked you to remain, I feared that perhaps something had happened with respect to Thorald, or even worse, Kentigern."

"No," she said. "There's nothing. He just wanted to speak with me about some changes he's been considering with the ducal tithes."

During the past turn, as he first started trying to win her trust, Paegar had wondered what powers the archminister possessed. If that was the most convincing lie she had to offer, he felt reasonably certain that delusion wasn't one of them.

"I see," he said. "Well, I'm relieved to hear it was nothing more." He smiled again and started toward the tower stairs. "Good day, Archminister."

"Good day."

He let her get almost all the way to her door before calling to her again. "I was on my way to the kitchen," he said. "I didn't eat before we spoke with the king. Would you care to join me?"

Paegar saw her hesitate. She even took a step back in his direction, before stopping herself.

"Thank you, High Minister. It's kind of you to ask." She paused again, chewing her lip. One might have thought he had asked her to leave Kearney and serve the emperor of Braedon. "I really should return to my quarters, though," she said. "I've a message to the duke of Tremain that I need to compose. Perhaps another time?"

It was just the response he expected. The only surprise was that she gave his offer so much thought.

"Of course, Archminister. Another time."

He turned away and descended the stairs, hearing her door open and close as he did. Only then did he allow himself a grin. To anyone watching, it would have seemed an insignificant encounter, a meaningless invitation politely refused. Paegar knew better, however. He had seen her waver as she weighed his proposal. He had seen her cheeks color slightly when she asked if they might sup together another time. She was starved for friendship and he had offered her sustenance. It would still take time, but already he felt certain that he had her. The greatest danger lay not in anything she might do, but rather in his own zeal. He couldn't rush this. She was lonely, to be sure, but she was also clever. He risked all by trying to ingratiate himself too quickly. Still, he had already begun to plan their next encounter, feeling certain that he could build on this one.

"Let the Weaver come," he whispered, crossing the castle courtyard to the kitchen tower. "I have a prize for him."

Chapter
Eight

✦

indreas stood atop the east wall of the castle gazing out over the city of Kentigern and the open land beyond its walls. The late-morning sun shone upon him from a sky of clearest blue, but it offered little warmth in the cold, steady wind sweeping across the face of the tor.

Beside him, Ennis, his youngest child and sole heir, kicked at the stone wall with a booted foot, making the barrel on which he stood wobble noisily. He was almost too big to stand on it anymore, though he wasn't yet tall enough to see over the wall without it.

"If you don't stop that kicking, you're liable to fall," Aindreas said.

The boy had never fallen before, of course, and he did this every time they walked the walls together. But Ioanna would have expected him to say something, and she would have his head on a pike if the boy did manage to hurt himself. When a mother lost one child, she grew ever more protective of those who remained.

"Yes, Father," Ennis said. He stopped kicking, but almost immediately began hopping from one foot to the other.

The duke could do nothing but smile. It was something he would have done as a child. Not surprising, really, since the boy favored him in almost every other way. He was bigger than most boys two or three years older than he, and his red hair, grey eyes, and round face were so like Aindreas's that even the castle guards had taken to calling him the Little Duke.

"Do you see him yet, Father?" the boy asked, sounding a bit more impatient than the last time he asked.

"Actually, I do," the duke said, marking the progress of a small company of riders on the road leading from Kentigern Wood to the city.

Ennis looked up at him, a smile brightening his ruddy face. "Really?"

Aindreas nodded and pointed toward the road. "See for yourself."

The boy rested his hands on the top of the wall and stared out at the riders. "I can see two flags," the said, "but I can't make out what's on them."

"There's a golden stallion on the red one. That's the banner of Thorald. And the blue one bears the crest of Shanstead, crossed swords over a rising sun."

"Which rider is the thane?" Ennis asked.

"It's hard to say from here. Probably the one riding just behind the men with the banners."

The boy looked up at his father, squinting against the sun. "Do you think he'll liance us?"

Aindreas couldn't help but grin. "Do you mean, Do I think he'll form an alliance with us?"

"Yes, that's what I meant."

Aindreas stared down at the riders again. "I don't know. Marston isn't the duke yet, and he can't do anything until he is. But I wouldn't have asked him here if I didn't think there was a possibility."

"Does he like the people who killed Brienne?"

The duke eyed the boy briefly, wondering whether to correct this as well. Ennis wasn't yet ten, but he was a bright boy, wise beyond his years. Perhaps he was ready to understand a more subtle explanation for Marston's visit.

"It was just one man who killed Brienne, boy."

"Lord Tavis."

Aindreas nodded and tried to say more, but the words stuck in his throat at the thought of his daughter.

"But you hate his father, too. And the king. I've heard you speaking of it with Villyd and the prelate."

The boy missed little of what went on around him. He'd make a good duke.

"Yes, I hate Javan of Curgh, and though I wouldn't say that I hate Kearney, I do believe that he betrayed us."

"How?"

"By giving asylum to that Curgh demon, and by turning Tobbar against me before I even had a chance to speak with him."

He glanced down again to find the boy staring at him, a puzzled look on his face. Maybe he wasn't ready for this after all.

"What's asylum?"

"It's when a noble gives protection to someone. Kearney guarded the boy after he escaped our prison and refused to return him to us."

Ennis frowned. "Why? Didn't he like Brienne?"

Aindreas almost ended the conversation there. He didn't want to have to admit the rest. But he was a duke and a father, and if the boy was to hear some of it, he had to hear all of it.

"Kearney doesn't believe Tavis killed her," he said. "Javan and his son claim it was someone else, and the king believes them."

"That's why you hate them."

He didn't miss anything. "Yes, I suppose it is."

Ennis nodded, facing the road once again. "That's why I hate them, too."

The duke placed a hand on the boy's shoulder and together they watched the riders approach the city gates. Once Marston and his company were inside the city, Aindreas and the boy left the wall and descended to the castle's inner ward.

"Go tell your mother the thane of Shanstead has arrived," Aindreas said.

"She won't want to see him. She never wants to see anyone."

The duke winced inwardly. Ennis was right about this as well. Since Brienne's death, Ioanna had hardly left her chambers, other than to pray in the cloister or take a brief walk through the castle gardens. In recent turns she had shown some signs of emerging from the darkness that gripped her, but the improvement often seemed painfully slow, like trying to see the movement of the moons as they arced through the night sky. At least she now managed to smile with Ennis and his remaining sister; at times Aindreas even heard her laughing.

"Tell her anyway," Aindreas said. "She'll want to know."

The boy shrugged and hurried off, leaving the duke to greet his guests. He had thought to do so alone, but a moment later he was joined by Villyd Temsten, his swordmaster, who led several hundred soldiers into the ward.

"One of the tower guards told me they had arrived," the man called to him. "I thought you'd want me here."

Aindreas grinned. He didn't trust many men anymore—he would never trust a white-hair again—but those who remained still served him well. "Thank you, Villyd."

The swordmaster nodded and ordered the men into neat rows, before taking his place just behind the duke, his stout legs planted squarely on the grass and his arms folded over his broad chest.

Marston arrived a few moments later, accompanied by two guards from the city gate who announced him to the duke. He looked older than Aindreas remembered, which wasn't surprising; it had been several years since last they met. But he appeared taller as well, and broader in the chest and shoulders. The duke had expected to see an unimpressive boy; instead he found himself facing a man who, despite his youth, looked very much like a thane, or even a duke. He resembled his father, just as his brother did, if Aindreas remembered correctly. All the Shanstead men seemed to share the same unremarkable but vaguely pleasant looks—straight brown hair, pale grey eyes, a straight nose and square chin.

Marston had come with eight of his men and his Qirsi minister, a young-looking man with close-cropped white hair and the same strange yellow eyes that all the sorcerers had. The thane introduced the man, but Aindreas missed his name, and didn't care enough to ask Marston to repeat it.

When they finished with the formalities, the duke had Villyd arrange for the housing of Shanstead's men and invited the thane, and with some reluctance his Qirsi as well, to join him for the midday meal. They kept their conversation light. Aindreas did not wish to discuss anything of substance in the company of the white-hair, nor did he wish to seem too anxious to speak of weightier matters. He had hoped that Ioanna might join them, but midway through the meal Ennis came to say that his mother was resting and would do her best to attend the evening meal.

"How fares the duchess?" Marston asked once Ennis was gone. "I've heard that she suffered greatly for the loss of your daughter."

"We all did, Lord Shanstead," Aindreas said pointedly. "My wife is doing as well as one might expect. As one parent to another, I can tell you that I wouldn't wish the loss of a child on my most hated enemy."

He regretted the words as soon as he spoke them, for the fact was he had done just that, fighting for the execution of Javan's boy. If Marston noticed the duke's error, he had the good sense not to comment on it.

"Of course not, my lord. You and your entire family have our deepest sympathies."

They lapsed into a difficult silence, which the Qirsi finally ended.

"This is my first journey to Kentigern, my Lord Duke. I wonder if we might walk the battlements when our meal is done. I've heard tales of them all my life."

Aindreas made himself smile. "It would be my pleasure, Minister."

A short while later they finished eating and ascended the steps of the nearest tower to the castle walls. The duke had walked the battlements with his guests so often that with barely a thought he could tell the history of Kentigern's various towers and the sieges they had survived. Still, the Qirsi seemed quite interested, as did Marston, who last visited the tor nearly eight years before, as a boy only a year or two past his Determining.

By the time they had come full circle back to Aindreas's private hall, it was nearly dusk. The thane and his minister left the duke to find their quarters and wash the road from their faces and clothes.

"If we're to meet the duchess," Marston said, "we ought not to smell like our mounts."

After making certain that his guests were escorted to their chambers, Aindreas returned to the castle's great hall to check on the preparations for the night's feast. Before Brienne's death, this had been Ioanna's task, but for the past several turns Aindreas had considered himself fortunate if she even attended a feast, much less planned one. He had become both duke and duchess, just as he had been forced to care for Affery and Ennis as both father and mother. At times like these, thinking of all that Tavis of Curgh had taken from him, the duke could barely contain his rage. The boy deserved to die, as did his father, the king, and everyone else who had aided his escape from Kentigern's dungeon.

To his surprise, his wife actually did come to the hall to join their meal, arriving just a few moments after Marston and the Qirsi. She wore a red velvet gown, one that Aindreas had always loved on her. But seeing her dressed so, jewels about her neck, and her hair combed and scented, the duke could only grieve. She had always been slight, but rather than looking elegant, she now appeared frail, as if the darkness that had consumed her mind had ravaged her body as well. Her once beautiful face had grown sallow and pinched; her large brown eyes seemed sunken and when she smiled, upon her arrival in the hall, she looked more like a wraith than a living woman.

Aindreas stood, offering her the chair beside him, and Marston and his minister bowed deeply to her, drawing another ghostly smile to her lips. Though pleased that she had come to the hall, the duke could not help worrying that she might embarrass herself. Her behavior since Brienne's death had been erratic almost to the point of madness. Aindreas didn't want it spread through the kingdom that the duchess of Kentigern had lost her mind, nor did he want his efforts to forge an alliance with Thorald and the other houses to be hindered by rumors that perhaps he was mad as well. Fortunately, Ioanna made it through the meal without any lapses. Indeed, the food and conversation seemed to do her good, leaving her more animated than she had been when the evening began. She lingered over the dried fruits, cheeses, and honey cakes served at the end of the meal, sipping her wine and speaking with Shanstead's minister about Sussyn, where, as it happened, both of them had spent their early childhood. Despite Ioanna's sickly appearance, Aindreas could not help but be pleased. In some small way, he felt that his wife had come back to him this night.

At last, the duchess announced that she had grown tired and wished to return to her chambers. Aindreas helped her to her feet and kissed her cheek.

"I'm glad you joined us," he said quietly, their eyes meeting for a moment.

"As am I." She turned to Marston. "Good night, Lord Shanstead. I've enjoyed your company."

"And I yours, my lady."

One of her ladies took her arm and led her out of the hall, leaving Aindreas alone with Marston and his minister.

"Shall we open another flask of wine?" the duke asked, smiling at the thane. "We have a good deal to discuss."

"Of course, my Lord Duke."

Aindreas motioned to one of the servants to bring more wine. He glanced for an instant at the Qirsi, before facing Marston again. "If you don't mind, I'd like for us to speak in private."

The thane looked for a moment as if he might object, but instead he offered a strained smile. "I don't mind at all." He turned to his minister. "It's all right, Xiv. We'll speak later."

The Qirsi nodded and stood. "Yes, my lord." He eyed the duke, his expression revealing nothing. "Good night, my Lord Duke. Thank you for your hospitality."

Aindreas nodded and made himself smile, but offered no reply.

"I hope you don't think me rude," Aindreas said once the man was gone. "Where some matters are concerned, I feel more comfortable addressing myself just to a noble."

"I don't think you rude, my lord. I think I understand your concerns."

"Good." Aindreas poured out the wine and raised his goblet. "To friendships, old and new."

"To friendships," the thane said, sipping his wine.

"I should have asked you earlier, Lord Shanstead, but how is your father?"

"He's well, my lord."

Aindreas raised an eyebrow. "I'm glad, though somewhat surprised. I had heard he was ill."

"It's a minor discomfort, my lord, nothing more."

"I see," Aindreas said, not entirely certain that he believed the thane. "Well, I hope you'll convey to him my wishes for a quick recovery."

"Yes, I will."

They fell silent, Marston sipping his wine again and the duke taking another honey cake, his eyes flicking toward the thane.

"I imagine you'd like to know why I asked you here," Aindreas said at last.

"I have some idea, my lord. Shanstead may be just a thaneship, but word of the major houses does reach us. You seek allies in your dispute with Curgh and you hope to convince Thorald to support you. My father has refused thus far, so you thought to learn where I stand, knowing that eventually the dukedom will be mine."

Aindreas couldn't help but grin. "You'll make a fine duke someday, Lord Shanstead." He drank some wine and placed his goblet on the table. "Yes, that's why I wanted to speak with you."

"I'll be happy to listen to whatever you have to say, my lord. But you must realize that as long as my father leads the House of Thorald, I can offer no promises one way or another."

"I understand," the duke said. "But surely you're free to express your opinions."

"That would depend. If you ask me to comment on any choice my father has made as duke of Thorald, I would say nothing save to agree with him. My duty to him, as both thane and son, requires no less."

Aindreas eyed the man for several moments, wondering if he had erred in inviting him to Kentigern. He had expected to find more ambition in the thane. Marston's father had become regent to Filib the Younger after the hunting mishap that claimed the life of the last duke of Thorald. But even after Filib's untimely death at the hands of road thieves, Tobbar could never be more than a duke, nor could his sons. The Rules of Ascension forbade any of them from becoming king. Marston's eldest son, however, had a claim to the jeweled crown, if only Glyndwr's line could be removed from Audun's Castle. Aindreas had thought to lure the thane into an alliance with the promise of placing his boy on the throne. He never intended to ask Marston to betray his father, but neither had he counted on the thane showing such strict loyalty to Tobbar's decrees. "I wonder, Lord Shanstead," he said, "if your father understands just what happened here during Elined's Turn. I wonder if you do."

He saw Marston hesitate, as if the thane knew that their conversation had taken a dangerous turn.

"I believe we do understand, my lord," he said, his voice and gaze both steady. "My house is no stranger to tragedy and loss."

"Has a daughter of your house ever been murdered in Thorald Castle by a visiting lord? Have other houses ever aided the escape of a prisoner from your dungeon, so that they might then offer the demon asylum?"

The thane looked down at his hands. "No, my lord."

"Then don't liken your losses to mine," the duke said, feeling his throat constrict. "No house of Eibithar has ever endured such indignities as those heaped upon Kentigern by Curgh and Glyndwr."

"None of us doubts that you and your family suffered terribly, my lord. To lose Brienne . . ." Marston shook his head. "I'm certain the Underrealm shines like the sky with her light. All the kingdom grieved with you, none more than my father. And then to have to fight off a siege as well. That you vanquished the army of Mertesse in spite of all that happened before bespeaks uncommon strength and honor, Lord Kentigern. That hasn't gone unnoticed in Thorald."

Aindreas nodded gruffly, his eyes still stinging with the memory of Brienne's death.

"I understand that your Qirsi betrayed you to the Aneirans," Marston said, running a finger along the rim of his goblet.

"Yes," the duke said. "One more injury among many."

"Do you think he was in league with this conspiracy we're hearing so much about in Shanstead?"

"I suppose it's possible. Certainly he was in league with Mertesse. I can only guess about the rest of it."

"But you're suspicious enough to have rid yourself of all your Qirsi ministers."

Aindreas shrugged. "One of them betrayed me. And not just any one, but my most trusted advisor. How am I to trust any of them after that?"

"I understand," Marston said. "In these times, we all should question the loyalty of our ministers. I've tried to impress this point upon my father, but with only limited success. I'm glad to see that you've taken it to heart. You even asked that my minister leave the hall before we spoke."

The duke narrowed his eyes, wondering where this was leading. "I meant no offense to you or your minister. But as you say, at times like these, we must use caution."

"Do you think it possible, my lord duke, that your daughter's murder and the attack on your castle were related in some way?"

"I think Mertesse knew of Brienne's death, if that's what you mean. I think he even knew of my intent to wage war on the House of Curgh. That's why he attacked when he did."

Marston chewed his lip for a moment. "That's not quite what I had in mind. Your first minister betrayed you to the Aneirans, perhaps as part of a larger Qirsi plot to weaken the kingdom. Isn't it possible that he arranged your daughter's murder as well, hoping to destroy the alliance that you were on the verge of forming with Javan?"

"You talk like a Curgh, Shanstead!" Aindreas said, glaring at the man.

"I'm merely speaking of what you already know to be true. The Qirsi—some Qirsi—may be trying to destroy the courts of Eibithar. Since one of these traitors was in this court at the time of Brienne's death, it seems logical to wonder if he had some role in her murder."

Aindreas shook his head, propelling himself out of his chair and starting to stalk around the perimeter of the hall. "No! It's not possible! Tavis was with her in that room! The door was locked from the inside! His dagger—" He choked on the word, pausing at an archway and slamming his fist against the wooden door. "It's not possible," he said again a moment later, his voice lower.

"I would have thought the same thing about my cousin Filib's murder nearly three years ago. We were all so certain that he was killed by thieves. His dagger and his gold had been taken. They even cut off his finger to get the gold ring that had once been the duke's. But in recent turns we've been forced to ask ourselves if we might have been wrong all this time, if in fact it could have been an assassination made to look like the work of common thieves. Where magic is concerned, my Lord Duke, nothing is absolute."

"Enough!" the duke said, whirling toward Marston. "I told you not to compare what happened in Thorald to what happened here. The two are nothing alike. Magic had nothing to do with my daughter's murder. It was lust and arrogance and evil."

The thane looked like he might argue the point further, but a moment later he seemed to think better of it.

"Perhaps so, my lord. Forgive me."

"I expect you'll be leaving Kentigern in the morning, Lord Shanstead," Aindreas said, ice in his voice. "I've learned all I need to know about Thorald's intentions."

Marston straightened in his chair, but he didn't stand or give any indication that he was ready to leave the hall.

"With all respect, my lord, I don't believe you have."

"What's left for me to know? You and your father have obviously allied yourselves with Curgh and our new king. You would have saved us both a good deal of time and effort had you simply informed me of that when I sent the message asking you to come."

"We've allied ourselves with no one, Lord Kentigern, nor do we intend to any time soon. The kingdom will be safer if we take no sides in this matter."

"But you do take sides, with all this talk of the Qirsi and their so-called conspiracy. That's just what Javan wants the whole kingdom to believe."

"To be honest, my lord, my father and I don't know what to believe. Javan is so convinced that his son is innocent that he won't even allow the possibility that Tavis killed Lady Brienne. And you're no better, refusing to consider any other explanation for her death. This land may yet go to war with itself, and if it does, you and Curgh will share the blame."

"You forget yourself, sir!"

The thane looked away, his face coloring. "Forgive me," he murmured, sounding anything but contrite.

For some time, neither of them spoke.

"Do you honestly believe the king plotted against you?" Marston asked at last, still not looking at Aindreas.

"Why shouldn't I? He harbored the boy rather than returning him to my prison, where he belonged."

"My father tells me that you and Kearney's father were once friends."

"What of it?"

"Don't you wonder why the king was willing to believe Tavis? Doesn't it say something that he would risk his own reputation and that of his house to guard Javan's son, even though Glyndwr and Curgh have never been on good terms?"

Aindreas had heard enough. Still standing at the archway, he reached for the door handle and pushed the door open. "Frankly, Lord Shanstead, I don't know what it says, nor do I care. Any ties that Kentigern once had with Glyndwr have been sundered. My allies live now in Galdasten and Eardley, in Rennach, Domnall, and Sussyn. I had thought to find them in Thorald as well, but I see that my hopes were misplaced. Our conversation is over. You may return to your quarters for the night. I'll have the stablemaster prepare your horses so that you can be on your way back to Shanstead as early as possible."

Marston stared at him a moment. Then he rose from the table, a thin smile on his face. He drained his goblet and made his way to the door, stopping just in front of the duke.

"You may not believe this, my lord, but I came here today as a friend, just as my father instructed. The House of Thorald bears you no ill will, nor do we owe any allegiance to Javan and his allies. Our duty is to the kingdom, and it was in that spirit that I journeyed to Kentigern. I'm sorry if in my devotion to Eibithar and my desire to save the land from civil war I gave offense. My father thought you invited me here to speak of such things. I told him I thought you were merely hoping to find another ally in this foolhardy conflict with Javan. I've never been so sorry to be right."

He stepped past the duke into the corridor and made his way to the nearest of the towers. Aindreas should have stopped him. He should have railed at the man for his self-righteousness. Under the circumstances he would have been justified putting him in the dungeon. A thane did not say such things to a duke, certainly not in the duke's castle.

Yet he couldn't bring himself to do anything more than watch Marston walk away. Even after the thane had entered the tower stairway, disappearing from view, the duke continued to stare down the corridor trying to summon anger or indignation or even hurt; anything other than the strange hollowness he felt.

At last he turned back to the table, eyeing the wine. But rather than filling his goblet again, he left the hall and made his way to the upper corridor of the castle, where the private chambers were found. He passed a pair of guards along the way, the men nearly jumping to salute him as he walked by, but Aindreas hardly noticed.

The duke heard the midnight bells ringing in the city just as he reached the door he sought—apart from his guards and Marston, he might have been the only person in the castle not yet asleep. Still he didn't hesitate to knock. When no one answered, he pounded on the door a second time. Silence. He raised his fist to hammer at the door a third time, but in that instant he heard a voice from within.

"This had better be important! I've got my sword, and I'm mad enough to use it."

"I'm armed as well, swordmaster," the duke said. "So I'd sheath your weapon before you open the door."

The door flew open, revealing Villyd, bare-chested, his hair tousled with sleep, and his eyes blinking in the torchlight. He carried a sword, though he held it point down, as if he had forgotten it. "Demons and fire! Forgive me, my lord. I didn't know it was you."

"You're forgiven, swordmaster." Aindreas looked past the man and saw Villyd's wife still asleep in their bed. "Why don't we go elsewhere, some place where we can talk."

"Of course, my lord."

The swordmaster ducked back into his chamber, emerging a few moments later wearing a shirt and strapping on his belt and weapon.

"I trust your conversation with Lord Shanstead went well, my lord?"

Aindreas frowned. "Actually no. That's why I wanted to speak with you."

The man gave him a puzzled look. "My lord?"

"Tell me again where we stand. What's the state of our army?"

"We're still down several hundred men, my lord. We lost some at the Heneagh during our battle with the army of Curgh, and a good many more in the siege. The lesser nobles are doing their best to fill the ranks, but it's going to take some time."

"And what of the castle?"

Villyd shrugged. "The repairs go well. The Tarbin gate is nearly at full strength again, though the last portcullis is not yet in place. The inner gates still need a good deal of work."

Aindreas nodded. "What about Galdasten?"

"They lost more than two hundred men to the pestilence just before the harvest. From what I hear, I believe they've replaced more than half of them, but even at full strength, Galdasten's army is no larger than ours."

Aindreas shuddered at the mention of the pestilence. The lords of Galdasten had long prided themselves on their ability to control the outbreaks with the burnings that accompanied their Feasts. But nearly eight years before, a commoner—a madman—brought infected vermin to the Feast, spreading the disease throughout the court. Not only did the duke and his family die, but so did much of his army and hundreds of the common folk living in Galdasten City. This past year, when the pestilence returned, the new lords of the house chose to weather the outbreak rather than resorting to the burnings again.

"And the others?"

"The others, my lord?"

"Eardley, Sussyn, Domnall," he said impatiently. "The others who stand with us against the king."

"They're minor houses, my lord. Each has six hundred men; Eardley may have eight hundred, but no more."

They reached Aindreas's chambers and the duke opened the door, leading the swordmaster inside.

"That's not enough men, is it?"

"For what, my lord?" the man asked, dropping himself into one of the chairs as Aindreas stepped to the hearth. "I have to confess that I don't understand what you hope to accomplish with this alliance you're forming.

I know that you feel Curgh and Glyndwr conspired to keep you from the throne, but that's done now. If you wanted the throne for yourself, you should have moved against them before Kearney's investiture."

It was not a tone Aindreas would have tolerated at most other times. But it was late, and he had roused Villyd from his bed.

"I don't want to be king," the duke said.

Villyd raised an eyebrow, drawing a grin from Aindreas.

"All right, let me put it this way. It's not the crown I seek, not right now."

"Then what, my lord?"

"I want Kearney off the throne. He betrayed this house by granting asylum to Tavis, and in return, Javan gave him the kingdom. He may claim to have taken no sides in this dispute, but he owes everything he's become to Curgh. So long as he rules Eibithar, there will be no justice for Kentigern."

"Will you sacrifice the Rules of Ascension to destroy him?"

"Gladly, if that's what it takes."

The swordmaster nodded. It was hard to tell what he thought of the duke's aims, though Aindreas suspected that he disapproved. "If your aim is to challenge the king, my lord, then you haven't enough men. Not anywhere near. And I doubt you ever will. The king has not only his guard, but also the army of Glyndwr. Javan will join him as well, as will Tremain and Labruinn. And I assure you, if you move against the crown, Thorald and Heneagh will oppose you as well. Even if the other houses stand with you—and I'm not convinced that they will—it will not be enough."

"What if we had Thorald?"

Villyd looked at him keenly. "Do we?"

The duke turned away, gritting his teeth. "No."

"I'm not sure it would matter, my lord. Thorald might balance the scales, particularly if Tobbar brought Heneagh with him. But still it wouldn't be sufficient. Kearney has Audun's Castle. You'd need an overwhelming force to take it from him."

"You said before that you weren't certain the other houses would stand with me in such a fight. What about you, swordmaster? Would you fight beside me to break Kearney's hold on the throne?"

Villyd lowered his gaze, the light of the blaze shining like torch fire in his dark eyes. "I serve Kentigern, my lord. I gave an oath many years ago to follow you and your house, even if it led me to my death. If you command me to fight Glyndwr for the crown, I'll do so." He took a breath. "But I hope with all my heart that you'll not give that command."

It was a more honest answer than he had any right to expect, perhaps a more honest one than he deserved. No doubt if Villyd felt this way, his men did as well. Raising an army to fight the king would not work. Villyd's words made that clear, as had his own conversation with Marston.

But Shanstead had said something else this night that gave the duke reason to think there could be another way. A year ago he wouldn't have believed himself capable of considering such a thing. But a year ago Brienne still lived. A year ago the man who had harbored her killer did not wear Eibithar's jeweled crown.

Chapter Nine

✦

Bistari, Aneira

T he tavern was so empty, so quiet, that Rodaf could hear the sign out front rattling in the wind. He often heard it during the days, but by this hour on most nights enough people crowded the tables of his inn to make it hard to hear an order from a man standing right in front of him, much less any sounds from beyond the tavern walls. Not that he should have expected any better. It was his own fault for opening at all one night before Bohdan's Night. Aliya warned him it would be like this tonight, and though he had told her to keep her mind on her stitching, he had to admit that she had been right. He wouldn't bother opening tomorrow night, nor would he do this again next year. For now, however, he had little choice but to remain open and serve those who came in.

The Ironwood wasn't completely empty. Old Winso was here, as usual, as were a few of the others. And since he had already told the serving girls to go home for the night, it cost him nothing to keep his doors open. Still, it would have been nice to be back in his private room, sitting before a fire, sipping a dark Sanbiri wine. Knowing how much Aliya enjoyed a good blaze on a cold night, there was no telling where the evening might have led.

Rodaf couldn't help but notice the strangers as soon as they entered the tavern. Even on a regular night, when the inn was so choked with men and women that a person could barely move, they would have caught his attention. Such an unlikely pair could hardly expect to go anywhere without drawing stares, though it seemed clear to the innkeeper that they hoped to go unnoticed.

One of them was Qirsi, a tall, broad-shouldered man who looked more like a swordsman than a sorcerer. His eyes were the color of torch flame and his white hair fell loose to the middle of his back. The other—well, it was hard to say what the other was. Eandi, to be sure, with the fine features and graceful swagger of a court noble, and deep blue eyes to match. He looked young, though it was difficult to guess his age, for his face bore a lattice of dark, angry scars that made Rodaf, who had seen his share of wounds and scars, shudder in spite of himself. More than anything else, though, their clothes drew his eye. They were travel-stained and poor-fitting. Almost too much so. Rather than making the strangers look indigent, their filthy road coats and torn trousers simply seemed out of place. There was an old Aneiran saying, "A man is more than his clothes." But for these two, it was more than just an adage. In fairness to the travelers, Rodaf had spent much of his life observing people—he grew up as the son and grandson of innkeepers. Their clothes might have fooled others. Seeing such tatters might have kept another man from even bothering to look at their faces. But Rodaf couldn't help thinking that the two were running from something.

"Welcome to the Ironwood, friends," he said, raising a hand in greeting and forcing a smile.

The Qirsi nodded, glancing around the tavern as if searching for someone. "Thank you, good sir," he said, his eye coming to rest at last on Rodaf's face. The accent was subtle, and the innkeeper couldn't quite place it. "Might we get some ale and a bit to eat?"

"You have coin to pay?" Rodaf knew they did, but dressed as they were, the strangers would expect him to ask.

"Yes, we do."

The innkeeper waved a hand at the empty tables. "Then please make yourselves comfortable." He started back toward the kitchen. "I hope cheeses and dried meats are all right," he called to them. "I sent my cook home with the prior's bells."

The Qirsi said something he couldn't hear, but Rodaf didn't bother asking him to repeat it. These two wouldn't object to anything he served. To do so would have been to make themselves too conspicuous.

He brought them the cheese and meats as well as a half loaf of dark bread and two tankards of black ale. The men said nothing as he set the food and drink in front of them, but Rodaf felt them watching him. They made him uneasy, and he found himself hoping that they would move on rather than asking to buy a room for the night, despite the six qinde it would bring him.

"Is there anything else you need?" he asked, looking from the younger man to the Qirsi.

"Actually there is," the white-hair said. "We were hoping you might join us for a moment. We have some questions for you."

He shook his head. "I'm not one for answering questions. Not for strangers."

"I can understand that," the Qirsi said. "But there's gold in it for you if you'll talk to us."

Rodaf hesitated, twisting his mouth in a way Aliya would have understood. "Dressed as you are, I'm surprised to hear you offering gold. That's sure to make people take notice."

The white-hair grinned and turned to his companion. "See, I told you he was the one to find. Rodaf Wantaro of the Ironwood sees things other men miss. Didn't I say that?"

The other man nodded and gave a thin, unconvincing smile.

"Have we met, friend?" Rodaf asked, staring at the man, and feeling his stomach tighten.

"No," the Qirsi said. "But I've heard others speak of you. I gathered, from what they said, that we should talk to you."

"About what?"

The white-hair indicated an empty chair with a nod. "Please sit, Rodaf."

Reluctantly, the innkeeper pulled a chair up to their table.

"My name is Grinsa," the Qirsi said. He gestured at his friend. "This is Xaver."

Rodaf nodded at the Eandi, but the lad only stared at him.

"What is it you want to ask me?" the innkeeper asked, trying to sound like he had far more important things to do than sit with them.

"We heard of the garroting of your duke," Grinsa said, biting into a strip of dried meat. "There's talk of it all over the kingdom. People here must have been terribly angry."

Rodaf shrugged. "Some were. House Bistari and House Solkara have hated one another for centuries, and old Chago did nothing to win this king's affections. I suppose it was just a matter of time before Carden grew angry enough to send his assassins."

"So you believe it was the king's men who did this."

"Of course," the innkeeper said. "Everyone does."

"Did you notice any strangers in the city around the time your duke was killed?"

"We get strangers all the time." Rodaf gave a small smile. "Even the evening before Bohdan's Night. Bistari sits at the edge of the Great Forest, on the shores of the Scabbard, and between the Kett and the Rassor. During the course of a single turn I see peddlers and merchants from almost every dukedom in every kingdom in the Forelands. Asking me if I've noticed a stranger is like asking a Wethy trader if he noticed a five-qinde piece."

"You might remember this man," the Qirsi said. "He's a musician. Long black hair, beard, pale blue eyes. He's slightly taller than I am, lean but powerfully built."

Rodaf shook his head. "I don't think I've seen anyone like that, at least not recently."

"Think harder," the younger one said.

"Xaver—"

"Well, he didn't even consider it," the lad said, turning to Grinsa. "He just said no."

Rodaf looked the boy up and down. The odd clothes made more sense now. He recognized the accent.

"You're from Eibithar," he said, the words coming out as an accusation.

"South Wethyrn actually," the Qirsi said quickly. "We both are."

The accents were similar. For some it was easy to confuse Jistingham and Glyndwr. But Rodaf knew better. As he'd said a moment before, running an inn in Bistari, he met men from every part of the Forelands, including Eibithar. He wasn't mistaken, and he could see from the look in the boy's eyes that his companion had warned him not to speak.

The innkeeper stood. "You're free to finish your meal," he told them. "But you won't be buying a room. Not here, not tonight."

The Qirsi grabbed his arm. "Wait. You said you hadn't seen anyone like the man we described, and then you said, 'at least not recently.' What did you mean?"

Rodaf pulled his arm free, glaring at the man. For a moment he considered just walking away, or better yet, demanding that they leave the Ironwood immediately. But Grinsa pulled a ten-qinde round from his pocket and tossed it on the table, where it sat glittering with the glow of the candles that lit the room.

After eyeing it briefly, the innkeeper picked it up. "There was a man like the one you describe who used to sing in one of the festivals. It's been a few years now, but it could be the same man."

"Do you remember his name?" Grinsa asked.

Rodaf searched his memory for some time. "No," he said at last. "I've forgotten."

"Corbin, perhaps?"

The innkeeper raised an eyebrow. "Yes, that was it. I guess it was the same man."

Grinsa nodded. "Thank you, Rodaf. We'll leave after we've eaten, and we won't return. You have my word."

Rodaf turned away and walked back to the bar, wondering if he had been rash in telling the men to leave. The boy might have been from Eibithar, but he certainly didn't look like the northern kingdom had treated him well. The innkeeper was just about to tell them that he had reconsidered, and that they could stay the night, when the door to the inn opened again and four of the duke's soldiers stepped in from the wind and cold.

Immediately, both Grinsa and the boy lowered their heads, as if intent on their food and ale. The guards glanced at them as they made their way to the ale tap, but they showed no sign that they were actually looking for the pair. Grinsa stared after the men, his head still down so that he could watch the soldiers without being too obvious. Whatever had brought them to Bistari, Rodaf wanted no part of it. Let them find beds at one of the other inns. He considered pointing the pair out to the soldiers, but though the lad was a northerner, he immediately thought better of it. He didn't want trouble, and he couldn't afford a reputation as a man who couldn't be trusted by his patrons. Nothing ruined a tavern's business faster than that.

The soldiers didn't stay long. As they did most nights, they drank their ales and returned to the castle. Once they were gone, Grinsa and the Eandi boy pushed back from their table. The boy stepped to the door, but the white-hair walked over to Rodaf and handed him another five qinde, more than enough to pay for their food and drink.

"That's a lot of gold you've given me," the innkeeper said. "I told you before, I can't tell you anything else."

"I realize that. But you could have pointed us out to those men, and you didn't. I'm grateful."

Grinsa held his gaze a moment longer, then turned to go.

"What is it you want with the singer?" Rodaf called after him.

The Qirsi faced him again. "He killed a friend of ours and left the boy to take the blame. We'd like to discuss that with him."

Rodaf nodded, wishing he hadn't asked. He didn't start to breathe again until the door closed behind them, and he found himself alone with Winso and the others.

*   *   *

It seemed to have grown colder just in the short time it took them to eat supper. The wind still howled through the city streets, carrying the chill, damp scent of the Scabbard, and a fine rain had begun to fall. Tavis couldn't imagine how it didn't turn to snow, so frigid was the air.

He and the Qirsi walked through the streets of Bistari, skirting the marketplace so as to keep their distance from Castle Bistari.

"I told you not to speak," Grinsa said, his voice tight, as if he were fighting to control his temper. "What's the good of using a false name if you're going to give away the fact that we're from Eibithar?"

"I'm not certain there's any good in it at all," he said. He had never liked the idea of using an alias. He was Tavis of Curgh, son of a duke and heir to one of the great houses of Eibithar. Why should he have to hide his true name like some road brigand on the moors? Using Xaver MarCullet's name helped a bit. At least this way he could honor his friend and liege man, maybe even atone in some small way for the knife wound he gave the boy after his terrifying Fating several turns back. Still, he would have preferred to stop hiding and travel the countryside openly as a noble. Let the Aneirans be damned.

"We've spoken of this before, Tavis," the Qirsi said wearily. "You're an Eibitharian lord in the heart of your kingdom's most bitter enemy. Your scars already make you an object of interest."

Tavis looked away. He didn't need the gleaner to tell him that. Everywhere they went he felt the stares, and each day he cursed Aindreas of Kentigern for the torture that had so marked him.

"Using your real name would be far too dangerous," Grinsa went on. "All we need is for one person to recognize you and all would be lost."

"If you're so worried about others noticing us, perhaps you should stop throwing my father's gold around like a drunken baron. You gave that man fifteen qinde for old meat, hard cheese, and stale bread. You learned nothing from him of any importance."

"Actually that's not true. I learned that Corbin had been here before, albeit not necessarily when Chago died. And I satisfied myself that the man we're looking for and the man we're describing are one and the same. It may not be much, but it's something. It's more than we had before we went in." He grinned. "And you forgot the ale. Your father's gold bought that as well, and I thought it was rather good."

Tavis had to smile. "It was all right," he admitted, "for an Aneiran brew." They walked in silence for a few paces and he glanced at the gleaner, trying to gauge his mood. "Where are we going now?"

"To another tavern, one where we'll be able to get a room."

"How do you know?"

"It's a Qirsi inn. The Silver Marten."

The boy nodded, but said nothing. He had grown used to this by now—sleeping and eating among white-hairs. They stared at him as well, but at least in the Qirsi taverns he could convince himself that they did so because he was Eandi, rather than because of the marks on his face.

"You still think Corbin killed Bistari's duke?" he asked. "The innkeeper seemed certain that it was the king's men."

Grinsa shrugged, his eyes trained on the street. "I don't know. We've been searching Aneira for more than three turns now, and we've yet to find Brienne's killer. I had hoped that following the Western Festival would lead us to him, but that didn't work. I had hoped to find something in Tantreve, even though the marquess there died more than a year ago. That turned out to be a wasted journey as well. This just seemed like the most likely place to look next." He let out a slow breath. "Maybe we need to try something new."

Tavis knew what would come next. Grinsa wanted to look for Shurik, once the first minister to Aindreas of Kentigern, who betrayed his duke to Rouel of Mertesse. The gleaner hoped that Shurik could help them find those leading the Qirsi conspiracy, which he believed had paid for Brienne's murder. Tavis didn't doubt that all this was true, but he felt that finding the assassin and proving that he killed Brienne would take far less time than thwarting an entire conspiracy. Since he couldn't reclaim his place in the Order of Ascension or his birthright as heir to the House of Curgh until he proved himself innocent of Brienne's murder, he had insisted that they follow Corbin rather than the renegade Qirsi.

"We don't need something new," he said in a flat voice. "We need to keep looking for the assassin. It may be that he's left Aneira by now. For all we know he's back in Eibithar."

"At least we know that Shurik's not. He would have sought asylum in Mertesse. He must still be there."

Tavis gave a silent curse. He might as well have been arguing the gleaner's cause for him.

"One more turn, Grinsa," he said, though it pained him to do so. "If we've found nothing by the Night of Two Moons in Qirsar's Turn, we'll start north for Mertesse."

The Qirsi looked at him with unconcealed surprise. "Do you mean that?"

He nodded. "We've found nothing so far. I'm no closer to taking back my name than I was when we left Eibithar. Whatever you think me, I'm not a fool."

"Not usually, no."

Again Tavis smiled, though he also shook his head. No one had ever spoken to him as Grinsa did, not even Xaver, who had been his best friend for as long as he could remember. From any other man, the gibes Grinsa dealt him would have seemed impudent. But with the help of Fotir jal Salene, his father's first minister, the gleaner had freed him from Kentigern's dungeon. In doing so, he revealed himself as a Weaver, the most powerful kind of Qirsi sorcerer, and the most feared and hated by the Eandi. Not only had he saved Tavis's life, he had trusted the boy with his own. No one had done so much for him or asked so much of him. Theirs remained a difficult partnership. Grinsa made no secret of the fact that he thought Tavis spoiled, thoughtless, and childish, nor did he hesitate to point out other faults in the boy as he noticed them. For his part, Tavis often resented the Qirsi's attempts to order him about, as if Grinsa were his surrogate father. But Tavis relied on the man as he had few others, and he sensed that he had begun to earn Grinsa's trust as well.

They reached the Silver Marten a short time later. Pausing briefly on the threshold, his hand on the door handle, Grinsa looked back at him, a plea in his yellow eyes.

"Don't say a thing."

"I won't." When the gleaner continued to stare at him, he smiled, adding, "You have my word."

Tavis followed Grinsa into the tavern, the warm air and aromas of cooking meats and stews wrapping themselves around him like a blanket. There were a few more people here than there had been at the Ironwood, but still the inn was nearly empty. All the faces he saw were pale, all the eyes yellow. Who could have imagined that he would ever spend so much time with sorcerers? Looking around the tavern, however, another thought came to him.

"You know," he said softly, "if Corbin was hired by a Qirsi, he might have come here. And he would have stood out like a Revel tumbler in a cloister."

Grinsa gave him that look, the one that always came to his face when Tavis surprised him with an insight. It almost seemed to say, *See what you can do when you think?*

"Choose us a table," the gleaner said. "I'll buy two ales and speak with the barman."

Tavis nodded and walked to the back of the tavern. He sensed the inn's patrons watching him, but he tried to ignore their stares. A few moments later, Grinsa joined him.

"He's going to bring our ales and sit with us for a time. Remember—"

"I know," Tavis said. "Say nothing."

"It may be even more important here, Tavis. These people may trust me because I'm Qirsi, but they'll be wary of questions, particularly if they think we're enemies of the movement. For all we know, this is the man who paid for Chago's blood."

Before Tavis could respond, the Qirsi bar man emerged from behind the bar, carrying two tankards. He smiled at them, but Tavis could see the man staring at the scars on his face. *Talk about standing out,* he thought, wishing he could hide under the table.

"Looks like you've had a rough time of it, my young friend," the man said, setting the tankards on the table and sitting beside Tavis.

At least he was honest enough to talk about the scars. Better that than the silent, sidelong glances Tavis had endured for the past several turns.

"He met up with some thieves a while back," Grinsa said. "We were in Caerisse at the time, the Paalniri Wild. He doesn't really like to speak of it."

"I should think not." The man leaned closer to examine the wounds. "Looks like he's healed well," he said, glancing at Grinsa. "Your work?"

"I'm not a healer. I found someone in Enharfe to help him."

The bar man nodded. "I see." He gazed at the scars a moment longer, then faced the gleaner. "You said you had questions for me."

"We do. We're wondering if you've seen an Eandi man in the last turn or so. A singer." Grinsa described the assassin briefly.

"Yes. I've seen him."

Grinsa blinked. "What?"

"I've seen him," the barman said again.

The gleaner just stared at him, as if unable to believe what he was hearing. "You've seen him recently?"

"Yes. He came in for an ale one night during the last waning."

Tavis and Grinsa shared a look. That was just around the time the duke of Bistari was killed.

"Did he speak with anyone?" Grinsa asked, leaning forward.

"As I remember it, he did."

"Who?"

The man faltered. "What is it you want with the singer?" he asked. He eyed Tavis briefly. "Is he the one who did this to the boy?"

The gleaner shook his head. "No. I assure you he's not."

"Then why are you so eager to find him?"

"Let's just say that he owes us something. We need to find him so that we can collect on an old debt."

The barman seemed to consider this.

"Now please, who was it he talked to?"

"I misspoke before," the man said, his eyes flicking about the tavern uneasily. "I remember now. He didn't speak with anyone."

He was lying. Tavis didn't need to be a gleaner to see that. He almost challenged the man, but Grinsa beat him to it.

"But a moment ago you said—"

"I was wrong. He sat alone the whole time he was here. I'm sure of it." His face had turned ashen and his brow was suddenly damp. It almost seemed that he felt a dagger at his back.

"So you're telling me that an Eandi singer came into your tavern, drank an ale, and then left without speaking to anyone."

"That's right."

Grinsa shook his head. "I don't believe you. Most Eandi would rather take off an arm than sit among white-hairs."

"Believe what you will. Your friend here seems happy enough to drink my ale. Why would the singer be any different? He was with the Festival—maybe he was used to our kind." He pushed back from the table and stood. "If there's nothing else, I've a tavern to run."

Grinsa looked up at him, his yellow eyes holding the man's gaze. "We've no other questions, if that's what you mean," he finally said. "But we'll need a room for tonight. Two beds."

The barman didn't look at all pleased with the notion that they'd be staying the night, but he nodded before walking off.

"That's it?" Tavis asked. "You just let him go?"

"There's nothing to be gained by asking him more questions," Grinsa said calmly.

"But he was lying."

"Yes, he was. And he was going to keep on lying no matter what we asked him."

Tavis looked away, pressing his lips in a thin line, much as his father often did. Grinsa was right. Again.

"We learned all we needed to," the gleaner told him, his voice dropping nearly to a whisper. "Corbin was here when Chago died, and because our friend at the bar is such a poor liar, we know as well that he spoke with someone. Given how he reacted to our questions, I think we can assume it was someone this man fears."

"Maybe," Tavis said. "Or maybe he fears us."

"What do you mean?"

"You said before that for all we knew the barman was with the conspiracy. What if he's not, but he thinks we are? We're looking for an assassin, because, in your words, 'he owes us something.' With all that's happened in the Forelands in the past few turns, and with all the talk of Qirsi plotting against the courts, that would be enough to scare me."

Grinsa's white eyebrows went up. "A fair point. If you're right, I certainly don't think we should do anything to disabuse him of the idea. Having him afraid of us could be helpful."

Tavis glanced around the large room. "Should we talk to anyone else? It may be that others noticed the singer as well. A patron may be more willing to talk to us than the barman."

"I'd rather not let it be known too widely that we're looking for him. He may still be nearby; we shouldn't do anything to scare him off."

The boy smiled. "It seems we won't be going north to find Shurik after all."

Grinsa gave a reluctant nod. "Not yet, at least."

After finishing their ales, Grinsa paid the barman for a room and he and Tavis ascended a creaking wooden stairway to the tavern's upper floor. Their room was the first one on the hallway. In most ways it was no different from every other room in which they had stayed since leaving Eibithar: small, dirty, smelling slightly of must and stale sweat.

"I hope we didn't pay too much for this," Tavis said, eyeing the beds doubtfully.

"It wasn't a lot, though it was more than the room's worth."

"How much of my father's gold—?"

He never finished the question. From the streets below the room's lone shuttered window, Tavis heard shouts and, after a moment, a loud cheer. Grinsa strode to the window and threw open the shutters.

A large group of men had gathered in the lane, many of them bearing torches. There was a good deal of laughter, and Tavis could hear shouts and cheering from further off, as if the scene was repeating itself throughout the city.

"What is it?" he asked.

The gleaner shook his head. "I don't know." He shuttered the window again and crossed to the door. "But we should find out."

They hurried back down the stairs, and finding the tavern empty, stepped out into the street. The barman was there, as were his Qirsi patrons. But it was the Eandi who were making most of the noise, shouting back and forth to each other, most of them grinning.

"What's happened?" Grinsa asked.

The barman looked at him for a moment, as if unsure whether or not to speak with him.

"A messenger just arrived from Solkara," he said at last, watching the Eandi once more. "The king is dead."

Grinsa gaped at him. "What? How did he die?"

"The man didn't say."

Tavis looked at the gleaner, their eyes meeting briefly. Had the king been murdered as well?

"Did he refuse to say, or did no one ask?"

The barman offered a dark smile. "Look at them," he said, gesturing toward the people in the street. "They don't care how the man died. They care only that their duke has been avenged. He had Chago garroted, and now the Deceiver has taken him as well. Songs will be written of this day."

"He was your king," Tavis said.

The boy regretted speaking the moment the words passed his lips, and Grinsa cast a withering look his way. But with all the noise from the revelers, the barman did not seem to notice his accent.

"Perhaps he was your king," the man said. "But in Bistari, he was just another Solkaran tyrant."

"So it's like this here every time a king dies?" Grinsa asked.

"I was just a boy when Farrad the Sixth died. I don't remember it that well. But when Tomaz died, people danced in the streets, yes. Maybe not like this—Carden was more hated than most of the Solkaran kings, and he dies without an heir, which gives the people here some hope that another house will claim the throne."

Tavis couldn't have said for certain how old Carden the Third had been. Not old, though. He knew that much. He had died young, with no heir, and of some cause alarming or private enough to be excluded from the message announcing his death. Abruptly, the young lord knew where he and Grinsa would be journeying next.

"Will Bistari challenge for the crown?" Grinsa asked.

The barman shook his head, apparently eager to talk now that the conversation wouldn't affect his business. "Hard to say. If the old duke were still alive I'd think so, but Silbron, his son, is only just past his Determining, and he and his mother still grieve."

"Then who?"

"Dantrielle might try, or Mertesse. Maybe even Orvinti. In the end, though, the crown will fall to Grigor."

"Grigor?"

The man turned to look at Grinsa once more. "The oldest of the king's brothers. You're not Aneiran, are you?"

"We're from Wethyrn," the gleaner said. "Jistingham, to be precise."

"You've come a long way to look for your singer."

"We're eager to find him. Eager enough to pay for the names of those he met in your tavern." Grinsa glanced around them for a moment. "Your customers are gone now," he said, lowering his voice. "My friend and I are the only ones listening. And we've got gold."

The man gave a thin smile. "I told you already: I never saw him with anyone."

"Very well." Grinsa started toward the tavern again. "Come, Xaver," he said, beckoning to Tavis with a wave of his hand. "There's nothing more we can learn here."

The young lord followed him back into the inn.

"He refused gold," the gleaner said as they climbed the steps again.

"I heard."

"That tells me it wasn't us he feared, but rather the person he saw with the assassin."

"A minister, perhaps?"

Grinsa glanced at him. "Perhaps."

"Since when are you so interested in the affairs of the Aneiran houses?" Tavis asked him, once they were back in their room. "By revealing that we weren't from Aneira you might have made him even more suspicious than he already was."

"True, but it was worth the risk. Knowing who stood to gain the most from Carden's death may tell us where to go next."

"After Solkara, you mean."

The gleaner nodded. "Yes. After Solkara."

Chapter
Ten

✦

lay another, lad!" one of the men called to him, drawing shouts of agreement from the others. "Do you know 'Tanith's Threnody'?"

Dario shook his head, though he continued to look down at his fingers as he plucked idly at the strings of his lute. "No," he said. "Never learned it."

It was a lie, of course. Every lutenist in Aneira knew the threnody, because it was all anyone ever asked them to play. He had already played it this day, and he heard snickers in the far corner of the tavern, probably from someone who had heard him perform it earlier.

"Then play anything," the man said.

Dario's fingers throbbed—he had been playing since just after the ringing of the midday bells. They were barely paying him enough to make eight or nine songs worth his while, and he had already done more than a dozen. The tavern shouldn't have even been open. For one thing, this was the day of Bohdan's Night, when men should have been with their families rather than drinking at a bar. Most of the men who frequented the Red Boar, however, had no families. More to the point though, with the king dead, every other tavern in the city had been shut down. The duke's guards never came to the Red Boar, however. They were afraid to. So it remained open, as if nothing had happened, as if it were just an ordinary day in Dantrielle.

One of the serving women put another ale before him and gave him a warm smile.

"They like you," she whispered.

"Another song or two and my fingers will be bloody."

She glanced around the tavern and nodded toward the men who crowded the tables and bar. "If you stop now, they're liable to bloody a good deal more than your fingers."

She had a point. It was never a good idea for a musician to anger a tavernful of listeners, and this was particularly true in the Red Boar.

"One more," he said. "And then I need to drink my ale."

"Fair enough," another man said. "The lad deserves a bit of rest."

The others nodded, and Dario began to play. It was one of his own pieces, as the last several had been. He had made up so many that he stopped titling them long ago. But he still remembered where he found each one, and in his own mind he called them by those names. This one was "Moors of Durril," where he had been early in the last harvest when he first played it.

Each element of the piece was fairly simple—the melody line he plucked from the upper strings, and the bass counterpoint he played on the lower ones. But together they created an intricate pattern that recalled for Dario the grasses of the moor, dancing in a light wind, and the brilliant sunset Morna had offered him that evening. The melody turned three rounds in the piece, each a bit lower in pitch and slower in tempo than the last, before the delicate ending climbed upward once more. It was Dario's best, and he always saved it for the end of a performance.

Despite their rough appearance and cruel reputations, the men of the Red Boar appreciated good music. They cheered lustily when he finished, and several of them offered to buy him ales, though he had barely touched the one he carried, along with his lute, to the rear of the tavern.

"Fine playing, lad!" the first man said, clapping him on the back as Dario walked past. "You can play for me anytime."

Dario smiled and nodded, but he didn't stop to talk. He might have been a musician, but he also had a profession, just as they did, and he had been living on a lutenist's wage for too long.

He took his customary seat near one of the back windows and laid the lute carefully on the chair beside him. After taking a long drink of ale, he pulled his father's old pipe from his pocket, filled the bowl with Trescarri leaf, and lit it. He leaned back in his chair, blowing a great cloud of smoke toward the ceiling and closing his eyes.

He remained that way for some time, only opening his eyes again when he heard the chair across the table from him squeak.

A man was sitting there, one Dario had seen in the Red Boar before.

Like so many of the others, he had the look of a road brigand to him. He hadn't shaved in several days, and he wore his black hair long and untied. He was built like Dario, neither brawny nor tall, but lean and muscular, like a festival tumbler. Even though they were both sitting, the lutenist could tell that the man could handle himself in a fight.

"Is there something I can do for you?" Dario asked him, puffing on his pipe again.

The man stared at him with dark eyes, a small smile on his thin lips. "Crebin sent me to tell you that he wants his gold, and that he's tired of waiting."

Dario frowned. "I think you have the wrong man. I don't know anyone named Crebin."

"He also told me that you'd say that. We've all enjoyed your playing, lad. None of us wants to see you floating facedown in the Rassor with a blade in your back."

"Well, I'm glad to know that we're in agreement on that point," Dario said, eyeing the man as he would a new instrument. He had never seen the man fight, so he didn't know his tendencies or his weaknesses. Dario was near the back of the inn, but he wasn't against the back wall. If he moved fast enough, he could stand and kick away his chair, clearing himself some room to draw his dagger and meet an assault. He opened his hands, as if to show the man that he held no weapon. "There's obviously been some misunderstanding, but I'm sure that you and I can work it out. Perhaps you can start by telling me what this Crebin looks like."

"Don't try my patience, boy. You may think you can handle yourself in a fight, but you've never fought me."

"You know, I'm tired of people calling me lad and boy all the time," Dario said, his hand snaking down toward his calf, where he held his spare blade. "I'm seven years past my Fating, and still everyone treats me like I'm little more than a child." He cocked his head to the side, just as the fingers on his throwing hand unfastened the strap that held the blade in place and closed around the smooth wooden hilt. "Recently I've thought of letting my beard grow in. Do you think that would help?"

"I think you should stop what it is you're doing, before you get yourself hurt."

"I don't know what you mean."

The man looked past him for just an instant, and too late Dario realized that there was a second man behind him. Before he could do anything with his own blade, he felt the point of another weapon pressing against the back of his neck.

"Bring your hand up slowly," the second man commanded. "And lay the blade on the table."

Dario did as he was told, cursing himself for his carelessness.

"And the other one."

He pulled his better blade from his belt, and placed it on the table beside the other.

"Now, let's try this again," said the man sitting before him. "Where's Crebin's gold?"

"I tell you, I don't know anyone named Crebin. Nor do I have any gold to speak of. Do you think I'd still be playing here if I did?"

The man shook his head slowly. "You're a fool. Men like Crebin aren't to be trifled with. Nor are we."

He nodded once to his friend, who grabbed Dario by the hair and pulled him to his feet, all the while keeping the tip of his dagger firmly against the lutenist's nape.

"Say there!" came a voice from the front of the tavern. "What are you doing with the lad?"

Several of the older men in the tavern came toward them, led by the man who had patted Dario's back earlier.

The man holding Dario shifted his blade so that its edge pressed against Dario's throat.

"Stay out of this, old man," the bearded one warned. "The boy stole gold from a man who doesn't take such things lightly. If he pays us what's owed, he'll be back to play for you again. If not . . ." He shrugged. "But if you get in our way, I swear to you, we'll kill him where he stands."

The man looked past the brigand to Dario. "You want us to help you, lad?"

"I think you'd better not. But I'll remember the offer, my friend. You can count on that."

The man nodded. He cast a dark look at Dario's two assailants, but then he and his companions backed away.

"We'd better go out the way you came in," the bearded one said. "We'll never get through that crowd."

The man holding Dario began to drag him toward the tavern's rear door.

"Wait!" Dario said. "My lute and pipe."

"You won't have much use for them as a corpse, boy." The man looked at the instrument briefly. "But we'll bring them just the same. They may fetch a few qinde in the markets when we're through with you."

The man stuffed Dario's pipe into his pocket and grabbed the lute roughly, banging it against a chair as he did. As an afterthought, he also picked up Dario's daggers off the table. Then he gave a nod to the other man, who turned toward the corridor leading to the rear door. He still held a fistful of Dario's hair, and had shifted his dagger once again so that it now pushed against the center of the lutenist's back.

Dario racked his brain trying to think of any way he could break free of the men and flee, or better yet, kill them before they killed him. He hadn't much time. The narrow byway just behind the tavern was dark and usually deserted, even at midday. If they did it there, no one would find his body for hours. It might have helped him had he known who this Crebin was, or why he thought Dario had his gold. But the only gold pieces Dario could call his own were the ones still owed to him by the owner of the Red Boar for this day's performance.

"What's a lute worth?" the man holding Dario asked.

"I don't know," the bearded one said. "This one looks to be a bit worn, but I'd wager we could get eight or ten qinde for it."

"Eight or ten?" Dario repeated incredulously, stopping so abruptly that the man's dagger jabbed painfully through his shirt. "It's worth thirty qinde if it's worth one!"

"Keep walking!" the man said, shoving him forward. They were near the end of the corridor. The door stood just before him, slightly ajar. So Dario did the one thing he could. Stumbling as if from the force of the man's push, he fell to his knees, wincing when the brigand failed to let go of his hair.

"Get to your—!"

Before he could finish, Dario threw his elbow back with all the force he could muster, catching the man fully in the groin. This time the man did let go, grunting in agony and falling against the corridor wall. The lutenist scrambled to his feet and sprinted toward the door, throwing it open and racing out into the byway, just as the bearded man would expect. He had no intention of running far, however, not so long as the brigand had his lute. He pressed himself against the outside wall of the tavern, just to the left of the door, praying to all the gods he could name in that moment that the bearded brigand was better with his right hand.

It seemed the gods were with him.

The man burst through the door, Dario's lute in his left hand and a blade in his right. Immediately the lutenist grabbed the arm and hand that held the lute, using the man's own forward motion to swing him in a swift arc into the wall, his head hitting the wood with a dull thud.

The brigand staggered back for an instant, just long enough for Dario to grab his other hand—the one with the blade—and hammer it into the man's gut, steel first. The bearded man gasped, his eyes widening and holding Dario's gaze for a moment before rolling back into his head as he collapsed to the ground.

Dario retrieved his lute and examined it closely. There were a few new scratches on the underside, but otherwise it appeared to be fine. He placed it carefully on an empty ale barrel that stood nearby. Then he returned to the corridor and dragged the other man into the byway.

"Your friend's dead," he said, kicking the man in the stomach. "If you ever come near me again, I'll kill you, too. Understand?"

The brigand looked up at him and nodded weakly.

Dario took his pipe and daggers from the dead man, picked up his lute, and went back into the Red Boar.

Another man had taken his seat at his table, so Dario chose one near it and started to sit.

"You handled that well," the stranger said, watching him, a mild smile on his face. He was lean and tall, but broad in the chest and shoulders, like a warrior. He wore a beard and his long dark hair was tied back. But it was his pale blue eyes, the color of the sky on a frigid day, that held the lutenist's attention. Dario had never seen eyes so cold.

"Thank you," he said after a moment.

"I take it both men are dead?"

"Only one of them. I let the other go. I doubt he'll bother me again."

The dark-haired man frowned. "I'm sorry to hear that. I had hoped to retrieve my gold, but I can only assume that the one who survived has already taken it and fled."

Dario narrowed his eyes, feeling his body grow tense. "You're Crebin?"

"It's a name I use. Some know me as Corbin. My friends call me Cadel."

The lutenist nodded, though it struck him that a man with such eyes couldn't have many friends. He stepped free of the table and pulled out his dagger once more. "Why did you send them for me?"

Cadel looked at the dagger and shook his head, his face hardening. "Don't be a fool. I'd kill you even more easily than you killed the man in the alley."

From another a man it might have seemed an idle boast. But something in Cadel's tone and expression convinced Dario that in this case it was true. After a moment he slid the blade back into its sheath.

"Answer me," he said. "Why did you send them?"

Cadel opened a hand, indicating the chair across from him, the chair in which Dario had been sitting before all this began. The lutenist took a slow breath and sat.

"Forgive me," Cadel said, smiling once more. "I sent those men as a test."

"A test?"

"Yes. I've heard you play, and you're very good, just as your reputation said you would be. Your reputation as a hired blade is a bit less sure. I wanted to see for myself how you'd handle such a situation."

"A test," Dario said again, shaking his head. "Who in Bian's name are you?"

"Someone who can make you very wealthy very quickly."

Dario knew he should have been suspicious—a man who would send murderers after him and then call it a test was not to be trusted. But his pockets were empty, and he didn't want to spend the rest of his life playing lute in the Red Boar.

"You have a job for me?"

"I might have several, though not as you're thinking of it. I'm not looking to hire you. I'm looking for a partner, someone to guard my back and help me with more difficult tasks."

"So you're a blade yourself."

"Yes, I am."

"And you're making enough to make me wealthy?"

"I've made over four hundred qinde in the last five turns," he said in a low voice. "I expect I'll make nearly as much in the next five. My partner's share of that would be somewhere around one hundred and fifty."

Dario gaped at him. One hundred and fifty qinde! That was more gold than he had made in the last four years. And here Cadel was offering him the chance to make that much by the plantings.

"I'd say you've found yourself a partner," he said with a grin.

Cadel smiled thinly. "Not yet, I haven't."

"I don't understand."

"Well, for one thing, I still haven't decided that you're the man I want."

Dario sat forward. "But your test! I bested both men without so much as a scratch from either of them."

"And then you let one of them go."

"You wanted me to kill them both?"

"Not necessarily. But I want to know that you didn't kill the second man for the right reasons. I agree with you that this man posed no threat to you. Seeing what you did to his friend, he'll probably be happy never to meet up with you again. But another man, a more accomplished killer perhaps, would almost certainly come after you again, either to finish the job he'd been hired to do, or to avenge his companion. By letting him live you could have been endangering your own life. And if you did something similar as my partner, you'd be endangering my life as well." He watched Dario for several moments, then raised an eyebrow. "So? Why did you do it?"

It would have been easy to lie to him, but for some reason, Dario decided against it. Maybe he didn't want to cast his lot with this man, even if it did mean wealth beyond his imaginings. Or maybe he just sensed that Cadel would know if he lied.

"I didn't want to kill him," he admitted. "So I let him live. I was confident that he wouldn't attack me again tonight, but I can't say that I gave much thought to tomorrow or the next day."

Cadel nodded. "I see. That's not really the answer I wanted to hear, but neither is it the lie I might have expected from a man hungry for gold. And when it comes to choosing a partner, I'll trade ruthlessness for honesty any day."

"Does that mean we're partners now?"

"It means I'm convinced that I could trust you. But before you agree to join me, there are a few things you should know."

"Like what?"

"Well, to start, I travel the land as a musician, joining festivals, including the one in Sanbira and the Revel in Eibithar. I know that you play alone, but I don't know if you've performed with a singer before, or if you're inclined to do so now."

"You sing?" Dario asked.

"A little bit, yes," Cadel said, smiling in a way that made Dario think he must be quite good.

Dario gave a small shrug. "I have no objection to performing with you. What else?"

"You should know that my last partner was killed trying to protect me. That's why I'm looking for someone new."

"I assumed as much, just as I assume that the partner before him died the same way."

"There was no partner before him. I worked with Jedrek for almost seventeen years."

Dario felt his face reddening. It wasn't the first time he had created trouble for himself by saying something stupid, but it might well have been the most inopportune. Not only had the man sitting before him promised to make him rich, he was also a paid killer. Either way Dario looked at it, this was not a man he wanted to make angry.

"I'm sorry," he said, looking away.

"It doesn't matter," the assassin said, his voice flat. After a brief pause, he went on. "The last thing you should know is that the gold we're talking about comes from the Qirsi."

"What do you mean?" Dario asked, looking at the man again. A moment later it hit him, and his eyes widened. "You mean the conspiracy?"

"Yes."

Dario sat back again, shaking his head. No wonder Cadel had made so much gold.

"It's an assassin's dream," the younger man said. "Steady work, good pay, jobs scattered throughout the Forelands so that you have to keep moving. What more could you want?"

Cadel smirked. "That's what I thought."

"Hasn't it turned out that way?"

"I guess. I've made a good deal of gold, I've had jobs in Eibithar, Aneira, Caerisse, and Sanbira. So all you say is true."

"Then why do you sound like you're trying to warn me away from this?"

"Have you spent much time with the Qirsi?" Cadel asked, his eyes locked on Dario's.

"Not really."

"Neither had I. It never occurred to me that their appearance and their magic would bother me so, but they do."

Dario started to say something, but Cadel raised a hand, stopping him.

"It's not just that," he said. "I used to think that this profession gave me freedom. As long as I had some gold in my pocket, I could work when and where I chose. Now that I work for the Qirsi, that's gone. They tell me what to do, which jobs to take, how the kills are supposed to be done. They pay me well, better than anyone else ever has. But their gold has a price."

He wasn't certain that he understood all that the assassin was trying to tell him, but the solution seemed obvious. "So stop killing for them."

Cadel shook his head, looking away. "I can't, at least not yet. They know too much about me. If I try to free myself of them, they'll reveal me to every house in every kingdom in the Forelands."

"Can't you threaten to do the same?"

The assassin stared at him again, looking like a man who had just had his innermost thoughts laid bare. "I've thought of that," he said. "In time, that may be my way out. But if I tried it now, they'd hunt me down and slit my throat."

Dario exhaled through his teeth. "I see."

"Are you certain you want to work with me?"

"Not as certain as I was a few moments ago," he said, rubbing a hand over his mouth. "But gold is gold, and the Red Boar doesn't pay its musicians enough to keep me here."

Cadel extended a hand. "Then I suppose we're partners."

Dario stared at the assassin's hand briefly before taking it with his own.

"The first thing we should do," Cadel said, releasing his hand, "is rehearse some pieces. They don't have to be perfect at first, but we should have at least four or five songs that we can perform reasonably well."

"All right."

"If you'd like, I can pay you a bit now, and take it out of your share later. You can buy yourself a new instrument. That one looks like it's been through a war."

"It has," Dario said, not bothering to mask his anger. "It was my father's, and it was nearly destroyed in the attack on my home village that took his life."

Cadel's brow furrowed. "It would seem that it's my turn to apologize," he said quietly. "Your lute certainly has a good sound, and as for the rest, I intended no offense."

The lutenist gave a single nod. "It's all right."

Another performer, a piper, began to play at the front of the tavern.

The assassin stood. "Why don't we go somewhere we can play, and you can show me just how fine an instrument it is."

Dario looked up at the man, and after a moment he grinned. "Very well. I just need to collect my pay from the tavern keeper."

He stood, picking up his lute, and they began making their way among the tables toward the bar. But after taking only a few steps, Cadel stopped, his face hardening as he began to shake his head.

"Not so soon," he whispered. "They can't want me again so soon."

Following the direction of his gaze, Dario saw a Qirsi woman standing by the bar, speaking with the owner of the tavern. She looked vaguely familiar to him, though he couldn't say why. There could be little doubt as to why she had come, however. As Dario watched, the tavern keeper nodded and pointed toward Cadel. The white-hair looked at them, recognition in her bright yellow eyes. She said something to the man, handing him a gold coin. Then she started in their direction.

Seeds of Betrayal

* * *

She didn't need a message from Fetnalla to tell her that she should have seen to the matter already, though Evanthya wasn't surprised when such a message arrived at Castle Dantrielle that morning. Fetnalla had penned it herself—Evanthya would have known her hand anywhere—but the note itself was so brief as to seem almost cold. "Any news yet?" it asked. And then, simply, "Write me soon." Only the signature offered the slightest hint of what lay behind it. "Your Fetnalla."

They had signed their notes this way for years. Such a small thing, yet it was all they dared. This at least could be passed off as an error made in haste, rather than as a declaration of their love.

Deep as that love went, however, Evanthya could tell that Fetnalla was cross with her. The note itself had been intended as a rebuke, a reminder of how much time had slipped by since Chago's funeral. She could delay no longer, especially with Tebeo preparing to ride later that day to Solkara for the king's funeral.

After her daily audience with her duke, Evanthya made her excuses to the underministers, changed out of her ministerial robes, and left the castle, hurrying through the north end of the city to the marketplace. As much as she had dreaded doing this, she had not been completely idle since leaving Fetnalla in Orvinti. For years she had heard rumors of a tavern in Dantrielle that was frequented by assassins, brigands, and thieves. Most cities had such places, but the one in Dantrielle had long been said to be the most crowded in the kingdom, the one to which the most renowned men of this kind flocked. She now knew that it was called the Red Boar, and that it could be found just off the southern edge of the marketplace. She knew, as well, the name of one particular man whose talents matched her needs perfectly. The information had cost her nearly half a turn's wage, and had required that she tell the most appalling lies not only to her duke, but also to several guards, the other ministers, and one of the stableboys, who was now convinced that she had a secret lover on the far side of the city to whom she paid frequent late-night visits.

As it turned out, the Red Boar was more difficult to find than she had been led to believe. It was located on a narrow street near the south city gate, with a single small sign that she overlooked several times as she walked up and down the lane. It didn't help that the tavern looked fairly respectable from outside; she had expected that its appearance would match its reputation.

Once inside, however, the first minister was not disappointed. She had little trouble believing that the men crowding around the bar and laughing raucously from nearly every table were killers and rogues. Many of them stared at her as she approached the bar—she was the only Qirsi in the tavern—but they left her alone. The tavern keeper seemed reluctant at first to speak with her, but when she showed him a ten-qinde round, he gladly pointed out the man she sought.

His name was Corbin, a Caerissan singer with a reputation as a skilled though expensive assassin. He stood at the back of the tavern with a younger man, and it appeared that they were preparing to leave.

Evanthya glanced around awkwardly as she walked toward them, conscious once more of being the only Qirsi in the room.

"Are you Corbin?" she asked, stopping in front of the Caerissan.

He stared at her with unconcealed hostility. "Did the barman just tell you I was?"

"Yes."

"Do you have cause to doubt him?"

She bit back a retort, forcing a smile instead. "Perhaps we can sit," she said, gesturing toward the table the man and his friend had just left.

Corbin hesitated, looking briefly at his companion. After a moment he nodded, and they walked back to the table.

The younger man carried a lute, and Evanthya wondered if he was merely a musician or an assassin as well. She suddenly felt far beyond her depth.

"This is Dagon," the assassin said, indicating the younger man with an open hand.

Dagon smiled, glancing at his companion. It occurred to Evanthya that this wasn't his real name, that in fact Corbin's name was probably an alias as well. Which probably meant that the younger man was also a killer. She found this hard to believe. He looked terribly young, with a clean-shaven face and warm brown eyes. He could easily have been a new probationer in the duke's guard or even a court noble. Indeed, Corbin had the look of nobility as well. Perhaps this explained his success as an assassin.

"And your name?" Corbin asked after a brief pause.

"My name isn't important," she said, unable to think of an alias of her own.

"Fine," the Caerissan said, the look in his pale eyes turning cold. "Then what is it you want?"

"I had hoped to hire you."

"Don't you people understand that every time I do a job for you, it makes the next one that much more dangerous?" He glanced beyond her briefly, and when he began again it was in a near whisper. "There are risks to every kill, and if one follows too closely after the last, it increases the chances that I'll fail, or that one of you will be discovered."

The minister shook her head. "I don't understand. Has someone else from the castle spoken with you?"

He frowned. "The castle?"

The realization came to her so swiftly, with such power, that she almost began to laugh. There was really only one explanation for what he had said, though she could scarcely believe that it was true. And as she moved beyond the humor of the situation, she began to tremble, fearing for her life.

"You've been hired by Qirsi before, haven't you?"

He nodded, his eyes wide, as if he understood what had happened as well.

Evanthya swallowed, then stood. "I think I'd better go."

"No, don't."

She stopped, unsure at first if he was urging or ordering her to stay. If she needed, she could summon a mist to aid her escape, but her other powers—gleaning and language of beasts—were of little use to her here.

"I was wrong to come here," she said, not looking at him. "I just want to leave."

"You came to hire an assassin."

Evanthya nodded.

"And you're not with . . . You're not part of a movement."

She looked back at the man, meeting his gaze. "No, I'm not," she said, as if daring him to hurt her for her loyalty to the duke.

"Neither am I," he said.

The minister narrowed her eyes. "But you said—"

"I said I had worked for them. That doesn't make me party to their cause."

"Meaning what?"

"Meaning that if you want to hire me, you can."

"It's not that simple," she said, shaking her head. "I don't just want to hire you, I want to hire you to kill a Qirsi we suspect is part of the conspiracy."

" 'We'?"

Her face colored. "I."

A small smile flitted across the man's face. "Please, won't you sit again?"

"Why? I'd just be wasting your time, and my own."

"Not necessarily."

"You'd actually consider doing this?" she asked.

He gestured at the empty chair. "Please sit."

She returned to the table and slowly lowered herself onto the chair, her eyes never straying from the two assassins.

"Who is this person you want killed?" Corbin asked, his gaze steady.

In a far corner of her mind, Evanthya wondered that she could be discussing such things so calmly with a hired killer. She wanted only to serve her duke and her kingdom, like any other Aneiran. Yes, she had yellow eyes and possessed magics that the Eandi feared, but in other ways she was just like any of her duke's subjects. She had never wanted to be more than she was, and certainly she had never thought to plot the murder of another. But in these times it seemed that loyalty to Tebeo and the kingdom demanded more than simple ministerial duties.

"How is it that you can do this?" she asked the man. "How can you kill for the Qirsi movement, and then turn around and take my gold to kill one of them?"

"Their gold buys my blade, not my allegiance," he said. "Just as your gold does. I may kill for you today, only to turn my blade against you tomorrow. That's the nature of my profession."

The assassin's eyes bored into her own as he spoke, as if by saying the words to the minister he could reach every Qirsi in the land. There was more at work here than just avarice, though she couldn't be certain what it was.

"This person you want killed," he went on a moment later. "Can you give me a name?"

"No. I wish I could. I know that he once served a duke in Eibithar, Kentigern I believe. He recently sought asylum in Mertesse."

Corbin's face paled at the mention of Kentigern. "Why this man?" he whispered.

"You know him?"

"I know of him. Tell me why."

Because it's all we can do, she wanted to say. *Because we know so little of the conspiracy that just suspecting he might be involved makes him a threat.* Word of the man's escape from Eibithar had spread quickly through Aneira, as did descriptions of the siege that nearly captured Kentigern Castle. Most in the kingdom greeted these tidings predictably, mourning the death of Rouel of Mertesse, cheering the blow dealt to Kentigern and the

Eibitharians, and marveling at how close the Mertesse army had come to taking the great castle atop Kentigern Tor.

But with word of the battle and the defection came whisperings among some of a darker purpose behind the minister's actions. He betrayed his duke not to help Mertesse, these stories implied, but rather to further the conspiracy, whose leaders hoped to draw the two kingdoms into a full-blown war. The stories went on to say that he had a hand in the death of Kentigern's daughter, whose murder nearly precipitated a civil war between Kentigern and Curgh, two of Eibithar's leading houses. Most dismissed these last rumors, but not Fetnalla and Evanthya. These tidings fit too well with all the other strange events darkening the Forelands. A turn later, Fetnalla dreamed of the man, and though she had told Evanthya little of the vision, offering only vague answers to her repeated questions, she did make clear that it had convinced her of what they already suspected: the traitor from Kentigern had acted on behalf of the conspiracy. The murder of Chago of Bistari only served to deepen their certainty that the time had come to strike back at the conspiracy. In light of Fetnalla's vision, and all they had heard since the siege of Kentigern, the renegade minister seemed the logical choice as their first target. Evanthya still grew queasy at the notion of killing a man on the basis of rumor, suspicion, and a single dream, but Fetnalla argued that their only alternative was to wait for another murder or siege that might finally bring war and chaos to the land. The king's death only strengthened her point.

"Because we know of him as well," Evanthya finally told the assassin. She had said "we" again, but she pressed on. "The conspiracy has gone unopposed for too long. I don't expect that this man's death will stop it. It might not even slow its advance across the land. But those who lead it have to be made to understand that they will be opposed. Perhaps this is the way to convey that message."

"Perhaps it is," he said thoughtfully.

"You said that you know of this man. Do you know his name?" She wanted to ask if he knew for certain that the man was part of the conspiracy, but she didn't dare reveal her doubts. She felt that she was betraying Fetnalla even thinking it.

"I wouldn't say even if I did," he told her. "I'm not part of their movement, but neither am I their enemy. I'll tell you nothing about them. And I'll tell them nothing about you."

How could she argue? "Very well."

"You have gold for me?"

Evanthya took a breath and pulled Fetnalla's pouch from within her riding cloak. She had added some of her own money to the sixty qinde Fetnalla had given her. The pouch felt heavy as she placed it in the man's large hand.

"That's ninety qinde," she said. It seemed a lot to her, but given the look that passed between Corbin and his young companion, she guessed that they usually demanded more. Her heart sank, and she expected the assassin to hand back the pouch.

"That's fine," he said instead.

The younger man started to say something, but Corbin laid a hand on his arm and shook his head.

"We'll see to this matter," he said, holding her gaze. "You may not place much faith in the word of men like me, but I promise you, the man in Mertesse will be killed, and no one will learn from us who bought his blood."

"Thank you," she whispered, her throat abruptly dry.

"Now I'd suggest you go, before your duke misses you."

Evanthya felt the blood drain from her cheeks.

"Don't be afraid," he said, smiling at her. "As you've seen, I don't betray those who buy my services."

She just sat there, knowing that she should leave, that she should run from the place and never return. But she wasn't certain that her legs would bear her. After several moments, she made herself stand and leave the table. She stepped to the tavern door, glancing back as she pulled it open. The two men were still at the table, but they were talking to each other. She glanced around the tavern one last time and then hurried out into the lane. She and the duke's company would be departing soon for Solkara, where, no doubt, she would see her love again, sooner than either of them ever imagined. Fetnalla would be pleased by what Evanthya had done, but that did little to ease the pounding of the minister's heart.

Cadel stared after the minister as she made her way to the tavern door. Taking her gold was dangerous, but he hardly cared. By making it clear to her that he knew who she was, he guaranteed that she wouldn't reveal him to others. And at last, he could strike back at these Qirsi who had controlled his life for so long.

"Why did you do that?" Dario demanded, sounding angry and terribly young.

Cadel looked at him. "She gave us gold."

"Ninety qinde, for a job that's going to take us the better part of a turn. Maybe longer. You can't expect me to believe that you've been accepting so little pay for other jobs."

"No, I haven't. But didn't you hear what I told you earlier about working for the conspiracy?"

"Yes, I heard," the young man said. "They know too much about your past. They can reveal you to every noble house in the Forelands. And if you try to stop working for them, they'll hunt you down. Demons and fire, man! What do you think they'll do to you when they learn that you're killing Qirsi who belong to the movement?"

"They won't find out. I've been doing this a long time now, and I've gotten quite good at it." He eyed the lutenist briefly. "If you don't want to do this, we can part ways now. I'll hold no grudges. You have my word."

Dario stared at him, as if weighing the offer. Then he shook his head. "No, I'll go with you." He rubbed a hand across his brow. "Ninety qinde," he mumbled to himself.

Cadel nearly laughed aloud.

"What's my share come to?" Dario asked.

Cadel thought for a moment. "Thirty-six qinde."

"Thirty-six. I suppose I should be pleased. That's more than I've got now." He peered into his empty tankard. "Still, I think it's only fair that you buy the ales."

Chapter
Eleven

✦

usaan strode through the white stone corridors of the palace, his red robe rustling like the cape of a king, his white hair dancing about his shoulders. He still seethed at the messenger's tidings, though he was certain that no one would have known it to look at him. He had learned long ago to keep a tight rein on his passions. In a few hours he would be free to loose his rage, but before then he had to endure an audience with the emperor. Surely Harel would be distraught enough for both of them.

He passed by one of the interior courtyards, its fountain gurgling noisily amid the blooms and shrubs growing in great carved marble planters. A pair of finches flew up from the water at his approach, alighting on a high ledge just below the white ceiling. Just beyond the courtyard, he turned to enter the broad, tiled corridor leading to the emperor's chambers. Guards stood on either side of the door, both of them dressed in gold and red, both holding pikes that gleamed in the sunlight from the glazed windows that lined the outer hall.

They bowed to him as he stepped past them and pushed open the door.

"Dusaan jal Kania!" another guard called out as Dusaan paused in the doorway. "High Chancellor to the Emperor of Braedon!"

Harel sat on his marble throne in the center of the chamber, his fleshy chin cradled in his hand, his small green eyes downcast. He looked utterly disconsolate, like a child trapped in his house by an untimely rainstorm. He wore white as always, his robe and cape fringed with red and gold. His jeweled crown sat upon his head in a nest of tight brown curls, and the

Imperial Scepter lay across his lap, its diamonds and rubies glittering, calling to Dusaan's eye like beacons in the night.

Like the hallway, the emperor's chambers were bright with sun. Even the great castles of Thorald and Solkara, Enharfe and Yserne, did not have glazed windows, Harel often reminded anyone who would listen. Only here, in the Imperial Palace of Braedon, could the leader of one of the Forelands' seven lands—the wealthiest and most powerful of them all—pass the cold months in the warm glow of the sun, rather than in the murky light of torches, lamps, and candles.

In the near corner of the chamber, a harper played a slow ballad, her slender hands moving like spiders over the strings. The empress's court ladies sat in a tight circle near the musician speaking in low tones, though the empress herself was nowhere to be seen.

Harel sat up straighter when Dusaan was announced, his round face brightening considerably.

"High Chancellor," he called, beckoning to the Qirsi with an outstretched hand.

Dusaan walked to where the emperor sat, dropping to one knee just before the throne and bowing his head.

"Your Eminence."

"Rise, High Chancellor."

Dusaan stood again, and the emperor regarded him gravely, as if they had both lost a dear friend.

"You heard?" Harel asked.

"Yes, Your Eminence. Word of the message reached my quarters not long ago."

The emperor shook his head. "Terrible business. I never would have thought that Carden could do such a thing."

Dusaan had to grit his teeth. "It's a great loss for Aneira," he managed to say. "And for all of us who considered the king an ally."

"I always liked Carden," the emperor said, chewing his lip, and staring off toward the harper. "He was a wise leader and a reliable friend."

Actually he was a fool and as poor a leader as ever ruled a kingdom of the Forelands, but Dusaan kept that to himself, nodding solemnly. He knew as well as Harel that the emperor's concerns lay elsewhere.

"We'll need to start again, you know, building an alliance with the new king, whoever that may be." Harel looked up at him. "Have you any idea who's next in line for the Aneiran throne?"

"No, Your Eminence, I don't. There was a daughter, but I can't imagine she'd be accepted as Carden's heir. Which leaves his brothers."

Harel frowned. "I don't like what I've heard about them. Particularly the eldest. What is his name?"

"Grigor, Your Eminence. And his reputation does leave much to be desired."

"I've no tolerance for brutes, High Chancellor, and I certainly don't wish to find myself allied with one. I spent a good deal of time and gold winning Carden's allegiance. Do you know how many ships I sent him? I believe it was fourteen. Fourteen ships at more than seven thousand imperial rounds each. None of that will matter to the new king. He'll just think of it as his navy, as if we'd done nothing at all to make it the strongest among the six. He'll know nothing of the weaponry we sent either, or the mercenaries. This man, this . . ." He shook his head, frowning once more.

"Grigor, Your Eminence."

"Yes, yes. This Grigor. Where is my mind today?" He looked past Dusaan to the harper. "You there!" he called. "That's enough music for today. Leave us." Then, looking at the ladies, he added, "All of you as well. Leave my chambers. I wish to speak with the chancellor in private."

The musician curtsied and stepped out of the chamber, leaving her instrument in the corner against the wall. The ladies followed close behind her, looking back at the emperor with frightened faces.

"This will delay the attack on Eibithar, won't it?" Harel asked, once they were alone.

"I'm afraid it must," the chancellor said, feeling his ire rise once more, and moving swiftly to quash it. "A new king, whoever it might be, will need time to consolidate his power. Even a man like Grigor won't rush into a war so soon. It will be several turns before we can act, at the very least."

"Several turns?" the emperor asked, looking relieved. "That's not so bad."

"At the very least," the Qirsi said again, pointedly this time. Sometimes the emperor seemed to him more child than man. Harel had held the scepter for more than half his life, taking the throne after his father died, just a year past his Fating. It often seemed to Dusaan that twenty-two years later he remained a frightened boy, out of his depth, foolish, and weak, even for an Eandi. "If Grigor does assume the crown, and if he can move quickly and decisively, then it will only be half a year," he explained, his patience strained. "But if he meets with resistance from the other houses it could take far longer. And if by some chance, Carden's death leads to war among Aneira's more powerful families, it could be years."

"Which means," Harel said, "that as soon as the king takes the throne, we must act quickly to back him, to make it clear to others in Aneira that the emperor of Braedon recognizes him as the legitimate successor to Carden."

"Yes, Your Eminence," the chancellor said, taken aback by the clarity of Harel's reasoning. "That's just what we must do."

"And in the meantime?"

Dusaan thought for a moment. "In the meantime, I believe we should continue with our plans as if nothing has happened. The training of the men should go on uninterrupted, and the bulk of the fleet should be divided between Ayvencalde and Bishenhurst. The longer the ships remain there, posing no threat to Eibithar, the greater the surprise when they finally cross the Scabbard. The delay is unavoidable, but perhaps in this small way we can use it to our advantage."

The emperor fairly beamed. "Excellent, High Chancellor! See to it, will you?"

"Of course, Your Eminence." He stood before the emperor another moment, neither of them speaking. "Is there more?"

"No," Harel said, looking troubled again. "No, nothing more."

"Very good, Your Eminence." Dusaan knelt again, then rose and started quickly toward the door.

"What makes a man take his own life?" the emperor asked, just as the Qirsi reached the door. "What could cause a king, with all his wealth and power, to take a dagger to his own heart?"

Dusaan stood unmoving, his back to the throne, biting down on his tongue until he tasted blood.

"Send the harper back in, would you?" Harel said after a moment. "And tell the kitchenmaster that I require my supper a bit early today."

"Yes, Your Eminence," Dusaan said, his voice thick. He faced the emperor again, sketching a quick bow. Then he left, fearing that the man would keep him there longer if given the chance.

After seeing to the harper and the emperor's meal, Dusaan returned to his chambers and summoned the other chancellors so that he could inform them of the tidings from Solkara and his conversation with the emperor. It was a waste of his time and theirs, but Harel expected it of him. Like all Eandi rulers, the emperor had a great number of Qirsi in his palace. Ostensibly they were here as advisors—most bore the title of chancellor, a few were ministers. But Harel rarely met with any of them, relying almost entirely on Dusaan. He collected Qirsi, just as he did swords from Sanbira and Uulrann, and horses from Caerisse. The more Qirsi he possessed, the wiser he appeared to both his people and his rivals in other kingdoms. Braedon was the most powerful of the seven realms—few would have argued the point, even in Eibithar. People here spoke of Braedon and the six, as if the other kingdoms were mere dukedoms standing in the vast shadow of the empire. Of all the realms, only Braedon dared call itself an empire, and in fairness to Harel and his predecessors on the throne, Braedon did have territorial holdings as far away as Enwyl Island, in the Gulf of Kreanna. So it was only natural that Harel should surround himself with Qirsi advisors.

From all that Dusaan could tell, Harel assumed, as did the other Qirsi, that the advice Dusaan gave the emperor was not just his own, but rather a compendium of the counsel offered by all the chancellors and ministers in their daily discussions. Dusaan, of course, did nothing to dispel this notion.

Most of the other advisors were typical of court Qirsi throughout the Forelands: blindly loyal to Braedon and House Curtell, almost pitiable in their desire to please the emperor and rise in his esteem, and disturbingly eager to try to surpass each other in this regard. With each day that passed, it became harder for Dusaan to meet with them without revealing the contempt in which he held them. A few showed signs of being more, of being capable of rising above their current station, with his help, of course, but the time for that had not yet come.

This day's discussion proved to be a somber affair, with the older chancellors and ministers falling over each other in their attempts to exalt the dead king. Dusaan had told them as little as possible about the emperor's plans to attack Eibithar, and now he said merely that the attack would be put off indefinitely.

Speaking of it served only to enrage Dusaan once again. He ended the meeting abruptly, dismissing the other Qirsi and locking the door to his chamber once they were gone. Stepping to his window, he pushed open the wooden shutters and gazed out over the ramparts of the palace and the swift waters of the River of Swords, which lay beyond. The windows in this part of the palace were not glazed, and a brisk wind stirred his hair and chilled his quarters. The sun had set, but the western sky still glowed orange and pink with the last glimmers of daylight. It would still be some time before he could do anything more than brood on his anger, and given the night that lay in store for him, Dusaan decided that he was best off using this time to sleep.

He closed the shutters again, lay down on his bed, and, closing his eyes, fell almost instantly into a deep, dreamless slumber.

The chancellor awakened to the sound of bells ringing in the city. The gate close, no doubt. He hadn't been asleep very long, but he felt refreshed and ready to speak with those who served him. He had taught himself long ago to sleep when he could and to arise when he needed. It didn't matter what thoughts filled his head; over the years he had disciplined his mind to shunt them aside, and to ward off dreams that might keep him from getting the rest he needed. He had mastered sleep, his own as well as that of others. As a Weaver who walked in the dreams of other Qirsi, he could hardly have done less.

He was most eager to speak with Pronjed jal Drenthe in Solkara, but it was early yet to find him sleeping, and it had been some time since he last visited with the woman in Kett.

Dusaan closed his eyes, drawing upon the vast ocean that was his power and reaching eastward with his mind. For a time he felt as a hawk must when it soars on a warm wind, unassailable and without equal, secure in the knowledge that even then, his consciousness gliding high above the Forelands, he had barely tested the extent of his magic. Soon he sensed the Caerissan Steppe looming before him and he reached downward toward Braedor's Plain and the city of Kett.

He found her quickly, and, touching her mind with his own, called forth the image of the moor that he used whenever he entered the dreams of a Qirsi. It was Ayvencalde Moor that he used, a desolate expanse of rocks and grasses that lay but a few leagues from the emperor's palace. But knowing as he did that those with whom he spoke always hoped to recognize the plain, and thus learn who he was, he darkened the landscape, making it impossible for them to see beyond the reach of his light. He had no intention of allowing his servants to divine his secret.

He liked to make them work to find him, situating himself atop a rise and making the climb arduous for those who had angered him. Later that night, Pronjed would face a daunting and wearying ascent. But for the woman, he made an exception. She was with child and had served him well as one of his chancellors. If Dusaan had his way—and he usually did—she would be his queen when he finally ruled the Forelands. When she opened her eyes to this dream, finding herself on the moor, Dusaan was already there standing before her, lit from behind by the great white sun he had conjured for these visions.

She looked even more beautiful than she had the last time they spoke. Her belly had grown larger, her breasts fuller with milk for her child. She stood before him in a simple shift, her fine white hair falling over her brow and down around her shoulders, her pale eyes bleary with sleep. Yet, for all Dusaan could tell, she might have been wearing glittering jewels and a banquet gown.

"You're well?" he asked at last, unable to say more.

She stared at the ground. "I am, Weaver. Thank you."

She feared him, of course. They all did. And though he hoped that someday she would love him, for now her fear suited his purposes quite well.

"You've been eating?"

A small smile sprung to her lips. "Yes, Weaver."

"You think me foolish for asking."

Her eyes snapped up, a frightened look on her face. "No, Weaver. You're very kind to show such interest in my baby and me."

"I may be a bit foolish," he admitted. "But as I've told you before, I foresee a glorious future for this child. And for you, as well."

The woman nodded. "Yes, Weaver. Thank you."

"I trust you've heard no news of the child's father?"

"No, none. All the talk here is of the king and who will take his place on the throne."

"I'm sure it is," he said, his voice tightening.

"The men who run the Festival are talking of going to Solkara, not for the funeral of course, but when the new king is invested. Do you wish that I remain here, or may I accompany them?"

"If you feel that you can make the journey, you're free to go. Assuming the man we seek is still in Aneira, he may be there also."

"I'd thought of that, as well," she said.

Dusaan narrowed his eyes, staring at her now. There was something in her voice and manner . . .

"Is everything all right?" he asked.

"Yes, Weaver. Everything is fine."

"And you're certain you've heard nothing?"

"Quite certain."

"You told me some time ago that you spoke to an assassin of this man, that the white-hair had killed this assassin's partner."

"Yes, Weaver. I remember."

"Is it possible that this assassin has already found him and killed him?"

And there it was, in her eyes, in the terror he sensed abruptly flooding her mind, like the surge of a storm tide. She still loved this man. She had seduced him for the movement, acting on Dusaan's instructions, and she had sent assassins for him twice now. Yet she still loved him. It shouldn't have surprised him so. Seduction was a difficult matter, and she was terribly young. Add the fact that she was carrying his child, and it would have been stranger if she had never loved him. But she served the Weaver and his movement. She was to be Dusaan's queen. That she should still carry such passion for this gleaner, that she could conceal this from Dusaan, made suspect all that she had done on the Weaver's behalf, and all that she had told him the past several turns. He could hardly contain the rage and jealousy that flared in his chest like Qirsi fire. He wanted to hurt her. Had it not been for the child, he might have. Then again, had it not been for the child, he might not have cared. Most of all, he wanted to kill this man, this Grinsa jal Arriet. Not through assassins and the dispensing of gold, but with his own blade, guided by his own hand. He wanted to feel the man's blood on his fingers. He wanted to watch as the spark died in his yellow eyes, leaving them empty and sightless.

"It is possible, Weaver," the woman said, though it seemed to Dusaan that her words came from a great distance. He could barely remember what he had asked her.

He just stared at her. She couldn't see his face for the light. She wouldn't know how his wrath twisted his features, how his eyes burned with his thirst for blood. Only his voice could give him away, and that he could control.

"Perhaps, it would be best if you didn't go to Solkara," he said, sounding bored, as if already tiring of their conversation.

"Weaver?"

He sensed her eagerness to go. This would be her punishment, though she might never recognize it as such. "The last time we spoke you seemed reluctant to travel to the steppe. It may be that you're best off remaining where you are." The child might still amount to something, even if he could never trust the woman again. Certainly he couldn't allow her to find the gleaner. "Yes," he went on, as if convincing himself. "Stay in Kett. I'll have others look for him in Solkara."

"But—"

Dusan reached out with his mind, placing an invisible hand over her mouth. He took care not to hurt her, but he saw from the widening of her pale eyes that he had frightened her. *Never forget what I can do to you if I choose.*

"My mind is set. You will remain in Kett. Do you understand?"

He removed the unseen hand.

"Yes, Weaver," she whispered.

"Very good."

His eyes lingered on her a moment longer, hungry for her despite the fire searing his heart. Then he released her mind, his consciousness hurtling back over Aneira and the Scabbard so swiftly that Dusaan felt as though he were falling. When he opened his eyes, he started violently, as one does awakening suddenly from a disturbing dream.

"Damn her!" he whispered to the darkness, gritting his teeth against a wave of nausea. "And the man as well."

He walked to the hearth and sat in the nearest chair, fighting desperately to ease his pulse and purge his mind of the visions abruptly clamoring for his attention. Images of Cresenne, her legs entwined with those of another man, and of his own fingers closing around her throat.

He took a slow, shuddering breath, staring at the flames dancing before him. Finally, after what seemed an eternity, he began slowly to take control of his thoughts once more. It was a long journey, and a difficult one, but he had spent years training his mind to retain its focus, to overcome his passions and the distractions foisted upon him by others. He was a Weaver. To do less would have been to risk discovery and execution.

Eventually, he was able to look away from the flames, and to think once more of the tasks that awaited him that night.

Pronjed would be sleeping by now, and if a residue of anger remained from his conversation with the woman, so be it. The Solkaran minister had earned Dusaan's fury as few ever had before.

The Weaver closed his eyes again, and sent his mind soaring eastward once more. He hadn't as far to travel this time and before long he sensed the Great Forest beneath him. He allowed his thoughts to spiral downward to Castle Solkara, where he found the king's archminister asleep.

Taking hold of the man's mind, he again called forth the image of the moor, this time placing himself atop a steep, unforgiving rise and leaving Pronjed a good distance from the base of the mount. He even raised a wind to blow down the slope, slowing the minister further. Let the man walk and climb. Let him enfeeble himself so that he might know how he had displeased the Weaver. And let him tremble with that knowledge as he dragged himself up the rocky slope.

The Weaver had a long wait, and though it was of his own making, he had little patience for the delay. He had to resist the urge to shorten Pronjed's climb, reminding himself again and again that he was punishing the man. When at last the minister reached the top of the rise, appearing in the distance as a small, slow-moving figure, Dusaan started toward him, his long strides covering the ground between them far faster than Pronjed could have on his own.

As they drew nearer to each other, Dusaan saw that the minister had indeed suffered in his ascent. Pronjed's bony face was flushed to a deep scarlet, and the sweat on his brow and cheeks shone in the Weaver's light. Still, though breathless, he wore a small grin on his thin lips, looking anything but contrite.

"Weaver," he said, stopping before Dusaan and bowing. He looked up, eagerness in his pale eyes. "You've heard?"

"What happened?" the Weaver demanded, his voice like a frigid mountain wind.

The grin vanished. "I don't understand."

"What is there to understand? I want to know why your king is dead!"

"But surely you're pleased. I'd have thought—"

"Tell me what happened!"

Pronjed licked his lips, the avid gleam in his eyes replaced now by something far more satisfying.

"There was a visitor. One of the dukes, one of Chago's allies. He gave the king a dagger the night of his arrival—"

"So you sought to make it a murder?"

"No, Weaver," the minister said, beginning to sound desperate. "A suicide. The king had seen the surgeon earlier in the day, and had learned that he was sterile. Carden was so galled by this that he had the surgeon garroted. So I saw an opportunity to—"

"You convinced the others that he was dying," Dusaan said, nodding. He could see the logic of what the minister had done, although he still wasn't ready to forgive the man's presumption. "And they believe it?" he asked.

"The queen believes it. What choice do the others have?"

"They can be suspicious. The king would have had to believe that Qirsi magic would fail to heal him. He would have had to believe beyond doubt that his line would continue to rule Aneira. And he would have had to believe that his death would spare his family suffering and humiliation. Failing any one of these, his suicide threatens to draw the attention of those who oppose us. All it takes is one doubter, one person with the persistence and courage to challenge you and the queen."

"That may be true elsewhere," the minister said. "But not here, not in Aneira. Those who knew Carden well enough to pose any threat to us, would realize that he was too vain and too callow to be stayed by the considerations of which you speak." He paused, seeming to realize abruptly that his tone had grown too familiar. "Though of course, for any proper king, you'd be entirely correct, Weaver. It was only Carden's vast shortcomings as a leader that allowed me to think I could do this."

"So you think I should be pleased," Dusaan said, "that I should be praising you for your bold actions."

The minister couldn't see his face and he appeared uncertain as to what response the Weaver expected.

"Well, I . . . I think that . . . No one has raised questions regarding the king's death. And already there is talk of the coming struggle for the throne."

"You assume that because I hoped for civil war in Eibithar, I want it in Aneira as well?"

Pronjed swallowed, his eyes widening. Clearly he had. "You had the duke of Bistari killed," he said quickly. "You made it look as though Carden had ordered the assassination. Didn't you wish to sow dissent among the other houses?"

"Dissent is one thing, you fool! Open conflict is another! If you're too dull to know the difference, I may have to reconsider the faith I've placed in you."

Pronjed opened his mouth to speak, but Dusaan stopped him, clutching his throat with the same power he had used to silence the woman.

"Did it never occur to you that I might want the king alive, that indeed I might need him? Do you believe that I tell you everything? Do you presume to think that you understand all that I have in mind for the Forelands? Or is it that you think you know better than I what our movement should do next?"

The archminister shook his head, trying to speak, as a look of panic crept into his eyes.

He tightened his grip on he man's neck. "Don't you think that if I had wanted Carden dead I would have commanded you to kill him long ago? Have you decided that you don't need me telling you what to do anymore? Is that it? You long to rule the Forelands yourself and so you've taken it upon yourself to make such decisions."

The minister's eyes began to bulge from his head, and he clawed at his throat like a beast trying to free itself of chains.

"The movement is mine, Pronjed. Never forget that. Only I have the power to speak with all of you any time I wish. Only I have the ability to combine our magics and make the Qirsi the most powerful force in the Forelands. The Qirsi of the seven realms need a Weaver to lead them. Any one of the rest of you can be replaced."

He thought of the woman then, and her child, wondering if this last applied to her as well. Surely it should have, but he couldn't say for certain that it did, and this disturbed him.

Pronjed dropped to his knees, his face turning a dull blue.

"Your actions have greatly complicated my plans," the Weaver said. "You've cost me a good deal of time and an even greater amount of gold. Only time will tell if the damage you've done will prove even more severe, but for now this is enough. I could let you die, and it wouldn't matter at all. It would satisfy my anger, and Qirsar knows it would be justified. I want you to know that so that later you can thank me for the gift of your life. Do you understand?"

The man managed a nod.

Dusaan smiled, letting him struggle a moment longer before finally releasing him.

The minister fell forward with a loud gasp and lay panting on the ground, his eyes closed as his color slowly returned to its usual shade of white. The Weaver let him lie there for a time before ordering him to his feet again.

"So now that it's done, who is to be the next king?"

"That remains to be seen, Weaver," the man said, his voice ragged. "The queen hopes to place the king's daughter on the throne, but fears giving Carden's eldest brother the power of a regent. I've encouraged her and promised my aid in guarding her child against the brother's ambitions."

"Will Aneira's dukes consent to being ruled by a queen?"

"Some of them may; others may decide the time has come to end Solkaran rule." He faltered. "If you like, I can try to persuade the queen to take a different course. Giving the kingdom over to the brother may be the safer course. He'd make a poor king, but he will be easy to bribe."

"No," Dusaan said. "That won't be necessary." The truth was that while Carden's death forced the emperor to postpone his attack on Eibithar, it did weaken Aneira considerably, particularly if his successor, whoever that might be, did not enjoy the support of all the land's houses. When the time came, other kingdoms might be more willing to come to Eibithar's defense if the armies arrayed against the northern kingdom were less formidable. And the wider this war grew, the better for the Weaver and his movement. He wasn't about to let Pronjed know any of this—better to let the man think that each time they spoke his life hung by a wraith's hair. "Let the queen do as she wishes. If she succeeds, you'll have her gratitude, and if she fails, we can see to it that the brother is made king. Either way, we'll have some influence with the throne. That should mitigate the costs of your recklessness."

Pronjed lowered his eyes. "Yes, Weaver."

"When is Carden's funeral?"

"Not for several more days, Weaver. Aneira's nobles are just beginning to arrive in Solkara."

"And when will the next king—or queen—be chosen?"

"It's hard to say. I expect the decision to be made in the days after the funeral. I doubt the dukes and Carden's brothers will leave the city until the matter is settled. Unless, of course, they intend to go to war."

"I'd prefer that didn't happen, Pronjed. A civil war would complicate matters greatly. If Aneira's houses go to war, I'll hold you responsible."

The minister paled. "Yes, Weaver. I'll see to it that they don't."

"It seems you've suddenly become a patriot," Dusaan said, grinning. "How curious."

Pronjed nodded, but said nothing.

"Is there anything else?"

"No, Weaver."

Dusaan nodded. "Very well. I don't want to have to hurt you again, Pronjed. But I feel it necessary to impress upon you how important it is that you not take matters into your own hands. As it were."

Taking hold of the minister's magic as only a Weaver could, Dusaan used the man's shaping power to shatter the bone in his thumb.

Pronjed clutched his hand with a shriek, doubling over in pain. So great was his agony that the Weaver had to strain to hold their connection a moment longer.

"I'm sure you'll find a healer in the castle who can attend to that," he said. "But it should serve to remind you never to trifle with me again. I hope we understand one another."

"Yes, Weaver," Pronjed said through gritted teeth.

Dusaan nodded his satisfaction, then released his hold on the man's mind, allowing him to awaken to his pain and his darkened chambers in Castle Solkara.

It occurred to the Weaver that Harel would want to attend Carden's funeral, something Dusaan could not allow. None of the men and women who served him had ever actually met him outside of a dream—this was why he had yet to turn any of the Qirsi in the emperor's palace—and though he thought that he could disguise his voice and, by tying back his hair, his appearance as well, it was not a risk he was willing to take. More than that, the emperor's appearance in Solkara might further inflame the situation there. Even in Aneira, which was regarded as Braedon's closest ally among the six, the emperor was not well liked. Such was the price of ruling the wealthiest and most powerful realm in the Forelands. His appearance at Carden's funeral might be perceived as a gesture of support for the queen and her daughter. This, in turn, would increase the likelihood that several of the dukes, in particular Noltierre and Dantrielle, would oppose the girl's investiture.

He would have to advise the emperor against making the journey. Fortunately, Chago's death and Harel's constant fear of assassination promised to make this rather simple.

His conversations with Cresenne and Pronjed had wearied him. Even the power of a Weaver had its limits. Usually he limited himself to no more than one or two visitations in a night. He had his chancellors to give instructions to the other Qirsi who served him. But because of what he had learned speaking with the woman, there was one last conversation he needed to have this night. After that he would rest.

For a third time he reached out across the Scabbard to the kingdom of Aneira. This time, however, he stayed to the north, his consciousness descending toward Castle Mertesse. Usually he found two of his servants sleeping side by side, but on this night he found just the one. It took him a moment to remember that Yaella would be near Solkara by now, accompanying her duke to the funeral. Her absence would actually make this easier.

Since the failure at Kentigern during the growing turns, he had made this one endure an arduous climb, much as he had just done to Pronjed. On this night, though, he was eager to be done so that he might enjoy a few hours' rest. Before long, the renegade stood before him, bowing and offering an obeisant greeting.

"They didn't take you to Solkara, Shurik. I'm sure you must be terribly disappointed."

The man gave a thin smile. "I never expected to go, Weaver. You know the saying. 'The traitor walks a lonely path.' "

"How did Mertesse's duke take the news of the king's death?"

"As you'd expect. He was struck speechless at first, and a moment later he was asking his minister how he might turn the tragedy to his advantage." Shurik hesitated. "We'd heard that Carden took his own life. Were we misinformed?"

"Do you honestly think I'd tell you one way or another?"

The man frowned, looking like a chastised boy. "No, Weaver."

"So Mertesse covets the throne for himself."

"Of course," Shurik said. "He's Eandi. But he knows better than to risk much in trying to win it. Instead, he seeks to curry favor with Carden's most likely successor."

"And who does he think that is?"

"Grigor, the eldest brother."

Dusaan nodded. "I see. How would the duke feel about a regency, with Grigor ruling until Carden's heir took the throne?"

"But Carden had no—" He stopped, his yellow eyes widening comically. "You mean the daughter?"

"That's what the queen wants."

Shurik seem to weigh this briefly, shaking his head. "I'm certain the duke has never even entertained the notion," he finally said. "I don't know how he'll feel about it. I'm sorry, Weaver. I'm afraid you'll need to speak with Yaella about that."

"It's no matter. That isn't the reason I've come to you tonight."

The renegade regarded him warily, straining as all of them did to see beyond the shadows, to catch just a glimpse of his face. "It's not?" he asked.

"No. I remember speaking with you just after your failure at Kentigern. You offered then to search the Forelands for this other man, this Grinsa jal Arriet, whom you believed to be another Weaver."

"I remember as well," Shurik said. "You forbade me to go after him. You told me to remain in Mertesse with Yaella."

"At the time, it was the best course to follow. Now circumstances have changed. I want you to find him for me. If you have the opportunity to kill him, you may. But hear me well, Minister. If you try to kill him and fail, thus revealing to him that I want him dead, I'll see to it that *you* die a slow, agonizing death. Is that clear?"

The renegade blanched, but he managed a small, mirthless smile. "Quite clear, Weaver. Where would you have me begin this search?"

During his previous conversation with Cresenne, before their troubling talk this night, the woman told him that she believed Grinsa was still in Aneira. At the time, he dismissed this as little more than a wish on her part. She didn't want to leave the Festival or brave the cold winds of the steppe, and so she chose to think that the gleaner remained in Carden's kingdom. Knowing what he did now, however, Dusaan was forced to consider that she might have been right.

"I wouldn't be surprised if he's in Solkara," the Weaver said. "Or at least on his way there."

Shurik made a sour face. "It would be . . . awkward, if I were to go to Solkara just now."

Dusaan nodded. "I agree. Start south in a few days, but stay out of the royal city. Once the funeral is over and the mourners begin to return to their homes, you may enter Solkara. That way you won't embarrass your duke, and you may still be able to track him."

"And if it turns out he hasn't been to Solkara?"

Dusaan felt a muscle in his cheek begin to jump and was grateful the man couldn't see his face. "If he's not in Solkara, I can give you the name of a woman to follow. I have a feeling she might lead us to him."

Chapter
Twelve

✦

Solkara, Aneira

etnalla was already awake and dressed when she heard the knock at her door. It was early still—the sun had yet to rise, though the night had given way to the ghostly light of morning—but she had slept poorly. Any day now, Evanthya would reach the royal city, and the anticipation had begun to affect her sleep. Nevertheless, she was surprised to learn that others were awake as well, and more surprised still when she called through the door to ask who had come.

"It's the archminister."

She and Pronjed had done their best to avoid each other for the past several days as preparations continued for Carden's funeral. For him to come now to her quarters so early in the morning seemed strange indeed. What choice did she have, however, but to let him in?

Opening the door, she found him looking ill. He was sweating and his face looked ashen, even for a Qirsi. He appeared to be trembling, and he cradled his right hand against his chest as if it pained him greatly.

"Forgive me for disturbing you, First Minister," he said, his voice weak. "But I'm wondering if you're a healer, or if there's one in your company."

"Of course, Archminister," she said, forgetting everything else as she helped him into her chamber. "I'm a healer."

"Thank you," he said, managing a smile.

She led him to a chair by the window and knelt before him, taking hold of his forearm and examining his hand. He winced as she turned the palm toward the light of a lamp resting on a nearby table.

"I'm sorry," she whispered.

He shook his head, but said nothing.

His hand looked terrible. The base of his thumb was swollen to nearly twice the size it should have been, and the entire thumb and much of the palm had turned a deep, angry shade of purple, like the color of storm clouds during the harvest. Clearly the bone had been broken, but what puzzled her was that it seemed to have occurred several hours before.

"What happened?" she asked.

He gave a small shrug, wincing again. "I fell while putting some wood on the fire in my quarters."

"Just now?"

The minister looked at her briefly. "No, earlier. I awoke in the middle of the night to find my chambers had grown cold. I got up to put more wood in the hearth, but I tripped. I must have been a bit addled with sleep, and I simply went back to bed, not realizing how badly I had hurt myself."

"Well, it looks to me as if you've broken the bone in several places." She laid her other hand on his and closed her eyes. "Hold still. I'll see what I can do to mend the bone."

Probing his hand with her mind, Fetnalla found that there were three breaks in the bone. Fortunately, the fragments hadn't moved much and setting the bone in his thumb was fairly easy. Still, the minister gasped at the pain and she feared for a moment that he would pass out.

When the bone pieces were in place, she drew upon her magic, allowing it to flow through her hands into his. At first all she sensed was warmth, as if her hands were a gentle fire. But after a time, she felt the bone beginning to heal and she smiled. As a minister in the court of Orvinti, she rarely had the opportunity to use her healing powers. It was, she realized, the magic she liked best.

"You've a deft touch, Minister," Pronjed said. "It's already feeling better."

"Thank you. It will take some time still."

They fell silent, the archminister seeming to relish the easing of his pain and Fetnalla concentrating on healing him. After some time, however, she started to feel that she should have been saying something.

"I'm surprised that you came to me," she told him at last, opening her eyes for just a moment. Pronjed was staring at the hearth. Some of the color had returned to his narrow face.

"Are you?"

"I'd have thought that you'd go to one of the castle's healers."

"The castle has none."

Again she opened her eyes. "None?"

"Carden never liked the idea of using magic to keep himself well. He welcomed Qirsi with other powers, those that could help him rule. But he allowed only Eandi surgeons to treat him and his family."

"That may be why he's dead now." As soon as the words crossed her lips, she regretted them.

"What?"

"Forgive me, Archminister. I only meant that perhaps a Qirsi healer could have found a way to help him."

"Yes, of course," Pronjed said, looking toward the fire again. "I'd considered that as well."

They lapsed into another silence, and this time Fetnalla did nothing to break it. She still feared this man and though he hadn't taken offense at her last remark, she might not be so fortunate with the next one.

The dawn bells rang in the city and a few moments later she heard footsteps in the corridor outside her chamber.

"That will be the day guards taking their places," Pronjed said. His voice sounded stronger.

Fetnalla removed her hands from his and looked at the injured thumb. It was still discolored and swollen, but not nearly so much as it had been before. He moved it slowly and smiled.

"That's much better," he said. "Thank you, First Minister. You've done me a great service. I won't forget it."

"I'm happy to have been able to help, Archminister. I might be able to do more, perhaps bring down the swelling a bit further. Do you want me to try?"

He shook his head. "That won't be necessary. Time will do the rest."

"Very well."

Pronjed stood, as did the first minister.

"Next time, you might want to have one of your attendants see to the fire," she said, smiling to soften the gibe.

"What? Oh yes, of course." He smiled in return, though she could see that it was forced.

Once again, she feared that she had offended him.

The archminister stepped to the door, pausing with his hand resting on the door handle to turn and face her again.

"I'd prefer—" He stopped himself shaking his head. "It's not important."

"I won't speak of this to anyone," she said, as he started to turn away. "It's not a healer's place to talk of such things."

He smiled again, and this time it seemed genuine. "Thank you again, First Minister. I believe the queen intends to speak with your duke later today. I'll look forward to seeing you then."

He opened the door and peered out into the hallway. Apparently seeing no one, he nodded to her once and left her chamber, pulling the door closed behind him.

Long after he was gone, Fetnalla continued to stare at the wooden door. Something about their conversation bothered her, though she couldn't say what it was. His explanation of what happened to his hand had seemed perfectly logical at the time, but thinking back on it now, she couldn't imagine how he could have slept with such an injury. It was almost as if—

Abruptly, the conversation she had with her duke about Carden's death came back to her. She had speculated at the time that a Qirsi with delusion magic might have been able to make the king turn his blade on himself. And just now, the king's archminister had convinced her of something that made little sense.

Another knock at her door made her jump.

"Who is it?" she called, closing her eyes for a moment and trying to steady her pulse.

"Your duke," came Brall's voice.

Fetnalla hurried to the door and opened it. "My lord. Good morrow."

He stepped past her into the chamber, looking about, as if searching for something, or someone. His silver hair was slightly tousled, and his broad face was pale, as if he too had slept poorly.

"I heard voices in here a short time ago. I awoke to them."

"Yes, my lord. Someone came to me with an injury. I healed the wound and the person left."

He completed a circle of the room, stopping just in front of her. "Who was it?"

A part of her wanted to answer. She was more convinced than ever that the archminister had a hand in the king's death, and she needed to find some way to share her insights with Brall. But she had given an oath, and she was tiring of the duke's lingering suspicions. He spoke to her of trust, of how important it was that they rely on each other during their time in Solkara awaiting Carden's funeral and the selection of his successor. Yet he showed no faith in her loyalty. "I can't say, my lord," she told him, knowing that this would anger him and further fuel his doubts. "I gave my word as a healer that I would not."

"Was this person Qirsi?"

"I won't tell you that, either."

Brall frowned, shaking his head slowly. "Very well," he said, turning away, the words coming out as a growl. "I'm on my way to the king's hall for breakfast," he said, leaving her chamber. "You're welcome to join me or not as you see fit."

Fetnalla didn't move. She wanted to scream at him, but it was all she could do to keep herself from crying. She deserved better, she had decided some time ago. But in the end, all she could do was follow him through the corridors and down the winding stairs to the hall.

As Pronjed had foreseen, a messenger came to the hall as they ate to tell the duke that the queen wished to speak with him. It had been days since they had even seen Chofya, so consumed had she been with plans for the funeral and whatever matters Carden had left unfinished.

"I wonder what it is she wants," Brall said quietly, after the messenger had gone.

"You're a guest in her castle, my lord. She may feel that she's neglected you for too long."

He shook his head. "No, it's more than that. The day we learned of the king's death she indicated that she wished to enlist my help with some cause. I believe that matter, whatever it may be, is what she wants to discuss."

Fetnalla had forgotten this, though reminded of it now, she felt certain that the duke was right.

They quickly finished eating and made their way to the king's chamber, which Chofya now used as her own. The guards at the door admitted them immediately, nodding once to the duke as he stepped past, and ignoring Fetnalla.

The queen sat at her husband's writing table, her hands folded before her and a smile fixed on her lips. She wore a simple black dress, a cape bearing the royal seal, and the circle of gold that rested as always upon her brow. There were lines on her face that Fetnalla did not remember from just a few days before, but otherwise she looked as she usually did: beautiful, formidable, and just a bit sad.

"Your Highness," Brall said, kneeling.

Fetnalla kneeled as well.

"Rise, Lord Orvinti, First Minister. Be welcome. I trust you've been comfortable these past few days."

"Yes, Your Highness. Quite."

"I'm glad. I hope you'll forgive my lack of hospitality. I've attended to so many things since the king's death that I'm afraid I've failed you as a host."

Brall smiled. "Please don't trouble yourself, Your Highness. This is the finest castle in all the Forelands, thanks in large part to you and your skills as queen. Our stay here has been most satisfactory. We only wish it hadn't been necessary."

"You're very kind, Brall."

"Is Your Highness well?" the duke asked, his smile giving way to a look of concern.

"As well as one might expect."

"And the Princess Kalyi?"

Chofya lowered her gaze. "She grieves for her father, of course. She was terribly young to lose him. But she has his strength."

"And yours, I'm sure, Your Highness. She seems a most extraordinary child."

The queen gave a strange smile. "I'm glad to hear you say so, Lord Orvinti. I believe she is extraordinary. Indeed, she's the reason I've asked you here today."

"Your Highness?"

"I won't weave mists with my words, Brall. I want Kalyi to succeed her father as Solkara's ruler. I realize that she's still just a child, so I'll assent to a regent. But I want my daughter on the throne."

To his credit, the duke reacted mildly. His eyebrows went up for an instant, but otherwise, he held himself still. Fetnalla stole a glance at Pronjed, but the archminister appeared intent on the queen. She did notice, however, that he held his injured hand out of sight, behind his back.

"I needn't tell you, Your Highness," Brall said after a lengthy silence, "that Aneira has had no queen in over two hundred and fifty years."

"I'm well aware of that, Lord Orvinti."

"And are you aware, as well, of how close the kingdom came to civil war the last time a woman sat on the throne?"

It was a period of Aneiran history known as the Time of Queens, which began with the investiture in 537 of Edrice, eldest daughter of Tomaz the Sixth. She wasn't the first queen in Aneira's pantheon of leaders. Indeed, she wasn't even the first queen from House Solkara. Her great-grandmother, Tanith, ruled the land only fifty years earlier. But like her father, Edrice had no male children and so passed the crown to her daughter Tanith the Second. The younger Tanith did have a son, but he died before his Fating, and when the queen died, she was succeeded by her only surviving child, Syntalle. By this time, the other Aneiran houses had begun to chafe at what they saw as a burgeoning matriarchy, not unlike that of Sanbira. Syntalle had only one daughter and three sons, but the girl was the eldest, and the queen made no secret of the fact that she was preparing her for assumption of the throne. Led by Bistari and Dantrielle, the other houses objected, and when Syntalle grew ill and frail after one of the longest reigns of any monarch in the history of the land, they threatened to wrest the crown from House Solkara rather than accept another queen. Defiant to the end, Syntalle abdicated on her deathbed so that she could see her daughter, Edrice the Second, invested as Ancira's fourth consecutive queen.

Unlike her mother, however, the younger Edrice had no appetite for power. With the armies of Bistari, Mertesse, Dantrielle, and Noltierre advancing on Castle Solkara, fearing for herself, her family, and her realm, Edrice abdicated to her eldest brother, Farrad. In exchange for the crown, Farrad agreed to name Edrice's son, who happened to be the first Carden, his heir. The king remained true to his word, and twenty-two years later, upon Farrad the Fourth's death, Carden took the throne, completing what became known as the Queen's Bargain.

"I know Aneiran history, Lord Orvinti," Chofya said, her voice growing cold. "I'm not attempting to foster a matriarchy, nor am I doing any less than a widowed queen and mother ought to do. Kalyi is Carden's only child. Isn't it just that she should claim her father's crown for her own?"

"I suppose it is, Your Highness," he said, his voice low. "What is it that you want of me?"

The queen twisted her mouth in disapproval. Clearly this conversation had not gone as she hoped it would.

"I had thought to ask you to help me win the support of the other houses," Chofya said. "It seems I was wrong to assume that I'd have your support."

"I promised to do anything in my power to help you, Your Highness, and I am a man of my word. I do have some questions, though."

"Of course, Lord Orvinti. I'll tell you anything I can."

"Do you have someone in mind to serve as regent?"

The queen looked briefly at the archminister before answering. "I intend to ask the marquess of Renbrere, Kalyi's uncle."

"Grigor," the duke said.

The Jackal, he was called. Actually he was one of two jackals, but as the elder, and the more powerful of the two, Grigor was far more dangerous than his brother Henthas. It would be madness to give him the power of a regent. Brall had confided to Fetnalla his distaste for the man and his fear that he would succeed Carden. In a way, though, a regency was worse, for he could work his mischief and blame it all on the whims of the child queen.

"I know what you're thinking, Brall," the queen said. "I don't trust him either. But in this matter I have no choice. In the eyes of many, Grigor has the most legitimate claim to the throne. Already I've received messages from him indicating that he intends to take the crown for himself and his sons."

"Then how can you want him as regent for your daughter? At his first opportunity, he'll try to have both of you killed."

"That's why I need the support of the other houses." She stood and walked to the hearth. "The realm is poised on the edge of a blade right now. Grigor is hated and feared throughout the land. If he takes the throne, House Solkara will be swept from power, though only after a long a bloody war."

"The same could happen if you force your daughter on the land as its queen."

Fetnalla expected Chofya's anger to flare again, but instead the queen merely nodded. "I know that. But in this way, Grigor helps us. I intend to use fear of the Jackal to keep the dissenting houses from rising against Kalyi. And I believe I can use Grigor's fear of the houses that support us to keep him from attempting to steal the crown. It's a fine balance, Lord Orvinti, but I'm certain that it's my only hope for keeping House Solkara in power."

"You're dancing with wraiths, Your Highness. One misstep will cost you everything."

"Then I'll have to be exceedingly careful, won't I? But you, Lord Orvinti, have the power to end this dance before it even begins. All my planning is predicated on my desire to keep the crown in Solkara. If you have ambitions for your house and your children, then I'll have to look elsewhere for support."

Brall smiled, though not with his eyes. "Were I to admit such ambitions, would I ever leave this castle alive?"

The queen faced him. "You have my word that you would."

They eyed each other for a moment. Then Brall nodded once. "As I've told you once, Your Highness, I have pledged myself to your service. And as it happens, I have no yearning to be king. I'm an old man, and I wish to spend my last years living in peace by Lake Orvinti. I've no stomach for war."

"What of your son?"

"I believe my son is content with his marquessate and the dukedom that awaits him when Bian calls me to his side."

Hearing these words from another duke, Fetnalla might have been skeptical. But she had been with Brall long enough to know that he was telling Chofya the truth. As a younger man, he might have seen in Carden's death an opportunity for House Orvinti. But not now.

"Then you'll support me?" the queen asked.

"What will you do if Grigor refuses? Will you fight him?"

"We don't think he will refuse," Pronjed said from his perch near the shuttered window.

Brall glanced at the man before swinging his gaze back to the queen. "Why wouldn't he? You said yourself that a number of dukes expect him to be king. Faced with the choice between a queen or Grigor, a good many houses may opt for the latter. The marquess knows this. I doubt that he'll give up the throne so easily." He paused. "I also can't help noticing that he hasn't arrived yet, though it's less than a day's ride from Renbrere to Solkara."

Fetnalla had been thinking the same thing. Henthas, Carden's second brother, had been in Solkara for days now, as had Numar, the youngest brother, the one they called the Fool. But there had been no sign of Grigor.

"We expect Grigor today or tomorrow," the queen said. "I had a message from him yesterday. As for the rest, I already told you, Brall, I need help to make this work. I don't need the support of all the other houses, nor do I expect it. But if I have Orvinti and Dantrielle behind me, and perhaps Kett, if Ansis can be swayed, that would be a start." She gave a small smile. "Don't you see, Lord Orvinti? You are the answer to your own questions."

The duke nodded, though he didn't look pleased.

"Think on it for the rest of the day, Lord Orvinti," the queen said, walking to stand before the duke and extending a hand. Brall knelt again, taking her hand and pressing it to his forehead for an instant. "We'll speak of this again tomorrow."

"Yes, Your Highness."

He stood and started toward the door, glancing back at Fetnalla and gesturing for her to follow. The first minister looked at Pronjed and found him watching her, a look of concern on his narrow face. He still had his hand hidden, but she sensed that his injury was the last thing on his mind. He almost appeared to be asking for her help with his small yellow eyes, and not knowing why she did it, Fetnalla gave him a small nod, bringing a smile to his lips.

The duke led her out into the corridor and back toward their rooms, saying nothing. She was glad for the silence. Though she agreed with Brall that the queen was risking a great deal in trying to put her daughter on the throne, she felt that the risk was justified. It seemed to Fetnalla that all other paths led to war. Pronjed appeared to feel the same way, and the first minister was unnerved to find herself agreeing with him.

The company from Dantrielle came within sight of Castle Solkara and the royal city late in the day, emerging from Aneira's Great Forest into the golden sunshine and cold winds of the Solkaran farming villages just as the faint ring of the prior's bells from the city gates drifted among the grasses. They had but a league left to ride, but Tebeo chose to dismount and walk his horse down the riverbank so that the beast might drink. Evanthya was so eager to reach the city and find Fetnalla that she would gladly have covered the remaining distance on foot at a full run, but she could do little but join the duke by the waters of the Kett.

The windows of all the houses in sight were shuttered, not only against the cold, but also as a sign of mourning for the lost king. Atop the castle, the yellow and red banner of Aneira flew from the base of its staff rather than from the top. The flagstaffs that usually held the black, red, and gold banners of Solkara stood empty and stark against the bright blue sky. Even with the sun shining, it seemed that shadows lurked everywhere and Bian's hand hung like a storm cloud over the great fortress.

She sensed that her duke feared what the next several days would bring, but they had not spoken of it beyond making plans for their departure from Dantrielle. Though she had done everything in her power to demonstrate her good faith, she knew that Tebeo still did not trust her. No doubt as the conspiracy continued to spread and claim more lives, more and more Qirsi ministers across the Forelands would find themselves in similar circumstances.

"We'll ride on shortly, First Minister," Tebeo said after some time, not even bothering to look at her.

"Yes, my lord."

"You're eager to reach the city."

She grinned. "I'm eager to spend a few days away from my mount, my lord. I'm eager to stand beside a fire, rather than huddling in my riding cloak."

"You don't travel well, First Minister," the duke said, grinning as well.

"No, my lord. I never have."

He glanced at the soldiers and servants standing nearby, then walked a short distance along the riverbank. Evanthya followed. When they were far enough from the men to speak without being overheard, he said, "I thought perhaps you were anxious to reach the city so that you could see Orvinti's first minister."

Evanthya felt her mouth go dry. "My lord?"

"You thought I didn't know."

What could she say? "Yes, my lord," she said, staring at the river, knowing that her cheeks must be crimson. "I feared that you wouldn't approve."

"I'm not certain that I do, but I learned long ago that Adriel can be stingy with her gifts. We all must take love where we can find it."

She looked up at him, her surprise and relief mingling until she felt that her heart would burst. "Thank you, my lord," she whispered, her voice barely carrying over the gentle rush of the river.

"You realize, of course, that if Brall and I ever have a falling-out, this will become a problem."

"Yes, my lord."

He nodded, then gazed up at the castle again. "We should ride. Night approaches and I'd like to be in the castle before dark."

The duke started to lead his horse back toward the soldiers, but Evanthya called to him, making him turn once more.

"I fear that Lord Orvinti would not be as . . . as understanding. Fetnalla has told him nothing of our love." She stopped, unsure of how to speak her mind without sounding impertinent.

"Don't concern yourself, First Minister. Brall will hear nothing of this from me." He started walking again, then halted to look back at her a second time. "You're right, though. He wouldn't be happy at all."

The rest of their journey passed quickly. Soon all the riders from Dantrielle were within the castle, and Evanthya was warming herself before the great hearth in the king's hall.

After allowing his men time to eat and rest, Tebeo ordered them to offer their swords to the captain of the Royal Army for the remainder of their stay. It was a customary gesture, and judging from the many colors worn by the men guarding the gates and corridors of the castle, it was clear that other nobles had done the same. Evanthya had been pleased to see a large number of men wearing the green, blue, and white of Orvinti. Fetnalla was already here and the first minister longed to find her.

As if in answer to Evanthya's desires, a horn rang out from the nearest doorway of the hall and a herald announced the queen. An instant later Chofya entered the great room, followed by the dukes of Rassor, Mertesse, and Orvinti, several lesser nobles, and their ministers, including Fetnalla. Tebeo knelt before the queen, as did Evanthya, although she couldn't keep from looking at her love, who was already watching her.

Fetnalla looked as she always did, tall and graceful, her face as white and soft as Panya's light reflected on the waters of the Rassor. She had her hair pulled back and she wore her long ministerial robes rather than riding clothes. It seemed she had been here at least a full day. She was smiling as she gazed at Evanthya, but there was a troubled look in her eyes.

The formalities seemed to take forever, with the queen presenting each of her guests to Tebeo, and the duke, in turn, presenting Evanthya to all the gathered nobles. At last, however, they finished and the queen called forth more food from the kitchen and flasks of wine from the cellars, inviting all her guests to partake of a feast.

Brall and Tebeo chose to dine together, giving Fetnalla and Evanthya an excuse to do so as well. They were surrounded by the most powerful men and women in Aneira, so they could do nothing more than sit, speak, and eat. But just being this close to Fetnalla made Evanthya's skin tingle as it did just before a thunderstorm on a warm evening.

"You look well, First Minister," Fetnalla said. "I trust you had a pleasant journey."

"Yes, thank you. And you?"

"We've been here some time now. Ten days, I believe. But the journey was pleasant enough."

Evanthya gaped at her. "Ten days?" she breathed. She thought a moment. "But that means you were here when—"

"Yes," Fetnalla said, her voice falling to a whisper. "Carden died our first night in Solkara. The blade that killed him was a gift from my duke."

"Demons and fire!"

Fetnalla cast a quick look at the others sitting with them at the table. "Perhaps we'll have an opportunity to discuss these matters later," she said, "when we can speak more freely."

Evanthya nodded, wishing they could steal away immediately. "I'd like that. I have tidings as well."

A strange look came into Fetnalla's eyes. "You've done it, haven't you?"

It took Evanthya a moment to realize that she was speaking of hiring the assassin. She nodded, glancing around the table, much as Fetnalla had a moment before. Brall and Tebeo were deep in conversation.

Fetnalla just gazed at her, shaking her head slightly, as if not quite believing it was true. "I want very much to hear about that." She gave a small laugh. "I wish I had seen it. You in a place like that." She shook her head again.

"It wasn't funny," Evanthya whispered, feeling her color rise. "I was terrified, and one of the men knew me."

The smile vanished from Fetnalla's face. "I'm sorry," she said. "I shouldn't have laughed." She looked as if she might say more, but at that moment, the horn sounded again, and the herald stepped into the hall.

"Grigor, Marquess of Renbrere!"

Every conversation in the hall stopped and all eyes turned toward the doorway. For a moment they waited. Then a man stepped past the herald into the great room, his satin cape swirling. For just an instant it seemed to Evanthya that she looked upon a wraith, so much did the marquess resemble his brother the king. Like Carden, Grigor was tall and powerfully built, broad in the chest and shoulders, with muscular forearms that he left uncovered, even in the last days of Bohdan's Turn. His hair was golden, his eyes were dark, and his features were so fine that they almost appeared womanly. He didn't have Carden's swagger, but moved instead with an effortless elegance that made him seem even more impressive than the king ever had.

She had heard others speak of the man more times than she could count, always referring to him as the Jackal. But seeing him now, Evanthya couldn't help thinking that he was more like a great wolf. There was a nobility to him that Carden never possessed.

After a moment's silence, the others in the hall rose and bowed to him, though many of them, Brall and Tebeo included, were of higher rank.

Chofya did not bow. She didn't even stand. After her guests took their seats once more, Grigor walked to where she was sitting and knelt before her.

"Your Highness," he said, his voice as clear and strong as the ring of a smith's hammer on hot steel. "You have my sympathy for your loss."

"And you have mine for yours," the queen answered. "Carden was as much your brother as he was my husband."

Grigor looked up at that, his eyes dancing with torchlight. "That may be so." The queen shifted uncomfortably, drawing a grin from the man. He stood, though Chofya hadn't yet given him leave to do so. Glancing around the hall, he spotted his brothers sitting together at a nearby table. He nodded to them, but remained where he was, continuing to survey the room. The other guests were still watching him silently, waiting for him to speak or sit or, perhaps, claim the throne right then and there. "Where are the other dukes?" he finally asked of no one in particular. "Noltierre, Tounstrel, Bistari, Kett. They should be here by now."

"I expect them in the next day or two," Chofya said after a brief pause. "The funeral is in three days. I'm sure they'll arrive in time."

"We should have a new king by then."

The queen straightened in her chair. "Aneira's new leader will be chosen after the funeral, as custom dictates."

Grigor turned to her once more, his eyes narrowing.

Evanthya had noticed as well. *Aneira's new leader,* Chofya said. Not, *Aneira's new king.*

She turned to Fetnalla, a question in her eyes, but the minister shook her head.

"Not now," she whispered. "I'll explain later."

"Do you plot for the throne, Your Highness?" Grigor asked, with a small laugh. He made a sweeping gesture, turning neatly on one foot as he did so as to indicate the entire hall. "Do you honestly believe that the men in this room would accept you as their sovereign? Was your father even a baron?"

The queen sat unmoving, her color high, her eyes darting about the hall as if she were gauging the reaction of the other nobles. "This isn't a matter to be discussed just now, Lord Renbrere."

"With my brother's death, I am now duke of Solkara," Grigor said sharply. "I should be addressed as such."

The queen's mouth twisted for just an instant, as if she realized that she had erred. "Of course, my lord. Forgive me."

Whatever game Chofya was playing, she had started poorly. Evanthya could only guess that she had miscalculated. Grigor was a dangerous foe; even seeing him for the first time this day, she could tell that much.

"She can't think to oppose him for the crown," Evanthya said quietly.

Fetnalla gave a small nod. "She does, though not as you think."

"Please, Lord Solkara," the queen began again. "Sit with us. Raise your glass and join us in our feast. These matters can wait, and it's been long since we last dined together."

The man gave a thin smile. "Thank you, Your Highness," he said, his voice dripping sarcasm. "But I came to honor my brother, the king, and to ensure the continued reign of House Solkara. My place is with my brothers."

With everyone still watching him, Grigor walked to where Henthas and Numar sat, leaving Chofya sitting by herself, looking small and defeated.

"He'll crush her," Evanthya said softly.

Fetnalla turned to her, her face looking paler than usual, her lips drawn tight. "We can't let that happen," she said. "He'll ruin us all."

Chapter
Thirteen

✦

hey're all staring at you," Numar said, looking amused as he watched Grigor take his seat at their table.

Grigor nodded, looking from one of his brothers to the other. It took some effort to keep himself from grinning, but he managed it well enough. He didn't need to look around the hall to know that Numar was right. He sensed their eyes upon him, and he relished the feeling.

"They're looking at their new king," he said softly to his youngest brother. "How can they help but stare?"

Henthas gave a short sharp laugh. "You think you've won already? You're a fool. Carden's whore won't give in to you so easily."

"When all is said and done, she'll have no choice," Grigor told him. "But rest assured, brother, I've no intention of declaring victory yet."

Henthas looked away and drained his goblet of wine. "Actually, I almost wish you would," he said, as a servant poured him more. "I'd enjoy watching her humiliate you."

"In that case you'll be disappointed."

His brother grunted, his eyes on the queen. Grigor knew that Henthas was trying to anger him, as he so often did. But on this night it wasn't going to work. Not with Carden's crown so close at hand.

If he could have done this without his brothers he would gladly have done so. Neither man was of much help to him, and Ean knew that the three of them had little affection for one another. Mostly Grigor needed to control both men, to keep either of them from undermining his intentions.

He would have had to be deaf and blind not to know how the three of them were perceived throughout Aneira, indeed, throughout the Forelands. The Jackals and the Fool. The names weren't flattering, to be sure, particularly to poor Numar, but they did offer the brothers Renbrere a certain notoriety. As it happened, though, they were hopelessly inaccurate. Jackals were pack hunters, like wolves. Grigor and Henthas had never been bound by any common interest. Grigor had always been guided by ambition and his unwavering belief that his fate would one day match his formidable talents. Henthas dreamed of nothing, loved nothing, and feared nothing. He was the third son of House Solkara; power lay too far from his grasp to give him purpose. Even after Grigor took the throne, Henthas would gain only the marquessate in Renbrere, a small step up from the viscountcy he held already. The Solkaran dukedom would go to Grigor's eldest son, leaving nothing for the brother or his boys. Grigor did not believe that Henthas had designs on his life, though he couldn't risk ignoring the possibility. He thought it more likely that the man would oppose him, either openly or in secret. For while ambition didn't drive Henthas, bitterness and envy did. He would gladly trade the marquessate and its small luxuries for the pleasure of seeing Grigor fail. And if that failure cost Grigor his life, all the better.

No, Henthas was no jackal. A viper perhaps, or some demon from Bian's realm. But the name they had given him implied social skills that the man simply did not possess.

Calling Numar a fool made even less sense. True, he had little more ambition than Henthas. He seemed perfectly content with his viscountcy and he rarely involved himself with any matters of state beyond its boundaries. But to mistake his reticence for simplicity carried risks as well. He had a keen mind and a troublesome sense of moral propriety. If he chose to oppose Grigor's bid for the crown, he would, Grigor knew, be a far more formidable foe than Henthas, if for no other reason than because Grigor had little sense of what tactics he might use. Whereas Henthas could always be counted on to resort to lies, betrayal, and brutality, Numar relied on reason and persuasion. He'd seek out allies, building bridges to Aneira's other major houses. In doing so, he'd try to show the entire kingdom that he was no fool, that in fact, he was the Solkaran they most wanted to see on the throne.

The Jackals and the Fool. It was an illusion, but one he needed to maintain. Though he and Henthas hated one another, the notion that they worked together aided his cause. Grigor had utter confidence in his ability to win the crown for himself, by himself, but so long as the kingdom's other nobles saw him as part of a deadly pair, they'd be less likely to challenge him. And so long as they dismissed Tomaz's youngest son as a dullard, they wouldn't realize that they could choose as their king someone other than Grigor without risking war with House Solkara.

"She must have the support of the dukes," Henthas muttered. "She wouldn't dare oppose you otherwise."

Grigor glanced toward the front of the hall, where Tebeo of Dantrielle and Brall of Orvinti sat together. "She may have some of them," he said. "I can't imagine that Mertesse or Rassor has offered support. And with Bertin, Vidor, and the boy-duke still not here, I would guess that Noltierre, Tounstrel, and Bistari are hoping that Carden's death will end Solkara's rule. They're not about to support her either. Kett might, but Ansis is easily cowed. I can win him over. That leaves Chofya with Dantrielle and Orvinti."

Henthas faced him again. "Both are major houses. If she can win Bistari over, you'll have no chance at all."

"I just told you—"

"She's not Solkaran. Not by birth, anyway. Her father held land in a barony near Tounstrel. It may be that Vidor will back her for that reason alone. And with all his father's old allies backing the queen, the new duke of Bistari—the boy-duke, as you call him—might very well do the same."

It was a point worth considering.

"Even without Bistari," Henthas went on, "she has Solkara's army, along with Tebeo's and Brall's. You can't fight such a force and hope to win. I know that Renbrere is strong for a marquessate, but it's not that strong."

Grigor frowned. "You don't really expect the army of Solkara to follow her, do you? Not if they know that I've laid claim to the crown."

Henthas smiled darkly and shrugged. "I wouldn't want to say one way or the other. Who knows what goes through a soldier's mind when his kingdom is divided? It does raise interesting possibilities though, doesn't it?"

The man was enjoying himself far too much for Grigor's taste. The duke turned to his other brother, who was watching them both with interest, though he had kept his silence.

"And what do you think of all this?" Grigor asked.

Numar stared back at him impassively, absently running a finger around the rim of his goblet. "Do you really care?"

"Enough to have asked."

The younger man shrugged, his brown eyes flicking toward Chofya for just an instant. "I think you're both misjudging her."

Henthas raised an eyebrow and grinned. "Do you?"

"You're thinking of her as you would another noble, a duke or a marquess."

"She is queen, Numar," Grigor said. "She may not have been born to a noble family, but she's been in the courts now for a good many years."

"No doubt. But I believe she's a mother before she's a noble. That's where her ambitions lie."

Grigor sat forward. "With the daughter?"

"You live up to your name, brother," Henthas said, shaking his head. "The girl can't yet rule. Chofya would have little choice but to name one of us as regent. Probably Grigor."

Numar appeared to ignore Henthas, keeping his brown eyes fixed on Grigor instead.

Grigor said nothing, though he didn't look away either. Numar was right. A regency for the girl made far more sense than a direct challenge from the queen. Chofya had no real claim on the throne, but as Carden's only child, Kalyi did. Mertesse, Rassor, and some of the others might be reluctant to accept a queen under any circumstances, but for those who distrusted the men of Solkara, the child would seem preferable to both Grigor and a protracted struggle to establish a new supremacy.

"Do you know this for certain?" Grigor asked, his voice low.

Numar shook his head. "It's just a guess."

Grigor nodded, a thin smile touching his lips and vanishing. "A good one, I'd say. Do you think she already has Tebeo and Brall?"

"You can't seriously believe she'd try such a thing," Henthas said, his voice rising.

Several of the nobles sitting nearby looked over at them. Grigor glared at him. "Quiet down!" He faced Numar once more. "Well?"

"I expect that she has Brall's support. He's been in Solkara for several days now. Tebeo only arrived this evening, and this will take some time, even for those who hate you."

"They all hate me, Numar. You know that as well as anyone."

His brother sipped some wine, but said nothing.

"And where do you stand?" Grigor asked. "Will you support me or the girl?"

"Does it matter? Either way, no one listens to a fool."

Grigor frowned. This was definitely not the answer he wanted.

"I would think," Numar continued a moment later, his voice dropping to a whisper, "that you'd find regency a most attractive proposition. It would give you time to consolidate your power, make pacts with the other houses, and win over the army's commanders. Eventually, you could have the girl killed and assume the throne with no fear of opposition."

The duke narrowed his eyes. Such a scheme would have sounded perfectly natural coming from Henthas or himself. But he had never known Numar to think this way.

"Do you really think I'd do such a thing to a mere child, my niece, no less?"

Again the man shrugged, lifting his goblet to his lips once more, and leaving Grigor to wonder if he hoped to be named regent himself.

A regency did have its advantages, most of which Numar had described quite succinctly. Ridding himself of the girl when the time came would present difficulties, but none of them were insuperable. The greatest danger lay in the fact that Chofya herself would remain in the castle with Grigor and the girl, as would Carden's Qirsi. Even if they chose Grigor as regent, which custom dictated they should, these two would know better than to trust him. Any plan to kill or exile Kalyi would have to make provisions for them as well. Better to claim the throne as his own now.

"I think in this case, Henthas is right," Grigor said at last. "Aneira isn't ready for a queen, even if she is Carden's daughter. In the end, I'm certain that most of the dukes will agree with me."

Numar nodded and smiled, though the look in his eyes remained grim. "Then you've nothing to fear."

Once more, Grigor wasn't sure what to make of his younger brother's words, but before he could say anything more, Carden's Qirsi approached them, his narrow face looking pale and birdlike in the glow of the torches.

"May I sit with you a moment, my lords?" the minister asked, stopping just beside Numar and hovering over them like a harrier.

"If we had wanted to speak with you, we would have sat with your queen," Henthas said, not bothering to look up at the man.

Grigor would have liked to laugh aloud. With Henthas nearby, spitting venom at everyone he met, Grigor could appear civil and reasonable without making himself seem weak.

"Please sit, Archminister," the duke said, waving a hand at an empty chair. "You'll have to forgive my brother. He's deeply saddened by Carden's death, as we all are."

"Of course, my lord," the minister said, lowering himself into the seat, his gaze alighting on one brother after another until it came to rest at last on

Grigor. "All Aneira suffers as you do. Which is why we need to settle the matter of Carden's successor as quickly as possible."

Grigor nodded. "I quite agree. As soon as the other dukes reach Solkara, we should meet with them and make it clear that, even though Carden had no heir, the Solkaran Supremacy will continue."

The Qirsi licked his thin lips, looking uncomfortable. "Before that happens, Lord Solkara, the queen would like a word with you. A private audience. Tomorrow morning? Just after the ringing of the midmorning bells."

He looked around the table. "Surely she can't think that I have anything to hide from my brothers."

"Of course not, my lord. But it is a matter of some . . . delicacy."

Now Grigor was certain that Numar was right. Chofya had to have her mind set on a regency for the girl. What else could she want to discuss with him? If she intended to take the crown herself, she would have been plotting against him, not trying to appease him. The question was, should he speak with her alone, or insist that his brothers join him? Henthas could be of value in such a meeting, but Grigor couldn't be certain what Numar might do.

"I'm not sure that I see the point in such a conversation," Grigor finally said. "But she is our queen, and it would be inappropriate for me to refuse her." He offered a smile to the minister. "Tell Her Highness that I'll speak with her at her convenience."

"What?" Henthas said, before the Qirsi could reply. His face had reddened, and there was rage in his dark eyes. "This affects our entire house, not just you! I will not be left out in the corridors of my family's castle like some child!"

Again, Grigor couldn't help but be amused and pleased. Had Henthas been wise enough to know how much he was aiding Grigor's cause, he would surely have shut his mouth.

"In this case, I must agree with my brother," Numar broke in, his voice so soothing after Henthas's shrill tones that the archminister merely stared at him, seemingly amazed that a man he knew only as the Fool could sound so sensible. "With Carden dead, the three of us are the only heirs House Solkara has left." He smiled. "At least the only heirs of age. All of us should be included in any discussions bearing on the future of the Supremacy."

There was little in Aneiran royal tradition to support such a statement. The eldest son controlled the family's destiny, and if that son died, the next oldest assumed leadership of the house. It would have been entirely within Grigor's prerogative to ignore his brothers' wishes and meet with Chofya alone, particularly since she had requested through her minister that he do so.

But with both Henthas and Numar having voiced their opposition, he couldn't defy them without weakening himself. If he wanted Chofya and the nobles to fear the Jackals, he couldn't openly break with Henthas their first night in Solkara. Henthas wouldn't have thought of this; he had spoken out of pique and wounded pride. But Numar knew just what he was doing. Grigor felt certain of it. The Fool, indeed. Numar was, as far as Grigor could tell, the most dangerous man in the royal city.

He made himself smile as he opened his hands. "As you can see, Archminister, I have little choice in this matter. I'm happy to speak with the queen, but she'll have to see all of us."

The Qirsi looked displeased, but he nodded as he stood again. "Very well, my lord. I'll convey this to the queen." He turned and walked away.

"You were really going to speak to her without us?" Henthas demanded in a fierce whisper as soon as the minister was gone.

Grigor ignored him, glaring at Numar.

"You look angry, brother," the man said mildly. "Did I upset your plans?"

"Don't cross me, Numar. This is no game we're playing. This is for the crown, and I won't allow anyone to keep me from claiming it as my own. Not the queen, not our niece, not even you."

"All I did was ensure that Henthas and I would be party to your conversation with Chofya. Surely you can see how having us there might work to your advantage."

Grigor glanced at Henthas, who was eyeing him with obvious mistrust.

"You wanted to meet with her alone, didn't you?" he said. "I want to know why."

"I was afraid you'd muck it up, Henthas," Grigor said wearily, "as you muck up everything. I don't want a war with Chofya, though I'll fight one if I have to. The last thing I need is you sitting in her presence chamber, insulting the queen and making idle threats."

"A threat is only idle if the man making it is weak. It seems more likely that you'd be the one to ruin things, with your arrogance and your pride."

Grigor looked at Numar, who was already watching him, the expression on his youthful face seeming to say, *See? If you want to control him, you need me on your side.*

"What is it you want?" he asked the younger man.

"I want what's best for House Solkara," Numar said. "Just as you do."

Grigor couldn't tell if he was being sincere, which scared him a good deal. He felt fairly certain, however, that Numar didn't honestly believe that he had the family's best interests at heart.

"And what would that be?"

Numar shrugged. "I don't know yet. That's why I want to hear what you and Chofya have to say to each other."

The feast promised to go on well into the night, but Grigor left the hall a short time later with both brothers just a step behind him. It almost seemed that their mistrust of one another ran so deep that each was unwilling to allow the other two out of his sight. Chofya had seen to it that their quarters were together, and long after he entered his chamber and locked his door, Grigor continued to listen for any sign that either of his brothers was wandering about the castle. Only when he had satisfied himself that they weren't going anywhere did he lie down to sleep. For some time, however, he lay awake in his bed, staring at the dim shadows cast onto his walls by the low fire in his hearth, and thinking back on what had just happened in the king's hall.

He realized now that having heard Numar dismissed as a fool for so long, he had begun to believe it himself, though he should have known better. More than that, he had always assumed that Numar did not share his own lust for power and wealth. He couldn't say why. Wasn't Numar Tomaz's son, just as the rest of them were? Perhaps, as the youngest, he had merely been clever enough to know that power would never be his so long as Carden sat on the throne. Now, however, with the king dead and the land teetering on the edge of upheaval, he could allow his ambitions to guide him. Having never tasted true power, Numar might have been even hungrier for it than Grigor, which only served to make him that much more dangerous.

Grigor had threatened his brother tonight. It had been vague to be sure, but a threat nonetheless. But now, lying in the dim orange glow of the dying fire, he wondered if he could really kill his own brother. And for the first time, he wondered if that brother—the youngest, the Fool—was capable of killing him.

They were lying in each other's arms, their pulses just starting to slow, their breathing still quickened, a fine sheen of sweat on their bodies and faces, when they heard knocking at the door.

Evanthya stared into Fetnalla's eyes, feeling panic rise in her chest.

"Whose room are we in?" she whispered. "I've forgotten."

Fetnalla grinned, her eyes luminous in the candlelight, and kissed her lightly on the throat. "Yours."

Evanthya pulled away and sat up. "Who's there?" she called.

"Your duke."

The minister sighed with relief. She wasn't about to open the door, but at least it hadn't been Brall or one of the other Qirsi ministers staying in the castle.

"Yes, my lord?" she said, quickly pulling on her clothes.

She heard him clear his throat, something he often did in awkward circumstances.

"I wish to speak with you," he said. "Please come to my chambers as soon . . . when you can."

"Yes, my lord. It will just be a moment."

She turned to look at Fetnalla, who was smiling at her, having made no effort at all to dress. Evanthya frowned.

"You said he knew," Fetnalla said with a shrug.

"Brall will be looking for you, too. And he doesn't know."

She made a sour face. "Maybe it's time he did," she said. But she began to put her clothes on as well.

In a few moments they were both dressed, and Evanthya stepped to the door.

"Wait a few moments after I'm gone, then slip out and return to your chambers," she said, her hand resting on the door handle.

Fetnalla gave a small grin, tilting her head to the side. "Yes, my lord."

Evanthya smiled and walked back to where Fetnalla stood. Rising to the tips of her toes, she kissed the woman gently on the lips.

"Forgive me."

"Of course. You always get this way when you leave me to see your duke."

Evanthya paused, gazing into her eyes. "Do I? I'm sorry."

Fetnalla kissed her brow. "I've grown accustomed to it. I even find it charming in a way."

They kissed one last time. Then Evanthya left the chamber, walked to Tebeo's door, and knocked once.

"Come in!" the duke called immediately.

The minister stepped into the duke's room, finding Tebeo and Brall seated by the hearth, both of them looking glum in the bright glow of a crackling fire.

"I thought Fetnalla was with you," Brall said, scowling at her.

"She was, my lord. When Lord Dantrielle called for me, she went to find you, thinking that you might wish to speak with her." The lie came to her easily. She only hoped that Fetnalla would tell the same story.

Brall nodded and turned to the fire again, leaving Evanthya and Tebeo facing one another.

"You called for me, my lord?"

"Yes, First Minister. You saw what happened in the hall tonight, between the king's brother and the queen?"

"I did, my lord."

"Chofya and Grigor are to meet tomorrow morning. The queen wanted a private audience, but Grigor has insisted that his brothers be there as well. The queen, in turn, has asked Lord Orvinti to attend on her behalf, and she's asked me as well, hoping perhaps that I will support her position."

"For the regency, my lord?"

The duke of Orvinti turned at that. "You've been talking to my first minister."

Fetnalla had spoken to her of how suspicious Brall had become. Hearing his tone now, seeing the distrust in his pale blue eyes, Evanthya understood that her love had not exaggerated the matter.

"I told you I had, Lord Orvinti. Your first minister guessed that you would enlist my duke in the queen's cause, and she thought I should be prepared to advise him."

"And what counsel would you offer?" Tebeo asked.

"Fetnalla seems to feel that any other course will lead to civil war."

"This one might as well," Brall told her. "I'm not certain that we wouldn't be better off handing the throne to Grigor. He won't make a very good king, but he might be able to keep the peace, albeit through fear and the threat of violence."

"I thought you supported the queen, Lord Orvinti."

The duke shrugged. "When Carden died, I gave her my word that I would aid her in any way I could. This is what she asked of me. But I've no illusions as to the difficulties a regency presents." A knock at the door stopped him.

"Enter!" Tebeo said.

The door swung open and Fetnalla walked into the room.

"There you are, my lord," she said, offering a small bow to Brall. "I searched for you after Lord Dantrielle came for the first minister."

Evanthya breathed a small sigh of relief. Usually they worked out their story before they parted, but they had been in too much of a hurry this night. She wouldn't let them forget again.

Brall nodded to her, but said nothing.

Instead, Tebeo gestured at an empty chair. "Make yourself comfortable, First Minister. We've been discussing a request from the queen that your duke and I attend a meeting tomorrow between Chofya and the new duke of Solkara."

Fetnalla raised an eyebrow, glancing at Brall. "Strange that she'd want you there."

"Grigor will have his brothers with him," Brall said, his voice flat. "She wants us."

"Do you support a regency, Lord Dantrielle?" Fetnalla asked.

Tebeo rubbed a hand over his face. "I'm not certain. Either way it seems that we'll have to contend with Grigor. I just can't decide whether he's more dangerous as a regent or as king in his own right."

"Does the queen have to name Lord Solkara as regent?" Evanthya asked. "Can't she choose anyone she wants?"

"She doesn't have to name Grigor," Brall said. "But there are few other choices. Henthas would be no better, and no one expects her to ask the Fool. And if she goes outside of House Solkara, she risks war with Carden's brothers and challenges from the other houses. Grigor is really the only one she can ask."

"And you expect he'll refuse." Tebeo offered it as a statement, but he stared at the other duke as if awaiting a reply.

Brall shrugged. "He wants to be king. He made that much clear tonight in the hall. But I believe that he'll look to the other houses before he decides whether to turn her down or not. If he senses that Aneira's nobles will oppose a queen, he'll claim the throne as his own. If, on the other hand, he sees that most of us support Chofya and will oppose his claim, he may accept her offer." He gave a wan smile, though it was fleeting and appeared forced. "In either case, however, he has his heart and his eyes fixed on the crown. I'm certain of it. Even if he becomes regent, it won't be long before he moves against Chofya and the girl."

Fetnalla looked from one of the dukes to the other. "Am I correct in assuming that if Chofya succeeds in establishing a regency for her daughter, she can have a hand in choosing the girl's ministers?"

Tebeo glanced briefly at Brall before nodding. "I believe that's correct, though I'd have to consult the Volumes of Pernandis to be certain. It's been over a century since the last regency."

The Volumes of Pernandis had been compiled during the First Bistari Supremacy, nearly six centuries before. According to legend, they were written by King Pernandis the First, whose reign of forty years was still the longest in Aneiran history. The volumes listed most of the ruling customs established over the first two hundred years of the Aneiran monarchy, and though written by a Bistari, to this day they continued to guide all the courts of the kingdom, even House Solkara.

"We should find out for certain," Fetnalla said. "If I'm right, it leaves us little choice but to back the queen."

Brall looked at her skeptically. "Why?"

"Because she can name Pronjed as one of the girl's ministers."

The duke looked at Tebeo for an instant, the frown on his face deepening. "I thought you feared the archminister. I thought—" He hesitated, his eyes flicking toward the other duke once more. "I thought you suspected him of having a hand in the king's death."

Tebeo's eyes widened. "Is this true?" he asked, staring at Evanthya.

"This is the first I've heard of it, my lord," she said.

Fetnalla had mentioned to her an encounter with the archminister, but they had fallen into each other's arms before having a chance to discuss it.

"I had a conversation with Pronjed this morning," Fetnalla said, speaking to the three of them, though her eyes remained mostly on Evanthya. "I have reason to suspect that he may possess delusion magic."

"What reason?" Tebeo asked.

"I can't say, my lord. I swore an oath to the archminister that I would share our conversation with no one."

"So it was Pronjed who was in your chambers this morning," Brall said, looking frightened.

Fetnalla exhaled slowly. "Yes," she admitted.

"And he asked you to heal an injury?"

"I cannot say more, my lord. Please try to understand."

Brall propelled himself out of his chair and walked to the hearth, his body seemingly coiled like that of a wild cat. "You ask me to understand, but you tell me nothing. You warn me about how dangerous this man is, and then you suggest that we support the regency so that he can serve the girl as her archminister." He threw up his hands. "Why should I trust your counsel?"

"Because I've given you no reason to doubt me," Fetnalla said, raising her chin proudly, despite the reddening of her cheeks. "Because Grigor is your enemy, not I."

"And what about Pronjed? A few days ago you told me that you were afraid of him."

"I still am. But he's no friend of Grigor, and I don't believe he wants civil war."

"But he might," Brall said. "If he has delusion magic as you say, there's no way to be sure, is there. Not even for you."

Fetnalla opened her mouth, then closed it again. Finally she shook her head. "No, my lord. If his powers run that deep, I can't be certain."

The two of them fell silent, though they continued to stare at each other, the duke's mistrust and Fetnalla's dismay making the room's air heavy as a winter fog.

After some time, Tebeo looked up at Evanthya, who still stood in the center of the chamber, uncertain of what to do.

"What say you, Evanthya?" he asked softly. "Do you know anything of the archminister?"

Evanthya swallowed, her eyes meeting Fetnalla's for just an instant. She feared that Fetnalla might begin to cry at any moment, and she would have said nearly anything to prevent that. But her duke had asked her about Pronjed, and she feared the archminister nearly as much as Brall did, nearly as much as she always thought Fetnalla had as well.

"I know that he's a formidable man," she said, choosing her words with care. "I've heard him called ruthless by some. He was always said to be a perfect match for his king."

"But do you know anything of his powers?"

"No, my lord. Nothing at all."

"Would you trust him if you thought he had this delusion magic?" Brall asked. "Would you be willing to place the fate of Kalyi's regency in his hands?"

Evanthya forced herself to keep her gaze fixed on the duke, though she longed to look at Fetnalla. Brall knew nothing of their love affair, so he couldn't have understood the difficult position in which he had placed her. This was small consolation, however.

"I suppose I would be reluctant to trust him, Lord Orvinti," she finally said.

Brall nodded, looking at Tebeo and then Fetnalla. "There, you see?"

"I wouldn't be eager to put my faith in the duke, either," she added quickly. "Rather than arguing over which man poses less of a threat to the kingdom, I believe we'd be better served by looking for other possible solutions."

"All other solutions lead to civil war," Tebeo said.

"That may be. But at times such as these, men of influence must decide whether war is preferable to a tyrant."

Evanthya chanced a look at Fetnalla, and regretted it immediately. The minister was staring at her as if she had just announced her intention to marry another. Her cheeks were scarlet and her pale eyes appeared red-rimmed, so that one might have thought she had been crying all this time.

"You'd actually counsel us to challenge House Solkara?"

Evanthya wanted to say something, to send some sign to Fetnalla that she was sorry, that she hadn't intended to hurt her. But the woman looked away before she could, and Evanthya had to force herself to face her duke again so that she could reply.

"I would, my lord," she said, struggling to keep her thoughts on the matters at hand. "If the crown stays with House Solkara, it will end up on the head of a man hated and feared throughout the land, or it will fall to a child whose best hope for surviving her regency rests with a Qirsi minister none of us trusts. Surely better choices lie elsewhere."

"And what of the girl?" Brall demanded. "Are we just to wrest her father's legacy from her grasp?"

"She is ten years old, Lord Orvinti. With Grigor as her regent and Pronjed as her archminister, do you really expect that she would survive the next six years? The regency is a death sentence for the child. All of us know that."

"So we're to ignore her mother's wishes?"

"Yes," Evanthya said, knowing how cold she sounded. "That's my counsel."

Both dukes stared at her for some time, saying nothing. At last, Tebeo gave a small nod.

"Very well, Evanthya. Thank you. You and the first minister are free to go. Brall and I have a good deal to discuss."

"If I may, my lord," she said. "If the two of you decide that you agree with me, I would strongly urge you to find some way to hide your decision from the duke of Solkara and the archminister. Perhaps even from the queen as well. In a sense, the war for the throne began this evening in the king's hall, and Grigor probably thinks he's already winning. He may not want to be regent, but he'll see in it a possible path to power. Either way, he believes the crown is his. If he senses that the two of you intend to oppose House Solkara, he'll want you dead. And since we can't leave the city for several days more, he'll have ample opportunity to have you killed."

Brall narrowed his eyes. "What are you suggesting?"

"That until we're safely away from Solkara, you should continue to talk and act as if you support the queen in this matter."

"What?" the duke said. "If we support the regency now, we'll appear to betray Chofya when we oppose House Solkara later." He shook his head. "I won't do it! It may not bother a Qirsi to be called a traitor, but I won't bring such shame on House Orvinti!"

"That's enough, Brall," Tebeo said in a low voice, his gaze still fixed on Evanthya.

"You're not actually going to listen to her, are you?" the duke asked.

Tebeo turned at that. "She's my first minister. I listen to all her counsel, and I accept that she has my best interests and those of my house at heart."

"But—"

"You may think that loyalty means nothing to the Qirsi, Lord Orvinti," Evanthya said. "But you're wrong. Fetnalla serves you faithfully, just as I do, my duke. You may not like the counsel I've just given, but I assure you that I offer it out of concern for my lord's life as well as for my own. You said before that you suspected the king might have been murdered. This was the first I had heard of such a possibility, and I don't know whether to believe it or not. But you must ask yourself, if someone was willing to kill the king, would they hesitate to kill a duke as well?"

"Thank you, First Minister," Tebeo said again.

She faced her duke, hearing in his voice a request that she leave. He nodded to her once, as if to say that he would be all right without her.

After a moment, she bowed to him. "Very well, my lord."

She walked to the door, sensing that Fetnalla was just behind her, and that the dukes were watching them both.

Even after the two ministers had stepped into the corridor and pulled the door closed behind them, they said nothing. Fetnalla regarded her briefly, the hurt still evident in her eyes. Then she started back toward her chamber, leaving Evanthya little choice but to follow.

Only when they stepped into Fetnalla's room and Evanthya closed the door did her love turn to look at her.

"How could you do that to me?" she said, flinging the words at Evanthya like a dagger, and finding her heart with the blade.

"I'm not allowed to disagree with you?"

"Not in front of my duke! Not about this! I told you how suspicious of me he's become, and still you made it sound like I was telling him to put his trust in a demon."

"Because I honestly don't trust Pronjed, and neither did you until now. What happened this morning? Why do you suddenly think he's the kingdom's best hope?"

Fetnalla looked away. "I'm not sure I can explain it," she said, her voice lower.

Evanthya took a step toward her. She wanted to place a hand on Fetnalla's shoulder. She wanted to take the woman in her arms. But she didn't dare.

"Can you try?" she asked instead, gently, as one might speak to a child.

"I just don't think that he wants a war," Fetnalla said with a shrug.

"I'm sure he doesn't. His fate is tied to House Solkara, Fetnalla. A war is the last thing he wants, because it may very well bring an end to the Solkaran Supremacy."

"That's what you want, isn't it?"

Evanthya took a breath. "I don't want a tyrant."

"I don't either. But I'm more afraid of a war."

She tried to smile. "Maybe together, we can find a way to avoid both."

But Fetnalla shook her head. "I don't think so. We're working at cross-purposes. I don't see any way for us to help each other."

Evanthya thought she might cry. "But—"

"You should go. I'm tired, and I'm sure you must be as well."

She had never heard Fetnalla's voice sound so flat, so devoid of love.

"Will I see you tomorrow?" she asked. She was the child now, small and frightened.

"I expect our dukes will keep their audience with the queen. I'll see you then."

Their eyes remained locked a moment longer. Evanthya wanted to say more, or more to the point, to hear Fetnalla say more. They hadn't parted without speaking the words for so long, she hardly knew how to do it anymore. But Fetnalla kept herself still, and after a painfully awkward silence, Evanthya turned and left the room. Once in the corridor, she fell against the stone walls, stifling a sob with an effort that made her chest ache.

I love you, she wanted to cry out. *I love you as I've never loved anyone.*

But the stillness stopped her. Leaning closer to Fetnalla's door, she felt her heart wither. She heard nothing, nothing at all. Not even the sound of tears.

Chapter
Fourteen

hey had come within sight of the royal city late the previous day, following the waters of the Kett away from the setting sun, through fishing villages, farmlands, and patches of dense forest. They could have entered the city at any time, but as he usually did when they arrived somewhere new, Grinsa chose to wait for morning, when the peddlers and shepherds would file through the city gates and make their way to the city marketplace. As two travelers entering Solkara, or any other Aneiran city, Tavis and he couldn't help but draw the attention of the city guards. As part of the horde flooding the city each morning, they could avoid close scrutiny. Every city to which they journeyed presented risks, none more so than the royal city in the wake of Carden's death, with every Aneiran noble and his best soldiers walking the streets. But short of abandoning their search for the assassin and his Qirsi allies, such small precautions offered the most safety for which the gleaner could hope.

Standing amid the beggars and merchants waiting for the ringing of the morning bells and the opening of the gates, Tavis stamped his feet in the cold and muttered to himself impatiently. He wore an old woolen riding cloak with its hood drawn up to hide at least some of his livid scars.

"Any other city in the Forelands would have let us in already," he said with petulance. "Certainly they would have in C—" He stopped, glancing about as if to see if anyone was listening. "At home," he continued a moment later, lowering his voice.

Grinsa had to smile. The morning had brightened considerably, and the boy was probably right. The bells should already have been rung. But it was a matter of moments. As much as Tavis had matured in the half year since his Fating, he remained terribly young, as only a noble could.

"It won't be long now," Grinsa said, gazing up the city lane through the iron grating of the gate. "Here come the morning guards now."

A murmur went through the crowd as the soldiers approached. Tavis wasn't the only one growing cold in the early-morning air.

The guards unlocked the gate, pulled both sides of it open, and waved the men and women into the city.

"Keep your head down," Grinsa whispered.

Tavis gave a quick glance, glowering at the Qirsi. "Yes, I know!" he answered. "Nod my head a lot and say 'good morning,' though not so loudly that the guards can hear my accent. You don't have to tell me every time!"

Grinsa smirked. "But I enjoy these conversations so."

Tavis glared at him a moment longer, before smiling himself and shaking his head. "I should have gone to Glyndwr when I had the chance," the boy said, the grin lingering on his lips. "Exile would be better than this."

Grinsa nodded, facing forward. "For both of us."

They passed the guards without incident and began to follow the crowd toward the marketplace. But before they had gone far, the gleaner heard the jangling of a sword and the scuffling of a soldier's boots.

"Stop right there, you!" came a hard voice.

Grinsa kept walking, and gestured for Tavis to do the same, but his heart was pounding at his chest like a fist.

"I told you to stop!" the guard said.

A sword was drawn, the morning air ringing with the sound of steel.

"Another step and you die!" the man warned.

Grinsa froze, putting out an arm to stop his companion as well. He turned slowly, only to see the guard pressing his blade against the throat of the man walking just behind him.

"What's this," the guard said, removing a two-handed sword from a baldric on the man's back. "Peddlers don't usually need such fine blades."

"I carry it for safety, good sir," the man said, his voice quavering. "There are thieves on the roads throughout the forest."

"That may be," the guard said. "But you don't carry such a blade into Solkara unless you're a noble or a soldier in the service of one." He paused, glancing over at Grinsa and frowning. "What are you looking at, white-hair? This doesn't concern you."

"Of course not, good sir," the gleaner said quickly, lowering his gaze. "Forgive me."

He hurried on, Tavis beside him, but for some time his pulse continued to race, as if he had just come through a battle. He looked forward to
the day when they could leave Aneira for Caerisse, or Wethyrn or Sanbira.
Any place where Tavis's lineage wasn't grounds for immediate execution,
and where his accent didn't draw the unwished-for attention of everyone
from castle guards to innkeepers.

"They stopped that man just for carrying a sword," Tavis said quietly.
"No wonder my father hates the Aneirans so."

"We're in their royal city, Tavis. Their king has just died and one of
their dukes was murdered barely a turn ago. Houses will by vying for the
throne, old rivalries will be rekindled. This is a time for vigilance. I
wouldn't assume that the guards always treat strangers that way."

Tavis eyed him briefly. "Why do you always take the part of those I
dislike?"

"I'm not taking their part. I'm merely trying to make you see the
world from someone else's perspective. A good king can see through his
enemy's eyes as well as his own."

The boy gave a short, sharp laugh. "You still think I'm going to be
king?"

"I don't know," Grinsa said. "But the same qualities that make a good
king, can make a good man."

Tavis seemed to consider this as they walked on, wandering slowly
among the stalls and peddlers' carts of the city marketplace. There was little for them to learn in the city streets, though they could certainly ask some
of the sellers about the assassin. But it was far too early in the day for them
to go to taverns and inns, where their chances of learning something useful
were far greater.

Grinsa couldn't say what it was about the woman that caught his attention. While there were more Eandi in the marketplace than Qirsi, there
were enough white-hairs about to keep one from standing out. From a distance, her clothes appeared ordinary—a simple brown cloak, hooded like
his own, and clasped at the neck with a plain silver chain. It was only when
she drew nearer that he saw the hem of her robe and realized she was a
minister in the court of an Aneiran noble. She was pretty in a plain way,
with a thin face, bright yellow eyes, and fine white hair that she wore loose
so that it hung past her shoulders to the middle of her back. But she wasn't
beautiful, like Cresenne or even Keziah, his sister.

Perhaps it was the expression on her face that made him notice her, the
deep sadness in her eyes, as if she had just lost a parent. Grinsa found him-

self wondering if she had been minister to the king and still mourned his death.

She was walking directly toward Grinsa and Tavis, gazing about the marketplace, but seeming to see nothing at all. Not knowing why he did it, Grinsa remained in her path so that when she drew near she had to step to the side to avoid him.

"Good morrow, Minister," he said, bowing to her.

She hesitated a moment, looking at him with surprise. "Good morrow," she said, her voice low. Glancing at him a second time, she continued past, pulling her cloak tighter around her shoulders.

Grinsa stood in the middle of the lane and watched her walk away. A few seconds later she seemed to turn her head again, as if sensing his gaze. After a time, he lost sight of her amid the carts and the city folk.

"Do you know her?" Tavis asked.

The gleaner shook his head. "No. I've never seen her before."

"Then what?"

"I don't know. There's something . . ." He shook his head again, unable to find the words. He wanted to follow her, and he had learned long ago to trust his instincts on such things.

"Come with me," he said, starting after her.

At first he couldn't find her again, and he felt his frustration mounting. Just as he was ready to give up, however, Tavis pointed to a lone figure entering a small tavern.

"There," the boy said. "I think that's her."

"Why would a noble's minister go to a tavern so early in the day?"

They walked quickly to the building, entered the tavern, and took a seat in the middle of the room, not very far from where she sat, alone, with her back to the door.

The tavern man appeared a few moments later, carrying a plate of breads and cheeses to the minister. He was Qirsi. Grinsa hadn't even thought to check the name of the inn, but he felt certain that it must be one of the city's Qirsi establishments.

"Good day, sirs," the man said, stepping to their table. "Can I bring you some breakfast?"

"Please," Grinsa said, though they had already eaten once, before entering the city.

"Bread and cheese?" His eyes lingered a moment on Tavis's face, but he had the good grace not to comment on the boy's scars.

"That will be fine."

The innkeeper nodded and hurried away to fetch their food, leaving Tavis and Grinsa to sit in silence, occasionally glancing over at the woman. She showed no sign of having noticed them. She merely ate, though even this she did slowly, seemingly with little enthusiasm.

"Are you going to speak with her?" Tavis asked in a whisper.

"Patience," Grinsa said.

The innkeeper returned carrying two plates of food, which he laid on the table. Grinsa pulled out a five-qinde piece and held it in his palm for the man to see.

"I'm wondering if you've noticed a man in your tavern. A singer. Eandi, with long black hair, a black beard, and blue eyes. He's tall and broad."

The man stared at Grinsa briefly, then looked at the coin, wetting his lips. "I'm afraid not," he said.

Grinsa closed his fingers over the gold piece. "I see." He started to put the coin away, then stopped. "Would you have a room available for the night?"

"Again, I'm afraid I don't. With the king's funeral just a few days away, I've sold every one."

Grinsa nodded. "A pity." He made a point of looking around the empty room. "All your guests must be heavy sleepers."

"They are," the man said, turning to walk away. "They also know better than to ask questions of a tavern man."

The gleaner gave a shrug and glanced toward the woman, only to find that she was already watching him. Their eyes met for just an instant before she turned back to her food. But that was enough. She knew the assassin. Grinsa felt certain of it. He could only assume that she was part of the conspiracy, and it seemed likely that she thought the same of him.

"Greetings again, Minister," he said. "I didn't realize that was you."

She stiffened. After several moments, she finally turned to look at him again. "Have we met?"

"I'm not certain. I knew you were a minister from your robe, but now that you ask, you do look familiar." He stood and walked to her table. "My name is Grinsa jal Arriet," he said, bowing to her once again. He indicated Tavis with a wave of his hand. "My friend there is called Xaver."

The woman nodded to Tavis, smiling weakly. "I'm Evanthya ja Yispar," she said.

"Your name is familiar as well. Do you serve one of the major houses, Evanthya?"

She faltered. Clearly she wanted no part of this conversation. "Yes," she finally answered, the word coming out as a sigh. "I'm first minister to the duke of Dantrielle."

Grinsa grinned. "Of course! I'm a gleaner, and I often travel with the festivals. That must be where I've seen you." He pulled a chair over to her table and sat beside her. "I love Dantrielle. It's a beautiful city."

Her eyes flitted about the room uncomfortably. "Yes, it is."

"If you're first minister to one of the land's most prominent houses, shouldn't you be staying at the castle?"

"I am," she said, looking down at her food. "I just needed . . . I wanted to get out for a time."

"Yes," Grinsa said, nodding sagely. "I can imagine Castle Solkara is a rather grim place just now." He felt certain that something other than mourning for the king had driven her from the castle walls, but he didn't want to push her too hard on this point, not when there were others of far greater importance that he wished to pursue.

They fell silent, Grinsa watching her from the corner of his eye, and the minister toying anxiously with her food. He sensed that she was readying herself to leave.

She looked at him at last, opening her mouth to speak, no doubt to offer some quick farewell. Grinsa didn't give her the chance.

"I couldn't help but notice you watching me as I spoke to the tavern man," he said. "It almost seemed to me that you know the man I was describing."

She looked away again.

"Do you?" he asked.

"I really ought to be going," the woman said, reaching into her cloak and pulling out two silvers to leave on the table.

"It's important that we find him," Grinsa said. He was going to tell the familiar lie about the singer owing them money, but he knew she wouldn't believe this, not if she had ever had dealings with the man herself. Instead he pointed over at Tavis. "You see the boy there. You see the scars on his face. The man I described is responsible for those wounds." It was close enough to the truth. Tavis averted his gaze, his cheeks reddening, but he made no attempt to hide his face.

"I'm sorry for the boy," she said, "but I don't know the man you're talking about."

Grinsa read the lie in her eyes and in the twisting of her slender hands.

"Did you know that this man was in Bistari just before the duke was killed?"

She stared at him, the color abruptly draining from her face. Then she quickly looked down again. For a moment Grinsa thought she would cry.

"Were you in Bistari for the duke's funeral?" he asked, knowing that she must have been.

The woman nodded.

"Did you see this man there?"

"I told you, I've never seen him before. I don't know him."

"Have you seen him here? Did he come for the king's funeral? Or did he leave once the king was dead?"

Her eyes flew to his face once more. "You think he killed the king?"

"Do you?"

She started to object, but he raised a finger, silencing her. "Yes, I know," he said. "You know nothing of this man."

"I really must go," the minister said, though she still did not stand.

There was one other possibility. He had heard men speaking of it in one of the northern cities. Had she been from any other house, he wouldn't have mentioned it, but she had said Dantrielle, and so it was worth trying.

"There's a tavern in Dantrielle, I believe it's called the Red Boar. Did you—?"

Before he could finish she was on her feet, having nearly toppled over the table as she stood.

"Who are you?" she demanded, leveling a trembling finger at him. "Who sent you?"

Grinsa stood slowly, holding up his hands as if to show her that he carried no blade. "No one sent me," he said gently. "I've already told you, my friend and I are looking for this man."

She backed away from him. "And I told you, I don't know him! Now stay away from me! If you come near me again I'll have you both arrested. I swear it."

The minister glared at him another moment before turning and walking swiftly to the tavern door. She looked back at the gleaner once, as if assuring herself that he wasn't following her. Then she hastened into the street.

"Are we going to follow her again?" Tavis asked, standing.

Grinsa walked slowly back to their table, shaking his head. "No. I don't think she can actually have us arrested, but I don't want to chance scaring her any more than I have already."

"You think she knows him."

"I'm sure of it," the gleaner said. "Just as I'm sure that she met him in that tavern in Dantrielle."

"Do you think she's with the conspiracy?"

"I suppose," he said.

Tavis narrowed his eyes. "You don't sound very certain."

"She seemed terribly uneasy, not at all like someone who's been plotting against the Eandi courts for any length of time."

"Perhaps she hasn't been," the boy said with a shrug. "If their movement is growing as we fear, they have to be adding new people. She must be one of them."

Grinsa nodded, though he remained unconvinced. Something about the woman's behavior troubled him, but he couldn't explain it, and even a Weaver could place too much trust in his instincts. She knew the assassin and had worked very hard to conceal this from him. That should have been all the proof he needed.

"If she is with the Qirsi movement," Tavis said, "and if she has allies in the castle, our lives are in danger."

Again, the boy made sense. Yet the gleaner's doubts lingered, like the scent of rain after a storm has passed. "Perhaps," he said, sitting once more. "But I don't think she has many friends in the castle. If she did, she wouldn't have been here."

She must have looked back over her shoulder a thousand times between the tavern and Castle Solkara, expecting at any moment to see the two men from the tavern coming after her. Her heart was laboring so hard that her chest ached, and she wasn't certain she could keep down even the small bit of her breakfast she had managed to eat.

Evanthya knew that the closer she drew to the castle gates, the safer she was, but that did little to ease her fears. It was bad enough that the assassin had guessed that she was a minister the day she hired him, but to have strangers in the royal city asking about Corbin and the Red Boar was too much. She longed to run to Fetnalla. If anyone could calm her, her love could. But such comfort lay beyond her reach now.

She could barely remember why they had fought, it all seemed so foolish and far away. She knew though that Fetnalla would not have forgotten. The woman was brilliant and loving, but she could also be as stubborn and proud as an Eandi noble.

Once inside the castle, Evanthya did manage to calm herself. Unable to confide in Fetnalla, and unwilling to risk a chance encounter with her duke, she retreated to her chamber and lay down. By the time the midmorning bells tolled, she felt composed enough to attend the audience with the queen.

She reached the castle's presence chamber just as Tebeo, Brall, and Fetnalla arrived from the opposite direction.

"First Minister," her duke said, regarding her closely. "We missed you at breakfast."

"Yes, my lord," she said, forcing herself to look at the duke so that her gaze wouldn't stray to her love. "I took a walk in the city. It's not often that I get to the Solkaran marketplace."

The duke nodded, although he didn't look entirely convinced. "Indeed" was all he said.

Brall knocked at the door and when the queen called for them to enter, they pushed open the door and stepped into the chamber.

Chofya stood before a grand table, dressed in a long red velvet gown with a high neck. She wore a circlet of gold on her brow and a long golden necklace, from which hung a brilliant green gem. With her black hair tied back from her face and her dark eyes shimmering in the light of several oil lamps, she looked both beautiful and forbidding, like a woman born to power.

Pronjed stood behind her, as pale as Chofya was dark, as austere as she was elegant, yet no less formidable. There were several guards in the chamber as well, but Grigor and his brothers had yet to arrive.

"Lord Orvinti, Lord Dantrielle," Chofya said, offering a tight smile. "I'm grateful to you both for being here. I know that you both have . . . misgivings about the arrangement I propose. You do me a great service by your presence."

"We're honored that you asked us, Your Highness," Tebeo said.

The queen gestured at a long table and several chairs that stood by the great hearth. "Won't you sit? The duke should be joining us shortly."

The dukes and their ministers stepped to the far side of the table and sat. Evanthya was glad for the warmth of the fire at her back, and grateful as well that both dukes sat between herself and Fetnalla. Pronjed and the queen continued to stand, though Chofya stepped closer to the table and the great throne that had been placed at the end of it, favoring them with the same uneasy smile.

"I trust you all slept well?" she said after a brief pause.

"Yes, Your Highness," Brall answered for all of them. "And you?"

Chofya let out a small laugh. "I've hardly slept since my husband died, Lord Orvinti. Last night was no better or worse than any other."

"I'm sorry, Your Highness."

She shook her head. "Don't be. Once these matters are resolved I'll have plenty of time to rest. Until then, this is my lot, and I accept it as such."

The duke nodded, but gave no reply, and a difficult silence settled over the chamber. Even with the windows shuttered, Evanthya could hear Solkara's master armsman shouting commands at his soldiers in the castle ward below. Perhaps the sound would serve to remind Grigor of the army Chofya had at her command. Evanthya wondered if the queen had that in mind when she called this meeting for midmorning.

The minutes dragged by. No one spoke, though the queen looked repeatedly toward the door, clicking her tongue impatiently every few moments. If the king's brother hoped to anger her, he had already done a fine job of it.

"Carden always said that even time could be a weapon, if used properly," Chofya murmured after some time. "He learned this from his father. Apparently his brothers were listening as well."

Still they waited. The soldiers finished their training. They heard footsteps in the corridor outside the chamber and Chofya straightened, facing the door. But no knock came and after a time, the queen seemed to sag.

Pronjed cleared his throat. "Perhaps I should send a guard for him."

"No," Chofya said. "He's doing this for a reason. I will not have him see that he's angered me."

"Yes, Your Highness."

So they sat, doing nothing. Evanthya began to listen for the midday bells, sensing that they couldn't be far off. Chofya wandered around the chamber, straightening paintings that already hung straight, and smoothing tapestries that had no creases.

When the knock finally came, it sounded so loud that Evanthya started.

Chofya crossed to the throne and sat. "Come!" she called, her voice icy.

The door swung open and Grigor strode into the chamber, followed by his two brothers. He looked much as he had the previous evening, elegant and graceful, and as broad and muscular as the hero of some childhood tale. He was dressed in warrior's garb, a dun shirt and matching trousers, black boots and belt. From the belt hung a fighting sword on one side and a matching short sword on the other, both with jeweled hilts. He had only been duke of Solkara for a few days, yet he looked as much like a king as Chofya did a queen, and by comparison he made the other two dukes appear to be little more than courtiers.

Positioned behind him, his brothers served as such perfect complements to his appearance that Evanthya had to believe the effect was intended. To the left stood Henthas, powerfully built like his brother, but with darker hair and harder features that made him appear grim where Grigor was jaunty. To the right stood Numar, slighter than his brothers and with a kind, open face that made the trio seem somewhat less imposing.

"Forgive us if we kept you waiting," Grigor said lightly, leading his brothers to the table, lowering himself into a chair, and indicating with a nod that the two of them should do the same.

Chofya waited until they were seated before speaking. "I didn't give you leave to sit, Lord Solkara, nor did I see you bow to me as is proper."

Grigor regarded her with a look of utter innocence. "With Carden dead, I'm duke of Solkara. I didn't think I had to ask permission to sit in my own castle." He furrowed his brow. "Unless you intend to vie for my dukedom as well."

Henthas chuckled.

"As for failing to bow to you," Grigor went on, "please forgive me." He half stood and sketched a small bow that was really nothing more than a nod. "Now, can we please be done with all this foolishness and discuss the matter at hand?"

Chofya glowered at him, her color high. But after a moment, she gave a curt nod. "Very well," she said. "By the matter at hand I assume you mean the selection of Carden's successor."

"Actually, no," the duke said, all traces of a smile vanishing from his face. "I mean the making of plans for my investiture as king. I do hope that you and your daughter will feel free to remain in the castle until the celebrations are complete."

"This castle belongs as much to Kalyi and me as it does to you!"

"There's no Solkaran blood in your veins, Your Highness," he said, his tone contemptuous.

"What about the girl?" Brall asked. "Surely you don't intend to deny her bloodright."

"This is a big castle," Numar said, before Grigor could respond. "I can't imagine that there isn't room here for Kalyi and her mother, no matter who is chosen to lead Aneira."

Grigor cast a venomous look at his brother, but after a brief pause, he nodded. "I suppose there's room."

The queen was gazing at Numar as if seeing him for the first time. Clearly she hadn't expected him to take her part. In light of his reputation, she might not even have expected him to speak.

"Now, as to my investiture," Grigor began again. "I'm willing to wait a few more days—"

"There will be no investiture," Chofya said. "Not until all the dukes have arrived and selected Carden's successor."

Grigor shook his head. "The crown belongs to House Solkara. We decide who rules, not the dukes."

"The Council of Dukes has always met to select a new king," Pronjed said.

"The Council is a formality, a way of presenting our choice to the other houses. You know that as well as I."

"As I understand it," Tebeo said, "the Volumes call for a vote."

Grigor closed his eyes, as if struggling to keep his composure. "That's true, but as I said, the vote is a formality. The Council hasn't actually chosen a king in hundreds of years."

The archminister shrugged, a small smile on his lips. "That's only because there hasn't been a dispute within the royal house that required resolution by the Council. Now there is."

"We will not allow the Solkaran Supremacy to be ordered about by outsiders!"

"If you try to defy the Council, brother," Numar said mildly, "the other houses may see fit to do away with the Solkaran Supremacy. None of us wants that, do we?"

Grigor balled his hands into fists, until his knuckles were white as Qirsi hair. But when he spoke, his voice remained even. "What is it you propose, Chofya? Surely you don't want the crown for yourself."

"No," she said. "As you're so fond of pointing out to me, I'm not Solkaran. Kalyi is Carden's rightful heir. I want her to be queen when she's of age. Until then I propose a regency."

"Who would you select as her regent?"

The queen hesitated, but only for an instant. She even managed a small smile. "You, of course. You're the eldest of Carden's brothers. It seems appropriate that you should guide her through the early years of her reign."

"You actually trust me with this?"

"Shouldn't I?"

A smile stretched across the man's face. "Of course. But you've shown little faith in me or my motives in the past. I find it strange that you'd suddenly see fit to entrust me with instructing your daughter in the ways of statecraft."

"Kalyi is ten years old, Lord Solkara. If I could make her queen without your help, I would. But under the laws of the land I cannot. Since I doubt that you'd agree to a regency with anyone else as regent, I'm willing to place Kalyi in your hands for the next six years. I'll be here to help as I can, and I intend to have her appoint Pronjed as her archminister. You won't be doing this alone."

Grigor looked from the queen to the archminister, nodding slowly. "Actually, it's not clear that I'll be doing this at all."

Chofya paled. "Does that mean that you intend to oppose her?"

"I've made no secret of the fact that I wish to be king, that indeed I feel entitled to the crown. As you say, I'm Carden's eldest brother, and therefore the logical choice to be Aneira's next king. We came close to establishing a matriarchy in the Time of Queens and the other houses nearly rebelled. I doubt that the Council will be eager to tread that path again."

"What if they are?" Tebeo asked.

"As I've indicated already, I don't recognize the Council as the final authority on this matter."

Brall stared at the man. "Are you saying you'd defy the other houses, that you'd risk a war?"

"I'm saying that I'll do what I feel is necessary to preserve the Solkaran Supremacy. If the other houses dare to challenge me, they'll be the ones starting a war."

"Don't take the other houses lightly, Lord Solkara," Tebeo said. "Yours may be the most powerful house in Aneira, but if she stands alone, she'll be crushed."

Grigor smiled. "My lords, please. We're getting ahead of ourselves. The Council has yet to meet, and I've done nothing but state my belief that I am the rightful heir to the throne." He looked at Chofya, who still sat on the throne, looking too small for it. "I'll consider your proposal, Your Highness. If the Council supports Kalyi's claim to the throne, we can meet again to discuss the form such a regency might take."

"That's not good enough," the queen said. "I want your word right now, in front of these men, that you'll respect the will of the Council."

Grigor stood, and after a moment, Henthas and Numar did as well. "I'm afraid I can't make that promise," the duke said. "Had he been in my position, your husband wouldn't have either. But I don't have to tell you that, do I, Chofya? You know it's true." He glanced at his brothers. "Let's go," he said, starting toward the door. "This discussion is done."

Henthas looked at Chofya and the dukes, a smirk on his lips, and then he followed. Numar offered a small bow to the queen.

"Your Highness," he said, without a hint of irony, before leaving as well.

When Carden's brothers had gone, closing the door behind them, Brall pushed himself out of his chair and began to pace, as Evanthya had seen him do so often.

"The impertinence of that man is galling," he said. "I had my doubts about the regency before, Your Highness. But having seen what the kingdom would have to endure instead, I'm ready to do whatever I can to see that your daughter is made queen. I only wish you'd reconsider your choice of Grigor as regent."

Tebeo let out a breath. "I have to agree, Your Highness. The man is set on being king. Giving your daughter over to him is far too dangerous. She won't survive the first turn."

"What about Numar?" Fetnalla asked, looking around the room and even allowing her gaze to alight briefly on Evanthya.

"He does seem a more reasonable man," Tebeo said. "And not at all the dullard we've been led to believe he was."

Chofya shook her head. "Grigor wouldn't stand for it."

"Forgive me, Your Highness," Evanthya said. She felt all of them watching her, even Fetnalla, but she kept her gaze fixed on the queen and hoped that her voice would remain steady. "But why should we care what Grigor thinks? He's willing to defy the Council, he treats you and all those around him with contempt, and he obviously cares for nothing but his own ambitions. He doesn't deserve your concern."

"He's a powerful man, First Minister," the queen said. "If we anger him, we risk war."

"He's intent on war already, Your Highness. If you truly wish to put your daughter on the throne, you'll have to defeat Grigor first."

"I'm afraid my first minister may be right," Tebeo said. "In which case all turns on the Council. It's not enough that you win the support of a majority of Aneira's dukes. You need enough of them with you to defeat Grigor in battle."

Brall drew his sword. "You'll have my blade, Your Highness."

"And mine," Tebeo said, raising his weapon as well.

The queen managed a smile. "My thanks to you both."

Evanthya looked at Fetnalla, and found the minister already staring back at her, an apology in her eyes. When she next glanced at Pronjed, however, she saw something quite different. He was staring at her as well, his face deathly pale and his eyes filled with rage.

*   *   *

Grigor was walking so fast his brothers could barely keep pace with him. He said nothing, fearing that others might hear—he knew that once he loosed his ire he would be unable to control it.

He led them out of the castle to a remote and deserted corner of the gardens, which had long since turned brown. Only then, when he was certain that he was beyond the sight and hearing of all in the castle, did he whirl toward his youngest brother, his short sword drawn.

"I should kill you here and now!" he said, laying the blade along the side of Numar's neck. "How dare you oppose me in front of Chofya and her little dukes!"

"I didn't oppose you, brother," Numar said, looking and sounding maddeningly calm. "I merely tried to point out that the castle is large enough to accommodate both you and the queen."

"There was more to it than that!"

"Yes, there was. I also tried to make you see that by angering the Council, you invite rebellion. Strong as our house may be, we cannot stand against all the dukedoms of Aneira. You may be the oldest, Grigor, but that doesn't mean I'll stand by and let you ruin House Solkara in your pursuit of the throne."

"I've warned you once, brother. Don't get in my way, or I'll destroy you."

Numar smiled. Even with the sword still at his throat, he actually smiled. "I'm not afraid of you, Grigor." He glanced at Henthas. "I'm not even afraid of the two of you together. You need to convince the Council that you can be trusted with the kingdom. If you kill me, you'll be undermining all that you've worked for."

Grigor glared at him a moment longer before lowering his sword and grinning.

"You may be right, Numar," he said, sheathing the blade again. "But that only protects you now. Once I'm king, there won't be anyone in the Forelands who can save you, and there won't be anywhere you can hide."

Numar gave a small shrug, the smile still on his lips. "Then I'll just have to see to it that you never take the throne."

Chapter
Fifteen

✦

he funeral of King Carden the Third began with the tolling of the dawn bells on the eighth day of Bohdan's waning. Nobles from across the land crowded into the wards of Castle Solkara to watch as the king's body was carried forth from the castle cloister, set upon an ornate golden cart, and pulled toward the city streets by four white Caerissan steeds.

As the cart passed through the castle gates, beginning its long winding procession through the streets of Solkara, the nobles fell in step behind, like soldiers following their king to war. Out of the castle they walked, and into streets that were lined six deep on both sides for as far as the eye could see.

Fetnalla saw few tears on the faces of those braving the cold to watch the procession; Carden had been feared, perhaps respected, but he was never loved. Mostly, she thought she read apprehension in the sunken eyes and begrimed faces of Solkara's people. One didn't have to be a duke or minister to understand that the kingdom faced a time of profound uncertainty. A prolonged struggle for the crown seemed imminent, war seemed likely. And though the people in the city streets might not have known precisely what was coming, or even the names of those most likely to shape their futures, they appeared to be steeling themselves for the worst.

The procession moved slowly, stopped more than once by mourners placing dried flowers in the path of Carden's cart and bards standing in the lane to sing an elegy that they hoped would bring them fame and the good grace of Aneira's ruling family. It was late in the morning, almost midday, before Carden's final journey ended where it began, at the base of the castle's cloister tower.

As the last of the nobles entered the castle ward once more, eight Solkaran soldiers in full battle raiment lifted the pallet holding the king's body and bore it into the castle's great hall. Inside, Solkara's prelate led the kingdom's most powerful men and women in prayer for their fallen leader. When the ceremonies ended, Carden was carried back out to the ward and placed upon a great pyre. Chofya and her daughter stepped forward, each bearing a lighted torch which they tossed onto the mountain of wood. Grigor, Henthas, and Numar followed, and finally the eight surviving dukes added their torches to the blaze. Soon the fire raged like a storm, warming the entire courtyard, bathing the stone walls with its yellow glow, and claiming the body of the dead king in a maelstrom of flame and smoke.

A feast followed the funeral, as was customary, but the mood in the hall seemed even more glum than one might have expected. Great platters of food sat uneaten on the tables as dukes and marquesses gathered in small groups around the periphery of the great chamber, speaking in hushed tones and eyeing rival nobles warily.

Tebeo and Brall stood together, as they always seemed to do under such circumstances, watching the rest, concern etched on both their faces. Usually, Fetnalla would have taken some comfort in having Evanthya nearby, but they had barely spoken since their fight several nights before. They stood as far as possible from one another; they didn't even allow their eyes to meet.

Fetnalla knew that she had been wrong. Evanthya had every right to disagree with her. Had it not been for Brall's persistent distrust of everything she did and said, she never would have reacted as she did. But having lost her temper, having dismissed Evanthya with such cold disdain, Fetnalla didn't know how to heal the rift she had created. She had always been stubborn. Her mother had told her so in her youth, and Evanthya had done the same in the beds they shared. Now that willfulness and pride had cost her the one love she had ever known.

"Do you see how Grigor moves from one cluster of nobles to the next?" Brall asked quietly. "Before the night is over, he may have won over all the houses he needs to claim the throne."

"Perhaps we should be doing the same," Tebeo said.

"To what end? We have nothing to offer, no reason to make them listen to us."

"We speak for the queen and her daughter. Isn't that reason enough?"

Brall shook his head. "It's the queen's place to speak for herself. And instead she sits with Kalyi, drying the child's tears."

"Isn't that what she should be doing, Lord Orvinti?" Evanthya asked. "Wouldn't you expect the same of your duchess, were this your funeral?"

Brall eyed her briefly, then nodded, looking away. "Yes. I suppose I would."

Grigor did not bother to speak with the dukes of Orvinti and Dantrielle, no doubt knowing that their loyalties lay firmly with the queen. Fetnalla noticed as well that he didn't circle the room in the company of his brothers. Henthas and Numar stood at the far end of the hall, watching Grigor, but keeping themselves apart from all the nobles. At least for a time. After Grigor stepped past Brall and Tebeo, an icy smile on his lips, Numar left his middle brother and approached the dukes.

"A word, my lords?" he said quietly, his gaze flicking from one of them to the other.

"Of course, Lord Renbrere," Tebeo answered.

Numar glanced over his shoulder, as if making certain that Grigor wouldn't hear him. "I wish to apologize for my brother's behavior during our conversation the other day. His disrespect for the Council and his indifference to your concerns was inexcusable."

"He seems a difficult man," Brall said.

"Where his ambitions are concerned, he's ruthless. You shouldn't doubt for a moment that he'll do anything he feels is necessary to gain the throne."

"Nor should he doubt that we'll oppose him with all the might at our disposal in order to protect the queen and the king's heir," Brall said. "I hope you'll make that clear to him."

Numar gave a chagrined smile. "It was Carden and Grigor who first called me the Fool, Lord Orvinti. I'm afraid my eldest brother has little regard for anything I tell him. But I will try." He hesitated, though only for an instant. "I also wanted to say that if by some chance Grigor does agree to the queen's proposition, you should all remain diligent in your protection of the girl. To be honest, I think Grigor a poor choice for her regent."

"We agree," Tebeo said. "But the queen seems to feel that she has no choice in the matter. A lord from another house would refuse to become entangled in the affairs of the Solkarans, fearing for his life."

Numar nodded. "She may be right."

"What about you, Lord Renbrere?" Brall asked. "Would you be willing to serve as regent for the girl?"

A strange look came into the man's eyes and then was gone. "If it was the only way to preserve the Solkaran Supremacy, then yes, I would. But

I'm afraid my brother would find the idea of me as regent even more distasteful than he would a regent from another house."

"Your brother's preferences in this matter are of little concern to us," Tebeo said. "I'm asking you about yours. If the Council supports the queen, we may find it necessary to suggest someone other than Grigor as our choice for regent."

"Let me think on it, Lord Dantrielle. You do me a great honor even to suggest this. But I must decide if I'm ready to break with my brother publicly."

"Of course. I understand."

They stood a moment in silence. Then Numar offered a small bow. "Thank you, my lords. We'll speak again soon."

He hurried back to Henthas's side, just as Grigor stepped past the dukes a second time.

Once the older brother had gone by, Tebeo looked at Brall, raising an eyebrow. "We might have just found a way to avoid war."

The feast finally ended late in the day with a last prayer offered by the prelate. Later that night, the Council was to meet in the king's presence chamber with Grigor and Chofya, but for a time at least, Fetnalla had nothing to do. Usually, she and Evanthya would have taken such an opportunity to steal away together, to bed perhaps, or at least to enjoy a walk on the castle grounds. But Evanthya walked out of the great hall with her duke, leaving Fetnalla with Brall.

"I'll be in my quarters if you need me," the duke said, starting away from her. "I'll expect you to meet me there shortly before the Council is to meet."

Fetnalla nodded, but Brall didn't bother to look at her. "Yes, my lord," she called to him.

He raised a hand in a vague gesture of acknowledgment, but he didn't turn or slow his gait. In a moment, she was alone.

The minister would herself have liked to leave, but with Brall having just walked away from her, and Evanthya before him, she felt foolish doing so, as if all those remaining in the hall would notice how they had left her. She was almost ashamed of how grateful she was when Pronjed approached her.

"First Minister," he said, the look on his bony face even more grave than usual. "I'm glad I found you."

"Yes, Archminister. How can I help you?"

"I saw your duke leaving without you and I wanted to make certain that you would be accompanying him to the meeting of the Council later tonight."

Fetnalla nodded. "Yes, I'll be there."

"And will your friend as well? Dantrielle's first minister?"

She swallowed, feeling her chest tighten. *What have I done?* "I assume she will be. Why?"

"You need to ask?" he said with a frown. "She speaks of civil war as if it were inevitable, as if it were something to be anticipated and enjoyed."

"Evanthya doesn't seek war, Archminister. And I assure you, no one abhors killing more than she."

"One wouldn't know it to listen to her."

"She's a brilliant woman who serves her duke well. She may not want war, but she's wise enough to understand that we may have no choice in this instance."

"You must think very highly of her."

Fetnalla looked away. "I do."

"I would think so, since she's already convinced you to fight Grigor as well."

"Evanthya has convinced me of nothing," she said sharply. *Such pride.* "At least not yet," she added, dropping her gaze once more. "She's merely made me see that we can't rule out war, just because it strikes us as distasteful."

"It's more than that!" Pronjed said with a fervor Fetnalla had never seen in him before. "War will be the ruin of us all, of Aneira itself. I'm certain of it." This time it was the archminister's turn to avert his eyes, his lips pressed thin. "You must help me find another way. Please."

"I'll do what I can, Archminister. I don't want war. Truly I don't. But wouldn't we be fools to rule it out entirely? Doesn't that weaken us in our discussions with Lord Solkara?"

Pronjed opened his mouth, rage in his pale eyes. Then he seemed to stop himself, though clearly it took an effort. "Yes," he finally said. "I guess you're right." He looked over his shoulder at Chofya. "I should return to the queen. Thank you, First Minister."

"You're welcome."

He spun away from her in a manner that told her he was still angry, and returned to the queen's table. After standing where she was for another moment or two, Fetnalla left the hall and hurried back to her chamber. She was lonely and would have preferred to walk the gardens, or better yet the marketplace. But with alliances being formed and broken all around her, and Grigor collecting supporters as a quartermaster gathers weapons, she felt safer in the solitude of her room.

The time passed slowly, and Fetnalla was ready well before she began to hear voices of the other dukes and their ministers in the corridor outside her room. Still, when she stepped out of her chamber and over to Brall's door, Tebeo and Evanthya were already there, and Brall was frowning at her as if she were hours late.

"At last," he said, striding past her into the hallway.

Fetnalla cast a quick look at Evanthya, who offered a sympathetic smile. She smiled in return, feeling her face redden slightly. She shouldn't have let the woman see how much a simple smile could please her, but just then she didn't care. Pride be damned, she wanted her love back.

Most of the dukes had already arrived by the time Brall, Tebeo, and the two ministers reached the chamber. A servant was pouring Sanbiri red into goblets on a small table by the door while the nobles and their Qirsi took seats at a second, larger table in the center of the room. Grigor and Chofya were already sitting, one at either end of the table, their goblets already filled and resting before them. The queen sat with Pronjed, but Grigor was alone. Henthas and Numar were nowhere to be seen. Apparently, the duke of Solkara did not wish to have his brothers speaking for him on this night.

After several moments, the queen stood, lifting her wineglass. Grigor stood also, as did the others in the room. Servants brought the wine to the table, so that soon all were holding their goblets for a toast.

"Welcome, all of you," Chofya said. "I know it's been a long, wearying day, and I'm grateful to you for coming here tonight. Our kingdom has been without a leader for too long. The time has come for us to decide this matter once and for all. Let us hope that we can find the wisdom to keep Aneira at peace with herself."

Grigor nodded, a thin smile on his lips. "Well said, Your Highness. But I would add that we must also keep Aneira strong, so that we do not invite challenge from our neighbors, particularly the kingdom to our north."

Several of the dukes nodded their approval. This promised to be a difficult night for the queen.

Chofya gave a low sigh. "It seems we can't even agree on a toast, Lord Solkara. Shall we drink simply to our realm then?"

The duke nodded. "Agreed. To Aneira."

"To Aneira," the dukes and ministers repeated.

Fetnalla took a sip of wine, then belatedly glanced toward Evanthya, who was watching her, still holding her glass. They had done this for several years, sharing a private silent toast whenever they attended such events together. Fetnalla smiled and raised her glass a second time.

Even as she did, however, she became aware of a queer sensation in her throat. She heard a strangled cry come from the queen, and then another from one of the dukes. Brall, who had started to sit, lurched back to his feet, staggered backward, and began to retch. But all Fetnalla could do was stare at Evanthya. The feeling in her throat was spreading down through her chest, making it difficult for her to breathe.

Evanthya was gaping at her, hands trembling until her wine started to spill. Aware suddenly of the goblet she was holding, Evanthya threw it away, as if it had abruptly become too hot to hold.

Fetnalla felt her stomach heave.

"Evanthya?" she called. Or tried to. The name came out as softly as a sigh.

Still Evanthya seemed to hear her. And as Fetnalla convulsed, vomiting violently onto the table, her love was at her side, her slender hands gripping Fetnalla's shoulders.

All around them was turmoil and panic. Shouts of "See to the queen!" and "Someone help my lord!" filled the chamber. Fetnalla sensed people running to and fro all about them, but all she could do was stare at Evanthya's face. Her chest burned like a smith's forge and she struggled to draw breath.

"Evanthya," she whispered.

There were tears on Evanthya's face and a wild look in her eyes, such as a horse gets on a stormy night. "Yes, love. Yes. I'm here."

"I'm so sorry."

"I know. Be still now. Someone's gone to fetch the surgeon."

Fetnalla nodded, and with an effort, she tried to gaze around the chamber. Several dukes were on the floor, as was Chofya. Servants were screaming to each other, terror on their faces. She could hear people vomiting, and she felt her own stomach rise again.

Turning the other way, she saw Grigor still standing at the end of the table, his face ashen, his dark eyes as wide as a frightened child's.

Fetnalla raised a hand, the effort almost more than she could bear, and pointed at him.

"You did this," she mouthed, unable to make a sound.

The duke shook his head. "No," he said, his voice quavering. "No, I swear."

She wanted to call him a liar. She wanted to scream at him. But instead she felt herself convulse again. And as consciousness began to slip away from her, like a memory or a dream, she felt Evanthya's arms easing her down to the floor.

"Where's the surgeon?" Evanthya screamed again, through the tears running down her face.

No one answered, of course. Everyone who hadn't been poisoned was seeing to someone who had. All of the servants had escaped harm, saved by their low station. A few of the ministers had waited for their dukes to drink before doing so themselves, and thus had been spared as well. Pronjed appeared to be fine, and though this raised Evanthya's suspicions, she was hardly in a position to make accusations.

Still, she felt certain that Fetnalla had spoken for all of them when she accused Grigor. Pronjed had barked an order to the castle guards, and four of them now stood around the duke of Solkara, swords drawn and pressed against his back and chest.

Fetnalla was still breathing, but barely, the rise and fall of her chest nearly imperceptible in the torchlight. Tebeo was on his back as well, but still conscious. He had taken but a small sip of the wine and had been in the process of swallowing when the queen cried out. He managed to cough up most of what he drank, and had emptied his stomach of the rest. If any of those who had taken the wine were to survive, the duke would be one of them. Evanthya had gone to his side after laying Fetnalla on the floor, but he had waved her away.

"I'll be fine, First Minister," he had whispered. "Tend to the others. Tend to Brall and Fetnalla."

Brall had collapsed to the floor some time before and had not moved since. One of the servants was laying wet cloths on his brow, but Evanthya feared the worst.

At last, the master surgeon burst into the room, followed by a number of his assistants, an older man who had to be the castle herbmaster, and several Qirsi. *Let them be healers*, Evanthya prayed silently, knowing that Carden had no Qirsi healers in the castle, but hoping that at least one of the gods might hear her.

The master surgeon hurried to the queen, but the other surgeons and the Qirsi began to move among those lying on the chamber floor. One of them, a young Qirsi wearing ministerial robes, knelt beside Evanthya and looked down at Fetnalla.

"Are you a healer?"

"Not by trade, but I have the power. How is she?"

"She's having trouble breathing. She's barely moved in some time." Evanthya started to say more, but then began to cry.

"All right," he said. "Let me see what I can do."

She made room for the man and watched as he closed his eyes and laid his hands on Fetnalla's chest and stomach.

One of the Eandi surgeons was kneeling beside Brall, a deep frown on his face. But he wasn't giving up on the duke, and Evanthya took that as a good sign.

"What was it?" the master surgeon called out.

Looking up, Evanthya saw the herbmaster sniffing at one of the goblets.

"I can't be certain," the old man said. "But if I had to guess, I'd say it was oleander."

"Oleander? That doesn't even grow here. You'd have to go south of Noltierre to find any in Aneira."

"Not today, you wouldn't," Evanthya heard herself say.

Both men stared at her.

"The funeral. It was all over the great hall and the cloister."

The herbmaster nodded. "Of course."

Oleander was also known as Bian's Rose because it was used so often in funeral settings for kings and queens. Despite its noxious qualities, it was a beautiful shrub that remained green throughout the year and could be made to bloom even during the snows if taken inside and cared for properly.

"In that case, herbmaster," the surgeon said, "bring me all the pink madder you have. That may be the only way to keep the palsy from their lungs."

The old man nodded and rushed away. The surgeon turned to one of the servants. "Bring tea. Uulranni, if you have it. Otherwise Caerissan will do. Make it strong and make a lot of it."

This man too offered a quick nod and then left to do the surgeon's bidding.

Evanthya turned back to the young Qirsi healer kneeling beside Fetnalla. "Is she going to . . . ?" She stopped, unsure of what she wanted to say, and almost afraid to hear his reply to any question she might ask.

He shook his head, his eyes still closed. "I don't know yet. A healer's touch only goes so deep. She'll probably need the madder and tea, just like the others."

Evanthya began to nod, then stopped herself, realizing that he couldn't see her anyway. As she continued to kneel there, watching the healer, Pronjed walked past her to where Grigor still stood, surrounded by the guards.

The duke of Solkara's face had regained little of its color, but he held himself straight-backed and proud, as befitted a man seeking the throne.

"You honestly believed you could do this and go unpunished?" Pronjed said, stopping just beside him. "You thought you could poison the queen?"

"I've poisoned no one," Grigor said, gazing straight ahead.

"Come now, Lord Solkara. You want us to believe that you came through this ordeal unharmed by sheer good fortune?"

He did turn at that, a sneer on his fine features. "You're fine, Archminister." He gestured at Evanthya. "So is she. Several Qirsi survived this," he went on, looking around the chamber. "I don't hear you accusing them."

"None of the Qirsi in this room seek to take the throne from the queen and her child. None of us has sworn to defy this council."

"Perhaps not, but all of us know of the conspiracy. And all of us know that poison in the weapon of a Qirsi. An Eandi uses his sword and his strength. I have no need for magic and potions."

Evanthya saw at least one of the guards waver.

"Hold your place!" Pronjed commanded, seeing it as well. "You serve the queen, not this man!" He lifted Grigor's goblet and sniffed it. Then he held it out to the duke. "Drink this."

"Are you mad?" the surgeon said from across the room. "I've already got more patients than I can handle. I won't allow you to poison another man, no matter what you think he's done."

A cold smile touched Pronjed's lips. "He won't be poisoned, you fool. That's the whole point. There is no poison in this cup."

"Then you drink it," Grigor said.

Pronjed raised an eyebrow. "Very well." Throwing back his head, he drained the goblet, wiped a drop of wine from the corner of his mouth, and returned the cup to the table. "You see?" he said. "No poison."

"How did you know?" the surgeon asked, his voice low.

Pronjed didn't take his eyes off the duke. "I saw him drink with the others just after the toast." He stared at Grigor briefly. "Tell me, Lord Solkara. You're so convinced that a Qirsi is behind this. Are you willing to drink from my cup as I just have from yours?" He gestured toward Evanthya. "Will you drink from this woman's, or from any of the others meant for Qirsi lips?"

Grigor swallowed and looked away. "No," he whispered.

"I see."

"But I'm telling you," the duke said a moment later, raising his eyes again, "I didn't poison anyone. I had no need. A majority of the Council was prepared to support me."

"But if they hadn't been, then you would have killed them. Is that what you mean?"

"Of course not. I'm just saying—"

"I've heard enough," Pronjed said, turning his back on the duke and returning to the queen. "Take him to the prison tower. He's a duke, and should be treated as such. Don't put him in the dungeon, but be certain to chain him to the wall, feet and hands. He has allies in this castle, and I don't want them winning his freedom."

Two of the guards sheathed their weapons, grabbed the duke's arms, and started dragging him toward the door.

"Release me!" Grigor shouted, struggling to break free. "I didn't poison anyone!"

Pronjed didn't even look at him again. None of them did.

"Let go of me!" he yelled, as the soldiers pulled him into the corridor. "I didn't do this! I swear it on the memory of my brother!"

"The man knows no shame," the archminister said in a low voice, as the duke's cries continued to echo through the castle halls. "He'll hang before long."

Evanthya had little sympathy for Grigor, but she couldn't help feeling that his denials had the ring of truth to them. Again she found herself wondering if there might have been more to Pronjed's escape than mere good fortune.

In the next instant, the herbmaster returned bearing several vials of ground madder root, and almost immediately after, several servants arrived with steaming pots of tea. The surgeon had the herbmaster mix the root right into the tea, and then directed the servants and healers to administer the tea to all who had ingested the poison.

Evanthya helped the young Qirsi lift Fetnalla into a sitting position and held her there as the man gently spooned tea into her mouth. At first the tea just dribbled down the woman's chin, staining her ministerial robes. She felt cold to the touch, and Evanthya feared that they had lost her already. Finally, though, Fetnalla seemed to swallow a small amount. A moment later she began to cough and retch. But her eyes fluttered open briefly, and when the healer offered more tea, she swallowed.

"Gods be praised," Evanthya whispered.

The healer glanced at her. "Indeed."

An Eandi surgeon tending to Brall called for assistance, and the healer handed the spoon to Evanthya.

"But I don't know—"

"There's no secret to it. Just keep giving the tea to her. As much as you can make her drink." He smiled kindly. "You'll do fine."

After a moment, she nodded. She began to feed Fetnalla the tea, which was the color of rusty iron and smelled slightly bitter, though she couldn't tell if that was the tea itself, or the madder root that had been added to it. For a long time she gave little thought to what was happening around her, giving all her attention to Fetnalla and the tea. The color started to return to the woman's face, and her breathing gradually grew less labored. She didn't open her eyes again, nor did she say anything or give any indication that she knew Evanthya was there. But she was alive, and with all that had happened, Evanthya could hardly ask for more. Eventually, Fetnalla refused more tea and Evanthya allowed her to lie down once more. She gazed at Fetnalla's face for a few moments, then rose, her knees stiff and sore, and walked to where the healer and a surgeon were spooning tea into Brall's mouth. The duke was drinking as well, though his face remained deathly pale and shiny with sweat.

"She stopped taking it," Evanthya said. "I think she looks better."

The healer glanced quickly at Fetnalla. "You're right, she does. Well done."

"How's the duke?"

The man shrugged. "He's taking the tea, which is something."

"Do you need my help?"

"No, but others might. Go ask the master surgeon."

She walked to the end of the table, where the master surgeon was overseeing the care of the queen. There were two other surgeons there, as well as a Qirsi healer. Circling the room once, she found that all those who had survived the poisoning thus far were being treated. She returned to Tebeo, who was still on his back, his eyes closed, and a hand resting under his head.

"My lord?"

He opened one eye. "Yes, Evanthya. What news of the queen?"

She sat beside him. "The master surgeon says it's too soon to know. She takes the tea, but her breathing is still weak and her face is grey."

"Demons and fire," the duke muttered. "What about Brall and Fetnalla?"

"The duke is much the same as the queen. Fetnalla took some tea and has better color than before."

"I suppose that's something at least. And the others?"

"Lord Tounstrel is dead, my lord, and Lord Noltierre is failing."

Tebeo closed his eyes. "Vidor and Bertin. No one hated the Solkarans more. Except maybe poor Chago, and they already took care of him."

"The first ministers of Kett, Rassor, and Bistari are dead as well."

"I'm sorry, Evanthya," he said, opening his eyes again. "Did you know them well?"

"Not very, my lord."

"Still. This will be remembered as one of Aneira's darkest nights. I expect such things from the Eibitharians, but for one Aneiran noble to do this to others . . ." He let the thought go unfinished, shaking his head.

"Have you had enough of the tea, my lord? I know that you're better off than most, but you did drink some of the poison."

He made a sour face. "I've had more than enough. I never liked Uul-ranni tea to begin with. The madder root just makes it worse."

Evanthya smiled, as if at a complaining child. "The taste is secondary, my lord."

"I know, Evanthya. I've had plenty. I promise."

"Very well." She started to stand again, then stopped herself. "My lord, thank you for letting me go to Fetnalla. I'm sure she would have survived anyway, but I was able to help her. I'll always be grateful to you for that."

"You're welcome."

She tried to stand a second time, but the duke grabbed her arm.

"Grigor will hang for this, First Minister. I'll see to it. I swear it to all the gods who'll listen, he'll hang."

They had placed Grigor in the topmost chamber of the prison tower, manacles on his wrists and ankles holding him to the stone wall facing the iron door. The room was semicircular, with two narrow windows at opposite ends of the arcing wall and a single sputtering torch mounted on the wall just to the left of the door. The room was clean and smelled only of torch smoke and his own sweat. Still, there could be no mistaking it for anything but what it was: a prison. As boys, he and Carden had often played in the tower, pretending to be archers in this very room. Never in his wildest imaginings, though, had he thought to be a prisoner in the castle of his ancestors.

He felt certain that Chofya's Qirsi had done this to him. Who else could hope to gain so much by turning the entire Council against him?

Chofya herself, perhaps. But while she might have harbored ambitions for her daughter, or even herself, he knew she wasn't capable of this. It had to be the archminister.

Knowing this did little to help him, however. Unless he could convince someone else, someone other than his brothers, he would be executed before the end of the waning.

He heard footsteps on the tower stairs and strained to see through the small barred grate at the top of the door.

After a moment a guard appeared, and with him Numar.

"I'll have to take your weapons, my lord," the soldier said.

Numar nodded. "Of course."

Grigor heard the ring of steel as his brother drew his sword and dagger and handed them to the man. The door swung open and Numar stepped into the room. After a moment the door closed again and the lock was thrown.

"I'll be at the base of the tower if you need anything, my lord."

"Yes, thank you," Numar said, walking slowly around the chamber. He stopped at one of the small windows and stared out into the night. "I remember this window offering a fine view by day," he said, looking over at Grigor for just an instant.

"I sent for Henthas," Grigor said. "Where is he?"

Numar gazed out the window for another few seconds, then resumed his pacing. "Ah, poor Henthas. He thinks you might really have done this, though he's not certain. And he fears that the soldiers will come for him as well, seeing him as your closest ally in Solkara. At this point, he doesn't know whether to raise the Renbrere army and attack this tower, or disguise himself as a cloister adherent and flee the castle." He faced Grigor again. "How is it that I became the Fool and not him?"

In that instant Grigor knew. He felt as though he had been kicked in the groin.

"It was you," he breathed.

"I don't know what you're talking about," Numar said with a grin that gave the lie to his denial.

"You killed all those people, just to keep me from the throne."

"First of all, I doubt very much that I killed all of them. I used a fairly light hand. Some of the older dukes might die, and a few Qirsi. But Chofya ought to survive, and most of the Council."

"You're mad."

"Second of all," he went on, ignoring Grigor for the moment, "there was more to this than just keeping you from the throne. I expect they'll make the girl queen now, and who do you think they'll trust with her regency. Henthas? He's another jackal, just like you. But I'm only a fool. And when they realize that I'm really quite intelligent, they'll probably beg me to serve."

"They'll find out. You won't be able to hide this forever."

"Why not? You think they'll listen to you?"

"Someone will." But even saying the words, Grigor knew it wasn't true.

"You know better," Numar said. "You made this possible for me years ago. You and Carden, and even Henthas, I suppose. The Jackals and the Fool. You've hanged yourself, Grigor. It's not just that the other nobles believe you're capable of poisoning those dukes. It's that they want to believe it. You've spent so much of your life making them fear you, that you never thought to make them like you." He smiled again. "They despise you, brother. Bards will write songs of the day you hang. People will dance in the streets. It hardly matters who put the oleander in their goblets. You tied your own noose years ago."

His brother had planned it perfectly, Grigor realized. Like a Qirsi magician entertaining children, he had deceived all of them, making them see just what he wanted them to see.

"What is it you want, Numar?" he asked, feeling the metal bite at his wrists, desperate now for anyway out of this.

"The same as you. I'm Tomaz's son, too, remember? I want to sit on Father's throne. The difference between us is that I'm patient enough to allow the girl to get me there."

"If you kill her as well, someone's bound to figure out all of this."

"It won't matter by then. I'll have the Council, and I'll have the army."

"I can help you with that. No one will ever trust me with the throne now, or the regency. But they still fear me. They will even more after this. With me at your side, no one will ever think to challenge you."

Numar stepped closer, stopping just in front of him, the smile still on his lips. "I'm sorry, Grigor, but I know you too well. You could never bring yourself to accept me as your king. Sooner or later you'd try to have me killed. For now, you're much more valuable to me in chains. And though I hate to see another Solkaran die, I'll feel a good bit safer once you've been executed."

Screaming his rage, Grigor launched himself at the man, only to find that the chains held him fast. Numar stood just beyond his reach.

"As I said, you're much more valuable to me in chains."

He turned away and walked to the door.

"Guard!" he called.

"I'll stop you, Numar. I'll find a way. And when I do, I'll kill you myself."

Numar glanced back at him and grinned, saying nothing.

"The man's a murderer!" Grigor shouted as the guard appeared. "He poisoned your queen and the Council of Dukes! Don't let him out of here!"

The guard unlocked the door and opened it for Numar.

"Thank you," Numar said. He stopped in the corridor outside the door, gazing back at Grigor as the guard locked the door again. "Take care of him," he said. "I know what he's done. But he was once a noble of House Solkara. Even with the shame he's brought upon us, we must never forget that."

"Yes, my lord."

"He's lying! He's betrayed our house, our realm! You must believe me!"

The guard didn't even look at him, and Grigor's words echoed through the tower like a rumble of thunder that brings no rain, the desperate, empty cries of a condemned man.

Chapter
Sixteen

✦

City of Kings, Eibithar

he snows came to southern Eibithar just after dawn on the tenth day of Bohdan's waning. Unlike most years, when the new season arrived with screaming winds and a blinding, frenzied swirl of snow, this year it came softly and silently.

Keziah was still in bed when the snowfall began, though she was awake, her eyes wandering her room as she summoned the courage to leave the warmth of her blankets. Hearing laughter rise to her chamber from the ward below her window, she climbed from bed, wrapped herself in a robe, and stepped to the window. Opening the wood shutters, she saw tiny white flakes falling from a sky of deep somber grey and covering the castle grounds as sawdust coats the floor of a carpenter's shop. The air was perfectly still, and she could hear the light scratching of the icy snow alighting on the castle walls and roofs.

She was shivering. With the window open and her fire having burned out during the night, her chamber quickly grew as frigid as the kitchen-master's cellars. Still, the minister couldn't bring herself to close her shutters again. Instead, she sat on the sill of her window and watched the snow fall, remembering how she and Grinsa had played in drifts on the steppe as children. Like the other castle children, they had spent much time throwing balls of snow and ice at one another, their hands growing numb and sore long before they tired of the sport. At other times, though, when they were alone, they practiced their magic on the pure white fields of Eardley's outer wards. Young as they were, they hadn't the power to shape wood. But they could trace patterns in the snow with their minds, drawing flowers, horses, and portraits of each other. As in everything else, Grinsa was better at this than she, though he was always quick to praise her efforts. They spent hours this way, alone, laughing and learning together. And when they were done, fearing that they might be punished for using their powers before their apprenticeships, they would stomp through the snow, erasing all evidence of what they had done. The Qirsi shortened their lives just a bit every time they used their magic, and the danger was greatest for children who had no training in how to control their power and use it sparingly. Had their parents learned of what they were doing, they would have forbidden the children from playing in the snow at all, or worse, kept Keziah and Grinsa apart from each other until the thaw. Such was the danger of the games they played.

Thinking of Grinsa, her mind turned southward, to Aneira and all that she had heard recently of events there. It had been some time since her brother last entered her dreams, and Keziah wondered where he was and whether he and Tavis of Curgh were any closer to finding Brienne's killer. She still wished that Grinsa hadn't gone with the boy. For all her brother's power, she didn't like the idea of him tracking a hired blade.

Someone knocked at her door, forcing her abruptly from her musings and memories. Pulling her robe tighter around her shoulders and passing a hand through her tangled white hair, she faced the door.

"Who's there?"

"It's Paegar."

Keziah smiled. In a castle and city that had long seemed empty of warmth and companionship, the high minister had in recent days become her closest friend, really her only friend. They had spent a good deal of time together since the waning began, talking as they walked through the corridors and wards, and laughing in the kitchens over midday meals. The night before, they had left the castle for a Qirsi tavern Paegar knew in the northern quarter of the marketplace. Keziah hadn't been to a tavern in years. In Glyndwr, as Kearney's first minister and lover, she had rarely left his side, much less his castle. Though she missed terribly the nights they spent together, she had found herself reveling in the freedom of being able to leave the confines of the castle walls and breathe in the life she found in the city. For too long, Keziah realized the previous night, she had allowed herself to steep like tea leaves in the grief that followed Kearney's ascension and the end of their love affair. Without saying a word, perhaps without even knowing it, Paegar had helped her see this. All it had taken was a friend inviting her to live again, to find mirth and good company without the man with whom she had shared her bed. She hadn't known how to thank the minister, and in a sense, she didn't have to. It was enough that they enjoyed their time together.

"Come in!" she said. Then remembering that the door was bolted, she crossed the room and unlocked it.

"Good morning, Paegar," she said, waving him into the room.

He smiled. "And to you, Archminister." Noticing her robe, he halted, his face falling. "Did I wake you?"

"Not at all. I was watching the snow."

He raised an eyebrow. "That would explain why yours is the only chamber in the castle in which I can see my breath."

Keziah gave a small laugh. "I know. I should start a new fire." She turned to face the window again and sighed. "But isn't it lovely? I've missed the snows."

"Spoken like a woman raised on the steppe. To me the snows are a bother. I never feel so old as I do in the cold turns."

She walked back to the window to push the shutters closed again. "You're not old, Paegar," she said, glancing back at him. "Not even for a Qirsi."

The high minister had stepped to the hearth and was piling new wood for a fire. "You're most kind, Archminister, but I'm a good deal older than you and far closer to the end of my life than I am to the beginning of it."

Bolting the shutters, she turned to look at the man. In many ways he reminded Keziah of her father. Like Dafydd, and unlike most older Qirsi, he had a full, healthy face. To be sure, there were lines around his eyes and the corners of his mouth, but his cheeks weren't sunken like those of some, and his color remained a healthy white, rather than the sallow yellow that crept into the faces of Qirsi nearing the end of their lives.

"I'd say you have some years left," she told him with a grin. "I expect you to be showing me the city's better taverns for a long time to come."

"Hardly a pursuit worthy of the king's ministers." Paegar placed one last log in the hearth and sat back on his heels. "The wood is ready, Archminister, but I'm afraid I don't have fire magic. Only gleaning and mists and winds." He gestured toward the hearth. "Can you?"

She shook her head. "I'm afraid not. Gleaning, mists and winds, and language of beasts. How embarrassing. Here we are, two of the king's most trusted Qirsi, and between us we can't even light a fire."

Paegar grinned. "Indeed." He glanced around the chamber, but Keziah kept no candles or lamps burning during the night.

"Wait just a moment," Keziah said. She stepped into the corridor, lit a tinder with the torch mounted by her door, and, returning to the hearth, handed it to the minister.

Watching him light the fire, she had to smile at what had just passed between them. She usually told no one what powers she possessed. Grinsa knew, of course, and Kearney, but that was all. Since Paegar had confided in her, however, she felt that she should do the same. More than that, though, she wanted to tell him. She viewed it as a measure of how quickly their friendship was deepening that they could share this so soon.

Which raised another point. "You need to stop calling me Archminister, Paegar. Please."

"It wouldn't be appropriate for me to call you Keziah in front of the king or the other ministers," he said, standing once more.

She considered this. "All right, but certainly there's no harm in it when we're alone."

Paegar shrugged, looking uncomfortable. "I suppose not."

In a few moments, the fire in her hearth was burning bright and hot, warming the chamber.

"Thank you, Paegar," she said. "But I can't imagine you came here only to build a fire for me."

His ears turned red, though he managed a smile. "No, I didn't. I was hoping you'd join me for a quick breakfast in the kitchens before we meet with the king."

"Of course," she said. "I need to dress first. Will you wait for me?"

His color deepened, and for the first time it occurred to Keziah that the minister might be taken with her. She felt her chest tighten. Nothing could ruin their friendship faster. Much as she already cared for him, she knew that she could never love him. She still loved Kearney; she probably always would. When she looked at Paegar she saw her father, someone to whom she could turn when her lingering love for the king became more than she could bear. She could no more fall in love with him than she could with Grinsa.

"I'll be in the hallway," he said. "Take your time."

Keziah nodded and watched him leave, feeling as though she might cry. At last she had found a friend in the City of Kings, and already she was on the verge of driving him off.

She dressed quickly, splashing cold water on her face and brushing out her hair before putting on her ministerial robes.

"Maybe I'm wrong about what he's feeling," she whispered to herself. *Maybe you're not.*

She joined him in the corridor and they walked to the kitchens, neither of them speaking.

As always the kitchens bustled with activity, even early in the morning of a day when no feasts were planned and no guests were expected to arrive. The scents of spices, baking breads, and roasting meats filled the air. People, animals, and birds ran or flew in every direction, the kitchenmaster shouted instructions to cooks and servants, and guards tried to sneak tastes of fresh loaves of bread and simmering stews.

"What do you want?" the master demanded, seeing Paegar and Keziah. "Are you here for the king or for yourselves?"

Few people spoke to Qirsi ministers in such a tone. But here, amid the food and the cooking flames, the kitchenmaster was king. He spoke to everyone with disdain and impatience. He might even have done so with Kearney, had the king the courage to venture down here.

"Ourselves," Paegar said. "We're just looking for a bit of breakfast."

The man frowned and shook his head. "Fine," he muttered. "Take what you want and get out of my kitchens."

Paegar nodded, a small grin on his face. "Of course, kitchenmaster."

The ministers gathered some breads and cheeses, and a few pieces of dried fruit, before retreating into the king's hall to eat.

"I don't think I've ever seen that man smile," Paegar said as they took seats in a corner of the hall. "He reminds me of the swordmaster in that way."

"Oh, Gershon smiles sometimes," Keziah said. "Just not at anyone with Qirsi blood."

Paegar nodded. "I see. I sensed that the two of you don't like each other, but I never understood why."

Keziah shrugged, taking a bite of bread. "There's a bit more to it than that," she said casually. Then she stopped herself, realizing where this was headed.

The high minister stopped chewing and looked at her closely. "Is something troubling you? It's the swordmaster, isn't it? I'm sorry, I shouldn't have said anything."

"No," she said, shaking her head. "It's not . . ." She shook her head a second time. "It's nothing. There are just certain things I don't think we should talk about."

Paegar dropped his gaze. "Of course. I understand."

She could hear the hurt in his voice and she cursed her own stupidity. She wasn't handling this well.

"Paegar, there's a great deal about my life in Glyndwr that you don't understand, and that I'm not certain I could ever explain."

The minister kept his eyes fixed on the food sitting before him. "I didn't intend to make you feel that you had to."

Keziah sighed, closing her eyes. Grinsa would have done this far better. "You didn't," she told him. "But I sense that you . . . that you harbor some affection for me."

He looked up at that, the bright red of his cheeks confirming her suspicions.

"I'm flattered," she went on. "Truly I am. But I've been friendless for so long, and I've so enjoyed the time we've had together these recent days. I don't want to risk losing you so soon."

"How do you know you'd lose me? Perhaps you'll fall in love with me as I have with you."

She smiled sadly. "Perhaps I would. But after all I've been through this past year, I'm not ready to try. My heart still belongs to another, and though he and I can't be together, I don't really want to stop loving him."

"Even though it pains you?"

Abruptly there were tears on her face and an ache in her chest and throat. "Yes," she whispered. "Even so."

To her amazement and her profound relief, the man actually smiled at her. "Well, I certainly hope he's worth all this. I'd hate to think that such an extraordinary woman was wasting her love on a fool."

She almost told him everything then. About Kearney and their forbidden love, and the distrust this had sown in her relations with Gershon. About how Kearney's ascension to the throne had forced them apart, though their love continued to burn, like the smouldering remains of some great fire. She longed to speak of it with someone, and it had been so many turns since she last walked in her dreams with Grinsa. But she couldn't bring herself to say the words. Maybe it was too soon after the awkwardness of the morning, or maybe, after all that she and Kearney had shared, she still felt that she owed the king her silence.

In either case, all she could do was smile at Paegar and say in a soft voice, "You're a good man, High Minister."

He gave a small shrug, looking down again. "I'll take your word for it."

They sat wordlessly for a time, Keziah taking a few bites of her meal, though she was no longer hungry. Occasionally she felt Paegar gazing at her, but she didn't look up.

"So has the king heard anything from Shanstead yet?" he finally asked.

She met his gaze, smiling gratefully. "Not yet, no. But I only sent the king's message late in the waxing. We may be well into Qirsar's Turn before we hear anything."

"You're more patient than I. I'd spend each day on the ramparts searching the horizon for any sign of a messenger."

"Actually, I'm more interested in knowing what Marston and Aindreas talked about when the thane was in Kentigern."

Their conversation went on this way for some time, until Keziah almost forgot the uneasy moments with which their meal began. Despite her earlier fears, the minister could not help but think that their friendship would survive this day, and—dare she hope it?—even grow stronger for it.

Eventually they heard the midmorning bells summoning them to their daily discussion with the king, and they left the hall to make their way to Kearney's chambers.

As they walked through the corridors, Paegar glanced at her, a shy grin on his lips. "How did you know?" he asked.

"Know what?"

"That I was falling in love with you."

Keziah smiled. "Your face gives you away, Paegar. I'm afraid you don't keep a secret very well."

"Really?" he said, looking surprised. "I'll have to remember that."

All through their audience with the king, and well after, as he walked the castle grounds alone, Paegar tried to convince himself that it was all for the best. Yes, he loved her. Keziah's efforts to discourage him that morning had done little to change the way he felt for her. Indeed, the entire time they sat in Kearney's presence chamber, he could barely take his eyes off her. She wore her hair loose this day, as she had the past two or three days, and it fell over her brow and around her shoulders like fine strands of white gold. Perhaps aware of his staring, her cheeks had more color than usual, making her pale eyes appear almost white. He had never seen her look lovelier.

He knew, however, that the wound she had inflicted on his heart would heal with time. What mattered most was that their friendship continue so that one day soon he could deliver her to the Weaver. In a way all of this would help him. From this day forward, any discomfort she sensed on his part, any dissembling that failed to deceive her, she would attribute immediately to his unrequited affections.

He would pay a price for this, he knew, but pride was the least of his faults, and the cost seemed small enough given the rewards that awaited him. Besides, once Keziah joined the Weaver's cause, Paegar would become superfluous. Two ministers in the court of Eibithar's king was a luxury even the Weaver could not afford. No doubt he would have Paegar leave for another court, one where he would be of greater value. Any love affair that might have grown from his friendship with the archminister was doomed to end quickly. Better it shouldn't begin at all.

Still, convincing her to join the Qirsi movement promised to be far more difficult now, relying on occasional conversations in castle corridors and courtyards, than it would have been in the intimacy of a lover's bed. He would have to proceed more slowly than he had first hoped, and of course, he would need to make certain that no one overheard their discussions.

Why couldn't she love me?

What disturbed him most was the possibility that the Weaver would come to him before he had a chance to turn her. He had little doubt that the Weaver would approve of his plans, but as soon as the man learned of them, he would hurry Paegar along. As powerful as he was, and as discreet as he must have been to hide his identity from those around him as well as from those whose dreams he haunted, the Weaver lacked patience. Paegar still recalled how he pushed for the murder of Aylyn the Second during the growing turns, heedless of the difficulties faced by those who had to do his bidding.

Paegar could see Keziah's conversion to the Weaver's cause taking many turns, perhaps as much as a year, not only because he saw in the process the opportunity to be with her, but also because it was bound to work better if she came to it on her own, with only gentle prodding. The Weaver, however, would expect him to take the quickest path to the same end. *Why take six turns,* he would wonder, *when it can be done in two?* And Paegar would have no answer to offer, except the one the Weaver was least likely to understand. *Because, when all is said and done. I want her to love me. Because if she senses that I befriended her on behalf of the movement, I'll lose even the small piece of her that I have now.*

The more the minister considered this, the more agitated he grew, until at last he felt that he needed to flee the castle entirely or give himself away by his pacing and his muttered curses. Striding swiftly to the nearest gate, Paegar left the castle and descended the sloped lanes to the city. Once there, he simply wandered, passing shops and taverns, peddler's carts and flocks of sheep driven toward the markets by shepherds. He walked the city's outer streets, passing all four of the sanctuaries. He briefly considered leaving the city altogether, and meandering for a time in the grasses and farmlands that lay beyond the city walls.

But as the day wore on, marked by changes in the rate of the snowfall, and the occasional tolling of the gate bells, Paegar grew increasingly uneasy. At first he merely thought it the lingering effect of his talk with Keziah. As the feeling continued to mount, however, he realized it was more than that. He might not have been the most powerful Qirsi in the castle, but he was a gleaner, and he knew this sense of foreboding had to be more than the product of a pained heart.

Stopping just at the gates of Elined's Sanctuary, he turned and started back toward the castle, walking as fast as he dared. By the time he had climbed the lane back to the castle's north gate, he was breathing hard, sweat dampening his brow in spite of the cold and snow. He hurried through the outer ward, into the castle's inner courtyards, and finally into the shelter of the corridors. Of course Keziah was the first person he saw.

"I was just coming to look for you," she said. "I was hoping we might have supper together."

He didn't even alter his stride. "Tomorrow perhaps. I've other matters to which to attend this evening."

"You don't look well, Paegar," she called to him as he walked on. "Are you all right?"

"I'm fine, Archminister. I promise. I've been out walking and I'm eager to warm myself by my hearth."

He turned a corner before she could answer, ran up the nearest stairway, and continued on to his chamber without meeting up with anyone else. His heart was pounding as he reached for the door handle, as much with fear as with the effort of returning to the castle. He hesitated a moment, then pushed open the door and stepped inside slowly.

He saw it immediately, though someone else might have missed it. A part of him had known all along what awaited him here. His thoughts had been carrying him on this path the entire day.

There on his bed, barely visible against the dark brown of his blankets, lay a small leather pouch. He wanted to leave, to turn away from the bed and hurry back out of the castle as if he had never seen the pouch, as if he had no idea what it contained or what it meant.

Instead he closed the door and sat on the bed beside it, staring at it for several moments as if he expected it to move. At last he lifted the bag into his hand, hearing the muffled ring of the coins within. It felt heavy. It must have held fifty qinde, at least. He could judge such things now. He had no idea where the movement got its gold, or how they managed to leave it in his chamber without anyone noticing. But he could gauge the contents of a leather pouch simply by its weight.

He untied the drawstrings and poured the coins onto the bed. Eighty qinde. The Weaver would be coming to him tonight, no doubt to give him some new task. Maybe he knew of Keziah already and wanted her to join the movement. Perhaps he had decided that Kearney had to die. Paegar would know soon enough.

Staring at the gold pieces lying on his bed, glimmering in the murky light of his room, Paegar didn't know whether to laugh or cry. He had no need for more gold. As high minister, his food and bed were provided by the king and he received a handsome wage as well. On occasion he liked to spend a few qinde on a good meal and ale in the city, but he avoided extravagance for fear of drawing attention to himself and his wealth. He still had more than one hundred qinde hidden away in a small wooden box in his wardrobe, gold he had yet to spend from the Weaver's previous payments. The minister served the Weaver not to gather riches, but to stay alive. The Weaver had sought him out and in so doing had tied Paegar's very survival to the success or failure of the Qirsi movement. The gold he received had become little more than a harbinger of his conversations with the Weaver.

His stomach felt empty and sour. It occurred to him that he had eaten nothing since his breakfast with the archminister.

A knock on his door made him jump. It had to be Keziah. No one else ever came to his room.

He returned the coins to the pouch as quietly and quickly as he could, and hid the bag under his pillow—*no chance of her finding it there,* he thought ruefully. He stood and took a step toward the door. Then, as an afterthought, he placed a log on the embers of his fire.

Opening his door at last, he found the archminister in the corridor, looking pale, her lips held in a tight line.

"Keziah." It was all he could think of to say.

"You're angry with me."

"No, I'm not."

She shook her head. "Don't lie to me, Paegar. You're angry about what happened this morning. I could tell by the way you rushed by me just now."

He had to smile. Just as he had expected, this was going to make it easier for him to conceal his betrayal. "I'm not angry, Keziah. I'm disappointed, and perhaps a bit embarrassed—"

"You shouldn't be," she said, her eyes growing wide. "There's no shame in this, Paegar. I just can't love you. I can't love anyone right now."

"I understand, Keziah. Honestly I do. And I'm not angry with you. I'm just not ready tonight to dine with you again. Perhaps tomorrow."

She nodded, looking sad. "Of course. I probably shouldn't have come. I just . . . I need you, Paegar. I need your friendship."

"You still have it. I assure you."

Again she nodded, turning away as she did. "Thank you, Paegar. Good night."

"Good night, Keziah."

Paegar watched her walk back toward her chamber. He had hours yet until the Weaver would come to him, and belatedly he wished that he hadn't sent the archminister away. Not that he was at all hungry, but he longed for her company.

"Keziah, wait," he called to her, just as she reached her door. "I'm being foolish. I would like to dine with you. Why don't we go back to the tavern? I'll even pay for your dinner."

She eyed him doubtfully. "Are you certain?"

"Yes." He had decided earlier in the day that his pride was to be the first casualty of his effort to win her trust. Perhaps it would take a toll on his heart as well. But that was a small price to pay for being with her. He retrieved the pouch, pulled out two gold pieces, and placed the rest in his wardrobe beside the wooden box.

He and Keziah left the castle and walked through the city streets to the Silver Maple, the Qirsi tavern in which they had eaten the previous night. The barman nodded to them as they entered and a serving girl with the white and black hair of a half-blood and bright yellow eyes led them to a small room at the back of the building. A few moments later, she returned with two tankards of ale and two steaming plates of the same spicy stew they had enjoyed the night before.

For a long time they ate in silence, looking up at each other once or twice and smiling awkwardly. Knowing that he would be speaking with the Weaver in just a short while, Paegar searched his mind for ways he might begin to broach the subject of the movement. None came to him. In the end, though, Keziah did it for him.

"Do you enjoy serving the king, Paegar?"

He looked up, surprised by the question. "Do I enjoy it?"

"Yes. You seem so solemn much of the time. I wonder if you're happy in the castle."

The minister made a show of considering the matter for several moments. "I suppose I do," he said at last. "I've never been a favorite of the kings I serve. Aylyn relied mostly on Natan and Wenda, and Kearney turns mostly to you and to Gershon. But I'm paid well, and I lead a comfortable life." He frowned. "I imagine that sounds terribly ungrateful. There are Qirsi throughout the Forelands who would gladly trade their lives for mine."

"Do you doubt that Kearney appreciates your counsel?"

"Not at all. But he's known you far longer than he has the rest of us. Like most Eandi nobles, he probably sees his other Qirsi as faceless sorcerers who aren't to be trusted."

"Kearney's not like that!" she said, her voice rising. She looked to the side, her lips pressed thin. "I'm sorry," she said a few seconds later, her voice calm once more. "But I know the king, and he's not like other Eandi. He may not know the rest of you very well yet, but he trusts you and he listens to what you tell him."

Paegar made himself smile, struggling with an unexpected bout of jealousy. "I'll take your word for it. As I've already said, you know him better than I. But I've served several Eandi nobles in my life, and in my experience, they have little regard for their Qirsi." He took a sip of ale, gazing off toward the fire burning on the far side of the room. "Just once, I'd enjoy the chance to serve in a Qirsi court." He glanced at her. "Wouldn't you?"

"I've never considered it," she said coldly.

"Oh, come now, Keziah. All of us have at one time or another."

"I'm telling you, I haven't."

"Not even when you were a child?"

She hesitated. "Well—"

"You see? I knew it!"

Keziah shook her head. "That's different."

"Why? Because you were too young to know any better? Nonsense. In many ways the dreams of our childhood are more honest, because as children we haven't been taught yet which dreams are permissible and which aren't."

She eyed him warily. "It seems you've given this a good deal of thought, Paegar."

He smiled broadly, ignoring the slight flutter in his chest. "Not so much, really. When I was younger I thought often of going to the Southlands, to see what the Qirsi homeland is like. But that's a long way from here, and at this point I'm a bit old to try crossing the Border Range."

"That's not what I meant, and I think you know it. We've all heard the rumors, Paegar. There are those here among us who would like to remake the Forelands in the image of the Southlands. And you should make no mistake, if I learn that you're one of them, I'll destroy you."

He laughed. "You believe I'm with the conspiracy?"

Her gaze didn't waver for an instant. "I didn't say that. But I want you to understand that I don't take lightly talk of Qirsi courts and serving Qirsi lords. We live in the Forelands. The kingdoms belong to the Eandi. Given the history of our people in the seven realms we're fortunate to serve them as we do."

"I'll remember that, Archminister."

She didn't correct him. And for a long time, she kept her gaze fixed on her food.

"I'm feeling tired," she finally said. "I think I'd like to return to the castle now."

Paegar nodded. His stomach had balled itself into a fist, and his head was pounding. Clearly he had miscalculated badly, and in a short time he would have to face the Weaver, far less certain of the prize he intended to offer the man than he had been just a short time before.

They made their way back to Audun's Castle without a word passing between them. He walked her to her door, where they stopped and faced each other.

"This has been a difficult day," she said, her voice so low he could barely hear her.

It's not over. Not nearly. "I'm sorry for that."

Keziah shook her head. "Don't be. It's not your fault. Sleep well, Paegar. Tomorrow can only be better."

"Goodnight, Keziah."

He left her there and returned to the darkness of his chamber, locking his door behind him. The fire had burned down again, though the embers still glowed an angry red. He put wood on the coals and then lay on his bed, not bothering to undress. His mind raced, and a part of him wondered if he could stay awake through the night, postponing at least for one day his encounter with the Weaver. As he lay in the shadows cast by his fire, though, feeling the chamber gradually grow warmer, Paegar's fear of the Weaver began to give way to weariness. A difficult day, she had called it. Indeed it had been.

He didn't realize he was asleep until the dream began, and he found himself stumbling over boulders on the grassy plain. Soon he reached the slope and started to climb. The ascent was not long this time, although he was winded when he reached the summit and saw the Weaver approaching, his body a living shadow against the brilliant light. The same dream every time, yet filled with so much uncertainty that Paegar trembled.

"You were paid?" the Weaver demanded, stopping before him.

"Yes, Weaver. Thank you."

"Good. You've heard of the death of Aneira's king?"

"Word of it reached the castle several nights ago."

"There is a fight looming for the throne, just as you might expect. Carden's only heir is a girl, not yet of age. Carden's brother seeks the crown as his own, but the other houses fear him and may challenge the Solkaran Supremacy. I want you to counsel your king to make overtures to the other houses. Tell him that the end of Solkaran rule could bring peace to the Tarbin. With all that Eibithar has been through in the past year, the idea should interest him."

"Do you believe any house in Aneira would be moved by overtures from Eibithar's king?"

"That's my concern," the Weaver said, his voice edged with steel.

"Of course, Weaver. Forgive me."

"You understand what I want?"

"Yes, Weaver."

The man nodded once.

"I've befriended the king's archminister!" Paegar said quickly, fearing that the Weaver intended to end their conversation. Immediately he wished that he had kept silent. Keziah would never join the movement. But he had been planning this for so long, and if the Weaver believed there was any chance the minister could win her over, he might leave Paegar alone for a time.

"Well, by all means, seek her help in this matter," the Weaver said, sounding impatient. "Such counsel will carry more weight coming from two of you."

"You misunderstand, Weaver." He winced at his choice of words, but forced himself to continue. "She was once the king's lover. Before, when he was duke. And now she's not. She has few friends in the castle—the other ministers were angered when Kearney made her archminister instead of Wenda. They treat her poorly."

"What is your point?" the man asked, biting off each word.

"With time, I think she could be persuaded to join the movement." He was lying to a Weaver. He must have been a fool.

For several moments the Weaver said nothing. Then, "You believe Kearney's archminister can be turned?"

"I do."

"I sense something else in your thoughts."

Paegar swallowed, fearing that he was about to die.

"You love her."

He would have to remember to say a quick prayer of thanks to Adriel when this night was over. "Yes, Weaver. Very much."

"But she doesn't love you."

Paegar shook his head.

Again the Weaver fell silent, standing motionless for so long that the minister began to wonder if he thought this a worthless pursuit, born of Paegar's fruitless love. But the man surprised him.

"Such things are never easy," he said softly. "Do what you can with the minister. We'll speak again soon and you can tell me what progress you've made. Maybe we can turn her together."

His blood turned cold at the thought of enduring another of these dreams so soon, but all he could do was nod. "Yes, Weaver. Again, thank you."

He expected to awaken then, as he always did when his dreams of the Weaver ended. But the two of them continued to stand there, almost as if the Weaver had forgotten him.

And perhaps he had. For in the next instant the brilliant light blazing behind the Weaver dimmed, so that rather than blinding him, it offered a softer glow by which to see much that he had missed before. It lasted only a moment, but that was enough. Or rather, it was too much. For just an instant, no longer than the flicker of a single lightning strike on a warm night, Paegar looked upon the Weaver's face. A square face, golden yellow eyes like those of a wild cat, straight nose and full lips. All framed by the wild white hair that always danced in the wind of this plain. This plain, which ran eastward to the Scabbard and overlooked the dark mass of Eibithar beyond the water. Ayvencalde Moor.

Paegar gasped. The Weaver's eyes widened. The light flared again, but too late. Both of them knew it.

"Stand," the Weaver said.

"I am standing, Weaver," he whispered.

"Only in this dream. Stand up from your bed."

Without knowing how he did it, Paegar felt himself stand up, though his mind still saw only the plain and the Weaver. Ayvencalde Moor, and a man with golden eyes.

"The woman of whom you spoke, what's her name?"

"Keziah. Keziah ja Dafydd."

"Thank you." The Weaver seemed to hesitate. "I'm sorry for this," he said. "Truly I am. Your love for this woman reminded me . . . I was careless, and now you must suffer for that. You've served me well. Take that with you."

Paegar didn't know what to say, and even if he had, terror and grief would have held his tongue.

"It will be quick."

Almost before he understood what the Weaver had said, he felt himself being grabbed from behind. He didn't know who or what had him; the Weaver hadn't moved. The unseen hands held him still for an instant; then he was thrown forward and down with dizzying force. He plunged toward the ground, but then suddenly found himself back in his room in Audun's Castle. And instead of the grasses of the plain rising to meet him, he saw the blunt stone edge of his hearth.

Chapter
Seventeen

✦

fter their strange conversation in the tavern the previous night, Keziah was relieved not to see Paegar when she emerged from her chamber the following morning. She managed to avoid him in the kitchens and hall as well, eating a light breakfast before returning to her room. When the midmorning bells tolled from the gates of the city wall, their sound muffled by the thin coating of snow that now lay over the City of Kings and Audun's Castle, she made her way to Kearney's chambers, expecting at any moment to hear the high minister calling to her. Still she didn't see him, and Keziah began to wonder if she had angered him with her passionate defense of the Eandi.

It was only during the ministerial audience with the king that Paegar's absence began to concern her. Even if he was angry with her, even if his pride still suffered from her rejection of his advances, he would have attended the audience. True, she had known him only a few turns, but in that time she couldn't remember him missing a single discussion with Kearney.

No one else appeared to notice. They spoke of the thane of Shanstead, and word from the west that Kentigern's captains were mustering in hundreds of new soldiers from the countryside surrounding the tor. But no one commented on the fact that the high minister had not joined them.

Finally, at the end of the discussion, as the other ministers stood to leave, Keziah asked, "Has anyone seen Paegar this morning?"

The king, who had already returned to his writing table to look over some recent messages, glanced up at her, a slight frown on his face. "Isn't he here?"

"No, Your Majesty," she answered, unable to mask entirely her exasperation. "I haven't seen him at all today."

"Nor have I," Wenda said.

The others shook their heads.

Kearney raised his eyebrows. "Perhaps you should go to his quarters, Archminister. He may be ill."

Keziah nodded. "Yes, Your Majesty. I'll go right away."

By the time she reached his room, Keziah was truly frightened. She tried to tell herself that he was probably avoiding her, or maybe even punishing her with his absence. She sensed, however, that there was more to it than that. She couldn't say why; it was just a feeling. Such was the magic of a gleaner. Among her powers, it was the one she liked least. It might warn her of danger, but it often brought grief and fear before she knew why.

She knocked on his door with a trembling hand. No answer came. She tried the handle, but it was locked.

"Paegar?"

Nothing.

She ran to the nearest tower and called for a guard. In moments, two of Kearney's men answered her summons and followed her back to the high minister's quarters.

"It's locked," she told them, her voice quavering.

One of the men pounded a fist on the door. "High Minister?" When Paegar didn't answer, the guard tried the door, then looked at Keziah. "Perhaps he's gone, Archminister."

"Gone?"

"Maybe he's left the castle."

It was the one possibility she hadn't considered, but she dismissed it almost immediately. He wouldn't have gone to the city if it meant missing the audience with Kearney. And he wouldn't have left for good without a word, or at least a note, for her.

She shook her head. "No. He's in there. You have to open the door."

"We haven't a key, Minister."

"Then find one," she commanded, her voice rising.

One of the men ran off. Keziah leaned against the wall by the door, her arms crossed in front of her chest. She tried to calm herself, to stop the shivering and the fluttering of her stomach, but her apprehension only grew.

After what felt to her like hours, the guard finally returned with two more men, one of them carrying a ring of keys.

"It might be one of these," this man said. "I'm not certain."

He began trying them one by one, a process that had Keziah ready to scream in frustration after only a few moments.

"This is ridiculous!" she said. "For all we know he could be dying in there." *He could already be dead.* "Open this door right now!"

"But, Archminister—"

"Break it if you have to, but I want it open!"

The guards looked at one another briefly. Then one of them shrugged. "All right," he said. "You heard her."

The others moved away, and he rushed the door, crashing into it with his shoulder. It took four or five blows, but finally the bolt gave way, the corridor echoing with the sound of rending wood.

"Demons and fire!" the man breathed, staring into the room.

Keziah pushed past him, then fell to her knees with a sob.

Paegar lay facedown upon his hearth, his head resting in a pool of blood, his arms lying at his side, palms up.

The guard stepped forward cautiously, as if afraid the high minister might suddenly move. He squatted beside Paegar and slowly turned him over, exhaling sharply through his teeth. Keziah turned her head away, though not before seeing that the impact had crushed the minister's face right across his eyes and the bridge of his nose. She felt her stomach heave and had to clamp her mouth shut to keep from being sick.

"Oh, Paegar," she whispered, her tears staining the stone floor like raindrops on a city lane. "I'm so sorry." What had she said to him the previous night? *Tomorrow can only be better.* She'd never been more wrong about anything in all her life.

The guard lowered the minister's body to the floor again so that it lay just as it had when they entered the room.

"Better get the surgeon," the guard said. "And the swordmaster as well. He'll want to see this."

Other guards stepped into the chamber, but Keziah remained where she was, on her knees in the middle of the room. The men walked around her, seeming to know better than to ask her to move. Eventually she heard a familiar voice and realized that Gershon had come, and with him the master healer.

The swordmaster bent down to look at the body, rolling Paegar over much as the guard had a short while earlier. After a few moments he glanced at Keziah.

"You didn't hear anything?"

She shook her head and wiped the tears from her face. "Nothing at all."

"When did you see him last?"

"Last night. We went to a tavern in the city." She closed her eyes. "I should have come for him before meeting with Kearney."

"It wouldn't have mattered."

She opened her eyes again.

"Look at the blood," he said, pointing to the dark edges of the stain on the stone floor. "It's already drying. This happened hours ago. He probably awoke in the night to a cold room, got up to add wood to his fire, and fell."

"That must have been some fall," the surgeon said, standing over them and gazing down at Paegar's face.

"What else could it have been?" Gershon asked. "The door was locked from the inside. . . ."

Even as he spoke the words, the swordmaster seemed to falter. Keziah knew why. The words came back to her as well. Lady Brienne of Kentigern had been murdered in a locked room as well, and though her father blamed Tavis of Curgh, Grinsa had convinced Keziah, Kearney, and Gershon that the boy was innocent, and someone else to blame.

"Could this have been done with magic?" Gershon asked her.

She considered the question for several moments. "I don't see how."

Gershon looked up at the surgeon. "Is it possible someone hit him with something, then put him here to make it look like he had fallen?"

The man shook his head and knelt beside Keziah. "Look at the way the blood has splattered here," he said, pointing to the edge of the hearth. "That's where his head hit. I'm sure of it. I didn't mean to say he couldn't have fallen—I think it likely that he did. I just meant that I've rarely seen a simple fall result in such a severe wound."

Gershon nodded. "I see." Keziah could tell, though, that he still had his doubts. He took a breath and looked at the archminister again. "I should inform the king. Are you all right?"

She hesitated, surprised by the question. "I will be."

He glanced at the body once more, then left the room. The guards continued to step around Keziah, and she decided that she should leave as well. There was little she could do here but get in their way.

She returned to her chamber and sat on her bed. She felt that she should have been crying again, but the tears wouldn't come. She was just cold and terribly tired, though she had slept well the previous night. After a time, she lay down again and almost immediately fell into a deep sleep. She dreamed of Paegar, not bloody and ruined as she had just seen him, but whole and smiling as he had been such a short time before. She saw herself with him, as if she were looking from outside her own body. They were in the castle gardens together, talking and laughing. She strained to hear what they were saying, but the wind was rustling the brown leaves on the shrubs and ivy, and birds were calling from overhead. She couldn't hear any of it. She called to Paegar and the dream Keziah to wait for her, to let her walk with them, but they ignored her, still laughing.

The minister awoke to pounding on her door, unsure of how long she had slept. Running her hands through her hair, she rose and crossed to the door.

"Who is it?"

"Gershon Trasker."

She unlocked the door and pulled it open.

"Good thing you answered," the swordmaster said, frowning at her. "I was about to think we had to break in another door."

"What do you want, swordmaster?"

"The king wants to speak with you. I think he's called for all his Qirsi."

"All right." It almost seemed like she was still dreaming, so fogged was her mind. "What's the time?" she asked as they started walking toward Kearney's chambers.

"It's almost time for the prior's bells."

Keziah took a breath. She had slept away much of the day.

The other ministers were already with the king when they arrived. Kearney looked up when Keziah and Gershon walked in, his eyes meeting hers. She read his concern in the furrowing of his brow, and she nodded, as if to say that she was all right.

She sat, as did Gershon, and the king stepped to the center of the room.

"By now you've all heard what's happened," he began. "Paegar jal Berget, our high minister, fell in his quarters last night, hit his head on the hearth, and died." He looked at each of the ministers. "I'm not as familiar with Qirsi custom as I should be, and so I'd like to leave it to you who knew him best to plan for his funeral. You shall have the full cooperation of all who live in this castle, the swordmaster, his guards, the kitchenmaster, and everyone else. I'll also see to it that the prelate makes the cloister available to you, though I realize you'll probably wish to work with the sanctuaries in the city." He hesitated. "Did Paegar have any family?"

For a moment no one answered.

"No, Your Majesty," Keziah said at last. "He had a brother, but he's long dead, as are his parents."

The king nodded, looking somber. "Then I'll leave it to you to see to his quarters, Keziah. I know how close you two had become recently."

"Yes, Your Majesty."

She could feel the other ministers staring at her, and she knew what they were thinking. They had known Paegar for years, she for but a few turns. What right did she have to lay sole claim to his friendship? It didn't matter that she had done nothing, that this had been Kearney's doing. They hated her. They had never stopped hating her. Paegar's friendship had only made it seem that way. Without him, she was alone again, an outcast in the king's court. Kearney didn't appear to notice. Her eyes stinging, Keziah stared at the floor, refusing to look at any of them. She would not give them the satisfaction of seeing her cry, not even today.

After a bit more discussion, Wenda agreed to take charge of the funeral plans, and Dyre said that he would meet with the prior in Bian's Sanctuary. In another few minutes, the king dismissed them. Keziah knew that he'd want her to stay so that they could speak in private, but she just wanted to be alone. She kept her gaze lowered so that he couldn't catch her eye and followed the others into the corridor.

She made her way back to Paegar's room, pushing the door open and peering inside, as if expecting to find someone there. His body was gone and the floor still wet from where servants had mopped up the blood. They had left the window open, probably so that the stone would dry, and the room had grown cold. The soft snow of the day before had given way to a harsh, windy storm, the kind that usually came to the upper Forelands this time of year, Taking a steadying breath, Keziah stepped inside, closing the door behind her.

For a long time, she merely wandered in slow circles. It felt strange to be in another person's chamber, looking at his belongings. Even with a cold wind stirring the air, it still smelled like Paegar. Keziah had expected the full weight of her grief to fall upon her as soon as she stepped into the chamber, but instead she found it comforting to be among his things, his scent, his home. It felt like a warm blanket on a snowy night. After some time, she stepped to his small writing table where she found a quill and ink, wax and a brass seal, and a number of papers. She stared at them a moment, then stepped away, crossing her arms over her chest. Maybe the others were right, maybe she had no business going through his things.

Thinking that perhaps his clothes would be an easier place to begin, Keziah moved to the wardrobe standing by his bed. Inside she found several ministerial robes, not only those he had worn in Audun's Castle, but also several bearing the crest of Rennach, and others bearing crests she didn't recognize, most likely from lesser houses in the Rennach dukedom. There were other clothes as well. A riding cape, trousers and shirts she had never seen him wear, even a leather jerkin. A sword with a plain leather hilt rested upright against the inside of the wardrobe and a swordsman's belt sat beside it.

Behind these, almost completely hidden from view, she found a small pouch and a wooden box. Keziah hesitated, then picked up the pouch. It rang with the sound of coins. Untying the drawstrings, she emptied the pouch onto the floor and stared with amazement at what she saw. There had to be at least fifteen gold pieces there, nearly an entire year's wage for a minister. She picked up the wooden box, and knew from its weight and the jingling she heard from within that it held gold as well. More than one hundred qinde, as it turned out.

Keziah leaned her back against Paegar's bed, gazing at the money lying before her. She wasn't sure she had ever seen so much gold in one place, save for the Glyndwr treasury, where she had gone once with Kearney many years before.

Paegar hadn't ever struck her as being extravagant. Before last night, he had never even offered to buy her a meal. Certainly he had never given any indication that he possessed so much gold. And since he kept the coins hidden in the back of his wardrobe, she had to assume that he wished to keep his wealth a secret.

Abruptly, Keziah found herself thinking once more of their conversation in the Silver Maple the night before. He had laughed away the idea that he might be a part of the Qirsi conspiracy. But how else could she explain this?

She heard voices, and in an instant her heart was in her throat. It took her a moment to realize that the sound came from below rather than from the corridor. Guards no doubt, walking across the ward below Paegar's window. Still, she quickly returned the gold coins to the box and pouch. It would be dark soon, and in spite of everything, she found that she was hungry.

She started to put the box and pouch back in the wardrobe, but then stopped, unsure whether that was wise. What if others found the gold? What if someone in the movement came looking for it, someone who had heard Kearney tell her to see to Paegar's belongings? It might be safer for her if they found the gold. Then again, if a guard found it, or someone else loyal to Kearney, all would learn of Paegar's betrayal. Keziah didn't want that. In the end she took the gold back to her chamber, shaking as she hurried through the corridor. The distance between her quarters and Paegar's had never seemed so great.

Once the gold was hidden to her satisfaction, in the back corner of her own wardrobe, she stepped out into the corridor again, making certain to lock her door. Then Keziah went in search of the one person with whom she knew she had to share what she had learned of her friend.

On most nights, Gershon and his wife ate with the king and queen in the king's hall. Kearney, both as duke and king, had never been one to rest once the sun went down, and during most suppers, while their wives chatted and their children ate and played, the king and his swordmaster spoke of the state of Kearney's army, or the advantages of various alliances, or, as in recent days, the prospects for war.

Tonight, though—with Kearney's permission, of course—the Trasker family ate alone. Kearney even allowed them to use his presence chamber for the meal, an offer Gershon accepted after only a moment's consideration. Sulwen, a smile on her ageless face, her brown eyes sparkling with the light of candles and torches, had been taken completely by surprise, but she was a clever woman and didn't need to ask him why they were doing this.

A man had died today, not from poisoning or the point of a blade, but from a simple fall in his bedchamber. It was at once comic and tragic, ludicrous and deeply frightening. On this day, life seemed to Gershon as fragile as the wings of a butterfly, and he wanted to be with those he loved most. He wanted to eat and laugh with his children. He wanted to raise a glass of wine with the woman he loved, and, when the children were asleep, make love to her until they were both weary and sated.

Which is why when he heard the knock on the chamber door, he chose to ignore it. A few seconds later it came again, louder this time, more insistent. Still he did nothing, though by now Sulwen was staring at the door, knowing, as she always did, that it was just a matter of time. For a third time, the intruder knocked.

"It doesn't sound like whoever it is intends to go away," Sulwen said, facing him again.

"Maybe not yet," Gershon said, getting to his feet and striding to the door. He yanked it open, only to find the archminister, quite possibly the last person in the entire castle he wanted to see just then. "You." He shook his head. "I should have expected this."

"I need to speak with you."

"I'm sure it can wait until morning."

"If I wait until morning, you'll rail at me for not insisting that I tell you tonight."

He faltered, narrowing his eyes. She had his attention, he had to give her that.

"This had better be important," he told her at last. He glanced back at his wife. "I'll return in a moment. I swear it."

She merely smiled, the way she always did when he made promises he couldn't keep.

He frowned, but stepped into the corridor anyway, closing the door so that he and the Qirsi were alone.

"What is it? Quickly, woman."

She ran a hand through her white hair. "I don't want you sharing this with anyone yet. Not even Kearney. Do you understand?"

"I make no promises to you, not when it comes to what I tell the king."

She shrugged and started to walk away. "Very well."

Gershon would have given anything to let her leave. But she had him now, and they both knew it. He swore loudly. "Fine, you have my word."

The woman nodded and walked back to where he stood. "I believe Paegar was a traitor. I think he was involved with the conspiracy."

Gershon gaped at her. "*What?* Are you certain?"

"Certain enough. I was going through his belongings, as the king asked me to do, and I found a good deal of gold."

"How much?"

"Nearly two hundred qinde, all of it hidden in the back of his wardrobe."

The swordmaster whistled through his teeth. That was more than two years' wages for a minister, or a swordmaster for that matter.

"That's a lot of gold, I'll grant you. But I'm not sure you can assume that he was a traitor just because he was wealthy."

"Last night, Paegar spoke to me of the conspiracy. Not in so many words, but I'm sure that's what was on his mind. He wanted to know if I had ever dreamed of serving Qirsi nobles and he made it sound as if he had. When I accused him of working for the conspiracy, he denied it, but by then I had made it clear that I didn't approve, and that I'd have him imprisoned."

"You think he was trying to turn you against the king?"

She seemed to weigh this. "Possibly. He had confessed to me earlier in the day that he was in love with me. If he was with the conspiracy, he would have wanted me to join as well."

"It's also possible that he was telling you he loved you to get you to join."

"I suppose."

Gershon looked away. "Did you . . . ? Were you in love with him?"

"No. I told him the truth, that I still love someone else."

The swordmaster nodded, though he still wouldn't look at her. He had never approved of the love she and the king shared, and for a long time he had questioned whether she truly loved Kearney, or had only been using him to exert her influence over the House of Glyndwr. In recent turns, however, as Kearney was faced with Lord Tavis's plea for asylum, his own unexpected ascension to the throne, and the need to end his love affair with the minister, Gershon had been forced to accept that her love for the man was genuine and powerful.

"And what of his efforts to turn you? Were you tempted to join him and his allies?"

"What do you think?" she asked, her voice rising. "Do you really believe I'd be speaking to you right now if I had been?"

Gershon winced, regretting the question almost as soon as the words passed his lips. "You're right, I—"

"I know that you hate me, swordmaster," she said, her pale eyes blazing in the torchlight. "To be honest, I don't care. But I am tired of you questioning my loyalty to Kearney and this land! I'm no more inclined to betray him than you are."

"You're right," he said again. "It was a foolish question. But then I must ask you, why do you want me to keep this from the king?"

"Paegar was my friend, and while I know that his treachery makes him little better than a demon in your eyes, it's not that simple for me."

It was the swordmaster's turn to grow angry. "Well it ought to be! You tell me that you love the king, that you're loyal to him and to Eibithar. Yet you seek to protect a traitor."

"He's dead, swordmaster."

"It doesn't matter! He betrayed the land! If he had left a wife or children, that would be one thing. But you said yourself earlier today, he has no family. There's only the high minister, and he deserves neither your concern nor my consideration. He sold his kingdom and king for gold."

"Gold he never spent. Gold that sat hidden in his wardrobe until the day he died."

Gershon couldn't believe he was hearing this, even from a Qirsi. "First of all, you don't know how much of it he spent! It may be that he received thousands of qinde from his friends in the conspiracy. The gold you found may have been merely the crumbs of a much grander feast."

"Two hundred qinde?"

"It's possible, isn't it?"

"I can't believe—"

He raised a hand, stopping her. "I only asked if it was possible. And it is, right?"

She opened her mouth, then closed it again. After some time, she nodded.

"Second," he went on, fighting the urge to gloat, "what the man did with the gold is of no importance to me. It's enough to know that he was a traitor. Nothing else matters. And I refuse to protect his name for no reason other than your grief at losing a friend."

The woman glared at him. "Yes, he was my friend. I didn't know him long, but I was beginning to understand him, to have a sense of what kind of man he was."

"Yet it was only when he died that you realized he had betrayed you and everything you work for."

"Yes. He deceived me. Is that what you want me to say, swordmaster? That he left me feeling foolish and dull-witted? There, I've said it."

"All I want is to understand why you're speaking to me of this at all. You're wasting my time, and I've had enough of it!"

He reached for the door handle, fully intending to return to Sulwen and his children.

"Please, wait," the Qirsi said, closing her eyes and rubbing a hand across her smooth brow. She looked weary and pale. Whatever his feelings about Paegar, Gershon could not deny that the man's death had taken a toll on the archminister.

"What I'm trying to tell you," she said, "is that while Paegar betrayed us, and was paid to do so, I believe that he was coerced into it somehow. I don't believe he had the heart of a traitor."

"Does that matter?"

She glowered at him again, but only briefly. Gershon had tried to keep his tone mild. He wasn't trying to goad her, only to grasp what it was she was telling him. After a moment, she seemed to realize this.

"I think it might," she answered. "In fighting the conspiracy, wouldn't it be helpful to know how its leaders go about spreading its influence? Wouldn't you like to know what it is they hope to accomplish and how they intend to do it?"

"Of course, but—"

"As I told you, swordmaster, Paegar spoke to me of the conspiracy, perhaps hoping that he could convince me to join. It's possible that he also spoke of me to those who paid him."

"What makes you think that?" Gershon asked, surprised by how much this alarmed him.

She shrugged, a slight smile on her lips. "Call it the instinct of a gleaner."

Gershon merely nodded. He didn't trust the Qirsi, nor did he like to rely upon their magic any more than was necessary. But over the years, he had come to respect the power that dwelled within them.

He waited for her to go on, but she said nothing more. She just watched him expectantly, as if at any moment he might offer some reply.

"So, you think he told his allies about you," Gershon said at last, still not certain what she was telling him.

"Yes. In which case, they may decide to lure me into their movement just as they did Paegar."

And finally it all made sense. "You want to join them, don't you?"

"Well," she said, grinning now, "not really, no. But how else can we learn who they are and what they want?"

"And you don't want me to say anything to Kearney because if they know we've discovered Paegar's betrayal, they might be wary of approaching you."

The smile lingered on her lips, though the swordmaster saw something else lurking in her eyes. "That's why I don't want you to say anything to the others," she told him. "Someone had to be giving Paegar his gold, and that person could very well be here in the castle."

"What if that person killed him?" Gershon said, as much to himself as to the minister.

She nodded, seeming to shudder at the suggestion. "I'd thought of that."

"Yet you're still willing to pretend that you've embraced their cause?"

"Would you go to war to protect Kearney?"

"Of course," the swordmaster said.

"How is this any different?"

Gershon considered himself an intelligent man, perhaps not as brilliant as the king, but capable certainly of matching wits with any foe on a battlefield. Yet, every time he spoke with this woman she seemed to be one stride ahead of him. "I don't suppose it is," he said. "I'll let you do this, if you'll promise to keep me informed of everything that happens."

She arched an eyebrow. "I intend to do this whether or not you let me."

"Must you always be so difficult, woman? All I meant was, I'll agree to keep Paegar's treachery a secret, but I want to know who you're speaking with, and what they have in mind to do."

"And I'm telling you that might not be possible."

"It will have to be!" Gershon let out a long breath, trying to control his temper. He often wondered if she tried to anger him. "The king trusts me with the safety of everyone in this castle, including yours." *Especially yours.*

"If you're going to attempt something this dangerous, I have to be certain that I can protect you. Paegar's dead. Now, it was probably an accident, a simple fall in a dark chamber. But it might have been more than that, and I'd be failing my king if I didn't do everything in my power to keep you from the same fate."

"I'll be trying to convince these people that I'm a traitor," she said. "If they see me speaking with you, they'll know it's a lie. In trying to protect me, you'll really be endangering my life."

"Then we'll have to make it appear that I'm interrogating you, that my questions are born of mistrust rather than concern."

She smiled, her eyes dancing. "That should be easy for both of us."

He had to smile as well. She had more than a little courage. To be fair, she was braver than many Eandi warriors he knew. She was brilliant as well, and though he found the Qirsi strange-looking, with their pure white hair and yellow eyes, he had to admit that she was prettier than most. Perhaps for the first time, he understood why his king had loved this woman; why, in all likelihood, he still loved her.

"I guess it should," he said. He heard one of the children laugh from inside the presence chamber. It sounded like Ula, his youngest. Sulwen would be wondering where he had gone and whether he intended to come back at all. "So it's agreed then?" he asked. "You'll keep me informed?"

She nodded. "Yes. You have my word." She smiled again. "Now go back to your wife and children, swordmaster. Forgive my intrusion."

She turned and started walking away. Still, Gershon stood there, watching her.

"You never told me why I shouldn't tell the king," he said at last. He kept his voice low, so that no one else would hear, but still the words reached her.

After a moment she turned to face him again.

"I see why we have to keep this from the others," he went on. "But why the king? Surely Kearney can be trusted to keep this to himself."

"Isn't it obvious?" she asked. "Even now, after so many turns apart, do you really believe Kearney would allow me to risk my life on his behalf?"

There was nothing Gershon could say. The answer was as plain to him as the single tear rolling down Keziah's face. Kearney would never have let her do it. Not even with Gershon protecting her. Not even if it meant saving his kingdom.

Chapter
Eighteen

✦

Mertesse, Aneira

My dearest Yaella,

By the time you find this I will be far from Mertesse, sent on an errand by a mutual acquaintance. I don't know how long I will be gone or where my journeys may take me, but know that you will never be far from my thoughts.

What few possessions I have, I leave to your care, hoping that if I do not return they may offer some comfort to you.

I love you more than you can know.

Shurik

He left the note on her bed, tucking a corner of the parchment under her pillow. Then he glanced about the dark room one last time before slipping back into the corridor and making his way out of the castle. Several days had passed since his conversation with the Weaver and though some delay in his departure had been in keeping with the man's instructions, Shurik now felt anxious to be on his way lest the Weaver come to him again and question why he had waited so long.

It was awkward enough having to leave with Yaella and the duke away from Castle Mertesse. As an exile from Eibithar, granted asylum by Rowan after the failed siege at Kentigern, Shurik lived in the fortress at the duke's indulgence. No matter when he ventured forth from the castle it was bound to raise eyebrows. Had he left the morning after his vision of the Weaver, only a few days after Rowan's departure for Solkara, it would have appeared that he had been awaiting just such an opportunity. Instead he remained in Mertesse for some time, and was fortunate enough to receive a message from Yaella midway through the waning. It was a brief note—she said merely that she missed him and looked forward to her return. But that was enough. As far as the duke's mother and the castle guards were concerned, it might has well have been a frantic request for him to join Rowan's party. Shurik never said to anyone that it was, but neither did he give them any cause to believe it wasn't.

Upon receiving the message, he returned immediately to his chamber, placed a few items in a small satchel, and sent a servant to the stablemaster with instructions to have his mount ready before dawn the following day. No one questioned him. He never gave them the chance.

He steered his mount through the castle's southern gate, riding away from the Tarbin and toward the distant, dark mass of Aneira's Great Forest. The sun had not yet risen, and the damp cold air of night still lay heavy over the farms and open plains. A light snow had coated the land overnight, whitening the roofs and roads and settling among the grasses like sugar on some confection from Kentigern's kitchens. The sky had cleared, and a few bright stars clung stubbornly to the night, as if defying the silver light that had begun to spread from the eastern horizon.

It had been several turns since Shurik last rode outside of a city, and longer still since he had done so alone. Indeed, he couldn't remember having left Mertesse since Rowan's grant of asylum. He felt free, and he savored the stillness of the morning and the simple beauty of the land. At the same time, he also felt more vulnerable than he had in years. He saw how the soldiers of Mertesse regarded him. He heard the contempt in Rowan's voice whenever they spoke. He was a Qirsi traitor and none of the Eandi in Castle Mertesse would ever see him as anything more. Still, he had been granted the protection of the house, and he never feared for an instant that any of the revulsion he engendered would spill over into violence.

Alone on the open road, however, he had no one to protect him. In Eibithar he had always traveled with Aindreas, who never left Kentigern without at least a small company of soldiers. Even in Kentigern City, he had worn robes announcing to all who saw him that he served the duke. No one had dared threaten him.

He no longer wore ministerial robes. Rowan accepted his counsel from time to time, and allowed him to accompany Yaella to most of their discussions, but the duke had not seen fit to accept him formally as a servant of House Mertesse. Outside the castle, in the brightening glow of the Aneiran morning, he was neither minister nor traitor. He was merely a Qirsi rider.

He still spoke with the accent of Eibithar, but since leaving Kentigern he had learned to mask it. Road thieves, of which the Great Forest sheltered many, usually left his kind alone, as did soldiers, particularly those of the lesser houses. But in the end, he was only as safe as his sword and his magic could make him.

The ride from Mertesse to Solkara promised to be an easy one. The cities were less than twenty leagues apart, and even if the weather turned bad, the forest would offer him some shelter. The greatest danger lay not in anything he might encounter along the way, but rather in the man he would seek once he reached the royal city.

Shurik hadn't seen the gleaner since the day Rouel's siege of Kentigern failed. That day, when talk of the siege turned to the ease with which the Aneirans had defeated Kentigern's famed gates, Fotir jal Salene, Curgh's first minister, suggested that they had been weakened by shaping magic. Of course Shurik denied that he possessed such power; he had kept it from Aindreas for nearly ten years and wasn't about to reveal the truth just then. As it happened, he didn't have to. He still remembered, with a clarity that made him tremble, how Grinsa had looked at him, seeming to see right through his denials as only a Weaver could. Shurik had no choice but to flee the castle that very day. Had he not, he felt certain that the gleaner would have revealed his treachery.

In all, he spent no more than a few hours in the man's company, but he would never forget Grinsa jal Arriet's face, the high cheekbones and wide mouth, the pure white glow of his skin. As tall as he was and as powerfully built, he looked healthier and stronger than most Qirsi ever did. No, finding him would not be terribly difficult. On the other hand, if he truly was a Weaver, killing him would be nearly impossible. Not only could the Weaver sense any magic he might have, he could reach into Shurik's mind and keep him from using that power, or worse, force him to use it against himself instead. As a younger man, he might have had the strength to resist a Weaver's power, at least briefly. But Shurik was old now, at least for a Qirsi, and since exhausting himself in his efforts to weaken Kentigern's great gates before the siege, he had found that his powers were diminished, his body quicker to tire. In more ways than one, he had paid a heavy price for his betrayal.

"If you try to kill him and fail," the Weaver had told Shurik in his dream, "I'll see to it that you die a slow, agonizing death."

He wasn't foolish enough to think this an idle threat. Which meant that all he had to do was find Grinsa and track him until the Weaver came to him once more. The Weaver had said nothing to him of money, nor had he paid him in advance, as he sometimes did. Still Shurik had little doubt that if he succeeded in this, his reward would be substantial.

The sun peered above the horizon a short time later, huge and orange, casting long shadows across the landscape and making the snow glitter like tiny shards of glass. Shurik stopped for a quick meal at a small inn by the road, before riding on. By midday, a new line of clouds had appeared in the west, advancing on the land like a grey army. The wind increased, and before long it was snowing again, the hard, sharp flakes biting at Shurik's face like blackflies during the growing turns.

Long before he wanted to, Shurik was forced to stop again, at a village inn that appeared from the outside to be barely more than the unkempt home of a poor farmer. He had come no more than three leagues from Mertesse, and already the Qirsi was bone-weary. He longed for the comfort of his small chamber in Castle Mertesse, and he found himself wondering if he had grown too old to be of any use to the Weaver.

Reluctantly leaving his mount with a small boy who didn't look old enough to reach Shurik's saddle, much less know how to remove it from the beast, he stepped into the inn. Inside, the house held a bit more promise than it had from the road. A fire crackled in the hearth and the common room smelled of roasting meat and baked bread. An old Eandi woman emerged from the kitchen at the sound of the door, and eyed him warily. Shurik pretended not to notice, wiping the snow from his riding cloak and shaking it from the satchel he carried. Sensing that she was about to tell him that they didn't rent rooms to Qirsi, he pulled out a pouch of coins and poured its contents into his hand, as if counting the gold and silver pieces.

Then he looked up, smiling. "I had hoped to stay the night," he said. "Do you have any rooms free?"

The woman licked her lips, her rheumy eyes straying briefly to the coins he held. "I suppose. It'll cost you nine qinde."

It was a lot, far more than he would have paid at a Qirsi inn in one of the cities. But he could hear the wind howling outside, and he had no desire to look elsewhere.

"That includes a meal tonight, and breakfast in the morning?"

She hesitated, then nodded.

"And feed and water for my mount?"

"I guess."

Shurik smiled. "Done." *I intend to eat a lot, woman, and I hope my horse grows fat on your grain.*

She took his coins, counting them twice to be sure he hadn't cheated her. Then she led him up the creaking stairway to a cramped room with two small straw beds and a pitcher and washbasin, both of them empty.

"I'll bring water shortly," she said. "When you hear the bell ringing below, that means supper is ready. I only serve it once, so don't keep me waiting."

"Of course."

She nodded once, looking around the room before leaving him, as if to make certain she hadn't forgotten anything.

Shurik sat on one of the beds, which was only slightly more comfortable than the floor would have been. It was a good thing the Weaver had paid him so well over the years. Had he been forced to pay so much for such a room on only a minister's wage, he would have already been on his horse again, braving the storm and searching for another inn.

To be fair, the room seemed clean, and smelled only of fresh straw. No doubt he could have done far worse this night.

Shurik didn't have to wait long for the bell announcing the evening meal. Descending the stairs, he found the woman waiting for him at the table, already in her seat. To his great surprise, his was the only other place set. She watched him sit, a sour look on her face, then muttered a quick prayer and began to eat the roasted fowl and steamed roots she had prepared.

The food was pleasant enough, though bland, and there was water but no wine on the table. But again, Shurik had to remind himself how much worse this day could have ended.

Most disturbing to him was the silence. The woman ate and drank, refusing to look at him, much less speak. Perhaps he shouldn't have minded—how interesting a conversation could such a woman have offered? But he had been without Yaella for nearly half a turn, and aside from a passing word to the guards and stableboys that morning and this woman and the boy upon his arrival at the inn, had not spoken to anyone all day.

"You live here alone?" he asked, when the silence became too much to bear.

She regarded him a moment before nodding.

"What about the boy who tended my mount?"

"Grandson. He lives with my daughter and her husband in the house out back."

"You've no husband?"

"Did once," she said, still chewing. "He's dead now."

"I'm sorry."

"Shouldn't be. If he was here, you'd still be looking for a place to sleep." She cackled, her mouth wide so that he could see her yellow, broken teeth. "Used to grow flax. I made our clothes myself and sold the rest at market in Mertesse. But then he died, and I couldn't work the land myself. So I opened the inn. Do a good business, too. There aren't many places between here and Solkara. If that's where you're going, you'll have a hard time finding food this good before you're inside the walls."

Though he was loath to admit it, Shurik had little doubt that she was right. Once more, he wondered if he had been foolish to think he could make this journey during the snows. He was about to ask her if she could give him the names of any other inns as comfortable as hers between here and the royal city. Before he could, however, there was a hard knock at the door.

The woman clicked her tongue once, then stood, hobbled to the door, and pulled it open.

A man stood there, gripping the doorframe as if it was all he could do to stay on his feet. Snow clung to his cloak and ice hung from his eyebrows and half-grown beard. His cheeks and brow were as red as the Eandi moon. It almost seemed that the frigid wind had burned his skin as might a planting sun. He was plainly dressed, except for the sash that hung across his chest, which was red, black, and gold. The colors of Solkara. The man was a messenger.

"Get the door," the woman said to Shurik as she helped the messenger to an empty chair. "I'll get you some food and make up a spare bed," she told the man. "We haven't much room, but we'll be all right."

The Solkaran shook his head. "I can't stay," he said, his voice ragged. "Just some food. Then I'll be on my way." He looked from the woman to Shurik. "How far is it to Mertesse?"

"Three leagues," Shurik said.

The woman frowned. "It's closer to two."

"You've a message?" Shurik asked, unable to mask his concern.

"For Lady Mertesse," the man said, "the duke's mother."

"Has something happened?"

The man just stared at him, saying nothing.

"I'm one of the duke's underministers." Under the circumstances it seemed a small lie, and a necessary one. "I've just come from Mertesse this morning."

"You wear no robes."

"I've been riding all day. You think a minister wears his robes on horseback in this weather?"

282

Still the Solkaran didn't look convinced.

"Rowan journeyed to Solkara with his first minister, Yaella ja Banvel, and a company of thirty men." His voice shook as he spoke Yaella's name, but he pressed on, hoping neither of them would notice. "He rode a large bay with white on its nose and rump. Now, tell me what's happened."

The man looked at him a moment longer. "After the funeral, the queen and the king's brothers met with the Council of Dukes. Grigor, the eldest, poisoned the wine."

"Demons and fire!" Shurik breathed, suddenly feeling unsteady on his feet.

He heard the innkeeper utter another prayer.

"How long ago?" he asked, his voice flat.

"Two nights," the messenger said.

Two nights. Solkaran messengers usually rode faster than that. Perhaps the snow had slowed him, and no doubt there had been much confusion in the castle. Chances were, he hadn't left right away.

"The duke of Mertesse lives," the man said, as if he thought Shurik should have asked already. "He remains weak, though."

"What of the queen?" the woman asked.

"She lives as well, but only just. When I left it was too soon to say if she would survive."

"The first minister, is she all right?"

The messenger looked at Shurik again. "You mean of Mertesse? I'm sorry. I have no news of her. Only the duke and queen. I know that several ministers died, as did the dukes of Tounstrel and Noltierre."

"Gods save us all," the woman said. "What's to be done with the brother?"

"He's a traitor to the kingdom. He'll be hanged, drawn, and quartered."

Shurik gazed toward the door. He longed to ride for Solkara, though he could still hear the wind buffeting the house and snow clawing at the wooden shutters like some taloned beast. Yaella might be dead. At the very least she had been poisoned. He should have been with her.

The innkeeper had gone to the kitchen to bring food for the messenger. Shurik wasn't hungry anymore, nor was he tired, though he knew he would have to sleep soon so that he could ride south with first light.

"Are they letting people in and out of the city?" he asked the man.

"They have their murderer. They have no need to lock the gates."

Of course. The guards wouldn't bother even a Qirsi traitor. In spite of his concern for Yaella, a part of him couldn't help but wonder if the

Weaver had been behind this as well. It sounded so much like something he would do.

"The castle might be another matter," the messenger went on a moment later. "Though if you're one of Mertesse's ministers, I'm certain they'll let you in."

Shurik nodded. It would be a problem, but one that was best dealt with in Solkara. For now, he needed only to ride.

"Have the boy saddle my mount at dawn," he told the woman as she returned from the kitchen. "Instead of that breakfast you promised, you'll have to pack me some bread and cheese."

"All right. I might have some salted meat, as well."

He started up the stairs. "That would be fine. My thanks." He looked at the messenger. "Ride well, Solkara. I'm grateful for the tidings."

"Ean guard you, Minister," the man said.

Shurik felt his pulse quicken. Minister. If the duke or his mother learned of this, he'd never be able to return to Mertesse. For now, though, that seemed the least of his concerns.

He slept poorly. It was still dark when he awoke to the keening of the frigid wind and the pounding of his heart. He should have been tired, but he felt restless and eager to be riding again.

Dressing quickly and closing his satchel, the Qirsi descended the stairs expecting to find a pouch of food on the dining table. Instead he found the innkeeper waiting for him, with the food she had promised and a piece of fresh bread covered with melted butter. Shurik wondered if she had slept at all.

"I still wake early, even though we haven't farmed in years," she said, as if reading his thoughts. "The old ways die hard, especially when you've lived as long as I have."

"You have my thanks," Shurik said, pulling out his pouch of money and offering her five qinde more.

The woman shook her head and grinned. "I asked too much for the room. We both know it. See to your duke and that minister you were asking about."

He bowed to her and saw her blush in the candlelight. "Again, my lady, you have my thanks."

He put the food in his satchel, ate the bread without bothering to sit, and stepped out into the storm.

Neither the wind nor the snow had abated during the night. Indeed, the snow seemed heavier than it had when Shurik reached the inn the day before. Still, the boy was standing in front of the inn with Shurik's mount, waiting for him much as his grandmother had. The child looked cold and small in the murky grey light as he handed the Qirsi the reins. Shurik gave him the five qinde.

Swinging himself onto the mount, he steered the horse to the edge of the road. He paused there long enough to remind himself of which way he had come the day before, then started south toward Solkara.

The wind cut through his cloak and clothes like a scythe through young grain, and the snow stung his eyes and cheeks until he had little choice but to cover his face with a tippet and trust that his horse would keep to the road. He didn't drive the mount too hard, but neither did he take much time to rest along the way. When he was hungry, he reached back into his satchel and ate in the saddle. When he needed to drink, he stopped only long enough to eat some of the newly fallen snow and to allow his mount to do the same. The muscles in his back and legs were screaming for a respite by midday, but Shurik rode on, drawing on strength he hadn't known he possessed. Late in the day, the snow finally slackened, though not the wind. Still he didn't stop. The Great Forest of Aneira loomed before him like a dark mist, and he swore silently that he wouldn't stop until he had entered the wood and found a village in which to pass the night.

He reached the great trees of the forest just as daylight began to wane. Even with their limbs bare, the trees offered shelter from the wind, and without the gale, the air didn't feel nearly as cold. Shurik was so relieved to be out of the worst of the storm that he continued past the first village he encountered. When it grew too dark to see, he raised his dagger and summoned to its blade a small, bright flame by which to ride. Coming at last to a second village, he dismounted, leading his horse on foot past a few modest shops and a small, empty marketplace. He soon found a small inn, rented a room, and, after a supper that left him longing for the food of the old woman, climbed the stairs to his room. His mind was still filled with thoughts of Yaella, but after riding the entire day, he fell into a deep sleep almost as soon as he lay down.

The next two days went much as this one had. Shurik rode from dawn to nightfall, stopping only briefly, and finding a small village in which to rest at the end of each day. The skies remained a somber grey, but this far south, the snows gave way to a frigid, soaking rain that left him even more miserable than had the snow. Still, by the time he stopped on that fourth night in a small town by the banks of the Kett, Shurik hardly noticed. He was less than two leagues from the walls of Solkara. He would have ridden through the Weaver's fire to reach Yaella's side.

He awoke early again the next day and followed the river road to the Solkara bridge. Crossing over the roiling waters of the Kett, Shurik soon came to the east gate of the royal city. The guards there let him through without so much as a question. In fact, they barely looked at him. Glancing around, Shurik saw that there were a great many of his people in the city, more than one might usually find in even the southernmost cities of the Forelands. It took him several moments to realize why.

In his single-minded haste to find Yaella, he had lost track of the days. Tonight would be Pitch Night, the last night not only of this turn, but of the year as well. Tomorrow began the turn of Qirsar, god of magic and creator of the Qirsi. Few cities in the Forelands honored Qirsar with a sanctuary—Adlana in Caerisse, Listaal and Prentarlo in Sanbira, and Olfan in Wethyrn—but on the first day of Qirsar's turn, Qirsi flocked to whatever sanctuaries they could, to pay homage to all the gods, and to Qirsar in particular. A Qirsi hoping to slip unnoticed into one of the kingdom's walled cities could not choose to do so on a better day. Truly the gods were with him.

Shurik rode through the marketplace, but soon decided that a Qirsi on horseback was more likely to draw someone's attention than one on foot. There was a good chance that Grinsa was here, not to mention the company of soldiers who had ridden with Yaella and Rowan to the king's funeral. He had already taken a terrible risk by coming here. He might be able to convince his duke that he had left Mertesse only after hearing of the poisoning, but he hoped that wouldn't be necessary. Glancing about to see if anyone was watching, he dismounted and led the horse the rest of the way to the castle.

He found a smithy just outside the castle walls and offered the man seven qinde to shoe the beast. The horse probably didn't need to be reshod, but this way Shurik could leave the animal with the smith and enter the castle alone.

As he expected, the guards at the castle's outer gate stopped him before he even reached the wicket door.

"Where do you think you're going, white-hair?" one of them asked.

Shurik briefly considered saying that he had been summoned by the castle's master healer, but he remembered at the last moment that Carden had no Qirsi healers. He shivered at the thought. *Let her be alive.*

Instead, he told the man the truth.

"I've come to see one of the ministers who was poisoned. Her name is Yaella ja Banvel; she's first minister to the duke of Mertesse."

The guard eyed him closely, looking doubtful. "And who are you?"

"I'm her brother." The truth had its limits, and "I'm her lover" wasn't likely to get him through the gate.

The man stood there another moment, considering this. "I'll have to speak with my captain," he finally said.

Shurik nodded. "That's fine. Just hurry, please. I'm . . . concerned for her."

The guard stepped away from the wicket gate, disappearing from view. The other guards remained there, watching Shurik but saying nothing. After what seemed an eternity, the first man returned.

"All right," he said. "You can go to her. But if you have any weapons you have to leave them here with me."

"What good will that do?" one of the other men asked. "He's a sorcerer."

"That's what the captain told me to do," the man said with a shrug. "Talk to him if you don't like it."

Shurik handed the guard his dagger. "Where is she?"

"All the ministers who survived the poisoning are in the chambers on the north side of the inner keep. If she's alive she'd be there."

The Qirsi swallowed, feeling his hands start to tremble. He hurried through the gate, to the north end of the castle, and climbed the tower stairs two steps at a time. He was badly winded when he reached the upper corridor, but he didn't stop to rest. Finding the nearest guard, he asked where Yaella could be found. Not surprisingly, the man couldn't answer.

"I know they're ministers and all," he said, "but I don't know one Qirsi from another."

"Well, have you seen the duke of Mertesse up here?"

"He came up here earlier today." He pointed to one of the doors. "He was in there for a while."

Shurik turned, not even bothering to thank the man, and strode to the door. He hesitated a moment, wondering if he should knock. But in the end, he merely opened the door quietly and stepped into the chamber.

She was lying on the bed, her eyes closed, her skin so white she might well have been dead, her lips pale and dry. Her face looked far thinner than it usually did, and her hands, which were resting at her sides, appeared tiny and frail, like those of a small child. Shurik walked carefully to the chair by the side of her bed and gazed down at her, relieved to see her chest rising and falling.

The chair creaked when he sat, and she stirred, turning toward the sound.

When she saw him, she smiled, her eyes widening.

"What are you doing here?" she said, her voice barely more than a breath of wind.

"I came to see you, of course. How are you feeling?"

"Weak still, but better than I was." She sat up.

Shurik shook his head. "You should be lying down, Yaella."

"It's been six days since the poisoning. You really think this is the first time I've sat up?"

Her voice sounded stronger now. It occurred to Shurik that he had probably woken her from a sound sleep.

Yaella frowned. "You shouldn't be here. If the duke finds you—"

"If the duke finds me I'll tell him I rode south upon hearing of what had happened. He may be angry, but I don't very much care. I wanted to make certain you were all right." He leaned forward and kissed her forehead, which felt cool and smooth against his lips.

She smiled again. "I'm grateful. Truly. But now you need to get back to Mertesse."

Shurik looked away. "I'm not going back to Mertesse, at least not for some time."

"What?" He heard the shock in her voice and could imagine the way she was looking at him, a pained expression in those deep yellow eyes.

"I had already left Mertesse when I encountered the messenger sent from Solkara. The Weaver came to me just after you and the duke left the castle, and instructed me to find the Revel gleaner, the one who I thought might be a Weaver himself."

"Why does he want you?" she asked dully.

"Because I know this man. I know what he looks like, and I'm the one person, aside from you, who knows that he might be a Weaver. I guess our Weaver has finally realized how important I am." He chanced a look at her and made himself grin.

Yaella's expression didn't change. "If he really is a Weaver, he's just as dangerous as our Weaver. You could be killed."

"I'm only supposed to find him." *If you have the opportunity to kill him, you may.* That seemed unlikely. If all went as Shurik hoped, Grinsa would never see him, and all he would have to do was wait for his next dream of the Weaver and tell the man where the gleaner could be found.

"Where do you think he is?"

"I wouldn't be surprised if he were here, in Solkara. But I don't plan to begin my search for another few days. For now, I only care about sitting with you and seeing to it that you recover fully from this."

She nodded, taking his hand.

"Do you think Grigor did this to you?" he asked her after a brief silence.

Yaella shrugged. "I don't know. The archminister seems to think so, as does my duke."

"How is your duke?"

"He's fine. It helps to be young and strong."

And Eandi. Neither of them had to say it; Shurik knew they were both thinking it.

"What of the queen?"

"She'll live, but the poison was very nearly too much for her."

He nodded, still thinking about Grigor. "Do you think it's possible that the Weaver was responsible for this?"

She stared at him for several moments. "I've been asking myself the same question."

"And?"

"I don't know, Shurik. The poison killed more Qirsi than it did Eandi, but they were all ministers. I don't know if the Weaver would care that he was killing them."

"He wouldn't have wanted to kill you."

"I suppose not. But if for some reason he was intent on keeping Grigor from the throne, I'm not sure that sparing me would have been reason enough not to do this."

They both fell silent again. Eventually, Yaella began to shake her head. "The Weaver wouldn't have done this, not if he wanted to weaken the kingdom."

"Why not?"

"Because Grigor would have been a terrible king. The dukes would have hated him; given time, they might even have rebelled. Now it seems that they've turned to Numar, the youngest of Carden's brothers, to be regent for Chofya's daughter. Strange as it may seem, Aneira is stronger for this having happened."

"Well, good," Shurik said. "I'd rather that this was the act of a madman. I would have been forced to hate the Weaver had I thought he had poisoned you."

Yaella gazed toward the hearth. "You mean the way I hate him now for ordering you away from Mertesse?"

"I won't be gone long. I'll make certain of it."

She nodded, but still wouldn't look at him.

"You don't know when he's going to come to you, Yaella. It's too dangerous to hate him."

"He'll never know."

Shurik gave her hand a squeeze, making her meet his gaze. "I'm serious. This isn't important enough to risk making him angry. I'll find the gleaner, tell the Weaver where he is, and that will be the end of it. With you still recovering, and Grinsa probably in Solkara, I may be back in Mertesse before you are."

"That's not what you said before. You said it would be some time before you came back to me."

He let out a breath, rubbing a hand across his brow. "I should let you rest. And I should find an inn before nightfall. I've ridden a long way, and I've yet to have a decent meal or sleep in a comfortable bed."

She said nothing.

"You'll be all right?"

"Yes."

"I'll return in the morning. Now that the guards have seen me once, I shouldn't have any trouble getting in again."

In spite of everything, she smiled at that. "I'll look forward to it. Just try to avoid the duke."

"Of course."

He kissed her brow again, then rose and left her, closing her door as softly as he could. In just a few moments he was out of the castle. He stopped at the smithy to retrieve his mount and pay the man, then began leading his horse back toward the city marketplace. He knew that there were at least three or four Qirsi inns in the city, one of which was supposed to be quite good. He had forgotten the name, but he knew that it was in the southeast corner of the city, near the Sanctuary of Morna, and he followed the broad lanes in that direction.

He hadn't gone very far, however, when something—or rather, someone—caught his eye. At first he saw nothing familiar in the face; instead it was the scars that drew his attention. Long, angry, dark gashes marking the youthful face, like muddy lanes in a field of golden grain. But then he saw the young man's eyes, and he knew. They were so much like those of the lad's father that there could be no mistaking them. This was Tavis of Curgh.

An instant later, Shurik spied the gleaner as well, and doing so, he marveled that he hadn't seen him sooner. He was tall and broad, and he stood out among the other Qirsi as Uulranni steel stands out among lesser blades.

Grinsa and the young lord were standing in the entrance of an inn—fortunately, not the one Shurik had in mind—the boy looking up at the gleaner, and Grinsa scanning the marketplace as if looking for someone. *If you try to kill him and fail* . . . Watching the gleaner now, his heart hammering in his chest like that of a hunted stag, Shurik knew that he would never be able to kill this man, not without help. He was equally certain, however, that this was no lowly gleaner. Power seemed to flow from the man, just as it did from the Weaver. Regardless of whether this man was a Weaver as well, he was definitely more than he claimed to be.

Shurik was still trying to decide if he should try to follow the man when Grinsa's gaze fell on him. To his relief, Grinsa didn't appear to recognize him. One moment he was staring right at Shurik, and in the next he was looking past him. An instant later, however, the man's eyes widened and flew back to Shurik's face. He said something to Tavis and the two of them began walking in Shurik's direction.

Not knowing what else to do, Shurik tried to climb onto his mount and get away. Before he could grasp the saddle, however, the horse suddenly reared, neighing loudly and kicking with its front feet. Shurik looked once more at the gleaner, feeling panic grip his throat.

The man wore a fierce grin as he strode across the marketplace. The language of beasts. Grinsa had done this, somehow covering the distance between them with his magic. He had to be so much more than just a gleaner. Shurik had only one hope. The Weaver would be angry—he had never imagined that he might find himself caught between two Weavers—but what choice had Grinsa left him?

"Guards!" he shouted, looking wildly around the marketplace for any Solkaran uniform and pointing toward Tavis and the gleaner. "Soldiers of Solkara! That man is an Eibitharian lord, come to kill our queen! Arrest him!"

Chapter
Nineteen

✦

Solkara, Aneira

ebeo paced the room restlessly, like a Sanbiri mount held too long in a stable. He looked healthier than he had at any time since the poisoning. His face remained wan and thin—though he had his strength again, he had not yet regained his appetite—but the very fact that he was on his feet once more marked much improvement from just a few days before.

Evanthya watched him, waiting for the questions he had posed every day since that awful night in the queen's chambers. How was the queen faring? Brall? Fetnalla? The others? It had become a ritual of sorts, a way, no doubt, for the duke to feel that he was more than just another victim of Grigor's twisted ambition. He was, among all the dukes, the one who had most fully recovered, and though he could not help but be thankful for his good fortune, Evanthya sensed that he felt guilty as well.

Eventually the questions did begin, and the minister told her duke what she knew of the others who had drunk the tainted wine. It now seemed clear that all those who survived the first night after the poisoning were going to be all right. Brall had recovered enough to leave his bed that morning and take a slow stroll through the corridors of the castle. Fetnalla was improving quickly, though she was still weakened, as were most of the other afflicted Qirsi. Even the queen, who hovered near death for so long that many feared she would never regain consciousness, had finally opened her eyes the day before and now appeared to be gaining strength with each hour that passed.

They had been fortunate, if such a word could be used in these circumstances, to lose only the two dukes—Bertin of Noltierre and Vidor of Tounstrel—and the first ministers of Kett, Rassor, and Bistari, all of whom died that first night.

"Has there been any word yet from Numar?" the duke asked, when Evanthya had told him all she knew about Grigor's victims.

"No, my lord. None. I believe he may be waiting until Grigor's fate is decided before he formally offers himself as regent."

"Grigor's fate was decided the night he poured that wine."

"Of course, my lord. But he lives still, and so long as he does the house is his to rule."

Tebeo's face twisted sourly, but after a moment he nodded. "What do you think he'll do?"

"I believe he'll wait until Grigor has been executed, and then he'll grant our request. If he intended to say no, he would. He only waits because he intends to say yes."

The duke's expression brightened somewhat. "I suppose you're right. Has the queen said when she intends to have Grigor put to death?"

"Not that I've heard, my lord. Soon, I believe."

"I'd like to know for certain. I want to be there. I want to see it." He took a breath, as if trying to calm himself. "Can you speak with the arch-minister?"

Evanthya wavered, though only briefly. "Of course, my lord."

"You seem reluctant."

He hates me, and I fear him. "No, my lord. I'll speak with him and let you know what I've learned." She rose from her chair. "Is there anything else, my lord?"

"No, Evanthya. Thank you."

She crossed to the door, but before she could open it, the duke spoke her name again. Evanthya turned to face him once more, waiting. He had stopped pacing.

"Do you distrust the archminister because he came through this atrocity unscathed?"

The minister smiled, though she felt herself begin to tremble. "I did as well, my lord. I can hardly blame Pronjed for his good fortune."

"But I sense that you do anyway."

She wanted first to speak of this with Fetnalla. She would have already, had the awkwardness that began before the poisoning not still stood between them. They had spoken in recent days, and Evanthya had spent a good deal of time in Fetnalla's chamber, sitting with her and feeding her when Fetnalla was too weak to feed herself. But their conversations remained difficult and they had not yet been able to speak of Pronjed, Grigor, and the matters that first caused their quarrel.

Tebeo, for all his fine qualities, was still an Eandi noble, proud, but easily frightened by talk of the conspiracy. He had also proven himself to be a friend, however, and she owed him an honest answer.

"I find it strange that he never drank from his glass. I didn't drink . . ." She paused, feeling her cheeks redden. "Fetnalla and I always toast each other at such occasions. She forgot that night, I didn't. But I don't know why Pronjed hesitated."

"You think he may be a part of the conspiracy."

"I have no proof of this."

"But you suspect it."

She paused, then nodded.

Tebeo took a step toward her. "Evanthya, I need to know everything you can tell me about this Qirsi movement. Even if it's not responsible in this case, the very fact that you're wondering about the archminister tells me the time has come to speak of this with the Council of Dukes and the queen."

He was right, of course. Indeed, it was well past time. Yet, what could she tell him? That she had hired a man to kill the one Qirsi she knew of in the movement? That she and Fetnalla had taken it upon themselves to combat the traitors among their people? Just a turn ago it had seemed a necessary step, a dark but justifiable way of striking a blow for those Qirsi who called the Forelands their home and considered the Eandi their friends. But in the wake of all that happened since, her doubts had grown too great. She could hardly bring herself to speak of it with Fetnalla, much less her duke. Too many people had died. This murder she had purchased, as one might buy cloth in the marketplace of Dantrielle, now seemed as cruel and arbitrary as the poisoning. She felt like an archer who looses an arrow, only to wish vainly that she could call it back to her bow.

"I know so little about the conspiracy, my lord. I've already told you what I can."

Tebeo looked disappointed, but after a moment he nodded. "I thought you had, but I felt I should ask."

She wanted to help him. Seeing how Brall treated Fetnalla, particularly recently, during their stay in Solkara, Evanthya had come to appreciate her duke more than ever. Which might have been why she didn't simply let the matter drop.

"I can tell you, my lord, that those who lead the conspiracy have a good deal of gold. I've heard that those who work on their behalf are paid very well." She still remembered the look on the assassin's face when she paid him—ninety qinde, all the gold she and Fetnalla had between them. And clearly the assassin had expected far more.

"Do you know where this gold comes from?"

"No, my lord."

"We should find out. Knowing that would certainly tell us much about the leaders of the movement."

"Yes, my lord."

They stood in silence briefly, Tebeo appearing lost in thought, and Evanthya waiting for him to grant her leave to go. At last he looked up at her again.

"My thanks, First Minister. I look forward to speaking with you again later."

She offered a small bow. "Yes, my lord."

Leaving him, she followed the turns of the castle corridors to Fetnalla's chamber, knocking once before letting herself into the room.

Like all of the chambers on this end of the castle, this one was small and dark, with a single narrow window, and a fire in the hearth that didn't quite manage to warm the chamber sufficiently.

Fetnalla was sitting up in her bed, a candle burning on the table beside her. She was staring toward the small window, a far-off look in her pale eyes. Seeing Evanthya, she smiled and gave a slight shake of her head, as if rousing herself from a dream.

"Am I disturbing you?"

"No. I was just thinking."

"What about?"

Fetnalla shrugged. "Earlier today Brall spoke with the castle surgeon about the poisoning. He was here a short while ago, telling me what he had learned."

Evanthya sat on the edge of the bed. "Did the surgeon tell him anything interesting?"

"Not really. Nothing beyond what we already knew. There was oleander in the wine, not a lot, but enough to kill some of us."

"That's odd. Why wouldn't Grigor use more than that?"

"Maybe he couldn't find more. Maybe he's not familiar with poisons."

Both seemed possible. Still, she could not keep from thinking back to that night in the presence chamber and remembering Grigor's denials. Even then, she had sensed that there was more to them than the desperate, hollow claims of a guilty man. This information about the poison only served to feed her doubts.

"You have that look again, Evanthya."

She looked at the woman, unable to keep from smiling at the sound of her own name. "What look?"

"Like you're readying yourself to stir up trouble. You don't think Grigor did this, do you?"

"Can you forgive me?" Evanthya asked abruptly, ignoring the question at least for the moment. "Can you . . . Can you love me again?"

Fetnalla placed her hand over Evanthya's. It felt cool and smooth, just as Evanthya remembered. "I never stopped loving you. You should know that. And as for the rest, I think I should be asking your forgiveness, not that other way around."

Evanthya leaned forward and kissed her lightly on the lips. She wanted to hold her, to kiss her far more deeply than this. But not here, in this room where Fetnalla had almost died.

"I've missed you," she whispered.

"I know. I've missed you, too."

They kissed again.

"Now answer me," Fetnalla said, grinning, her head tilted to the side as always. "What about Grigor?"

She took Fetnalla's hand, needing to be touching the woman in some way. "I'm not certain what I think. Tebeo asked me if Pronjed could be part of the conspiracy, and I had to admit that I thought it possible."

"Brall has asked me the same thing, just as he did when Carden died. I suppose I think it's possible as well."

"Then Grigor may not be lying when he says he's innocent."

"True," Fetnalla agreed. "But remember, Grigor is saying far more than that. He claims that Numar did this, not Pronjed. And I don't think anyone in the castle believes that."

Evanthya shook her head. "I'm confused. You still believe Grigor did this?"

Fetnalla hesitated, as if searching for the right words. "I think that with all that's happened in the Forelands over the past several turns, it's easy for us to forget that sometimes those who appear guilty really are guilty."

"Then what about Pronjed?"

"As you yourself pointed out some time ago, it may be that neither man can be trusted. Would it really surprise you to learn that one of them was a murderer and the other a traitor?"

Evanthya felt her cheeks burning. Fetnalla was referring to the night of their fight, when she had disagreed with Fetnalla in front of both their dukes. "No, I don't suppose it would."

"It would be nice to know for certain, though," Fetnalla went on, her tone light. Having brought up their disagreement, she seemed eager to move beyond it. "It's time we found a way to determine which Qirsi we can trust and which ones we can't."

Such a simple statement. It was nothing that Evanthya hadn't thought herself a dozen times before. Yet in this instance, it struck her so powerfully that she actually found herself standing, though she didn't remember getting to her feet.

"What is it?" Fetnalla asked, eyeing her with concern.

She even knew where to look. With any luck at all, the man was already looking for her.

"There might be a way," she said breathlessly. She stooped quickly, kissed Fetnalla on the brow, and strode to the door. "I'll be back later."

"Where are you going?" Fetnalla called, as Evanthya stepped into the corridor.

"To the city, to continue a conversation I began several days ago."

As far as Tavis was concerned, they had already been in Solkara for too long. The assassin wasn't here. He might have been once, though they had found no proof of this. No one among those they questioned even knew of the assassin. That is, no one except for the Qirsi minister Grinsa and he met their first morning in the royal city. And she denied knowing the man. Still, the gleaner seemed certain that she was lying, that in fact she had spoken to the assassin in her home city of Dantrielle. It was this, the vague instinct of a Weaver, that kept them there, spending Curgh gold for a room in a Qirsi inn where Tavis's father would never have deigned to sit, much less sleep, and waiting for a chance to question the minister again.

It had been several days since they saw her last. That same night, the queen, several of Aneira's dukes, and many of their ministers had been poisoned. For all Tavis and the gleaner knew, Dantrielle's first minister was dead, a victim of Grigor's ambition.

Tavis raised this possibility with Grinsa as word of the atrocity spread through the streets, but the gleaner dismissed the suggestion with a shake of his head, his eyes rising to the castle towers as if he could see the minister through the grey stone walls.

"Everything we've heard tells us that those who died, Eandi and Qirsi, were older. Evanthya is a young woman. Even if she was stricken, I'm sure she survived. Besides," he added, glancing at Tavis, "this is no time for an Eibitharian noble to be captured sneaking out of Aneira's royal city."

How could he argue?

So they remained in the city, wandering the marketplace by day, and haunting the taverns at night, making themselves familiar to those who frequented the inns, and, they hoped, gradually earning their trust. They didn't ask about the assassin again, at least not for several days. But Grinsa suggested to Tavis that he stop trying to hide his scars.

"Let them see you," he told the young lord. "Let them wonder about the wounds and the blade that caused them."

At first, Tavis found their stares and questions almost impossible to bear. Every eyebrow that went up at the sight of his face, every whistle through gritted teeth that greeted him as he entered an inn, every thoughtless remark—"Lad looks like he's been through a war"; "I've never known road thieves to have such a heavy hand"; "A pity, seems he might have been fair of face once"—brought back his grief at losing Brienne and dark memories of the horrors he endured in Kentigern's dungeon. Still, he understood the reasoning behind Grinsa's request. Convincing the men and women they met in the taverns to talk about the assassin had been difficult. If he and the gleaner could win their trust, and at the same time make them believe that the singer was responsible for Tavis's injuries, they just might learn something about the man or his whereabouts.

As of yet, however, on the last day of both the turn and the year, they hadn't gleaned anything new. Still weary after another uncomfortable night in the tiny bedchamber they were renting, Tavis's patience had run out.

"Father's gold isn't going to last much longer," he said, not bothering to conceal his annoyance as they walked past the peddler's carts. "And we've nothing to show for all the qinde we've spent here."

Grinsa scanned the marketplace, as if too intent on his vain search for the minister to bother looking at him. "If we weren't spending the gold here, we'd be spending it elsewhere," he said. "Unless you're ready to start sleeping in the wood rather than in a bed."

"The snows are almost on us," Tavis said. "No doubt they've begun already to the north. And you speak of sleeping in the wood?"

Still the gleaner didn't look at him, though he did grin. "As you say, your father's gold can't last forever. Eventually you're going to have to choose between sleeping on the ground and working to earn more gold."

Tavis shook his head and muttered a curse. Neither possibility appealed to him.

"Let's just find the assassin and be done with it. If I'm going to suffer through the snows, I'd just as soon do it in my own castle."

They both knew that wasn't likely to happen this year, perhaps not ever again. But Grinsa had the grace and sense not to say anything.

They passed much of the morning walking the length and breadth of the marketplace, nodding to those they recognized from the taverns and stopping to greet peddlers with whom they had spoken before. Once again, neither Tavis nor Grinsa mentioned the assassin, or asked questions of any sort. Despite his concerns about their gold, Tavis sensed that the gleaner had no intention of leaving Solkara any time soon. He could also see that Grinsa continued to search the marketplace with his eyes, even as he spoke and laughed with the sellers.

By midday they had covered much of the city, and they paused as the bells rang, trying to decide whether to return to the inn at which they were staying, or buy a small meal from one of the food vendors.

Tavis's feet ached, and he told the gleaner as much, hoping he could convince Grinsa to go back to the inn.

"It will cost us less to eat in the marketplace," the Qirsi said. "If you're truly concerned about your father's gold . . ." He didn't bother to finish. He didn't have to.

Before Tavis could respond, however, they heard a light footfall behind them.

"I'd have thought you'd be harder to find. Men such as yourselves should travel the city with care."

They both turned to see the minister standing before them. She held a dagger in her hand, though she held it close to her body so that others in the marketplace wouldn't see. Her bright golden eyes were fixed on Grinsa and her expression was grim.

"I'm glad to see that you're all right," the gleaner said. "I was concerned when I heard of the poisoning."

The woman actually laughed, though the look in her eyes didn't change. "Were you?"

"Yes. I trust your duke is well?"

A moment's hesitation, then, "Yes. Thank you."

Grinsa's gaze wandered to her dagger. "Is that intended for us?"

Her face blanched, even as her blade hand remained steady. "I carry it to protect myself."

"From us."

A pause, then, "Yes."

"Would you believe me if I told you that you don't need it, that we bear you no malice?"

"No, I don't think I would."

The gleaner shrugged, but Tavis could see that he was troubled.

"Very well," he said. "Is this a chance meeting, or have you come looking for us?"

"The latter. I want to ask you some questions."

"Can you give me any reason why we should answer? You show no trust, you doubt me when I say that I was concerned for your safety, and you stand before us bearing a blade. Are you offering anything in return, Minister?"

"I offer your continued freedom," she said. "I could just as easily have you arrested as members of the Qirsi conspiracy. I have no doubt that the men in Solkara's dungeon would have no trouble getting answers to the same questions I wish to ask. But their methods are sure to be far less gentle than mine. An hour with them, and this blade will seem a trifle."

At the mere mention of the dungeon, Tavis felt himself begin to tremble and sweat. He was certain that hers was an empty threat, but his memories of Kentigern were still too fresh in his mind.

Grinsa laid a hand on his shoulder, his eyes still on the minister. "I don't think you have any intention of having us arrested. You have no evidence that we're part of the conspiracy, unless you refer to our inquiries about the Eandi singer. And if that's the case, you'd have to explain your own knowledge of the man, which I can't imagine you want to do."

The woman opened her mouth, closed it again. The hand holding the blade fell to her side.

"As it happens, Minister, we might be willing to answer your questions, but only if you agree to answer ours in return."

"I can't do that," she said.

"Then you'd best call for the Solkaran army, or prepare yourself to use that dagger. Because you have no other means of compelling us to tell you anything."

The minister glared at him, seeming to weigh her choices. Her grip on the blade tightened, whitening her knuckles, and Tavis sensed that she was ready to summon the castle guard. After what seemed a long time, however, her expression softened somewhat. She glanced down at her blade, then sheathed it.

"I can't tell you everything," she said, her voice low. "But I will answer some of your questions."

"Fair enough," Grinsa answered after a moment's pause. "Where shall we go?"

She glanced about, appearing unsure of herself.

"You don't want to be seen or heard speaking with us at any length, but neither do you trust us enough to go somewhere private."

The minister met his gaze again. "You understand me quite well, don't you?"

"I know how I'd feel. Why don't we return to the inn at which we met the first time? We'll have some privacy there, but the innkeeper can guarantee your safety."

"Very well." She gestured toward the far side of the marketplace. "After you."

They walked to the inn in silence, the minister a few steps behind them, as if she expected them to flee at any moment. Tavis wasn't certain that he trusted her any more than she did the two of them. Not only did she have a blade at the ready, but she was also Qirsi. Who knew what powers she possessed? Grinsa appeared perfectly willing to keep his back to her, however, and not for the first time, Tavis was glad to be traveling in the company of a Weaver.

The inn was called the Grey Dove, named like other Qirsi establishments, for the pale sorcerers who came there to eat and drink among their own kind. Entering the tavern just after the ringing of the midday bells, they found it far more crowded than it had been several mornings before. They couldn't help but be seen together, but with the crowd came a din that would keep others from listening to their conversation. They waded through the mass of white-hairs to an empty table near the back of the great room. The minister appeared uncomfortable, and she continually looked around, as if expecting at any moment to be recognized by one of the inn's patrons.

"Would you rather go elsewhere?" Grinsa asked, his voice just loud enough to carry over the noise.

The minister shook her head, tight-lipped and wary. She sat, as did Grinsa and Tavis, but for some time none of them spoke. Eventually a serving girl came to their table, bearing bowls of stew and a loaf of dark bread. A second girl came a few moments later, and placed three cups of red wine on the table. Tavis began almost immediately to eat, but the two Qirsi merely sat, the minister staring at her food, and Grinsa watching her.

"You think we're with the conspiracy," the gleaner said at last, drawing her gaze.

"Aren't you?" she asked, sipping her wine.

"You think this because we were asking about the Eandi singer. The one who is also an assassin."

The minister returned her cup to the table with a quivering hand, spilling some of her wine. She fumbled for her napkin, but Grinsa wiped away the wine before she could reach it.

"I sensed the day we met that you might know this man as well," Grinsa went on. "Does that mean that you're part of the conspiracy?"

"No!" she said, looking up. "I have nothing to do with it."

"Why should we believe you?"

"I'm first minister to the duke of Dantrielle. I've served him loyally for more than five years now."

Grinsa gave a small shrug. "You wouldn't be the first Qirsi minister to betray her duke."

"But I haven't—" She stopped, staring at him with narrowed eyes. "You don't really believe I'm with the conspiracy, do you?"

"What makes you say that?"

"Answer me."

After a few moments Grinsa shook his head, a smile touching his lips. "No, I don't. But you've assumed from that first day that we were, and I thought this would be the best way for me to answer your suspicions."

"So you still maintain that you have nothing to do with the movement either?"

"It's the truth," Grinsa said. "I'd even go so far as to say that we're enemies of the Qirsi who lead it."

The woman looked at Tavis, making no effort to hide her curiosity about his scars. He resisted the urge to turn away, suffering her gaze as best he could.

"That morning you told me that the singer did this to the boy. Is that true as well?"

The gleaner hesitated. "In a manner of speaking. I believe I said that the singer was responsible for his scars, which is closer to the truth."

"Now you're weaving mists with your words."

"Perhaps," Grinsa admitted. "But I can't tell you more. Not without endangering the boy's life, and my own."

"I see. Then it seems we've nothing more to say to each other."

"You still don't believe me," he said.

"Actually, I do. I'm not certain why; I suppose I've no choice but to trust my instincts. And they tell me that you're not a traitor."

"Then why would you assume that our conversation is over? Unless you don't consider yourself allied with those who oppose the conspiracy."

"Of course I do. But I needed information about the movement, about those involved with it. Obviously, you don't have any knowledge of this."

"No," Grinsa said, "I don't. But you can still help us. I'm no friend of these renegade Qirsi, and neither are you. We're partners in this struggle, and I need information. The singer—the assassin—has killed on behalf of the conspiracy. My friend and I need to find him."

The woman turned away. "I can't help you with that."

"You can tell me where you saw him, where he was going. Anything you can tell us might prove to be of value."

"You don't understand," she said. "I don't want you to find him."

"What?" The gleaner sat back, looking for the first time like she had truly surprised him. "Why—?" He stopped, his eyes widening. "Are you lovers? Is that it?"

The minister burst out laughing so loudly that others in the tavern paused in their conversations to stare at her. The gleaner's face reddened, but the woman didn't appear to notice.

"No," she said, when her laughter finally subsided. "We're definitely not lovers."

"Then what?" Grinsa asked.

She fell silent again, refusing to look at either of them. Tavis assumed that she would refuse to answer, but he was wrong.

"I'll tell you," she said at last, her voice so low that both Tavis and Grinsa had to lean closer just to hear her. "But I'll give you no details, no names, no places. You'll just have to trust that I'm telling you the truth, and that I have the best interests of the land at heart."

Grinsa nodded. It seemed to Tavis that the gleaner didn't know what else to do.

"I've hired him. I've sent him to kill someone we believe is part of the conspiracy."

"What?" Tavis said, unable to stop himself. "Are you mad?"

The minister's eyes narrowed once more. "You're from Eibithar! I'd know that accent anywhere."

Tavis felt himself flush.

"Yes, he is," Grinsa said, sighing. "Our search for this man has brought us far. But that's not important now. I need—"

"Not important?" the minister repeated, her voice rising. "One moment you tell me that we're allies in a struggle against the conspiracy, and the next I learn that you've brought an enemy of my realm to the royal city."

"He's not an enemy of your kingdom!"

"Of course I am," Tavis said.

Grinsa winced and shook his head.

"At least one of you is being honest, gleaner," the minister said.

"The man we seek is an enemy of Qirsi and Eandi alike," the young lord continued, facing the woman. "He's an enemy of Eibithar, but he also may have killed your Lord Bistari, which I believe makes him an enemy of Aneira as well. Isn't it possible, Minister, that in this instance the interests of our two kingdoms, indeed, of all the seven, are the same?"

She eyed him closely, as if trying to see beyond his scars. "Who are you?"

Tavis almost told her then. For just an instant, for the first time in what seemed an age, he felt like a noble again, like a man whose life revolved around the courts and the exigencies of statecraft. Before Kentigern he had given little thought to what it actually meant to be a noble. Only now that his title was gone, and with it his future, did he realize that he had lost more than comfort and wealth and power. He had trained all his life to be duke and perhaps king. It was his calling, the one trade at which he might have excelled.

"His name isn't important," Grinsa said, gently placing a hand on Tavis's arm, as if reading his thoughts. "But he makes a good point."

The minister looked from one of them to the other, before finally nodding. "Yes, he does. Unfortunately, there's nothing I can do to stop the singer now. I've given him gold and asked him to kill. I have no way to contact him again, and even if I did, I'm not certain that I would. We're at war with the conspiracy, and I'll not quibble about fighting my battles with a bloodied weapon."

"Can you at least tell us which direction he's gone, so that after he's served your purposes we can find him?"

"How do I know you won't find him too soon? Do you intend to engage him in conversation before seeking your vengeance?"

The gleaner frowned, but said nothing.

"I thought not. I've sent him to one of Aneira's houses, but that's all I'll tell you."

"You've told us nothing at all," Tavis said.

"Of course I have. You know now that he's still in this kingdom. That should help you quite a bit."

Tavis started to argue the matter, but Grinsa tightened his hold on the young lord's arm, silencing him.

"Can you tell us anything about this person you sent him to kill?" the gleaner asked.

She faltered. "Like what?"

"You said before that you believe this person is part of the conspiracy. You're not certain though, are you?"

"I'm certain enough."

But Tavis could tell from the tightness of her voice, and the way her hands began to tremble again, that she had doubts.

"If you tell me this person's name, I may be able to put your mind at ease, or perhaps offer to track the assassin and stop him, before he murders an innocent."

The minister's face turned white, but she shook her head. "I can't. As I said, I'm certain enough."

Grinsa let out a breath and sat back. "Very well."

"I should leave," the minister said. "I'll be missed in the castle."

"Of course."

She stood, but did not move away from the table, her eyes fixed on her cup of wine as if she were searching for something lost.

"Neither of us was very forthcoming, and I apologize for my part in that. But I want you to know, I do accept that we're allies of sorts and I hope you find your singer eventually."

"Thank you, Minister. Gods keep you and your duke safe."

Still she didn't leave.

"That first morning, when you followed me to this tavern, you made a point of asking the innkeeper about the singer in a way that allowed me to overhear. Why?"

Grinsa shrugged, a small smile on his lips. "I shouldn't have to explain to you what it means to be a gleaner. I saw you walking the streets of Solkara in your ministerial robes. I saw you enter a tavern in the early morning when you should have been enjoying the hospitality of the queen. It seemed clear to me that you were a person I needed to meet."

She appeared to weigh this. After some time she nodded. Her eyes strayed to Tavis and she seemed to consider saying something. But in the end she merely offered a small smile and walked away.

Tavis and the gleaner remained at their table, silently watching her go. Even after she left the tavern, they didn't speak, choosing instead to eat their food and drink their wine.

Only when they had left a few silvers on the table and stepped back out into the street did Grinsa say, "Well, it seems there's no longer anything holding us in Solkara."

"Are you serious?"

The Qirsi glanced at him. "I expected you'd be relieved."

"I suppose I am. I'm just surprised."

"The singer isn't here, and even if the person Evanthya wants dead is, no assassin would attempt a murder in the royal city, not after all that's happened."

"All we need to do is retrieve our things from the inn and buy some food, and we can be on our way."

He stood scanning the marketplace for a moment, as if trying to decide from which of the peddlers to buy their stores.

An instant later, however, his eyes widened. *"Demons and fire!"*

"What is it?"

Grinsa started striding away so quickly that Tavis nearly had to run to keep pace with him.

"What is it?" he asked again, his voice rising.

"It's Shurik."

"Shurik? Here? Are you certain?"

But the gleaner didn't answer.

Tavis heard a horse neigh and looking toward the sound, saw a beast rearing, kicking out with its front legs. A thin Qirsi man struggled to calm the animal, but his gaze kept flitting toward Grinsa and Tavis. It took the boy a moment, but he did recognize the man. Kentigern's first minister, the one who betrayed Aindreas to the duke of Mertesse.

There was terror in the man's pale eyes, and he looked about the marketplace as if seeking shelter or aid. But nothing could have prepared the young lord for what he did next.

"Guards!" he shouted suddenly, pointing a bony finger at Tavis and the gleaner. "Soldiers of Solkara! That man is an Eibitharian lord, come to kill our queen! Arrest him!"

Grinsa froze in midstride. "This way!" he said, pushing Tavis to the left and leading him through a knot of peddlers, carts, and buyers.

There hadn't been any guards nearby, and though Tavis could still hear Shurik shouting for help, he saw no uniforms.

"Where are we going?" he asked, struggling to keep up with the tall Qirsi.

"We haven't time to make it to the sanctuary. But the south gate isn't far. Perhaps we can make the wood before word spreads to the guards on the city wall."

They reached the edge of the marketplace, crossed a small lane, and cut across a common plot where sheep and goats huddled together against the cold, chewing the brown grasses. Tavis still heard cries, and an instant later a bell began to toll.

He could see the gate now, an arched opening in the grey wall surrounding the city. But with the sound of the bell, several soldiers had gathered there, swords drawn. A few seconds later, the bell at this gate began to ring as well.

"Damn him!" Grinsa said, stopping and looking around.

The guards at this gate wouldn't know why the bells were ringing, or for whom they should be looking, but they weren't likely to allow anyone to leave the city.

"Stay close to me," the gleaner said. "Take hold of my cloak."

Almost before the words had left his lips, ghostly white tendrils of mist began to rise from the ground, swirling around them like Bian's wraiths until Tavis could see nothing of the wall or the soldiers.

Tavis grasped the man's riding cloak, and the two of them started forward. He could only assume that they were making their way to the gate—the soldiers' voices were growing louder—but he kept silent and allowed the gleaner to lead him.

Grinsa drew his dagger, and Tavis did the same. Seeing this, the gleaner stopped, leaned close, and whispered, "Only as a last resort. I'd rather get through without them knowing we've passed."

Tavis nodded, and the two of them walked on.

After a few moments, Tavis felt a slight breeze brush past his cheek, stirring the mist, and thinning it for just an instant. They were at the gate. Four soldiers had positioned themselves in the opening, swords drawn, their eyes wide as they attempted to see through the cloud.

"There!" one of them cried, pointing his blade at Grinsa and Tavis.

The wind died away and the mist closed around them again, hiding the men from view. Grinsa whispered a curse. And then Tavis heard a strange sound, or rather, four of them in quick succession. The shattering of steel.

"Hit them low," Grinsa said quietly, his voice taut.

He rushed forward and Tavis did the same, lowering his shoulder as he did. Suddenly a guard loomed before him, tall and muscular, and far bigger than Tavis. In a fair fight, Tavis wouldn't have had a chance. But the man was gaping at the useless hilt of his sword. He didn't even see Tavis until it was too late. The young lord crashed into the man's chest, driving him to the ground. Tavis stumbled for an instant, but kept his balance and ran. Grinsa was beside him, still drawing mist from the earth, and now summoning a wind that howled like a demon. Tavis felt the air moving past him, but it didn't slow him. Somehow, the gleaner had managed to raise a gale and then shield the two of them from it.

"That should slow them!" the Qirsi shouted over the roar of his tempest. "Follow me to the wood!"

"Where are we going?"

"Away from Solkara."

Tavis rolled his eyes. "Of course. But then where?"

Grinsa didn't hesitate. "North, to Mertesse. I want to be there when Shurik returns."

Chapter
Twenty

✦

Thorald, Eibithar

arston had hoped to reach his father's castle in Thorald long before the end of the waning. Indeed, he had promised his wife and children that he would be back in Shanstead by Pitch Night. That now seemed unlikely. The ride from Kentigern to Thorald measured nearly a hundred leagues and would have taken the company from Shanstead nearly half a turn even in the best weather. The return of the snows slowed them as they crossed the Moorlands, as did the rising of a cold north wind as they forded Binthar's Wash. As the waning progressed, Marston feared that they would not ford the Thorald River until Qirsar's Turn began, and with it the new year.

Entering the North Wood, however, they found the forest roads muddy but passable, and they were able to quicken their pace. For the next four days, Marston pushed the men and their mounts, resting only when absolutely necessary and riding well into the night by the weak glow of the two moons. They came within sight of Thorald's famed walls and double moat the day before Pitch Night. Most of the celebrations were over by then. Marston had long since missed Bohdan's Night, the Night of Two Moons in the god's turn, when family and friends exchanged gifts and shared in great feasts. But at least he and his men would not be abroad on the last night of the waning.

As the Pitch Night legends went, Bohdan's Turn offered little to fear. Pitch Night in the god's turn was a night of quiet contemplation after the festivities of the turn. But even the bravest of men preferred to be safely housed on any night when neither moon shone.

After leaving the mounts with the castle's stablemaster, and making certain that his men were given rooms on the east corridor, where the castle's guests were always lodged, Marston walked across the upper ward to his father's quarters. A light snow fell on the brown grasses and empty gardens of the ward, and a cold wind blew over the castle's ramparts, carrying the scent of Amon's Ocean and the ghostly cry of a single gull.

Usually, Marston would have brought Xivled, his Qirsi minister, to such a meeting. But Aindreas had insisted that Xiv be excluded from their conversation in Kentigern, and though the man had been uncompromising in his condemnation of the king, and unreasonable in the demands he placed on Thorald, Marston thought it best to honor his demand for privacy, even here. He also hadn't seen his father in some time, and given how quickly the illness was spreading through Tobbar's body, there was part of him that feared seeing the duke again. Best that he be alone.

As it happened, he had also asked Xiv to attend to another matter while they were in Thorald, one that needed to be addressed discreetly.

Entering the tower at the north corner of the ward, Marston hesitated, unsure as to whether to go to Tobbar's presence hall or his chambers.

"He's in his bedchambers, my lord," one of the guards said, his voice low.

Marston turned to the man. "Is he worse, then?"

The guard stared at him for a moment before lowering his gaze and nodding.

Marston took a breath, his stomach tightening. *I'm not ready to be duke. I'm not ready to lose my father.* "I see. Thank you."

He climbed the stairs to the upper corridor and walked quickly to his father's chambers. Marston and his brother had been raised in Shanstead; his father only came to Thorald seven and half years before when Filib the Elder, duke of Thorald and next in line after old Aylyn to be king, was killed in a hunting accident. Marston and Chalton hadn't even been of Fating age then, but the duke's son, Filib the Younger, needed a regent, and since he was then heir to the throne, his needs outweighed those of Tobbar's sons. Tobbar returned to Shanstead quite often during the next several years, but still Marston felt that he had been robbed of his father. His resentment of his cousin Filib festered like an untreated wound until he found himself lying in his bed in the dark of night, wishing for the boy's death.

By the time Filib was killed, several years later—everyone assumed at the time that his death came at the hands of common road thieves—Marston had outgrown his childish jealousies. He was seventeen by then, past his Fating. He had assumed the thaneship in Shanstead and so had come to understand the workings of the Eandi courts and the demands placed by the Rules of Ascension upon all the major houses, but especially Thorald.

Still, those nights he had spent cursing Filib's name haunted him, and he couldn't help but feel some guilt about the boy's death. To this day, walking through the corridors of Thorald Castle disturbed him. Despite the Thorald blood flowing in his veins, despite the many years his father had lived here, this fortress had never been his home. He would be duke before long. Chalton would take the thaneship and Marston would move to Thorald. But he doubted that he would ever feel comfortable in this place. His heart lay in Shanstead.

Pausing in front of his father's door to take a long breath and offer a quick prayer to Ean, Marston knocked.

"Come in!" Tobbar's voice sounded strong, giving the thane some hope.

He pushed the door open and stepped into the room. A fire burned brightly in the hearth and the windows were shuttered, making the chamber far too warm for Marston's liking. But Tobbar was seated by a low table, rather than lying in bed, a small scroll in his hands. His face appeared far too thin and pale, the round ruddy cheeks Marston remembered from just a year ago nothing more than a memory. But his grey eyes sparkled with the glow of the fire, and a smile lit his face. He even managed to stand as Marston crossed the chamber to embrace him.

"I expected you days ago," the duke said, releasing his son and waving a bony hand at a nearby chair.

Marston pulled the chair over next to his father's and sat.

"I know. If the snows had held off for another half turn, we would have been here sooner. As it was we were lucky to make it here when we did."

He glanced around the chamber and was pleased to see that his father was alone, save for a pair of servants. Usually his first minister was with him. Enid ja Kovar had served Tobbar for several years now, and though his father still trusted her, even with all the rumors of Qirsi betrayal spreading across the Forelands, Marston did not. As his doubts about Filib the Younger's death mounted, he had begun to question whether the minister might have been involved in the young lord's murder. Tobbar rejected the notion, and had grown angry the last time Marston raised the matter. But the thane still preferred to avoid her. At this point, he distrusted most Qirsi. Xiv was the son of his father's first Qirsi advisor. The two of them had spent much of their youth together. Had he not agreed to serve as Marston's minister, the thane would have none at all. As it was, he did not plan to take on more ministers when he became duke, though most dukes had several underministers in addition to their first ministers. He had little doubt that as word of the Qirsi conspiracy continued to spread, more and more Eandi nobles would follow his example.

"Tell me of your visit with Kentigern."

Marston gave a wan smile. "I'm afraid it wasn't much of a visit. I was there only one night before he as much as ordered me from his castle."

Tobbar's eyes widened. "What did you say to him?"

"Nothing that you wouldn't have, Father. I promise you."

The duke looked away, his expression troubled. "I believe you. Tell me what happened."

Marston described his conversation with Aindreas, making certain not to leave out any details, not even those he knew would displease his father.

"You shouldn't have brought up Brienne's murder," Tobbar said when he had finished, shaking his head and staring at the fire.

"I didn't bring it up, Father. Aindreas did. We could hardly expect him not to. It lies at the root of everything."

Tobbar faced him, his eyes bright and angry. "But to tie it to the conspiracy. Demons and fire, Marston! What were you thinking?"

"His first minister betrayed him less than a turn after the girl's death, Father! You may be willing to accept that the two had nothing to do with each other, but I can't. The conspiracy is real, and it has been for longer than any of us—"

"We're not going to have this conversation right now!"

"It has been for longer than any of us want to admit!"

"I won't listen to this again!"

"Damn your stubbornness, Father! You have to listen!"

The duke was glaring at him, his cheeks looking unnaturally flushed, and his chest rising and falling rapidly, as if just arguing the point demanded too great an effort.

"Nobles are dying, Father," he went on a moment later, his voice lower. "Eandi nobles. Not just in Eibithar, but all through the Forelands. I know that Aindreas's Qirsi betrayed him to the Aneirans, but even with the minister weakening Kentigern's gates, an assault on the tor could have only hoped to succeed with the duke away, fighting with the Curgh army."

"Maybe the Qirsi was in league with the Aneirans for a long time, but only arranged the siege after Brienne's murder. Maybe he was taking advantage of an opportunity."

"You know as well as I that a siege of that size requires more planning than that. Aindreas's minister didn't take advantage of an opportunity, he created one."

"Have the Qirsi done anything like this in the other kingdoms?" Tobbar asked. "It's one thing to assassinate a noble, but have they killed other young girls and implicated their paramours?"

"Not that I've heard of. But," Marston added quickly, "they have killed nobles and made it seem the work of court rivals or thieves. I'm sure they've even tried to disguise their handiwork by making a murder seem to be nothing more than an accident."

Tobbar narrowed his eyes. "Is that what you think has happened here in Thorald?"

He shrugged. "I don't know anymore. All I can say is that Eibithar has been on a path to civil war for some time now, longer than any of us realized at first. It began with that incident in Galdasten all those years ago, at the Feast. When Uncle Filib was killed, and Filib the Younger after him, it ensured that grandfather's death would give the crown to Javan of Curgh. And Brienne's death made it likely that Javan's ascension would bring war."

"And you believe this was all the work of the conspiracy? The incident in Galdasten? My brother's death? Your cousin's?"

"It's possible."

"What happened in Galdasten was nothing more or less than the act of a madman, a villager who had lost his wife to an illness, and his son to the pestilence."

"That may be so. But the rest—"

"The elder Filib was thrown by his mount. Had he landed one fourspan to the right or left of that stone, he would have survived. You think the Qirsi did that as well?"

"There's a magic known as the language of beasts—"

"His swordmaster was with him!" Tobbar said, his voice rising. "He saw the mount rear! There wasn't a white-hair within a league of them!"

He should have known better than to pursue this matter. Each time he and his father spoke of the conspiracy, it came to this. Tobbar refused to accept that his Qirsi could be involved, and Marston remained just as adamant in his refusal to believe that all the events of the past few years were unrelated. With his father weakened by illness, he should have let the discussion end, but his fears, and perhaps his pride, wouldn't allow it.

"Nobody witnessed Filib the Younger's death," he said. "Will you at least allow that there may have been more to his murder than we first thought?"

He expected his father to rail at him again, but the duke surprised him. "I don't know what to believe about the boy. The Revel was in Thorald at the time, and I warned him that there were thieves about."

"But there were Qirsi here, as well."

Tobbar eyed him briefly before turning his gaze on the fire again. "Yes." He frowned. "That doesn't mean the conspiracy killed him. Whoever it was cut off his finger to get the Thorald signet ring. I still think it was probably thieves."

"But?"

His father looked at him again, the corners of his mouth twitching. "But with all that's happened since, I have to wonder if someone wished to have the House of Thorald removed from the Order of Ascension."

Marston started to agree, but his father stopped him with a raised finger.

"That doesn't mean I'm ready to send away all my ministers," he said. "As you say, the Revel was here, and with it all its gleaners and fire conjurers. If the Qirsi were behind his death, it would have been one of them. I'm certain of it."

Once more, Marston wanted to argue the point, but his father had already admitted that Filib's murder might have been an assassination, rather than a simple act of thievery. Marston had never thought the duke would come that far. Continuing the discussion was only likely to anger him further.

"Perhaps you're right."

Tobbar raised an eyebrow. "Are you humoring me, whelp?"

Marston grinned. "Maybe I should go. You look tired."

"I am tired. But you can't leave yet." The duke lifted a scroll off the table and handed it to him. It was tied with two satin ribbons, one tawny, the other black. The colors of Tremain.

Marston looked at his father a moment before unrolling the scroll.

"It arrived at Shanstead a few days ago. Your brother brought it to me, thinking it might be too important to keep until your return. Forgive me, but I read it, though it's addressed to you."

"Of course," Marston said absently, beginning to read the message.

It was from the Lathrop, duke of Tremain. He wished to know where Marston stood in the conflict between Curgh and Kentigern, and he offered to ride to Shanstead to discuss the matter.

The message was brief and rather vague, but the last line caught Marston's eye.

> With the kingdom at the very precipice of war, it behooves all
> of us who honor the Rules of Ascension and cherish the peace
> they have brought to our land, to stand with the king. I hope
> you will agree.

"It seems Aindreas isn't the only one interested in cultivating an alliance with you," Tobbar said, as Marston began reading the message a second time. "I get the feeling they don't expect me to live much longer."

Marston looked up. "Father, no. I don't think they—"

"It's all right," Tobbar said, smiling. "I'd do the same, were I in their position. You are the future of this house, you and your brother."

"Did Chalton read this as well?"

"No. He left it with me, stayed just the one night, and returned home."

Marston nodded, eyeing the message again. "Why would Lathrop write to me? He's yet to take sides in this matter, and yet asks me to do just that."

"I'd imagine Kearney asked him to do it."

"But why. If the king wishes to ask one of his thanes where he stands on a matter of such importance, surely he can send the message himself."

"Think, Marston. You're going to be duke someday. It's time you began to see the world through a noble's eyes. Kearney has sent me several messages since his ascension. I've already spoken for the house, and I've made it clear to him I won't commit Thorald to either side of this fight. But he needs to know what will happen when I'm gone. If he were to send a message to you directly, it would be an affront to me, an indication that he no longer considers me Thorald's leader."

"Is Tremain's message any less of an affront?"

"He's the duke of a minor house, and as you said, he hasn't sided with either Javan or Aindreas. Under the circumstances, he was an appropriate choice. Strictly speaking, I'd be justified in taking offense, but as a practical matter, Kearney needed to get a message to you, and this was the best, quickest way for him to do so." He gazed at Marston for several moments, a slight smile on his pallid face. "The question is, how are you going to respond?"

The thane shrugged. "Just as you have, and just as I told Aindreas I would. Thorald wants no part of this fight."

"Are you certain?"

"Surely I don't have to convince you of this, Father. If we commit Thorald's army to either side, it will embolden one of them and bring us to war. You've said so yourself a dozen times."

"Yes, I have," Tobbar said, nodding. "But I'm too old for a war. You're not. And it may be that there's something here worth fighting for."

"What? You can't be serious."

"Do you want Davin to sit on the throne?"

The question silenced him. What man of Thorald didn't dream of seeing his son crowned as king? The Rules of Ascension didn't allow Marston or Chalton to aspire to the throne, but with Filib's line dead, their sons could rule. Though only if Glyndwr relinquished the crown.

"Of course I do," he answered at last. "But I won't destroy the kingdom to put him there."

"Is that what it would take?" his father asked mildly.

"Yes. Kearney has a son. And someday the younger Kearney probably will as well. Glyndwr won't give up the throne. It would have to be taken, and that means war. It also means defying the Rules of Ascension. And if we abandon the rules, then even when Glyndwr's line does fail, Thorald may need to fight to reassert its supremacy." He shook his head. "Much as I'd like to see Davin as king, the price is too high. I won't choose between Javan and Aindreas, and if one of them challenges the king, they'll have to defeat our soldiers as well as the King's Guard. I'll lead the army myself."

Tobbar nodded, the smile still on his lips. "Very good, Marston. Very good, indeed. The house will be in good hands when I'm gone."

"You're not fooling me, old man. You're too stubborn to die."

He grunted, facing the fire again. "Hardly. I'm tired, boy. The healers have given up on me, and I haven't the strength or the will to fight this battle alone."

Marston felt a strange tightening in his throat and he had to blink his eyes to keep the tears back. He wondered if his father had said any of this to Chalton.

"You needn't grieve," the duke said, firelight in his grey eyes. "I've had a good life. I've been in love, I've seen my boys grow to manhood, and I've ruled the land's finest house. Few men can say as much. I would have liked to have more time with your mother, but Bian wanted her for himself." He glanced at Marston, the smile touching his lips again for just an instant. "I'm eager to see her, even if it is in the Underrealm."

Marston tried to grin. Failed. "Isn't it enough to see her on the Night of the Dead?"

Tobbar shook his head, looking away once more. "I want to hold her hand. I want to kiss her. You can't hold a wraith in your arms."

He searched for something to say, but nothing came to him. "Perhaps I should leave you, Father. We can speak again later, when you've had some time to rest."

The duke nodded.

Marston leaned forward and kissed his father on the cheek, something he hadn't done since he was a boy. He stood and started to walk away, but Tobbar caught his hand, giving it a quick squeeze before letting him go.

Stepping out of the warmth of his father's chamber into the cool air of the castle corridor, Marston paused. He was hungry, and he would have liked to lie down in a comfortable bed. But first he wanted to speak with the castle surgeon. *I'm not ready to be duke.* He needed to know how much time he had to prepare.

Xivled remained in his chamber long enough to give his thane time to reach Tobbar's quarters. Then he left, descending the tower stairs to the ward, and crossing to the north end of the castle, where the ministers had their rooms.

"Ask her about the messages Father has exchanged with the king," Marston had instructed. "Father could probably tell me himself, but with his illness worsening, this is something the two of you can discuss. I'm sure she'll understand."

It was a simple enough task, one that was appropriately handled by ministers.

But in this case, Xivled hoped it would be merely a pretext for another conversation.

The minister half expected to find her chambers empty. She rarely left the duke's side, and he thought it likely that she'd be with him this day as well. It seemed, however, that the gods were with him. Knocking on her door, he heard a rustling of scrolls and then footsteps approaching the door. An instant later, the door opened, and Enid ja Kovar stood before him, her ministerial robes hanging on a frame that appeared to be more bone than flesh.

She had once been a pretty woman. Xiv remembered thinking so during his first few visits to Thorald as Marston's minister. Youth and beauty could be fleeting among his people, however, and Enid had grown old more quickly than most. She still wore her white hair tied back from her face, and her pale eyes still held the same look of keen intelligence and barely suppressed amusement he remembered from earlier visits to the castle. But her face had grown even thinner and more sallow than it once had been, making her resemble a cadaver more than a living woman.

"Cousin," she said, obviously surprised to see him. "I didn't know the thane had returned. Otherwise I would have been with the duke."

"We reached the castle just a short time ago."

She said nothing for several moments, as if expecting him to speak. When he didn't, she gave a forced smile. "Well, have you come to fetch me, and bring me to the duke's chambers?"

"Actually, no. I believe the thane wished to have some time alone with his father. He asked me to find you and learn what I could of his father's correspondence with the king."

She raised an eyebrow. "Can't he ask his father just as easily?"

"With the duke ill, my lord thought it best that he trouble Lord Thorald as little as possible with such matters. But if you prefer, I can seek out one of the underministers."

This time her smile appeared genuine. "No, that's not necessary. I can't remember the last time I entertained such a charming young man in my bedchambers."

Xiv gave a small laugh, hoping it would mask his discomfort.

"Please come in, cousin," the first minister said, stepping to the side and waving him into her room.

He took a seat in a lone chair by the hearth. The minister walked to her writing table and sat, eyeing him with unconcealed curiosity.

"So you wish to know about Tobbar's correspondence with the king."

"My lord does, yes."

She gave a slight frown. "I'm afraid there's not much to tell. The king sends a brief message nearly every turn, stating his belief that the conflict between the lords of Curgh and Kentigern threatens to tear the kingdom apart, and asking the duke not to commit himself or his army to either man."

"Does he tell the duke much of events in Curgh or Kentigern?"

"No. Indeed, I expect Lord Shanstead knows more of what is happening in Kentigern than does his father. For that matter, I imagine you know more than I do. Perhaps you can tell me something of your visit to the tor."

"Of course, First Minister, though we were in Kentigern for less than a day."

She let out a small breathless laugh. "Less than a day?"

"When the thane made it clear to Aindreas that he agreed with his father's decision not to commit Thorald's army to Kentigern's cause, the duke demanded that we leave."

"I see."

"You've told me of the king's messages. How does Lord Thorald respond to them?"

"As any dutiful Eandi noble would. With assurances of his continued fealty to the crown and promises that he will do as the king asks."

Xiv smiled inwardly at the opening she had given him. "You don't approve, First Minister?"

She smiled again, her small, sharp teeth looking as yellow as her eyes in the light of the fire. "It's not my place to approve or disapprove. I merely offer my counsel."

"But you speak of Lord Thorald's sense of duty to his king as if it's a fault."

She regarded him silently for several moments, as if trying to gauge how much she could say.

"Speaking Qirsi to Qirsi," she finally said, "I do find the blind devotion with which Eandi nobles follow their king somewhat . . . disturbing."

"You'd rather your duke joined Aindreas of Kentigern in challenging the king's authority?"

"Of course not. Don't be a fool. I merely believe that the Eandi are so concerned with honoring the nobles above them that they do their leaders a disservice. The king would be much better served if his dukes could express themselves honestly, without fear of being branded traitors."

"Do you think Lord Thorald wishes to respond differently to the king's messages than he has?"

She shook her head. "I don't believe so. My lord is a good man, but he doesn't think boldly."

Xiv nodded. "It seems the son doesn't step far from his father's shadow."

"Really? I always thought the thane an intelligent young man."

"He is, for an Eandi." Xiv met her gaze. "That is what we're talking about here, isn't it? The difference between the Eandi and the Qirsi?"

"I'm not certain I understand what you mean," she said, smiling in a way that told him she did.

Xiv gave a small shrug and stood. "Forgive me. I thought you would."

He started toward the door, but before he was halfway across the room, she stopped him.

"Perhaps I do understand. Sit, cousin." She hesitated, then added, "Please."

After a moment's pause, Xiv returned to his chair.

For a long time she just stared at him, as if she expected to read his thoughts from what she saw on his face. At last she stood and walked to the hearth, bending to place another log on the fire.

"You've known the thane for a long time, haven't you?"

"Since we were boys in his father's court."

"I would think that after all these years, you'd be loyal to the man. Few of us have friendships that last half that long."

"It's because of how long I've known him that I feel no loyalty to him whatsoever."

"What do you mean?"

Xiv looked away. "Our friendship is nearly as old as memory, yet he treats me like a servant. He's known the captain of Shanstead's army for three years, maybe four. But the two of them hunt together, their children play

319

together, their wives speak to one another as sisters. All because they're Eandi. Just once, I'd like him to address me as—" He stopped himself, exhaling loudly through his teeth. "The years we've known each other mean nothing to him," he said, his voice low. "Why should they mean any more to me?"

She nodded. "You're right; they shouldn't. Has anyone contacted you yet?" she asked, picking up a poker and stirring the embers. "Have you received any gold?"

"No, nothing."

She glanced at him. "Then what is it you want from me?"

"To join," he said. "With all respect, First Minister, neither you nor your duke can live forever. With the thane assuming leadership of the House of Thorald, I feel certain that I'd be a valuable addition."

Enid smiled thinly. "I'm delighted to hear my failing health has created such a wonderful opportunity for you."

"I didn't wish this on you, First Minister. But you've lived a full life, and I'd be a fool to let this chance slip by. I needn't tell you that there's a good deal of gold at stake."

"This is about more than gold," she said, her voice hardening. "This is about bringing Qirsi rule to the Forelands. It's about allowing our children to dream of being more than court servants and Revel fools. You'd do well to remember that if you're to join this cause."

"Of course. Forgive me. I only meant that—"

"I know just what you meant. A few years ago, the gold meant a good deal to me, too. But as I've grown older, as my capacity for enjoying wealth has diminished, I've come to realize that the riches mean nothing next to the advancement of the Qirsi people. The W—" She stopped abruptly, her face coloring. "With time, you'll understand this as well."

"You were going to say something else."

The minister shook her head. "It was nothing." She paused, then, "You're wrong about one thing though. I haven't lived a full life. It may surprise you to learn that I'm only in my thirty-seventh year."

Xiv couldn't keep his eyes from widening. He would have guessed she was at least five years older than that.

She smirked. "Yes, I know. I appear far older. My mother died young, even for a Qirsi. It seems we share that fate."

"I'm sorry." He wasn't certain what else to say.

"Don't be. I regret only that I won't see this movement bear fruit." She straightened and returned to her chair by the table. "Return to Shanstead with your thane. You'll receive your first payment in the next turn or two, and soon after you'll be contacted."

"By whom?"

"It's not my place to say," she told him. "You may be given a task to complete, or you may be told to wait. Not long ago, there was a great deal happening here in Eibithar. Since Aylyn's death, however, and the events in Kentigern, the movement has turned its attention to the southern kingdoms."

Xiv shuddered, as if a frigid wind suddenly had swept through the chamber. "Was the . . . the movement responsible for Aylyn's death?"

"Again, it's not my place to say."

"What about all that happened in Kentigern? Brienne's death, the siege?"

"If you want to be welcome in this movement, cousin, you'll stop asking questions. Each of us knows little of what the others do. Those who lead us prefer it that way. You'll know what's expected of you, and for now that should be enough."

"I understand. It's just that I know so little of the movement, and I want to be prepared when I'm given my first task. I don't want to fail."

"No," she said. "You don't." She picked up a scroll, unrolled it, and began to read. "Leave me now. As I've told you, you'll be contacted."

He hesitated, then stood and walked to the door. Pausing on the threshold, he turned back to her. "What have they asked you to do?"

She didn't even look up. "Close the door behind you, cousin. The corridors are terribly cold this time of year."

Xiv had to smile. "Goodbye, First Minister. Thank you."

She raised a hand.

Closing the door, Xiv hurried down the stairs of the nearest tower, crossed the upper ward once more, and returned to the castle guest chambers.

He stopped in front of Marston's door and knocked once.

"Enter!"

Opening the door, he found the thane still in his riding clothes and boots, lying on his bed, his eyes closed.

"Forgive me, my lord. I didn't mean to disturb you."

"Not at all, Xiv," Marston said, sitting up. "I must have dozed. What's the hour?"

"I'm not certain, my lord. I haven't heard the bells in some time."

Marston nodded, rubbing a hand across his face and yawning. "You spoke with the first minister?"

"I did."

"And?"

Xiv smiled. "You were right about her."

"She admitted it?" he asked eagerly.

"Not right away. But once she was convinced that I hated you, and wanted to join, she said that she would have someone contact me."

"What else did she tell you?"

"Not as much as we would have liked. I couldn't get her to admit to anything, nor would she tell me what the Qirsi movement had to do with what happened in Kentigern."

Marston frowned. "I was hoping she'd tell us something of Filib's murder. And Brienne's as well."

"She made it sound as if she knew little of the movement's activities outside of Thorald. And she warned me about asking a lot of questions. I'm sorry I couldn't learn more."

The thane shook his head. "Don't apologize. You've done well, Xiv."

"I could do more if you'd let me join. This might be an opportunity for us to learn a great deal about the conspiracy."

"No. I don't want to give her time to tell anyone about you. It's more important that we prove to my father that she's a traitor. If we can convince him, he might be able to convince Aindreas that the Qirsi were behind Brienne's death." He smiled. "Besides, do you really think Tamah would ever forgive me if I let something happen to you?"

"I think you're making a mistake," Xiv said. "Enid told me that the Qirsi leaders have turned their attention to the southern kingdoms. There's little happening in Eibithar right now. The danger to me would be minimal."

"You don't know that."

He faltered, but only briefly. "Not for certain, no. But it makes sense."

"Maybe it does, but I'm not willing to take that chance. Aindreas has already shown that he won't listen to me, but he can't ignore my father as easily. We have to tell the duke what we know, and we need to do so now, while he's still strong enough to speak with Kentigern." He managed a smile, though it seemed to Xiv that there were tears in his eyes. "We can't stop the conspiracy on our own, Xiv. But we might be able to prevent a civil war. We just have to do it quickly, before my father dies."

Chapter
Twenty-one

obbar stared off to one side, his face burning with rage and humiliation and grief. If what his son and the boy's Qirsi were telling him was true, he had been a fool for more years than he cared to count. Worse, it was possible that through carelessness, and his blind willingness to trust, he had allowed Filib the Younger's death.

"I don't believe any of this," he said, his voice low. *Or at least I don't want to.*

"You think Xiv would lie about such a thing?"

"He's Qirsi, too. Who's to say that he's not the traitor here?"

"Father!"

The duke looked up at the young Qirsi, who stood near the hearth, silent and withdrawn, his gaze lowered. Tobbar knew that he should apologize to the man, but he couldn't. "What gave you the right to speak with my minister in the first place?" he demanded instead. "In my castle, no less."

"I asked him to, Father," Marston said, forcing Tobbar to look his way. "If you want to rail at someone, rail at me. Xiv did this on my behalf."

"Then you answer me. What gave you the right?"

Marston straightened, taking a breath. "I had no right. I feel that what we've learned justifies how we learned it, but you're right. It wasn't my place to send Xiv to your first minister without your approval. Forgive me."

Damn the boy. Perhaps he knew more of statecraft than Tobbar realized. With his apology he forced Tobbar to look beyond the transgression to what their actions had revealed. Enid was a traitor, a part of this conspiracy that seemed to be everywhere. Ean knew how long she had been lying to him, and what other things she had done to weaken Thorald.

"This isn't a night for such things," he said, sounding, he knew, like a peevish child. "Pitch Night in Bohdan's Turn is a night for reflection and prayer, not for . . . for this."

"Is there ever a good time for this? Will you be any more willing to speak with her tomorrow than you are tonight?"

Tobbar looked away once more. "Tell me again what she said."

Xivled cleared his throat. "She told me that I would be contacted, that they'd probably give me gold first and that I might be instructed to carry out some task."

"She didn't say who would contact you?"

"No, and she warned me against asking too many questions."

"Did she give you any sense at all of who her superiors were?"

"None at all. At one point she started to say something more, but she stopped herself and wouldn't reveal anything when I pressed her on the matter."

Tobbar nodded, still not looking at either of them. *She betrayed me.* Try as he might, he could think of no reason why Xivled would lie about this. If he wished to be Thorald's first minister he had only to wait. Certainly, if he belonged to the conspiracy himself, he gained nothing by drawing attention to the alleged treason of another Qirsi. Nor did he appear to be lying. Tobbar couldn't sense such things, of course; none of the Eandi could, which was why so many of their nobles were dying. He had only his instincts, and though his faith in them had been badly shaken, he wasn't ready to abandon them entirely.

"What would you have me do?" he asked at last, making himself meet Marston's gaze.

"Simply speak with her, Father. I'm not asking you to accept what we're telling you on faith."

"Of course you are. You want me to summon my first minister to this chamber so that I can accuse her of betraying our house."

Marston's jaw tightened, but he didn't answer. How could he?

"That is what you want me to do, isn't it? Confront her with what your minister has told us, and ask her to defend herself?"

"Yes," Marston said. "That's what I want you to do."

"And what if Xivled is wrong? Enid has served me—has served this house—for nearly seven years. How do I repair the damage I'm about to do to my friendship with this woman? How do I justify accusing her of this?"

"If she truly is your friend, Father, she'll understand. Surely she's heard of the conspiracy just as you have. She can hardly blame you for asking where her loyalties lie?"

"Would you be so understanding?" the duke asked, looking past his son to the Qirsi.

"This isn't worth discussing," Marston said before his minister could reply. "Xiv isn't wrong, and bruising Enid's pride should be the least of your concerns." He stepped to Tobbar's chair and knelt before the duke, forcing Tobbar to look him in the eye. "She betrayed us, Father. All of us. I have no doubt that she had Filib killed. We need to know what else she's done. We need to know if there are others in the castle who have helped her. And then we need to imprison her and plan for her execution."

He stared at his son, wishing at that moment that he could abdicate. Regardless of whether or not Marston was right, he didn't want to face this. He was dying. Why couldn't the gods simply let him go? Why couldn't all of this have happened a year from now, when he was dead, or too ill to care anymore?

He knew the answer, of course. It echoed in his mind like thunder in the highlands. *Enid was your choice. You brought her to this house. Her betrayal is your failure.* He could no more escape blame than she could.

At last he nodded, closing his eyes against a throbbing pain in his head. "Summon her." He rubbed his temple, listening as Marston crossed the room to the door and instructed one of the guards to bring Enid to the chamber.

A moment later his son closed the door again then returned to Tobbar's side.

"Are you all right?"

The duke opened his eyes. "No, I'm not all right. I'm old and I'm dying, and I don't know who to trust anymore."

Marston recoiled as if Tobbar had struck him.

"I didn't mean you," the duke said quickly. "You know that."

His son regarded him briefly, his lips pressed thin. Then he nodded, though Tobbar could see in his eyes that he was still hurt.

Marston stood once more and began pacing the room. Xivled remained by the hearth, and the duke sat motionless in his chair, gazing at his own hands, wondering how they had grown so thin. None of them spoke.

Finally the duke looked up at Marston's minister. "I owe you an apology, Xivled. I shouldn't have said what I did before. Your father served me for more than ten years and never did I have cause to question his loyalty or his courage. Our families have been tied to each other for too long. You deserve better than my suspicion."

"Thank you, my lord. My father always spoke of you as a friend, and your son has always treated me as no less."

They fell silent again, waiting for Enid. It seemed to take her hours to answer his summons. When at last the knock came at the door, Marston halted and looked toward the duke, as if suddenly unsure of himself.

"Enter," the duke called.

The door swung open and the first minister walked in, appearing terribly frail. It struck Tobbar that this was a waste of all their time. He and his minister would both be dead before long. Why not let this pass?

But he knew better. Seeing her now, allowing himself to wonder if she had indeed betrayed him, the duke felt anger welling in his chest. In spite of everything he had said to Marston a few moments earlier, he wanted to know the truth. And if she had killed his nephew or paid others to do so, he wanted her dead.

"You called for me, my lord," she said, glancing at each of the three men.

"Close the door, Enid."

The minister hesitated, perhaps sensing from his tone that this was to be no ordinary conversation. She pushed the door closed and took her customary seat by his writing table.

"How may I serve, my lord?" she asked, a brittle smile on her lips.

"The thane's minister was just telling me of a conversation he had with you in your chambers."

"Yes. He asked me to tell him of your correspondence with the king. I thought it an odd request, since your son could just as easily have asked you, but I saw no reason to keep anything from him. Would you have preferred that I say nothing?"

"That's not the conversation to which I was referring."

"Then I'm afraid I can't help you, my lord. It's the only conversation we've had."

She looked and sounded as calm as ever. Even searching for some sign that she was lying to him, Tobbar saw none.

"According to Xivled, you offered to put him in touch with the leaders of the Qirsi conspiracy. You even promised him gold."

The minister laughed. "Did I offer as well to make him emperor of Braedon?" She looked over at Marston, as if expecting to hear him laugh with her. When he didn't—when none of them did—she sobered, facing the duke again. "You're not serious, my lord."

"You deny it?"

She paled. "Of course I do. I know little more about the conspiracy

326

than you do, my lord. I've certainly had no contact with anyone involved with it. And I have no gold to promise."

"You're lying!" Marston said, striding toward her.

"Be quiet, Marston!" Tobbar eyed her for several moments, trying to decide how to proceed. "So you're telling me that the two of you spoke only of the messages I've exchanged with the king? There was nothing more?"

Enid glanced at Xivled, looking uncomfortable. "That's not entirely the case. I'm reluctant to say anything that might harm the reputation of another Qirsi, but your son's minister spoke of the thane in terms that can best be described as insulting. He questioned Lord Shanstead's judgment and intelligence, and expressed great bitterness at the treatment he had received from the thane." She turned in her chair to look at Marston. "Were I in your position, my lord, I would be reluctant to place much faith in this man. I believe in time he will betray you."

"As you've betrayed my father?"

"I've done no such thing, Lord Shanstead. If this minister of yours has told you otherwise, he's a liar."

"I know him too well to believe that," Marston said.

"Apparently the years you've spent together mean little to him, my lord. He's yet to deny that he said those things about you."

Marston grinned darkly. "I don't expect him to deny it. I told him to speak to you so, knowing that you'd reply by asking him to join the conspiracy."

Enid glared at him for a moment before looking at Tobbar again. "You knew about this?"

"No," the duke said. "They did this on their own, and I've already chided them for it. But what Xivled told me about your conversation disturbed me greatly. I was hoping you could explain."

"So you believe I've betrayed you. You're willing to take this man's word over mine, though I've served you well for all these years."

" 'This man,' as you put it, is the son of my former first minister, the Qirsi you replaced. I've known him longer than I've known you." Tobbar exhaled heavily. "But still, I don't know who to believe. One of you must be lying, and so one of you must be a traitor. So what is your counsel, First Minister? How am I to decide?"

For the first time, he saw her falter, as if she thought the question itself a trap. In truth, Tobbar hadn't intended it as such, though he realized now that it placed her in an awkward position. If she had betrayed him, she could only offer more denials and accusations.

"It is a difficult matter, my lord," she said slowly. "You must consider all that you know of both of us. You may have known the minister's father, but do you know him? Do you know all that you should about his feelings for your son? For while he may hold you in esteem, his opinion of the thane may be more difficult to fathom."

"To be honest, Enid, I can't claim to know either of you, at least not as you suggest. The Qirsi may have magic that allows them to see into a person's heart and mind, but I'm just an Eandi noble."

"Perhaps the minister will allow us to search her chambers," Marston suggested.

"To what end?" Tobbar asked, facing his son. "What would we be searching for?"

"Gold," Xivled said.

They all looked at the younger minister.

"If she's allied with the conspiracy, they'll be paying her. From what I've heard, the leaders of this movement have a good deal of gold and pay their underlings quite well."

"Where does this wealth come from?" the duke asked.

Xivled shook his head. "I don't know, my lord."

Tobbar eyed Enid for several moments. "What do you think of that, First Minister. May we search your chambers?"

"Who will search his?" she demanded, pointing at Marston's minister.

"I will," Marston said. "As soon as we return to Shanstead. You have my word."

"Well, Enid?"

"This is foolishness," she said, refusing to look at the duke. "I've told you already, I have nothing to do with this conspiracy. If there had ever been gold lying around in my chamber, I'd have spent it long ago."

Marston opened his hands. "Then you have nothing to fear from letting us examine your quarters."

She sat motionless in her chair, her eyes trained on the floor, wide and wild, like those of a treed wildcat.

And in that instant, Tobbar knew. Marston had been right all along. Enid had betrayed him for the Qirsi conspiracy. Somewhere in her chambers lay a pouch of gold that would prove beyond doubt that she was a traitor, an enemy of every Eandi in the Forelands. A part of him wanted to strike her; a part of him wanted to weep as he hadn't since Liene's death. Until just then, he hadn't realized how much he valued Enid's friendship—or rather, the illusion of friendship she had offered him all these years.

Which might have been why he deigned to give her one last chance at redemption.

"If you tell me everything," he said, his voice so gentle he might have been speaking to a lover, "I'll spare your life. You can live out your last days in the prison tower. I promise you comfort, meals, warmth in the colder—"

Enid began to laugh, a chilling sound that made the duke shudder and flinch away.

"You offer me the comfort of an Eandi prison?" she asked. "And knowing what you do now, you expect me to accept?" The woman shook her head, a harsh grin frozen on her face. "You're an even greater fool than I believed. I'd sooner endure the tortures of your pitiful dungeon than tell you anything. You might as well kill me here, Tobbar."

"You could at least tell me why," he said. "I never did anything to you but offer you my trust, my friendship, and the opportunity to serve this house."

" 'The opportunity . . . '?" she repeated, laughing again. "Could you truly be such an ass? The only opportunity you ever gave me was the opportunity to strike a blow at the Eandi courts of this kingdom. I came to you a traitor, you fool. I have been true to my heart since the day I first set foot in this castle. I am grateful for your trust and your friendship, but only because they enabled me to serve my people so well for so long."

Tobbar stared at her, groping for something to say. It almost seemed that she had transformed herself before his eyes from his minister to some demon from Bian's realm. He no longer knew her. If she was to be believed, he never had.

Enid cast a withering glare at Xivled, her yellow eyes like ward fires in a besieged castle.

"You think you've struck a great blow against the movement, cousin. You've done nothing. I'm an old woman, a relic from a time when the movement sought to cripple Eibithar. We've already done that. You're too late. This is a war, and the important battles are now being waged elsewhere. You may have beaten me, but there will be no spoils from this victory."

"You'll tell us what you know," Marston said, standing over her. "We'll at least learn what you've done and who you serve. We can start with Filib's murder and your role in that. Then you can tell us about what happened in Kentigern earlier this year."

She crossed her arms over her chest and stared straight ahead. "I won't tell you anything."

"In all your years in Thorald Castle, have you ever been in her dungeons? Have you ever seen what torture does to a prisoner?"

Enid smiled, allowing herself to look up at him once more. "As I said, Lord Shanstead, I'm an old woman. My body will fail long before my will. If I must die to serve my people, so be it. It will be a far more glorious death than I had any right to expect."

Marston opened his mouth to say more, but Tobbar stopped him with a raised hand.

"I've heard enough," he said, his voice flat. "Guards!" he called, the word echoing through the chamber like the meeting of swords.

The door opened, and two of Thorald's soldiers entered the room.

"Yes, my lord?" one of them said.

"Take the first minister to the dungeon."

The two men exchanged a look. "My lord?"

"You heard me. She's to be taken to the dungeon and placed in chains. I don't want her hurt—at least not yet—but beware. She's Qirsi, and therefore dangerous." He racked his mind, trying to remember what powers she possessed. But he knew only that she was a gleaner, as were most of her people.

Looking as frightened as probationers facing their first battle, the two man walked to where Enid sat.

Enid eyed them both before gazing once more at the duke, the smile lingering on her face. "This is a useless, spiteful gesture, Tobbar. It doesn't become you at all."

"Perhaps not, Enid. But you leave me no choice. You don't want to be imprisoned in the tower. Would you be willing to talk if I offered you a quick, painless death?"

She seemed to consider this, though only for an instant.

"No. Though you may not believe it, honor means a great deal to me. I have sworn to serve my people, and I'll carry that oath to the Underrealm."

"May you be thrown to the flames and demons there," Marston said, refusing to look at her. "May the Deceiver torment you until the end of time."

The first minister stood, glancing at the two guards. "You heard your duke," she said. "Take me to the dungeon. I grow tired of this company."

The guards didn't move, appearing uncertain of what to do, until Tobbar nodded to them. Each man took hold of one of the woman's arms and led her away. She looked like a waif between them, tiny and harmless. One last deception among so many.

* * *

She would have liked to strike out at all of them, to use her powers to destroy all of Thorald. Even having betrayed Tobbar, she had never hated him. He had never struck her as being worthy of such intense feeling. In the wake of this, however—having been ensnared by Marston's whelp of a minister and humiliated by the duke before his guards—she found that she could hate him after all. This is a war, she had told them, and for the first time in years, almost since she arranged the murder of Filib the Younger near the woodland sanctuary where the boy's father died several years earlier, she felt like a soldier in the service of the Weaver. She was ashamed—not of being a traitor, but rather of being foolish enough to let Tobbar find out—and she knew that before long she would be broken, but at least she was fighting again, striking at the Eandi for her people.

She had spoken the truth to the young Qirsi earlier that day: there was far more to be gained from serving the movement than merely gold pieces. Wealth might have been enough for the young; it had been for her. But though she was too old now to enjoy fully the gold given to her by the Weaver's chancellors, she drew greater satisfaction than ever before at furthering their cause. If only she could have done more.

Her powers had never been great. She was a gleaner, and she possessed as well the magics of fire and language of beasts. Not many Qirsi wielded three magics, but only that last, language of beasts, was thought of by her people as one of the deeper powers. None of them was capable of shattering the walls of this castle, or killing its inhabitants. Even had she been a shaper, she was too old to do much damage before the Eandi killed her. She couldn't remember the last time she had drawn upon her power. She still had gleaning dreams occasionally, visions that woke her from her sleep with their clarity and the certainty that they carried the weight of prophecy. But there was a great difference between gleaning in a dream and wielding magic as a weapon.

The two guards led her down the steps of the nearest tower into the cold air of Thorald's north ward. Clouds raced overhead, like grey mounts charging across the moorlands. A few stars shone in the deep black of the night sky, but this was Pitch Night, the last of the year. Neither moon shone upon them. Torches from the ramparts lent a dim glow to the ward, and the dry snow crunching beneath their feet seemed to gather the starlight and torch fire so that it gleamed like a moonlit lake. A stiff wind carved across the ward, making Enid shudder. Apparently the guards thought she was trying to wrench herself out of their grasp, and they tightened their hold on her arms until she thought they would bruise her.

"The duke told you not to hurt me," she said.

"He also said you were dangerous, Minister," one of them said. Still, a moment later, they relaxed their grip once more.

They continued past the castle's great hall, through the central ward, until the prison tower loomed above them, dark and ponderous, like some great black creature from the Underrealm.

Seeing the tower, shivering once more from the cold, or from fear, Enid felt herself waver. *My body will fail long before my will,* she had said. A boast. She would happily die if it meant protecting the movement and the Weaver. But standing before the castle prison, she no longer felt so certain that she could endure the duke's torturers.

At the entrance to the tower, a soldier stopped them. In the dim light, it took her a moment to recognize the captain of the guard.

"What's this?" he asked, looking briefly at the minister before facing the older of the two guards.

"The duke told us to put her in the dungeon."

The captain raised an eyebrow. "The dungeon? You're sure he didn't mean the tower?"

"He said the dungeon, all right. He wants her in chains. Seems she's a traitor, and the duke wants to know something of her allies."

The man exhaled, whistling through his teeth. "So it's to be torture."

"Can you torture a Qirsi?" the other guard asked.

The two men looked at him, the captain frowning.

"Well I've never heard of it," the man said, sounding defensive. "I thought maybe a sorcerer could keep it from hurting or something."

The captain eyed at her again. "No, you can torture them. Isn't that right, Minister?"

She regarded him for a moment, then looked away. Her pulse was hammering at her temples, and her hands trembled. Of course a Qirsi could be tortured. They felt pain like the Eandi; they bled, their bones shattered, their skin burned. Even a healer couldn't stave off pain forever. A shaper might shatter the manacles that held his wrists and ankles and neck, but no Qirsi as old and weak as she could fight off the Eandi forever. Except, perhaps, the Weaver, but he possessed powers that went far beyond those she had wielded in her youth. That was why they followed him; that was why she would die for him.

Please, Qirsar, she prayed silently. *Give me the strength to keep silent. Give me the courage to face their blades and torches.*

The captain led the men to the dungeon door, searching his keys for the proper one. Finding it, he unlocked the door and pulled it open. Stale, fetid air swirled up the dark stairs, hitting Enid like a gangrenous fist and making her gag. She tried to back away, but the men held her.

"It's not too late to tell us what you know, Enid," came a voice from behind them. "You don't have to go down there."

The guards turned, and the minister with them.

Marston stood in the tower doorway, the golden glimmer of the torches lighting his ruddy face and grey eyes.

"My father sent me to reason with you one last time. He's prepared to offer you a choice: life in the tower, or a quick, easy death. All you need do is talk to us. Answer our questions about the conspiracy, and you need never set foot in that dungeon."

It occurred to her then to lie to them. She had been lying for so long. A day more or less wouldn't mean anything. She could give them plausible answers to their questions and be done with it.

But as quickly as the thought came to her, she dismissed it. It seemed there was more to her silence than devotion to the Weaver and his cause. Here at the end, with every path before her leading to the Deceiver, she found strength where she least expected it. Pride. To feign a confession, to give the Eandi fools any information at all, faulty or not, was to surrender. Enid couldn't bring herself to do it. Even if it could have bought her freedom, rather than just a comfortable incarceration, the price would have been too high. She would sooner linger a year on the torturer's rack than give in to them.

Instead, she chose to fight, like a good soldier faced with an insuperable foe. This is a war. Yes. She needed time, however. Just a bit.

"Your father believes I would betray my people, just to save myself from a foul smell?"

"My father is a good man. Indeed, he's so generous in spirit, that it weakens him. He refuses to accept that others are not as honorable as he, even after they have proved themselves liars and cowards again and again."

"I see," she said, though she was barely listening to him. Rather, she was reaching for her power, despairing at how feeble her magic had grown with age and years of neglect. At first she thought there was nothing left, that she might have to face the dungeon after all. But at last, as Marston began to drone on again about her duty to the House of Thorald and his father, she sensed the magic still residing with her, like a shallow still pool. She remembered when it had flowed through her limbs and body like a torrent fed by the early rains, and she lamented the passing of her life, the withering of her body and mind.

Still, she reached into those still waters, carefully drawing forth what remained, like a child carrying the precious nectar of Bohdan's fruit in cupped hands. She would have but one chance, she knew. If she failed the first time they would kill her before she could try again. So she devoted her mind fully to this last act, as if she were a young Qirsi new to her apprenticeship, using her powers for the very first time. She closed her eyes.

"What is she doing?" she heard Marston say, fear in his voice.

She would have liked to strike at the thane as well, but she was so weak. It would have to be enough to attack the two who held her.

With a sudden, hard push of her mind that tore a cry from her chest, she threw fire at the two guards.

Enid heard them cry out, felt them release her. Opening her eyes, feeling the ground pitch and roll as if from an earth tremor, she saw that their clothes and hair were ablaze. She was stronger than she realized. Once again she considered using her magic against Marston as well, but already he was drawing his sword. She hadn't time. Instead she lunged for the nearer of the two guards, grabbing his dagger from his belt.

Other guards were coming at her. Marston had drawn back his weapon to strike. She sensed death closing on her from all sides, like an ocean fog. But still she had time enough to choose. Barely.

She turned, took a long step toward the stairs to the dungeon. Then a second and third. And then she leaped.

The fetor, the unseen fist, pounded at her senses, but she no longer cared. She felt herself falling through the blackness, knowing the impact with the foul stone floor would probably kill her. Still, she wanted to be certain. Slowly, as if she had an abundance of time, she placed the tip of the soldier's blade against her chest.

"For my people!" she cried.

And struck.

Chapter
Twenty-two

✦

Solkara, Aneira, year 880, Qirsar's Moon waxing

ake up, traitor!"

Grigor started, hearing the too-familiar jingle of chains. He opened his eyes and let out a soft moan. His legs and back ached from sleeping on the stone floor of the prison chamber. Or perhaps it was from the manacles that held his wrists and ankles, making it impossible for him to lie comfortably when he slept. He couldn't be certain anymore, nor did he care.

He smelled like the streets of Solkara on a hot day, having fouled himself more times than he could remember. His hair and clothes were matted with filth, his skin itched as if from a thousand bug bites.

They had spared him the dungeon—a grace offered because he was duke of the royal house. But Grigor could hardly imagine that the dungeon would be worse. He had two windows in this chamber, though each was as narrow as the flat side of a sword, and he had not been tortured. Yet. But in every other way, this was his dungeon, his forgetting chamber.

"Get up!" the voice said again.

The voice of the yellow-haired guard. Grigor had come to know it well over the past several days. Aside from Numar and Henthas, the only people who had spoken to him since the poisoning were the night guard and this man, the day guard. They brought him water and food, such as it was, and they ordered him to keep quiet when they tired of hearing him complain or protest his innocence.

"I said, get on your feet!" The guard's voice echoed loudly off the stone walls.

Looking toward the door, Grigor realized that the man wasn't alone.

"Why?" Grigor asked. His lips and throat were so dry, he could barely make himself heard.

"Because I ordered it, traitor!"

He just grinned at the guard, not moving. "Why?" he said again.

"I believe he wants you to stand because I'm here," the other man said, stepping forward so that Grigor could see his face through the small iron grate on the chamber door.

Pronjed jal Drenthe, Chofya's archminister. There was a small smile on his bony face, a look of amusement in those ghostly pale eyes. Had Grigor been armed and free to move, he would have lunged at the door, blade in hand.

In truth, he would have liked to stand. His knees throbbed and he longed to stretch the night from cramped muscles. But he refused to give the Qirsi that satisfaction.

"What is it you want?"

The minister shrugged, his smile broadening. "I was about to walk down to the city—"

"And you wanted to know if I could come?" He shook his chains, making them ring like tiny bells. "A kind offer, Minister. But as you can see I have other matters holding me here."

Pronjed regarded him for several moments, the smile growing forced and brittle. "You have a singular humor, sir. I suppose some might even mistake it for courage. No, I was going to say that I'm on my way to the city to announce your execution, which is planned for tomorrow. I thought it only fair that I tell you first."

He tried to sustain his own grin, but failed. He needed water. "What day is this?"

"The third of the new waxing."

Grigor frowned. He had thought it the second. The Deceiver awaited him; in less than a day he would journey to the Underrealm to face whatever eternal fate Bian had chosen for him. And he fretted over losing count of the days. Was it mere vanity to worry now for the soundness of his mind?

"That's all?" the Qirsi asked. "Just a simple inquiry about the day? A moment ago you jested bravely; now you can't find your tongue. Is it the prospect of your death that gives you such pause?"

Grigor looked away, saying nothing.

"Surely you expected this."

"As I told you that first night, Minister, I didn't poison anyone. I suppose I trusted that Ean would save me from an unjust death. It would seem that my faith was misplaced."

"It's a terrible thing to face death in the absence of one's faith."

He faced the door again, searching the white face for some sign that he was being mocked. Seeing none, he finally stood.

"I'm innocent, Minister. You must believe me. I have never shied from raising my sword to strike at my enemies, nor have I ever lied about doing so. For this reason I have long been hated and feared throughout the kingdom. You know this. And I am telling you now, I did not do this thing. I have been betrayed by my own brother, who poisoned the queen and her guests and deflected blame to me. He admitted as much to me that very night."

"Ah, yes," Pronjed said, obviously unconvinced. "I had heard that you were blaming Lord Renbrere for this. I found it interesting that you chose to blame the Fool. Henthas would have seemed a much better choice."

"This is not a ruse, you idiot!" he said, straining against his chains. "Numar poisoned the wine! He seeks the regency, and when the time comes, he plans to kill the girl!"

"I see. And he saw fit to tell you all of this?"

Grigor closed his eyes, his entire body sagging. The Fool. It was almost funny. His one consolation was that House Solkara would prevail. He wouldn't live to see it, but all Aneira would suffer for taking Numar too lightly. Just as he had. "Yes, he told me. He knew there was no danger in it." He opened his eyes once more. "So, I'm to be hanged?"

"Hanged, drawn, and quartered. Your head will be impaled on a pike, and left in plain sight on the east wall of the castle. The pieces of your body will be carried by four horsemen to the far corners of the kingdom and left for the ravens and dogs and vultures to eat. In this way, Queen Chofya hopes to show all Aneirans what becomes of traitors." He spoke the words in a flat voice, reciting them as a new adherent in the cloisters might his litany. "Because you have been a duke in this house, however briefly, and because you were brother to her king, the queen has mercifully offered to grant you a final meal of your choosing. You can make your request now or speak to one of the guards later. Don't wait too long, however. The kitchen will need some time."

His stomach felt like a river stone, cold and hard. He wondered if he would ever be hungry again, then nearly laughed aloud, realizing with the certainty of the damned that he would not. An instant later he was blinking back hot tears, wincing at the pain of ironies that cut too deep.

This is what it's like to face death.

"I don't care what I eat," he said. "But I want a change of clothes and a basin of water in which to wash. My death may be a spectacle for the people of Solkara, but I'll not walk to the gallows looking like a common brigand. As you say, I was duke of Solkara, and before that a marquess."

Pronjed considered this a moment, before nodding. "I'll have to ask the queen, of course. But it seems to me a reasonable request. I'll advise her to grant it."

It was a small kindness, but when one's life was reduced to a matter of hours and moments, even the simplest courtesies carried some weight.

"My thanks, Minister."

The Qirsi turned, as if to leave.

"Minister, wait," he called. He wasn't certain how to ask the question that burned within, nor was he confident that Pronjed, who was facing him again, waiting, would be willing to answer. But in the end his curiosity proved more powerful than these other concerns. "How many died that night?"

The man's expression hardened, and for several moments Grigor thought that Pronjed would rail at him rather than offering any response.

"I guess there's no harm in telling you," he finally said, his tone icy. "Perhaps you'll even be disappointed. You killed five, two Eandi, three Qirsi."

"The two Eandi, they were dukes?"

Pronjed nodded. "Tounstrel and Noltierre."

Vidor and Bertin. Along with Chago of Bistari, who, rumor had it, died at the hands of Solkaran assassins, these two had been Carden's most stubborn opponents; no doubt they would have given the kingdom's new regent much trouble, had they lived. Numar had accomplished so much in that one night, perhaps even more than he knew.

"I can't tell if you're pleased or disappointed."

"I'm neither," Grigor said. "I've told you: I didn't poison anyone, so I have no stake in who lived and who died."

The Qirsi smiled thinly. "An assassin couldn't have said it any better. You tell me that you didn't poison them, yet you care nothing for the lives lost, nor do you take any satisfaction in knowing that we saved a good number."

Maybe he should have argued. There might have been some small chance that a sign of compassion now could still save him from execution. But he was beyond caring. The Fool had won, the queen and dukes had long seen him as ruthless and cruel; Numar had merely given them further reason to see him as such. Like any good swordsman, his brother had taken Grigor's greatest strength—his fearsome reputation—and turned it to his own advantage.

"You're right, Minister. I don't care about the lives lost or saved. I'm to be killed myself in the morning. I asked out of curiosity, nothing more." He turned his face away. Had he been free to turn his back on the door, he would have done so. "Now leave me. I grow tired of your company and your judgment."

He expected the Qirsi to say something more, to level one last verbal blow at his heart. All he heard, however, was the scrape of the man's boot as he turned to go and the slow retreat of his footsteps as he descended the tower stairs.

The yellow-haired guard entered the chamber and placed a small plate of food and a cup of water on the floor at Grigor's feet. Grigor didn't look at him, nor did he stoop to eat. He would have liked to ask the man to return and allow him a moment at one of the windows. He cared nothing for the cold anymore, but he would dearly have liked to see the sky and clouds, to feel the cool, clean touch of a snow-laden wind. But he couldn't bring himself to speak, and he had no confidence that the soldier would do as he asked.

He merely stood there, held by his chains, staring at the stone floor, his eyes wandering the seams between the stones. He didn't actually think about dying, though the fact of his impending death was never far from his thoughts. Rather, he thought of his father and mother, of his childhood spent chasing after Carden and the older boy's friends, of being bullied by them until he cried, only to find himself visiting the same cruelties on Henthas and Numar a short time later. He thought of his wife and his many mistresses, and he thought of his sons, who fought among themselves just as he and his brothers once had. He had sent word to Renbrere that they were not to come here, not even to see him die. But, he now realized, a part of him had hoped they would come anyway, just so that he could see them one last time. Others wouldn't believe in his innocence, but perhaps they would have.

Mostly though, he thought of nothing at all. He just listened to the sounds of the castle. The sharp crack of wooden swords as soldiers trained in the ward below the prison tower; the whistle of the wind as it swept through the ramparts above his chamber; the distant echo of the bells tolling in the city, marking the slow, inexorable march of time toward his hanging.

Even hearing the bells, he had no idea of the time when the sound of boots on the tower steps reached him once more. He heard voices as well, and so knew who had come before his brothers' faces appeared in the door grate.

"Do you want me to let them in?" the guard asked.

Grigor nodded. "Would you take the food away, as well?"

The soldier didn't answer, but after letting Henthas and Numar into the chamber, he removed the plate, though he left Grigor's water.

His brothers removed their swords and daggers, handing them to the guard as he left the chamber.

"Go to the base of the tower," Numar said, as the man stepped back into the corridor. "We wish to speak with our brother in private one last time."

"No, don't," Grigor called to him. "Stay where you are. Anything we have to say to each other we can say in front of you."

Grigor saw the guard falter, and for an instant he thought that the man might actually stay.

Numar must have seen this as well. He gestured at Henthas. "This man is your duke now, and I am to be regent to the new queen. You take your orders from us, not from the traitor. Do you understand?"

"Of course, my lord." The guard cast a quick look at Grigor before closing the chamber door and scurrying to the stairs like a frightened boy. It might have been a trick of the light, the bright sun from the narrow windows mingling with the glow of the torches burning in the corridor, but it seemed to Grigor that there had been an apology in the man's eyes.

"You didn't actually think I'd let him overhear my confession, did you?" Numar asked, when they could no longer hear the guard on the stairs.

Grigor looked quickly at Henthas, gauging his reaction.

"He knows, brother," Numar said with a grin.

Henthas leered at him, looking every bit the jackal.

"He was horrified at first, but when I offered him the dukedom, he recovered quite quickly." The younger man glanced at Henthas, his eyes dancing. "I think he plans to make an attempt on my life at some point, hoping to take the regency as well. At which point I'll have to kill him. But for now, we're both content to watch you hang."

"You'd really let him do this?" Grigor asked, ignoring Numar for the moment.

Henthas shrugged. "Why shouldn't I? The regency was never going to be mine. At least with you gone, I can claim Solkara as my own."

"Only as long as he lets you. If he's willing to do this to me, what's to stop him from having you killed so that he can take the dukedom?"

"You forget, brother," Numar broke in, "Henthas is doing this to you as much as I am. He may not have conceived the plan, but he's certainly embraced it as if it were his own."

"I don't think you and Carden ever grasped just how much I've hated you both," Henthas said. "Perhaps now you do."

Grigor stared at one of them, then the other, not knowing what to say. Henthas, with his fine features and dark blue eyes, looked very much like their father. So had Carden, and so, he had long been told, did Grigor himself. But though Numar favored their mother—lean and tall, his hair the color of wheat, his eyes a warm, rich brown—he was most like Tomaz in temper and intellect. While the older boys had toyed with swords, playing at being warriors, Numar sat on their father's knee and learned what it meant to be a noble, to command armies, and to survive in the courts. In the world of children, where strength of body was everything, he had been the weakest. But over the years, he had honed his mind into a weapon that none of them could match. Grigor, standing with his arms and legs in chains, felt as if he were seeing his youngest brother for the first time.

"Look at him, Henthas," Numar said, the grin still on his youthful face. "He has no answer for you. You've managed what I could not. You've silenced the Jackal."

Still Grigor stared at him, until Numar's smile faded, leaving an expression of vague discomfort.

"What is it you're looking at?" he asked, his voice tight.

"A man I thought I knew, but didn't. A brother who has managed to become more than I ever was. But mostly, I expect I'm looking at Aneira's next king."

At that, the smile returned. "Yes," Numar said. "I believe you are."

The door to the prison tower of Castle Solkara opened just as the dawn bells began to ring in the city. Two guards emerged from the arched stone doorway, followed by the traitor, and then a second pair of soldiers. Chofya stood just in front of the doorway with her daughter, the future queen, beside her. The traitor's brothers stood behind her, and Brall and the rest of the dukes with their ministers stood in a line behind them. More than a thousand soldiers, most from Solkara, but many from Aneira's other dukedoms were also there, blades drawn, their young faces grave. It was a cold, still morning. The sky was the color of dull armor and a few small flakes of snow fell softly upon the castle and its wards.

Grigor wore a soldier's garb—a dun shirt, matching trousers, boots, and an empty scabbard on his belt. He held himself straight, his head raised, defiance in his eyes. Stopping before the queen, with soldiers on either side of him, he appeared to tower over her, as if he were an inquisitor, and she the prisoner. For her part, Chofya looked to have recovered sufficiently from the attempt upon her life. Her face remained as colorless as a Qirsi's, and she appeared thin almost to the point of frailty. But she stood without aid and when she spoke it was in a voice both clear and strong.

"Grigor, duke of Solkara, marquess of Renbrere, you are hereby accused of murder by poison, treason against the queen of Aneira, and violence against the Council of Dukes. Do you wish to be heard before sentence is passed?"

"Only to repeat what I have already said. I am innocent in this matter, made to appear a murderer by those who have the most to gain from my execution. I speak of my brothers, though it grieves me to say so. I'm as much their victim as you are, Your Highness. Indeed more so, since you will survive this day, and I will not."

An angry murmur swept through the formation of soldiers.

"Hang him now!" one man cried.

Several of the others cheered.

Chofya allowed herself a grim smile. "As you can hear, your denials carry little weight with the men of Aneira. You are not fit to be king, nor even to walk among the living of this great kingdom. Thus, with the consent of the Council of Dukes and the support of my people, and in the sight of Ean and his servants here in the living world, I decree that you shall be hanged as a traitor, then drawn and quartered as all are who betray the crown and the land. May Bian show you mercy."

Grigor's expression did not change, but his face blanched, and his knees appeared to buckle, so that the guards standing on either side of him had to keep him from falling.

Chofya nodded once, then turned, and taking her daughter's hand, started walking toward the castle's city gate. Numar and Henthas followed, as did the guards escorting Grigor, the dukes and ministers, and finally the soldiers.

"Have you ever witnessed an execution, First Minister?" Brall asked Fetnalla, who was walking next to him.

"No, my lord."

"I find them . . . disturbing. Even in a circumstance like this one, I believe there's little satisfaction to be found in them."

"Yes, my lord."

The procession slowed as the dukes began to file through the gate.

"I couldn't help overhearing you, Brall," Tebeo said from behind them. "Do you mean to say that you don't think Grigor should be put to death?"

The duke shook his head, though he didn't look back at Dantrielle. "I don't mean that at all. I just don't believe there's anything to be gained from making his hanging into a public event. It's an execution, not a festival."

Tebeo nodded, falling silent. In another few moments they passed through the gate and into the city of Solkara. Even here, on the steep incline nearest the castle, people lined the street, shouting obscenities at Grigor and cheering the queen, her daughter, and the dukes.

Brall couldn't help but frown, even as city folk waved to him or reached out to touch him, as if he were some sort of hero. He could understand the importance of punishing a traitor, particularly one as dangerous as Grigor. But he found the fevered behavior of the throng unsettling.

"You've seen many executions, my lord?" Fetnalla asked.

"I've seen a few. I wouldn't say many."

"Do the condemned always maintain their innocence to the very end?"

He glanced at her. She was watching him, looking surprisingly young.

"Some do, most really. Not all. Why?"

The woman shrugged, facing forward again. "The duke seems determined to accuse his brothers, though he has nothing to gain from this anymore."

"You think him innocent?"

"I haven't before today. I just expected him to relent. Faced with . . . with this, I thought he would confess and make peace with the gods."

"You can't expect this man to behave as you or I would, Minister. He's a murderer and a traitor. Perhaps you heard that an Eibitharian spy was found in Solkara a few days ago."

"Yes, my lord, I had heard."

"All along we've wondered if there might have been more to what happened in the queen's chamber than we realized. I think it's clear now that there was, though not as we thought at first. Grigor wasn't working with the Qirsi conspiracy, but rather with our enemies to the north."

"Has Grigor admitted this?"

Brall turned once more. Tebeo's first minister was watching him with widened eyes.

"No," the duke told her. "He hasn't."

"Have the soldiers found the . . . the spies yet?" she asked.

Again, Brall shook his head. "Not yet. But I'm confident that they will."

Evanthya nodded. "Of course, my lord."

It seemed to the duke that Tebeo's Qirsi was disappointed, that she wanted Grigor to be in league with the conspiracy rather than the Eibitharians, as if one were any better than the other. He couldn't imagine why she might feel this way, but he no longer pretended to understand any of the white-hairs, even his own. In recent days he had come to believe once again that Fetnalla was loyal to him, though he remained wary. Beyond that, as far as he was concerned, they were unfathomable, an unfortunate necessity in a land whose courts had come to rely too heavily on magic and dubious visions of the future.

"The point is, Fetnalla," he said, turning his attention back to his minister, "we can't hope to understand a man like Grigor. It may be that he still holds out hope of redemption. Perhaps he believes, by some perverse logic, that his acts are justified and that the gods will reward him for his defiance. Whatever his reasoning, I'm certain that the land will be safer after he's dead."

"Yes, my lord."

They continued toward the marketplace in silence. Well before they reached the first of the peddler's carts, Brall saw the gallows standing on a broad wooden platform and towering over the crowded lanes and stalls. It looked solid, if crudely fashioned, the warm tones of the fresh wood a stark contrast to the cold grey sky. Hordes awaited them there, chanting for the traitor's death and cheering loudly at their first glimpse of the queen and her child.

Soldiers rushed forward to clear a path though the throng for Chofya, Kalyi, and the dukes. They were also forced to beat back the city folk, who, catching sight of Grigor, attempted to drag the man away from his escort.

It took some time, but at last, Pronjed, the castle prelate, and the four guards led Grigor up a long flight of wooden steps to the gallows. Amid screams from the people below, the prelate offered the traitor a final opportunity to confess. When he refused, tight-lipped and ashen, the crowd jeered him lustily and shouted for his death.

The executioner, a tall, burly man in a brown hooded robe, climbed slowly to the platform, and as he did the soldiers tied Grigor's hands behind his back and slipped the noose around his neck. The cheers grew louder.

Fetnalla turned away.

"An execution can be difficult to watch," Brall told her, "particularly the first one. But none of the people here is likely to forget this. Other trai-

tors will think twice before taking on the royal house, and those who seek
vengeance for what was done to their queen and the Council of Dukes will
leave here satisfied that justice was done."

The Qirsi offered no response.

At the base of the gallows, the executioner grabbed hold of the rope
and, with a quick glance toward Pronjed, who nodded once, gave a mighty
pull. Grigor was lifted off the platform, to the roared approval of the
crowd. The traitor kicked his feet several times, his body swinging back
and forth, his eyes squeezed shut and his teeth bared. The executioner left
him up there for some time, until his features started to slacken. Only then,
when the man was broken, but not yet dead, did the executioner lower him
again, removing the noose and cutting the bonds that held his hands. They
laid him down on the bare wood platform, and brought forth the knives.

Even Brall had to look away after that, though from the shouting, and
the cries of some, he knew that they were disemboweling him. At last he
heard the executioner call out the ritual words, "See in my hand, the heart
of a traitor." It was nearly over.

In another few moments, the guards descended the steps again, each
one of them bearing part of the man's body. The executioner followed,
carrying Grigor's head on a pike. The horsemen who were to bear the traitor's body to the four corners of the kingdom waited just beyond the mass
of people, and already some were leaving the marketplace for the castle, so
that they might see the man's head mounted there.

"Justice," it was said, "is both patient and swift, curative and cruel,
equitable and absolute."

Never had Brall thought the words more apt that they were this day.

With the execution ended, Brall and Fetnalla followed Chofya back to
the castle. There, just after midday, in the queen's presence chamber, the
Council of Dukes met for the first time since the poisoning.

Chofya was there, of course, as were her daughter and Grigor's two
surviving brothers. Henthas, Brall was disturbed to see, wore the red, black,
and gold of Solkara and took a seat at the table with the rest of the dukes.
Numar stood at the head of the table with the queen, Pronjed, and Kalyi.

When all the dukes and their ministers had arrived and were seated,
Chofya stood. "After the darkness of the past several days," she began, "I
am pleased to have tidings of a different sort. Numar, marquess of Renbrere, youngest brother of my husband the king, has agreed to serve as
regent to my daughter Kalyi when she is invested as queen of Aneira."

Brall glanced at Tebeo, who was already looking his way, relief written
plainly on his round face.

"He has agreed to accept Carden's archminister, Pronjed jal Drenthe, as his archminister, and he has already sent word to his home in Renbrere to have his possessions brought here so that he might live in the royal city."

She stepped to the side as Numar stood, a smile on his face.

"I am honored that Queen Chofya has deemed me worthy to serve as regent to her daughter until our new queen is old enough to rule Aneira on her own. With all that's happened since we first arrived for my brother's funeral, it would have been only natural for this council to turn away from House Solkara and toward the uncertainty and dangers of civil war. I'm grateful to all of you for your patience and your commitment to peace. I hope that I prove myself worthy of your trust."

"Forgive me, Lord Renbrere," the duke of Rassor interrupted, "but I must ask why your brother is here. We bear you no ill will, but Henthas has always been at Grigor's right hand. He has no place in this council."

Several of the others nodded in agreement, including both Ansis and Tebeo.

"I assure you, my lord duke, Henthas had no part in Grigor's crime. He gives me his word as both my brother and a noble of Solkara, and I believe him. I intend to devote myself wholly to my duties as regent, and will have little time for the Solkaran dukedom. As none of my brothers nor I have sons who are of age, the title of duke must fall to Henthas."

Rassor still did not look pleased and though Brall had little affection for the man, he had to agree with him in this instance. Numar seemed to sense that the other dukes remained unconvinced as well.

"My lords, please. You have entrusted me with the well-being of your kingdom and the care of your child-queen. This is but a trifle by comparison. My brother and I will be living together in this castle. I give you my word that I will see to it that he rules Solkara with a steady hand."

Henthas appeared to bristle at this.

"I'm not some horse to be tamed and fitted with a bridle," he said, his voice low and bitter. "I'm the oldest living son of Tomaz. By all rights, the kingdom should be mine. Isn't it enough that I've given that up and the regency, too? Would you have me throw down my sword as well?"

Numar turned to his brother, a smile on his lips, obviously forced. "You make your point plainly, brother. As always."

"I don't like him being in the castle with the girl," Rassor said. He glanced at the queen. "Forgive me, Your Highness, but I fear for her safety."

"We all do, Lord Rassor," Chofya said. "Not because of Henthas, but because she is a child, and the kingdom has many enemies. That's why I'm so pleased that Numar has agreed to be her regent and to keep Pronjed as archminister. I trust my husband's brother in this matter, as in all matters. I have no doubt that Henthas will be a fine duke and that House Solkara will flourish under his leadership."

With that, the queen effectively ended their discussion. Many of Brall's doubts remained, and he felt certain that he wasn't alone in this regard. But Chofya had spoken. To press the matter further would have been to question her judgment, and none of the dukes was willing to do that.

"Kalyi's investiture will take place in the morning," the queen said a moment later. "All of you are invited, of course, as are the people of Solkara. After the ceremony, I assume most of you will be returning to your realms. It's been nearly a full turn since Carden's death. The time has come for our kingdom to end its grieving. As I said a moment ago, Aneira has many enemies. They will be watching us, looking for signs of weakness. We must show them none. Go home to your people. Tell them they have a new queen and that she will be guided by a strong, capable regent."

For a moment, the gathered dukes said nothing. Then Brall stood, and following his example, the others did as well. Even Henthas.

"As you wish, Your Highness," Brall said.

They all bowed to her and to her daughter in turn. The girl smiled, looking embarrassed and terribly young, and Brall felt himself grow cold.

The dukes and their ministers began to leave, Brall and Fetnalla with them. Once in the corridor, the two of them stopped to wait for Tebeo and Evanthya. Then they all made their way out to the castle ward, where they could speak freely.

"What do you think?" Dantrielle asked, his breath making clouds of vapor. "Do we have cause to fear Henthas?"

Brall exhaled heavily. "I think Henthas is the least of our problems. We're placing our kingdom in the hands of a child and a man who, until recently, was known throughout the land as the Fool."

"Numar is no fool, Brall. I feel certain of that."

"I know he's not. But he's younger than Ansis. He's barely older than the new duke of Mertesse. He knows nothing of leading a kingdom."

"He's Tomaz's son. And he'll have Chofya and Pronjed to help him. Besides, even if he were a fool, and without anyone to offer him guidance, I'd still rather he was regent than most anyone else."

"Yes," Brall said reluctantly. "I feel the same way." He'd heard many of the dukes speaking this way in recent days. Better a Fool than a Jackal, they were saying. It had become an aphorism of sorts. And though he could not argue with them, neither could he bring himself to feel at ease with the thought. Not with the conspiracy spreading its influence across the Fore-lands and agents of Eibithar abroad in the kingdom.

This had all begun with his dagger, the crystal blade he had given the king upon his arrival in Solkara, so long ago that he barely remembered the day. He hadn't guided the king's hand, of course. Carden had done this to himself and to the kingdom. But the duke still remembered Fetnalla's suspicions of the archminister, doubts that Tebeo's first minister echoed later. Now they were trusting Pronjed to help Numar lead the land, and they were hoping that this young noble could stand fast if the minister proved to be faithless. The fate of Aneira had never seemed so uncertain. And he couldn't help thinking that he had let this happen, that something vital had escaped his notice.

Chapter
Twenty-three

vanthya had never attended an investiture before, though she had heard tales of the grand celebration that followed the crowning of Tomaz the Ninth. From all that she saw, however, and from all that Tebeo and Brall told her, she had the sense that Kalyi's coronation was a modest affair. Aneiran nobles wore their ceremonial garb and gathered in the great hall of Castle Solkara, just as they had for the funeral of the girl's father. The kitchens prepared the finest of foods and the cellarmaster provided flask after flask of Sanbiri wine. But to Evanthya the celebration felt muted, as if those who had come to wish the new queen well were all too aware of the difficulties that lay ahead and the dangers facing this child.

The Eandi nobles would begin the long journeys back to their realms the following morning knowing that for the first time in two and a half centuries, the land had no king. It was a realization that seemed to weigh heavily on all of them.

Many of the lesser nobles left early, offering obeisant farewells to Chofya, the new queen, and Numar. Seated as they were with the Solkaran royalty, Brall and Tebeo had little choice but to remain until the end of the feast. But as the sound of conversations in the great hall gradually diminished and the grand chamber emptied, Fetnalla gazed toward Evanthya and mouthed the words "Let's walk."

Evanthya nodded, quietly excused herself from the table, and left the hall. She walked slowly through the corridors and into the cold, crisp air of the courtyard. The clouds had thinned, and she could see both moons turning their slow arc across the night sky. Panya, white and luminous, though barely more than a thin, curving blade, hung just above the western wall of the fortress, while Ilias, not quite halfway through his waxing, hung overhead, bathing the castle in his red glow. This was Qirsar's Turn, and of all the moon legends, none were more important to the Qirsi than those tied to the god of magic. In just a few more nights, on the Night of Two Moons, her power would be greater than it was any other night of the year. And on Pitch Night, the last night of the turn, when neither moon shone, she would be unable to wield her magic at all. All Qirsi went through this, and the effects of Pitch Night lasted just the one evening. But still she shuddered at the thought.

The air was still, as it had been earlier in the day, and Evanthya could smell smoke from the fires burning in hearths throughout Castle Solkara. She pulled her robes tighter around her shoulders, still shivering. In a few moments she heard footsteps behind her, and turning, saw Fetnalla emerge from the nearest of the stone archways.

The woman stopped in front of her and they both paused, then shared a quick, awkward kiss.

"Walk with me," Fetnalla said, indicating the gardens with a slender hand.

They began to walk, following their dim shadows along the stone pathway. For some time, neither of them spoke. With all they'd been through since her arrival in Solkara, Evanthya wasn't certain what to say or what to expect from Fetnalla. The fight they had before the poisoning seemed a small matter now and so far in the past as to have been almost forgotten. But clearly both of them still felt uncomfortable speaking of it, and they hadn't lain together since the night she and Tebeo arrived.

"I don't know when we'll see each other again," Fetnalla said at last.

Evanthya gave a thin smile. "Careful. The last time one of us said something like that, the king was dead less than a turn later."

Fetnalla nodded, but her expression remained grave. "We wasted so much time—I wasted it. I'm sorry."

"We've spoken of this before. All's forgiven, on both sides."

"I know. But there's so much we should have been discussing. And now there's no time."

"We have time right now."

Fetnalla halted and faced her, Ilias's light in her eyes. "All right. This man you spoke to in the city. Are you certain he wasn't with the conspiracy or sent by the lords of Eibithar?"

Evanthya had expected this. She told Fetnalla about her conversation

with the gleaner on Bohdan's Pitch Night, just hours after leaving the Qirsi
man and his young companion in the tavern. They had been forced to
speak quietly and choose their words with care. After word of the Eibitharian spy and his stunning escape through the south gate spread through the
city, every guard in the castle had been called to duty. Even in Evanthya's
chamber, with the servants dismissed and the door locked, they feared
being overheard. Considering what they needed to discuss, even a stray
word or phrase could have convinced a soldier that they were traitors. She
had done her best to put Fetnalla's fears to rest, but she sensed that every
reassurance she offered only served to heighten the woman's concerns.

"I'm as certain as I can be," she said.

Fetnalla frowned. "That's not very comforting."

"I don't think they were spies. When the younger one spoke, and I recognized his accent, the gleaner didn't deny that he was Eibitharian. And
their interest in the assassin seemed genuine. They didn't ask me about
anything else, as members of the conspiracy might have. They knew I was
first minister in Dantrielle, but they didn't press me for information about
my duke or the queen, other than to inquire after their health."

"Still," Fetnalla said, "he told you he was a gleaner. But if they were
the ones who fled the city, he was far more than that."

"Even gleaners have other powers."

"Mists and winds? Shaping? You heard what the gate soldiers said.
This was no mere gleaner, Evanthya. This man is at least as powerful as
we are."

Evanthya could hardly argue the point. She had thought much the
same thing herself. Regardless of where their loyalties lay, these men were
more than they claimed to be. She sensed this about both of them, the
Eandi boy as well as the Qirsi.

"Do you think the assassin made an attempt on the boy's life and
failed? You said he bore scars."

Evanthya shook her head. "The scars were on his face, and they didn't
appear to be the work of an assassin. Besides, from all we heard of the
singer before we hired him, it doesn't seem likely that anyone could survive
his assault." She pushed her hair back from her brow, then crossed her
arms over her chest. "The gleaner was quite mysterious in speaking of this.
He didn't say the assassin gave him the scars, but rather that he was responsible for them. In fact, he said that twice."

"A strange distinction to make," Fetnalla said.

"I thought so as well." Even as Evanthya spoke the words, however, a
thought came to her that stole her breath. Hearing of events in Eibithar

during the warmer turns, none of them had thought to question whether the conspiracy might have been involved. But in light of what the gleaner had said, and the young man's unmistakable accent, she was forced to consider a most remarkable possibility.

"What is it?" Fetnalla asked, eyeing her closely.

"What if it's not such a strange distinction after all?" she said, by way of reply. The more she thought back on her conversations with the gleaner and the Eandi, the more convinced she became. There had been something about the boy; he had struck her as both impressive and overly pampered, as only an Eandi noble could.

Fetnalla shook her head. "I don't understand."

"The Eibitharian spy?" Evanthya said, meeting her gaze. "I think it may have been Lord Tavis of Curgh."

"The one who killed the girl in Kentigern?"

"The one who was accused of killing her. The one who was tortured by her father in Kentigern's dungeon."

"You honestly believe he'd come here?"

"Maybe," she said, "if he was desperate enough to find the man who really murdered that girl. The gleaner said that he couldn't tell me more about what the assassin had done without endangering the boy's life. At the time I didn't know what to make of that, but if this was Tavis, it makes a great deal of sense."

Fetnalla shook her head. "You're assuming that he's innocent, and that he's free to wander the Forelands. The last I'd heard, he was an exile in Glyndwr, friendless and hated by his own people."

"I heard that he never went to Glyndwr, but I don't think any of us knows for certain. As to his innocence, we've seen our own kingdom thrust to the brink of civil war, perhaps by the conspiracy, perhaps not. Much the same thing happened in Eibithar just a few turns ago. Doesn't that strike you as odd? Isn't it at least possible that the conspiracy has been behind all of this? Isn't that why we hired the singer in the first place?"

Fetnalla seemed to weigh this, glancing up at the red moon. "I suppose it is." She looked at Evanthya again. "Tell me once more what you said to him about the assassin."

"I told him very little," Evanthya said. "Just that we had hired him to kill a man we felt certain was part of the conspiracy."

"Did you tell him where the man was?"

"No. He asked me, but I refused to answer."

Fetnalla stepped closer to her. "You're absolutely certain?"

"Yes. Why?"

"Because if this was Lord Tavis, and the gleaner was from Eibithar as well, they'd know of the traitor in Mertesse, and so they'd know just where to go to find the assassin."

Perhaps this should have frightened her. Clearly it alarmed Fetnalla. But Evanthya, feeling certain that she was right about the Curgh boy, merely shrugged.

"You're right, they would. But they might also be pleased to see the traitor dead."

It was very late when Kalyi and her mother finally returned to their quarters. Kalyi still wore her father's gold crown on her head, though it felt heavy and fit her poorly. She was queen now, which struck her as quite strange. For as long as she had lived, her mother had been queen. She didn't understand why her father's death should change that.

Usually her mother had Nurse help her into her sleeping gown and put her to bed, but tonight her mother did it herself. Her mother looked sad and tired, the way her father used to before he died. When Kalyi was in bed, her mother sat with her for a time, stroking Kalyi's hair and gazing at her in the candlelight. She still looked tired, but at least she was smiling now.

Kalyi glanced over at the golden crown which sat on the dressing table beside her wardrobe.

"Do I have to wear Father's crown all the time?" she asked.

"You're queen now. You lead Aneira. The crown tells people that you're our leader."

"Can't I wear your circlet instead? I'm queen like you were, and I think it would fit me better."

Her mother let out a small laugh. "Your father's crown has been worn by Aneira's leaders for centuries, and it's far more beautiful than my circlet."

"I don't think so."

"We can speak of this in the morning. We'll see what the archminister and your uncle Numar have to say. Perhaps we can let you wear the circlet for now, until you grow into the crown."

She leaned forward to kiss Kalyi's forehead and started to leave.

"Don't go yet," Kalyi said, grabbing her arm. "Please."

"I'm tired, Kalyi. And it's late."

"I know. Just a little while longer."

Her mother smiled and nodded, running her fingers through Kalyi's hair again.

"Will I have to go to war now?" Kalyi asked.

"I certainly hope not," her mother said, raising her eyebrows.

"Well, Father always said that one of the things a king did was lead his armies to war."

"Kings do far more than fight wars, child. I think your father forgot that sometimes."

"But if we had to go to war—"

"If we had to go to war, your uncle Numar would lead the army, not you. He's your regent, which means that for the next few years he'll be helping you rule the land and teaching you how to be queen so that you can lead on your own when the regency ends."

"When will that be?"

"After your Fating."

"My Fating?" Kalyi said, widening her eyes. "That'll be forever."

Her mother laughed. "Hardly."

"Will Uncle Numar protect me, too?"

The smile vanished from her mother's face. "Why do you think you need protecting?"

"Because of what that man said today, that he feared for my safety."

"That man was the duke of Rassor," her mother said, frowning and taking a breath. "And he should have held his tongue."

"You agreed with him. You said that all of you were afraid for me."

"Did I?"

Kalyi nodded. "Why are you? Is it because of Uncle Henthas? That's what the duke said."

Her mother smiled, though Kalyi thought she didn't look happy. "I don't think Henthas will hurt you. Truly I don't. But you lead the kingdom now, and we have enemies in the Forelands."

"Like in Eibithar?"

"Yes, the Eibitharians are our enemies. And others as well. They may see how young you are and think that the kingdom is weak because it's led by a child. That's why we have Numar here. And that's why we all need for you to be very strong and very brave. Do you think you can do that?"

Kalyi nodded, and this time her mother's smile seemed real.

"Do you think Uncle Grigor would have hurt me?"

"Peace, child. Please. It's time for sleep, not questions."

"I'm sorry, Mother. Goodnight."

But her mother just sat, staring at the candle. "Grigor was a bitter, cruel man," she finally said. "He wanted to be king, and he didn't care who he had to hurt or kill to reach the throne."

"I'm glad he's dead," Kalyi said. She knew it was a bad thing to say, but it was the truth, and both her mother and father had always told her to speak the truth.

Her mother looked at her sharply, but then looked away again. "So am I," she whispered.

A moment later, she leaned forward again, kissed Kalyi on each cheek, and blew out the candle. "Goodnight, love."

"Goodnight, Mother."

She watched her mother leave, then bundled herself in her blankets so that she could barely move her legs and arms. With the windows shuttered, the only light in the chamber came from the fire burning low in the hearth. It gave an orange glow to everything she could see, and cast strange dancing shadows on the walls and ceiling.

We all need for you to be very strong and very brave. She didn't feel strong. She felt young and terribly small. Her father's crown was too large for her; the throne she had sat upon during the ceremony earlier this day had seemed immense, as if she were just a baby sitting on a soldier's stallion. She had been the only child at her investiture, she was certain of it, because she looked for others, even when she should have been listening to the prelate. Other children lived in the castle, some Qirsi, some Eandi. Most of them were her friends—because she was the daughter of the king, all the children wanted to play with her and see where the king lived and slept and planned for wars. But none of them had been invited to the ceremony. Or none had chosen to come.

Kalyi hadn't seen any of her friends since her father died. She spent most of her days with her mother, or with Nurse, or with the prelate, who made her pray in the cloisters whenever he saw her. Before all this began, she had been tiring of her lessons, but now she couldn't wait to get back to them. She wondered if she'd still have lessons now that she was queen. More than that, she wondered if the other children would still want to be her friends. They might not like having to bow to her and call her "Your Highness." She would have been happy to tell them not to do any of that, but she didn't know if she was allowed to. There was a lot she didn't know about being queen. That was why she needed Uncle Numar.

The one thing Kalyi did know was that she could be brave. She might not have been strong like her father or the soldiers in her army, but she wasn't going to be afraid. She had cried the morning her mother told her that Father was dead, but she hadn't cried since, and she didn't intend to.

Nor did she intend to let the Eibitharians frighten her. There had been a spy from Eibithar in the city a few days earlier. Kalyi had heard of it from the guards. And though everyone else in the castle seemed scared, including her mother, Kalyi was not. Father had told her many times that a soldier had to learn to master his fear. She hadn't understood at first what that meant, but her father explained it.

"Everyone has times when they're afraid," he told her one bright afternoon, as they walked along the battlements facing the river. "But a good soldier is able to see beyond his fear, to conquer it in his mind the way he conquers his enemies in battle. If you fear defeat, you make plans for victory. If you find yourself fearing death, you think of how you will fight to avoid dying. A soldier who marches to battle thinking he's going to die, probably will, just as a king who leads his army into a war expecting to lose, has little chance of winning."

Kalyi knew that she was not a soldier, but she sensed that her father's advice worked just as well for princesses and queens. The dukes of Aneira were afraid that Henthas wanted to kill her and that the spies from Eibithar wanted to destroy the kingdom. But Kalyi was queen now, and she refused to let those things happen.

She still needed to learn how to be queen, how to protect her land from its enemies. But Numar and Pronjed and her mother would help her. And as for Henthas, she would just stay away from him. If she had to see him, she'd make certain that someone else was always with her. Either way, she wasn't going to be afraid of him, because then he would hurt her. Her father had told her so.

The one thing Kalyi didn't understand was her father's death. Her father, she was quite certain, was not afraid of anything or anyone. Yet he was dead, killed, she had heard someone say, by his own hand. Kalyi knew what that meant, just as she knew that taking one's own life was a violation of one of Ean's doctrines, though she couldn't remember which. But it seemed to her that a person only killed himself if he was terribly afraid of something. Her mother said he did it because the castle surgeon told him he was dying, but Kalyi knew that her father wasn't afraid of death. He had told her so. Which meant that there must have been another reason. She was going to find out what it was. She couldn't really be queen yet, because she was too young. But she could be strong and brave, like her mother said, and she could discover why her father had died.

* * *

Yaella eyed her duke cautiously from the chair near the hearth, gauging his anger. He stood before the fire, glowering at the flames, his back to her and his hands behind his back. One hand was fisted so that the knuckles had turned white; the other held that one by the wrist, as if to keep it from reaching for a weapon.

"I did tell him not to come," Rowan said, his voice hard. He turned briefly, glancing back at her. "I remember doing so."

"I remember it as well, my lord." She tried to keep her tone neutral. As always, she was forced to tread a fine line between defending Shurik and not offending her duke. "But I daresay a lot has changed since then."

"Not my wishes in this matter. The man is still a traitor. I may have granted him asylum for helping my father, but I did not make him a minister in my court. He seems too eager to forget that, and he has since the day he arrived in Mertesse. That hasn't changed either."

He was his father's son in so many ways. Not just the sky blue eyes and jutting brow, but also the pride and willfulness, the quick temper and enduring anger. If anything, Rowan's youth made him more difficult than Rouel had been. In the last years of his life, the old duke had come to recognize his flaws and had learned to laugh at them. Rowan was not ready even for this.

"Forgive me, my lord, but this is more my fault than Shurik's. In the time since he has been living in Mertesse, he and I have grown rather . . . close. I believe that when he heard that we had been stricken by Grigor's poison, his concern for me outweighed his sense of duty to you. You have my deepest apologies."

It was a risk, but a small one. She and Shurik had not been as discreet as they should have been, and as a result she felt fairly certain that Rowan already knew of their affair. Even if he didn't, it was only a matter of time before he would. Best then that he hear of it from her.

The duke kept his back to her, as if embarrassed by her admission. "That still doesn't excuse it," he said. But Yaella could tell from his voice that she had succeeded somewhat in blunting his anger.

"Of course not, my lord. I'm certain that Shurik realizes his error and will apologize for it. But he still needs your protection." *Now more than ever.* "I'd hate to think that his affection for me might cause you to withdraw your offer of asylum."

At that Rowan did turn. "No, First Minister. I won't make him leave." His expression soured. "Just keep him as far from me as possible. You'll pardon me for saying so, but I don't care for the man. Not at all."

Nor he for you. "I understand, my lord. If you like, Shurik and I will ride back to Mertesse at the rear of our company."

He nodded. "That would be acceptable. He knows to meet us outside the city gates?"

Yaella felt the color drain from her face. "The city gates?"

"Yes, of course. I don't want anyone in Solkara seeing the man in my company." He narrowed his eyes. "Is there a problem, First Minister?"

"Yes, my lord. I told Shurik to meet us outside the castle gates, not the city gates. I don't know if I've enough time to get another message to him."

Rowan pressed his lips in a tight line. "You should have known better, Yaella. I've made my feelings for this man very clear. It seems he's not the only one who's allowed his judgment to be clouded by his affections."

Yaella lowered her gaze, as he'd expect. "Yes, my lord."

He shook his head, his gaze traveling the room, but avoiding her. "Very well," he said at last. "I don't suppose there's anything to be done about it. Just keep him far from me, and try not to draw any attention to yourselves. We'll be leaving later than most of the other nobles. Perhaps he won't be noticed."

"Yes, my lord. Again, my apologies."

"I'd like to be out of the city before the ringing of the midday bells. Please see to it that the men are prepared to ride and that our horses are saddled."

She stood, eager to leave him. "Of course, my lord. I assure you, everything will be ready."

He nodded once and faced the fire again, saying nothing. It was something his father might have done, though from Rouel it would have seemed more forceful, far less like the silent brooding of a peevish child.

Yaella bowed to the duke and left the chamber, relieved to be away from him.

At last she understood why Shurik had been so eager to serve the Weaver and why he had worked so hard to convince her to do the same. Her betrayal of House Mertesse had begun several years before, when Rouel was still alive, but it had troubled her then. Though aware of the old duke's faults, she harbored a certain affection for him. She still remembered seeing him die in Kentigern Castle during the siege several turns before, the image so clear that it still made her shudder. Her grief at losing him had subsided, but it had yet to vanish entirely. She wasn't certain it ever would. She had made her decision to join the movement in spite of Rouel, not because of him. Had she served Rowan at the time, rather than Rouel, it would have been a far easier choice to make.

She found the soldiers of Mertesse in the castle courtyard, watching the Solkaran army train, speaking and laughing softly among themselves. They fell silent as she approached. Eandi men always did, though Yaella still wondered if this was because she was Qirsi, or a minister, or a woman. No doubt all three had something to do with it.

"The duke wishes to leave before the midday bells," she said, stopping in front of them. It sounded abrupt to her own ears, but even after living among the Eandi for so long, she felt no more comfortable with them than they did with her. "Make certain that you're ready, and that our horses are waiting."

"Yes, Minister," said the highest-ranking of them.

She hesitated, then nodded and started away.

"Are you well, Minister?" the man called after her.

Yaella turned again, staring at the man in wordless surprise. He was broad in the chest and soldiers, thick-necked and tall, like all of Mertesse's soldiers, indeed, like all the Eandi warriors she had ever seen. It sometimes seemed to Yaella that they were all the same man, created over and over again so that dukes and kings would have soldiers to fight their wars. Yet here was one of them asking after her health like an old friend.

"Forgive me," he said, perhaps mistaking her astonishment for ire. "But we'd heard that some of the Qirsi were slower to mend than others."

"It did take me some time, but I'm feeling much better, thank you." She felt that she should say more, but she couldn't find the words. "It was kind of you to ask," she finally said, then cringed at how foolish it sounded.

"Not at all, Minister. We'll be ready before the bells."

"Thank you," she said again, before hurrying away.

She had always thought of her betrayal of House Mertesse as being a betrayal of its duke. But walking away from the men of Mertesse, Yaella could not help thinking that her deception went far deeper. She had ridden to war with the Mertesse army. For all she knew, the men with whom she had just spoken had been with her in Kentigern, taking shelter in the mists she raised, and protecting her life with their blades and shields. Hadn't she betrayed them as well?

Shurik would have laughed at her, she knew. They were Eandi, just like Rowan. Probably they were worried for her health because they knew the company might need her mists on the ride back to Mertesse. There were brigands on the roads of the Great Forest, some of them riding in large groups. The soldiers merely wished to know how much magic she could wield on their behalf. This, at least, is what she told herself.

The fact was, however, the man had seemed genuine in his concern for her. She almost wished that he hadn't.

The minister walked back to her chamber and gathered the few items she had brought with her to Solkara in her satchel. Then she returned to the courtyard and the castle stables. Her mount was there already saddled for her, white and glorious in the morning sun. Rowan had not yet arrived, but the rest of his company was there, awaiting their duke in the cold.

When Rowan did finally arrive, he did so in the company of Chofya, Kalyi, the archminister, and the brothers Renbrere. The Solkarans said a brief farewell, as did Rowan, though awkwardly. Yaella found it difficult to believe that he was but a few years younger than Numar, so great was the difference between her duke and this refined man who would lead the kingdom.

Within just a few moments, Rowan had climbed onto his mount and was leading the company of Mertesse out of Castle Solkara. As she had promised, Yaella rode at the rear of the company, expecting to see Shurik awaiting them just beyond the castle walls. Fortunately, he understood the duke even better than she. Rather than waiting for them in the open, where Rowan and others watching the duke's departure might spot him, he remained concealed until he saw Yaella. He caught up to the riders of Mertesse just as they reached the city marketplace, pulling abreast of Yaella without fanfare.

"I take it you're riding back here so that your duke doesn't have to be near me," he said, smiling thinly, his voice low.

She would have liked to deny it, to soften the blow. But she wouldn't have fooled him, and he probably was just as happy to ride with her behind the others.

"That's about right."

"Was he angry with me for coming?"

"Very. But I told him that your passion for me had clouded your mind."

Shurik glanced at her, grinning. "Did you really?"

"I might have said 'affections' rather than 'passion,' but otherwise, yes, that's what I said."

"And what did he have to say?"

She smiled. "Very little."

"Well, that must have been a welcome change."

Yaella laughed, drawing scowls from the soldiers riding a few fourspans ahead of her.

The company reached the north city gate and passed through, the Solkaran guards there raising their swords in honor of the duke.

When they were through the gate, and on the road running alongside the river, Shurik asked, "So has he demanded that I leave the castle?"

"No. I think he might have had it been his decision to grant you asylum. But because his father promised to protect you, he feels compelled to honor that pledge." She looked away, following the flight of a raven that soared overhead. "Would it matter if he had made you leave? I seem to remember you telling me when you first came to Solkara, that our . . . friend has instructed you to go elsewhere."

"Our friend told me to find Grinsa," Shurik said, his voice dropping to a whisper. "Since then, Grinsa has found me."

Yaella faced him once more. He was staring straight ahead, his expression bleak and his jaw tightening. He had told her briefly of his encounter with the gleaner, but with his visits to the castle so short and secretive, they had yet to speak of it at length. She knew that Lord Tavis of Curgh had been with the gleaner, and that they had escaped through the south gate of the city wall, but that was all.

"You don't have to tell our friend that," she said softly, watching the soldiers riding in front of them for some sign that they could hear her. "Simply tell him that you found Grinsa, just as he asked."

"It's not that easy," Shurik said. "I have no idea where he's gone. Finding him means nothing."

"Surely he didn't think you could keep Grinsa here against his will, not if this man really is what we suspect."

Shurik looked over at her. "He is that. He used mists and winds to escape the guards, and he shattered their blades. He may even have whispered to my mount, trying to make the beast throw me. This from a man who claimed to be a gleaner and nothing more. He must be a Weaver."

"All the more reason for our friend to forgive you. You couldn't hope to stop him."

"I shouldn't have let him see me at all. That's what he'll say. Grinsa escaped because I feared for my life and so called for the Solkaran guards." He shook his head, a haunted look in his pale eyes. "I've failed him again. Last time he almost killed me. He won't hesitate this time."

Yaella felt herself begin to tremble. Just after the failed siege in Kentigern, when Shurik came to Mertesse, he dreamed of the Weaver. She and Shurik were in her bed at the time, and she awoke to find him thrashing wildly, clawing at his eyes as if he were in agony. She had been unable to wake him, and so had just sat beside him, helpless and horrified as he endured the Weaver's wrath.

"You said yourself that he needs you," she said, trying to convince them both. "You told me that he's finally realized how valuable you are. You're still the one person in the . . . among us who knows what this man is and can recognize him."

"Actually, I doubt that. I know that our friend turned to me, but I can't imagine I'm the only one who knows Grinsa. If he wishes to kill me, there's really nothing to stop him."

"What if you can find Grinsa again? I want you to come back with me to Mertesse, but maybe you'd be better off searching for the gleaner. If you can find him, our friend will never need to know what happened here."

"I already know where Grinsa's going to be," Shurik said. "He'll be coming to Mertesse. He has to now. I recognized him, and I know what he did to escape. I know that he's a Weaver, and he must realize that. He has no choice but to kill me."

"Then don't come back with me."

"It doesn't matter!" he said, his voice rising. The soldiers glanced back at them once more. "It doesn't matter," Shurik repeated, more quietly this time. "Don't you see, Yaella? If one of them doesn't kill me the other one will. Either our friend will punish me for failing, or Grinsa will kill me to guard his secret. Either way I'm dead. For all I know, there are only two Weavers in all the Forelands, and I've managed to make enemies of both of them."

She couldn't think of anything to say. If Shurik was right, there was no place he could hide. Not even the walls of Mertesse could protect him from men who walked in his dreams.

"I shouldn't return to Mertesse," he said, the words so soft that she had to lean closer in her saddle to hear him. "I should go as far from you as possible. Just because I'm going to die doesn't mean you have to as well."

Yaella shook her head. "I think you're wrong. You don't know that our friend intends to kill you, and in spite of everything, you can't be certain that Grinsa is a Weaver. You're safest in the castle. It will be hardest for Grinsa to reach you there. Our friend can find you anywhere, but not the gleaner."

"What about you?"

"Grinsa doesn't know anything about me, and the other can't afford to rid himself of both of us. Don't worry about me. It's most important that we keep you safe, and we can do that best in Mertesse." She gave a grim smile. "I'm Qirsi, just like you are. We may not be Weavers, but perhaps together we can keep each other safe."

She reached out her hand and he took it for a moment, squeezing it gently and returning her smile. A moment later, though, he let her hand drop, his expression turning grave again.

"I don't know how this happened, Yaella. These men are leading us all, Qirsi and Eandi alike, toward a war unlike any ever seen in the Forelands. A war between Weavers. And somehow I've managed to put myself between them."

Chapter
Twenty-four

✦

Curtell, Braedon

ll color drained from the emperor's face as he read the message, a hand coming up to cover his mouth as if he feared he might cry out at the tidings from Aneira.

"Ean save us all!" he breathed. He looked up at Dusaan for a moment, horror in his small green eyes. "They're animals, High Chancellor! We've allied ourselves with brutes and demons!"

Dusaan would have liked to rip the parchment from the man's fat fingers so that he might read it himself. But there was nothing for him to do but wait while the emperor read the message a second time and fretted like a spoiled child.

"Perhaps if Your Eminence allowed me to read the message . . ." he suggested when he could stand it no longer.

"What?" Harel said looking up. "Oh, yes. Of course."

He held out the scroll to Dusaan. After the chancellor took it from him he slumped back in his chair and closed his eyes. One would have thought the very act of reading the message had overwhelmed him.

Dusaan read of the poisoning and Grigor's execution without reaction. The deaths of the two dukes didn't trouble him, nor did the loss of three Qirsi ministers. By serving Eandi nobles, they had betrayed their people. Their lives meant as little to him as the lives of the Eandi. That is, until he realized that one of the dead Qirsi was the first minister of Bistari, one of those who served him. He had lost too many of his underlings recently—he could ill afford to lose another.

"Demons and fire," he muttered.

Harel nodded. "I know."

At least the queen had survived, and her daughter as well. Had Grigor succeeded in killing off all the leaders of House Solkara, it would have so weakened the Supremacy that civil war might have become inevitable. As it was, the selection of the girl as Carden's successor, and Numar of Renbrere as regent, promised to bring some stability to the kingdom. He couldn't know if Pronjed had any involvement in these events, but somehow, through skill or plain dumb luck, the archminister had managed to keep Aneira from descending into civil war. A good thing; with so many Qirsi dying, Dusaan would have hated to have to kill another.

He handed the scroll back to the emperor, keeping his expression grim.

"Do we really wish to ally ourselves with such people, High Chancellor?"

"These tidings are disturbing, Your Eminence. They are proof once more of why Braedon is destined to rule all the Forelands. Such depravity and wickedness on the part of the six can only lead to their decline and our glory."

"Indeed," the emperor said, brightening. "Well said, High Chancellor."

"Awful as these events may seem, however," Dusaan went on, keeping his tone light, "they should not change our plans substantially."

"No?"

"House Solkara still rules, and though Lord Renbrere may need some time to earn the trust of his dukes and the army, particularly after his brother's crime, I have no doubt that he will welcome any overtures from the empire."

Harel sat forward once more, obviously interested in what Dusaan was telling him. "What of this girl, and Carden's wife?"

"They are nothing, Your Eminence. Numar rules Aneira, if not in name, then in fact. We need only win his trust to assure our success."

"Then the invasion can go on as we planned."

"In time, yes. Numar will not be ready for several turns. We thought half a year when we heard of Carden's death, and that still seems right to me. Six or seven turns, perhaps a few more. But we need not wait much longer than that."

The emperor nodded, but even as he did, his gaze fell to the scroll once more.

"Poisoning is a terrible thing," he said, his voice low. "It's a coward's way." He started to say something else, then stopped himself, glancing uncomfortably at the chancellor.

Dusaan knew what he was thinking. "Poison is the weapon of a Qirsi." The saying dated back to the early years of the empire, when memories of the

Qirsi Wars and Carthach's betrayal were still fresh, and even men who coveted Qirsi magic for their courts spoke of the sorcerer race with contempt.

"Dusaan," the emperor said, sounding almost shy, as if what he was about to say frightened him, "have you heard the rumors of a Qirsi conspiracy?"

He had been expecting this for some time now and so had no trouble keeping his composure. In truth, he had thought the fat fool would raise these questions long ago, and he had wondered if answering them would make him uneasy. As it turned out, he had to struggle to keep from laughing at the man.

"Yes, Your Eminence, I've heard them."

"Do you give them much credence?"

"I think it would be imprudent to do otherwise, Your Eminence. Don't you?"

"Are you alarmed by what you've heard?"

Such blind, foolish trust. It was as if the emperor never even considered the possibility that Dusaan could be involved, much less the movement's leader.

"Alarmed?" The chancellor shook his head. "No. But I think it's fair to say that I'm listening carefully to all that I hear of this conspiracy, lest there come a time when rumor gives way to reality."

"Yes, of course," the emperor said, nodding so vigorously that the flesh under his chin shook. "No doubt that's very wise."

Dusaan narrowed his eyes. "Are you wondering if the poisoning was the work of these Qirsi?"

"It had crossed my mind. After all, it was poison. . . ."

And Ean forbid that an Eandi would be cowardly enough to put oleander in the queen's wine. "Yes, Your Eminence, it was."

"Not that all Qirsi would do such a thing," the emperor added. "Not that you would. But it does give one pause."

"Of course. If you'd like, I'll ask the other chancellors and ministers what they've heard of this conspiracy and whether they think it may be responsible for recent events in Aneira."

"Yes, Dusaan, that would be fine."

The Weaver made a half turn toward the door, as if to go, hoping that would be the end of their conversation. But the emperor didn't dismiss him.

"Have you noticed, High Chancellor, that most of the killings attributed to the conspiracy have taken place elsewhere? The empire has largely been spared. It's almost as if the weakness of the six invites such tragedies, while our strength keeps us safe."

Again, he had to keep from laughing. Braedon had been spared because Dusaan chose to spare it. The last thing he wanted was for the emperor to grow suspicious of his Qirsi before Dusaan had the chance to turn the empire's army and fleet to his purposes. Eventually, he would command enough Qirsi warriors that he would no longer need the emperor's soldiers, but that time had not yet come.

"I hadn't noticed, Your Eminence. But now that you bring it to my attention it seems clear that you're correct. These Qirsi may believe they can weaken the other kingdoms, but they would not dare make an enemy of the empire."

Harel smiled, looking far too satisfied with himself. "Quite right, High Chancellor. But still, I feel the time has come to take some precautions."

"What kind of precautions?" Dusaan asked, his stomach tightening.

"Well," the emperor began, suddenly sounding a bit less sure, "I think we should stop bringing new ministers and chancellors into the palace. I've enough Qirsi advising me now."

The Weaver felt himself relax. "That seems wise, Your Eminence."

"I also think we should watch those Qirsi who already serve me a bit more closely. There may be some among them who wish to betray the empire."

"Again, a most prudent decision."

"And finally, I feel that I must make more decisions without consulting any Qirsi at all." He glanced quickly at the chancellor, then looked down again, toying absently with the Imperial Scepter. "Even you, Dusaan. I realize that I've come to rely on you a great deal. Perhaps too much."

He would have liked to slap the man, to leave a crimson imprint of his hand on the emperor's fat face. It was bad enough that Dusaan should still be forced to serve such a man publicly, bowing to this overgrown child and lavishing him with undeserved praise. But to be reminded just now that his own fortunes and those of his movement were still subject to Harel's whims and petty fears was almost too much for him to bear.

"As you wish, Your Eminence," he managed to say, his voice sounding thick. "If you like I'll leave the planning of the invasion in your hands." He could hardly imagine the emperor agreeing to this—the very idea of leading this war seemed to terrify Harel. But Dusaan wouldn't have minded if by some chance he did agree. The chancellor wanted Braedon at war with Eibithar. If the emperor led that war incompetently, all the better. The weaker the Eandi armies, the easier it would be for his Qirsi army to conquer them. Better Harel should take control of the invasion than the treasury. Dusaan needed access to Braedon's gold in order to continue paying those who served him.

"The invasion?" the emperor asked, shifting uncomfortably in his throne. "You've worked so hard on it already. I'd hate to . . . to deny you the pleasure of seeing it to its completion."

"Not at all, Your Eminence. This invasion promises to be the crowning achievement of your reign as emperor. The pleasure of completing it should be yours as should the glory that will follow from it."

"The invasion," Harel said again, as if considering it. He licked his lips. "I had in mind some of the more mundane matters that I leave to your discretion each day."

"Well, of course, Your Eminence, if you wish to concern yourself with such trifles you may. The empire is yours and I but serve. But it seems to me that the man who will soon lay claim to the entire northern half of the Forelands has better ways to pass his day than bothering with the collection of tithes, the enforcement of warrior quotas, and the mediation of inconsequential disputes among your lords."

The emperor perked up at that. "There! Mediating disputes among my lords. That's just the sort of thing I mean. That, it seems to me, is the responsibility of an emperor, rather than his high chancellor. You understand, don't you, Dusaan?"

The Qirsi shrugged, feeling himself relax once more. "I suppose I do, Your Eminence. If you feel it necessary to handle these matters, I'm more than happy to defer to you. To be honest, I'll be glad to be done with them. With all respect to the lords who serve you, they seem almost eager to quarrel with one another. They take offense like overly tender children and threaten war over the smallest, most desolate scraps of land."

"Yes, I suppose they do," the emperor said, nodding sagely. "But you have to remember, Dusaan: they don't know what it is to rule an empire. Their realms are small, and so even the merest threats to their power seem great. These matters must be handled with care lest they grow into civil conflict." He nodded again, as if convincing himself. "I think it best that I mediate all future disputes among my lords."

"Of course. Your Eminence is most wise." He hesitated, watching the emperor closely. He was eager to leave Harel's chambers, but he needed to be certain that his control over the treasury remained safe. "Is there anything else, Your Eminence?"

"No, Dusaan. You may go."

The chancellor bowed and started toward the door.

"You will remember to speak with the others?" the emperor called to him, just as he reached for the door handle.

Dusaan halted, but didn't turn. "The others, Your Eminence?" he asked, struggling to keep his impatience from seeping into his voice.

"The other Qirsi. You said you'd speak to them about the conspiracy."

He faced Harel. "Of course. Forgive me, Your Eminence. I had forgotten. I'll summon them to my quarters immediately."

The emperor frowned. "Are you all right, Dusaan?"

"I'm fine, Your Eminence."

"It's not like you to forget such things."

"I've a good deal on my mind. And I think I find the very idea of the conspiracy so disturbing that I didn't want to remember this particular task." He forced a smile. "But I'll see to it right away."

"Very good, Dusaan. Thank you."

The Qirsi bowed again, let himself out of the chamber, and walked quickly back toward his quarters.

There were certain risks in speaking of the conspiracy with the other Qirsi. Skilled as he was at masking his true feelings, he would be hard-pressed to endure the righteous denunciations of his movement that he expected from Harel's fawning underchancellors and ministers. But rather than dreading this discussion, he was actually looking forward to it. At some point, sooner rather than later, he would have to begin gathering allies from within the emperor's circle of advisors. As the time for the uprising neared, his need to remain anonymous would give way to a greater need to build his army of sorcerers. While he had nothing but contempt for several of Harel's advisors, he saw promise in some of them, and recognized that several others wielded powers that would be of use to him in the coming war.

Not that he intended to begin today to lure some of them into the movement. Rather, he hoped to learn from what he saw in their responses who among them were most likely to be receptive to his overtures when the time came. He had little doubt that all of them had heard talk of the conspiracy, and he felt certain that at least a few of them—perhaps more—harbored sympathies for his cause. He had only to watch and listen.

He passed one of the emperor's pages in the palace corridor—a Qirsi child, probably the son of one of the other Qirsi advisors. He stopped the boy with an outstretched hand.

"Y-yes, High Chancellor?" the lad said, staring up at him with wide, frightened eyes.

Dusaan reached into a pocket and pulled out a silver piece. It was only one qinde—an imperial at that—but to the boy it would be a treasure. "Summon the other chancellors and ministers for me, boy. Tell them to meet me in my chambers at the ringing of the prior's bells."

The boy stared at the coin and nodded. "Yes, High Chancellor."

Dusaan handed him the silver and walked on. Normally he would have entrusted only a guard with such a task, but he had no doubt that the boy would do as he was told. His fear of the high chancellor made that certain. And by paying him, Dusaan made a friend, one who might be of use to him later. "A well-placed coin," it was said in the Braedon courts, "pays for itself tenfold." In light of the success he had enjoyed in turning Qirsi all across the Forelands to his cause, the Weaver could hardly argue the point.

Returning to his quarters, Dusaan locked his door and pulled out the treasury accounting. He carried the volume to his writing table and lit a nearby oil lamp with a thought.

The past several turns had been difficult ones for him, the worst he had encountered since he first began bringing other Qirsi into his movement. First there was the failure in Kentigern during the growing turns when all his gold and hard work not only failed to bring war, but actually fostered an alliance between the houses of Curgh and Glyndwr in Eibithar. And now Pronjed's rash decision to kill the king of Solkara had led to this poisoning and the death of Bistari's first minister. By necessity, Dusaan had to rely on Qirsi who served in the Eandi courts. In order to win control of the Forelands, he had to defeat the Eandi nobles, and who better to help him with this than their most trusted advisors.

But while his ability to turn these men and women to his own purposes had been, thus far, his greatest strength, it had also revealed itself recently as his most dangerous vulnerability. He had come to Curtell to serve the emperor knowing already that he was a Weaver, and intending to use his influence and his powers to wrest control of the court from the Eandi. Most of those who had joined his movement, however, had once aspired to the positions they now held. They served him now, but once they had chosen to serve their Eandi nobles. They were, at root, just the sort of weak-minded traitors to the Qirsi people he most despised. He couldn't succeed without them, yet as Shurik had shown in Kentigern, and Pronjed had made glaringly clear in Solkara, he might find eventually that he couldn't succeed with them, either.

He couldn't blame all of his troubles on others, he knew. His own carelessness had forced him to kill the high minister in the City of Kings. He still didn't understand how he had managed to let the man see his face.

"Of course you do," he murmured to himself, pausing over the accounting and rubbing his brow.

It was the woman. Cresenne. He had allowed himself to imagine her as his queen, though it should have been clear to him that she still loved this other man, the one who had fathered her child. Hearing Paegar speak of his love for Kearney's archminister, Dusaan had been reminded of his own unrequited affections and his pain and rage at learning that she still longed for the gleaner. Before he understood fully what had happened, the light behind him had faded and Paegar had looked upon his face, he had seen the plains of his dreams for what they were, the moors near Ayvencalde. There had been nothing for Dusaan to do but kill the man.

Which meant that he needed someone new in the royal city of Eibithar.

Paegar had given him a name before he died. Keziah ja Dafydd. Another minister, another Qirsi who had pledged herself to the service of an Eandi noble. Still, the Weaver sensed that this one might be different, that she might be more. For one thing, she was a woman, and he had found over the years that among the ministers, the women served him far better than did the men. Enid in Thorald, Yaella in Mertesse, Abeni in the court of Sanbira's queen, in Yserne; all of them had proven their worth time and again. Even Cresenne, who had caused him so much anguish as of late, had been more valuable to him than the most powerful men he had turned. Keziah, he believed, would serve him just as well as the others.

But not only was she a woman, she was also, according to Paegar, the king's lover. At least she had been before he took the throne. Theirs had been a forbidden love, which meant that it most likely had been a deep love as well. Even for a duke and his first minister, the risks of an affair between a Qirsi woman and Eandi man would have been too great for it to be anything less. Losing him had to have been a terrible blow, enough perhaps to leave her bitter and eager for vengeance. Such had been Paegar's hope, and Dusaan found that he wanted to prove the man right, as a way of honoring him. He smiled at the thought. These were not sentiments he would usually have allowed himself, but in this instance they seemed justified.

Still, though she might hate her king now, enough perhaps to betray him without other incentive, the Weaver needed to be prepared to pay her. He had noticed that most of the women he turned did not have the same voracious appetite for gold that he observed in so many of the men. But neither did they refuse it when it was offered to them.

Finding gold in Braedon's treasury had never been a problem for him. The challenge lay in turning the gold to his own purposes without raising the suspicions of the emperor or his other Qirsi. Fortunately, an empire as vast as Braedon had no shortage of expenses. By adding a few extra qinde to the allocation for the Braedon garrison on Enwyl Island, in the Gulf of Kreanna, for instance, or increasing slightly the allowance for the naval presence near Mistborne Island, at the top of the Scabbard, he could make the accounting look reasonable while creating a pool of gold which he could use without drawing attention to his activities. He never sent the garrisons or naval forces less than they needed, so no one ever complained. And since requests for gold came directly to him, no one else ever noticed the discrepancies.

Dusaan sent this extra gold to a sea merchant who frequented the ports of Ayvencalde, Bishenhurst, and Finkirk. For centuries, the empire had used merchants as spies to keep watch on the other six kingdoms of the Forelands. None of the emperor's couriers would have thought twice about delivering gold to this man. That he was Qirsi would have seemed to them a curiosity and nothing more.

His name was Tihod jal Brossa and he was the one man in the world whom Dusaan considered a true friend. They had grown up together in valley of the Rimerock River near Muelry. Their fathers, unlike most of the Qirsi in Braedon, had refused to work in the Eandi courts or in Braedon's Carnival. Instead, Tihod's father farmed and Dusaan's father served the nearby villages as a healer. Neither man ever grew wealthy. Indeed, there were many times when Dusaan's mother pleaded with her husband to seek a position in one of Muelry's lesser courts. But throughout their lives, both men maintained a stubborn pride in their ancestry and in their powers as well, limited though they were. They instilled this same pride in their sons, telling them tales of the ancient Qirsi warriors at bedtime, and taking it upon themselves to begin training the boys in the ways of magic well before their Determinings. While so many Qirsi children grew up ashamed of their white hair and yellow eyes and slight builds, Dusaan and Tihod saw these as signs of dignity. The rest of the children, Qirsi and Eandi, called them arrogant, but the boys didn't care. They were inseparable, like brothers; they had no need for other friends.

When their formal training began, and Dusaan learned from his Qirsi master that he was a Weaver, he told Tihod, but no one else, not even his father. To this day, his friend remained the only one who knew.

Generally he sent Tihod between one thousand and two thousand qinde at a time, placing a reserve of gold in the merchant's hands to speed payments when necessary. These were imperial qinde, which were accepted throughout the Forelands but were held to have less value than the qinde used in the six kingdoms. One thousand imperial was worth about seven hundred qinde in the six. Tihod exchanged the gold pieces at a rate somewhat more favorable to himself, usually sending five hundred qinde on to those who served Dusaan for every one thousand imperial he received from the Weaver. It was a steep price Dusaan was paying, but since he was using the emperor's gold, he gave it little thought. In return for all this gold, Tihod delivered the payments to ports throughout the Forelands, making certain that they found their way into the right hands. He had even created a web of couriers who carried the gold from the ports to the inland cites, where it could be left in specified places for Dusaan's most trusted servants—his chancellors, as he called them. Dusaan didn't know any of these couriers by name, nor did Tihod know the names of those who served the movement. The Weaver told Tihod how much gold to send and where to have his couriers hide it. He then told his underlings where to find the payments. In all other respects Tihod's web and Dusaan's movement remained utterly separate from one another.

In this way, the Weaver could pay his underlings in common currency rather than in imperial coin, making it far less likely that any of them might trace the gold back to Braedon and thus learn his true identity. At the same time, his friend made enough gold through these transactions to ensure that he would do nothing to upset Dusaan's plans. The Weaver trusted Tihod, but he found it comforting to know that the merchant had other incentives beyond their friendship to keep his secret. A Weaver could never be too careful.

It took Dusaan but a short while to allocate enough gold to make his first payment to the archminister of Eibithar. He had decided to give her one hundred qinde, or rather to have Tihod give it to her out of his reserve. Dusaan wanted this done quickly. One hundred, he hoped, would be enough to lure her into the movement, but not so much as to seem that he was trying to buy her loyalty. He needed to impress upon her that this was more than merely a way to grow rich. The movement offered her a chance to bring glory to her people, to redeem the Qirsi from Carthach's betrayal. And perhaps, if Paegar proved to be right about this, the Weaver might also convince her that by joining his movement she could strike back at the Eandi king who had spurned her when he placed the jeweled crown on his brow.

He returned the volume containing the accounts to the shelves and sat back in his chair, rubbing his eyes. He had not slept well since killing Paegar, and because he spent many of his nights entering the dreams of others, he found that he was constantly weary. Tonight he would have to speak with Tihod, but, he hoped, no one else. He heard bells ringing in the city, and it took him a moment to remember that the tolling would soon bring Harel's other advisors to his chambers. He was in no mood for this meeting.

The first knock came at his door just a few moments later, and over the next several minutes the emperor's Qirsi entered his chamber in a steady stream, bowing to the high chancellor and taking seats around his hearth. As always, the young ministers reached his chamber first, eager to serve and afraid to offend by arriving late. Watching the Qirsi as they came in, young and old, men and women, ministers and chancellors, Dusaan could not help but feel that his search for allies would be largely a waste of time. Yes, a few of them showed promise, particularly some of the younger ones. But so many more of them struck him as foolish and weak, and far too old to be of much use to the movement.

The last of them finally reached his quarters and Dusaan had this man close his door.

"Is it true that there's been a poisoning?" one of them asked, a young minister named Kayiv. Of all the Qirsi in Harel's palace, he was the one Dusaan thought most likely to join the movement. He possessed three magics—gleaning, shaping, and language of beasts—making him one of the more powerful of the emperor's advisors.

"Yes," Dusaan said. "Though not here. It happened in Solkara during the last waning."

"How bad was it?" one of the older fools asked.

Dusaan described briefly what had happened, telling them of the few who had died, and of Grigor's subsequent execution.

Kayiv eyed him, looking vaguely amused. "Is this why you've summoned us? Has all this convinced the emperor to further delay his invasion?"

Dusaan shook his head. "We don't think that will be necessary. After Carden's death we thought we'd have to wait half a year. That, we believed, would give the new Aneiran king time enough to prepare, provided there was no civil war." Just speaking of it rekindled Dusaan's anger at Pronjed. The man was lucky events unfolded as they did, though the Weaver still would have liked to kill him for his stupidity. "With Numar of Renbrere taking the regency," he went on, "civil war has been averted. A half year still seems about right."

Another chancellor shook his head. "Do we really wish to ally ourselves with these people?"

"The emperor has asked the same question."

"What they do to each other seems of little consequence," Kayiv said. "We need them for their swords and their ships. We don't have to dine with them."

A few of the others laughed, as did Dusaan. He could work with this man.

"Well put."

The older chancellor shook his head. "I don't think this is a question we can just laugh away. The empire has avoided formal alliances for centuries. Abandoning that course now strikes me as dangerous, particularly if it means casting our lot with the Aneirans."

"The emperor feels otherwise. Despite their recent troubles, the Eibitharians are stronger now than they've ever been." Again Dusaan felt his rage returning. Too many of his underlings had failed him. "We may be able to defeat them on our own, but an alliance with Aneira ensures our success. That outweighs all other concerns."

The older Qirsi nodded, unwilling to challenge Dusaan again. They might not know that he was a Weaver, but the other Qirsi in the palace still deferred to him. He had the emperor's ear and as high chancellor was, after Harel, the most powerful and most feared man in all of Braedon.

Kayiv sat forward, as if preparing to stand. "Is there anything else, High Chancellor?"

"Actually, there is. The emperor wanted me to ask all of you what you had heard of the so-called Qirsi conspiracy."

The minister sat back again, his eyebrows going up. The others just stared at Dusaan, as if too frightened to speak.

"How did you answer him?" a woman asked at last.

It was a clever response, and Dusaan had to smile. Her name was Nitara, and she was another of the young ministers who had impressed him. He often saw her with Kayiv—they were sitting together now—and he wouldn't have been surprised to learn that they were lovers.

"I told him that I had heard rumors of the conspiracy and that I thought it wise to take these stories seriously, lest they prove to be true."

"That's all?"

"He didn't ask for more, and I felt it prudent not to alarm him unnecessarily. As it is, the emperor has decided not to bring any more Qirsi to the palace."

"He thinks Qirsi were behind the poisoning." Kayiv. He looked as angry as Dusaan had felt while speaking to Harel. This was definitely a man who could be turned to the Weaver's cause. It almost seemed to Dusaan that he was looking for an excuse to betray the emperor.

"He thinks it's possible," Dusaan said. "Like so many, he sees poison as a Qirsi weapon."

The younger man opened his mouth, then closed it again, looking away. The chancellor sensed his fury.

"Do you think the conspiracy was behind it?" Nitara asked.

"No, I don't. Grigor hanged for the crime. I trust that Aneira's queen knew what she was doing when she ordered his execution."

"Did you say so to the emperor?"

He considered this for a moment. Then he shook his head. "Perhaps I should have. Qirsar knows I wanted to. But there are times when we must allow the Eandi their prejudices, foolish though they may be. The emperor fears the conspiracy. He might even fear us, at least more than he once did. To argue the point would have been to alarm him further. I didn't wish to give him cause to question my loyalty or that of his other Qirsi. A good chancellor is one who recognizes both the strengths and flaws of the noble he serves and tempers his remarks accordingly. It's hard to dissuade our emperor from his beliefs once he's made up his mind, no matter how wrong he may be, and it can do more harm than good to try."

He had never spoken so of Harel in front of the other Qirsi, nor had he ever before suggested that he was less than candid in his conversations with the emperor. Some of the older chancellors frowned in response to his admission, but most of the Qirsi offered little by way of reaction. Maybe he had given them too little credit over the years. Wouldn't it have been ironic if all this time they had thought of him as the weak one, the Qirsi who demeaned himself by his unquestioning service to the Eandi?

Kayiv faced him again. "You said before that the emperor doesn't intend to bring any more Qirsi to the palace. Does that mean he doesn't trust us? Did he send you here to ask about the conspiracy as a way of testing our loyalty?"

"He's Eandi, Minister. I think it likely that he's never trusted us entirely. But I believe he sent me here to do just what I said, to find out what you've heard about the conspiracy. I doubt there was more to it than that." *He's not clever enough to think that way.* He wanted to say it. Faced now with the possibility that they thought him just another fawning chancellor, Dusaan was tempted to tell them what he really thought of Harel.

A lengthy silence ensued, broken at last by Nitara.

"Well, I've heard little of the conspiracy beyond that it seems to be real enough. Some of the peddlers I've talked to in the marketplace believe that it might have been behind the murders in Kentigern and Bistari, but they have no proof of this."

One of the others spoke up as well, noting, as the emperor had, that the movement had been far more active in the six than it had been here in the empire. For some time, Dusaan simply listened as rumor chased rumor around the chamber. Many of the tales were laughable. One minister had heard that the conspiracy was, in fact, a continuation of the original Qirsi invasion that began nine centuries before. It had gone unnoticed in the intervening centuries, but had been behind the early civil wars in Eibithar, Amnalla's Rebellion in Aneira, and Valde's Rebellion in Caerisse, all of which dated back nearly six hundred years.

Other rumors, however, proved disturbingly accurate. According to several of the chancellors, there was talk among the merchants that Filib of Thorald had not been killed by thieves, but instead was the victim of an assassination by the conspiracy. And Kayiv offered his own opinion that the king of Aneira had died at the hands of a Qirsi.

"Well," Dusaan said, when the discussion had run its course. "I'm not certain how much of this to believe, but I'll leave that for the emperor to decide. I have no doubt that he'll be grateful to all of you for your counsel on this matter."

"Do you really think so?" Kayiv asked. "Or do you think it will just scare him anew, and make him trust us even less?"

The young Qirsi sounded hurt, angry, bitter. If he hadn't been susceptible to the Weaver's overtures before, he certainly would be now. The same could probably be said of Nitara and a number of the others. Harel might have thought that he was protecting himself by suggesting this meeting, but all he had done was make it easier for Dusaan to win the loyalty of the palace Qirsi.

"To be honest, Minister, I don't know how the emperor will respond. As I said before, he's Eandi. It may be that he never trusted us. For now all we can do is serve the empire, as we've sworn to do. But there may come a time when our choices are clearer, and we have the opportunity to prove ourselves. When that time comes, I for one hope that the emperor will be watching."

Kayiv grinned, a gleam in his bright yellow eyes. It almost seemed to the Weaver that the man understood him.

Chapter
Twenty-five

✤

Mertesse, Aneira

ad they been eager to reach the walled city of Mertesse, they might have made the journey from Dantrielle in less time. It was fifty leagues, and with the weather turning worse with each day that passed, progress didn't come quickly, even on the well-traveled roads of Aneira's Great Forest. Still, Dario and Cadel might have made it to Mertesse before the beginning of the new year.

Instead, they stopped frequently at inns along the road, playing music in exchange for meals and rooms. They never remained in one place for long, but neither did they hesitate to stop, even if they had paused at another inn only an hour or two before. Musicians in the Forelands rarely turned down opportunities to play, particularly if it meant free food, or, better yet, gold. To have done so as they made their way north would have been to risk raising the suspicions of the innkeepers at those establishments they bypassed. More than that, though, Cadel realized that they needed the practice.

Dario played the lute beautifully. Cadel actually preferred the pipes, finding their sound richer, more soothing. But he had to admit that his new partner coaxed a sound from his instrument that few of the lutenists Cadel had encountered before could match. Despite his skill, however, and Cadel's own talent as a singer, their musical tendencies were not compatible, at least not at first. Dario had been performing on his own for so long that he had little sense of how to match his cadence to someone else's singing. Cadel had the impression whenever Dario took up his instrument that he would have preferred to play one of his own compositions rather than accompanying Cadel as he sang. He knew the notes to play for pieces like the *Paean* and "The Elegy for Shanae," but he never played them the same way twice. Cadel could only hope that he was more disciplined as an assassin than he was as a musician.

For his part, Cadel was willing to admit that he could be uncompromising when it came to music. He and Jed sang together for seventeen years. They knew what to expect of each other. They performed most of these pieces so many times that their performances became as natural and constant as the rise and fall of the moons. Jedrek understood that when it came to music, and to killing, Cadel always strove for perfection.

The problems were apparent to both of them from the start, but, predictably, Dario was far less disturbed by them than was Cadel.

"They're going to pay us anyway," the younger man said one night, after their fourth or fifth failed attempt to practice "Tanith's Threnody."

They were in a small village at the time, near the mouth of the River Orvinti, just a few days' journey from Solkara. The king had been dead for nearly half a turn and they were still thinking that they might stop in Solkara for Carden's funeral and the investiture of the new king. Most of the land's musicians would be there, Cadel knew, and there was a good chance the Qirsi man they had been hired to kill would be as well.

"Getting paid is beside the point," Cadel had answered, not bothering to mask his exasperation. "Music isn't just a source of gold, and it isn't just something we do for amusement. It's our disguise, it's what allows us to move about the land without drawing attention to ourselves. To those who listen to us, it has to appear to be our passion as well as the source of our livelihood. If it appears to be anything less, it will raise their suspicions. Do you understand that?"

"Yes," Dario said. "But I don't see what's wrong with them knowing that we've just started playing together. With all the festivals and revels in the Forelands, musicians are always moving around and finding new partners."

We sound ragged, like tavern singers in some Caerissan farming village. Jedrek would have understood. And perhaps that was the point. Cadel hadn't sung with anyone since Jedrek's death; he had barely sung a note by himself. He wasn't looking for a new partner, he realized. He was trying to replace Jedrek, which was unfair to Dario. When it came right down to it, the young man was right: musicians in the Forelands changed partners quite frequently. Though Cadel and Jedrek remained together for years, they performed with literally dozens of different singers and players. Indeed, they had been together so long, they might have risked drawing attention to themselves in that way.

Cadel was frustrated because of the way he and his new partner sounded, and because he worried that a man as young and blithe as Dario might get him killed when they turned from music to their more important trade.

"I suppose you're right," Cadel finally admitted. "We don't have to sound perfect, at least not yet. But I still think it needs work."

The young man shrugged, tuning one of the strings on his lute. "All right. It's not like there's anything else to do."

As they continued northward, performing at inns and practicing well into the night, their playing improved. A few days after their conversation near Orvinti, as they came within sight of the royal city, word of the poisoning reached them. After a brief discussion, they decided to continue on toward Mertesse. After such an event, the guards in Solkara were likely to be more vigilant than ever. Even if the Qirsi man they sought was there, and even if he had survived the poisoning, they were unlikely to get close enough to him to earn their gold. Better to travel directly to Mertesse, where they were most likely to learn of the Qirsi's fate. They would find regular work at a tavern in the city and wait for an opportunity to kill the Qirsi.

Cadel was so intent on improving the sound of their music that they spoke of little else throughout their travels. Only when they began to cross the narrow plain that lay between the Great Forest and Mertesse did he begin to wonder how Dario had come to his other, truer calling. Still, he didn't ask at first. Their conversations tended to go much as did their practices, even when they weren't speaking of music. Perhaps it was the difference in their ages. Perhaps it was Cadel's fault for starting the partnership with his test of Dario's fighting skill. Whatever the reason, nothing they did together came easily, and though neither of them had shown any sign of wanting to abandon their young partnership, there was, as of yet, no friendship between them.

It began to snow during their third day on the plain, fine white flakes dancing and whirling in the cold wind that blew from the west. A heavy blanket of snow already lay over the land north of the wood, so that it seemed the only colors left in the world were grey and white. Even the road they were on, no doubt a muddy brown every other time of year, was covered with a thick grey carpet of half-melted ice and snow that made for slow walking.

As the snowfall increased, Dario halted to check on his lute. He always kept it wrapped in a soft cloth when they traveled, and now he added a second layer of animal skin.

"The cold's bad enough," he muttered as he tucked the skin snugly around his instrument. "But this snow will damage the wood."

"We won't go much farther," Cadel told him. "Just another league or two."

The lutenist looked up. "We can make the gates tonight if we keep at it."

Cadel hesitated. The truth was, he didn't want to reach the city just yet. There were matters he and the younger man needed to discuss first. "Perhaps, but I'd rather not stay out in this cold for too long. I feel a bad throat coming on." He grimaced. "If I can't sing, we'll have to pay for a room." It was a lie, but under the circumstances a necessary one.

Dario eyed him a moment longer, then gave a small shrug, his answer whenever they disagreed.

There were few inns anywhere along the road between the Great Forest and Mertesse, and fewer still as one drew nearer the city. The two assassins journeyed farther that day than Cadel had intended, stopping at last at a small farmhouse just beside the road that looked too small to be an inn, but had a sign swinging in the wind out front. They couldn't have been more than two or three leagues from Mertesse—Cadel thought he could just make out the walls of the castle looming above the plain in the distance, stark against Mertesse Forest, but shrouded in the swirling snow.

The innkeeper was an old woman, a widow, with rheumy eyes and yellow teeth. She had only one room for rent, which made it unlikely that she would give them their beds in exchange for a performance, but Cadel was determined to stop before they reached the city.

After haggling with them briefly, she agreed to six qinde for the room and their meals, provided they would play for her, and her daughter's family, after supper. It seemed a fair price. Cadel paid her and she led them up a narrow stairway to the room. Their quarters were quite small, as were the straw beds, but the chamber was no worse than others they had stayed in since leaving Dantrielle.

The woman left them, saying that their meal would be ready before long. Dario sat on one of the beds and began carefully to unwrap his lute.

"What are you doing?" Cadel asked.

He didn't even look up. His yellow hair fell over his brow, hiding his eyes and much of his face. But Cadel could imagine his expression as he said in a flat voice, "I assumed you'd want to practice. We're to perform tonight, and you still don't seem happy with how we sound."

Cadel frowned. As difficult as he found the younger man, he had to admit that he had handled things poorly since they started traveling together.

"I'm sure we'll be fine," he said, drawing the other man's gaze. "I'd rather we talked for a bit."

Dario looked uncertain, but he laid his lute gently on the bed. "All right."

Faced now with the prospect of actually carrying on a conversation with Dario, Cadel found that he didn't know how to begin. He started to say something, then stopped himself, realizing that he hadn't the words. After doing this several times, he rubbed a hand over his brow, exhaling through his teeth.

"What's this about?" Dario asked, narrowing his eyes. "Is there something else I've done wrong?" Almost immediately he shook his head. "Actually that couldn't be it. You never have trouble telling me that."

"You've done nothing wrong," Cadel told him, ignoring the gibe. "Before we reach the city, I . . . I feel that we should know more about each other. We want to convince people that we're . . ."

"Friends?"

"Yes."

"We've talked about this before."

"No, we haven't."

"Sure we have. It's no different from what I said before about our performances not being perfect, and about musicians finding new partners. If we don't know everything about each other nobody's going to notice."

Again, the lutenist had a point, but Cadel didn't care. He'd had enough of the younger man challenging him at every turn. Cadel was the one who would be doing the killing. It was his reputation that had gotten them this job in the first place, just as it would get them every subsequent job they were likely to have. Dario would do as he said, or Cadel would find himself another partner.

He was ready to say as much, but then thought better of it. It might make him feel better to tell Dario how angry he was, but it certainly wouldn't help matters. He was about to kill a Qirsi, and he needed a partner for that. Would he have preferred Jed? Of course. But Jed was gone, and for better or worse, he had chosen this man to take his place. Driving him away now would have been folly. Still, he did need to make Dario understand which of them was in command.

"Nobody else may notice," he said, managing to keep his voice even.

"But I think we should talk anyway. We're about to enter Mertesse. We're not just musicians learning to play together anymore. We're assassins, and we're hunting a sorcerer. I expect you to guard my back, to keep me from getting killed or captured while I find this man and earn our gold." He grinned. "I think I'd feel a bit more comfortable with that if I knew for certain that you wanted me to come out of this alive."

Dario's expression didn't change. "So you do the killing? Always?"

"Most of the time. Certainly when we've been hired to kill a Qirsi. That's the way I've always worked. When I find a partner who's my equal with a blade, I may change my mind. But that hasn't happened yet."

The other man nodded and looked away.

"Depending on the job, we might be able to work differently," Cadel said after a brief, awkward silence. "But not this time. This is our first job together, and as I said, we're hunting a Qirsi." He regarded the lutenist for a moment. "Have you ever killed a white-hair?"

Dario faced him again, seeming to search for some sign that Cadel was mocking him. "No," he admitted. "Have you?"

"Seven times."

"All right," Dario said, turning away again. "I guess this one's yours."

"They're all mine," Cadel said pointedly, "unless I decide differently."

Silence.

"Tell me how you became a blade."

Dario shrugged. "It just happened. I needed gold, and I couldn't wait for my apprenticeship to end."

"Why did you need the gold?"

He gave a small laugh, looking at Cadel again. "All right," he said. "If you really want to know, I needed the gold to take care of my sister and brother. I grew up on the Plain of Stallions, south of Tounstrel. People who live in the Great Forest think they have trouble with road thieves, but that's nothing compared with what we used to face. The thieves down there roam in large groups, usually on horses they've broken themselves. Mounted raiders we call them."

He picked up his lute and plucked two of the strings. "One day they attacked our village. It was early, the sun wasn't even up yet. They attacked us in our homes—in our beds, really—stealing what they could, killing those who fought back, and burning our houses and barns. My family didn't have much—a bit of gold, a silver ring my father had given my mother, and my father's lute. When the raiders tried to take the ring, my father fought them. He was killed, as was my mother. One of them tried to cut off my mother's finger to get the ring, and another grabbed the lute. Before I knew it, I'd grabbed a meat knife and killed them both. They hadn't even noticed me."

He played a few more notes, then put the lute down again, though he continued to stare at it. "With my parents dead, it fell to me to take care of my sister and brother. We had no money, and the raiders had also killed the smith to whom I'd been apprenticed. After the raid I knew I could handle a dagger, and killing the raiders hadn't bothered me at all." He looked up, meeting Grinsa's gaze. "So here I am."

"How old were you?"

"Fourteen."

"And where are your sister and brother now?"

"They're still on the plain, in a village just north of Tounstrel. When I'd made enough gold, I took them to live with my father's sister. I go to see them sometimes, though it's been a few years now." He took a breath and smiled, though clearly it was forced. "Is this like singers' night in a tavern? I've sung mine, now it's your turn?"

Cadel rarely spoke of his past. He had told Jedrek a little bit, and a Qirsi woman in Thorald, the first person with the conspiracy to hire him, had somehow known a great deal. But having heard Dario's story, he could hardly refuse to tell him anything.

"I come from a noble house," he said quietly, "though not one of any importance. When I was still young, I fell in love with a girl. She preferred another, and in a rage I killed him. Rather than bringing disgrace to my house and my father, I feigned my own death and fled. Like you, I'd found that killing didn't trouble me, and that I was good at it."

"And how old were you?"

"I was just shy of my Fating."

Dario raised an eyebrow. "Then we've that in common as well."

"What?"

"Well, if you fled your village before your Fating, and you wanted your family to believe you were dead, I can't imagine you would have risked having a Fating somewhere else."

"You're right, I didn't."

"Neither did I. I wonder what that means. Neither of us has faced the Qiran a second time. We're men without fates, Cadel."

Cadel shook his head. "If the Qiran really can reveal a man's fate, I've no doubt as to what I would have seen at my second gleaning. I was destined for this life long before I killed that boy. I sense the same is true of you."

"Maybe."

Cadel heard a footfall on the steps below their room and he held up a hand to keep Dario silent.

"Your supper is ready," the old woman called them. "It's best hot, so don't dawdle."

"We'll be down shortly," Cadel answered. "Thank you."

The woman mumbled something that he couldn't hear before descending the steps once more.

He would have liked to continue his conversation with Dario, but the younger man had stood at the mention of food. Perhaps they had talked enough for now. Already Cadel felt better about their partnership. He wasn't certain they would ever be friends, certainly not the way he and Jedrek had been. But he could work with Dario, he could trust the man to watch his back. He'd have to be satisfied with that. There was one matter, however, that could not wait.

Dario took a step toward the stairs, but Cadel held out a hand, stopping him.

"From now on, you're to call me Corbin, even when we're alone."

Dario nodded. "I'd forgotten. I'm sorry."

"What about you? Is there a name you've used before?"

"I've always just gone by Dario."

"I referred to you as Dagon in the Red Boar."

The man grinned. "I know. I didn't like it."

Cadel clicked his tongue. He would have preferred an alias, but if Dario hadn't used one before, particularly if he had performed under his given name, changing it now would be dangerous.

"All right, Dario will have to do. You don't give your family name, do you?"

"I never have."

"Good," Cadel said, nodding.

They found the innkeeper already seated at her table, eating the stew she had prepared.

"It's probably half cold already," she said, as the two men sat.

Cadel glanced at Dario, who grinned in return.

"I have no doubt that it still tastes wonderful, my lady," Cadel said.

The woman paused with her spoon just in front of her mouth, peering at him from beneath wisps of white hair. "I never said it didn't."

He suppressed a laugh, and both men began to eat. The stew wasn't bad, nor was the bread she had baked to serve with it, though Cadel expected that they would find better of both in the city. She had placed no wine on the table, but for six qinde he couldn't bring himself to complain.

None of them spoke for some time. The woman seemed content to eat in silence, and Cadel saw no reason to risk unwanted questions by striking up a conversation. Eventually, though, the innkeeper finished her meal, and, with both men still eating, she remained at the table, eyeing them both.

"So, you're musicians," she said. "Are you any good? Or did I give up two qinde for nothing?"

The two men exchanged another look.

"We're good," Dario said. "With a bit more practice we should be good enough to play for the duke himself."

The woman sniffed. "I don't know that the duke cares for music. The older one did, his father. But this one . . ." She trailed off with a shrug. "Besides," she went on a moment later, "he's not even at the castle. I think he's still in Solkara, though he could be on his way back by now. Word is he came through the poisoning all right."

"I'm glad to hear that," Cadel said.

"We had one of the queen's messengers here not long ago," the innkeeper said, as if she hadn't heard. "And one of the duke's ministers, too."

Cadel cast a quick look at Dario. Whether the lutenist had intended it or not, his boast about playing for the duke might have been a stroke of genius. "A minister?" he repeated, trying not to sound too interested. "Then was the duke here as well?"

She frowned. "No. This was after the duke and his first minister had gone south. Though it wouldn't surprise me at all if Rowan himself stopped here on the return."

Cadel felt his interest growing by the moment. "If the duke had already passed by, why would another of his ministers be stopping here?"

"I don't presume to guess at such things. But he was interested in the duke, and even more so in the duke's first minister, when the messenger was here, telling us of the poisoning. Wouldn't surprise me if he and that minister were a pair, if you know what I mean."

"So he had already left the castle when he heard of the poisoning?" Dario asked, putting down his spoon.

She nodded. "Oh, yes. Seemed rather bothered by it, if you ask me. Because of the minister, in particular. Left in a hurry the next morning. I didn't like him at first. I don't take well to white-hairs. But he was kind enough, for one of them."

"What did he look like?" Cadel asked. When she looked his way, eyeing him warily, he added, "I've sung in many of the taverns in Mertesse, including the Qirsi ones. I might be able to put a name to the face, tell you which minister had been here."

She still appeared doubtful, but after a moment she gave a small shrug. "He looked to me like every other Qirsi. He was lean, thin-faced. I had the impression that he was a bit old for one of them, but other than that, there wasn't much to distinguish him."

"What about his accent?"

Her eyes widened slightly, but quickly narrowed again, as if the question had only heightened her doubts about him. "Now that you ask, he did speak a bit strangely. I couldn't place the accent, but it seemed to me that he was trying too hard to sound Aneiran." She paled. "You don't suppose he was a spy."

No, he was a traitor. Cadel was certain that this was the man he and Dario had been sent to kill. He could only hope that the Qirsi intended to return to the castle with the duke and Mertesse's first minister. "No," he said, making himself smile. "He wasn't a spy. One of the duke's ministers was born in Eibithar. But he serves Aneira now. No doubt this was the man who stayed here."

"Well, gods be praised for that. A Qirsi is bad enough, but a Qirsi spy . . ." She shook her head. "I don't need any brutes or lawbreakers coming to my inn."

Cadel and Dario nodded their agreement and finished their meal. Cadel was eager to return to their room and discuss with the younger man what they had learned of the Qirsi. But almost before he had swallowed his last bite of stew, the innkeeper reminded them of their promise to sing for her and her family.

Dario retrieved his lute from their quarters, and the innkeeper went out the rear door of the house to fetch her daughter, leaving Cadel to ponder why the Qirsi would have left Mertesse Castle if it hadn't been because of the poisoning. Perhaps he had gleaned what would happen in Solkara, and had only feigned his shock or surprise upon hearing the messenger's tidings. Or maybe he had left Mertesse for some other purpose and had no intention of actually riding on to Solkara. If this was the case, their journey north had been in vain, and they had a long search ahead of them.

Dario came back down the stairs, glancing about quickly to see if the innkeeper had returned.

"You think it was the one we're after?" he asked, seeing that she hadn't.

"Yes. That was well done, mentioning the duke that way."

The lutenist grinned. "I thought so. I wasn't certain it would do us any good, but I saw no harm in trying."

Cadel nodded. Dario might have been difficult, but he was clever as well. If Cadel was to be honest with himself, he would have to admit that Jedrek never would have thought to try such a thing.

Before they had time to talk more, the innkeeper stepped back into the house, followed by a man, a woman, and a small boy. They sat at the table, the older woman looking expectantly at Dario and Cadel.

"I've told them you want to play for the duke," she said. "We'll let you know if we think you're good enough."

"Mother!" the other woman said, looking appalled.

Once more, Cadel had to keep himself from laughing.

Though Cadel would have preferred to speak with Dario about the Qirsi, he could not help but be pleased with how they sounded almost as soon as they began their first piece. His voice felt good, and Dario's playing was more controlled than he had ever heard it. They went through nearly their entire repertoire—the threnody, "Elegy for Shanae," "Ilias's Lament" from *The Paean to the Moons*, and several folk songs, both Caerissan and Aneiran. They knew some old Eibitharian songs as well, but thought better of playing them in the Mertesse countryside.

By the time they were on their last piece, even the innkeeper was smiling and singing along, her voice surprisingly sweet. Their small audience applauded appreciatively and the innkeeper disappeared into her kitchen only to emerge a few moments later with a plate of sweet rolls, a jar of honey, and a flask of light wine.

"Music like that deserves a reward," she said, grinning at Cadel.

"I take it," he said, "that it was worth the two qinde."

Her face reddened, but she merely raised her eyebrows and said, "I suppose."

The two musicians could hardly refuse the wine and food, so they remained with the innkeeper and her family a while longer, until the rolls were gone and the flask nearly empty. Then they walked up the stairs to their room.

"If he's not in Mertesse—" Dario began.

But Cadel raised a hand and shook his head, silencing him. He had noticed earlier in the day that the woman's bedchamber was almost directly beneath theirs. They would have to wait until they were on the road once more to speak of the minister.

The next morning dawned fair and unusually warm. Before Cadel

and Dario had finished their breakfast, they could already hear water dripping from the melting snow atop the roof. The innkeeper was eating with
them again, humming one of the songs they had sung for her the night
before.

They finished their meal quickly and, having already packed their
satchels, started toward the door, offering their thanks to the old woman.

Before they could leave, however, she stopped them, hurrying into her
kitchen and returning with a sack of food, which she held out to them.

Cadel took it from her, his brow furrowing. "What's this?"

She blushed. "You asked me last night if your music was worth the
two qinde I took off the price of your room. In fact, it was worth more."
She nodded toward the sack. "It's not much really—some dried meat, a
piece of cheese, some bread. But it should keep you full while you walk the
rest of the way to Mertesse."

"Thank you," Cadel said. He took her hand and bent to kiss the back
of it.

Her color deepened and she looked away, though she didn't pull her
hand from his. "Stop it," she said, not quite managing to sound cross. "You
better get moving before this weather changes its mind and turns to snow
again."

"You have our thanks, my lady. If anyone asks, we'll have nothing but
kind words to say about your inn."

She dismissed the remark with a wave of her hand. "You'll just be
making more work for me." Then she smiled. "But if you're ever coming
this way again, I'd welcome another performance."

Shouldering their satchels, the two men stepped out into the cool air
and bright sun to resume their journey north. The road was already growing too soft with melting ice and snow; it promised to be slow going. On the
other hand, with the day so fair, Cadel could clearly see the city walls and
the great towers of the castle. They had even less distance to cover than he
had thought.

The two men walked for some time without speaking. They saw few
people on the road, though they did pass a small contingent of soldiers
wearing the black-and-gold uniforms of Mertesse and bearing weapons
that glittered in the sunlight. The guards stopped briefly to ask Cadel and
Dario where they were headed and what business they had in Mertesse.
But when Cadel told them they were musicians and Dario pulled out his
lute, the men let them go on.

"We'll get more of that now," Dario said when they were walking
again. "With the new queen in Solkara, and nobles looking for poison in

every cup of wine they raise, we'll be lucky if we get anywhere near the castle."

"I've thought of that."

"Do you have a plan in mind?"

"Not yet."

Dario twisted his mouth, but gave a small nod. He didn't remain silent for long, however. "Have you thought of what we're to do if the old woman is right, and this Qirsi we're after isn't in Mertesse?"

"I expect she is right," Cadel said. "The question isn't whether he's gone, but rather if he's coming back. What concerns me most is the fact that he had already left Mertesse when he heard of the poisoning. That makes me think that he was leaving for some reason that had nothing at all to do with his duke."

He didn't say it, but Cadel could only assume that if he wasn't serving Mertesse, he was acting on behalf of the conspiracy.

"If that's the case, there's no telling where he might have gone."

"True. But I'm hoping that the poisoning changed his plans." He gestured over his shoulder in the direction of the inn. "Our friend back there seemed to think that he was in love with the duke's first minister. If she's right, then I imagine he'll be returning with Rowan. Provided the first minister didn't die in Solkara."

Dario regarded him a moment, then shook his head slowly. "You're placing a good deal of faith in an old woman who may know nothing at all."

"Not really," Cadel said, smiling. "Though I suspect she knows more about people than you might think. Mostly I'm just acknowledging what we both know to be true. We're going to be here for some time. If the Qirsi doesn't come back, I have no idea where to begin looking for him. So our best hope is to wait for the duke's return and hope that both ministers are with him."

"And if the one we want isn't with the duke?"

Cadel shrugged. "We'll walk back to Solkara and start searching again, hoping that he really did go there after leaving our innkeeper."

"Are all your jobs like this?" Dario asked.

"Like what?"

"So uncertain, so dependent on good fortune."

Cadel shook his head, gazing toward Mertesse. The castle looked bigger than he remembered, more formidable.

"No," he said at last. "This job is unlike any I've ever had before. I rarely agree to kill without out knowing the name of the one I'm hunting, and without being certain I know where to find him." He hesitated, thinking suddenly of Brienne of Kentigern. "Or her." He shivered, though the sun felt warm on his back and legs.

"You also rarely kill for so little money," Dario said quietly. "You really were eager to strike back at the conspiracy, weren't you?"

Cadel eyed him for a moment, but said nothing.

"Do you regret it now?"

"No. Not even a little."

Dario nodded, but at least he had the sense not to say anything more. The truth was that while Cadel didn't have any qualms about striking at the conspiracy, he wished that he had found a different way to do it. Usually he liked to have a job planned well in advance or, failing that, to have at least a few alternatives in mind. Right now, he had no sense of how he was going to kill this man, or even get close enough to him to try. He could almost hear Jedrek railing at him for being so rash as to take gold from the woman who had hired them. *Never take a job when you feel anything for the one you're supposed to kill, be it love, hate, anger, or pity.* It was one of the first rules Cadel had taught Jedrek, and he here he was violating it. It seemed he had learned nothing at all in Kentigern.

"So what do we do when we get to Mertesse?"

Cadel took a breath, then squinted up at the sun. They'd be in the city before nightfall.

"We find work," he said. "There's no shortage of taverns in a city this large. One of them is bound to need musicians."

"And then?"

"And then we hope that the gods are with us."

But he could hear Jedrek again, asking the question he couldn't answer. *Are the gods ever with an assassin?*

Chapter
Twenty-six

✤

City of Kings, Eibithar

S he could always tell when Kearney was unhappy with her. The signs were subtle, like the scent of snow in the highlands before a storm. The silver-haired king had spent too long in the courts of Eibithar's nobles to reveal much, and few others would have noticed anything at all. Except, perhaps, for Gershon Trasker. But to Keziah, who had loved him for so many years, the indications were as clear as a bright morning in the cold turns. The way he avoided her gaze; the expression on his face, a boyish mix of hurt and resentment; the restless pacing as he listened to the counsel of his other ministers. She had seen all these things before, usually after she angered him with some cutting remark about the queen, or overstepped with her teasing about the Glyndwr traditions.

Until now, though, she had never actually tried to make him angry.

The other ministers did not appear to have noticed what she was doing. If they had they were certainly keeping it to themselves. Clearly, though, they believed that she was angry with the king and she could only assume that they would delight in seeing her influence with Kearney wane. More to the point, she wondered if one of them might see in this an opportunity to exploit.

Unlike the ministers, Gershon was watching everything she did with complete understanding and and—dare she think it—more than a little admiration. They hadn't spoken in private since the night after Paegar's death, when she went to his quarters to tell the swordmaster of the gold she found in the high minister's chambers. All who lived in Audun's Castle knew of their enmity, and would have taken note of seeing them together. But she had learned to read Gershon's expressions as well. He had long been her chief rival for Kearney's ear, and even loving the man she served, she had not been entirely above court politics. Gershon was watching her, gauging the progress she made in alienating the king, and offering his approval with raised eyebrows and barely concealed grins.

She felt his gaze upon her now, as she watched the king pace before his writing table, and she sensed the swordmaster's concern. Before this day, she had opposed Kearney only on small matters, trifles really, that would trouble the king without compromising the safety of the kingdom. With this meeting of Kearney's council of ministers, matters had abruptly grown far more dangerous.

"You're certain of these tidings, Your Majesty?" Dyre asked, his yellow eyes fixed on the king. "Might there be some mistake?"

Kearney shook his head. "There's no mistake, Minister. This information came from our own men. It wasn't purchased and it didn't come from those who might oppose us."

"First he goes to Kentigern, and now he sends a messangeer to Curgh," Wenda said. "Could it be that Marston is trying to broker a peace?"

Kearney stopped, glanced at Keziah, then faced Gershon. "Swordmaster?"

Even the other ministers couldn't help but notice that. The king almost never asked Gershon questions of this sort. He was Kearney's most trusted advisor on tactics, arms, and war, but not on matters of statecraft and mediation. Until recently, he would have asked Keziah before anyone else. It was working. The archminister's chest felt tight, and she feared she would cry, right here in the king's chambers.

Gershon cleared his throat and straightened in his chair. "I would think it possible, Your Majesty. We did have Tremain send Marston a message, asking him for help."

Dyre shook his head. "We asked only to know where he stood in this conflict. We certainly didn't ask him to mediate it." He looked at Keziah. "Did we, Archminister? After all, it was you who penned the message to Lathrop."

"As you say, High Minister," she answered coolly, "we asked only where he stands."

"Maybe he took it upon himself to do more," Gershon suggested.

A cue.

She turned to the swordmaster, arching an eyebrow. "Maybe he's decided to sell his loyalties to the highest bidder. He wouldn't be the first noble to do so."

He glared at her. "The buying and selling of loyalties is a Qirsi trade, Archminister. It has been for centuries."

"That's enough!" Kearney said, his voice like a blade. He looked from one of them to the other, but his eyes came to rest on Keziah. "Marston's no traitor, and his house is the strongest in the land. What could Curgh or Kentigern possibly offer him?"

She regarded him as if he were simple. "The throne, of course. He's probably trying to decide which of them will make the stronger ally, and which alliance will cost him the least."

"So what would you counsel us to do, Archminister?" Gershon, with another cue. His voice was heavy with sarcasm, but she read the concern in his blue eyes. If Kearney took her words to heart, it could lead them all down a path to civil war. She doubted, however, that her king would ever again take seriously any advice she gave him. At least, he wouldn't if her plan worked.

"I'm not certain there's anything you can do," she said. *You* rather than *we*. None of the rest would hear it, but Kearney would. Before long, his displeasure with her would be as obvious to all of them as it already was to her. "You thought that by taking the throne for Glyndwr, you could avoid a civil war, but you were wrong. Curgh and Kentigern are still at each other's throats, and the other houses are choosing sides. All you've done is put Glyndwr in the middle of the conflict. You should never have come here, and now that you have you're even more powerless to keep the peace than you were. Glyndwr can't mediate anymore. Everything the king does is seen as a ploy to keep the crown. Nobody trusts him." She felt Kearney staring at her, but she refused to meet his gaze. "Now that he's king," she said, her voice dropping, "everything has changed."

For a long time no one spoke. Keziah knew they were watching her, as if waiting for her to weep, or run from the room, or berate the king. But she merely sat, staring at her hands, her face crimson and her heart aching as if from a dagger's blow.

"That's rubbish," Gershon finally said, sounding angry, just as all of them would have expected. It seemed strange that with Paegar gone, the swordmaster, who had hated the Qirsi all his life and had hated her most of all for sharing a bed with Kearney, should become her closest confidant in the castle. Even stranger, he best served their growing alliance by continuing to treat her with disdain and hostility, just as he always had. "We saved this kingdom—the king did really—and everyone in Eibithar knows it except Aindreas and you. Just because you'd rather be back in Glyndwr doesn't mean the rest of us feel the same way."

"I said that's enough!" Kearney broke in again. "It doesn't matter anymore what any of us wishes had happened. I am king, and I'll do everything I deem necessary to hold this kingdom together. So, assuming for just a moment that Marston isn't trying to broker an agreement between Aindreas and Javan, that some darker purpose lies behind these journeys he's making, what should we do?"

"Tobbar is still alive," Wenda said. "He may be ill, but he still speaks for the House of Thorald. Perhaps we should send a message to him. He may not even know what his son is doing, in which case maybe he can get Marston to stop."

"And if he does know?" the king asked.

The high minister hesitated, though only for a moment. "Then I'm afraid the archminister is right. There's nothing more we can do. If Thorald is intent on opposing us, we can only hope that the armies of Curgh and Glyndwr, when combined with the King's Guard, will be enough to hold off the other major houses."

Kearney shook his head. "I won't accept that. There have to be alternatives. I will not allow Marston's betrayal—if that is in fact what he has in mind—to destroy the kingdom."

"Your resolve is admirable, Your Majesty," Dyre said cautiously. "But it would be . . . dangerous not to prepare ourselves for the worst. It may not be a fight we want, but it is one in which we can prevail, provided that we ready the army."

"Yes, fine," the king said, sounding impatient. "Gershon, you'll continue to work the men, even through the snows. Do whatever you feel is needed to keep them battle-ready."

"Of course, Your Majesty."

"Wenda," Kearney went on, turning to the high minister, "I want you to draft a message to Tobbar, informing him that we're aware of Marston's activities and asking him if Shanstead is making these overtures on his behalf."

She glanced uneasily at Keziah. Usually Kearney would have had his archminister write such a message. "Yes, Your Majesty," the older woman said. If she took any pleasure in Keziah's fall from the king's grace, she showed no sign of it. Rather, she appeared uncomfortable.

Yet, Kearney wasn't finished with her. "When you're done," he said, "bring the message to me. Then meet with the rest of the underministers and come up with a better answer to my last question. There have to be other ways to combat any betrayal by Thorald than just sending my army north. Now go."

The high minister stood and bowed to him. "Yes, Your Majesty."

The other ministers stood as well and started toward the door, Keziah among them.

"Be quick about it, High Minister," Kearney called to her. "We may not have much time." Then, "Archminister, I'd like you to remain for a moment."

Keziah halted in midstride, her face coloring again. The other Qirsi looked at her briefly, then left.

"You'd better go as well, Gershon," the king said.

Keziah hadn't turned to look at Kearney or the swordmaster, but she could imagine Gershon's nod, the grave expression on his blunt features as he said, "Yes, Your Majesty."

The swordmaster brushed past her on his way to the door, but, of course, kept his silence.

"Please sit," Kearney said, his voice colder than she had ever heard it when they were alone.

She would have given anything to avoid this conversation, but she realized that by asking her to remain, the king had done more to help her than he could ever know. This was not the time to weaken.

The minister turned and walked slowly back to her chair, eyeing the king as she did, and trying her best to look insolent.

"Yes, Your Majesty?" she asked, her voice flat as she dropped herself into the seat.

"Perhaps you'd like to tell me what that was all about."

She raised her eyebrows. "I don't know what you're talking about."

"Demons and fire, Kez! You've never spoken to me as you did just now! I've never known you to accuse anyone without cause the way you did Marston, and I've certainly never heard you speak of 'Eandi nobles' with such contempt."

She looked away. *I'm sorry!* she wanted to say. *I have to do this! I have to convince them that I can be turned, that you've hurt me so much my loyalties are no longer so certain. Don't you see? I have to do this for you.* Instead she regarded him coolly and lied. "Just because I never said it before, that doesn't mean I haven't thought it."

"So you believe that Eandi nobles are quick to betray their allies?"

"Yes, I do."

"Does that include me?"

She knew she had to hurt him. Even speaking with him in private, she couldn't afford to waver from her purpose. But she couldn't bring herself to speak the words. She merely shrugged, leaving the question unanswered, and so answering it in his mind.

Kearney swallowed. "I see." He stepped around to the far side of the table and sat, as he often did when she made him angry or sad. It almost seemed at such times that he needed to put something solid between them. "Have you felt this way very long?"

"I didn't when we were in Glyndwr, if that's what you mean."

"So you feel that I've betrayed you."

"I said what I did about Marston of Shanstead, not about you. Why do the Eandi always make everything about themselves?"

He just stared at her, as if she had told him she was an Aneiran spy. After a few moments, his eyes narrowed. "This all started after Paegar died, didn't it?"

"Did it?" she asked. She didn't want their discussion turning in this direction, but she felt powerless to stop it.

"Do you believe I wronged him in some way? Was his funeral too modest? Or was there more to your friendship with him than I knew? Was he your lover? Is that it? Did losing him remind you once more of the love we lost?"

"He wasn't my lover." *How could I ever love anyone other than you?* "This has nothing to do with Paegar."

"Then what is it, Kez? What's happened to you?"

"Nothing has happened to me, Your Majesty. I merely expressed an opinion. I believe that Marston intends to betray you."

"Because that's what Eandi nobles do."

"Because this Eandi noble has every reason to, and because your hold on the throne may appear tenuous to Eibithar's other houses."

Kearney shook his head again. "I think there's more to it than that. You're angry with me. I can always tell."

"Well, Your Majesty, it may be that you don't know me as well as you thought."

His jaw tightened, the way it did when he was trying to control his rage. "Yes," he said thickly. "That may be. In which case the question becomes can I still trust you to serve as my archminister."

Keziah's breath caught in her throat. It was one thing to convince others in the castle that she and Kearney were estranged. It was quite another to lose her position and with it her influence. The conspiracy would have no interest in her if she didn't still serve Eibithar's king. Losing what she had left of him in this way was bad enough, but to do so in vain would kill her.

Yet the only way to keep him from sending her away was to goad him further. "I merely expressed an opinion, Your Majesty. Am I to understand that you wish to be served only by those who will agree with all you say, and offer counsel that pleases you?"

"Not at all," he said, his voice hardening. "I've never asked my ministers to be anything less than honest! But neither have I demanded from them anything less than their respect and their courtesy! If you feel you can serve me in a manner that befits both your station and mine, then you may remain in my castle! Otherwise I expect you to pack your things and return to Glyndwr! Is that clear, Archminister?"

She was sobbing, her cries for forgiveness tearing at her chest. But only within. She couldn't imagine where she found the strength, but somehow she kept her composure, so that all Kearney saw was the coloring of her cheeks and the trembling of her hands. And those he would have anticipated.

"Yes, Your Majesty," she managed, the words as soft as falling snow. "Is that all?"

"No, it's not. I'm tired of this foolish bickering between you and Gershon. I want you to speak with him, and finally put this nonsense to rest. Regardless of Marston's intentions, I can't tolerate this any longer. There's too much at risk."

It was more than she could have asked for. She had been eager to speak with the swordmaster for days, and now the king had given her just the excuse she needed. Still, Kearney would expect an argument.

"But, Your Majesty—"

"I know it's been both of you all along. But in light of your behavior recently, I'm placing the onus for this on you. Find a way to work with the swordmaster, or leave."

You would choose Gershon over me? Have I really hurt you that much?
"Yes, Your Majesty."

"That's all. You may go." He picked up a scroll from his table and began to read, as if his words had not been enough of a dismissal.

"Yes, Your Majesty. Thank you."

She stood and left the room quickly, not trusting herself to look back at him. Once she was in the corridor, she could at least close her eyes and take a long steadying breath. But two of Kearney's guards stood near the door, and though they would not have been able to make out all she and the king said to each other, they would have heard Kearney's tone when he raised his voice. They eyed her with unconcealed distaste, their stares forcing her to walk away.

She thought briefly of returning to her chamber. She would have liked nothing more than to splash warm water on her face and lie down for a long sleep. It was more important, though, that she speak with the swordmaster. She hurried to Gershon's quarters.

Reaching his door, Keziah hesitated, as if suddenly unsure of whether or not to knock. Gershon might be her only ally in the castle now that Paegar was dead and she had alienated Kearney, but they remained wary of one another. Even now, working together to combat the conspiracy, the concerns that bound them to each other were matched—nearly overmatched—by their long history of hostility and distrust.

She almost turned away from the door. But then she remembered that Kearney had ordered her to speak with the man. Eventually, she would have to do this. Better to do it now, with her courage high.

She knocked twice, the sound echoing loudly in the corridor.

In a few seconds the door opened and Gershon peered out into the corridor. Seeing her, his eyes widened, and he quickly looked down the hallway in both directions.

"Are you mad?" he asked in a loud whisper. "Did anyone see you come here?"

"The king asked me to speak with you, swordmaster," she said, allowing her voice to carry. "He fears that our disagreements are weakening the throne, and he wishes for us to discuss our differences so that we might put them behind us."

Gershon looked at her, as if trying to gauge whether she was telling him the truth. "All right," he said at last. "Here? Or do you want to walk?"

"Better we speak in your quarters," she said quietly. "Even with the king's blessing, it would be best if others didn't see us together."

He nodded and stepped to the side, gesturing for her to enter.

Stepping into the chamber, Keziah saw that the swordmaster's wife was there, as were their four children.

Sulwen Trasker nodded to her. "Archminister," she said, her tone neither warm nor cool.

"Good day, my lady." Keziah turned back to Gershon. "Should I come back later?"

"No." He looked past her to his wife. "This might be a good time for their devotions," he said, nodding toward the children. "I'll meet you at the cloister shortly."

Sulwen's eyes strayed to the minister again, but she nodded and called to the children to stop their playing. It took several minutes to get all of them out of the chamber, but eventually Gershon and Keziah were alone.

"They seem like fine children," Keziah said, taking a seat near the hearth and stretching her hands toward the fire to warm them.

Gershon frowned, as though uncomfortable accepting compliments from her. But after a moment he muttered, "Thank you," and took a seat across from hers. "I wouldn't have thought that you like children."

"Why not?"

His frown deepened and he looked away. Keziah sensed that he wished he hadn't spoken at all. "You were with Kearney all those years, loving a man who couldn't give you children. I just assumed."

"I like children very much, swordmaster. I just loved Kearney more."

More than anything she had wanted to have children with her duke—her king. But doing so would have revealed their forbidden love to the world, and the first labor probably would have killed her. Her kind weren't strong enough to bear even half-bloods.

"The king truly wanted us to speak?" Gershon asked, breaking a brief, strained silence.

Keziah took a breath, clearing her mind. "Yes. He said he was tired of our bickering."

"Is that why he asked to speak with you?"

"Hardly," she said, a wan smile springing to her lips. "He had me stay so that we could discuss my recent behavior."

"So, it's working."

"I suppose it is."

He looked at her, searching her eyes. "You don't sound pleased. Wasn't this your idea?"

"Yes, swordmaster, it was my idea."

"Then what's the matter?"

She turned her gaze to the fire. "I guess I didn't realize how difficult it would be. I still love him, and to see the way he looks at me now, to hear him threaten to send me back to Glyndwr—"

"He did that?"

Keziah nodded, still staring into the bright flames. "He also told me that he would hold me responsible if you and I continue to fight. He told me to find a way to bridge our differences, or leave." She smiled again, though it felt brittle. "You should be happy: our king has chosen you over me. If you wish to rid yourself of me, you can do so now. I know you've wanted to for a long time."

She glanced at Gershon, only to find that he had looked away once more. He appeared uneasy again, though she couldn't tell if it was because he no longer wanted her gone, or because he still did.

"I don't think he'd really have you leave the castle," he said, his voice low.

"You didn't hear him today, nor did you hear everything I said."

"Is it possible that you're pushing him too hard?"

"Do you think I am?"

He shrugged. "Maybe. You said some things about Marston today that struck me as too strong. He's not a traitor, and by suggesting that he is, you make it harder for Kearney to trust him. That could be dangerous."

"I was trying to make it seem that my anger at the king had made me distrustful of all Eandi."

"Well, you did that."

"Don't worry, swordmaster. After today, the king isn't likely to place much faith in anything I say. Our ties to the House of Thorald are safe." She felt a single tear rolling down her cheek and she swiped at it impatiently, hoping that Gershon hadn't seen.

"You're doing the king a great service," he said, his voice more gentle than she had ever imagined it could be. "He may not know it now, but when all of this is over, I'll tell him. I swear it."

She nodded, but couldn't speak for the tears that were now coursing down her face. After keeping such a tight hold on her emotions for so long, it was all Keziah could do just to breathe amid her sobbing. Her anguish overwhelmed her; she felt like a child caught in the sudden tumult of a great ocean wave. Indeed, the only thing that saved her, that allowed her to stop crying at last, was the look of utter panic on the face of the poor swordmaster. He had found a kerchief and was holding it out to her. But he seemed at a loss to do more than that.

"Forgive me, swordmaster," she managed, taking the kerchief and dabbing at her tears. "As I said before, this is more difficult than I had expected. Do you have any water?"

He nearly leaped to his feet, so anxious was he to do anything other than sit before her watching her cry. He went to a pitcher near the small window, poured her a cup of water, and carried it to her like a server at a banquet.

"Is there something else I can do?"

She shook her head. "I'll be fine. Thank you. Just tell me, did you hear any of the other ministers speaking of today's discussion?"

"Yes," he said. "I made a point of walking with them briefly, at least until they reached the stairway leading to their chambers. They're very much aware of the change in your behavior, and they trace it to Paegar's death."

She winced. "I've been too obvious."

"No, it's all right. A number of them . . ." He stopped himself, his face turning bright red.

Keziah smiled. "They think that Paegar and I were lovers."

"Yes."

"Kearney suspected the same thing, though I told him it wasn't so."

"Why? Where's the harm in it? It makes all of this much more convincing."

"I don't want him thinking that, no matter how much it might help us."

Something in her voice must have reached him. He stared at her a moment, then nodded. "Very well."

"But the ministers do think it," she said, prodding him.

"Some of them do. And at least one of them remarked on the growing discord between you and the king. If it was your aim to make the castle's Qirsi think that your loyalties might be compromised, you've succeeded."

She made herself grin, though she suddenly felt a chill, as from a north wind. "Well, I suppose I should be pleased then."

Gershon continued to stare at her, a look of genuine concern in those hard blue eyes. "Are you certain about this? It's not too late to stop. You can attribute it all to your grief at Paegar's death, apologize to the king, and go back to advising him as you always have. No one would ever know but me, and I wouldn't think worse of you for making that choice."

"Careful, Gershon. Treat me with such kindness too often, and I may yet mistake you for a friend."

He frowned again. He was the only man she had ever met on whom a frown seemed more natural than a smile.

"I'll take that to mean that you still intend to go through with this," he said.

"I do, unless you've thought of a better way to learn what we need to know about the conspiracy."

She knew that he hadn't of course. There was no other way. Had there been, she would have jumped at the chance to end all of this.

Keziah stood. "Your family will be awaiting you in the cloister, swordmaster. You should join them."

He made a sour face. "I think I'll see to my men instead."

The minister laughed. "Perhaps you should join me in the sanctuaries one day. Devotions don't have to be as tedious as the prelate makes them."

Gershon actually grinned. "Good day, Archminister." He pulled his door open and held it for her. "I hope this can be the beginning of better understanding between us," he said, letting his voice carry into the corridor. "I pledge to do my best to make it so."

She stepped into the hallway and turned to bow to him. "As do I, swordmaster. Thank you."

He nodded once, looking for just an instant like he wanted to say more. But after a moment, he merely shut his door again, leaving her alone in the corridor. Had Keziah not known better, she would have thought he was going to tell her to be careful.

She walked quickly back to her chamber, passing guards as she went, and enduring their stares as best she could. She passed Wenda as well, just a few steps from her room. Seeing her, the high minister paused, clearing her throat awkwardly.

"Yes, Wenda?" she asked, not bothering to mask her impatience.

The older woman faltered, then shook her head. "It was nothing, Archminister. Good day."

Keziah resumed her walking. "And to you, High Minister."

Entering her room, she shook her head, cursing herself for not being more courteous. She might have learned something from Wenda. She thought about leaving the room again and finding the high minister, but it wouldn't have been in keeping with her recent behavior. And she was just too tired.

She walked to her bed intending to lie down, but a dark shape on her blanket caught her eye. For a moment she stood utterly still, staring at this thing, afraid to move, as if thinking it might scurry away at her approach. Then she realized what it was, and fear gripped her heart like the clawed hand of some great beast of the Underrealm.

He should have gone to the cloister. Sulwen would be expecting him, and even knowing how he felt about the devotions, she would chastise him for failing to join her and the children there. After speaking with the archminister, however, Gershon couldn't even bring himself to walk to the ward, where the guards were training. He just sat, watching the fire burn, wondering how he had allowed the Qirsi woman to talk him into this. He had known from the start that her plan carried risks, and he had weighed them carefully. What he had neglected to consider, though, were the other costs—the archminister's heartache, and the king's as well.

Kearney's love affair with his minister had been a mistake. Gershon had wanted to say so to Kearney a thousand times while they still lived in Glyndwr. Despite having misgivings about his duke taking the throne in the midst of the conflict between Curgh and Kentigern, the swordmaster had at least found comfort in the knowledge that Kearney's ascension would end this foolhardy affair. But though the king and the Qirsi no longer shared a bed, it seemed to Gershon that their love continued to color all that happened here in Audun's Castle. It made the archminister's deception possible, by making believable her alienation from the king. Yet it also increased the dangers of what she was doing. By angering Kearney, by adding to the pain he had already suffered by losing her, Keziah risked not only her life, but the safety of the entire kingdom.

The swordmaster finally trusted her. Any doubts he had harbored about her devotion to Kearney and Eibithar had vanished when she agreed to seek out the conspiracy. But he thought her terribly young, and he had seen her put Kearney in harm's way too many times. Gershon still remembered, with a vividness that made his sword hand tremble, how enraged he had been when she allowed her friend, the gleaner, to bring Tavis of Curgh to Tremain where the Glyndwr army had stopped on its way to the Heneagh River. At the time, the boy was still a fugitive from Aindreas's dungeon, and Kentigern and Curgh were on the verge of war. No harm came of what she had done, and Kearney granted the gleaner's request to give Tavis asylum. But Keziah had taken a terrible chance, placing at risk both the House of Glyndwr and the House of Tremain. Despite trusting her, despite knowing how much she loved the king, Gershon couldn't help but feel that she remained the greatest threat to everything he held dear. That she was also their greatest hope of learning how to defeat the conspiracy only served to deepen his fears.

He made himself stand, and reached for his sword, intending to join his army in the castle courtyard. Before he could strap the scabbard to his belt, however, he heard a knock at his door. He pulled it open, only to find Keziah standing before him once more, her face deathly pale and her eyes wide, like those of a child who has just awakened from a frightening dream.

She held out his kerchief to him. "I forgot to return this to you," she said, a flutter in her voice.

He took it from her, watching her closely. Clearly, this wasn't all that had brought her back to his door.

"Do you want to come in again?"

She nodded and hurried past him to the center of the room.

Gershon closed the door and turned to face her. "What—?"

He stopped, staring at what she held in her hands. It was a simple leather pouch, brown, tied with a thin black cord, but he understood instantly that it signified far more than that. He crossed to where she stood and took the pouch from her. It was heavy with coins.

"You've counted it already?"

Keziah nodded. "One hundred qinde."

He handed it back to her quickly. "You shouldn't have come here. They may be watching you."

"I know. I was scared. It thought that by returning the kerchief—"

"You wanted this, Archminister. You've done all you could to draw their attention, and now that you have it, you must keep your nerve. If you give them cause to doubt you, they'll kill you."

Any other day such a remark from him might have brought a cutting response about how he had never cared so much for her safety before. It would have been a joke, of course, though with an edge. But abruptly, even this humor was denied them. None of this was funny anymore.

"You're right. I'm sorry." She started for the door. "I'll leave."

"How much did Paegar have?" Gershon asked, stopping her again just short of the door. "I don't remember."

"One hundred and ninety qinde."

He turned to face her, whistling through his teeth. "Even if he spent none of it, that's nearly three hundred qinde they've spent here alone. That's a lot of gold."

"Yes, it is."

"I know of nobles in Eibithar and Aneira who couldn't afford to pay so much. Not just barons, mind you, but thanes and marquesses. That may be the way to find them, Archminister. If we can trace that gold to its source, we can find the leaders."

Keziah nodded again, still wide-eyed. "I'll do what I can."

"And I'll do everything necessary to keep you safe. You may not see me, you may not even believe that I can see you. But I'll be watching just the same. You have my word."

The Qirsi woman gazed at him a moment, then hurried back to where he stood and brushed her lips against his cheek. "Thank you," she whispered.

A moment later she was gone, and Gershon was forced to wonder if he had judged her too harshly a short time before. It wouldn't have been the first time. She might have been reckless, as only someone so young could be. But standing alone in his chamber, contemplating what she was about to do, he thought her the bravest soul he had ever known.

Chapter
Twenty-seven

✦

Thorald, Eibithar, Qirsar's Moon waning

ven after Enid's death and all that it implied, Marston's father had been reluctant to speak with Eibithar's other dukes of what they had learned. Tobbar and Marston had argued the point for the better part of two days, Marston telling the duke that the other houses had to be informed of Enid's betrayal.

"It changes everything, Father," he said at the time. "It brings into question all that we've assumed about Filib's murder. With Lady Brienne's murder still threatening to tear apart the kingdom, we have to speak with the others."

To which his father replied simply, "This is a humiliation for our house. I'll not make matters worse by telling all our rivals throughout the land."

Though angry, and desperate to make Tobbar see that they couldn't keep this a secret, Marston was no fool. "This is not a humiliation, Father, not for Thorald, and certainly not for you."

Tobbar looked up at that, grey eyes glinting like a blade in the firelight. "I brought her into this castle," he said, his voice dropping to a whisper. "Had my brother lived, she might never have become Thorald's first minister. If all you say is true, I'm responsible for Filib the Younger's death."

Marston shook his head. "No. The conspiracy killed him, you didn't. It may be true that Enid wouldn't have become first minister had it not been for the elder Filib's death, but not for the reasons you think. I believe the Qirsi sought to throw the kingdom into turmoil, turning the Rules of Ascension to their purposes. Whether or not the conspiracy was behind

Filib the Elder's hunting accident, it was his death that made my cousin a target. If the duke lives, the Qirsi have no cause to kill the boy."

Tobbar nodded, seeming to see the logic of this. "Still, I trusted her. I allowed her—I allowed the entire conspiracy—to turn this house to their purposes."

"Kentigern did the same thing. He was betrayed as well."

"But this is Thorald!" Tobbar said, his voice rising. "This is the house of Binthar, the house of the Golden Stallion. We are the leading house in Eibithar; where other houses fail, we must stand firm. Kentigern's shame does nothing to ease the sting of our own."

"Perhaps not. But as the leading house in the kingdom, don't we have a duty to keep other houses from suffering the same fate? The treason of Kentigern's first minister nearly allowed Mertesse to take the tor, and for all we know, it cost Lady Brienne her life. What if there are traitors in the other houses as well? What will be the price of their betrayal? We have to tell them, Father. We have to warn them. How can the house of Binthar do anything less?"

At the time, his father turned away, refusing to answer and effectively ending their conversation. Finally, as their silence dragged on and the fire in Tobbar's hearth burned low, Marston left the chamber, returning to his own quarters, weary and discouraged.

He was awakened the following morning, however, by one of his father's pages, who told him that the duke wished to speak with him as soon as possible. Thinking that perhaps his father's health was failing, Marston dressed quickly and hurried through the corridors to the duke's chambers. He knocked on the door and was relieved to hear his father call for him to enter, his voice sounding clear and strong.

"What would we say to the other houses?" Tobbar asked, before Marston could even close the door behind him.

"I hadn't thought that far ahead," he admitted, taking a seat near his father's bed.

The duke was sitting up, leaning back against a pair of pillows. He looked no worse than he had when Marston first arrived in Thorald, but he looked no better either. His face was still pallid, his cheeks still gaunt, as if the skin hung lifelessly on his cheekbones.

"Surely you've given some thought as to what you'd put in such a message."

The thane grinned. "I didn't expect you to change your mind. Composing a message seemed unnecessary."

His father didn't return the smile. "I'm not certain that I have changed my mind. But I do agree that we have to warn them. Perhaps if a message were worded properly I would feel better about telling the other houses what's happened."

"What would you think of speaking with them in person."

"What?"

"Though I believe that we have to inform the others, I do share your concerns about revealing Enid's betrayal. Not so much to the dukes, but if such a message were to fall into the wrong hands—Qirsi hands—it might prove quite harmful to the House of Thorald, indeed, all of Eibithar. If instead we invite the dukes here, where we can discuss this conflict with them, we might be able to accomplish far more than would a simple message."

Tobbar narrowed his eyes. "Go on."

"Right now, the other houses are lining up behind Javan and Aindreas, choosing sides as if in anticipation of civil war. Even if we remain neutral, there's a chance that either Curgh or Kentigern will eventually decide that he has the advantage, that war is preferable to peace. I want to isolate them. If we can convince the other houses that the conspiracy is behind all of this, and that neither Javan nor Aindreas is at fault, perhaps we can stop them from taking sides. It may not keep Curgh and Kentigern from going to war again, but it may keep their war from spreading throughout the land."

Tobbar regarded him silently for several moments, until Marston began to wonder if he had somehow angered the duke. "You thought of all this on your own?" the older man asked at last.

"Yes."

His father gave a small laugh and shook his head. "Your grandfather would be very proud. Many nobles go an entire lifetime without mastering the finer points of statecraft. And here you are, younger than I was when I became thane, and you're already a better duke than I've ever been."

"That's not true, Father. I merely—"

"It's all right. I'm pleased." He rubbed his hands together, as if chilled. "Send your messages. Invite the dukes here. With the snows falling, I doubt many of them will make the journey, but we can address that when the time comes."

Marston stood, unable to keep the smile from his face. "Yes, Father."

"We can't expect the king to make the journey, nor should we even presume to ask him. So you should send a separate message to him, telling him just what's happened. Give that message to our best horseman, and send eight guards with him."

"It will be done, my lord," Marston said, bowing to the duke.

Tobbar frowned. "Don't call me that."

Returning to his quarters, Marston sat at the small table by the hearth and began writing his missives. Confronted now with the task, he found that the words did not come nearly as easily as he had hoped they would. He wished to tell the dukes enough to convey his sense of urgency, without revealing so much that he risked the reputation of his father and their house. In the end, he decided it was better to be too vague than too specific.

> My dear dukes,
> I write to you at the request of the duke of Thorald. Information has come to us recently that sheds new light on the tragedies that occurred in Kentigern during the growing turns. As the conflict between Curgh and Kentigern still threatens to sunder our kingdom, we wish to discuss these tidings with you as soon as possible.
> To that end, Tobbar, duke of Thorald, invites you to be his guest in Thorald Castle at your earliest convenience.
> May Ean guard you and guide you safely to our gates.
>   Marston, thane of Shanstead

Marston dispatched the messengers later that day and spent the rest of the waxing waiting impatiently for the other houses to reply. He should have known better than to expect to hear from any of them quickly. Even Eardley Castle, which was closest to Thorald, stood twenty-five leagues to the east. Pushing his mount to its limits, the messenger sent to the coast of the Narrows would have to ride three days in each direction. Still, only a few mornings after his conversation with the duke, Marston was already pacing the battlements of the castle, watching for Thorald's riders to return.

It was not until the ninth day of the waxing, just before the ringing of the twilight bells, that the first rider returned. As it happened, the first reply came not from Eardley, but from Galdasten, the nearest of the major houses.

Seeing the rider approach, Marston bolted down the stairs of the nearest tower and across all three of the castle wards, so that he might meet the man by the west gate.

The messenger looked haggard, his face an angry shade of red from the cold and wind.

Dismounting, he could barely stand without the help of two guards.

Marston should have given him a chance to rest and eat and warm himself by a fire, but his impatience overmastered all other considerations.

"Well?" he demanded, approaching the man.

The rider shook his head. "The duke of Galdasten instructed me to tell you he has no interest in being a guest of Thorald's duke. He said as well that he doubted Thorald had any more information than Galdasten, and he had heard nothing to change his mind about Lord Tavis's guilt."

Marston closed his eyes briefly, cursing himself for not saying more in his message.

"That's all?" he asked, looking at the man again. "He wrote no reply?"

The rider gave a thin smile. "He didn't even allow me into his castle, my lord. He kept me waiting at the gate, and sent his Qirsi to convey his response."

The thane wiped a hand over his face, shaking his head. "Very well," he said. He glanced at the nearer of the two guards. "Get him some food and some hot tea. Make certain he's made comfortable."

"Yes, my lord."

The rider bowed to him. "Thank you, my lord."

The three men walked slowly toward the kitchen tower, leaving Marston alone by the gate to struggle with his rage and frustration.

Domnall's answer came the following morning. Shamus, the duke there, showed Thorald's messenger far more courtesy than had the duke of Galdasten, but his answer was no different.

"The nobles of Domnall have the highest regard for the duke of Thorald," he wrote in his reply. "But we have little doubt that Lord Tavis of Curgh killed Lady Brienne, and if there is to be war between those two houses, we cannot in good conscience offer Aindreas of Kentigern anything less than our full support."

Sitting with his father a short time after the messenger's return, Marston could not mask his bitterness. "It's almost as if they want a civil war," he said. "Don't they understand what it would do to the kingdom?"

"Shamus might not have thought it through so carefully," the duke said from his bed. "But I have no doubt that Renald knows precisely what he's doing and where it might lead."

"You think Galdasten wants war?"

"I believe he wants to see Kearney driven from the throne, and if war comes, undermining the Rules of Ascension, all the better."

"So he covets the crown."

Tobbar gave a grim smile. "Would that surprise you? The lords of

Galdasten have been removed from the Order of Ascension for eight years now, and their exclusion will continue for four generations, all because a madman brought the pestilence to their castle. It's true that we have no claim to the throne until your sons reach Fating age, and even then, Glyndwr will retain the crown. Kearney is a young man, and he has a son. But at some point Glyndwr's line will fail, and when it does, the crown will revert to Thorald. Galdasten must wait decades longer, and still, Renald has no guarantee that his grandson's grandson will rule.

"The other houses have always resented Thorald's supremacy in the Order of Ascension, Galdasten most of all, perhaps because it ranks second only to our house. Such resentments have lain at the root of nearly every civil war fought in Eibithar's history. And though hostility to the rules can't be said to have caused this one, if it comes to war, they will fuel its fury. No doubt Renald sees this as an opportunity to end our supremacy, and Aindreas may feel the same way."

"I suppose you're right," Marston said. "But doesn't that mean that we should cast our lot with Kearney and Javan? So long as we uphold the Rules of Ascension, we preserve our status as the kingdom's preeminent house."

"That may be so. But none of us benefits from a civil war. As long as our neutrality continues to keep the peace we shouldn't take sides."

Later that day, the riders sent to Eardley and Labruinn returned bearing the first hopeful word Marston had received. Neither Elam, the duke of Eardley, nor Caius, Labruinn's duke, wrote a formal reply, but both men told their messengers that they would be riding to Thorald in the next few days.

Even more surprising, two days after hearing from the minor houses, Marston received word from Javan of Curgh. He was leaving immediately for Thorald, riding with his first minister and a small company of soldiers. Barring a storm, he hoped to reach the castle before the Night of Two Moons.

"Don't go thinking you've saved the land just yet," Tobbar warned, no doubt sensing how much Curgh's reply had pleased Marston.

"He's riding more than fifty leagues to come here, Father. That must mean something."

"It only means that Javan is as desperate for allies as Aindreas. And don't forget, Curgh has every reason in the world to blame the Qirsi for all that's befallen Eibithar in the last half year. He may agree with everything you say, but that doesn't necessarily make him a friend."

Marston knew his father was right, but he couldn't help thinking that if a few other dukes chose to come as well, these discussions might actually do some good.

Unfortunately, Javan's was the last response he received for several days. And when the riders finally returned from the other houses, they bore discouraging news. Lathrop of Tremain didn't care to brave the snows for such a long journey, nor did the dukes of Sussyn and Rennach. Or so they said. Marston couldn't help but wonder if they had other reasons for staying away. Aindreas, as Marston had expected, refused to hear Thorald's messenger at all. The king offered to receive Marston anytime he wished to ride to the City of Kings, but he would not be coming either. The thane had expected this as well; Eibithar's king could hardly be expected to ride to Thorald at his request, or even Tobbar's.

Perhaps he should have been pleased that any of the dukes had agreed to come—certainly his father thought so—but as Marston awaited the arrival of Caius and Elam, he felt his bitterness returning.

Eardley and Labruinn reached Thorald's gates the same morning, arriving within an hour of one another. Shortly after, a single rider approached the castle from the west, wearing the brown and gold of Curgh. It was one of Javan's soldiers, and as he strode across the castle ward to where Marston stood, the thane feared that he had brought word that Javan would not be coming after all. Instead he announced that the duke of Curgh's company was but two days' ride from Thorald, and would reach the castle the first day of the waning.

"You invited Curgh?" Elam asked, upon hearing this news in Thorald Castle's great hall.

"We invited every duke in the land," Tobbar answered, "and the king as well. Most have declined our invitation, but we would have welcomed all with equal warmth."

"If we're to discuss this conflict between Curgh and Kentigern, it would be best if Javan and Aindreas were elsewhere. Clearly, the duke of Kentigern understands this. It's unfortunate that Javan does not, and it surprises me that you don't either, Tobbar." The duke of Eardley glanced briefly at Marston, his lip curling. "Perhaps you've placed too much faith in your son's youthful judgment."

Elam was one of Eibithar's older dukes, a tall man, with silver hair, square features, and dark green eyes. He had grown heavy with the years, but he still looked more like a king than the lord of a minor house. He and the elder Filib had been friends, but after the duke of Thorald's death, and the murder of Filib the Younger, Elam had done little to cultivate a friendship with Tobbar. Marston believed it was because Thorald no longer wielded as much power within the kingdom. His father chose to be more generous, attributing Elam's distance to his grief for Filib. Still, Marston found it very easy to dislike the man.

Tobbar smiled, though clearly it took an effort. "I believe, Lord Eardley, that any attempt to end this crisis must include both Javan and Aindreas. I view Curgh's response to my invitation as the appropriate one. As long as Lord Kentigern keeps himself apart from the rest of us, he places the kingdom at risk."

"I had thought Thorald was neutral in this matter, my lord duke."

"We are," Tobbar said. "But we're no less concerned for our impartiality."

With Javan expected to reach the castle within two days, Tobbar thought it best to delay their discussions until the duke's arrival. He instructed his servants and guards to make Caius and Elam as comfortable as possible, but steadfastly resisted Eardley's attempts to wring from him the information mentioned in Marston's message.

As promised, Javan and his company reached the castle gates just after the ringing of the midday bells on the first day of the waning. Travel-stained, and obviously weary, the duke nevertheless declined Marston's offer of rest and a meal.

"I've come a long way, Lord Shanstead," he said, following the thane through the castle wards to Tobbar's chambers. "And with all that's happening in Eibithar just now, I don't want to be away from my home for long."

Marston remembered Javan as a dour man, though formidable. The years hadn't changed him much, though his hair was more grey now than brown, and his face was deeply lined. He still carried himself with grace, straight-backed and lean, like a swordsman.

"I understand, my Lord Curgh. My father awaits you."

"Have others come?"

"Only Eardley and Labruinn."

Javan raised an eyebrow. "I'd have thought that Renald would make the journey, and Shamus as well."

"I had hoped they would, my lord," Marston said, staring at the path before them.

"They remain committed to Aindreas."

"Yes, my lord."

The duke nodded. His Qirsi walked just a stride or two behind them, and Javan glanced back at the man now. "It seems Hagan was right."

"He seemed quite certain of himself, my lord," the Qirsi said.

"He usually does."

The minister grinned. He was taller than the duke and slightly built, like so many of the sorcerer race. He wore his white hair tied back, making his face appear narrow and long. Unlike most Qirsi, he had a beard and mustache, though they were so pale as to be barely visible. His eyes, however, gleamed in the bright sun, as yellow as Uulranni gold.

They made their way to Tobbar's presence chamber, finding the door open and the dukes of Eardley and Labruinn already seated by the hearth. Marston's father sat across from the other dukes. Away from his bed, dressed in soldier's garb, he looked better than he had in several days. Still Marston could only imagine how he appeared to Javan, who hadn't seen the duke in many turns.

"My Lord Duke," Tobbar said, climbing stiffly to his feet as Javan entered the room. "Be welcome in my home."

Marston noticed that the other dukes also stood, though Elam's mouth twisted sourly.

Javan crossed to Tobbar and embraced him gently. "My Lord Thorald, you honor me with your offer of hospitality."

"I would have liked to greet you at the gate," Tobbar said, releasing him and sitting once more. "But I don't climb the towers as well as I used to."

"Your son did me the honor, and acquitted himself nobly."

Marston bowed. "My lord is too kind."

Javan turned to Caius and Elam. "My Lord Dukes," he said. "I'm pleased to see you both."

"And I to see you, my Lord Curgh," Labruinn answered, stepping forward to embrace Javan in turn.

Elam remained where he was. "Curgh" was all he said, adding a small bow, almost as an afterthought.

Javan gave a thin smile, but said nothing to the man. After a moment, he faced Tobbar again. "Forgive my haste, my Lord Duke, but as I've already told your son, I'm loath to be far from Curgh for very long. I was hoping that we could begin immediately to speak of whatever tidings led you to issue your kind invitation."

"That suits me as well, Tobbar," Eardley said. "Caius and I have waited long enough. Javan's here now. Let's get on with it."

Tobbar nodded. "Very well." Turning his gaze to Marston, he asked, "How do you wish to proceed? This was your idea."

The thane took a long breath, feeling far less sure of himself than he had at the beginning of the turn, when he wrote the messages.

"Xiv?" he said, facing his minister.

"Of course, my lord." The Qirsi stepped to center of the room and made himself smile. "If the other ministers would follow me, we can speak of these matters on our own while our lords talk among themselves."

"Is that necessary?" Labruinn's first minister asked.

"It's all right, Ottah," Elam said. "Go with the other ministers. I'll be fine."

"As you wish, my lord." The minister didn't sound pleased, but he followed Xiv and the others from the chamber, closing the door as he left.

Elam eyed Tobbar briefly before turning to Marston. "Now, what's this about, Shanstead?"

"Won't you sit, my lord?" He glanced at the other dukes. "The rest of you as well. Make yourselves comfortable."

Elam and Caius returned to their seats and Javan sat beside Tobbar.

"I notice that your first minister is nowhere to be seen, my Lord Duke," Curgh said. "Is this about her?"

Elam's face reddened. He had been in Thorald for two days, and it seemed he had failed to realize this.

"It is," Tobbar said, his voice flat, his cheeks coloring as well. "Enid is dead, killed by her own hand, though not before she admitted to being a traitor and party to the conspiracy of which we've all heard so much."

"You have my sympathy," Javan said. "I'm certain that I speak for my fellow dukes when I say that each of us fears he'll be the next to learn that one of his Qirsi is a traitor."

"Indeed," Caius agreed, passing a meaty hand over his brow. "None of us is immune."

"Have you had a minister betray you, Labruinn?" Elam asked.

"Not yet. At least not as far as I know. But I must admit that I rely on them far less than I have in the past. Ever since Kentigern—" He stopped abruptly, his eyes flicking toward Javan.

"It's all right, Caius," the duke said, actually managing to laugh. "You can speak his name in my company."

"Well, I was just going to say that we were all alarmed when we heard about his Qirsi."

Elam sat forward. "I'm sure her betrayal must have been difficult for you, Tobbar, but I fail to see how this warrants calling us all to Thorald."

"That was my idea," Marston said. "Enid's treason did far more than cost my father a friend and a trusted advisor. It's forced us to question many of our assumptions regarding events in Thorald over the past several years."

Caius let out a small gasp. "Filib!" he whispered. "You think she had something to do with his death."

"I believe it's possible."

"Which Filib?" Javan asked.

"The Younger," Tobbar said. "Enid hadn't yet come to Thorald when my brother died. I made her my first minister a few years later. It now seems that was the greatest mistake I've ever made."

"It was a mistake any duke might have made," Eardley said, surprising Marston.

"Thank you, Elam," Tobbar said, sounding like the man's kindness had caught him unprepared also.

Caius shook his head. "I'm afraid I'm still a bit confused. Even if Filib was killed by the Qirsi rather than by thieves, why ask us here?"

"Because of Kentigern's first minister," Javan said before Marston could answer. He turned to Tobbar. "Has Enid's betrayal convinced you of Tavis's innocence?"

Elam bristled. "One has nothing to do with the other."

"Are you certain?" Marston asked. "We've assumed for years that accidents of history placed Curgh in position to claim the throne. The act of a madman in Galdasten, my uncle's death during a hunt, Filib's murder at the hands of thieves—all separate occurrences that together removed Eibithar's two leading houses from the Order of Ascension. When Tavis was accused of killing Brienne, it seemed that Javan's house had squandered its one opportunity to rule the kingdom. But now it seems there were far darker forces at work here. Assume for a moment that Filib was murdered by the Qirsi, or people working for them. And then consider that the betrayal by Aindreas's minister came only days after Brienne's death. Suddenly these seem less like accidents of history, and far more like a Qirsi plot to bring civil war to our land."

Elam frowned. "You sound more like a Curgh than a Thorald, Lord Shanstead. Is this your thinking, or have you been speaking with Curgh and his allies?"

"I assure you, Lord Eardley," Marston said coldly, "this is the first time I've spoken of these tidings with the duke."

"I see. And can you offer any proof that your father's Qirsi had a hand in Filib's murder?"

Marston felt his cheeks growing hot. "No."

"Well, have you learned anything new about Lady Brienne's death that might support this wild theory of yours?"

"Nothing beyond what we've all heard."

"So you're just guessing then. Your father's first minister turns out to be a traitor, and so you assume that Qirsi conspirators are responsible for all the land's troubles. Is that about right?"

"It's more than that," Javan broke in. "We have many reasons to believe that Tavis was innocent of any crime, though Aindreas refused to acknowledge them. My minister and I have thought for some time that the Qirsi might have been behind Brienne's death and my son's suffering."

The duke of Eardley glared at him. "Don't speak to me of your son's suffering, Javan. Aindreas and Ioanna have suffered. I'll even allow that you and Shonah have. But not the boy, not after what he did. And as to these reasons of which you speak, I don't even want to hear about them. I'm not likely to give much credence to anything you have to say about the Lady Brienne or your son."

"That's your choice, Elam," Caius said pointedly. "I, for one, would like to hear what Javan has learned."

"Of course you would, Caius. You've already allied yourself with Curgh and Glyndwr. I'm sure you'd welcome any word that might justify that choice and cleanse the lady's blood from your house."

Labruinn stood, his hand straying to the hilt of his sword. "How dare you!"

"My Lord Dukes, please," Tobbar said, forcing himself to his feet once more. "We are all men of Eibithar, and we all want what's best for our kingdom. Surely that bond is stronger than any issue that divides us."

Elam was still sitting, but he stared up at the other duke as if ready to do battle.

"Please, Caius," Tobbar said gently. "Sit down."

After another moment, the duke of Labruinn nodded and lowered himself into his chair. His eyes never left Elam's face, however, and his expression did not soften.

"You saw my son at Kearney's investiture," Javan said to Elam, breaking a lengthy silence. "You saw the scars on his face. They were nothing compared with the marks Aindreas's torture left on his body. Yet he never confessed. Doesn't that tell you something? Doesn't it at least give you pause?"

"It tells me only that the boy is strong-willed to the point of stubbornness." Eardley gave a cold smile. "It comes as no surprise, really, given that he's a Curgh."

"You think willfulness is all a man needs to endure torture?"

"Maybe he knew that an attempt would be made to win his freedom, that all he needed to do was last a few days until his escape. Certainly such hope would sustain him through a good deal of suffering." Elam gave a small shrug. "To be honest, I don't know what kept him from confessing. But to assume, in the face of all the evidence against him, that his failure to confess makes him innocent seems to me the worst kind of sophistry."

Marston could barely contain his frustration. "So you refuse to accept that there might be any connection at all between Brienne's murder and the treason of Kentigern's Qirsi."

"In the absence of any evidence linking one to the other, yes, I do."

"Don't you see that by taking Kentigern's part, you weaken us? This is just what the conspiracy wants: a kingdom at war with itself, and a king without the support of his people. You're as bad as Enid and every other traitor to—"

"Marston!" Tobbar said, his voice like a war hammer. "That's enough!"

Elam looked around the chamber, shaking his head slowly, a dark grin on his lips. "I should have known better than to come here. It's not a discussion you want, Shanstead. You asked me here to turn me from Kentigern's side."

"That's not true."

"Then how is it that in a kingdom that leans heavily to Kentigern's point of view, I find myself his sole defender here in your castle? Did you send that damned message to anyone else, or was I the lone target of your efforts this time?"

"He sent the message to every house in the land," Tobbar answered. "Including Kentigern. The snows kept some of the others away, narrow-mindedness the rest. Aindreas wouldn't even allow our rider to deliver his message."

"Can you blame him? Demons and fire, Tobbar! You have children. Can't you see how the man grieves?"

"Of course I can. And I can even see why he hates Curgh so." The duke glanced at Javan. "Forgive me, but circumstances demand nothing less than complete honesty. Had it been my child, and your son's blade, I'd hate your house as well." He faced Elam again. "That said, the defection of my Qirsi would have given me cause to wonder, and so too would the boy's refusal to confess, even after the most severe torture."

Eardley shook his head again. "I expect such nonsense from Javan, and maybe from the thane as well. But you should know better, Tobbar. Your neutrality is a farce. You claim to fear for the kingdom, but you care only for your own power. You ally yourself with butchers and a false king so that you can maintain your precious supremacy." He stood and started toward the door. "If Ean cares at all for justice, the boy will hang, and the Rules of Ascension will cease to govern our land."

"Elam," Tobbar called. "I beg you not to go. My son had no right to say what he did. But his fears are justified. No matter what you think of the rules or of Javan, you have to see that civil war will weaken us."

Eardley had pulled the door open, but he paused now on the threshold, turning to face the duke. "Kearney weakens us. Demons like Tavis of Curgh weaken us. What is a kingdom without justice? If it takes war to make Eibithar whole again, then so be it. But I'll not allow Glyndwr's ambition and Curgh's lies and Thorald's lust for power to rule over my house."

With that he walked out, not bothering to close the door again, so that the click of his footsteps echoing through the corridor filled the chamber.

"Can he really be so blind?" Marston asked. "Doesn't he know that the Qirsi want us thirsting for each other's blood?"

"For centuries," Javan said quietly, "the Rules of Ascension have only barely masked the fact that Eibithar remains a loose confederation of clans. Over the course of our history we've been as eager to fight ourselves as we have the Aneirans." He looked at Marston. "The Qirsi seek to defeat us by attacking our greatest weakness as a kingdom. It shouldn't come as a surprise to any of us that their tactics are working."

Eardley's first minister dropped herself into a large chair by the thin slit of a window and looked up at Xivled, Marston's minister. "So tell us, cousin. Why has Thorald called our dukes to his castle? What are these tidings you're all so eager to share with us?"

"Yes, cousin," Labruinn's first minister added. "You and your thane have been terribly mysterious, and I grow tired of it. What could possibly justify asking us to brave the snows?"

Ottah was older than the rest of them. His pallid face was deeply lined and his white hair had begun to thin. Though his journey had been much shorter than the one from Curgh, and the path he and his duke followed through the North Wood more sheltered than Fotir's ride across the Moorlands, the Curgh minister had little doubt that the older man had found his travels quite arduous.

"My lord and the duke of Thorald wished to speak with Eibithar's other dukes about the Qirsi conspiracy," Xivled answered. "That's why they asked us to leave."

"But why now?" Cerri asked, playing with her braided hair. "Why wait for the snows? Or for that matter, why not wait longer, until the rains return?"

"Because we only learned on the last Pitch Night that the duke of Thorald's first minister was a traitor."

Fotir had expected something like this. His duke had noticed almost immediately upon their arrival that Enid ja Kovar was nowhere to be seen. Either she was dead, or she had left the castle. And if she had died without incident, Tobbar would have replaced her with one of his underministers. All signs pointed to her betrayal.

"My lord believes Enid may have played a role in Filib the Younger's death," the minister continued. "Perhaps in the elder Filib's as well."

"Where is Enid now?" Fotir asked.

"She's dead. We tried to imprison her, hoping to learn something of her allies in the movement, but she took her own life before we could."

"The movement?" Cerri asked, raising an eyebrow. "Is that what you call it when you speak with Shanstead?"

Xivled frowned. "The conspiracy then."

"I'm serious, cousin," Eardley's minister said. She looked at the rest of them. "When the rest of you speak with your dukes about these Qirsi, what do you say about them?"

Fotir shook his head. "I'm not sure I know what you mean."

"Of course you don't, cousin," Ottah laughed. "The great Fotir jal Salene doesn't concern himself with such trifles. No one would ever doubt where his loyalties lie. The rest of us don't have that luxury, though. We have to watch every word when it comes to the conspiracy." He looked at Cerri. "I know I do."

"So how do you handle it?" she asked.

The man shrugged. "I tread lightly. What else can I do? I always use 'we' when speaking of Labruinn, or the courts, or sometimes even the Eandi. And of course I refer to the Qirsi in the movement as 'they.' Lately I've found myself avoiding the use of my magic at all costs. Just half a turn ago, I had a dream that I'm quite certain was a vision. It wasn't anything too important—there were no lives at stake. But I saw something that may affect the next harvest in the Labruinn countryside. The point is, though, I've yet to mention it to my duke. I'm afraid that any mention of my powers will make me suspect in his eyes."

Fotir stared at the minister, not quite believing what he was hearing. "But that makes no sense. We're Qirsi. The nobles of Eibithar—indeed, of all the realms of the Forelands—have relied on our magic for centuries.

That's why your duke brought you to Labruinn in the first place, to wield your powers on his behalf."

"As I already said, cousin, I wouldn't expect you to understand."

"Why not? Am I any less Qirsi than you are? Are my eyes less yellow, my hair less white?"

"It's not your eyes and hair that concern us, Fotir," Cerri said. "It's your blood. From what I've heard, it runs more Eandi than Qirsi. It doesn't surprise me at all that you never worry about your duke's suspicions."

Fotir's cheeks burned, and he struggled to keep from storming out of the chamber. Such remarks about a sorcerer's blood dated to the days of Carthach and his betrayal of the Qirsi people during the early wars. Any white-hair at whom they were directed could not help but take offense. More to the point, however, they echoed similar comments made to him by Shurik jal Marcine, during their conversations in Kentigern during the growing turns, and by a Revel Qirsi named Trin the night of Tavis's Fating. Somehow, during his years of service to the House of Curgh, Fotir had acquired a reputation as a man more devoted to his lord than to his people. All he had done was serve Javan and his house loyally for nine years. Was there a crime in that? Certainly his father would have thought so. His father, who had cursed Carthach's name every day of his life, and had stopped speaking with his only son the night of Fotir's Fating, which showed him serving an Eandi noble. He could almost hear the man saying, *You see? This is what comes of serving the Eandi.*

"I don't fear my duke's suspicions," he said, measuring each word, "because he harbors none. And if he did, he'd bring them to me. There's no secret to my friendship with Javan. We speak with each other honestly. If you and your duke did the same, you could be true to yourself and your heritage."

He expected Ottah to respond in anger, but the minister merely laughed. "You truly believe that your duke harbors no suspicions of you?" He glanced briefly at Cerri, who was grinning as well, then faced Fotir again. "Perhaps you're more simple than I thought, cousin."

Xivled cleared his throat. "Actually, Ottah, I don't believe Marston is suspicious of me."

"Well, you've known him since you were children," Cerri said. "That's hardly the same thing."

"Isn't it? I'm Qirsi, he's Eandi. The way you and Ottah speak of it, one would think that nothing else matters. I'm forced to wonder if you're not the simple ones, assuming that every Qirsi minister feels about his or her noble as you do about yours."

Cerri pressed her lips in a thin line and stared at the fire. Ottah didn't respond either.

"How did you learn of Enid's betrayal?" Fotir asked after a lengthy silence.

"Marston and I contrived to have me speak with her in private. While in her chambers I led her to believe that I hated the thane and wished to join the conspiracy. She didn't believe me right away, but it didn't take me long to convince her. I gathered from what she told me that Thorald had once been a center of conspiracy activity, but that its time had passed. I think she believed that bringing me to the movement's leaders would enhance her stature once more."

"So you had an opportunity to join the conspiracy?" Fotir asked in amazement. The other two ministers were staring at Xivled, as if he had transformed himself into a Weaver before their eyes.

"Yes, I did."

"And what happened?"

The younger man looked away. "My thane and I exposed her treason to the duke that very night. She killed herself as they took her to the dungeon."

"A pity," Fotir said.

"I know. I said as much to Marston that night, but he wished to protect me from harm." He looked up again, eyeing Ottah and Cerri. "An irony, given our conversation. Wouldn't you say?"

Neither of them answered, and the ministers lapsed into silence again.

"So Enid was a traitor," Ottah finally said, shaking his head. "That's only going to make matters worse for the rest of us. My duke is likely to be even less trusting than before." He grinned at Fotir. "Who knows, cousin? Even Javan might have his doubts now."

Fotir merely stared at the minister.

"Come on, Cerri," Ottah said, pushing himself from his chair. "I don't know about our friends here, but I for one could use some wine."

"By all means," Xivled said, as Cerri stood. "Visit our cellars. Tell the cellarmaster I sent you."

Ottah pulled the door open and held it for Eardley's minister. "Thank you, cousin. We will." He nodded at Fotir. "First Minister."

A moment later they were gone. Fotir closed his eyes and exhaled through his teeth.

Xivled sat in the chair beside Fotir's. "I feel I should apologize for them, First Minister. They have no right speaking to you so."

"It's all right, Minister. It's not your fault, nor is it anything I haven't heard before." He regarded the other man briefly. "You should know that it's only a matter of time before other Qirsi speak of you as they do of me. You're in line to be First Minister to Eibithar's most powerful house, and you leave no doubt as to where your loyalties lie. Most other ministers will envy you. Some, like Ottah and Cerri, will compare you to Carthach, if not to your face, then when your back is turned."

Xivled gazed at the fire, looking thoughtful and quite young. "I suppose they might. You know as well as I that the jealousies of loyal Qirsi are the least of our worries."

"Usually I'd agree with you, cousin. But we live in strange times. Every conflict weakens us, no matter how petty it might be. Noble houses are threatening each other with war, not only here, but in Aneira and Sanbira as well. The Aneirans still threaten us from the south, and we've noticed a good deal of activity from Braedon's fleet. Eandi lords have grown afraid of their ministers, and now it seems Qirsi are hiding their powers to allay those fears. Ottah's envy may seem a trifle, but it's one more fissure in a kingdom that's already crumbling. I fear for us, cousin. We know so little about our enemies that we're turning on each other." He paused, unsure as to whether to give voice to all that he was thinking. "It may not be my place to say this," he went on at last, "but I wish your thane had allowed you to join the conspiracy."

The minister's gaze flicked in his direction for just an instant, but that was long enough for Fotir to see the pained expression in Xivled's pale eyes. "I could have learned so much."

Chapter
Twenty-eight

✦

Kentigern, Eibithar

T here might have been another way to accomplish his goals, had he only taken the time to look for one. Aindreas tried to tell himself that his choices were limited, that there was only so much a duke could do under such extraordinary circumstances. Indeed, there was more than a bit of truth to this. He couldn't tell Villyd what he had in mind, for the swordmaster would never have approved. He might even have forsaken his oath of service and left Kentigern for good, or worse, informed Ioanna of what Aindreas was doing so that she might dissuade the duke with her rage and disgust. Certainly Aindreas couldn't have told Barret, his prelate, and the only other man in the castle he could trust. And he couldn't very well inquire in the city on his own, not without raising a swarm of questions.

The fact of the matter was, however, he was glad to be in the dungeon again, torturing once more. He had a thirst for it, just as he did for Sanbiri red. Even the stench of the place didn't bother him anymore. There was comfort to be found here: in the screams, in the smell of the torches, in the feel of his sword cutting into another man's flesh. If he closed his eyes, he could almost imagine that he was hurting Tavis again, exacting a measure of revenge for what the boy did to Brienne.

It was only when he opened his eyes, and saw yet another Qirsi face distorted with pain, that he remembered.

He didn't allow any of the guards down here with him. Not even they could know what he sought in the answers he wrung from the white-hairs.

He had started with his former underministers, the other Qirsi who served him when Shurik was still in the castle. It struck him as logical that the first minister wouldn't have been working alone, and where better to look for the traitor's accomplice than his own circle of advisors?

Only when he turned his attention to the first man, however—a young Qirsi named Goel—did Aindreas begin to realize how greatly torturing a sorcerer would differ from hurting an Eandi. He had kept records of all the Qirsi he brought to his castle as ministers, so he knew this man was a shaper, and he took elaborate precautions to protect himself and render the Qirsi helpless.

He invited the man to the castle, slipped some sweetwort into his wine, and after the minister lost consciousness, had him taken to the castle dungeon. There he bound the man's wrists and ankles with satin ties, which the Qirsi couldn't shatter as he could iron shackles. Aindreas then hung him by his hands and feet like a calf being carried to slaughter, and suspended him high over a fire. When the Qirsi awoke, he was as helpless as a babe. If he managed to shatter the chains from which he hung, he'd fall to the flames below.

Still, the duke soon discovered that the Qirsi had resources beyond his reckoning. Aindreas began to ask him questions about the conspiracy, and as the man denied having any knowledge of the renegade Qirsi or their activities, the duke used a windlass to lower him toward the flames. When the handle splintered in his hand, the sound of rending wood echoing sharply off the dungeon walls, Aindreas nearly shrieked like a frightened girl.

"Next time I shatter your skull," the man said. "I swear it. Now get me down from here."

Shaken and unwilling to risk asking any more questions, Aindreas fled the prison and sent eight of his archers to kill the man.

"No more shapers," he whispered to himself. "The others don't scare me, but no more shapers."

He soon found, however, that healers could be trouble as well. One woman healed herself for more than an hour as he tortured her with his blade, until at last she just failed, dying almost instantly. She answered not one of his questions. Another woman used magic to set his sleeve on fire and threatened to burn his hair and beard, before he ran her through with his sword. He learned nothing more from her than he had from the others.

After a time, however, he began to enjoy a bit more success. He found no conspirators, but he did learn that the Qirsi could be tortured, provided one was patient and imaginative.

He began to blindfold his victims, so that they couldn't anticipate his attacks or direct their magic at him with such ease. He also relied more heavily on torches and the breaking of bones, particularly with the healers, who seemed far more adept at closing cuts than soothing other injuries. Finally, he learned to use a lighter hand, for once their magical defenses failed, the Qirsi proved far more delicate than Tavis and other Eandi.

Still, even as he honed his skills, Aindreas learned little from those he brought to his prison. A few told him that they were with the conspiracy after he had hurt them for some time. But when he questioned them more thoroughly, he invariably found that they had been lying, hoping to end their misery.

Before long he had killed off all those Qirsi who once served in his castle, save for one minister who had shaping magic, and had begun to comb the city for other Qirsi to question. He began with the taverns, of course: the Silver Bear, the Grey Boar, and the rest of the establishments that catered to white-hairs. No doubt he was making enemies of all the local Qirsi, but he no longer cared. He was desperate to find someone from their damned movement, and he intended to spare no effort in doing so. As failure followed upon failure, however, he found himself losing hope as well as his appetite for torture. Perhaps Shurik had been working alone here in Kentigern. Perhaps there was less to this conspiracy than the nobles of Eibithar thought. Eager as he was to find a Qirsi who could tell him about their movement, this last possibility held some appeal for him, since it undermined the claims of Javan and others that the conspiracy was behind not only the weakening of Kentigern's defenses, but also Brienne's murder.

He was weighing these possibilities while using torches on a slight Qirsi man, with an uncommonly round face and close-cropped white hair. It was late in the day—he had already killed one Qirsi that morning—and this second man had denied repeatedly knowing anything about the conspiracy. The Qirsi's voice was growing ragged from screaming, and Aindreas sensed that he wouldn't last much longer, which was fine with the duke. The time had come to rethink his methods.

"If you'll tell me about the conspiracy," the duke said dully, "I swear to you, your suffering will end." The words had started to lose meaning for him, the way he thought a litany must for new adherents in the cloister. He held a torch to the man's back again. "Don't you want to stop the pain?"

The Qirsi wailed, tears streaming down his face.

"All right," he gasped, as Aindreas pulled back the torch. "Yes, I'm with the conspiracy. Ask your questions. Just don't hurt me anymore."

Aindreas had heard this too many times to allow himself much excitement. A tortured man would say almost anything when he reached the limits of his endurance. It was almost enough to make him admire Tavis of Curgh, who never confessed to Brienne's murder, though Aindreas inflicted far more pain on the boy than he had on any of these frail sorcerers.

"What do you do for the conspiracy?" he asked, his voice flat.

"Mostly I gather information," the man said, his voice scraped raw. "But I've also delivered gold and carried messages."

Aindreas gaped at him, scarcely believing what he had heard.

"What did you say?"

"I gather information. I carry messages and I deliver gold."

The duke just stood there, too astonished to speak. After some time the man began to flinch, as if expecting his torture to resume at any moment.

"You said you wouldn't hurt me anymore," he whimpered.

Aindreas grabbed at the parchment resting on the floor at his feet. The man's name was Qerle jal Brishta. He was a cloth merchant who frequented one of the taverns in the marketplace. He claimed to be a gleaner and nothing more, but Aindreas had learned in the past few days that an alarming number of Qirsi lied about their abilities. Many, it seemed, possessed more than one type of magic.

"You go by Qerle?" Aindreas asked.

"Yes."

"Did you ever bring gold to the castle, Qerle?"

"Yes, to your first minister."

"And messages as well?"

"Only written ones that were placed in the pouches of gold. Our leaders don't like us couriers speaking with the others."

"Do you know the leaders? Have you met them?"

"Never."

Aindreas waved the torch at the man's side.

"I swear it!" he screamed. "I've never met them. I don't know anyone who has, at least not so that they could see who it was."

The duke stepped closer to the man. "What do you mean by that? 'Not so that they could see.' "

The Qirsi hesitated and Aindreas swung his torch, making the flame flutter, like a windblown pennon. He didn't hold it close to Qerle, but the sound itself spurred the man to speak.

"There are rumors," he said. "Nothing more than that. But some say that the movement is led by a Weaver, and that he enters the dreams of his more trusted servants."

A Weaver. Maybe Aindreas should have been appalled, but after all that had befallen him in the past half year—Brienne's death, Shurik's treason, the siege by Mertesse that nearly cost him his castle—even the revelation of a Weaver didn't disturb him anymore.

"Has this Weaver ever entered your dreams?"

Qerle shook his head and grimaced. It took Aindreas a moment to realize that he was trying to smile. "The Weaver commands ministers throughout the Forelands. Compared with them, I'm nothing. You've captured a sparrow, Eandi. That's all you've done today."

"That remains to be seen," the duke said. But he burned the man's arm as punishment for his impudence.

"Where does the gold come from?" the duke asked, when it seemed that Qerle's newest pain had receded.

"I don't know."

"Well, when you paid Shurik, where did you get his money?"

"From another courier."

"And what was his name?"

"That I won't tell you. You can torture me until I die, but I won't give you the names of any others. I swear it on all that I have left in this world."

Aindreas briefly considered resorting to the torch again, just to see if the man was as brave as his words. He quickly thought better of it, though. There was much this Qirsi needed to do for him before he died and it struck the duke as foolish to waste this life in the pursuit of yet another sparrow, as Qerle put it. Besides, there was something almost admirable in the way he protected his comrades.

"Do you know where this man got the gold?" he asked instead.

"I believe it came from a merchant, but that's all I know."

The duke nodded. He had little doubt that this was true. The gold was the movement's weakness, the one path a determined enemy might follow back to its leaders. In all likelihood that path twisted and turned like a Revel dancer. No mere courier would know much about it. Indeed, Aindreas would have wagered a hundred qinde that even a man as important as Shurik knew little beyond what Qerle had just told him.

"Did you ever take a message from Shurik back to the leaders, or those who could contact them?"

"No, never."

"Would you know how to do such a thing?"

"Even if I did, I'd refuse. I already told you: I will not betray any of the others."

"That's not what I'm asking you to do."

"Then what?"

Abruptly Aindreas was trembling. For more than a turn, since his troubling conversation with the thane of Shanstead, he had pursued the Qirsi, arresting them, torturing them, and all the while, lying to Villyd and the rest about his reasons. Now, at last, he had the man he sought, the one who could lead him to the conspiracy and bring his plans to fruition. And Aindreas felt himself waver. Once he started down the road before him, there could be no turning from it. Certainly, he could never return to where he stood now. His house, his kingdom, would never be the same.

An image of Ennis entered his mind. His boy, his heir. Seeing that face, he shivered, and nearly reached for his sword to finish the Qirsi without speaking another word. But then another image came to him. Brienne. Not as he last saw her, a bloodied corpse on Tavis's bed, but rather as she had appeared the night before she died, golden and spirited and so beautiful that it made his chest ache. Her murderer was free, and the man who guarded his life when Aindreas sought vengeance now sat on the Oaken Throne. It was more than Aindreas could bear.

He took a step forward, extending a hand toward Qerle's head. The Qirsi flinched again, turning his face away and wincing in anticipation of more pain. Aindreas waited a moment, until the man relaxed. Then he removed the blindfold from Qerle's eyes.

The white-hair blinked several times, as if even the dim glow of the torches was too bright for him.

"Why did you do that?" he asked, regarding the duke warily.

"I want you to help me contact the leaders of your conspiracy."

"Why?"

"I want their help. And I think they might be interested in having mine as well."

"You can't be serious."

That of all things made the duke laugh. "You doubt that I'm serious? You, who I've tortured for the better part of a day?"

"You're mad."

"Perhaps I am. But my land is ruled by a king I hate, a king who offered refuge to the man who killed my daughter. Your leaders hate the Eandi courts, but can they deny the value of allying themselves with one as powerful as Kentigern? I'm offering them a chance to bring down Eibithar's king, and in exchange all I ask is that my court be spared, perhaps even given a place of influence in the new order their rebellion creates. Do you really expect them to say no?"

The Qirsi shook his head, his pale eyes wide, as if he feared Aindreas more now than he had when the duke was torturing him.

"I don't know what they'll say," he said softly. "But I'm sure they never even thought this possible."

"You have to convince them that it is. You have to make them believe that I can help their movement."

"So, you're going to let me go?"

"I need someone to speak with the Qirsi leaders for me. Who else is there? I'm willing to pay you quite handsomely if you succeed." He lifted one of the torches again. "But I want you to remember this day, and what I did to you. If you fail me, your next visit to this dungeon will make today's torture seem mild by comparison."

The man nodded. Aindreas could see hatred in his pale eyes.

"You'd like to kill me," the duke said. "I understand. I'd probably feel the same way, were I in your position. But you're going to have to swallow your anger. If you betray me, or if you attempt to flee Kentigern, I'll find you. My men will be watching your every movement, and they'll be watching your wife and children as well. From what I hear, it seems you have a lovely family. You wouldn't want to see any of them down here, would you?"

"You wouldn't," the Qirsi breathed.

"I've just told you I want to ally my house with the Qirsi conspiracy. You honestly think I'd hesitate to torture another white-hair or two?"

"The movement's leaders will think I'm luring them into a trap. They may kill me when they hear what I have to say, fearing that you intend to use me as a means of capturing them."

Aindreas shrugged. "You'll have to convince them otherwise."

"How?"

"I don't know, Qerle. Frankly, I don't care. These are your people, not mine. Talk to them. Tell them whatever you have to. But be persuasive. Your life, and the lives of those you love, hang in the balance." The duke hesitated. "I can offer you some token to prove to the others that your message truly comes from me—a gold round perhaps, or a piece of cloth bearing the seal of my house."

Qerle glanced down at the raw, angry burns on his arms and chest. "I think you've given me all the tokens I need, Lord Kentigern."

Aindreas raised an eyebrow. "Perhaps you're right. The scars you'll keep, but we can ease your pain a bit." He looked up at the prison door. "Guards!" he called, his voice pealing like sanctuary bells in the stone prison.

He heard his men hurrying to the door, and, after a moment, he heard the lock turn.

"Yes, my lord?" a soldier asked from the top of the stairs.

"It seems this man is not guilty of any crime. Remove the bonds from his hands and feet, and take him up into the tower. Then find a Qirsi healer in the city and have him or her brought here. I want this prisoner made whole again and released."

"A Qirsi healer, my lord?" the guard asked.

There hadn't been a Qirsi in the castle since Shurik's betrayal, at least not one who wasn't taken immediately to the dungeon.

The duke nodded. "I want his injuries mended as soon as possible."

Two guards descended the stairs, and began to release Qerle from the bonds holding him to the wall.

"I'll look forward to speaking with you again, Qerle," Aindreas said, as he started up the stairs. "Don't keep me waiting long."

"Of course . . . my lord."

Something in the man's voice made the duke pause at the top of the stairs. Looking back at Qerle, however, he saw that the Qirsi had his eyes closed, and his head tipped back against the wall. After a moment the duke left the prison, thinking that he must have imagined it.

Aindreas waited several days for Qerle to return, his patience strained almost from the start. Despite his warnings to the Qirsi, he knew better than to have his soldiers follow the man. The conspiracy's leaders had not enjoyed so much success by allowing themselves to be observed by the soldiers of Eandi nobles. If he had guards follow Qerle, the Qirsi would never speak with him. Instead, he had his men watch Qerle's home, and he didn't have them make any effort to hide themselves. As long as Qerle knew his wife and children were in danger, he wouldn't knowingly betray the duke.

This at least was what Aindreas told himself. After five days of waiting for the Qirsi to return to Kentigern Castle, the duke began to wonder if the man had fled anyway, or worse, if he had been killed as a traitor by others in his movement.

At last, just after dark on the sixth day, a knock at the duke's door interrupted his supper. He had taken to wine once again, much as he had in the days following Brienne's murder, and he was already on his third goblet, having barely touched his meal.

"What is it?" he called.

A guard opened the door and poked his head in the chamber, looking, for all his brawn, like a timid boy.

"There's someone come to see you, my lord. A Qirsi man. He says—"

Aindreas was striding toward the door before the fool could finish whatever it was he was trying to say.

"Where is he?" he asked, pushing past the man and into the corridor.

"We've held him at the gate, knowing how you feel about their kind. We were going to send him away, but he—"

"If you'd sent him away, I'd have had your head on a pike."

The man swallowed, then nodded. "Yes, my lord."

Aindreas walked swiftly to the north gate and through the outer ward, reaching the city gate several steps ahead of the guard, who was panting with the effort of keeping up with him.

Qerle stood alone by the wicket gate, flanked by soldiers and looking like a boy beside them.

The duke stopped a short distance from the Qirsi and regarded him cautiously.

"He's alone?" he asked the guards.

"Yes, my lord."

Aindreas frowned. He'd expected that Qerle would have at least one other Qirsi with him, though he now realized that he'd been foolish to think so. Why would they reveal more than they had to? Qerle was to be a messenger between the conspiracy and Kentigern. It made perfect sense, but the duke couldn't help but feel that he was in the weaker position. He had revealed himself to them, only to be denied a similar gesture on their part.

"Very well," he finally said. "Come with me, Qerle."

He turned and started back toward his chambers, sensing that the Qirsi was following.

"Shall we accompany you, my lord?" a soldier asked.

Aindreas didn't even turn. "If I'd wanted you to, I would have commanded it."

The duke and the Qirsi passed through the inner gate in silence and entered the nearest tower to escape the cold.

"I was in the middle of my supper. Are you hungry?"

"No."

The duke glanced at him. Qerle was staring straight ahead, his expression grim, his lips pressed thin. Aindreas saw no physical sign that the Qirsi had harmed him, but he sensed that the past several days had left their mark on the man.

They entered his chambers, and Aindreas ordered his servants to leave. Returning to his seat at the large table, the duke drained his goblet of wine.

"You're certain?" he asked, refilling the cup and breaking off a piece of bread.

"I have no desire to stay here any longer than I must."

"Fine. Then tell me what happened. What did they say?"

A bitter smile flitted across the Qirsi's face and was gone. "They didn't believe me at first. They threatened to kill me as a traitor, and when I insisted that I was telling them the truth, they sent me away. That night, after the gate closing, two of them came to my home."

The duke was reaching for his wine again, and now he stopped, his hand poised over the table. "Your home? My men told me nothing of this."

Qerle laughed, though harshly. "Your men probably didn't know. The movement has escaped the notice of Eandi nobles for years. It shouldn't surprise you that they can avoid detection by a few of your soldiers."

Aindreas rubbed a hand across his mouth, his brow furrowing. After a moment, though, he nodded, gesturing for the man to continue.

"One of the Qirsi was a shaper, and he threatened to shatter the bones in my daughter's hands unless I told them what really happened. Only then, when I still didn't change my story, did they finally believe me."

The duke searched for something to say, but in the end could only manage a quiet "I'm sorry."

"Why? It's nothing you haven't done. Somehow my children have been dragged into the middle of this foolishness. I can hardly blame the movement for that when your soldiers stand in the street outside my home."

He would have liked to strike this impertinent sorcerer, but instead he grabbed his wine and took a long drink. "What did your leaders have to say once they understood that you were telling them the truth? Are they willing to work with me?"

"Not yet. They want to know more about this alliance you're proposing. How do you intend to help us? Are you offering gold? Arms? If it comes to war, will you commit your army to the Qirsi side, or do you wish to maintain your deception until you're certain that we'll be victorious?"

"I can give you gold if you need it."

"We don't. But we need more than just your word. It's one thing to say that you hate the king and that you want to see him destroyed. But it's quite another to ask us to place faith in you as an ally. To be honest, those I serve don't trust you. To them, you're just another Eandi noble. Perhaps you're a bit more farsighted than the rest. You're clever enough to realize that if you don't make peace with us now, you'll die at our hands when we take the Forelands. But otherwise, there's little difference between you and Kearney or the lords of Thorald and Galdasten." Qerle grinned. "Or even Curgh."

Aindreas sensed that this was leading somewhere, and once again he fought to keep his anger in check. "What is it they want from me?"

"Nothing yet. Or at least next to nothing. I've been told to get a written pledge from you, of your support for our movement. It's to be penned in your own hand and sealed with the sigil of your house. Give it to me tonight, and I'll return tomorrow with an answer for you."

"This is a waste of time!"

"Those I serve disagree. You wish to do everything in secret, which means you make no promises to us. My leaders believe that I'm telling the truth, but they fear that you're lying to me, and thus to them as well. With this pledge, you tie yourself to us. If you fail us, it will find its way to the court of your king, where it will be evidence of your treason and grounds for your execution."

"You ask too much of me. What's to stop you from taking this to the king right away and having me hanged?"

"The movement doesn't want that, and you know it. Kearney is weaker with you alive and leading the dukes who would oppose him. If you were to be exposed as a traitor, it would unite the other houses and strengthen the crown." Qerle shook his head. "No, this would be a last resort and nothing more, a way of ensuring your good faith."

Aindreas could hardly fault the man's logic. Without meaning to, he realized abruptly, he had already been aiding the conspiracy. Perhaps this shouldn't have bothered him in light of what he was contemplating. For a number of reasons, however, many of them obvious, and one far less apparent, he found the very idea of it unsettling.

"I'd be a fool to agree to this," he said, staring at the Qirsi.

Qerle gave a small shrug and stood. "Very well. If you decide otherwise, you know where to find me."

He would have liked to let the Qirsi bastard go. A voice in his head—Ioanna's, or perhaps Brienne's—begged him to. *This was a mistake,* it seemed to say. *Let it end here.* But then he saw it all again, like some twisted dream haunting his sleep night after night. Brienne's blood, Tavis's blade, Kearney drawing his sword on the battle plain near Heneagh in defense of the boy. How could he surrender himself to this king?

Qerle was almost to the door when Aindreas called his name. He turned, a smirk on his pallid features. "My lord?" he said, and there could be no mistaking the irony in his tone.

Muttering a curse, the duke pulled a parchment scroll from a drawer and picked up his writing quill.

"What should it say?"

"That you pledge yourself to our cause and embrace the movement as an ally. Nothing elaborate. We want your meaning to be absolutely clear."

He sat a moment, staring at the blank parchment, wondering if there was a way to word this that would protect him. It didn't take him long to abandon the notion. No matter how carefully he chose his words, any document acceptable to the Qirsi would brand him as a traitor. His signature and the sigil made that certain. It almost didn't matter what he wrote.

"I, Aindreas of Kentigern," he finally wrote, "pledge myself to support the Qirsi movement and offer my allegiance to its leaders."

He signed the scroll, and sealed it in silver-blue wax with the signet of his ancestors. Maybe, he thought, with a message that short, he could claim that he had signed it under duress. He nearly laughed aloud at his foolishness. Once he handed the scroll to Qerle he belonged to them.

"I need something in return before I give this to you," he said, clutching the rolled parchment in his hand.

"We have nothing to offer. You came to the movement, Kentigern. You tortured me and countless others, looking for someone who could win this alliance for you. You have it now. But your cruelty to our people makes us leery of you, and demands that we have some measure of protection."

"And what of my protection?"

"I've already told you—"

"Yes, damn you, I heard!" The duke stood and began to pace his chamber. "I'm more valuable to you in power than in disgrace. Well, that's not good enough. I need something more."

"Like what?"

"A name." He said the words as quickly as he formed the thought. But he knew immediately that he had found the answer, the measure of assurance he needed. "Give me the name of one of your leaders."

"All right."

"All right?" the duke repeated, narrowing his eyes. "You're not going to argue with me, or tell me you need to speak with the men you serve?"

"They anticipated this."

Aindreas stared at the Qirsi, feeling like a dolt. Qerle had been waiting all this time for him to suggest such an exchange, and it had taken the duke their entire conversation to think of it. "So you have a name for me?"

"I do. Enid ja Kovar, first minister to the duke of Thorald."

Tobbar's first minister! His surprise was fleeting, however. He had turned away a rider from Thorald midway through the waxing. In all likelihood these were the tidings he would have read in the horseman's message.

"Not good enough," he said, shaking his head. "Tobbar has already learned of her betrayal. For all I know, she's dead by now."

434

Qerle's eyes widened for just an instant. "That's the only name they gave me."

Aindreas smiled, pleased to have the advantage at last. He returned the scroll to a drawer in his table. "Have them give you another," he said. "Return here tomorrow, and you can have the pledge I just signed."

What little color the Qirsi had in his face vanished. No doubt his superiors would not be pleased. He nodded and stood, stepping to the door.

"Qerle!" he called, stopping the man short of the door. "Tell them that if they try to deceive me again, there will be no alliance, and I'll bring the full weight of my house down upon them. I found you by torturing every Qirsi in that tavern of yours. If I have to, I'll destroy your movement by killing every white-hair in my realm. Make certain they understand that."

"Yes, my lord," the Qirsi said, his voice, at least for now, free of irony.

When the man had gone, Aindreas closed his eyes, rubbing his brow with a cold hand.

"You don't have to do this, Father."

He looked up, seeing Brienne before him. Again. She wore the sapphire gown, her golden hair falling to her waist like the waters of Panya's Falls at sunset.

"I do it for you. I do it to punish those who killed you."

"Are you certain, Father?"

"Who else would I do this for?"

She was so beautiful. More than anything he wanted to reach out and touch her face, her hair.

"I fear you do it for yourself. But I meant, are you certain they are the ones who killed me?"

"Don't!" he pleaded, squeezing his eyes shut.

"Poor Father."

For a long time, he refused to look at her. When at last he opened his eyes again, she was gone.

Qerle returned the following day, again just after sundown. Aindreas had instructed his guards to admit the Qirsi to the castle, so when the knock came at his chamber door, he knew it was Qerle. To his surprise, however, the man was not alone. A young Qirsi woman accompanied him into the room. She was slight and barely as tall as Affery, Aindreas's sole surviving daughter. She had bright golden eyes and wore her white hair loose to her shoulders.

"Who's this?" the duke asked, standing, but remaining behind his desk.

"My name is Jastanne ja Triln," she said in a strong voice. "Qerle says you wanted to meet me."

Aindreas frowned. "That's not quite right. I told him I wanted the name of one of your movement's leaders, as a way of ensuring that you won't betray me."

"I've just given you my name."

"You're a leader of the Qirsi conspiracy?" he asked, making no effort to conceal his doubts. "You look like you're barely old enough for a Fating."

"I'm twenty-four years old, my Lord Duke. That may not be old for an Eandi, but I've lived more than half my life already. For the last four years I've served the Qirsi movement, and for the last two, I've been one of its leaders."

"I'm not certain I believe you. The Qirsi have lied to me too many times."

She gave a wan smile. "It was a mistake to have Qerle give you Enid's name. My mistake. I apologize for that. I took a chance, thinking that you hadn't heard yet of her death. I wanted to give up as little as possible to win your support. I won't try such a thing again."

"Do you live in Kentigern, Jastanne?"

"No. I come here frequently, but my home lies elsewhere."

"Where?"

"I'd rather not say. I'm a merchant, my lord. I spend little time at my home. I have a ship called the *White Erne* that sails the coast of the Forelands from Rawsyn Bay to the Bronze Inlet. If you need to find me, just look for the *Erne*."

"You own a ship," Aindreas said, shaking his head. "I find it hard to imagine so slight a woman braving the Narrows or steering a vessel through a storm in the Scabbard."

"And I find it hard to imagine a man of your size climbing onto a horse, but I know you've done so."

He tipped his head, conceding the point.

"I've come here at considerable risk to myself and my cause, Lord Kentigern. I won't stay long. You told Qerle that you wish to ally yourself with our movement. I believe you said that you want us to help you drive Kearney of Glyndwr from the throne. Is that still your desire?"

Don't do this! Tell her to go and be done with it!

The duke stood and began to pace behind his writing table.

"He gave asylum to Brienne's killer!" he said, as if arguing with the voice in his mind. "How can I do nothing?"

Jastanne grinned. "I take it that means yes."

He blinked, staring at the woman. "Can you offer me proof that you're a leader of the conspiracy?"

"None that would satisfy you. We take great pains to leave as little evidence of our activities as possible. Usually we concern ourselves with proving that we're not with the movement. You have my word, and that of Qerle here. But I have nothing more to give you."

Aindreas weighed this a moment longer, then made his decision. Reaching into the table drawer, he retrieved the scroll he had placed there the night before.

"Here. My pledge to support your cause. As I told Qerle last night, if you betray me, I'll spend my last breath destroying you and your friends. I swear it in the name of my dead daughter."

She took the scroll from him and unrolled it. After a moment, she nodded and handed it to Qerle. "You needn't worry, Lord Kentigern. We have no intention of betraying you. We may not like you any more than you like us, but we understand the value of having you as an ally." She turned to Qerle. "Go now. You know where to take this?"

"Yes, ch—" His face colored and his eyes flicked toward the duke. "Yes, my lady."

"Good. We'll speak later."

Qerle turned and hurried from the chamber, clutching the scroll as if it were made of gold. Propriety dictated that he await leave from Aindreas to go, but the duke made no effort to stop him.

"May I sit?" Jastanne asked, once the man was gone.

"Of course."

She lowered herself into a chair and eyed his wine.

"Would you like some?" he asked, struggling with his impatience.

"Yes, please."

He crossed the room to get a second goblet, poured her wine, and returned to his seat.

"To allies," she said, raising her cup.

He hesitated, then raised his goblet as well.

"Qerle said you expect your court to be spared when the movement takes the Forelands. Is that right?"

"It seems reasonable, doesn't it? Now that we're allies."

The woman gave a thin smile. "That depends on what you bring to the alliance. You've offered only gold, and as Qerle already told you, that's one thing we don't need."

"I can offer arms as well."

She drank her entire cup of wine, then placed the goblet on her palm and held it before her. An instant later it shattered, shards of clay scattering on the floor like frightened vermin.

437

"What use would we have for your arms?"

The duke shuddered. Of course they would send him a shaper. "Then what is it you want of me?"

"Nothing that you haven't contemplated already, Lord Kentigern. It's known throughout the land that you hate your king, and that you've convinced other dukes to join you in opposing him. We ask only that you continue to foment rebellion."

Aindreas began to feel vaguely uneasy, just as he had the night before when Qerle spoke of his opposition to the king. He picked up his goblet, then returned it to the table without taking a sip. "We can't prevail in a civil war. Even with the support of the other houses, my army isn't strong enough to defeat Kearney and his allies."

"Leave that to us," she said. "Those I serve want civil war in Eibithar. Once that war begins, we'll do everything in our power to keep Kearney from defeating you."

Aindreas gripped the edge of the table, as if to steady himself. "But how do I convince the others to start a hopeless war?" he asked dully, his stomach turning to stone.

"I'll leave that to you." She smiled and stood, brushing slivers of clay from her cloak and dress. "We're allies, my lord. We have to learn to trust each other." She sketched a small bow and turned toward the door. "From now on we'll communicate solely through messages," she said over her shoulder. "Address them to my ship and put your seal on the scroll. I'll know they're for me."

She slipped out of the room, closing the door gently behind her.

Aindreas reached for his wine once more, then thought better of it and sat back in his chair, rubbing his eyes with an unsteady hand.

He had no qualms about opposing Kearney or even about waging civil war so long as he had reason to hope that he might prevail. Until he met Jastanne, he had been eager to do whatever was necessary to remove Glyndwr from the Oaken Throne.

Suddenly, though, his certainty had vanished.

Those I serve want civil war in Eibithar. The words repeated themselves in his head like the insipid lyric of a child's song, relentless and unwelcome.

He shouldn't have been surprised. Ean knew he shouldn't have been. For he had heard much the same thing said before, by Javan and by Kearney and by the strange Qirsi man who had saved Tavis of Curgh from Kentigern's dungeon. Before tonight, he had dismissed such claims as the desperate excuses of men who had embraced a killer and turned their backs on truth and honor. But it was another matter entirely to hear the words spoken by a leader of the conspiracy.

From the beginning, the duke had every reason to believe that Tavis had killed his Brienne. The dagger, the blood, the locked door. He had never thought to question his own assumptions. Certainly he had never considered asking Brienne about the murder. More than once he had considered going to the Sanctuary of the Deceiver in Kentigern City on Pitch Night so that he could see her. Ean knew how much he wanted to go, and also how much he feared the encounter. He never made the journey. It was too soon, he told himself each turn. I'm not ready to face her. Even on the Night of Two Moons in Bian's Turn, when his daughter's wraith came to him, Aindreas had been unable to do more than weep at the sight of her. But even had he managed to speak with her, he wouldn't have asked her about that terrible night so many turns ago. Tavis had killed her. He knew this.

Or at least he thought he did. *Are you certain?* she had asked him last night. It wasn't the real Brienne. He knew that of course. His mind wasn't so far gone. But the doubts voiced by this apparition that haunted him echoed his own, particularly now, with what the Qirsi woman had told him.

Those I serve want civil war in Eibithar.

He was bound to the Qirsi now, held fast by chains he had forged himself. He had thought to use them, to harness the power of their conspiracy to rid Eibithar of the demons in Audun's Castle. Now it seemed he was surrounded by demons, and he could find nothing to distinguish one from another.

Chapter
Twenty-nine

✦

Great Forest of Aneira

ith all that had happened in Aneira over the past few turns, Grinsa should have expected that a thick mist and strong wind would not be enough to keep the soldiers of Solkara from pursuing them. "That man is an Eibitharian lord, come to kill our queen!" Shurik had said, pointing an accusing finger at Tavis and calling for the royal guard. At any time, such a claim would have drawn the attention of soldiers and city folk alike, but with the king dead and Grigor's hanging still fresh in the minds of every man and woman in the realm, Shurik's words seemed to awaken all of the Solkaran countryside.

Just an hour after their escape through the south gate of Solkara City, Grinsa and the boy crouched in the shadows of the Great Forest and watched as guards poured from the castle, fanning out in every direction.

"Is that all for us?" Tavis whispered, face grim and eyes wide.

"I'm afraid so. By now Shurik has probably told them who it was he saw. Tavis of Curgh, who murdered Lady Brienne and came to Solkara to do the same to the new queen. He may even have told them that I'm a Weaver."

"They'll kill us both."

The gleaner nodded. "If we give them the chance, yes, I expect they will."

A few moments later, they were on their way again, running through the wood like hunted elk. Grinsa wanted desperately to go north toward Mertesse, where he suspected Shurik would be headed. But with the soldiers following, he didn't dare give away their true intentions so soon.

Instead, he led Tavis to the south and east, toward the Rassor River and the shores of the Scabbard, hoping their pursuers would believe they had a ship awaiting them in one of the inlet's many hidden coves.

For several days they continued in this direction, sleeping in what natural shelter they could find in the forest, and eating Osya's root and what remained of the harvest berries growing along the forest road. They built no fires, and they wasted no time hunting for more substantial fare. Most of the guards sent after them were on foot, and though Grinsa sensed that they were still following, he and Tavis saw no sign of them. On two occasions, however, smaller parties of mounted soldiers nearly found them. Once, two days out from Solkara, they managed to avoid the soldiers by concealing themselves in a dense and uncomfortable copse of holly until the men had passed. The second time, caught in a portion of the wood that was relatively open, Grinsa had no choice but to raise a mist. He coaxed strands of fog from the earth as slowly as he dared, hoping the soldiers would take it for a natural mist rather than an act of magic, but judging from the way the men drew their swords, peering through the fine grey cloud and bare tree limbs, he felt certain that he hadn't fooled them. After a time, Grinsa summoned his power a second time, snapping a large limb from a nearby oak so that it crashed loudly to the ground. To their credit, the horsemen didn't flee, though several of their mounts reared, whinnying nervously. But they did retreat at last, allowing Tavis and Grinsa to hurry away from this section of the wood.

The next morning, the two fugitives turned north and west, away from the Rassor, and toward the center of the forest. Almost immediately, they encountered a large group of soldiers on foot, and only barely managed to evade them. Once again, however, they were forced to turn southward, at least until Grinsa convinced himself that they had put some distance between themselves and the Solkarans.

Two nights later, trudging among the trees by the dim light of the moons, they caught a glimpse of a fire burning a short distance ahead. It was too small to warm more than one man, so Grinsa and Tavis approached, feeling sure that they were not putting themselves in danger. As they drew nearer, Grinsa heard a horse snort, and saw a small trader's cart. A moment later, he saw the trader himself, a diminutive white-haired Eandi with a long nose and sullen face.

"A peddler," he said to Tavis, keeping his voice low. "If we're lucky, we might be able to buy a warm meal and a night's sleep beside a fire."

The gleaner began to sing an old Sanbiri melody his father had taught him as a child. He had a poor singing voice, but he hoped to alert the peddler to their presence in the wood so that their appearance wouldn't startle him.

As it happened, the sound of his voice had the opposite effect on the man. Instantly, he was on his feet, dagger held before him as he stared into the darkness.

"Who's there?" he called.

"Friends," Grinsa answered, smiling as he and Tavis stepped into the firelight.

The old man shook his head and took a step back, fear in his dark eyes. "You're not friends of mine, Qirsi. I know who you are." He waved the blade at Tavis. "He's the Eibitharian who tried to kill the queen."

"I did not!" Tavis said.

Grinsa glared at him. "Be quiet!"

"You'd rather he thought that I tried to kill her?"

The gleaner shook his head and faced the man again. "Who told you this?" he asked.

"That's not your concern, Qirsi! Now leave me, or I'll be forced to use this blade!"

His hand was shaking so violently that Grinsa half expected him to drop the dagger and run. Certainly, he posed no threat to either the gleaner or the boy. Grinsa was more afraid that he would cry out for help, bringing any soldiers who might be nearby.

The Qirsi held up his hands to show that he had no weapon, and took another step toward the fire. "Come now, friend. We both know that you're not going to hurt us with that blade. We mean you no harm. My companion doesn't always know when to keep silent, but he spoke truly when he told you that we made no attempt on your queen, nor do we intend to."

"I don't believe you." His eyes flicked to Tavis and he backed away again.

"You see the scars on the boy's face?" Grinsa asked, beginning to circle the fire slowly. "We're looking for the man who did that. Our search took us to Solkara. He is from Eibithar, but we're not assassins, and we're not your enemies."

"Stay where you are!" the man said in a quavering voice.

But by now, Grinsa was close enough.

"Tell me where you heard that we tried to kill the queen," he commanded again. This time, however, as he spoke the words, he reached out with his magic and touched the man's mind lightly. He didn't like to use mind-bending power. It was by far the most intrusive of all Qirsi powers and in many ways the most dangerous. If he used too heavy a hand, he could impair the man forever. But in this case he felt that he had little choice.

Immediately, the peddler lowered his blade. "It's all over the wood," he said, his voice suddenly calm. "Everyone's speaking of it."

"You mean the soldiers?"

"The soldiers, village folk, everyone. Riders came from the castle to tell us. There isn't a town between here and Kett that will welcome you."

"Is there a bounty as well?"

"None that I've heard."

Grinsa glanced at Tavis. "They probably feel that they don't need one, that hatred of Eibithar will be incentive enough."

"We need to get out of the wood," Tavis said. "We're not safe here."

"We may not be safe anywhere in the kingdom."

"What about Bistari?"

Grinsa weighed this briefly. It was possible that the people of Bistari hated the Solkarans even more than they did Aneira's northern neighbor, but he wasn't certain enough of this to chance turning back to the west.

He looked at the peddler again. He still held the man with his mind, though he was tiring quickly. Magic so precise demanded a good deal of effort.

"What should we do with him?"

"We're not going to harm him," Grinsa said quickly.

Tavis frowned. "I know that. You really think that's what I meant?"

The Qirsi took a breath. "No. Forgive me." He rubbed his brow. "I don't know what we should do with him, but we need to decide quickly. I'm getting weary."

"Can your magic make him forget all of this?"

"Not all of it, no. He'll remember he met someone. I can alter the memory some, though if I try to change it too much I'll . . . I'll injure him."

Tavis appeared to flinch, as if the very idea of it made his head hurt.

"What do you sell?" Grinsa asked the merchant.

"Lots of things. Mostly pipeweed and spices this time of year."

"We'll take some pipeweed and any food you have to spare."

"I need my food."

Grinsa touched his mind again, harder this time, though he hated to do so.

"I can spare a bit of food. Dried meat, maybe some cheese."

"That will be fine." It was nothing short of theft, and it made Grinsa sick to his stomach. But they needed something other than roots and berries if they were to keep ahead of Solkara's soldiers.

The peddler pulled several pouches of dried meat from his cart, along with a small sack of Caerissan pipeweed and two large rounds of hard cheese.

"One will be enough," Grinsa said.

Tavis started to object, but the Qirsi silenced him with a stony look.

He gave the peddler ten qinde—far more than the food and pipeweed were worth, though that did little to assuage his guilt.

"Did the soldiers say where they thought we were going?" he asked the man.

"They said you were headed south, but that they expected you to turn north eventually, to return to Eibithar."

Damn you, Shurik! "Very well," he said, stepping closer to the trader and staring into his eyes. "I'm going to make you sleep now. When you awake, you'll remember nothing of the boy. You sold food and pipeweed to a Qirsi man and woman. They paid you five qinde. Do you understand?"

The old man nodded.

Grinsa led him to a blanket that lay on the ground beside his fire. "Lie down."

The man lowered himself to the ground and Grinsa found a second blanket to cover him.

"Sleep now," the gleaner said.

Immediately the man's eyes closed and his breathing slowed.

"It seems Aneira's new leaders are eager to find us," Tavis said, watching the man sleep.

"Yes. We might be better off heading east to the steppe."

"The steppe? That will take us a hundred leagues out of our way. We won't reach Mertesse for another turn."

Grinsa knew he was right. Truth be told, he didn't want to leave Aneira either. Now that Tavis had finally agreed to go after Shurik, the Qirsi was anxious to reach Mertesse and question the traitorous minister. He wasn't certain what he would do with Shurik after that—perhaps kill him, perhaps return him to Aindreas as a gesture of goodwill. That decision could wait—for now, he was consumed with merely finding the man. Already Tavis was beginning to talk once more of the need to search for the assassin, to avenge Brienne's murder and clear his name. It wouldn't be long before he began to chafe at the idea of going to Mertesse. Grinsa needed to get them there as quickly as possible. Every delay gnawed at him.

He also realized, however, that if they remained in Aneira, they would be taking a grave risk. Tavis needed to understand that. "At least in Caerisse, we can travel without constantly fearing for our lives," he said, eyeing the boy. "I don't know if we can avoid Solkara's soldiers forever."

"Better to try than to go running to the steppe. For all we know, they'll be expecting that. It's far closer than the Tarbin; the Solkarans are probably watching the slope already." He looked up at the gleaner. "Each day that I spend running means one more day in exile. I want to go home, Grinsa. I want to go back to Curgh. And at this point I'd rather fight off the entire Solkaran army than waste another turn seeking refuge on the steppe."

"Actually, I feel the same way, but I wanted to give you the choice."

They started north immediately, putting some distance between themselves and the peddler's camp before stopping for the night. The next morning they resumed their journey, avoiding the forest roads and staying close to the thicker groves of the wood. This slowed their progress, but it kept them far from most of the soldiers, and it allowed them to elude those they did encounter. They followed a meandering course through the wood to further frustrate those pursuing them, but still they reached the southern banks of the Kett only a few days after leaving the peddler. The waters were slow here, though Grinsa couldn't tell how deep the river might be. Not that it mattered. With the air this cold, they would have been fools to ford the waters, especially since he still feared attracting the soldiers' attention with a fire. Yet, he was certain that the Aneirans would be watching all the bridges. In the end, they decided to gather fallen logs and lash them together into a small punt using willow boughs. It took them much of what remained of the day, but they were able to cross the river without freezing or alerting the Aneirans. Once they were across, Grinsa shattered the boat with a thought, rather than leave it for someone to find.

With the Kett behind them, the two travelers continued north, though they began to angle westward once more. At some point they would have to cross the farmlands between the Great Forest and Mertesse, but Grinsa wanted to make certain that they spent as little time as possible in the open.

For a court boy who had enjoyed a comfortable childhood and still desired the comforts of a noble's life, Tavis was a surprisingly good travel companion. He rarely complained of being tired, and had no trouble matching the pace Grinsa set for him. When the gleaner complimented him on this, a few days after they had crossed the river, the boy smiled.

"You should save your praise for Hagan MarCullett."

"Xaver's father?"

"Yes. He's my father's swordmaster, and as many times as he's had me run the towers of Curgh Castle, I ought to have the endurance of an Uul-ranni mount."

They walked a short time in silence, before Tavis glanced at him again.

"What about you?" the boy asked.

"What do you mean?"

"I've always heard that Qirsi are weaker than the Eandi, yet you don't get tired as one might expect. When we rest it's usually for my benefit, not yours."

Grinsa shrugged. "I'm a Weaver."

"So Weavers are stronger than other Qirsi—physically I mean?"

"Usually, yes."

"Is that why my people are so afraid of your kind?"

The gleaner hesitated. Since the night he rescued Tavis from Kentigern's dungeon, with the help of Fotir jal Salene, first minister of Curgh, he and Tavis had rarely spoken of Grinsa's secret. When the boy asked him questions of this sort, he usually gave a terse answer, making it clear that this was not a topic he wished to discuss. Perhaps, though, the time had come to tell Tavis a bit more. They had been traveling together for nearly half a year now, and if the visions Grinsa had of the boy prior to Tavis's Fating proved to be accurate, they would be together for some time to come.

"What do you know about Weavers, Tavis?"

"Not much really. I know that Weavers led the Qirsi invasion of the Forelands, and that after the army of the Southlands was defeated all the Weavers were executed."

"But you don't know why."

"I'd guess it was because you're stronger than the other Qirsi, not only physically, but also in terms of your magic."

"You're right, we are. But that's not why we're feared. That's not why the Eandi have been executing Weavers for the last nine centuries."

"Then why?"

"Have you noticed how many different types of magic I possess?"

"Now that you ask, you do seem to have a lot. You healed me in Kentigern's dungeon, you shattered the guards' swords in Solkara and raised a mist. I've seen you conjure fires, and you made the peddler answer your questions when he didn't want to."

"That's five. I also made Shurik's horse rear in Solkara."

"Language of beasts."

"Yes. And you forgot the fact that I'm a gleaner."

"Seven," Tavis said. "Is that all the Qirsi powers?"

"There's one other. My people call it weaving and divining. It allows us to read the thoughts of other Qirsi, sometimes we can even enter their minds. Only Weavers have it."

"So Weavers wield every kind of Qirsi magic."

"Yes, but there's even more to our powers than that. Because we possess all the magics, and because we can touch the thoughts of other Qirsi, we have the ability to combine the magic of one Qirsi with our own and with that of others."

Tavis stopped walking. "I'm not sure I understand," he said, though judging from what he heard in the boy's voice, Grinsa guessed that he understood all too well.

"Weavers do just what our name implies. We weave together the magic of other Qirsi. A Weaver who leads an army of shapers, for instance, wields the power of all his soldiers as if it were his own. Fotir and I carved a hole in the wall of Kentigern Castle the night you escaped Aindreas's prison. With an army of shapers and a bit of time, I could have reduced the entire castle to rubble. With an army of fire wielders, I could burn this forest to the ground in a matter of days."

Tavis gaped at Grinsa, the expression on his scarred face a mix of awe and abject fear.

"How did the Eandi ever defeat you?" he whispered.

"The easy answer is that the Qirsi army was betrayed by one of its commanders, a man named Carthach. He told the Eandi how the magic of the Weavers worked."

"Why do you say that's the easy answer?"

The gleaner looked away, abruptly thinking of Cresenne, whose hatred of Carthach, and thus all Qirsi who lived in peace with the Eandi, had driven her to the conspiracy. The rifts that still divided his people and now threatened to plunge the Forelands into a maelstrom of murder and war could all be traced back to Carthach's betrayal. Talking about Carthach with other Qirsi was difficult enough. Speaking of the traitor with an Eandi was humiliating, even now, even for Grinsa. He should have known that any discussion of his powers would lead here.

"That's the easy answer, because it's not really true. By all accounts, the Eandi were already beginning to turn the tide of the war before Carthach betrayed the Qirsi army."

"But how could they?"

"Because our powers aren't truly meant for war. Woven properly, we can destroy a castle or burn a forest, or even turn a stampede of wild horses.

But as our power grows, it becomes more difficult to control, even for the most accomplished Weaver. The same shaping magic that can shatter a castle wall is nearly helpless to block a volley of arrows. Your people had begun to realize this and had changed their tactics." He started to walk again, as did Tavis. "We would have been defeated eventually anyway. I believe Carthach did what he did to save Qirsi lives." He glanced at the young lord. "I can say that even though I'm a Weaver, and even though since the time of Carthach's betrayal my kind have been hunted and killed by the Eandi."

"Are there other Weavers in the Forelands?"

"I would expect so," Grinsa said. "I doubt Weavers were ever common, but neither do I think that they were as rare as they seem to be now. Certainly nine hundred years ago there were enough in the Southlands for the Qirsi to send eight with the invading army. They wouldn't have done so had there not been at least that many in the army that remained to protect the Qirsi homeland. And I doubt that all the Weavers were used as generals."

"Then what's happened to them all?"

"What do you think?"

"Were they all killed?"

"Many of them were in the first century after the invasion failed. But one rarely hears of Weavers being killed anymore."

"Then where are they?"

Grinsa smiled, though it felt forced. "There just where I'd still be if I hadn't come to save you."

Tavis's eyes widened. "In the Revel?"

"In the Revel, in the festivals of Sanbira and Caerisse and Aneira, in Eandi courts. They could be anywhere, Tavis. They hide their powers, fearing for their lives and those of their fam—"

He halted suddenly in midstride, weathering a wave of nausea that nearly drove him to his knees. How could he have been so foolish? How could he have forgotten?

"What is it?" Tavis asked, his brow knitted with concern. "Are you ill?"

"How long has it been since we left Solkara?" Grinsa demanded, scouring his mind in his rush to count the days.

"What?"

"The day! What day is it?"

"I'm not certain. With all the walking we've done, I've lost count."

Grinsa closed his eyes. "We fled the city on the last day of the waning," he said more to himself than to the boy. "I haven't noticed the moons the last few nights. Damn!"

"It's been overcast," Tavis said. "The moons have been hidden. But I believe we're close to the Night of Two Moons. We may even be in the next waning already."

Grinsa nodded, exhaling heavily. "I think so, too. Demons and fire!"

"What is it, Grinsa? Why are you suddenly so concerned with the day?"

"I think Shurik knows that I'm a Weaver. Indeed, after what I did to evade capture at the city gates, I'm certain of it. For years I've been claiming to be a gleaner and nothing more, and yet, in the space of just a few moments, I shattered swords and raised a mist and a wind. Shurik is certain to have noticed."

"Yes. But surely you've thought of this before now."

"Of course. Yet, somehow I managed to forget about Keziah. I should have warned her right away."

Tavis still looked confused.

"In the past, it's not only Weavers who have been killed, but also their families. Wives, children, parents, even siblings. Different types of Qirsi magic tend to run in a family. You have your father's eyes and your mother's features. My children may have my powers, and so might Keziah's."

"But you said nothing to Shurik about Keziah. How would he know that she's your sister?"

"There aren't that many Qirsi in the Forelands, Tavis. For every Qirsi in Eibithar, there are ten Eandi, maybe more. No one knows that Keziah is my sister because I haven't given anyone cause to wonder if I have family. But our father was a minister in Eardley. Not a first minister, but a man of some importance. If Shurik believes me a Weaver, it will be a small matter for him to learn everything about my family."

The boy appeared to consider this briefly. "So you need to get a message to the City of Kings," he said at last.

Again the gleaner smiled. He had hidden this from Tavis during the warmer turns, when they fled Kentigern. But with all that he had told the young lord this day, there seemed little sense in preserving this last secret. "Actually, no. I need only wait until nightfall, and then I can speak with her."

"How?" Tavis asked, sounding like he didn't really want to know.

"I wouldn't know how to explain it. It's enough to say that the same power I use to wield her magic also gives me access to her dreams."

The boy paled. "Please tell me this only works with Qirsi."

Grinsa laughed and began to walk again. "It does. I promise."

For a long time they journeyed in silence. The gleaner sensed that Tavis was pondering all he had learned about Weavers and Qirsi magic. At some point the questions would begin again, but for now Grinsa was content to say nothing.

His fears might well have been unfounded. What he had told Tavis was true: if it occurred to Shurik to search for Grinsa's family, it wouldn't take him long to find Kezi. But that seemed unlikely, at least for now. The traitor had been so frightened at seeing Grinsa in Solkara that he had called for Eandi guards to save him. This was not a man who would go out of his way to draw Grinsa's wrath. Still, he owed it to his sister to warn her, and he should have done so days ago.

Late in the day, as the sun dipped low in the western sky, sending golden rays of light through the forest, like slender fingers of the goddess, Grinsa heard voices approaching from the north. Looking back at Tavis, he saw that the young lord already had his dagger in hand, and had slowed, dropping into a crouch. Quickly scanning the wood, the gleaner spied a thick cluster of smaller trees a short distance to the left. Drawing his own blade, Grinsa pointed toward the trees. Tavis nodded, and they made their way to the center of the copse, moving as quickly and quietly as they could. A few moments later, several soldiers came into view, all of them wearing the red and gold of Solkara. They made no effort to keep silent, and they walked in a loose formation, indicating to Grinsa that he and Tavis had strayed close to one of the forest roads.

When the men were well past them, the two travelers resumed their journey, angling slightly to the east again. Obviously they still needed to use caution while in the wood—there would be no fire again this night—but the fact that the men were headed southward, back toward Solkara, gave Grinsa some cause to believe that the worst of their troubles were over. It had been half a turn since they escaped the royal city. No doubt the Solkaran soldiers were beginning to lose interest in the hunt.

They stopped for the night just as darkness enveloped the wood, spreading their sleeping rolls on the forest floor before eating. Enough of the peddler's food remained to provide them with an ample meal, but tomorrow they would be forced to eat roots and berries again, unless they managed to find another trader or chanced a cooking fire.

Tavis had said little since their conversation earlier that day, but finally, after their meal, he cleared his throat awkwardly. His question, though, when it came, surprised the gleaner.

"Why did you save me from Kentigern's prison?"

Grinsa hesitated. "I've told you before. I saw in your gleaning that you had been imprisoned unjustly. I had to do something."

"I remember you saying that, and I believed you at the time. But that was before I knew how much you risked coming for me. If you hadn't done that, you'd still be a gleaner in the Revel. No one would know that you were anything more, and your sister wouldn't be in any danger."

"If I had done nothing, Mertesse would hold Kentigern Castle, and Aindreas and your father would be at war."

"So you saw that in my gleaning as well?"

Grinsa started to answer, then stopped himself. Along with the nature of his magic, Tavis's Fating had been one of the topics of conversation he had managed to avoid during their time together. Even now, he wasn't certain that the young lord was ready for the truth. More to the point, though, it seemed to the gleaner that Tavis had earned the right to make that choice himself. Grinsa had realized some time ago, several turns before Bohdan's Revel reached Curgh this past year, that his fate and Tavis's were tied to each other. Now the two of them were bound by circumstance and need as well; only the gods could say how long they would remain together. But surely the time for secrets had passed.

"I had a vision of your fate long before your gleaning, Tavis. I saw the two of us journeying together throughout the land, and fighting side by side against the conspiracy." He paused, straining to see the boy's face in the shadows. The moons were not yet up, and he could only guess at Tavis's reaction. After a moment, he went on. "What I showed you in the stone was your future, but not your fate."

"You said the same thing to me once before, in the dungeon."

"I remember."

"You wouldn't explain what you meant then, though I asked. Are you ready to now?"

"It's very simple really—it should be clear. You weren't fated to die in that prison, or even to spend very long there, though I'm certain it felt like an eternity at the time. It was your future, but you were destined to win your freedom, to join the fight against the conspiracy and search the land for Brienne's killer."

"None of that would have happened had you not freed me from the dungeon. Isn't it just as possible that what you showed me in the stone was my true fate, and you altered it by coming to Kentigern?"

Grinsa smiled. Here lay the burden of the stone, not only for the gleaner, but also for the child who peered into its depths, hoping to glimpse a promise of glory or joy. He had tried to explain this to Tavis as well, just after the young lord first saw himself in that wretched prison, but Tavis had been beyond reason then, already falling into the black despair that would lead him to raise his blade against Xaver MarCullet.

"Our fate changes all the time, Tavis. Every choice we make, every path we choose to follow, turns us toward a different future. The stone, for all the wisdom we ascribe to it, can only show us our fate at a single moment. More than anything, it serves as a signpost, a marker indicating the direction our lives might take. If we find hope or pleasure in the vision it offers, we make choices that will take us in that direction. If not, then perhaps it can warn us away from decisions that lead to darkness. That's what I hoped would happen when I showed you what I did. I intended your Fating as a warning, and I hoped that it would save you from the misery we both saw in that image. At the time, I had no idea how you would end up in that prison. I knew only that you were innocent, though you would doubt that yourself. Had I known that you were powerless to prevent what happened, I would never have done what I did. Certainly I never intended to cause you or Xaver such pain."

He had long expected that when he and Tavis finally had this conversation, the boy would respond to his revelations with outrage. But once more, Tavis surprised him.

"You altered my Fating to guard your secret," he said, his voice low. "If I had seen us fighting the conspiracy together, I would have known that you were more than a gleaner."

"Yes."

"And then you risked everything to save me."

"After what I'd done, I felt that I had to."

"A lesser man wouldn't have."

"A braver man would have shown you the Fating the stone intended."

Even in the darkness, Grinsa could see the boy shrug. "Maybe. I don't know that much about bravery. But I'm grateful to you just the same."

For several moments neither of them spoke. Tavis lay down on his sleeping roll, wrapping himself in a blanket.

"How soon until you can . . . go to your sister?"

Grinsa looked to the east. White Panya was just appearing above the trees, her pale glow seeping through the wood like a sorcerer's mist. Judging from how late she was rising and how far into her waning she appeared, he guessed that they had to be at least three nights past the Night of Two Moons. Perhaps four. Once again, he cursed himself for his carelessness.

"It will be a while yet, at least until Ilias is up."

Tavis nodded, yawned.

"Sleep, Tavis," Grinsa said, lying down also. "I intend to. I'll wake later and reach for her then."

Again the boy nodded. "Goodnight, gleaner."

In truth, Grinsa didn't expect to sleep at all, but it seemed the day's journey had wearied him. He awoke some time later to the call of a nearby owl. He hadn't slept long—Panya shone directly overhead and red Ilias hung low in the eastern sky—but he felt dazed from his slumber, as if he had drunk too much wine.

Sitting up and taking a drink of water from the skin that lay nearby, he rubbed a hand over his face and blinked his eyes, trying to wake himself up. Tavis stirred and turned over, but he didn't wake.

Grinsa sat for several moments, listening to the owl, and to a second bird that hooted in reply from farther away. At last, he closed his eyes and, drawing upon his magic, sent his mind north and east, across the Moors of Durril and the edge of the steppe, which was covered with fresh snow, to Eibithar's City of Kings. It took him only a few seconds to find her and touch her mind with his power.

He knew instantly that something was wrong. The plain looked as it always did when he went to her, the way it had when they were children living in Eardley. Except that the sky to the west was black, as if from a great storm, and a brilliant light shone at the center of the gloom. Grinsa thought he saw someone standing at the edge of the darkness, or more precisely, on the seam between the light he had brought to her dream and the storm he had found there. Keziah. It had to be. He started walking toward her.

The distance to her turned out to be greater than he had thought at first, but soon he could see her white hair twisting in the wind, and he recognized the sleeping gown she was wearing. Grinsa called to her several times, but she didn't answer. She didn't even turn to face him. His apprehension mounting by the moment, the gleaner hurried on until he was running toward her.

As he drew nearer, Grinsa began to hear voices, as if Kezi was speaking to someone else. He slowed, trying to make out what they were saying. Had he come to her in the middle of one of her own dreams? Such a thing had never happened before, but he couldn't say for certain that it was impossible. Or was he the one dreaming? His mind had been fogged with sleep—perhaps he hadn't really awakened at all and he was imagining all of this.

The gleaner shook his head. He could feel the magic flowing through his body and mind—this was no dream. And sensing Keziah's thoughts as he approached her, he understood that though she slept, the vision before her was as real as any he had offered her in the past. She was terrified, not only of what she saw in the darkness, but also of Grinsa. He could almost hear her screaming for him to leave. But all he could do was step closer. He moved slowly now, as if stalking game, and he strained his ears to hear her conversation.

". . . Others before you have fought me as well," he heard a voice say. A man's voice, deep and laden with power. "They suffered for their defiance. Is that what you want?"

"No," Keziah answered, sounding desperate. "I don't mean to defy you. But I've never had someone ask this of me before. I don't know what to do."

"Merely open yourself to me."

"I'm afraid. You have to give me a bit of time."

Something in her voice told Grinsa that she was speaking not to this other man, but to him.

"Kezi?" he whispered.

"There is no time. You received your gold, didn't you?"

"Yes, my lord."

"Call me Weaver. I'm not some dull-witted Eandi noble, and I won't be addressed as such."

"Yes, Weaver. Forgive me."

A Weaver! Abruptly it all made sense to him. Not just the strange appearance of the sky and plain, but also the man's mention of gold. He had often wondered who he would find at the head of the conspiracy. A powerful minister perhaps, or a wealthy Qirsi merchant. That this person should also be a Weaver shouldn't have surprised him. Who else could wield the power necessary to overthrow the courts of the Forelands? Who else could guide a movement that sprawled across so many kingdoms? What puzzled him, though, was the man's presence in Kezi's mind. Why would the leader of the conspiracy be speaking to her of gold?

"You have your payment," the man was saying. "Now it is time for you to give yourself to me and this movement."

"But—"

"*Enough!*" the Weaver roared.

An instant later, Keziah cried out, her hands flying to her face. Somehow Grinsa felt it, too. A great pressure on his eyes, as if the man was pressing his fingers into her skull.

"Give yourself to me!"

She whimpered, dropping to her knees.

"Kezi!"

"What was that?" the Weaver demanded, the pressure on Grinsa's eyes ending as suddenly as it had begun.

He wanted to remain there, to learn more about this man, and to repay him for the pain he had caused Keziah. He wanted to yell to her, to rouse her from her sleep. The conspiracy had to be stopped, but she risked too much by seeking out its leader alone.

All Grinsa could do, however, was leave her. As long as he remained he imperiled Keziah and himself. He heard them speaking again, but he didn't wait to hear any more. He merely whispered, "I love you," the words as soft as a planting breeze. Then, dread in his heart, he forced himself to leave her.

Opening his eyes, he felt the earth heave and spin. Even sitting, he nearly lost his balance.

"Are you all right?"

He squeezed his eyes shut briefly, then looked up at Tavis. "I will be," he said, his voice ragged.

"I heard you call your sister's name. You sounded scared."

Grinsa nodded, feeling a tear on his cheek. "I am."

The boy just stared at him, waiting.

"She was with another Weaver."

"What?"

"I think he must lead the conspiracy."

"Why would she be with such a man?"

Grinsa shrugged, though he knew the answer. She had always been too brave. He was the Weaver, the one who wielded unfathomable power. But Keziah had always been the warrior, fighting battles from which others shied. "She must think that she can learn something of him," he said at last. "By joining his movement, she seeks the means to destroy it."

For a long time, Tavis didn't reply. Finally, staring up at the red moon, he said, "That's either the most courageous thing I've ever heard, or the most foolhardy."

Grinsa could only shake his head. The boy often made such statements. Utterly unfeeling, and so honest as to leave no room for argument.

Chapter
Thirty

✦

City of Kings, Eibithar

o one doubted that the threat of a new war with Aneira loomed like a storm cloud over all Eibithar, and like the king's other ministers, Wenda had heard rumors of Braedon's naval activity at the north end of the Scabbard. Kearney would have been remiss had he not taken these threats seriously. Yet it struck her as a measure of how alarmed he was that the king would arrange a meeting between the dukes of Rouvin in Caerisse and Grinnyd in Wethyrn on such short notice and in the middle of the snows. Aylyn the Second, the old king, whom she served for fourteen years, would have issued invitations to the two men only after a good deal of discussion and planning.

This was not to say that she disapproved of Kearney's decision. On the contrary—she admired his boldness. But once more she could not help but notice the vast difference between the two kings she had served. Some of it sprang from Kearney's youth, the rest from contrasts in their natures. Regardless of the cause, however, Wenda still found herself questioning whether she was suited to serving this new king.

Under the best of circumstances, a meeting between the two dukes would have presented great challenges to their host. Caerisse and Wethyrn had long been enemies. Over the course of their history, the two lands had fought several major wars and dozens of smaller skirmishes. Their most recent conflict, the so-called Queen's War, had ended just over a century before and had led to an uneasy peace along Orlagh's River, the border between the two realms. Though both had strong ties to Eibithar, this had never been enough to overcome their mutual hostility, which was rooted in an ancient dispute over a narrow strip of land now held by Caerisse.

Kearney would need both as allies if there was to be war with Braedon and Aneira. Neither Wethyrn nor Caerisse was considered a major power in the Forelands. Caerisse had been great once, but it had been supplanted long ago by Eibithar, Sanbira, Aneira, and, of course, the Braedon Empire. But the Caerissan army would be of great importance in the event of a land war along the Tarbin, and Wethyrn's navy, while small, still enjoyed a well-deserved reputation as the finest among the six, second only to Braedon's in all the Forelands.

The dukes of both Rouvin and Grinnyd, though not of their realms' royal families, wielded great influence with the men who led the kingdoms. If Kearney could convince them that it was in the interests of Caerisse and Wethyrn to put aside their differences and form an alliance with Eibithar, they in turn, might convince their leaders.

Unfortunately, Kearney's already formidable task had been greatly complicated by recent events here in Audun's Castle. One needed only to look as far as the seating for this night's welcoming feast in the castle's great hall to perceive the depth of the king's troubles. Wenda, who would normally have been seated at a lesser table with the rest of the king's underministers, had been placed instead at the table of honor, just next to the archminister.

Perhaps it shouldn't have come as a surprise to her. Like the other ministers, Wenda had watched as the resentment and mistrust between Keziah and the king deepened. She even thought that she understood. There had been rumors about the two of them almost from the moment they arrived in the City of Kings. They had been lovers in Glyndwr, these stories said, bound by a passion so great that they defied the law of the land and risked the honor of Kearney's house for a forbidden love. Though Wenda disapproved of such scandalous talk, particularly where it concerned the king, she could not help but believe all that she had heard. It explained so much—not only the bitterness of their estrangement, but also the awkwardness that had come before.

Still, recognizing the source of this rift between Keziah and the king did not make her any less fearful of what it could mean for Eibithar. In recent days, Wenda had begun to find fault with much of the counsel Keziah offered the king. It almost seemed that the archminister wanted him to make bad decisions. On those few occasions when her advice made sense, Kearney ignored her, as if he no longer trusted anything she said. It would have been best for all concerned had he just ordered Keziah to leave his court—her service to him had all but ended anyway. Keeping her here benefited no one.

But Wenda sensed that Kearney was incapable of sending her away. Perhaps he still loved her, or perhaps his sense of loyalty for the years she had served him in Glyndwr prevented it. Whatever the reason, her continued presence in the castle endangered the king and all who served him faithfully.

The high minister had never liked Keziah—she and the other ministers had resented Kearney's decision to make her archminister, passing over Dyre and Paegar and Wenda herself, all of whom had served in Audun's Castle for years. Indeed, in some small way, their hostility to her might have contributed to her unhappiness. But though Wenda didn't care for the woman, she hadn't thought to question Keziah's loyalty, at least until now. With word of the Qirsi conspiracy spreading through the Forelands like smoke from a grass fire, it was both foolish and dangerous to allow this woman to work each day beside Eibithar's king. If the conspiracy's leaders hadn't already lured her into their movement, they would soon. It should have been clear to all of them. Certainly Gershon Trasker should have seen it. As swordmaster and leader of the King's Guard, he was responsible for Kearney's safety. Yet he did nothing.

The king's answer was to treat Wenda as a second archminister. He turned to her now as he once did to Keziah, asking for her counsel on all matters before anyone else's, and having her draft messages to his dukes and lesser nobles. She had never imagined that he would go so far as to seat her at the table of honor, but she should have known better. He couldn't rid himself of Keziah, but he couldn't trust her either.

"It's been many years since I last visited your castle," the duke of Grinnyd said, smiling briefly at Wenda before looking past her to the archminister. "I had forgotten how magnificent it is."

A brief, thin smile flitted across Keziah's face and was gone.

"Yes," she said. "I suppose it is."

The man cleared his throat and smoothed his black beard with a meaty hand before trying again. "Can you tell me what the banners signify? I know they must be for Eibithar's twelve houses, but which seal belongs to which house?"

He was still looking at Keziah, who was younger than Wenda, and far prettier, but the archminister merely sat there looking bored. After a moment, Wenda answered him, giving the history of each banner and naming the current dukes of the various houses.

"Curgh," the duke repeated, interrupting her as she started to speak of the great bear on Curgh's sigil. "That's where the boy is from, isn't it? The one who is said to have killed Kentigern's daughter?"

459

"Yes, it is," Wenda answered. "Though His Majesty believes the boy innocent and granted him asylum after his escape from Kentigern's dungeon."

"I had heard of this as well. That took a great deal of courage. Did your king think of this on his own, or did you counsel him to grant the boy protection?"

Wenda hesitated. "Actually, he was still duke of Glyndwr at the time and I still served Aylyn the Second, though he was quite ill."

"I advised him to do it," Keziah said. She took a drink of wine, then faced the duke. "It may have been the last counsel I gave him to which he paid any heed at all."

Grinnyd raised an eyebrow. "If one of my Qirsi spoke as you do, Archminister, I'd soon find myself questioning her loyalty."

"I'm not surprised, Lord Grinnyd. It's been my experience that Eandi nobles are often quick to do so."

"That's enough, Archminister!" Wenda said. She faced the duke, though not before casting a beseeching look at the swordmaster. "You must forgive the archminister, my Lord Grinnyd. She sometimes expresses her opinions too freely. I assure you, she meant no offense."

Wenda expected Keziah to berate her for presuming to apologize on her behalf, but instead the woman just raised her goblet to her lips once more, as if nothing had happened. The duke stared at the food sitting before him, his jaw tight.

A moment later Gershon joined them, a look of concern in his blue eyes.

"I hope you're enjoying your meal, my Lord Duke. There's an old saying in Eibithar, 'An empty stomach is a poor foundation for statecraft.'"

Grinnyd smiled, though clearly it took an effort. "The food is excellent, swordmaster. Thank you."

"I take it the ministers are good company."

"Perhaps 'interesting company' would be a more appropriate way of phrasing it."

"I see," Gershon said, frowning at Keziah.

The archminister glanced up at him, the same indifferent expression on her oval face. "You needn't worry, swordmaster. The high minister has already apologized for me."

"It troubles me that either of you had to apologize. I shouldn't have to remind you that the duke is a guest of our king."

"Of course, swordmaster," she said, sounding too obsequious. "I'll be certain to keep that in mind."

"I should hope so."

"You have my apologies as well, my Lord Duke," she said, lifting her cup again. "As the high minister said, I meant no offense."

"Thank you, Archminister." The duke smiled again, and this time it appeared genuine. "As long as you're here, swordmaster, perhaps you and the archminister can tell me something of your king. I never knew him when he was duke of Glyndwr, although I met his father once. If I'm to recommend to my archduke that we strengthen our alliance with Eibithar, I should first know something of the man who leads her."

"Then I suggest you speak with him yourself, my Lord Duke, though I'm happy to answer any of your questions. You'll find that Kearney of Glyndwr is a man without pretense. There's no trick to knowing him."

"High praise indeed for an Eandi noble," Keziah added. "Wouldn't you agree, Lord Grinnyd?"

"It seems high praise for any man, Archminister. Qirsi or Eandi. In these times especially, we're all desperate for people we can trust, no matter the color of their eyes."

"Well said, my Lord Duke," Gershon said pointedly, eyeing the archminister.

Before Keziah could answer, the king stood, raising his goblet in a toast, his silver hair shining in the torch fire and candlelight. "Once again, Leilia and I would like to welcome our guests and thank them for undertaking such arduous journeys, particularly at this time of the year. For centuries Eibithar has valued our close ties to both Caerisse and Wethyrn. I'm hopeful that in the days to come, we can use those ties as the basis for an even stronger partnership among all three of our kingdoms. I speak not of an alliance for war—though we must be able to rely upon one another if we find ourselves embattled—but rather of a union that will give us the strength to preserve peace throughout the Forelands no matter how we are assailed.

"Nine centuries ago, when invaders came to the Forelands, the ancient clans put aside their differences and joined forces to protect themselves and preserve their sovereignty. Out of their triumph grew the seven realms of the Forelands, and all that we have accomplished since."

He was speaking of the Qirsi Wars, of course, and though Wenda thought Aneira and Braedon greater threats to Eibithar than the Qirsi conspiracy, she could hardly blame the king for drawing on that chapter in the kingdom's history. She stole a glance at Keziah, wondering if the king's words would enrage her. But while the archminister looked wan and young as she watched the king, her expression revealed nothing.

"We have endured wars since," Kearney went on, "and times of darkness. But always we have prevailed, and through the centuries one truth has stood out above all others: never are we stronger than when we are united and at peace." He lifted his glass high and looked first at Rouvin and then at Grinnyd. "My Lord Dukes, I drink to friendships, old and new."

"To friendships!" the others in the hall echoed.

"We have more food and wine," the king said, smiling as he placed his goblet on the table. "And we have music to dance. I hope all will join us."

He nodded to the musicians standing near his table on the dais and they began to play. Then he took Leilia's hand and led her down the small stairway to the open floor just in front of his table. For a few moments, as was appropriate, others in the hall simply watched the king dance with his queen. Then, slowly, couples joined them on the floor.

"He does seem a fine king, swordmaster," the duke of Grinnyd said, regarding Kearney. "One cannot help but be impressed with him."

"He's been that way since I met him, my lord, and that was many years before he became duke of Glyndwr."

Grinnyd nodded. "You expect that he'll survive Kentigern's challenge?"

Wenda sensed Gershon bristling.

"I do," the swordmaster said, steel in his voice.

The duke turned to him. "Forgive the question, swordmaster. But before I ask my archduke to swear himself to an alliance with this man I must know that he'll still wear the crown a year from now. Wethyrn places great value on its ties to Eibithar. I daresay we rely on Eibithar's friendship more than you do on ours, even now. If we pledge ourselves to your king, only to find in a few turns that his place on the throne has been taken by a man who despises him, where will that leave Wethyrn?" His eyes strayed briefly to Keziah. "As formidable as Kearney may be, I see many perils in his path, some distant, and some quite near. We'll be watching to see how he navigates them." The duke smiled and faced Wenda. "High Minister, I find myself drawn to this music. Would you join me in a dance?"

Wenda returned his smile. She wasn't fond of dancing, but she could hardly refuse an invitation from one of the king's guests. "Of course, my Lord Grinnyd. It would be an honor."

The duke rose, pulling out Wenda's chair and taking the minister's hand when she stood. She didn't look back at Keziah and Gershon, but she felt their eyes following her as she left them alone together. She would have given all the gold Kearney paid her to be a mouse under the table during the conversation they were about to have.

She couldn't take her eyes off of them, though Qirsar knew she wanted to. It seemed that everyone in this shining hall was staring at the king and queen, though Keziah was certain that the sight of them dancing didn't do to others what it did to her. Kearney looked as he always did, wearing his usual battle garb, the Glyndwr baldric—silver, red, and black—strapped to his back. The silver in his hair and the youthfulness of his face made him appear ageless and regal, as a true king should. Leilia, on the other hand, looked even older and sadder than usual. Keziah had expected that the end of her affair with Kearney would give new life to the queen, but clearly it hadn't. Perhaps she realized now that Keziah hadn't destroyed their marriage or stopped Kearney from loving her; she had done all of that herself.

"What did you say to the duke?" Gershon asked in a low voice, his eyes on the king as well.

"Not much, really. I complained about Kearney not following my counsel and remarked that Eandi nobles were quick to question the loyalty of their Qirsi. Other than that I said nothing offensive, though I'm sure I proved a rather poor dinner companion."

"Do you think you might be taking this too far?"

"They've given me gold, but I've heard nothing from them since," she said. "This isn't a time to temper my behavior."

"Nor is it a time to get yourself banished from the king's court. You heard Grinnyd. He thinks that you're a threat to the king, and he won't hesitate to say so to Kearney."

"I know. To be honest, I don't know if I can stop myself anymore. I don't plan any of the things I say. They just come to me. It's almost as if I've actually started to believe them."

She knew that Gershon was staring at her, but she couldn't tear her gaze from the king.

"Are you a threat to the king?"

Keziah managed a small smile. "No, it's not that bad."

"Not yet."

At that she did look at him. "I'll do nothing to harm him or the kingdom. You have my word." Her eyes drifted to Kearney again. "I'm more a danger to myself than to anyone else."

She sensed him frowning. "What does that mean?" he asked.

"I don't know. Nothing." She closed her eyes. "Have I stayed long enough yet? I don't know how much more of this I can take."

"Yes, you can go. The way you've been lately, you're likely to draw more attention remaining to the end than leaving early."

"Do we need to have words first?"

"You've done enough tonight. I think a simple 'goodnight' will do it. Just make it convincing."

"That doesn't seem to be a problem. Be well, Gershon. We'll speak again soon."

He nodded, saying nothing.

Keziah stood abruptly, draining her goblet and setting it on the table smartly. "Goodnight, swordmaster," she said, her tone heavy with sarcasm. She turned and strode from the great hall, certain that most of those who remained were staring after her.

She returned directly to her chamber, only allowing the scowl to leave her face when she had closed and locked the door behind her. Crossing to her bed, she lay down and, as she had every night for the last half turn, began to cry, muffling her sobs with her pillow. She had thought that this deception would become easier with time, but it hadn't. Just the opposite was true. Every day that drove her further from Kearney brought new, deeper grief, until she began to fear for her sanity. She missed Paegar almost as much as she did her brother, though she knew that had it not been for the minister's treachery, she would never have found herself in these circumstances.

After a time, when she was too weary even to cry anymore, Keziah forced herself up, splashed some cold water on her face, and put on her sleeping gown. The fire in her hearth had burned down, and she added two logs before climbing back into bed.

She must have fallen asleep instantly, for it seemed the next moment she was dreaming.

She stood on a plain, a cold wind cutting through her sleeping gown and making her hair dance. Tall grasses bowed like novices in a sanctuary and hulking boulders loomed like great grey beasts in some child's tale. There was something both familiar and alien about the scene and for a moment she wondered if her brother had come to speak with her. Except that this wasn't the moor near Eardley, and in all the visions Grinsa created for her, there had been daylight. It was night here on this plain.

Or so she thought. Looking up at the blackened sky, straining her eyes to see something, she realized that there was nothing. No stars, no moons, no clouds. Just darkness, as absolute as death.

Keziah shivered. And in that instant, she heard a single word spoken. "Come." It brushed past her like the feathered seed of a harvest flower riding the wind. Before she understood what she was doing, she had turned and started walking toward the sound.

Confused and frightened, her arms crossed over her chest against the chill wind, she opened her mouth to call out Grinsa's name. At the last minute, though, she stopped herself, not quite understanding why.

Soon she was climbing a gentle slope. She had heard nothing more, but she knew this was the way, and even as the climb grew more difficult, she didn't stray. After some time, the ground became level again and she stopped, breathing hard.

The light that stabbed suddenly into her eyes made her cry out and cower, as if Bian the Deceiver had revealed himself to her. She didn't realize that she had dropped to her knees until the voice spoke again.

"Rise." His voice was deep, powerful, as she imagined a god's might sound.

Keziah stood slowly and, still shielding her eyes with a hand, tried to see who had come. A figure stood before her, tall and imposing, as black as the sky against that brilliant white glare. Wild hair twisted about his shoulders in the wind, and a long cape stirred like pine boughs.

"You believe you're dreaming," he said.

"Aren't I?"

"People often think so the first time they encounter a Weaver this way. You are asleep, but this is not dreaming as you know it."

Precisely because this wasn't her first encounter with a Weaver, Keziah knew immediately that he was telling the truth. She felt a fool for not anticipating this. Of course the conspiracy would be led by a Weaver, perhaps several.

"Do you believe me?"

"Yes."

"I sense no surprise on your part. You expected this?"

"No, I—"

"Then what?"

"This isn't the first time a Weaver has entered my dreams. My father was a Weaver. He spoke to me this way many times." The lie came to her easily. She'd been lying about so many things for so long—Grinsa, her affair with Kearney, and, most recently, her feigned resentment of the king and all the Eandi. At this point, she felt as comfortable with deceit as she did with the truth.

"Your father was an underminister for the House of Eardley."

She swallowed. How much more did he know about her?

"Yes. He never told anyone but my mother and me about the true extent of his powers."

Keziah held her breath, terrified that he would ask about her brother.

"I see. This pleases me. You bear a Weaver's blood and so your children might be Weavers."

She had thought of this many times. Even though neither of her parents had been Weavers, Grinsa's powers made it clear that there was Weaver's blood in her veins.

"Yes, they might."

"And you must also know that if they have the gift, and if their true powers are discovered, they will be killed and you with them."

Keziah nodded.

"Do you know why I've come to you?"

Before she could answer, she felt a strange sensation, as if she were being distracted by another sound, though there was nothing here but the wind and the Weaver. An instant later her head began to spin, and she nearly fell to the ground again.

"Well?" the Weaver said. "Do you?"

At first she thought the Weaver was doing this to her, and she tried to guard herself, as if from an assault. Then she heard another voice calling her name, as distant and soft as a whisper, but insistent and drawing nearer. Grinsa.

"The movement," she managed to say. "You lead the movement."

"That's right."

She sensed a light behind her, and though she didn't dare turn to look, she guessed that Grinsa had added his landscape to her dream. The Weaver didn't appear to notice—she couldn't imagine why, but she thanked the gods for her good fortune.

"Do you know how I found you?" the Weaver asked.

"Paegar. He told you about me."

"Yes, he did. He said that you were once in love with your king. Is that true?"

She considered lying again. At that moment she would have said nearly anything to end this dream before the Weaver learned of Grinsa and of all she had done to convince the movement that she could be turned against Kearney. But she had sacrificed too much to lure the man here. She could hardly drive him away now.

"Yes, it's true. I loved him, and he cast me from his bed as soon as they gave him the crown."

"You hate him."

Keziah hesitated. Even here, speaking with this man, she couldn't bring herself to say the words.

"It's all right," the Weaver said gently. "Perhaps it's too much to ask you to hate him already. But you long to strike back at him."

She heard Grinsa approaching and in her mind she shouted for him to leave her, to return another night. But he couldn't hear her any more than could the man standing before her.

"I do."

"I can help you," the Weaver said. "I can make you part of a great movement that will rid the Forelands of your foolish king and others like him. Already, throughout the seven realms, Qirsi like you are rising up against the Eandi courts. You can join us. You can punish the Glyndwr king for what he did to you, and assure your children of a glorious future." He took a step toward her. "All you must do is pledge yourself to my service and open your mind to me, fully, without reservation."

She faltered. How could she do such a thing without revealing too much?

"You resist," he said, his voice harder. "Why?"

Keziah sensed that Grinsa was close and she had to fight an urge to whirl on him and yell for him to leave her.

"I can't do this. Not yet."

"I have revealed myself to you, because you have made it clear with your actions and your words that you no longer wish to debase yourself in service of the Eandi. You have been chosen and you must join me now."

She felt his magic buffeting her mind and she struggled to hold him off, fearing that her defenses would fail her at any moment.

"Others before you have fought me as well," he said. "They suffered for their defiance. Is that what you want?"

"No," Keziah answered, her voice quavering. "I don't mean to defy you. But I've never had someone ask this of me before. I don't know what to do." This last, she intended for Grinsa. Surely he could hear the Weaver now. Couldn't he see that he had to leave her?

"Merely open yourself to me," the Weaver said.

"I'm afraid. You have to give me a bit of time."

"Kezi?" Grinsa whispered, as if standing just beside her.

Go! Please! I can't hold him off much longer!

"There is no time. You received your gold, didn't you?"

"Yes, my lord."

"Call me Weaver. I'm not some dull-witted Eandi noble, and I won't be addressed as such."

"Yes, Weaver. Forgive me."

"You have your payment," he said again. "Now it is time for you to give yourself to me and this movement."

"But—"

"Enough!"

Pain exploded in her mind, blinding, searing. He was crushing her eyes, though she hadn't seen him take a step toward her. She threw up her hands, trying to shield herself. She tried to draw upon her magic, but no power she possessed could protect her from a Weaver.

"Give yourself to me!"

Helpless, lost, she collapsed to the ground, writhing in agony.

She heard Grinsa cry out her name and abruptly, the pain ceased.

"What was that?"

Keziah managed to open her eyes, though for several moments she could see nothing at all.

"What, Weaver?" she said, her voice barely carrying over the sound of the wind.

"I heard a voice cry out. I think it spoke your name."

He was looking about, as if expecting to see someone step out of the darkness.

"I cried out, Weaver. But I heard nothing else."

"No, it sounded . . ." He stopped, shaking his head.

Keziah still felt Grinsa standing nearby, and now she heard him whisper again.

"I love you," he said, and then was gone.

She choked back a sob.

The Weaver faced her once more, his features still shrouded in shadow. "Stand up."

The archminister stood slowly, her legs trembling so violently that she barely trusted them to support her. Even with Grinsa gone, she realized that she could not open herself to the Weaver. She needed to conceal too much from him—her reasons for seeking out the conspiracy, her real feelings for Kearney, Grinsa's powers. Standing on that darkened plain, facing for the first time a man who might have been stronger than her brother, it seemed to Keziah that her entire life consisted of secrets that had to be guarded. She had never given a thought to what a Weaver might do to her through her dreams. There had been times in her dreams of Grinsa when he had put his arms around her, or kissed her brow, and she had felt all of it. It never occurred to her that he could hurt her as well. Why would it? But having felt the Weaver's wrath, she didn't doubt for a moment that he could truly maim her, perhaps even kill her. She thought abruptly of Paegar and shuddered. Had he angered the Weaver? Was that why he was dead?

"Are you ready to open your mind to me now?" the man demanded.

"I can't," she whispered, flinching at the mere thought that he might hurt her again.

"You know now what I can do to you."

"Yes, Weaver."

"Yet still you resist. Tell me why."

"I don't trust you." Even keeping herself closed to him, she sensed that lying to him again might be dangerous. So she sought refuge in those truths she could chance. "I'm archminister to the king of Eibithar. You may want me to join your cause, or you may wish only to learn from me what you can and then kill me. As you say, I know now what you can do to me. If anything I fear you more than I did before."

"I can kill you where you stand," he said, his voice like a drawn sword. "Yet I don't. Doesn't that tell you something?"

"It says only that you need something from me. I can't be certain what it is."

They stood in silence for several moments, Keziah staring at the black space where the Weaver's face should have been. She felt his eyes upon her, but she couldn't begin to guess at what he was thinking. She could only steel herself to endure more pain and hope that she could withstand another assault.

When he spoke again, he surprised her, as much with his words as the gentle tone of his voice. "I can see why Paegar loved you."

Her face grew hot.

"You do know that he did."

"Yes, Weaver."

"But you still loved your king."

She nodded, feeling fear rising in her throat. Had he found some way to read her thoughts without her consent?

"Those whom I hurt as I did you usually relent before I have to resort to pain a second time. That you continue to resist speaks well of your courage if not your sense."

469

"Thank you, Weaver."

"While I wouldn't go so far as to say that I need you, I will admit that winning the loyalties of Eibithar's archminister would be a great boon for the Qirsi movement. For that reason, I'll give you time to reconsider your decision to refuse me. I'll come to you again a few nights hence, at which point you will open yourself to me or die. I'm afraid there are no other choices. I have given you gold and I have revealed myself to you. Even granting you this small grace, I risk all. But I'm hopeful that with such a gesture I can convince you to trust me."

Keziah nearly laughed aloud. *You're threatening to kill me,* she wanted to say. *And this is supposed to make me trust you?*

Instead she lowered her gaze and said, "Thank you, Weaver."

He nodded once. "We'll speak again soon."

Keziah opened her eyes to find herself lying in bed, her sleeping gown, bed linens, and hair soaked with sweat. She sat up and felt her room lurch, as if from an earth tremor. For several moments she held herself utterly still, gritting her teeth against the bile rising from her gut. Then, surrendering, she rushed across her room to her chamber pot and vomited until her stomach was empty and her throat ached.

She washed her mouth and face with frigid water and sank to the hard floor, tears coursing down her face again.

More than anything, she wanted to go to Kearney, to confess all and seek comfort in the warmth of his arms. The king couldn't protect her, of course. Not from this enemy. Neither could Gershon, though she knew that she should go to the swordmaster and tell him of the Weaver. Keziah had felt the power of the man's magic—there wasn't an Eandi noble in all the Forelands who could stand against him. Few Qirsi could either. Certainly she couldn't save herself.

In her foolishness and her arrogance she had thought to defeat the conspiracy on her own. She felt like a general who leads an army to battle, only to find himself overwhelmed by the strength of his foe. True, there weren't thousands of lives to be lost here, at least not yet. There were only two. Her own and Grinsa's. But it might as well have been all the soldiers of the seven realms. For she was certain that if anyone could defeat this Weaver, it was her brother. And she feared that before long, the Weaver would know this as well.

Chapter
Thirty-one

✛

Mertesse, Aneira

heir first few days in Mertesse had been no better than their conflict-ridden journey north from Dantrielle. Despite the understanding Dario thought they had reached during the night they spent at the inn just outside the northern city, Cadel remained a difficult business partner, finding fault with nearly everything Dario did, not only musically, but also with respect to their other profession.

The lutenist thought he understood the cause of Cadel's dark moods. They still had not learned the name of the Qirsi they were to kill, they knew nothing of his powers, and they couldn't even be certain that he intended to return to Mertesse with the duke's company. Dario could not deny being on edge as well, and he wasn't the one who would have to kill the sorcerer when the time came. This had to be far worse for Cadel. Still, that didn't excuse the man for treating him this way. Young as he was, Dario was no child. There wasn't a lutenist north of Noltierre who could play with him, and while he might not have been killing for hire as long as Cadel or for as much gold, he knew how to use a blade and defend himself in a fight. Hearing how the singer picked at him, one might think that he was still apprenticing.

They did manage to get a job playing in the west quarter of the city, just a short distance from the marketplace. The tavern, called the Swallow's Nest, bore a disturbing resemblance to Dantrielle's Red Boar, though the clientele seemed a bit more respectable. They were paid six qinde for each night they played and given a room and all their food for free. They had to pay for their ales, but neither of them drank much. All in all, the

471

arrangement suited them well. It was a job, and getting it should have pleased Cadel.

Instead, it just made matters worse. Now that they had committed themselves to nightly performances, he grew even more critical of Dario's playing, until the lutenist began to wonder if any amount of gold could justify remaining with the man.

Cadel's mood finally changed for the better on the Night of Two Moons, though Dario couldn't really say why. The duke's company had not yet returned, and though their performance of *The Paean to the Moons* went quite well that night, the crowd was no better than any other.

When they returned to their room late that night, Dario asked Cadel why he seemed so pleased. The singer merely smiled mysteriously and said, "The wisdom of the moons, boy. At times the legends are worth more to men like us than Uulranni blades."

No doubt Dario should have tried to think through what the man meant, but he was so angry at being called "boy" that he barely heard the rest of what Cadel said.

Four days later, the duke finally returned to Mertesse. Few saw him enter the city. Coming north from Solkara, he entered the castle through the south gate, without passing through the city's marketplace. Word of his return spread quickly, however, as did rumors of the grave condition of his first minister.

The following morning, Cadel and Dario ventured into the city streets and, choosing a prominent spot among the peddlers' carts began to play. Dario did not like playing his lute outside, particularly with the air so cold, but he knew that Cadel had reasons for asking him to do so. They told the innkeeper at the Swallow's Nest that they were hoping to draw more customers to the tavern by giving the city folk a taste of their music. In reality, Cadel hoped to draw some of the castle guards into conversation between songs.

It worked. The first minister, one soldier told them, was not nearly as ill as some believed. She had suffered greatly from the poisoning and had slowed the company's return to Mertesse, but she would live and she continued to serve the duke.

"I had heard the duke has a new minister," Cadel said casually as Dario pretended to tune his lute yet again.

The guard shook his head. "The traitor you mean? No. The duke would never stoop to making him a minister, not even a lesser one."

The traitor! Dario forced himself to keep his eyes on the instrument in his hands.

"Why do you call him the traitor?"

"You don't know?" the guard said, obviously pleased to be the bearer of such fascinating news. "You must not be from here. Caerissan aren't you?"

Cadel smiled, though Dario could see that it was forced.

"Yes, I am."

"Thought so. I can pick any accent in the Forelands. Not just realms mind you. But even cities. I'd guess you're from Jetaya."

"Very good. That's quite close."

Actually, Cadel had once told Dario that he came from the Adlana dukedom, which was more than fifty leagues south of Jetaya, but if he didn't care to correct the man, Dario certainly wouldn't.

"The traitor?" Cadel prompted after a brief silence.

"Oh, right. He used to be first minister in Kentigern. They say he betrayed his duke during the siege and was given asylum here."

"And he lives in the castle?"

"He lives in the first minister's quarters," the man said with a wink. "If you get my meaning."

The singer gave the same thin smile and nodded. "I once met a minister in Kentigern. I performed there many years ago. Perhaps it's the same man. I believe his name was Bekthad jal Pors."

The guard shook his head. "No. I think this one's called Shurik jal . . . something. Those white-hair names give me trouble."

"Oh, well. It was worth a try." He glanced at Dario. "Are you tuned yet?"

The lutenist began to play another song, and eventually the guards moved off.

Shortly after, Dario and Cadel returned to the tavern. For the first time since their initial encounter in Dantrielle, the older man seemed truly pleased.

"I'm impressed," Dario told him over their midday meal. "That guard would have told you even more if you'd given him the chance."

"Probably," Cadel agreed. "He certainly would have kept talking. I'm not sure we would have been interested in anything else he had to say."

"So now we know where to find this Qirsi. How do we kill him?"

Cadel gave him the same mysterious grin he had offered on the Night of Two Moons. "We wait."

"For what?"

"Don't you know the moon legends?"

Dario shrugged. "Some of them. To tell you the truth, half the time I don't even know which turn we're in."

"Well, you should."

The lutenist cursed himself for his honesty. No doubt Cadel would see it as another occasion to lecture him.

"An assassin uses every weapon he can," Cadel said, "every scrap of information. What turn is this?"

Dario thought a moment. "Qirsar's."

"And what do the legends say about Qirsar's Moon?"

He shrugged. "I guess something about the Qirsi."

"Something about the Qirsi," Cadel repeated, shaking his head. "Yes, they say something about the Qirsi. On the Night of Two Moons, a Qirsi's magic is more powerful than on any other night of the year. And what about on Pitch Night?"

It came to him in a rush. For all Cadel's bluster, in this instance, there could be no arguing with him. Dario should have remembered. It was brilliant.

"On Pitch Night in Qirsar's Moon," he answered, so excited he barely managed to keep his voice low, "a Qirsi has no power at all."

Cadel nodded, sitting back in his chair. "Very good. Very good, indeed."

"We have more than half the waning to wait," Dario said.

"That's all right. We still have some planning to do. I doubt our friend will be venturing far from the castle, especially on that night. We'll spend our evenings singing and our days preparing for Pitch Night."

The lutenist nodded. It seemed a sensible plan.

That night, however, the Swallow's Nest was so crowded the two musicians had almost no room to perform. The innkeeper said he had never seen so many people in his tavern and he credited his success to the daytime performance they had given in the streets of Mertesse. He offered to raise their nightly wage to seven qinde, provided they agreed to return to the marketplace each day. Posing as wandering musicians, they could hardly refuse.

The day following his ill-fated attempt to speak with Keziah was quite possibly the longest of Grinsa's life. Of course he intended to reach for his sister again that evening, and the wait for nightfall nearly drove him to madness. Consumed by his fear and frustration, he set a punishing pace throughout the day, which Tavis managed somehow to match. They encountered no Solkaran soldiers and covered several leagues, stopping for the evening near a village that Grinsa knew to be only a day's walk from the northern edge of the Great Forest. If they continued to evade the royal guard, they would be in Mertesse in another four or five days.

Their meal consisted of roots and berries once again. Tavis grumbled about it, but Grinsa hardly noticed. He wasn't hungry and he had little to say to the boy. He just stared to the east, waiting for the moons to rise. After some time, Tavis lay down to sleep offering a curt "Goodnight."

Grinsa marked Panya's progress through the sky with an anxious eye, but it was Ilias he awaited. As soon as he saw the red moon top the trees, he closed his eyes and reached for Keziah.

Upon entering her dreams, he turned a full circle, scanning the plain for any sign of the dark sky he had seen the night before. Seeing none, he felt something loosen in his chest.

"Kezi?" he called.

She came into view an instant later, walking quickly toward him, her face as white as new snow, dark purple lines under her yellow eyes. Reaching him, she fell against his chest, sobbing like a hurt child so that her whole body shook. Grinsa merely held her, stroking her soft hair.

After a long time, she stepped back, wiping her tears, though more still flowed down her cheeks.

"Tell me," he said.

Swallowing, she looked away for a moment, as if she didn't want to talk at all. Once more, he was reminded of how she had looked as a young girl.

At last she began to speak, telling him first of Paegar and their friendship, and then of his death and the gold she found in his chambers. By the time she started to explain her idea for attracting the notice of the conspiracy, Grinsa understood everything he needed to know. At least he thought he did.

"I find it hard to believe that Kearney allowed you to do this," he said, not bothering to mask his anger.

"Kearney doesn't know."

Then, finally, he truly grasped all that she had endured. "Oh, Kezi," he breathed. "I'm so sorry. There's no one you can tell? Not even one of the other ministers."

"I've told Gershon everything, but no one else."

"Gershon?" he repeated. His expression must have been comical, because she smiled through her tears.

"Yes. He's actually been quite kind to me."

"He shouldn't have let you do this. He should have known how dangerous it would be."

It was the type of statement that would have drawn an argument from her a few turns before. This night, she only gave a small shrug. "Neither of us knew there would be a Weaver."

Grinsa hadn't thought of it either. It wasn't his place to fault his sister or the swordmaster.

"I felt what he did to you," he said. "Are you all right?"

"I am for now. That was the only time he hurt me."

"Did you finally do what he wanted?"

Her tears started to fall again. "Of course not. How could I? As soon as I open my mind to him he'll kill me. He'll know about you, he'll realize that I've been deceiving him." She shook her head. "Had I known that I'd be contacted by a Weaver, I never would have tried this."

"So end it now." But as soon as Grinsa spoke the words, he knew that it would do no good.

"Ending it does nothing, Grinsa. You of all people should know that. He knows who I am and how to find me. He told me he'd return in a few days and that when he did I'd have to open myself to him or he'd kill me." She faltered, looking away briefly. "Can he really do that? Can a Weaver kill someone through their dreams?"

He would have liked to lie to her, to put her mind at ease, but it would only have made matters worse, and she would have sensed that he was hiding the truth.

"Yes," he told her. "He can kill you, just as he hurt you last night."

"So what can I do? How do I deceive a Weaver?"

"I don't know," he said gently. "I've never had to try. I suppose you have to find a way to keep some of your thoughts from him while making him believe that your mind is completely open to him."

"But how? Is my mind open to you right now?"

"No. But I've never wanted it to be. I'm content to speak with you, and learn from you what you want me to know."

She raked a rigid hand through her hair. "I'm dead," she whispered.

"No, you're not. You're stronger than you think. You need only find your strength."

Keziah gave a small nod, but she wouldn't look him in the eye.

"Did you learn anything about the Weaver?" he asked. "His name, perhaps, or where he lives?"

"I learned nothing. He kept himself in darkness and summoned a bright light from behind. I couldn't see anything."

"I saw that he had darkened the sky, and I thought I saw something glowing at its center."

"How is that possible?" she asked, frowning. "The Weaver saw nothing of the sky you created. I did, but he didn't."

"You're certain?"

She nodded, then appeared to shiver. "He would have said something."

"Interesting," he said, allowing himself a small grin.

"Why are you smiling like that?"

"Last night, as I was walking toward you in the dream, I almost thought I could hear you calling to me, telling me to leave you."

"I was, but you wouldn't listen."

"I know. I should have. I'm sorry." He narrowed his eyes. "Did the Weaver hear those thoughts? Did he know I was there?"

"Of course not."

"Then there's your answer."

Keziah blinked. "I don't understand."

"You already know how to hide your thoughts from a Weaver. You allowed me to see what you were seeing, to hear and feel all that was going on in your dream, without revealing me to the Weaver."

"But my mind was closed to him."

"Not entirely, not enough to keep him from your dreams. The words 'opening your mind' offer an image, nothing more. There's no door in your head that keeps one set of thoughts separate from another. Opening your mind simply means allowing him to read all your thoughts rather than some of them. The secret lies in showing him what you need to while making him believe that there's nothing more."

"I don't know if I can do that."

"You did it last night."

"Maybe, but I don't know how."

He reached out a hand to brush the hair back from her brow. "Somewhere inside, you do. You have to find that knowledge, Kezi, and you have to trust your power. If I could do this for you I would. You know that. But this is your burden. You chose to carry it, and now you have to live with that decision." *Or die with it.* Grinsa didn't say it. He didn't have to.

She took a breath and nodded once more, a dull look in her eyes.

"I should let you sleep."

"Where are you?" she asked, as if she hadn't heard.

Grinsa winced. He'd almost forgotten again.

"We're near Mertesse. That's why I tried to contact you in the first place. To warn you. While we were in Solkara, we encountered Shurik jal Marcine, the minister who betrayed Kentigern during the siege. We escaped him, but I'm certain he knows I'm a Weaver. I had to reveal too many of my powers in getting away. I don't think he knows you're my sister, but if he decides to look for our family, it won't take him long to find you."

"You think he's back in Mertesse?"

"As certain as I can be."

"And what do you plan to do with him when you find him?"

Grinsa hesitated. "I was going to question him about the conspiracy. Beyond that . . . I hadn't decided."

"But you've considered killing him."

The idea of it still troubled him, but he could hardly deny it. "Yes."

"That's what you have to do, Grinsa. If the Weaver contacts him we're lost. Shurik will tell him, and the Weaver will learn in no time that we're related. Don't bother questioning him. I'll find out everything we need to know about the movement. Just kill him and get out of Mertesse."

He knew she was right, yet he couldn't believe that she could speak so casually of murder, even when it concerned a man like Shurik.

"You're surprised to hear me say such things."

"I guess I am."

She gave a small shrug. "This is the world we live in now. If Shurik had the opportunity to kill you, he wouldn't hesitate to do so. Which means you have to kill him first."

"I'm not arguing with you. I just worry that you're changing so quickly. The Keziah I knew a year ago would have had trouble speaking those words."

"I'm not the one changing, Grinsa. Eibithar is different, as are all the realms of the Forelands. A year ago you were traveling with the Revel, and Kearney and I were still in Glyndwr; Lady Brienne was still alive and Javan of Curgh was in line to be king." She looked away. "I'm archminister to the king. I no longer have the luxury of being squeamish. We both know that Shurik has to die. I just happened to be the first of us to say so aloud."

He gazed at her for several moments, though she continued to look away. Unable to think of any reply, he finally stepped forward and put his arms around her again.

She held him tight, pressing her cheek to his chest. "I'm afraid," she whispered. "Of everything."

"I'm afraid for you. But I know how strong you are. Trust yourself and you'll be all right." He kissed her forehead and gazed into her eyes for a moment. "I love you, Kezi. I'll see you soon."

He released her and a moment later broke the connection linking their minds.

Opening his eyes to the darkness of the Aneiran wood, he lay down near where Tavis slept and closed his eyes once more, falling almost immediately into a deep, dreamless slumber.

Grinsa and Tavis reached the north edge of the Great Forest late the following day and waited for nightfall before continuing onto the narrow open plain that lay between the wood and Mertesse. Grinsa was convinced that most of the Solkaran soldiers had returned to the royal city, but he didn't dare chance being mistaken. For the next several days he and the boy traveled by night and rested during the day, taking refuge in the darkened corners of barns and abandoned shacks. Leaving Tavis briefly on the second day, Grinsa ventured into a nearby village and bought them enough food to last the rest of their journey.

On their fourth night out of the forest, they came within sight of Mertesse. Even from a full league away, they could see torches burning atop the great stone walls and towers of the castle. Tavis wanted to try to reach the nearest entrance to the city before the ringing of the gate-closing bells. Grinsa agreed that they had time enough to make it, but he argued against trying.

"We'll be far more noticeable among the few who enter the city at night. We should wait for morning and enter with the shepherds, just as we did in Solkara."

Tavis looked unhappy, but he let the matter drop, something he wouldn't have done a few turns before.

They continued on until they were less than half a league from the castle before stopping for the night. There were no buildings nearby, but with thin high clouds covering the sky, the night didn't grow too cold. They slept in the open, rising with first light to complete their journey to the city walls. When the gates opened to the pealing of the city bells, Tavis and Grinsa were among the first to enter the city. They crossed through the gate in the company of several merchants, their hoods over their heads and their eyes fixed on the ground. None of the guards seemed to notice them. Apparently, word of their escape from Solkara had not spread beyond the forest.

Once in the city, they made their way to the marketplace, which was already filling quickly with peddlers and their customers.

"What now?" Tavis asked, his voice low.

"I need to go to the castle and see if I can learn where Shurik is. The duke and his company should have returned from Solkara several days ago. I want to know if the traitor was with them."

"And if he wasn't?"

479

"I'd rather not think about it. I expect that he was, in which case it becomes a matter of waiting for him to emerge from the castle."

"If he thinks you've followed him here, he's not likely to come out any time soon."

The gleaner nodded. "I know. Let's find out first if he's in Mertesse. Then I'll worry about the rest."

"What do you want me to do?"

"Remain in the marketplace. We'll find an inn later."

"All right."

"And stay out of trouble, Tavis," he added. "We're too close to Shurik to muck things up now."

The young lord opened his arms wide. "Why do you always think I'm going to find trouble?"

Grinsa frowned and started to walk away without responding. The answer seemed as plain as the scars on Tavis's face.

The journey back from Solkara had left her weary and weak. Even after five days resting in her chamber in Castle Mertesse, Yaella found that she wanted nothing more than to sleep, or to huddle in the great chair beside her hearth. She ate little—the mere thought of food or, even worse, wine, left her queasy—and she had only left her chamber twice, once to speak with the duke, and a second time to satisfy the castle surgeon, who urged her to walk the corridors in order to regain her strength.

She couldn't help but notice that Rowan, who had been poisoned as well, appeared to have made a full recovery already. Shurik assured her that this was simply a matter of his being Eandi.

"There's no question that they're physically stronger than we are," he told her, soon after their return to Mertesse. "The duke especially. He may be a dullard, but he's built like his father. Of course he's mended faster than you have."

Yaella feared that there was more to it than that, however. Except for the Night of Two Moons nine evenings before, when the god's gift of magic seemed to bolster her physical strength, she hadn't felt whole since first leaving Mertesse nearly a turn before. She wasn't a young woman any-more—at thirty-one the minister was only four years younger than her mother had been when she died. True, her father lived to be almost forty, but even if that proved to be her fate also, she was approaching the final years of her life. What if she never recovered fully from the poisoning? What if her near encounter with the Deceiver marked the beginning of a slow decline toward death? Notwithstanding what Shurik had told her, she didn't feel ill anymore. She felt tired. She felt old.

Shurik spent much of his time with her, encouraging her to eat and offering to make tea for her and fetch her something more from the kitchens. Though grateful for his company at times, now and again she would have liked to tell him to leave her. She understood, though, that he needed to care for her in order to keep his mind from his own troubles. He slept poorly at night, twitching like a sleeping cat and crying out at the demons that haunted his dreams. His face, always thin and pale, had a pinched, unhealthful look that worried her.

Having felt the power of the Weaver, having faced him in his wrath and awakened to find her heart pounding, tears on her cheeks, Yaella could hardly fault Shurik for his fear of the man. On the other hand, she didn't know what to make of his worries about this second man, whom he also believed to be a Weaver. She couldn't deny that it was strange for a Revel gleaner to conceal the fact that he possessed other powers. Yet neither could she say that this alone meant he was a Weaver. Weaving magic had not been bred out of her people, as some of the Eandi seemed to believe, but Weavers were rare and she remained skeptical that Shurik had managed to make enemies of two of them.

As a younger man Shurik had never allowed his fears to overmaster his good sense. But like her, he was growing older. Add to that his recent exile from Kentigern and his harsh treatment at the hands of the Weaver, and Yaella could see how he might imagine dangers at every turn. She didn't dare say any of this to him, of course. She listened as he ranted on about the ill will of the gods and how they had cursed him with bad fortune, and she tried to put his fears to rest.

On this morning, to her surprise and relief, he appeared to have forgotten both Weavers, at least for the moment. He wasn't even urging her to eat, though that would soon change if she didn't climb out of her chair and return to the breakfast he had brought her, which sat untouched on the bed. He merely sat near the hearth, staring at the patterned tapestry that hung on the wall. When he finally spoke, however, it became clear to her that the Weavers were anything but forgotten.

"It's possible that they caught him," he said abruptly, as if they had been talking all this time.

"Who?" she asked, knowing well who he meant.

"Grinsa, of course. The Solkarans might have him already, and the boy as well. That may be why word of their escape never reached the guards here in Mertesse."

"I've told you, Shurik. Solkaran guards would have ceased their search at the northern fringe of the Great Forest whether they had him or not. That's where Solkaran lands end and those of Mertesse begin."

"But surely soldiers of the royal house can ride where they please."

"Yes. But with Numar new to his power and fears running high throughout Aneira, they aren't about to stray too far from the royal city in pursuit of two men." She closed her eyes briefly, angry with herself for arguing the point. Better to let him believe that Grinsa was no longer a threat. "He may very well have been captured. I certainly hope that he was. But it's just one possible explanation. They may simply have decided that the gleaner and the Curgh boy weren't worth so much effort."

Perhaps he sensed more in her tone than she meant to convey. He stared at her a moment, a pained expression in his eyes. Then looking down, he asked, "Is that what you think?"

"No."

But he heard the hesitancy in her answer and his face colored.

"He's a Weaver, Yaella. I'm certain of it. I know it seems odd that I would have drawn the attention of two of them, but I have." He smiled grimly, the wounded look in his eyes remaining. "It seems I'm more important than either of us ever realized."

"I've never doubted that you're important, Shurik. You should know that. But I know that my own fear of the Weaver has made me wary of every new Qirsi I meet. You first encountered this man just after you weakened the gates at Kentigern, and you immediately thought that he knew somehow you had betrayed Aindreas. Isn't it possible that you allowed your fear of being discovered to color your impression of the man?"

Shurik stood, his lips pressed thin, his cheeks reddening further. "No," he said, his voice icy with rage. "It's not. And you should know better."

He stalked to the door.

"Shurik, please. I'm sor—"

The door slammed behind him before she could finish her apology.

A small part of her was glad to see him go, and she wondered if on some level she had meant to make him angry. She knew she should find him and apologize. If he was right, and this Grinsa was a Weaver, the Solkarans would have little chance of capturing him and even less of preventing his escape. She might have been tiring of Shurik's company, but she knew that he was safer with her than alone. Still, Yaella continued to sit before the fire, watching the flames dance and enjoying her solitude.

After some time, she stood, walked slowly to the bed, and made herself eat. Then she left her room in search of Shurik. She checked his quarters first, but the door was unlocked and the room empty. After that she walked to the kitchens and the great hall, but none of the servants in either place had seen him. An uneasy feeling came over her and she walked quickly through the corridors and out into the castle courtyard. Nothing. Almost running now, she stepped into the outer ward, circling it twice. He wasn't there either.

As she passed the city gate a second time, she thought she glimpsed a shock of white hair at the sally port. Rushing to the gate, she stared down the lane leading to the city, but she saw no sign of him.

"Who was that you were speaking to?" she asked the nearest of the guards.

The man stared at her blankly. "I wasn't speaking to anyone, First Minister."

"I thought I saw a Qirsi here. I was wondering if it was the . . ." She faltered. Since Shurik first arrived in Mertesse, a traitor from Kentigern seeking asylum in Aneira, she had not known what to call him when speaking with others. He wasn't a minister any longer, and she refused to call him "the traitor" as she knew most of the guards did. "I thought it might be my friend, Shurik. The Qirsi from Kentigern."

"I swear, First Minister. There was no one."

She turned toward a second guard, who stood a short distance from the gate. "Did you see him?"

"No, First Minister." He gestured toward the first guard. "Like he says, there wasn't anyone here. We would have noticed a whi—" He nearly choked on the word, his face turning crimson. "We would have noticed a Qirsi," he said a moment later.

Yaella gazed toward the city again, but still saw no one. She was so certain that she had seen the white hair of a Qirsi, but then again, she hadn't been well recently.

"My apologies," she murmured, walking back toward the inner gates. "I must have been mistaken."

She finally found Shurik some time later, standing alone at the top of the granary tower on the far side of the castle. The wind blew hard so high up, and Yaella shivered as she stopped next to him, looking out over the city walls toward the Great Forest.

"I'm sorry," she said softly, glancing at him, trying to read his expression. "You've never given me cause to question your word or your judgment, and I shouldn't start doubting you now."

"But you have. You think I'm wrong about Grinsa."

"I don't know what to think. I've never even seen him, so who am I to

483

say you're wrong?" She shrugged. "Maybe I just find the idea of facing two Weavers so frightening that I don't want to believe it."

He gave a wry smile. "I can understand that."

"For what it's worth, just now, when I thought you had left the castle, I was very worried." She briefly considered telling him what she had seen at the city gate, but that would have served only to make him more afraid, and for no reason at all. The guards wouldn't have lied to her. Certainly she had imagined it.

"I'm not about to leave the castle, Yaella. This is the only place I feel safe. At some point, the Weaver may order me to search for Grinsa again, but until then I'm staying here."

She hooked her arm through his and rested her head against his shoulder. "Good."

Shurik pressed his lips gently against the top of her head. Then he regarded her oddly, as if noticing her for the first time. "You're out of your quarters," he said, grinning. "Outside the castle corridors even. I can hardly believe it."

"I told you, I was worried."

"How do you feel?"

"Tired. A bit cold."

"Shall I escort you back to your chamber, First Minister?"

Yaella smiled. "Soon. I like it up here."

They stood there a while longer, watching thin, grey clouds glide over nearby farms and the bare trees of the Aneiran wood. Occasionally the sun broke through, casting stark shadows on the brown fields before vanishing again behind the grey. At last, as the clouds began to thicken and the wind increased, they retreated into the closest tower and descended a winding stairway to the corridors near Yaella's room.

"I have to ask you something," Shurik said, as they approached her door. "But I'm afraid you'll think me foolish again."

A pair of guards turned the corner in front of them and walked past. Neither of the Qirsi spoke until the men reached the far end of the hallway and turned out of sight.

"I don't think you're foolish, Shurik, and whatever else I may think of Grinsa, I don't doubt for a moment that he's a threat to you. Just ask me."

"All right. I know that the Solkarans pursued him and the boy. For all I know the two of them are a hundred leagues from here. But still I'd like you to ask the duke to alert his guards. I want the men looking for them, just in case Grinsa comes to the castle."

Yaella felt a strange tightness in her chest and once again she saw in her mind that head of white hair. *You imagined it. You're as unnerved as Shurik.*

"Of course," she said. "I need to rest right now. But I'll speak with him later today."

They stopped in front of her door, and Shurik turned to face her, looking anxious. "Do you think he'll do it? We both know how he feels about me."

"Regardless of his feelings for you, Rowan is smart enough to recognize a threat to his castle. If I tell him there are agents of Eibithar in the kingdom who wish you harm, he'll double the guard at every gate. I promise."

He nodded, even smiled. "Thank you," he said. He kissed her cheek. "I'll leave you now. Rest."

Yaella nodded. But as she lingered in the doorway, watching him walk away, she couldn't help thinking that the Qirsi man she had seen at the gate had looked a good deal taller than Shurik.

Chapter

Thirty-two

avis had circled once through the marketplace, stopping at the carts of a few peddlers to look at blades or travel sacks—his was badly frayed—before moving on again. Granted, they were well into the snows now, and in a kingdom like Aneira, which stretched southward all the way to the Border Range, the northern cities were bound to have a more difficult time attracting merchants during the colder turns. Still, the young lord could not keep himself from measuring this marketplace against the one in Curgh, and he noted with satisfaction that it fared poorly in the comparison.

Seeing no sign of Grinsa, Tavis had resigned himself to a second pass through the markets when he saw a knot of people forming in the distance. Curious, he started in that direction. Before he reached the growing throng, however, he heard the gleaner calling his name, or rather, Xaver's.

He stopped, turning to see Grinsa striding toward him.

"Where are you going?" the Qirsi asked as he drew near.

Tavis nodded toward the crowd, but said nothing. There were too many people close by and though he had been working to perfect his Aneiran accent, it remained less than convincing.

Halting just in front of him, Grinsa gave a quick glance toward the mass of people, his brow wrinkling for just a moment. "What is it?"

"I don't know," Tavis said quietly. "I thought I'd take a look."

"Another time perhaps. We need to find a room and talk." Grinsa faced him again, an avid look in his fire yellow eyes. "He's here, in the castle."

"All right, we'll go shortly. But I want to see what's happening over there."

Grinsa frowned. "Excuse me!" he called to a man hurrying past them. "What is it you're all rushing to see?"

The man looked at them over his shoulder, barely slowing down. "The musicians, of course."

"Musicians?"

The stranger gave an exasperated sigh and stopped, though clearly he would have preferred to leave it to someone else to answer their questions. "The ones from the Swallow's Nest." When neither Tavis nor Grinsa gave any sign that they understood, he went on, his tone growing more impatient by the moment. "They've played in the marketplace the past several days. I guess they hope to draw people to the tavern." He started away again. "They're better than any festival players I've ever heard."

"Thank you," Grinsa called after him. "There," he said, turning to Tavis again. "It's just musicians. Seems you'll be able to hear them tomorrow if you like. For now, we need to talk."

Reluctantly, Tavis followed the gleaner away from the crowd and toward one of the many narrow lanes leading off the marketplace. It took them some time to find an inn that would rent them a room, and more time still to haggle over the price. By the time they began to climb the steps to their room in yet another Qirsi inn, it was well past midday. Once they were alone, Grinsa told Tavis all that he had learned from the guards at Mertesse Castle.

Shurik had returned with the duke and hadn't left the safety of the castle since. He spent most of his time caring for the first minister, who was still recovering from the poisoning in Solkara. The new duke, though honoring his father's pledge to protect the man, despised him and had no intention of ever making him a minister.

"How did you get a soldier of Mertesse to tell you all this?" the young lord asked, when Grinsa had finished.

"You remember the peddler we met in the Great Forest?"

Tavis felt the blood drain from his face.

"With all the guard told me," the Qirsi went on a moment later, "I still have no idea how I can get close enough to Shurik to—" He fell silent, glancing uneasily at Tavis.

"To what?"

Grinsa stared at him briefly, his mouth twitching. Then he looked away. "To kill him."

"I thought you wanted to question him, to learn what you could about the conspiracy."

"I did. But with Keziah trying to join the movement, he's too great a threat, to her as well as to me. I don't have a choice anymore."

Tavis considered this for several moments before starting to nod. "All right. What do you want me to do?"

Grinsa smiled, looking relieved. "Nothing for now. Rest. Walk the marketplace. Enjoy the musicians. I still have a great deal to learn. It's been several years since I last visited Mertesse, and I don't remember much about the castle."

"You think we'll have to do it there?"

"I doubt very much that Shurik will give us the opportunity to do it anywhere else."

They spoke a while longer, Grinsa relating to Tavis those details he did remember about the castle and actually asking the young lord questions about the design of Curgh Castle, which apparently had been constructed at about the same time as Mertesse. Eventually they returned to the main room of the tavern to have a small meal and continue their conversation. Tavis was pleased to find that much of what he told the gleaner about his family castle seemed to interest Grinsa. So often in their time together—most recently when they had spoken of Grinsa's powers—Tavis had felt like a child learning from a master, or even a parent. He enjoyed speaking with the Qirsi as if, for once, they were peers.

When they finished eating, Grinsa walked back to the castle, though he remained vague as to what he planned to do there, and Tavis returned to the marketplace, hoping to find the musicians. They agreed to meet back at the tavern at sundown.

When the young lord reached the marketplace, there was no sign of the musicians or the crowd they had attracted. He did find some jugglers who were throwing knives back and forth with alarming speed, and he watched them for a while before wandering among the carts again. It had been some time since he last heard a performance by worthy musicians, and he briefly considered going to the tavern where they were said to play. What had the man called it? The Swallow's Nest. He knew, though, that Grinsa would think it a bad idea. With Shurik so close, Tavis sensed that the gleaner would have liked to lock Tavis in their room the entire day, just to keep him from being noticed. He couldn't, of course, but he had made it clear that the boy was to limit himself to their room at the tavern and the marketplace. In any other city, Tavis would have chafed at such constraints. But Mertesse, located only a league from the Tarbin and the border with Eibithar, was different. In his kingdom it was said that no Aneirans hated his people more than those in Mertesse. If someone here recognized his accent they might very well kill him where he stood. He would wait until tomorrow, when he could hear the musicians in the marketplace.

When Tavis and Grinsa met at the end of the day, the gleaner seemed weary and discouraged. He explained that he had spoken to six or seven more guards, using his mind-bending magic on several of them, but had learned nothing more about the castle, or where Shurik's quarters could be found. They ate their dinner in silence, then climbed the stairs to their room and slept.

The following morning, Tavis dressed quickly and was ready to leave the room before Grinsa was even out of bed.

"I want to find a good place to sit to hear the players," he said, as he pulled the door open.

"All right. Be careful. I'll be at the castle much of the morning, but I'll try to find you in the marketplace around midday. If you don't see me, come back here."

Tavis nodded and left. So eager was he to reach the marketplace that he didn't even stop to eat in the tavern. Instead he bought a round of bread from a baker and hurried on to where the musicians had played the day before. Even so, he wasn't the first to get there and within an hour of his arrival, he was surrounded by a mass of people. He could only hope that the musicians were as good as these Aneirans seemed to think.

"It looks like everyone in the city is here."

Tavis turned toward the voice, only to find a young, attractive red-haired woman looking at him. A frown flitted across her features as she traced his scars with her green eyes. But then she met his gaze and smiled. He gave a small smile in return and nodded, not wanting to risk a conversation.

"Did you hear them yesterday?" she asked.

He shook his head.

"I did. They were wonderful, of course. When was the first time you saw them?"

"Actually, I haven't seen them at all," he told her, trying his best to sound Aneiran.

Judging from the puzzled look she gave him, he could tell that he had failed. "You're not from Mertesse, are you?"

"No. I was born in Tounstrel, but I've . . . moved around a lot."

The woman nodded seeming to accept this. "Well, you're going to enjoy this. They're the best musicians to perform here in years."

"I've heard others say the same."

"I'm Rissa." She turned and surveyed the crowd, her frown returning. "My brother's here somewhere, but I don't see him right now."

"I'm Xaver."

"Are you here with anyone, Xaver?"

Before he could answer, the people far behind them began to cheer. It seemed the musicians had arrived. Tavis and Rissa turned to the sound, straining to see over the crowd, and slowly the sea of people began to part, revealing the players. He saw the lutenist first, a young man with golden yellow hair, warm brown eyes, and a square face.

Looking past him to the other man, Tavis felt his whole body grow numb with cold, as if Brienne's spirit had passed through him, borne by a wind from the Underrealm. There could be no mistaking that face. He had seen it in Curgh during the Revel, when he first heard this man sing, though it had taken Brienne's ghost to remind him. He saw it again in the great hall of Kentigern, when the man, then posing as a castle servant, handed him a flask of dark Sanbiri wine. He saw it a third time in Kentigern's Sanctuary of Bian, a vaporous image summoned for him by Brienne's spirit. And he had seen it a hundred times since, haunting his sleep like one of the Deceiver's demons, taunting him with a malevolent smile.

The smile appeared kinder now, as did the thin, bearded face. But those eyes—pale blue, and as cold as the north wind blowing off of Amon's Ocean—those eyes could only belong to a killer. Brienne's killer.

Tavis's first instinct was to reach for his blade, to finish it right here. But he knew he couldn't. Even if he could have managed to overpower the singer, the people around him wouldn't allow it. The man was a luminary here in Mertesse. And Tavis was an Eibitharian noble, an exile.

He looked around desperately, searching for Grinsa, or a castle guard, or anyone who might believe the truth about this man. *He's an assassin!* he wanted to shout. *That man is a hired blade! He killed the woman who was to be my queen! He killed the duke of Bistari and may even have murdered your king!* Again, though, nobody in the marketplace had any reason to believe him, and hearing his accent they would view him as the enemy, not the assassin.

The singer had almost reached him. In another moment he would see Tavis, and surely the scars and the stained travel clothes would not keep him from recognizing the young lord. Tavis had but one choice. Turning quickly and pushing his way through the thick ring of people that surrounded him, the boy fled.

"Xaver!" he heard Rissa call to him. "Xaver, where are you going?"

He ignored her, fighting his way through the crowd like a lone crow flying in the face of a gale. The Aneirans pressed against him, as eager to get closer to the singer as Tavis was desperate to get away from him. For several moments he wondered if he'd get through at all. He could barely move forward, and there was no going back. Feeling fear rise in his chest like the waters of the Tarbin in flood, he very nearly reached for his blade so that he might clear a swath through this mass of bodies. At last, however, he broke free, stumbling into the open street as if he had been shoved out of the throng.

He bent at the waist, his hands resting on his knees and his breathing labored. For just an instant he thought he might be sick, but the nausea soon passed, leaving him weary and tearful.

He straightened and began to walk back toward the inn, struggling to keep from bawling like a babe. The singer had been right in front of him. Had he but drawn his blade and waited a moment or two, he might have been able to kill the man. Yes, the crowd would have overwhelmed him. They might even have killed him. But at least the singer would be dead, and Brienne avenged. He had sworn to her spirit that he would strike the man down for her and though he had not spoken the words aloud, he had vowed to himself that he would not allow fear for his own life to stay his hand.

Now he had done just that.

"I am a coward," he muttered under his breath, tears stinging his eyes. "I always have been." The only time he had truly been brave was in Kentigern's dungeon, when he had endured the torture inflicted upon him by Brienne's father rather than confess to her murder. And all he had to show for those brief moments of valor were the scars on his face and body.

That would end here, in the half-frozen, mud-covered lanes of this city. He began to walk faster. The assassin hadn't seen him; the young lord felt certain of that. Which meant that the man would be as unprepared for Tavis's assault at their next encounter as he had been at this one. He had lost an opportunity, but nothing more. He would find this Swallow's Nest and kill the singer there. Let the Aneirans hang him. Better to be executed for the murder of a killer and reviled as a nobleman of Eibithar, than to waste away in exile with all the Forelands believing that he had butchered his queen.

By the time he reached the small lane that led to the inn at which he and the gleaner had taken a room, he was running, enlivened by his resolve. He threw open the door of the tavern, took the stairs two at a time, and rushed down the corridor to their room. Opening the door, he found that Grinsa had already gone.

He spat a curse and searched the room for a quill and a piece of parchment. Seeing none, he hurried back down the stairs to where the innkeeper sat, puffing on a pipe.

"Do you know where my friend went?" he asked, heedless of his accent.

The Qirsi man regarded him coolly. After a moment he shook his head. "I saw him leave just after you did, but he told me nothing."

No doubt he had gone back to the castle, hoping to learn something of its design and of Shurik's whereabouts.

"Do you have a quill, and something on which to write?"

The innkeeper gave him a sour look, but he stood and walked slowly back to his chamber, emerging a few seconds later with a quill, a stoppered vial of ink, and parchment.

Tavis grabbed them from him, tossing a "Thank you" over his shoulder as he ran up the stairs once more.

He sat on his bed and opened the ink, but then faltered with the quill poised over the vial. If he explained too much about what he intended to do, the gleaner would try to stop him. Grinsa would see only the danger. Tavis was more than willing to exchange his life for the assassin's, but the Qirsi would balk at such a trade. In the end, however, the young lord decided it was best to tell him everything and hope that Grinsa wouldn't have the chance to interfere. Someone should know what he had done. Someone should be able to explain to his parents that he hadn't died a coward, that he hadn't carried his shame to the Underrealm.

He kept his message to the gleaner brief and to the point, but he did include a final word of thanks for all Grinsa had done for him.

"Had it not been for your companionship, I would have spent these last several turns alone and friendless," the young lord wrote. "For that, I will always be grateful. Be well, Grinsa. May the gods keep you safe."

He placed the parchment at the foot of the gleaner's bed, checked to make certain that his blade was strapped securely to his belt, and left the room. His stomach felt hard and empty, but he didn't dare eat. Having made his decision to avenge Brienne here in Mertesse, he now needed to contrive a way to kill the singer without getting himself killed first, and without giving the gleaner time enough to stop him.

Their performance in the marketplace went quite well; better, Cadel had to admit, than had any of their previous ones. Not that the city folk would have noticed much difference from one day or evening to the next. Dario could have neglected to tune his lute, and Cadel could have reversed the lyrics of the *Paean*, and still the people of Mertesse would have cheered lustily for every note. Such was the power of the reputation they already enjoyed in this city.

Perhaps the singer should have accepted this as evidence that Dario was right: no one cared if they played perfectly. It was enough that they sounded good and pleased their listeners. But something about their performance this day left him troubled. More precisely, it was something about the marketplace itself, or perhaps the crowd that greeted them there. Cadel could hardly say which. He knew only that he felt the way he often did before a difficult kill, alert and a bit on edge. It almost seemed that his body was readying itself for a fight, though Pitch Night was still several days away. He couldn't explain it, but he had learned long ago to trust his instincts. He couldn't dismiss it either.

Yet there was nothing to be done about it, at least not until he had a better sense of what was coming. As they walked back toward the Swallow's Nest, Cadel found himself scanning the city streets for signs of trouble, one hand drifting time and again to the handle of his dagger.

Dario didn't appear to notice. "We sounded good, don't you think?" he said, a broad grin on his boyish face. "I bet there were people in Kentigern who heard those cheers."

"Your timing is still all wrong in the threnody, and the Caerissan folk songs are far too ragged in the refrains."

Cadel winced at what he heard in his own voice, and the smile vanished from the lutenist's face, leaving a hard, bitter look.

"We're so close to having it all just right," the singer began again a moment later. "We just need a bit more work."

Dario nodded, but said nothing.

He couldn't say why he treated the younger man this way. There remained much about their playing that bothered Cadel, and though they had practiced every song more times that he cared to count, Dario's playing had changed little. Nearly every compromise had come from Cadel, either with a specific change in his singing style, or a silent acquiescence to another of Dario's poor habits. But while Cadel found this exasperating, disagreements over their music hardly explained these outbursts of anger, which, at times, caught even him unaware. It almost seemed that he was directing at Dario all his lingering rage at having lost Jedrek.

"We won't practice very long," he said, trying once more to soothe the other man's anger. "Just once through the threnody and the folk songs ought to do it." *I need this,* he almost said. *I need to sing in order to keep my mind off of everything else.*

Dario gave no reply, and they walked the rest of the way to the inn without speaking a word.

They played the songs quickly and flawlessly, though without any of the feeling that usually marked their performances. The lutenist stared at his hands the entire time, as if refusing to look at Cadel.

If I'm not careful, I'll destroy this partnership before our first kill.

"That sounded good," he said when they had finished the last song. "All of them did."

"So that's what you want?" Dario asked, his voice as flat as his playing had just been.

"Well, that's the right pacing. As for the rest, we just finished a performance. We're both tired."

"So we're done here?"

Cadel nodded. "I think so."

Dario stood, wrapping his lute in its cloth, and stepping to the door.

"Where are you going?"

The lutenist shrugged, keeping his back to Cadel. "Away from here. That's all that matters."

"We still have a good deal to plan for Pitch Night."

Dario did turn at that. "You make the plans. Tell me what you want me to do and I'll do it. That's what you expect, isn't it?"

He didn't wait for an answer. Pulling the door open, he walked out of the room and closed the door firmly behind him. If the younger man hadn't left his lute on the other bed, Cadel would have wondered if he intended to return.

For a long time the singer merely sat and thought, trying to determine if he was angry with the lutenist or just weary of him. He needed someone to guard his back. He had been saying so for years. The truth was, however, he had always preferred working alone. Even when Jed was still alive, he had savored those kills he completed by himself. On a few occasions Jedrek had managed to warn him of danger. Perhaps he had even kept Cadel from being captured or killed. And though Jedrek died trying to protect him while Cadel rode to Kentigern, the singer couldn't ignore the possibility that Jed had delayed the Qirsi enough to save his life this one last time. Still, Cadel had to admit that he kept Jedrek around not for protection, but rather for the man's company during the many turns each year when they had no jobs, and all they had to do was wander the land and sing.

He could get by alone if he needed to. There were risks to working without a partner, but he was an assassin and risks came with the profession. Even with the added dangers, working alone had to be better than this. He had grown tired of fighting with the lutenist all the time, of working so hard to accommodate a man whose lute playing was so undisciplined and whose skill with a blade remained so uncertain.

Oddly, considering how much gold he had earned with his dagger, all that had stopped him from ending their partnership before now was his reluctance to kill the lutenist. Dario knew too much about Cadel and his work for the singer to let him live. If he wanted to work alone, he would have to kill his partner, and despite all his misgivings about working and singing with the man, Cadel wasn't certain he could bring himself to do it.

He shook his head, as if to clear his mind, and stood, stretching his legs and back. He heard the prior's bells ringing from the city gates, and he cursed himself for wasting so much time. More than half the day was gone—the sun would be setting in just a couple of hours—and he had yet to make his way to the castle. Playing in the city streets had seemed such a fine idea a few days before. Now it was a bother, one more obstacle keeping him from planning Shurik's murder. He had befriended a few of the castle guards, and had learned much from them about the Qirsi and the fortress itself. But what good were the guards if he found no time to speak with them? Cadel crossed to the door, pulled it open, and stepped into the corridor.

Instinct. There was no other way to explain how he managed to have his dagger in his hand so quickly. It almost seemed that he knew the attack was coming even before he saw the shadow spring at him from the corner of the dark corridor. Still, even with his blade ready, he could do little to defend himself. The attacker caught him off balance, crashing into Cadel's side and knocking the assassin to the floor. Cadel tried to stand again, but instantly the shadow pounced on him, pinning the singer's blade hand beneath his body. He tried to free his weapon, at the same time struggling to throw the attacker off of him. His assailant was strong, but not very big, and as they grappled on the wood floor, Cadel sensed that the stranger had little experience with such fights.

It didn't take the assassin long to loose his blade arm and he struck at the body on top of his, intending to plunge his dagger into the attacker's back. Just as he did, however, the stranger lashed out with his left arm, catching Cadel full on the wrist, so that his weapon flew from his hand, clattering harmlessly against the wall.

The assassin tried to reach for it, but in the next moment, he felt the cold edge of a blade pressed against the side of his neck.

"Don't move!" A man's voice, young and unsteady.

"What is it you want with me?" Cadel asked, his left hand snaking down toward the second dagger he always kept strapped to his calf.

"Vengeance. You took my queen, my title, my life. You're going to die for that."

One motion. That was all it would take. A simple arch of his back to throw the man off of him, then, using the force of that first move, he would roll onto the man, second dagger in hand and ready for the killing blow.

Even as the last word passed the attacker's lips, Cadel had braced one foot against the floor. Before he could move, though, a brilliant white light filled the corridor.

"Tavis, no!" came a voice from near the stairs.

Cadel froze, staring up at the scarred face looming above his own. He wouldn't have recognized the boy on his own, but there could be no mistaking those eyes, and the noble mouth and nose. This was Tavis of Curgh, one slash of his blade away from avenging Brienne's murder. Just as the girl's spirit had warned on Bian's Night in Solkara.

Grinsa returned to the inn a short time before the ringing of the prior's bells, weary but pleased. He had managed to find a lone guard whose mind he could touch without drawing the attention of anyone else. He had learned a good deal about the castle and about where Shurik was likely to be during the night. With any luck at all, he and Tavis could be out of Mertesse within a day.

Entering the inn, he nodded to the innkeeper who was smoking a pipe in the middle of the great room.

"Your friend was looking for you," the man called to him as Grinsa crossed to the stairs.

The Qirsi halted. "How long ago?"

"He's not from Aneira, is he?"

Cursing under his breath, Grinsa walked to the innkeeper's table and sat.

"He's from Eibithar."

"Yes," Grinsa admitted, his voice low, though there were no others in the room.

"You are as well?"

"Yes." He could have lied, but knowing the truth about Tavis, the man wouldn't trust them anyway. Better to fight the innkeeper's suspicions with honesty. "But we're not here as enemies of Aneira. We have business with one man, and when that matter is completed, we'll be leaving."

The innkeeper chewed his pipe, his bright yellow eyes fixed on Grinsa's. "Two more nights," he said at last. "Then I want you out. And I want five more qinde per night for these last two."

The room cost too much already, but if they had only two days left, they couldn't afford the time it would take to find a new inn. "Fine," Grinsa said. "How long ago was he looking for me?"

"A while ago, just around midday."

Grinsa stood and walked away, not bothering to look at the man again.

"Two days," the innkeeper called after him, as the gleaner started up the stairs.

He nodded, but didn't stop again. Reaching their room, he found a note lying on his bed and began to read.

> Grinsa,
>
> I've found Brienne's killer and have gone to avenge her death. Should I be killed in the attempt, or imprisoned afterward, tell my parents that I died restoring honor to the House of Curgh.
>
> Had it not been for your companionship, I would have spent these last several turns alone and friendless. For that, I will always be grateful. Be well, Grinsa. May the gods keep you safe.
>
> Tavis

"Demons and fire!" he muttered, throwing the parchment to the floor and bolting from the room.

It seemed lightning had flashed in his mind, illuminating shadows in which the truth had been hiding. Of course the assassin was here. The first minister of Dantrielle had sent him. Word of Shurik's betrayal had spread through all of Aneira, and while most in the kingdom saw it as a humiliation for Eibithar, it shouldn't have surprised Grinsa that a discerning few would see the traitor's actions for what they were: a failed attempt by the conspiracy to start a war.

"I've sent him to kill someone we believe is part of the conspiracy," Dantrielle's minister had said that day in Solkara. But there had been the barest hint of uncertainty in her voice, because she hadn't been sure—she had chosen to send the assassin north based on hearsay. As it turned out, she was right, but Grinsa should have seen her uncertainty for what it was: a clue pointing to the identity of the man Evanthya wanted dead. Shurik, of course.

"We're at war with the conspiracy," she had said. And so she had hired the finest blade in the Forelands to kill the man. Grinsa had been an idiot not to see this sooner.

Charging down the stairs, he called to the innkeeper. "The inn where the musicians play! Where is it?"

"The Swallow's Nest?"

"Yes! Where?"

"In the west quarter, on a small courtyard off Fisher's Lane."

Grinsa burst through the doorway, nearly knocking down an older Qirsi woman. He spun out of her way and sprinted through the streets toward the western end of the city. It had been hours since Tavis left his note. One or both of them might already be dead.

It took him some time to locate the inn, each moment seeming a lifetime. When he finally spotted it, he dashed inside, vaulting the steps to the second floor, heedless of the shouts of the innkeeper. He could hear them struggling even before he reached the corridor and leaping over the last three stairs he raised his hand summoning a dazzling white flame.

"Tavis, no!" he cried, seeing the boy's blade glint in the sudden light.

The Curgh boy looked up at him, his dagger still resting against the assassin's neck. In a distant corner of his mind, Grinsa wondered how Tavis had managed to overpower a hired blade.

"Leave us, gleaner!" the young lord said, his chest heaving. "I don't need your help."

"I'm not here to help you, Tavis. I'm here to stop you."

The boy gaped at him, and the assassin used this opportunity to wrench his body to the side, throwing Tavis off of him and raising a blade of his own, one Grinsa hadn't noticed until that moment.

With a single, desperate thought, the gleaner threw his power at the dagger, shattering it into tiny fragments. The assassin stared at him, his face blanching.

"I can do the same to your bones," Grinsa told him. "And I won't hesitate to do so."

Slowly, the singer nodded.

Tavis jumped to his feet, brandishing his weapon again.

"Hold, Tavis."

The boy rounded on him. "Why?"

"Because he's here to kill Shurik, and we have to let him do it."

"What?"

"Remember what Dantrielle's first minister told us. She hired the singer to kill a member of the conspiracy. Shurik's the one. Isn't that so?" he added, shifting his gaze to the other man.

The singer narrowed his eyes. "Who are you?"

Grinsa eyed the man briefly, noting his cold, pale eyes and his lean, muscular frame. Even having described the man to countless barkeeps and merchants during their search through Aneira, Grinsa realized that he hadn't known quite what to expect. There could be no denying that he had the look of a killer. The gleaner wouldn't have wanted to face this man without his magic.

"I'm a friend of the boy, and an enemy of the man you've been hired to kill."

"Tell me your name."

And then Grinsa understood. The assassin he had killed in Kentigern Wood, the one sent by Cresenne, had been this man's partner. So many paths converging on this one city, on this one day. It almost seemed that the gods had been guiding them all along, turning all of them to their purposes. Who was Grinsa to defy their will, whatever it might be?

"Grinsa jal Arriet."

The man's eyes widened.

"Yes," the gleaner said. "I'm the one."

"She told me you were more than a mere gleaner," he said.

Cresenne. So she had sent two assassins for him. He nodded, ignoring the ache in his chest. "She was right."

"And now you're saving my life?"

"So it would seem."

"No, he's not!" Tavis said, looking from one of them to the other, his face a mask of rage and pain. "He killed Brienne!" the boy said, his wild gaze coming to rest on Grinsa. "Because of him I was imprisoned, beaten, tortured! Because of this man, my father gave up the throne!"

"Not because of this man. Yes, he killed Brienne." He glanced at the singer. "You did, didn't you?"

The assassin hesitated, then nodded, as if sensing that there was too much at stake here to lie.

"But none of this happened because of him. He's a hired blade, a weapon. Nothing more. The conspiracy used him to kill Brienne and make you suffer. If it hadn't been this man, it would have been another. But they would have done this anyway."

"I promised her, Grinsa. I swore to her that I'd avenge her death."

"I know. But Shurik has to die, and I'm not certain that we can kill him. This man can."

As he was speaking, he saw the assassin eyeing a dagger that lay on the floor near where he knelt. "Don't do it," he warned the man. "I'd prefer that you survive this day, but I'll kill you if I have to."

"No, you won't," Tavis said. "I will. I can't let him live, gleaner."

"You have to. We need him, at least for now."

The boy raised his weapon again. "No," he said again.

Grinsa took a step forward. "I'm tired, Tavis. I've shattered his blade and I've been holding this flame for some time now. I can break your blade, too—I will if I must—but I might miss, and splinter your wrist instead. Please don't make me do that."

The young lord glared at him. "How can you do this to me?" he whispered, tears streaking his face.

"I'm sorry. Truly I am. But your need for vengeance is not as important as stopping the movement."

Tavis shook his head. "No!" he said savagely. "You mean it's not as important as protecting your life and your sister's! That's what this is about! Guarding your precious secret! You just don't want anyone else to know that you're—"

"That's enough!"

The boy looked away, his face reddening, his tears still falling.

Grinsa faced the assassin. "Tell me your name. Not an alias, the real thing."

Once more the man faltered. Then, "Cadel."

"Go, Cadel," the gleaner said. "While you can. My debt to you is paid. The next time we see you, I won't stop him. Do you understand?"

"Yes," the assassin said, climbing to his feet. "But you should understand that I have to protect myself, regardless of debts. I know you're here now. I know the boy wants me dead. If I have to kill him and you to keep myself safe, I will. And if you're here in Mertesse on Pitch Night, I'll hunt you down."

"We won't be." Grinsa paused. "Is that when you plan to kill Shurik?"

"I'm Eandi, and he's a sorcerer. If you were in my position, when would you kill him?"

The gleaner nodded. "Come, Tavis."

The boy faced the singer, hatred in his dark eyes. For a moment

Grinsa thought he would strike at the man, in spite of all that the gleaner had said. Instead he leveled his blade at the man's heart. "The next time I see you . . ." He trailed off, lowering his weapon again and walking away.

The assassin opened his mouth as if to speak, but then appeared to change his mind.

As Tavis stepped past him, Grinsa laid a hand on his shoulder. The boy shrugged it off violently and continued down the corridor to the stairs.

Grinsa looked at the singer again, their eyes meeting for just an instant.

"Don't fail," the Qirsi said.

"I never do."

They stood there, saying nothing. Then, with a sudden chiming that made the assassin jump, Grinsa broke the blade that lay at the man's feet. He gave a grim smile and let his flame die out before hurrying to catch up with Tavis.

Chapter
Thirty-three

✦

He was sitting in the back corner of the Swallow's Nest, sipping his fourth cup of Eardley bitters, when Dario returned to the tavern. Cadel saw the lutenist step through the door, but he merely watched as the younger man walked to the stairs and climbed to the upper corridor. He'd come back down soon enough, and Cadel wished to enjoy his solitude for just a moment longer.

It had been some time since he last drank this much. Certainly he had never done so on a night when he was to sing. But the lutenist never worried about the quality of their music, so why should he? The bitters wouldn't detract much from his performance anyway. Wine and ale clouded the mind. Bitters brought clarity. They had this night.

At no time during his struggle with Tavis of Curgh did Cadel truly fear for his life. He trusted all to his instincts, as he so often did in such circumstances, and he fought, assessing dangers and opportunities as they presented themselves. Only when the encounter had ended, as he stood alone in the darkened corridor, listening to the fading footfalls of the Qirsi gleaner, did he begin to contemplate how close he had come to dying.

Earlier in the day he had sensed that something was amiss, that a threat lurked somewhere just beyond his sight and hearing. Emerging from his room just a few hours later, however, he gave no thought to those premonitions. He merely stepped into a dark hallway, his blades sheathed and his mind wandering like that of a child. Had he taken the time to glance toward the corner as he did—a simple precaution that even the most inexperienced assassin knew to take—he would have seen the Curgh boy and killed him with ease. Instead, he found himself on his back, with another man's steel pressed against his throat. He deserved to be dead. Looking back on all that had happened, he was forced to conclude that he had been fortunate. Had the Qirsi not arrived when he did, Cadel might have managed to throw the boy off of him. But he couldn't be certain of that. It was just as possible that he would have died in the attempt. He shuddered at the thought, as if he could still feel the cold blade on his neck.

Assassins often spoke blithely of killing and being killed. No one who wielded a blade by profession could ignore the risks inherent in such a life. And no man, no matter his skill with a dagger, was immune to the passage of time. Cadel had plied his trade for more than eighteen years, not long for a farmer or smith perhaps, but an eternity for an assassin. He had always known that he would have to quit eventually, or be killed himself. But until today that time had seemed remote, a vague certainty, like the distant promise of the plantings in the middle of the snows.

His instincts had saved him this day, barely. But how much longer could he count on them? Next time he faced Tavis of Curgh, the boy would be older, stronger, more sure of himself with a weapon. And Cadel would be that much slower, that much more likely to fail and die.

Which brought him to the essence of the matter, the realization that had come with the clarity of his bitters. He wished to live. He had more gold than he could spend in a lifetime, some of it in a pouch he carried with him, the rest hidden in Cestaar's Hills, just outside of Noltierre. Before he died, he wanted to enjoy his wealth, to wander the Forelands without planning his next murder or his next escape. A few turns before, after facing the ghost of Lady Brienne, he had convinced himself that he needed a new partner. A few hours ago, he had decided that he wanted to work alone. Now he understood that what he wanted most of all was to be finished with killing altogether. There was enough blood on his blade; there were already too many wraiths berating him on Bian's Night. Brienne had told him that he wouldn't survive the year, and the prioress in the Deceiver's sanctuary had suggested that he find a new profession. It had taken far too long, but at last he had taken to heart the lessons of that harrowing night.

He wasn't foolish enough to think that the Qirsi would leave him alone for long, but he would find a way to avoid them and their movement. He could go east, to Wethyrn. The Wethy Crown had never held much appeal for him, but he had heard that the conspiracy was far less active there, no doubt because the eastern realm was the weakest of the seven.

Wherever he chose to go, he had made his decision. The time had come to end his life as an assassin. One kill remained, and then he would be free.

He saw Dario come down the stairs again and scan the tavern for him. It didn't take the man long to spot him and approach his table. Seeing the cup of bitters in front of Cadel, he frowned.

"You're drinking?"

"Yes. Care to join me?"

"We're performing tonight."

"I'm aware of that. You're concerned that I won't sing well?"

"No. I just . . ." Dario stopped, shaking his head. "This wouldn't have anything to do with the broken daggers I found in the corridor, would it?"

Cadel eyed the younger man for a moment, then looked away. "Yes, it would." It occurred to him that he was unarmed, for the first time he could remember. He carried extra blades in his travel sack, just in case he lost or broke one—a musician couldn't be seen purchasing daggers too often, not without raising suspicions. But he would have to remember to put them in the empty sheaths.

The lutenist leaned closer. "What happened?" His eyes widened. "Was it the white-hair?"

"A Qirsi broke my blades, but not the one you have in mind." He drained his cup and forced a smile. "It was nothing. A debt from the past come due. It's over now."

Dario regarded him closely, as if expecting him to say more. When he didn't, the younger man shrugged, seeming to dismiss the matter. He looked angry, however. Or maybe hurt.

"Fine then. If it's over, I won't ask about it anymore."

"Good."

"Do you plan to drink more, or is that over as well?"

Cadel stared briefly at the empty cup. "I think I'm done."

"Then there's something I want to talk about."

The singer gave a wan smile. *Of course there is,* he wanted to say. But he kept silent and waited.

"I've given this some thought," he began, his voice dropping low, "so I hope you'll listen to all I have to say before arguing with me. I understand that you've always taken care of the jobs involving Qirsi. I understand as well that your old partner accepted this, that it was just the way you two worked things out. I can even see that we should do things the same way, at least until I've proven to you that I can handle a kill on my own." He paused, appearing to gather himself for a fight. "But this job is different.

We're going into Castle Mertesse and we're doing it on Pitch Night in Qirsar's Turn."

"Your point?"

"Killing the Qirsi is going to be the easy part. Any other day of the year it wouldn't be, but that night he'll have no magic. He'll be no more dangerous than an Eandi. In fact, I expect he'll be weaker than most of the men you usually go after."

Cadel had to agree. "Interesting. Go on."

Dario grinned, but it lasted only a moment. "The castle guards are the real danger. So it seems to me that it makes more sense for you to guard my back while I take care of the white-hair."

It wasn't how Cadel had envisioned his last kill, but he hadn't survived eighteen years in this profession by being stubborn. Clearly, this would make things far easier for him, and that alone made Dario's suggestion attractive.

"All right," he said. "We'll try it your way. You take the Qirsi, and I'll watch your back."

Dario gaped at him, as if Cadel had offered him all his gold. "Really?"

The singer gave a shrug of his own. "As you say, killing the white-hair will be the easy part."

For all Qirsi, Pitch Night in the turn of Qirsar, god of their people, was a night of uncertainty and fear. Any Qirsi with even a bit of sense understood how much the Eandi hated the sorcerer race. Most of Shurik's people believed that only their magic protected them from constant persecution.

For one night each year, perhaps as a test of their strength and courage, perhaps as a cruel joke, Qirsar took away their power, their shield, and forced them to face Ean's children unguarded. The vast majority of Qirsi passed this night in the sanctuaries. There were few shrines devoted to Qirsar anywhere in the Forelands, but as the last bastions of the Old Faith, the sanctuaries of the other ancient gods offered some solace and comfort. They were considered sacrosanct, even by nobles whose courts had long ago turned to the Path of Ean. The Qirsi knew they were safe in the shrines. Even Shurik, who rarely visited the sanctuaries any other time of year, had spent Qirsar's Pitch Night in Kentigern's Sanctuary of Bian every year he served in Aindreas's court.

This year, however, he had no intention of leaving the castle. Not with two Weavers after him. Yaella had tried repeatedly to convince him to join her when she went to Elined's Sanctuary in the north quarter of the city, but he wasn't going to change his mind. If anything, the approach of Pitch Night only served to heighten his fears. By the last morning of the turn, he could barely bring himself to leave his chamber in order to have breakfast.

He couldn't say what he expected to happen. He had slept soundly the night before, without any thought of the Weaver, much less a dream of him. And the Mertesse guards weren't about to allow a strange Qirsi man and an Eibitharian lord into the castle. But as a gleaner, Shurik had no choice but to trust the sense of foreboding that hung over him like a demon's shadow.

He took his meal in the castle kitchen, eating quickly and retreating immediately to his chamber. Almost as soon as he returned to the dark confines of his room, he wished that he had forgone his breakfast. His stomach felt heavy and sour, and he expected to be ill at any moment. He had often heard of Qirsi fasting on this night and he wondered if this was the reason.

A knock at his door made him start and his heart race.

"Come," he called irritably.

Yaella stepped into the room. The sight of him brought a frown to her face.

"You don't look well."

"I'm not," he said. "I'll be glad when this night is over."

"It would do you some good to get out of this chamber, maybe even out of the castle. The sun's shining and it's not very cold. How about a walk in the gardens?"

He had to smile. "The gardens? In Qirsar's Turn?"

"Why not? There may not be much to look at, but at least you'd be doing something."

Shurik considered this for a moment, but then shook his head. "No. Thank you, but I'm happy to stay here."

She smiled coyly. "Well, would you like some company then?"

"That's a nice offer, but I think I'm better off alone."

The frown returned. "Now I'm really worried about you. You've never turned me from your bed before."

"I've never had two Weavers wanting me dead. Forgive me, Yaella. I'm not myself today. I'll be fine after tonight. I promise."

"You still won't come with me to the sanctuary?"

He gave a small shrug. "I'm sorry."

The minister tried to smile, but failed. "All right. Try to . . ." She shook her head, as if unsure of what to say. "I'll stop in later, before I go to the city."

He nodded. "Thank you."

Finding himself alone once more, Shurik sat on his bed and picked up

507

a volume of fables he had been reading the night before. He had purchased it from a merchant shortly after Rowan paid him for his betrayal of Kentigern. It had been a luxury, but one he could easily afford, and in the turns since, it had often rescued him from the boredom of his exile. On this day, the tales gave him little comfort, but at least reading passed the time. Occasionally he rose to put more wood on the fire in his hearth, but mostly he read, hearing the city bells toll in the distance every few hours. His stomach began to feel better late in the day, but he thought it best not to eat until morning.

Sooner than he expected, another knock broke the silence in his chamber.

"Come in."

Yaella pushed the door open and stuck her head into the room.

"You look better," she said, a smile on her lips.

"I told you I'd be fine. I just need some time alone. Come the morning you won't even recognize me."

"You're certain about the sanctuary?"

He nodded. "Quite."

"I'll see you in the morning then."

She pulled the door closed, the echo of her footsteps in the stone corridor receding slowly. For just an instant, Shurik considered hurrying to the door and calling for her to wait. Certainly the sanctuary would be safe, and he dreaded spending the entire night alone in his chamber. Still, his fear of the city streets overmastered his desire to be with her. Before long, he couldn't hear her footsteps anymore. He hadn't moved from the bed.

For some time he continued to stare at the book, though none of what he read reached him. Finally, he put the volume aside, stood, and crossed to the window. Staring out through the narrow opening in the stone wall, he shivered at the cold air that seeped into his chamber. The last faint glimmer of daylight still clung to the western corner of the sky, an orange so deep it was almost red. Above the castle, the first pale stars had begun to emerge in the gathering darkness.

Shurik tried to summon a flame, reaching for his power as a starving man grasps at offered food. He felt nothing. He could conjure nothing. For tonight at least, his magic was gone.

He turned from the window and began to pace the small room, pausing at the hearth to stir the fire and add another log. Once more, he thought of going to the sanctuary, but at this point he would have to make the journey alone, in the dark. He couldn't bring himself to try.

Instead, he lay down on the bed and closed his eyes, trying to calm his nerves.

He was awakened by a loud voice in the corridor, a man's voice. He was singing poorly, as if drunk. After a moment Shurik heard pounding on the door next to his.

"Shara!" the man called. He battered the door again. "Shara!"

Shurik sat up, rubbing his eyes. He had no idea of the time.

His door shook with the force of the man's knocking. Too late, the Qirsi realized that he hadn't bolted the lock before lying down.

"Shara!" came the voice again.

The handle turned and Shurik's door swung open, revealing an Eandi man who held a lute in one hand and a flask in the other. He was young, his face clean-shaven, his hair yellow. He stood in the corridor a moment, tottering in the glow of the torches. Then he took two unsteady steps into Shurik's chamber.

"Is Shara in here?" he asked loudly.

Shurik fumbled for his dagger, his hands trembling. "Get out of here!"

"I'm just looking for Shara."

"She's not here! Now get out!"

The man raised the flask to his lips and took a long drink. "Do you know where she is?" he asked a moment later. "I wrote a song for her. Would you like to hear it?"

He bent over and carefully placed the flask on the floor, nearly toppling onto his back as he did. Straightening, he began to pluck tentatively at the strings of the lute.

Shurik stood, still clutching his dagger. "Look," he said, trying to sound forceful. "I don't know who this woman is or where you can find her, and I don't want to hear your song. Now either you leave my chamber, or I'll call the castle guard."

The man shrugged. "Fine then." He stooped to retrieve his wine. But rather than picking up the flask, he laid the lute on the floor. And faster than the Qirsi would have thought possible, he stood, lashed out with his left hand to knock the blade from Shurik's grasp, and hammered his other fist into the Qirsi's throat.

Shurik fell back onto the bed in agony, clutching his neck and fighting for breath. The Eandi kicked the door closed and advanced on him, brandishing a blade of his own. Cowering away from him, Shurik tried to scream for help. But with his throat shattered, he could only manage a pathetic coarse sob that barely carried past the walls of his room.

* * *

In the end, they kept their plan as simple as possible. Cadel had spoken of scaling castle walls in Kentigern and killing a guard in one of the cities of Sanbira. Neither of those approaches seemed necessary here. The two of them were renowned throughout Mertesse City and had befriended several of the castle guards. No soldier of Mertesse would have any trouble believing that the musicians had won the affections of two court ladies, nor would they doubt that with the city taverns closed for Pitch Night, the two men would be eager to indulge in a more private performance. When Dario and Cadel arrived at the castle gate bearing wine and Dario's lute, the soldiers let them pass without question.

From there, it was a small matter to find the Qirsi's quarters. Once he had rendered the man helpless, Dario wasted little time. It might have been Pitch Night in Qirsar's Turn, and he might have spoken brazenly to Cadel of taking care of this kill on his own, but the lutenist was no fool. He strode to the bed, grabbed the white-hair by his throat, and thrust his blade into the man's heart.

The Qirsi's body went rigid, a small gasp escaping his mouth. Then he sagged, his eyes rolling back in his skull. Dario lowered him to the bed, and took a long breath.

He heard a soft footfall behind him and spun, dropping into a fighter's crouch. Seeing Cadel close the door behind him, he relaxed.

"What are you doing here? Shouldn't you be watching for guards?"

"He's not going to make any more noise, is he?"

Dario grinned. "No."

Cadel crossed to where the lutenist was standing, pausing for a moment to retrieve the Qirsi's dagger. Stopping next to Dario, he looked down at the white-hair's body. "I wanted to see how you did."

"I did fine, just like I told you I would."

"It seems you were right. Any trouble?"

"None. But I wouldn't have wanted to try this any other night of the year. Any sign of the castle soldiers?"

"No." Cadel glanced at Dario, a small smile on his lips. "Who is Shara?" he asked. "Is that your sister's name?"

"No, it's just a name I made up."

The singer gave a puzzled frown, gazing at the Qirsi again. "I was sure you told me your sister's name was Shara."

"No. My sister's name is Lettalle."

"Lettalle," Cadel repeated. "And what's your family name?"

"Hunfeurta," Dario said, staring at him. "Why?"

By the time it occurred to the younger man to be afraid, Cadel had already started to move. Grabbing a handful of Dario's hair, the singer ducked behind him. Dario tried to twist away, but then felt a sudden burning pain in his heart. Looking down with a strangled cry, he saw the Qirsi's dagger sliding up into his chest, just below his breastbone. He flailed at Cadel, desperate to free himself from the man's powerful grip. But already he could feel the life draining from his body.

"I'm sorry," Cadel whispered to him, easing Dario down onto the bed beside the Qirsi. "Truly I am. It wasn't my intention to do this when I found you in Dantrielle. But circumstances have changed. I need to end this, and I can't have you wandering the land knowing all you do about me, about my past and my ties to the conspiracy."

It seemed to Dario that Cadel was already leaving him, that his voice was receding like an ocean tide. He could barely see for the darkness of the chamber.

"They'll find you," he whispered. He was shivering, his legs and hands growing numb. He had never known the snows could bring such cold. "They'll find you and kill you. You'll be with me soon enough."

Cadel's face loomed above him, wraithlike and grim.

"I know," the singer said.

Dario wanted to say more. He wanted to close his fingers around the man's throat for what he had done. But the cold held him fast, and Cadel's face seemed to drift away, leaving only blackness.

He had only felt this way about a kill once before: in Kentigern, after murdering Lady Brienne. Cadel shuddered to think how he would suffer on Pitch Night in Bian's Turn for what he had just done. Facing Brienne had been bad enough. Now he'd have to face Dario as well.

He lifted the lutenist's body and draped it over the Qirsi's, staining the white-hair's blade hand with Dario's blood. Then he overturned the Qirsi's chair and picked up the flask Dario had left on the floor, only to drop it again so that it shattered, sending shards of clay and dark streaks of wine in all directions. Surveying the room briefly, he nodded to himself, satisfied with the way it looked. He took the lute, wiping it clean on the inside of his riding cloak, and opened the door quietly, peering out into the hallway before making his way to the nearest of the towers.

He descended the stairs to the first of the castle's two wards and hurried on to the gate.

The guards there waved and smiled. Seeing the lute in his hands, however, their smiles faded.

"Where's the lad?" one of them asked.

"He went off with one of the duchess's ladies. Last I saw him, he was carrying a flask of wine and telling me to take care of this."

The soldiers laughed.

"Guess his hands are full with other things," the first one said.

Cadel nodded and stepped past them to the wicket gate. "Just my luck. Serves me right for traveling with a younger man."

They were still laughing as he left Castle Mertesse and started across the city. He heard the gate bells ring on the city walls. Gate closing. Not that it mattered: he had never planned to leave Mertesse through the gates.

The city was quiet, like a great sleeping beast. He saw no one as he walked back to the Swallow's Nest, nor did he see the innkeeper as he crept up the stairs of the tavern. He took both his travel sack and Dario's, pausing in the room only long enough to write a brief message, before leaving the inn as noiselessly as he had come. With neither moon traveling the sky this night, he had little trouble scaling the city wall unobserved. Before long he had reached the edge of Mertesse Forest, which he followed west, toward the rocky shores of the Scabbard Inlet. At some point he would head back in the other direction, toward the Moors of Durril and the Caerissan Steppe, and, eventually, to the relative safety of the Wethy Crown. First, however, he needed to find a merchant, and short of remaining in Mertesse, the easiest way to do so was to visit the trading villages along the coast.

He walked through the night, setting a swift pace so that he might put as much distance as possible between himself and Mertesse. With first light of day, he slipped into the shadows of the wood, and continued to travel westward. They would be finding the bodies soon and Cadel knew that the castle guards would be interested in speaking with him. Best not to give them that chance.

Near midday, sooner than he had expected, Cadel spotted a peddler's cart approaching, following one of the sea-lanes toward Mertesse. He stepped out of the forest and raised a hand in greeting. Seeing him, the man reined his horse to a halt. He had steel grey hair, though not much of it, and his face was ruddy from the cold and wind. As Cadel approached the cart, he saw the man pull out a long bladed knife.

"Are you heading to Mertesse?" the singer asked.

"I am. I suppose you're wanting a ride."

"Actually, no. I was wondering if you would be willing to ride on to Solkara without stopping in Mertesse."

The merchant wrinkled his brow. "Why would I do that?"

"Because I'll pay you fifty qinde."

He chuckled. "You have fifty qinde?"

Cadel pulled out his money pouch and counted out the gold pieces, which glittered in the sunlight.

The merchant rubbed a hand over his mouth, his dark eyes fixed on the coins and the hand holding the knife falling to his side.

"What is it you want of me?"

Cadel swung the travel sacks and lute off his shoulder and knelt beside them, returning his money to his pocket. Rummaging through Dario's bag, he soon found the lutenist's pouch of gold and counted its contents. Then he added a bit of his own.

"This lute and travel sack belong to a friend of mine. He wants them taken to his sister in Tounstrel dukedom."

"Tounstrel! You said Solkara. It'll take me nearly the entire turn to ride to Tounstrel."

Cadel raised an eyebrow. "When was the last time you cleared fifty qinde in a single turn?"

The man clicked his tongue several times. "The girl's name?"

"Lettalle Hunfuerta. She lives in a village on the Plain of Stallions, just north of Tounstrel city." He pulled from his pocket the message he had written the night before. "On your way to Tounstrel, I want you to deliver this to Castle Dantrielle. Give it to the first minister there."

"You ask a lot."

Cadel strode to the cart and dragged the man down off of his seat. The peddler tried to raise his knife, but the singer slapped it away.

"What's your name?" Cadel demanded.

"T-Traver. Traver MarSint."

"Well, Traver, you're right. I do ask a lot. And I expect even more. There's forty qinde in that travel sack. If I hear from Lettalle that she didn't get the lute, or that even a single qinde is missing from the pouch in that sack, I'll find you, and I'll slit your throat. Do I make myself clear?"

The merchant nodded, his eyes wide, spittle on his chin.

Cadel released him, smoothing his overshirt. He took out his money again and paid the man his gold.

Traver tucked it away in a pocket without bothering to count it.

"You better get moving," Cadel said. "You've a long journey ahead of you."

The man eyed him briefly, then nodded again and climbed back onto his cart.

"Why don't you want me going to Mertesse?" he asked, picking up the reins.

Cadel started to walk away. "It's not safe," he said over his shoulder. "I hear two people died there just last night."

She sat on the floor beside Shurik's hearth, staring at the bloodstained bed, tears running down her face like melting snows off the steppe. Her love's body and that of the other man had already been removed, but Yaella couldn't bring herself to leave, even with soldiers and servants constantly stepping around her.

The castle guards said that the second man was a musician, a lute player of some renown, who had come to the castle to bed one of the duchess's ladies. But despite their certainty, and the broken flask of wine found in the middle of the chamber, she had no doubt that he was actually a paid assassin. She found it remarkable that Shurik had managed to kill the man, on Pitch Night no less.

Her chest ached merely thinking of how she had doubted him. For nearly an entire turn, he had spoken of his fears, of how two Weavers wanted him dead. Yet for all that time, she had tried to convince herself and him that the danger wasn't as great as he believed. She should never have left him alone. She should have stayed with him, or better yet, insisted that he accompany her to the sanctuary.

"I failed you in so many ways, Shurik," she whispered. "I'm so sorry."

One of the Weavers had arranged this. She felt certain of it. Sitting there in the chamber, Yaella resolved to learn which one. If it turned out to be her Weaver, the leader of the movement, she wasn't sure what she would do. The man could read her thoughts. He would sense her rage, her need for vengeance, and he would have her killed as well. But if it was the other one, this Grinsa jal Arriet, she would use every resource within her grasp to destroy him. She owed Shurik that much.

She heard the sound of boots clicking in the corridor, and looking toward the doorway, saw the duke walk in. Reluctantly, she stood and bowed to him.

"First Minister," he said, meeting her gaze before walking to the bed and shaking his head at the dark stains. "This is a terrible business. I don't understand how such a thing could happen in my castle."

Is that all you can think about? Your castle? "Yes, my lord."

"You must be terribly upset. I'm sorry for you."

Her tears starting to flow once more and she cursed herself. This foolish young duke had hated Shurik, yet she reacted to his smallest kindness as if he had put his arms around her.

"Yes, my lord. Thank you."

"I'm sure you'll want the funeral to be at the sanctuary, but you'll have whatever help the servants of this castle can offer."

"That's most generous of you, my lord."

He hesitated. "There is the matter of this chamber. There's no hurry of course, but at some point it will need to be . . . emptied. Will you want to do that, or would you like me to have the servants take care of it?"

Shurik had left most of his belongings in Kentigern when he fled Aindreas's castle after the siege, but there might be some gold in this chamber. The Weaver's gold.

"I'll see to it, my lord."

"Very well. As I say, there's no hurry." He glanced about the room once more, shaking his head. "I intend to find out how this happened, First Minister. No man, regardless of his race or how he came to be here, should fear for his life within the walls of Castle Mertesse." Rowan turned to leave, his cape swirling.

"Thank you, my lord," she said again, despising him.

Yaella remained in the chamber for a few minutes more, then walked back to her own quarters and curled herself into a ball on her bed, sobbing as she hadn't since she was a girl. Her stomach felt hollow, and no matter how tightly she wrapped herself in her blankets, she couldn't stop shivering.

Her mind was clear, however, and she thought of the two Weavers. If her Weaver had wanted Shurik dead, he wouldn't have needed assassins to kill him. He could have done it in a dream. It had to have been Grinsa, to whom Shurik would never have opened his mind. Yet, Yaella could not keep herself from blaming both of them. Had the Weaver who haunted their sleep not sent Shurik after Grinsa, this might never have happened. She had been more than happy to work on behalf of the movement when its enemies were Eandi, and Shurik fought by her side. But if one Weaver opposed the other, their war already claiming Shurik's life, how was she to choose between them? The Weaver had spoken of a glorious future, in which Qirsi ruled the Forelands and aspired to be more than festival performers and servants of Eandi nobles. And though she was drawn to such a vision, she increasingly found herself repelled by the thought that the Weaver she knew, the one who had bought her loyalties with gold and who held them with cruelty and the constant threat of a painful death, should claim the throne for himself.

She could never turn to this other Weaver as an alternative, not with

Shurik's blood staining his hands. But perhaps she didn't need to. Perhaps there was another way. Shurik was gone, and though she couldn't bring him back, she might be able to strike a blow on his behalf, one that would be felt by both Weavers.

Chapter
Thirty-four

Curtell, Braedon, Eilidh's Moon waxing

I t promised to be a long, difficult night. He needed to speak with several of the Qirsi who served him, and with one whom he hoped would pledge herself to him before dawn. Fortunately, Dusaan had slept well the previous night. He might have been a Weaver, but he could not escape the limitations placed upon Qirsi magic by the moon legends. Qirsar's Pitch Night affected him as it did all his people, and so, unable to reach for the dreams of others, he allowed himself a night of rest. He felt better for having done so.

The emperor had long since dismissed Dusaan for the night, taking to his bedchambers with one of his wives. Aside from the palace guards, the Weaver assumed that no others were awake. Still he waited, poring over the treasury accounting until he was certain that those he wished to contact were sleeping. Finally, as the midnight bells tolled in Curtell City, he put aside the treasury volume, added some wood to the fire in his hearth, and sat beside the blaze.

Closing his eyes, he sent his mind eastward, first seeking out one of his chancellors, a merchant who had last been in Kentigern. This promised to be the quickest of his discussions and so the easiest.

Usually he made his servants walk to him, requiring them to climb the rise on Ayvencalde Moor before they could speak with him. On this night, however, he hadn't time for such games. Dusaan allowed himself a smile. Well, perhaps there was time enough to make just the next one climb. But not the others, not tonight.

He found Jastanne's ship at the top of the Scabbard, just a few days' journey north of Kentigern. Touching the woman's mind, he summoned the vision of the plain, with its great white sun. He saw her appear before him, naked, as she always was when she slept, and seeing her there, he stepped forward so that she would see him, black as night and framed against the brilliance of his white sun. If she felt abashed speaking to him unclothed, she had never shown any sign of it. Nor did she have reason to, he had to admit. The woman was lovely.

"Yes, Weaver," she said, her voice strong. "How may I serve?"

"Did you hear anything more from Kentigern before you set sail?"

"No, Weaver. But neither did I expect to."

"You believe he intends to honor our agreement?"

"I believe, Weaver, that before speaking with me, the duke of Kentigern failed to grasp the power and scope of your movement. He thought to use it as a weapon against his king, whom he hates as we do the Eandi. I made him understand that we are no mere sword in his armory, that in fact we're more formidable than any Eandi court. He'll need some time to accept this, to alter his ambitions to match the reality of what we are. But his needs haven't changed, his hatred for Kearney is no less than it was. He'll serve you, Weaver. I'm certain of it."

"Very good," Dusaan said.

"Is there anything else, Weaver?"

He merely gazed at her, her fine white hair and golden eyes; her skin, as white and flawless as the stars. Without raising a hand, he caressed her cheek and the side of her neck. He had longed to make Cresenne his queen—if not for her lingering affections for the gleaner, whose child she carried, he might have already. But this woman who stood naked on the moor—eyes closed now, a small smile on her full lips—was, in her own way, even more perfect for him than the other. One needed only listen as she spoke of taming Lord Kentigern to know that.

He allowed his touch to travel down her shoulder and then to circle her breasts. Her lips parted and her nipples grew hard, but she did not flinch away as some women might. Yes, she would make a fine queen.

"You serve me well," he said, his voice rough.

He made himself stop touching her. It was to be a long night.

Slowly, she opened her eyes, her smile deepening. "Yes, Weaver."

"We'll speak again soon."

An instant later he withdrew from her dream, opening his eyes to the orange glow of the fire in his chambers. He sat for several moments, savoring the memory of her smooth, cool skin, before shutting his eyes once more and reaching toward Mertesse, where he expected to find Shurik jal

Marcine. This conversation would be a brief one as well, not only because he had but a few questions for the man, but also because he didn't care to be in Shurik's company any longer than was necessary. When he couldn't find Shurik in Castle Mertesse, he sent his mind southward to Solkara and then Dantrielle. Failing to find the man in either of those cities, Dusaan began to feel a familiar quickening of his pulse.

Less than a turn before, he had tried to reach for Enid ja Kovar in Thorald Castle, only to find that he couldn't perceive her consciousness there or anywhere else in Eibithar. A few days later, he received word of what he already suspected. The woman had died, her betrayal revealed to her duke. She kept faith with the movement to the end, taking her own life rather than submitting to her duke's torture, but her death disturbed the Weaver nevertheless. True, she had outlived her usefulness to him, but after having killed Paegar and lost the first minister of Bistari in the Solkara poisoning, Dusaan could scarcely afford to replace another minister.

Now it seemed something had happened to Shurik as well. It almost seemed that the gods were against him, though he refused to believe that. At least this time, he might not have to wait for word of Shurik's fate. Turning his mind back to Mertesse, he sought out the man's lover, Yaella ja Banvel.

As soon as he saw the woman, he knew. Her eyes were red and swollen, her face discolored. Judging from how she looked, Dusaan deemed himself lucky to have found her sleeping at all.

Finding herself in the dream, the woman turned to face him, but she kept her eyes trained on the ground in front of her.

"Tell me what happened," he said, as gently as he could. He hadn't liked Shurik, but he valued this woman, and if the traitor was indeed dead, he needed her more than ever.

She swallowed, her gaze still lowered. "I found him dead in his chamber this morning. There was another man there, dead as well. The guards say he was a musician, but I suspect he earned most of his gold as an assassin."

Dusaan felt his stomach knotting. On several occasions, the movement had employed an assassin who posed as a singer. Could this have been the same man?

"What did this second man look like?"

As soon as Yaella began her description, the Weaver knew it couldn't be the same man. Still, the very notion that someone would send an assassin for Shurik alarmed him. Under different circumstances he might have blamed his murder on the duke of Kentigern, whom Shurik betrayed. But in light of the duke's recent overtures to Dusaan's movement, this didn't seem likely.

"You're certain it was an assassin? Could there be any other explanation?"

She faltered. "We did find a flask of wine in the room."

"Shurik's?"

"No. It belonged to the other man."

Dusaan suppressed a smile, his relief palpable. "So, he might have been drunk."

"I suppose it's possible."

He had no desire to be cruel to the woman, but neither could he have her imagining threats where they didn't exist. "You'll forgive me for saying so," he began, softening his tone once more, "but if Shurik managed to kill this man on Pitch Night, it seems far more likely that he was a drunkard than a hired blade."

She looked up at that, anger in her deep yellow eyes. But then she clamped her mouth shut, as if afraid to speak her mind.

"It's all right," he said. "Say what you will."

"I disagree with you, Weaver. I think it very likely that this was an assassin."

"What makes you so certain?"

"Shurik went in search of Grinsa, as you commanded. He found him in Solkara and only barely managed to escape him. After their encounter, Shurik became convinced that the man is a Weaver and he feared for his life, not only because Grinsa would want to keep secret the extent of his powers, but also because he knew he had failed you by running from him."

This was the last thing Dusaan had expected.

"So you think I might have sent the assassin."

Her eyes flicked away. "I wondered," she said, showing more courage than he knew she possessed.

Usually he would have done nothing to dispel her doubts. Such uncertainty and fear could be more effective than gold in keeping his servants loyal. But under these circumstances he didn't want to risk driving Yaella away from the movement.

"I didn't," he told her. "You have my word."

She glanced at him, her gaze dropping again almost immediately. But she nodded and murmured, "Yes, Weaver."

"You don't believe me."

She was wise enough not to deny it. "Forgive me, Weaver. It's been a difficult day. I—I don't know my own mind."

He wanted to be generous with her but he could only tolerate so much. "I understand, of course. It must have been terrible for you, finding him like that. But," he went on, his voice hardening just a bit, "I expect that by the next time we speak, you'll have abandoned your mistrust. There's still a great deal to be done, and I must have complete faith in all who serve me. I'd hate to lose someone else so soon after Shurik's death."

The woman swallowed. "Of course, Weaver. Thank you."

Dusaan could tell that she wanted their conversation to end, but he kept her there as he pondered all that she had told him.

"Shurik indicated to me several turns ago that he suspected Grinsa might be a Weaver," he said at last. "Did something happen in Solkara to convince him further?"

"Grinsa escaped the city by shattering the swords of several Solkaran soldiers and shrouding himself in a mist. Yet, when Shurik first met him in Kentigern, he claimed to possess only gleaning magic."

Dusaan nodded. It didn't prove the man was a Weaver, but it certainly gave him cause to wonder.

"You were in Solkara at the time too. Did you see this man when Shurik did?"

"No, Weaver. I was still in my bed, recovering from the poisoning."

"Ah, yes. Forgive me, I'd forgotten. I take it you're well now?"

"I've healed, yes."

"Good," he said, nodding again. The Weaver had the impression that she was keeping something from him, though her mind seemed open. There was more at work here than mere grief. He would have liked to question her further, but he could feel himself tiring, and he still had more to do tonight, particularly now that Shurik was dead. "I'll leave you," he finally told her. "Rest well, and be ready to serve me the next time we speak."

"Yes, Weaver."

He released her mind and opened his eyes once more to his chamber in the Imperial Palace. He stood and poured himself a cup of water, which he promptly drained. He poured a second, sipped it, and returned to his chair.

With the traitor gone, there remained only one person who could help him find the gleaner. He was reluctant to turn to her, not only because she loved the man and carried his child, but also because she would be giving birth within this next turn, and any journey she undertook right now would be most difficult for her. But what choice did Dusaan have? If Grinsa was indeed a Weaver, and if he knew enough to send an assassin for Shurik, he threatened the entire movement. Eventually he might even become a danger to Dusaan himself. He had to be found and killed.

The Weaver explained much of this to Cresenne upon entering her dream. Even as he spoke, however, he could not keep his eyes from straying to her magnificent belly. He could hardly believe that one as lithe as she had been nine turns ago could have been transformed so completely. He could imagine how she must have looked beneath the simple shift she wore, her body as white and smooth and round as Panya on the Night of Two Moons. Yet her face remained just as he remembered it from the first time he walked in her sleep. A bit fuller perhaps, softer in the cheeks, but radiant nevertheless.

"You understand, I have to send you north," he told her, barely trusting himself to speak.

"Yes, Weaver."

Just a short while ago he had thought to claim Jastanne as his queen. He had touched her, wanting to do so much more. But now, staring at Cresenne, he couldn't even summon an image of the other woman's face.

"You're eager to find him," he said, unable to mask the rage in his voice.

Cresenne blanched. "No, Weaver. I just—"

Before he knew what he had done, she recoiled as if from a blow. An instant later a red imprint of his hand began to darken her cheek. He hadn't moved.

"You should know better than to lie to me. Now answer. Are you eager to see him?"

She dropped her gaze, nodding.

"You love him."

"I don't know."

He would have liked to slap her again, but he sensed that this time she wasn't lying. "Can you continue to serve me?"

Dusaan knew what she would say. All answers but one would invite death. Her fate would be decided not by what she said, but rather how she said it. Even as he waited for her to speak, though, he wasn't certain what he would do if he heard another lie. He had no desire to kill her; he wasn't even certain that he could.

"I'm devoted to this movement," she said. "I want my child to grow up in the world you have envisioned, Weaver."

A clever response, though not truly an answer to his question. He considered pressing her on the matter, but thought it best not to. He had just hurt her, and he didn't need his powers to see that she hated him for it. There seemed no sense in forcing her to lie, and thus forcing himself to kill her.

"Very well. You'll find a way north?"

"With the new turn, there should be peddlers coming to Kett. I'm certain one of them will agree to take me, provided I offer enough gold. I'll have to go up onto the steppe—crossing the Tarbin during the snows would be difficult. But Grinsa will do the same. He can't risk the Tarbin so long as the Curgh boy is with him."

Dusaan felt his rage returning. She had given this a good deal of thought. He wondered briefly if she had considered making the journey even without his approval. "Do you feel well enough to go?" he asked, keeping the rest to himself.

She appeared to falter for just a moment, a thin smile flitting across her face. "Yes."

"You were going to say something else."

"It was nothing."

"You wondered if it would make any difference if you told me you didn't."

Cresenne winced and nodded, seeming to brace herself for another blow.

The Weaver merely shook his head. "Probably not. You wish to serve the movement, to ensure your child a place in a better world. This is the cost you must bear for that glorious future. Believe me when I tell you that it's far less than others have paid in the past turn."

"Yes, Weaver."

"Can you kill this man if you have to?"

"I don't know," she said. "Twice now, I've sent assassins for him. But killing him myself..." She shrugged, looking young and frightened, although whether of Dusaan, or of having to kill Grinsa, the Weaver couldn't say for certain.

"Perhaps it will be enough if you can tell me where he is. If he is a Weaver, you'll have no more chance against him than the assassins you've sent. I may be the only one who can defeat him."

"I'll do my best to find him, Weaver. You have my word."

"I have far more than that. I have access to your dreams. No matter where in the Forelands you go, I can reach you. Never forget that, Cresenne. This man may love you as much as you love him. He may even possess the same abilities I do. But if I choose to kill you, he'll be powerless to stop me."

One of her hands had wandered to her belly, as if she sought to guard her baby from his threats. Her gaze remained steady, however. "I understand, Weaver."

"I'm glad. I've foreseen great things for you and your child. I'd hate for anything to keep the two of you from your true fates."

He released her then, sending the woman to the waking world with fear for her child fresh in her mind. Clearly he would never claim Cresenne's love as his own. But perhaps her terror would serve his needs just as well.

Even after becoming aware of his surroundings again, the gentle crackle of his fire and its warmth on his legs and face, Dusaan continued to squeeze his eyes shut. His temples had begun to throb and he rubbed them, taking long deep breaths.

He had no idea of the hour, but he guessed that little of the night remained. There was time enough for one last conversation, the most important of them all, though he could not let her know that. He had promised to kill her if she did not open her mind to him, but as with Cresenne, he didn't know if he could follow through on his threat. At any time, he would have leaped at the chance to win the loyalties of Eibithar's archminister, but with Paegar dead and the invasion looming, his need of her could not have been greater. If she refused him, he would find a way to compel her acquiescence, even if it meant returning to her dreams again and again, even it meant resorting to torture. Regardless of the cost to both of them, she would serve him.

Sending his mind eastward one last time, over the Scabbard and the bare-limbed trees of Kentigern Wood, the Weaver reached down into Audun's Castle, finding the archminister in her bedchamber. He could feel himself growing weary and though confident that his magic would not fail him before this last conversation ended, he vowed silently to rest the next night.

He made her walk a distance—not far, and not up the slope, but just long enough to convey the scope of this vision he had conjured for her. When she finally stopped, just a few steps from where he waited, her cheeks were slightly flushed. She had an oval face and long hair, which she wore tied in twin braids. The last time they spoke, he had failed to notice how pretty she was.

"I knew you would come to me tonight," she said, before he could speak. "I gleaned it in a vision last night, as I slept."

No one who served the movement had ever said such a thing to him before. He wasn't certain what it meant, but for some reason it pleased him.

"Did it frighten you to dream of me?"

"No. It convinced me that my destiny lies with your cause."

"So you won't defy me anymore?"

"No, Weaver. My mind is open to you."

So it was. Reaching further into her consciousness, embracing her thoughts and feelings as he would a lover, he felt her abandon her resistance. He sensed the doubts that lingered, and even the residue of fear she felt looking upon him. But they were obstacles no longer. He grasped the power of her love for Kearney and the depth of her pain at losing him. He tasted the grief she felt at losing Paegar and even saw that she suspected him of having a hand in the minister's death. Some shadows remained, darkened places she couldn't bring herself to show him yet, but this was true of every Qirsi whose mind he had touched. With time, the light of the white sun he brought to her dreams would illuminate even these murky corners. In all ways that mattered, though, she was his, fully and by her own consent.

"I'm pleased," he said after some time. "I know that you'll prove most valuable to our movement."

"Thank you, Weaver."

"Tell me, does your king still rely on you for counsel?"

Keziah began to toy with one of her braids, a great sadness in her eyes. "Not very much. He did for the first few turns we were here, but the last turn has been difficult. After Paegar died, I stopped trying to hide how angry I was. I've said and done things that Kearney might never forgive."

"You'll have to apologize. Blame your behavior on your grief. Tell him you love him still, and you said what you did to hurt him. Do whatever you think is necessary to win his confidence again."

"I don't know if I can."

"You must. You're of no use to me or our cause if you can't influence your king."

She chewed her lip briefly, looking like a child. "Yes, Weaver."

"It won't be easy, but you have to try. Think of it as a test, the first of many that you'll face in your service to this movement."

What he asked of her carried risks, not only for her, but also for the movement. As she regained Kearney's trust, she might also begin to rekindle their passion. There was a chance that she would question her loyalties again, that Dusaan might lose her to Eibithar's king. But as he told her, without the king's trust, she could offer nothing to the movement.

"Your king is aware of the threat from Kentigern?" he asked.

"Yes."

"And what does he intend to do about it?"

"He's trying to make Aindreas an outcast within the kingdom. He hopes to win the support of the other dukes. If Kentigern sees that he is alone, that civil war will bring only ruin, he might relent."

"Is it working?"

"Not as he had hoped. Several of the other houses, Galdasten among them, remain certain that Tavis of Curgh killed Aindreas's daughter. They think Kearney is in league with Javan, and they question the legitimacy of his reign."

"Is Kearney speaking with the lords of Galdasten?"

"Not since his investiture. He intends to invite the duke to Audun's Castle, but he'll wait until the snows end."

"It would be better for the movement if he didn't meet with Galdasten at all, but I suppose that can't be helped." He paused for a moment. "As you win back the king's trust, I want you to encourage him to take a firmer stance with Aindreas and his allies. Tell him that a king can't tolerate such dissent in his realm. Make him see that Kentigern is guilty of treason. Don't push too hard. You shouldn't actually call Aindreas a traitor. Just lead him in that direction. Kearney's pride will do the rest."

"Yes, Weaver. I'll begin right away."

"Good. Is there anything you wish to ask, before I leave you?"

"Yes. When might I expect more gold?"

The Weaver felt his smile fade. He had spoken of gold to many others within the movement, but had hoped that it would not be necessary with this woman. "Is that why you agreed to serve me? To grow rich?"

He read Keziah's retreat in the widening of her eyes and the coloring of her cheeks. "No, Weaver. I never—"

"This is a war, Archminister. We fight to free ourselves of the Eandi, to break their hold on the Forelands. We fight for our children and the generations that follow, so that they might grow up in a land where they can aspire to be kings and nobles rather than servants and Revel clowns. Service to our people should be compensation enough. Victory will be our reward."

"Of course, Weaver," she said, staring at the ground, looking abashed. "Please forgive me."

"You've already received a good deal of gold," he went on, softening his tone. "And in time you will receive more. Eandi nobles shouldn't be the only ones who know the joys of wealth. But you must be patient. When you've proven yourself to me, when I know a bit more about you, I'll be happy to send you more gold."

The woman looked up. "When you know more about me?"

"We've made a good start tonight, and as your service to the movement continues, so will our understanding of each other. I make it a point to learn as much as possible about those who serve me. The more I know about you, the better I can use you to achieve our goals."

He felt her apprehension flare like distant lightning. "This troubles you."

"I—I don't want others to learn that my father was a Weaver. I'm sorry, Weaver, but I fear for my life. I know that you live with this fear each day, but I thought when he died . . ."

"That the secret would die with him?"

She nodded.

"I understand. Rest easy, Archminister. Those upon whom I rely for such information know to be discreet, just as they know that if they fail me in any way, they'll die. You have my word, they will guard your secret. And of course, I will as well."

"Yes, Weaver. Thank you."

She was still afraid, but that would pass with time. He could offer her no more assurances. He sensed that dawn was approaching, and he knew that his magic would fail him if he remained with her much longer.

"The night is almost done," he said. "We'll speak again soon. For now, I want you to begin winning back the trust of your king. I'll have other tasks for you shortly, but none is more important than this. Do you understand?"

"Yes, Weaver."

"Until next time then."

He released her, and was aware once more of the chair and the fire and the sounds of the palace awakening. He opened his eyes and stood too quickly, so that the chamber pitched and rolled like a ship caught in a harvest storm. He had demanded too much of himself this night. He needed to rest, but already he could see the first light of day seeping through the shutters that covered his window. Harel would be awake soon, summoning him to the imperial chambers, forcing the high chancellor to listen to his foolish prattle. As far as Dusaan was concerned, the invasion and all that would follow couldn't come soon enough.

Feeling a bit more steady on his feet, he poured himself another cup of water and reflected on the conversations that had occupied his night. Only then did he grasp the significance of what he had done. Four dreams, four women. Among followers of the Old Faith, it was said that the gods always worked in fours. The world began with the four ancient ones, Morna, Bian, Amon, and Elined, and followed a cycle of four seasons, the snows, the planting, the growing, and the harvest. Determinings took place when a child turned twelve and Fatings four years later, at sixteen.

It was an omen, but for good or ill, Dusaan couldn't say. He saw great promise in all of them, but peril as well. If Jastanne found a way to control Aindreas, to make him a reliable tool for the movement, they might be able to bring civil war to Eibithar, their success atoning for Shurik's failure at the siege. Still, though he had much faith in Jastanne, Dusaan disliked relying on any Eandi, particularly one as dangerous as the duke of Kentigern.

Yaella had served him well for several years, but the Weaver could not help but wonder how Shurik's death would affect her. What if her suspicions of him lingered beyond this night? And what if Cresenne's love of the Revel gleaner proved more powerful than her devotion to the movement and her fear of Dusaan? He had little doubt that she would find Grinsa, but he couldn't say with any certainty what she would do once they were together.

All of which brought him to Kearney's archminister. Dusaan and Keziah had much in common. They were the highest-ranking Qirsi in the two most powerful realms of the Forelands. Both knew what it was to harbor a secret, one that would bring execution were it revealed. True, she wasn't a Weaver herself. But to be the daughter of a Weaver was no less dangerous. In many ways it was more so, since she hadn't a Weaver's powers to draw upon in case the Eandi learned the truth.

There remained so much that he didn't know about her, but that would change soon. Already one of his chancellors, another merchant captain who frequented the ports of the eastern Forelands, including those near Keziah's old home in Eardley, had begun to learn what he could of the woman. Dusaan suspected that before long, Keziah ja Dafydd would prove more important to the success of his movement than any other Qirsi in the seven realms.

Certainly one of them would. There had been four of them, and the gods worked in fours. One of these women would help him carry the Qirsi movement to glory. Even as he formed the thought, however, he heard an echo in his mind, as if the gods themselves were warning him. Perhaps to glory, their voices seemed to say. Or else to ruin.

Chapter
Thirty-five

✦

North edge of the Moors of Durril, Aneira

t had been five days since their encounter with the singer in Mertesse, five days since their hasty departure from the inn at which they had been staying, five days since Tavis had spoken a word to him. They had traveled a good distance in that time, skirting Mertesse Forest as they walked eastward, putting as many leagues as possible between themselves and the assassin. Tavis had made no effort to slow their progress, though Grinsa knew that the boy wanted to return to the walled city and face the singer again. Perhaps he realized that he had little hope of besting the man a second time, that if he tried again, he'd be killed. If so, he must also have known that Grinsa had cost him the best opportunity he might ever have to avenge Brienne's death. Whatever the reason, he walked when Grinsa asked him to, stopped when the Qirsi did, and ate what food he could find in his carry sack, all the while refusing even to meet Grinsa's gaze.

For his part, the gleaner had tried to justify his choice every waking hour since leaving the walled city. He did more that night than stop Tavis from taking his revenge and possibly reclaiming his place in the Order of Ascension. He kept the boy from killing an assassin, a man who was as certain to murder again as Ilias was to follow Panya into the night sky, a man who had sold his blade to the conspiracy and would likely do so again. And for what? So that this assassin might kill Shurik and preserve Grinsa's secret. The gleaner didn't need Tavis's bitter silence and smoldering glare to make him question the choice he had made. His own doubts were almost more burden than he could bear.

529

He tried to convince himself that Shurik's death had been necessary, if not for himself, then for Keziah. "If the Weaver contacts him we're lost," she had said several nights before, confirming what he already knew to be true. "Just kill him and get out of Mertesse." Little did she know that he would find a way to kill Shurik without having to raise the blade himself.

In recent days he had come to understand that it was this last point, his reliance on the singer, that lay at the core of his guilt. Not that he had let an assassin live, or that he had allowed a man to be killed, but rather that he had not killed Shurik himself. He didn't question that it had been the safest course, nor did he think that Keziah would fault him for his choice. He had no doubt that the assassin would find a way to enter the castle, kill the traitor, and escape with his life. His own chances of success would have been far less certain. Yet, he couldn't help feeling that he had taken the coward's way out, at a terrible cost to the boy.

Midway through this fifth day, it began to snow, in heavy, wet flakes that clung to their clothes and hair. Before long they were soaked and Grinsa was shivering with cold. Had they still been in the forest, they might have taken shelter among the trees and risked a fire, but the moor offered neither refuge from the storm nor kindling for a warming blaze.

"We should stop at the next village," the gleaner called to Tavis, who was walking a few paces ahead of him.

The young lord turned just slightly, not enough to allow Grinsa to see his face, but enough to indicate that he had heard. He gave a small nod, before facing forward again. A meager response, but more than he had offered in days.

Grinsa quickened his stride, so that he was walking just behind the boy. He had apologized countless times since Mertesse, to no avail. Still, he briefly considered asking Tavis's forgiveness once again.

"There are small towns throughout the moor," he said instead. "None is likely to have more than one or two inns, but we should be able to find somewhere to stay."

Nothing.

"I know it's cold, but can you walk a while longer, or do you need to rest?"

Again, no reply.

Grinsa dropped back again, and they continued on in silence.

Several hours later, with the sky above them growing dark, they came at last to a small farming village that sat along a narrow stream, most likely a tributary of the Tarbin. The village consisted of a few homes, a smithy, a wheelwright's shop, and a small marketplace that might have drawn a few peddlers in the warmer turns. In most of the Forelands, a village of this size would not have had an inn, but this one, located in an area of the moor crossed with some frequency by those traveling between Mertesse and the Caerissan Steppe, had a single tavern with a few rooms for rent.

The innkeeper, a ruddy-faced Eandi man who made little effort to conceal his distaste for anyone with yellow eyes, refused at first to rent them a room. Eventually, however, his wife prevailed upon him to relent, pointing out that the inn had not seen any paying guests in nearly half a turn.

Tavis and Grinsa changed out of their wet clothes and ate a surprisingly fine meal of mutton stew, steamed roots, and fresh dark bread. Still the boy didn't speak and Grinsa's weak attempts to force a conversation left him increasingly frustrated.

They returned to their room and climbed into their beds, though Grinsa wasn't at all tired. He left a candle burning, staring for a time at the sagging wooden ceiling. Stealing a glance at Tavis, he saw that the boy was awake also, his eyes trained on the small, bright flame.

"At least with you refusing to talk to me, I don't have to listen to your weak attempts at sounding like an Aneiran."

The young lord glared at him a moment, but didn't answer.

"What do I have to do, Tavis?" Grinsa demanded, too frustrated to hold his tongue any longer. "You want me to apologize again? Fine. I'm sorry. I know you want to avenge Brienne's death, but Shurik had to die, and I don't think I could have reached him without getting myself killed, and you with me."

Tavis let out a short sharp laugh. "So, you did it to save my life," he said, his voice thick with sarcasm.

"No. I probably would have left you at the inn. I did it to save myself, and Keziah. Is that what bothers you?"

The young lord turned away, his jaw tightening.

"I've tried to tell you all along that there's more at stake here than your life and your family's claim to the throne."

"What? Your life?"

Grinsa sat up. "Stop it! You're not nearly as stupid as you're making yourself sound right now. You couldn't be. You know of the conspiracy, you know what it's done. We have to destroy it. Don't you see that? Don't you understand that defeating these Qirsi is more important than any one of us?"

"The assassin killed for the conspiracy."

"Yes. But as I told you that day in Mertesse, he's nothing more than a hired blade. One day he kills for them, the next day he kills one of them. Shurik was the real threat."

"Only to you."

"Yes, to me! Who do you think is going to stop the conspiracy, you little fool? You? Your father? The movement is led by a Weaver, Tavis. *A Weaver!* And it's going to take another Weaver to destroy him."

He rubbed a hand across his brow, wondering how he could explain to the boy what it meant to go to war against his own people. The Eandi did it with some frequency though they didn't seem to realize it. They saw themselves as Aneirans and Sanbiris and Eibitharians. Grinsa's people, even those who served loyally in the courts, were Qirsi before they were anything else. This was how they viewed themselves; certainly it was how the Eandi saw them. Clearly, they weren't all willing to join the conspiracy, to abandon their friendships with the Eandi and their loyalties to the realms in which they lived. But the Eandi, including Tavis, his father, and Kearney, spoke of civil war as if it were an unimaginable horror, without seeming to understand that this was precisely where the Qirsi of the Forelands were headed: a war pitting Qirsi against Qirsi, perhaps brother against brother.

Not long ago, as they crossed through the Aneiran wood, Grinsa had told Tavis of Carthach's betrayal. He couldn't begin to explain to the boy, however, how one man's treachery, though well intentioned, had divided his people, how, nine hundred years later, it still divided them. Grinsa already hated the Weaver for what he had done to Keziah, yet he still didn't relish the notion of leading the Eandi courts to war against him. The man was Qirsi, a Weaver, just as was Grinsa. The gleaner wanted to believe that he was nothing like this man, who had used his magic to cause Keziah such pain, who had bought murders with his gold. But Grinsa knew better. They were more alike than they were different. Even without seeing the Weaver's face, he had seen his own reflection in the man's shadow. It had been distorted, twisted, to be sure, but it was still recognizable.

"I'm not even certain that I can defeat him," Grinsa said, his voice dropping. "But I'm the only one who has any chance against him." He looked up, meeting the boy's angry stare. "If the Weaver finds a way to destroy me first, everything else is lost. He doesn't know my face, at least I don't think he does. Shurik did, and so Shurik had to die, even if that meant denying you your vengeance and your name."

"So the fate of all the Forelands rests solely on your shoulders?" the boy asked.

"It depends on a great many people," he began again. "I—"

Tavis sat up. "No! That's not what you said. You've told me twice now that you're the only one who has any chance of defeating the Weaver. You really believe that, don't you?"

Grinsa clamped his mouth shut for a moment, struggling to keep his anger in check. He had no desire to yell at the boy a second time. "I suppose the armies of the seven realms could defeat a Qirsi army if they managed to put their differences aside and fight as one. But the loss of life on both sides would be great."

"So you're saving lives now." Tavis laughed again, though he was shaking his head. "You're keeping all the people of the Forelands from destroying themselves. I've never heard such rot! You're one man, Grinsa! I don't care what powers you wield, you're just one man. And I refuse to accept that you're any more important to this war than my father or the king!"

"I don't give a damn what you choose to believe! Nor do I care if you forgive me for what I did in Mertesse! I had thought that you were man enough now to grasp the significance of all that's happened to you over the past few turns, but obviously I was wrong! You were a spoiled fool of a boy the day I met you and you remain one to this day! This is not about you, or me. This is about fighting a war against a man whose powers you can't possibly understand, whose resources seem boundless, and whose army is unlike any fighting force seen in the Forelands for nearly nine centuries!"

He lifted his hand, summoning a bright golden flame to his palm. A moment later he raised a wind that swept through the small chamber like a squall in the planting turns, making the window shutters rattle, and threatening to overturn the small wardrobe in the far corner, all without disturbing the flame. As the wind continued to blow, and the flame still burned steady and unflickering in his hand, he shattered the wood of a small chair by the bed, sending splinters in all directions.

The young lord stared at him as if he had transformed himself into some great beast from Bian's realm.

"I'm but one man, Tavis," he said calmly over the roar of the gale. "Yet if I chose to do so, I could tear this inn to the ground in a matter of moments. And I could do it any number of ways. I could summon a wind that would rip the building off its foundation. I could shatter the walls and beams with shaping power, or I could conjure a flame that would consume it before your eyes." He let the wind in the chamber die away and extinguished the flame that had balanced on his palm. "A Weaver binds together the power of many Qirsi and wields it as a single weapon. Imagine what I could do with an army of one hundred Qirsi, or a thousand.

"The Weaver can do all that I can, perhaps more. And he *has* raised an army. He's gathered to his cause some of the most powerful sorcerers in the Forelands—not Revel Qirsi, but ministers from the courts, who wield two, three, maybe even four different magics. Even Cresenne, who did come to him from the festivals, wields three." He paused, groping for the right words. "When I say that I'm the only man who can defeat him, I'm not boasting, and I'm not trying to excuse my past actions. I'm merely stating what I know to be true. I'm a Weaver, and so I know what a Weaver is capable of doing and how he or she can be defeated. Kearney, your father, the other nobles, they're good people most of them, and they're formidable in their own way. But they've never faced an enemy like this one, and with all that's happened in the past few turns, the courts are weaker than they've been in centuries. You may not believe this right now, Tavis, but I am your friend. That said, I cannot allow our friendship to keep me from doing what I must to defeat the Weaver. You have to understand that."

For a long time Tavis kept silent, sitting motionless on his bed. Grinsa saw something glisten on the boy's face and realized he was crying.

"You threatened me," the young lord finally said, his voice so low that the gleaner could barely hear him.

"What?"

Tavis looked at him, wiping his tears on his sleeve. "At the Swallow's Nest. You said that you'd shatter my blade if you had to, and that you were tired enough that you might break my wrist also."

Grinsa closed his eyes briefly, wondering how he could be so thoughtless. Time and again, he found he had to remind himself that for all the changes he had seen in the young lord over the past several turns, despite the scars on his face and his arrogant bearing, Tavis was still a boy, less than a year past his Fating.

"I didn't mean it as a threat so much as a warning," the gleaner said. "I wasn't going to let you kill the man and if I couldn't persuade you to lower your blade, I would have had to break it. I swear to you, Tavis, I have never had any desire to hurt you. I've always done only what I felt was necessary. That's all."

He looked over at the boy, trying to gauge his reaction. Tears continued to fall from the young lord's dark eyes, but the expression on his face didn't change.

"I know that it seemed we were searching for the singer a long time," Grinsa went on. "But it was only a few turns."

"It was five."

He conceded the point with a small shrug. "All right, five. But that's still less than half a year. Now we know what he looks like. We know his name, or at least the name he uses. He'll be easier to find a second time."

"He knows we're looking for him now. Even if we find him, I won't be able to surprise him again."

"Maybe not. But then we'll find some other way. No matter what it takes, we will prove your innocence to all the nobles of Eibithar. I don't know what will happen with the Order of Ascension—the fate of the Glyndwr line lies beyond my control. But we will restore your name, that I promise you. You were born a noble of the House of Curgh, and you'll be a lord of that court again."

Tavis took a long breath and nodded, though he still looked grim. At last he spoke. "If all that you say is true, you risked a good deal more than your life freeing me from Kentigern's dungeon. You risked the future of the Forelands."

Grinsa was silent for a moment. "I suppose I did. I thought the risk was justified."

"I'm grateful. But my point is that if you're the only one who can stop this Weaver, then we have to do everything possible to keep you alive."

"Don't worry about me, Tavis. As I've already made clear, I wield many magics. I can take care of myself."

The young lord looked away. "But it might be helpful if you had someone with you, watching your back. Someone who was good with a sword."

Grinsa suppressed a smile. A joke came to mind, something about the lord becoming a liege man, but he kept it to himself. He had worked too hard trying to repair their friendship, and he sensed that this was important to the boy, that Tavis needed to feel that he had a role to play in the coming war, just as did his father and the king and Grinsa himself.

"Yes," the gleaner said instead, keeping his expression solemn. "I think you're right. I'd feel safer knowing such a person was nearby."

Tavis nodded. "All right then."

The gleaner watched him for a moment. "Does that mean you're going to start talking to me again?"

"Isn't that what I'm doing now?"

Grinsa frowned. "On second thought, I think I enjoyed your silence." He lay down again. "Sleep now. We've a long way to go and I'd like to cover at least three leagues tomorrow, notwithstanding the snow."

"Where are we going, anyway?"

Grinsa glanced at him, a smile on his lips. "Don't you know?"

The boy shook his head. "I've been occupied with other things. I know we're headed east, toward the steppe. I assumed you just wanted to get as far from Mertesse as possible."

"I did. But I have it in mind to cross into Caerisse and then turn north."

"North?"

"Yes. I thought it might do you some good to go home, to Eibithar."

"It would," Tavis said, smiling for the first time in days. Almost immediately, however, his expression sobered again. "But Aindreas still wants me dead. Except for Glyndwr, I'm not safe anywhere in the realm."

Grinsa summoned a small wind that extinguished the candle. "You haven't been safe in Aneira either," he said, closing his eyes. "And at least to the north you won't have to rely on that awful accent." He couldn't be expected to keep all of his jokes to himself.

Chapter
Thirty-six

✦

Dantrielle, Aneira, Eilidh's Moon waning

umar writes of overtures from the emperor of Braedon," Tebeo said, pacing the chamber as he always did when unsettled. "It seems he intends to strengthen our ties to the empire."

Evanthya looked up from the parchment she was reading, which bore the Solkaran seal. "Does this surprise you, my lord?"

"I suppose not. Carden had already begun the process."

"But it troubles you."

The duke gave her a quick look, a sour expression on his round face. "You don't think it should?"

"I only wish to understand why it does, my lord." Evanthya felt certain that she had finally put to rest Tebeo's suspicions about her loyalty, but their conversations remained difficult. It almost seemed that because her eyes were yellow, he blamed her for the Qirsi conspiracy, even as he convinced himself that she was not party to it. "As you say, the late king started us down this path some time ago."

"But it's more dangerous now than it was when Carden was alive. The emperor wants Aneira as an ally in the event of a naval war with Eibithar. The Eibitharians must know this, in which case we invite an attack by tying ourselves to the empire. With all that's happened in the past few turns, we can hardly afford a war on the Tarbin."

"With all that's happened we're more vulnerable than ever," Evanthya said. "Isn't it just as likely that an alliance with Braedon will keep the Eibitharians from attacking?"

"I'd considered that, First Minister," he said sharply. "I'm not simple."

"Of course, my lord," Evanthya said, looking away.

He stopped pacing and ran a hand over his beard. "Forgive me, Evanthya. You didn't deserve that. An alliance with Braedon may well give the Eibitharians pause. I'm sure that's what Numar thinks." He returned to the chair behind his writing table and sat, rubbing his eyes with a meaty hand. "I've never taken the threat from Eibithar lightly, and I never would. But I think you'll agree with me when I say that Aneira faces far greater dangers than King Kearney and his army. This is no time to go looking for a war. Rather, we should be trying to reach beyond old hostilities. If we're arrayed against one another, we have no hope of defeating the conspiracy."

Evanthya nodded, remembering that the gleaner's friend, the Eandi boy she believed to be Tavis of Curgh, had said much the same thing in Solkara. "Is it possible that the emperor is reaching out to Numar for just that reason?"

Tebeo gave a sad smile. "Have you ever met the emperor, First Minister?"

"No, my lord."

"I did once, at Carden's investiture. I barely spoke to him, of course. We sat near each other at the banquet that night, but Carden was so busy flattering the man that he left the rest of us little opportunity to say anything at all. Still, that one night was enough for me to see that he is a singularly unimpressive man. He thinks of war and of wealth, and of little else. I doubt very much that he's ready to lead an alliance against the conspiracy. More likely, he'll continue to follow his petty ambitions, even if they lead all the Forelands to ruin."

"Do you intend to speak with the regent then, my lord?"

"Perhaps, when the planting begins. Numar is still new to his power. I don't want him mistaking such a conversation for a challenge to his authority. He may not be as ruthless as Carden and Grigor, but he's still Tomaz's son."

"Very well, my lord."

"You think I'm foolish to wait?"

"I wouldn't presume to judge, my lord. I share your concerns about the conspiracy and about any possible conflict with Eibithar. But as long as the regent and the emperor aren't making plans for war, I'm not certain that I see the harm in building on our friendship with Braedon."

"As long as they're not planning a war, neither do I. I'm just not certain I trust either of them to maintain the peace."

There was a knock at the door, and a moment later the duchess stepped into the room. Seeing Evanthya, she faltered, looking uncertain.

"Forgive me. I thought the duke was alone."

Evanthya stood and returned the parchment to Tebeo's table. "I was just leaving, my lady." She faced the duke and bowed. "My lord."

"Thank you, First Minister. We'll speak of this again."

"Of course, my lord."

She let herself out of Tebeo's chamber and descended the stairs of the nearest tower to the castle's upper ward. It had snowed the night before, though only briefly, and a fine white powder coated the grass, like flour on a warm loaf of bread. The sun burned brightly overhead, and already the snow on the battlements and towers of the castle was melting, darkening the stone walls beneath.

Evanthya crossed the ward quickly, pulling her robes tightly around her shoulders. Before she reached the tower leading up to her quarters, however, she heard a guard calling to her from the lower barbican. She stopped and turned, waiting as the man strode toward her.

"A peddler just came to the gate, First Minister," the man said as he drew near. "He told me to give you this."

He handed her a small scrap of parchment.

Evanthya unfolded it and read the brief message scrawled in black ink. The words held no meaning for her.

"You say a peddler brought this?"

"Yes, First Minister."

She stared at the parchment, her brow furrowing.

"Did he say who it was from?"

"No. He said only that he had come from the north, and that it had been given to him just outside of Mertesse."

Her eyes snapped up, meeting his. "Mertesse?" she whispered.

"Yes, First Minister."

Of course. Abruptly the missive made sense, cryptic though it was. Evanthya's mouth had gone dry and her heart raced as might that of a soldier marching toward his first battle. She knew the guard was watching her, that he could see how her hand trembled. But she felt powerless to walk away, or even to dismiss him.

"Are you well, First Minister?"

"Yes, thank you." She made herself look up and smile.

The man nodded and, after a moment's hesitation, left her.

She should have hurried from the ward. Better to ponder the meaning of this note in the privacy of her quarters. Fetnalla would want to know as well. She would have to send word to Orvinti. But still she just stood, unable to look away from the message.

Three words. "It is done."

They could have meant anything, which of course was the point. Only she would know that "It is done" actually meant "Your gold has bought the blood of another Qirsi." Only she would understand that the traitor had died, simply because she wanted him dead. Only she would see this message for what it was: a proclamation of war. Just as the loosing of a single arrow high over a battle plain signaled the commencement of combat, so the death of this one man declared her intent to oppose the conspiracy, no matter the cost.

Terror and exhilaration warred within her, one gaining supremacy over the other, only to retreat in turn. Even with Fetnalla at her side, she knew that she could not stand against a movement that seemed to grow more vast by the day. Yet this first skirmish was theirs, and the taste of their success served only to make her hunger for more.

That she had taken the life of a Qirsi gave her pause. Her people would suffer greatly before this war was over. With each new betrayal, it became more likely that they would never again be trusted by the nobles of the Forelands. More to the point, it had been nine centuries since Carthach's betrayal, and still the Qirsi battled among themselves over what the traitor had done. This war she had taken it upon herself to wage would only deepen an age-old rift. She tried to tell herself that this couldn't be helped, that by striking at the Eandi courts, the conspiracy had made itself the enemy of all those who were loyal to the realms, no matter the color of their eyes. But she was a gleaner, and though she had glimpsed only vague images of what the future might hold for the Qirsi, she quailed at what she saw.

"It is done."

Only Evanthya could have understood so much from the assassin's simple words. Still, as she stood there in the brilliant sunlight, holding this token of her triumph, even she couldn't explain why her eyes stung with tears for the man she had killed.

About the Author

✦

DAVID B. COE grew up just outside New York City, the youngest of four children. He attended Brown University as an undergraduate and later received a Ph.D. in history from Stanford. He briefly considered a career as an academic, but wisely thought better of it. *Seeds of Betrayal* is the second volume of Winds of the Forelands. He is currently working on volume three, *Bonds of Vengeance*.

He has published four other novels and was the 1999 recipient of the William L. Crawford Memorial Fantasy Award. He lives in Tennessee with his wife, Nancy J. Berner, their daughters, Alex and Erin, and, of course, Buddy, the wonder dog.